APOLLO

Fame is the Spur

Howard Spring

⚠

APOLLO

Apollo Librarian | Michael Schmidt || Series Editor | Neil Belton
Text Design | Lindsay Nash || Artwork | Jessie Price

www.apollo-classics.com | www.headofzeus.com

First published in 1940.

This paperback edition published in the United Kingdom in 2017
by Apollo, an imprint of Head of Zeus Ltd.

1 3 5 7 9 10 8 6 4 2

A CIP catalogue record for this book is available
from the British Library.

ISBN (PB) 9781784976347
      (E) 9781784976507

Fame is the Spur

Introduction

"**We** come here for fame!" was how the Tory prime minister Benjamin Disraeli once explained the allure of the House of Commons to the liberal politician John Bright. "Bright earnestly insisted that he came there for no purpose of the kind," according to one observer. "Disraeli ceased to argue the point, and listened with a quiet half-sarcastic smile, evidently quite satisfied in his own mind that a man who could make great speeches must make them with the desire of obtaining fame."

Fame is the Spur is, at one level, the account of a Labour Disraeli, preternaturally attracted to climbing the greasy pole of politics only to confront the hollow reality of the Book of Matthew: "For what is a man profited if he shall gain the whole world and lose his own soul?" As such, it is often read as a stinging rebuke to the career of Ramsay MacDonald who, like our hero John Hamer Shawcross, chose to betray the Labour movement in 1931 by leading the National coalition into the General Election in the hope of retaining high office.

But, this being a socialist rather than Conservative story, a familiar tale of principles sold out for power is then overlaid with all the complexity of social class, lineage, education and even pronunciation, which so often suffuse the personality politics of the Labour movement. However, Howard Spring's engrossing work of fiction is so much more than a critique of radical firebrands turned establishment reactionaries. It is a richly absorbing account of the psychology of politics; a fiercely paced novel by a gifted journalist turned popular writer, with rich echoes of *The Forsyte Saga*; and an account of poverty, social injustice and the indignities of inequality that stands comparison with Robert Tressell's *The Ragged Trousered Philanthropists*, Disraeli's *Coningsby, or The New Generation* and Upton Sinclair's *The Jungle*.

The lineage of John Hamer Shawcross, whose journey takes him from the hunger, fragility and filth of backstreets Manchester to the red benches of the House of Lords, is both pure and sullied. He is, at one and the same time, the bastard child of an aristocrat (providing his sense of entitlement and ultimate corruption) and heir to Peterloo. His inheritance of a sabre from the bloodbath of St Peter's Field – where, in 1817, the Manchester and Salford cavalry cut down a peaceful gathering of democracy campaigners and proto-Chartists – links him umbilically to the ur-point of nineteenth-century socialism. Peterloo was the Martyrs' Memorial for the Victorian radical tradition and Shawcross begins his political odyssey endowed with its finest relic.

That is just the start. In an echo of his unknown, aristocratic breeding, the young Shawcross is trained, like a Derby winner, for the very heights of the Labour movement. Harold Wilson once reflected that the Labour Party owed more to Methodism than Marxism, but Shawcross has both. From his stepfather he learns his *Pilgrim's Progress*, *Life of Wesley*, *Methodist Hymn Book* and the cadences and rhythms of the chapel sermon – "the easy brilliance, the challenging eye, the persuasive gestures and the rise and fall of the voice that could plead, condemn, exhort." Naturally, he also discovers the work of the great republican puritan John Milton:

Fame is the spur that the clear spirit doth raise
(That last infirmity of noble mind)
To scorn delights, and live laborious days.

Then, from his stepfather's friend, the old Jewish bookseller Charles Suddaby, there came a schooling in socialism from the works of Cobbett, Voltaire, Rousseau, and Robert Owen. Only Michael Foot could have read more widely. Best of all, there is a Manchester cameo from Friedrich Engels: "His face was heavily bearded; his clothes were of stout, excellent broadcloth. And he earnestly hoped that perhaps this dead and damned and rotten old year is the last year men will know in poverty and squalor... It's like a rotten old shed. How it will blaze!"

Added to Shawcross's intellectual pedigree was the lived reality of poverty. Later crafted into a politician's narrative of empathy and struggle ("I can speak of a poor home smitten by sudden calamity, of the loaf dwindling in the cupboard, the oil failing in the lamp, the fire sinking low upon the hearth, and hope burning low in the soul"), Spring nonetheless describes how Shawcross's childhood, amidst want and misery, drives his political mission. In his account of Manchester soup kitchens, worries of respectable working-class life, and brutality of capitalism, this is a work to stand comparison with Dickens's *Hard Times*, Gaskell's *Mary Barton* and Tressell's *Ragged Trousered Philanthropists*.

Spring successfully explains the fury and agony of inequality, and a life lived at the whim of the propertied class: "They own you, body and soul. One word, and they put out the light for you. No clothes for your wife. No food for your children." There is the occasional lapse into socialist impatience at the stubborn incapacity of the proletariat to realize their historic function ("It makes you wonder whether they're worth saving"), but, in fact, Spring has a much deeper sympathy for the lives of the working class than Dickens or Tressell ever did. In his descriptions of the Shawcross parlour, the chapel, the workshop, and the Saturday afternoon outfits, there is an admiration for a provincial urban culture of richness and pride.

This, then, is the setting for Shawcross's ascent to the top. Whilst the very same circumstances produces his friend, and conscience, Arnold Ryerson, who flees Manchester for Bradford to work as a printer and become involved in the nascent trade union movement, it is Shawcross who retains the aura of mystery around his persona. Whilst Ryerson does the branch meetings and factory gate demos, it is Shawcross (supported by his doting mother and stepfather) who travels the world, then sweeps into West Yorkshire to take the parliamentary seat and steal the heart of the guiltily well-off socialist Ann Artingstall. There is a Carlylian transcendence around Shawcross's "energy and force" which Spring urges us not to trust. And, with it, a willingness to use and discard friends and family on his way to the top – even uprooting his own mother from her settled domestic circumstances in order to curtail some political flak.

The ascent of Shawcross provides the narrative arc for a broader history of the rise of the Labour Party and the strange death of Liberal Britain. In Spring's schema, it was to be a party as dedicated and selflessly committed to the interests of working people as the Tories promoted the rights of capital. And from Bradford to Manchester to the Rhondda Valley, Spring ably marks the movement's growth across working-class communities. Yet the cynical joy of *Fame is the Spur* is that a nascent politician like Shawcross instantly understands the particular merits of a new party. "A man might join the Conservative Party or the Liberal Party, old and slow-moving both of them, and in twenty years be where he was at the beginning. The party of the rising tide was another matter." On a spring tide of socialist solidarity and collective endeavour, Shawcross rises to personal fame with a knowingness around the political process which would have impressed the most world-weary Whig grandee. Like so many Labour leaders, he knows how to quote his Shelley ("You are many; they are few"), how to "make these people feel that they were crusaders, not mere voters," and "while appearing to have nothing but his country's interest at heart" he knows the real politician "must be an expert at appealing to panic, passion and prejudice. When these do not exist, he must know how to create them at the right moment." Only occasionally would the guard drop, such as when he finally reached Westminster. "'So this is it,' said Hamer at last [on entering the Commons]; 'this is what all the dusty work and drudgery means – to get through those doors.'" Forget all that rot about service and sacrifice.

Such is Hamer Shawcross's personal ambition and growing self-regard that he even opposes female suffrage on the grounds it might costs Labour votes and block his ascent to office. "'I am a politician,' he said bluntly. 'I want to see my party in power.'" This provides the unbridgeable fissure in the marriage between Shawcross and Ann, who joins with her progressive aunt Lizzie Lightowler and Arnold Ryerson's wife, Pen Muff, to become an active campaigner for women's votes – even if that meant disrupting Shawcross's own hustings. The battle for the suffrage provides a symbol of true political principles and personal sacrifice in the cause of a just ideal. It also means a cast of female characters of much greater depth and sophistication than is the case in most "socialist classics". Spring is at his most powerful as a writer when describing, in gruesome detail, the force-feeding of Ann by a team of nurses and doctors prizing open her mouth. "She felt steel forcing her lips apart, grating on her teeth. It searched along the line of clenched teeth, slipped, cut into her gums… She tried to draw her tongue back, retching."

Shawcross, meanwhile, is enjoying all the trappings of public life as one of the Labour Party's new MPs. "His quarterdeck was the terrace along the Thames, opposite the House of Commons. He loved to come here and walk and think. On one hand the blackened time-smoothed granite parapet with the lamps springing out of it. Beneath his feet the long stone pavement, running forward in a lovely vista." At Westminster, any remaining radicalism which still attached to "Shawcross of Peterloo" is stripped away. From his growing flirtation with the Countess of Lostwithiel to the smart, prep school education for his son, to his regular appearances in the newspaper society pages, London feeds his vanity and corruption. His growing disconnect from the working-class voters of West Yorkshire earns him a rebuke from the ascetic Keir Hardie: "'There's a certain virtue' – he smiled – 'in lighting your own fires, and cleaning your own boots, and cooking your own food, as I do in my wee place behind Fetter Lane.'"

But, for Shawcross, the allure of high office was too enticing and he proves willing to undertake any number of humiliating errands to get into power. As striking miners in South Wales threaten to undermine the energy supply for the Royal Navy during World War I, Shawcross is despatched as Minister of Ways and Means in the wartime government to get them back to work. Whilst his own son, Charles, is wounded on the battlefields of northern France, and Pen Muff suffers in a munitions factory explosion, Shawcross's national service is to ask labour to bend to capital. "Never before had he felt so furtive and ashamed... He believed that the miners were in the wrong, but that was not the point... His visit had been contrived by people who would have been against the miners wrong or right."

An official, governing mentality had by now subsumed all remnants of that socialist idealism that first spurred him into political combat – that initial aspiration to pull down the Lostwithiel seat of Castle Hereward and all the social injustice it stood for. "Beat a drum. Fire a rocket... There it has been since Domesday, running us, ruining us, milking us, arranging the wars we should fight in and the dens we should live and die in." Now Shawcross's political "reality" sees him condemn the Jarrow March of 1929; support austerity in the public finances ("'We are spending more than we earn, and I tremble to think what the consequence of that will be on our credit abroad'");

feel a terrible sense of national loss when Castle Hereward is put on the market in the aftermath of the crash; and, finally, heretically, sanction the destruction of the Labour Party by signing up to support the 1931 National Government. His reward is a Viscountcy.

As such, *Fame is the Spur* can be read as a denunciation of the "low, dishonest decade" of the 1930s and the fateful merging of Liberal, Labour and Tory ideology. Howard Spring had himself once complained of how "the formal distinctions had melted; the three old gangs were fused into one amalgam, one sort of man: just a politician." But for all the finely tuned contempt for Shawcross's self-regard, in the final chapters of the book Spring seems to offer the reader a slightly more generous consideration of his characters and motives. Unlike so many on the Left, including his son Charles, Shawcross never falls for the bleak Marxism of Soviet communism and, instead, makes a strong case for the progressive merits of social democracy. "'I've come to believe that there is more in life than bread-and-butter for what you call the workers, I believe they can have it – plenty of it – without destroying free art and science and letters.'"

Increasingly disillusioned with the ugly, righteous stridency of politics, Shawcross inherits from Ann a growing fondness for the meditations of Marcus Aurelius and his philosophy of contemplative Stoicism. Shawcross ends his days a lonely widower, distanced from his son, his Peterloo sabre now encased in glass, lamenting the vanity and hubris of man. Fame is no longer the spur. In fact, his one prayer is that "'for fifty years, politicians of all breeds would leave the people alone. We might then have a better world. We couldn't have a worse one.'"

The socialist who has done well for himself and enjoys the comforts of success has long been a familiar subject of ridicule in British popular culture. "There is nothing too good for the working class – or their representatives," as Labour MPs like to joke. And in the rise of Shawcross there is, yes, the example of Ramsay MacDonald (who rose as an illegitimate son of Lossiemouth to Lord President of the Council); but also shades of Roy Jenkins's Duchess and claret dinner parties; the suave career of Labour Attorney-General Sir Hartley Shawcross (widely ridiculed as "Sir Shortly Floorcross," for his abandonment of Labour); and perhaps even Anthony Powell's grotesquely ambitious anti-hero Kenneth Widmerpool, in *A Dance to the Music of Time*.

Fame is the Spur sits outside Howard Spring's canon of more family-based sagas, but brings to the study of politics a popular novelist's gift. He captures not only late-Victorian Manchester, and the suffragette struggle, but also the socialist, literary culture and Nonconformist sense of purpose which underpinned so much of the early Labour movement. In the chronicle of Shawcross, the Labour Party rises and falls with all the weakness of his own character faults – and, in the process, leads Spring himself to urge a broader retreat from politics. In fact, just five years after publication, the Labour Party was to surge to power in its own right and, under the leadership of Clement Attlee (who also believed in private education and the House of Lords), deliver a programme of radical change which still stands as a lodestar for contemporary, left-wing politics.

And what of today? This is a cynical tale, which can only cement the fervent convictions of Labour Party leader Jeremy Corbyn's followers, that the Parliamentary road to socialism is inherently flawed. Real change has to take place on the streets away from the *Vanity Fair* of SW1. Hamer Shawcross's fame-hungry journey from Peterloo to Parliament is a salutary tale of the Establishment embrace, from which true socialism needs always to immunise itself. But, at the conclusion of the book, for all the language of betrayal and "sell-out," Howard Spring, the idealistic Labour voter, seems to have some sympathy for Shawcross's stoical humanism. "'Go on demanding the Millennium, my boy,' said Hamer [to Charles]. 'God help us when we cease to do that. But don't expect to get it, and, above all things, don't try to shove it down other people's throats. If the Millennium pays a penny in the pound, you'll be lucky.'" Indeed.

TRISTRAM HUNT, 2017

Fame is the spur that the clear spirit doth raise
(That last infirmity of noble mind)
To scorn delights, and live laborious days.
—MILTON, *Lycidas*

When thou wast young, thou girdedst thyself, and walkedst
whither thou wouldest: but when thou shalt be old, thou shalt
stretch forth thy hands, and Another shall gird thee and carry
thee whither thou wouldest not.
—ST. JOHN'S GOSPEL, XXI: 18

For my son
David Howard Spring

A few men and women who have played some part in the history of our times are mentioned in this novel. These apart, all characters are fictitious and all scenes are imaginary.

As a newspaper reporter, I saw much of the war waged by women for the vote; but I should be less than generous if I did not acknowledge the sharp refreshment of memory from *The Suffragette Movement*, by Miss E. Sylvia Pankhurst, who herself suffered so much in that cause.

H.S.

Part One

Sabre on the Wall

Chapter One

When they buried the Old Warrior there was only one small wreath to go on the coffin; so, as the hearse stood there in the narrow street, with the two black horses drooping their heads under the leaden winter weather, someone ran back into the house and brought out the cavalry sabre that hung over the mantelpiece. This was laid on top of the flowers.

John Hamer Shawcross never forgot that moment. Years afterward, on the other side of a gulf wellnigh incredible, he watched a uniformed and bearded king place with a kid-gloved hand a wreath of flowers at the foot of a cenotaph gleaming whitely under the pale blue of a London winter sky. Soldiers in formal lines, and beyond the soldiers the dense press of the people in Whitehall; and here, in front of the cenotaph, an open space yellow as the seashore with clean strewed sand. The air was cold, and the sun shone palely, and so great was the silence that the whickering of banners could be heard, and the passage of a pigeon's wing. You could hear, too, the crunch of the spurred royal boot on the harsh texture of the sand as the king stepped forward a few paces, leaned the tall wreath against the tall white stone, stepped back, and saluted. And as he stood there with his colleagues of the government within the wide cleared space, dressed in his formal clothes, holding his silk hat in his hand, with the people away back there behind the barrier of the soldiers, with the king's sons here about him, and a queen and princesses looking on from a near-by window, the Right Honourable Hamer Shawcross saw again the day when he was twelve years old, and a meaner wreath than this lay upon the coffin of the Old Warrior, and someone ran into the house in Broadbent Street and brought out the cavalry sabre.

But there was no use in thinking back. He had got out of the habit long ago; and as the military bands broke suddenly upon the silence with their rich pompous music he threw up his handsome head with a characteristic gesture and allowed his eyes to rest upon the sky. All the people began to sing the hymn which the bands were playing.

> God, our help in ages past,
> Our hope for years to come,
> Our shelter from the stormy blast,
> And our eternal home.

The words came draggingly through the frosty air, indescribably moving, and Hamer Shawcross, his eyes on the sky, gave himself up wholly to the sensuous melancholy of the moment. Some remote compartment of his being was not displeased to find that the salt of unshed tears was stinging behind his eyelids. His eyes came down from the heavens, rested for a moment upon the hymn-sheets wavering in royal hands, and then, drawn by a play of the wintry sunshine, fell upon the wreath standing in strong colour before the white stone. It gleamed redly, and the thought burst upon his mind that it was made of poppies, the flowers of sensuous illusion, the flowers of forgetfulness. He brushed his hand through the shock of white hair that fell upon his forehead, as it were impatiently brushing away a reflection so incongruous and untimely. It floated away, as the thought of the Old Warrior's sabre had floated away, lightly as the white birds that passed ceaselessly to and fro down this broad highway between the Nelson column and the Houses of Parliament.

Soon the bugles were blowing Reveille, reminding the Right Honourable Hamer Shawcross, P.C., M.P., that there was so much to do, so much to do.

The house in Broadbent Street was very small. The houses were all in a row, with no division between them, and they had no gardens. The front doors opened right off the street, and if you went through one of them, you were in a narrow passageway with the stairs in front of you, going straight up between walls, with no handrails. Downstairs there were two rooms: the front room and the kitchen, and behind the kitchen was a back kitchen which you could hardly call a room.

Upstairs there were two bedrooms. Ever since he could remember, little John Shawcross – no Hamer about it in those days – had shared the back bedroom with the Old Warrior. His mother and Gordon

Stansfield, his stepfather, slept in the other. The Old Warrior had a large bed with fine brass knobs on the posts, and young John had a low pallet against the wall. Between them they filled the room. Often the child would awaken early and steal to the side of the old man's bed and gaze spellbound at the wild disordered beard spreading over the counterpane, and the gnarled hands, ridged with hard violet veins, sometimes clenching and unclenching, as though in sleep he were again engaged in the exploits because of which, while still living, he was already a legend.

There were not many people in Ancoats, then, whose memories went back to 1819. So far as the Old Warrior knew, there were none at all. He was within two years of eighty when he died. There had been a time when he would look round the circle in which he happened to find himself and see the nodding heads and hear the murmuring voices which confirmed his story. But for long now he had been taken on trust, and those who listened to him noted an embellishment here and there, as a man, looking back to the home of his childhood, will, as it recedes farther and farther down the years, add to the height of its trees and prolong the golden splendour of its summer evenings.

But of the main facts there was no doubt. They were written in history. Always, with a hand that increasingly trembled, old Etchells, or the Old Warrior as they called him, would prelude his story by taking down the sabre from the wall. It hung over the mantelpiece in the kitchen, which was the family living-room in Broadbent Street, the loop of the handgrip resting upon a nail, another nail supporting the end of its curved, shining length.

It was always to young John Shawcross a magnificent moment when the old man got up to unhook the sabre. It was usually when someone had looked in, for Gordon Stansfield was a hospitable man who liked to see a friend or two about him. It was a lovely home, that little house in Broadbent Street, for Gordon's wife, Ellen, who was John Shawcross's mother, would have worked her fingers to the bone for the quiet man with the brown twinkling eyes who had put that roof over her head when, God knows, she had needed a roof and love beneath it.

She had found that, and she made Gordon's house her Hallelu-jah Chorus, with its shining brass and steel, its scoured floors, its winking fire, its red curtains, which seemed, of a winter night, to be contentment's very wings, drawn and protective about the hearth. To one side of the fire was an old leather armchair, its crimson faded to a homely brown, its resilience undermined so that it no longer buoyed up a sitter but accepted him and absorbed him into its amorphous and decrepit amplitude.

Gordon bought the chair when the Old Warrior came to live with him. He was a brother of Gordon's mother, and he had out-lived most of his generation. He was beyond working, an old man who had never saved a penny, and no one cared whether he went to the workhouse or the devil. So Gordon bought the chair, and the big bed with the brass knobs that was now in the back bedroom, and then he invited old Etchells to make his home in Broadbent Street.

He arrived on a winter night, with a spare pair of boots and a clean shirt wrapped in a large red handkerchief, and the naked sabre gleaming in his hand. Before he would settle down, he demanded a hammer and two nails. He fixed the sabre over the mantelpiece, and there it had remained, for ten years now, undisturbed save when Ellen took it down every Saturday morning and laid it among the kitchen knives to be cleaned with a cork dipped in moistened powder of Bath brick, or on those occasions when the old man himself told the story of how he came to possess it.

Little John Hamer Shawcross would have found it hard to say whether the sabre or the Old Warrior fascinated him the more. There was the old man, his once large body now a deflated sack, sagging in the chair, his head sunk upon his chest, his great untended beard imparting an indescribable air both of grandeur and of ancientry, his old rheumy eyes, flecked with red haws like a hound's, turned upon some far-back memory, his blue-veined hands resting upon the chair's arms and occasionally rising and falling as if beating the cadence of a song sung long ago.

He was so old and done with and finished; and there was the sabre, as old as he was, shining with a bright menace like a flame that might yet begin a conflagration.

And sometimes the flame that was in the sabre would be in the old man's eyes when occasion led him to speak of 1819. He had told the tale so often that he never stumbled in its telling, not even now in the days of his last decrepitude. It ran down the grooves of his memory as easily as a ship launched on a greased slipway. He would evoke the gay break of the morning of that August day when he was a boy of twenty, a boy in love going out to meet his girl. He laid the sabre on the table under the lamp, and it shone like a curve of solid light.

"No, you wouldn't think it to look at me now, but I was a grand lad at twenty. There wasn't much to eat for the likes of me, I can tell you, in those days, but I had big bones, and I was six foot three."

He held out his thin, old man's wrists and looked at the hands dangling at the ends of them and shook his head.

"Emma had asked me to breakfast," he said.

He always used those words, and no one knew who that Emma was who had waited for her grand lad on the sunshiny morning so long ago.

"She wore gingham," he said, "a gingham gown, and there was a red ribbon in her hair. She didn't wear a hat. She was a little bit of a thing, not up to my shoulder, and when she wanted to kiss me she'd stand on my feet and then get on tiptoe. We worked in the same mill, but we didn't go to work that day. None of us did. It was like a holiday. That was the funny thing about it. It was like a holiday to begin with: all fun, what with the bands and the singing and us all wearing our best."

The Old Warrior paused and held out his transparent hands to the flames, and a look of wonder came into his eyes as though, even now, when nearly sixty years were passed, he could not get over that perplexity: the gay August morning, all fun, that was to close in so dark a night.

"Emma's mother wasn't up," he said. "We had breakfast just to our two selves, with a bit o' kissing, and then Emma pinned a rosette in my coat and we went to join the others.

"This was in Middleton, and there was Sam Bamford wearing green leaves in his hat and trying to shove everybody into order. 'Come on, you two handsome ones,' Sam said. 'You'll look a treat at the head of a column,' and he took me and Emma by the arms and stuck us in front of a lot of lads and lasses from our mill. 'Let's have law and order,' Sam said. 'March as if you meant it, an' sing as if you meant it, but behave yersens.'

"'What's it all about, Sam?' I said; and Sam said: 'Keep yer ear-oils open when you get there and you'll know.' And then, more quiet, he said: 'It's about bread, lad, and about liberty, an' that's why you've got to act like sensible chaps and behave yersens,' and, with that, off he goes and tells the band to begin."

So there they were, rolling down the gritty road to Manchester, the Old Warrior, young then in his strength, and his girl Emma who wasn't up to his shoulder and wore gingham and a red ribbon in her hair. It was a gay procession, with the band playing and the sun shining on the men in their Sunday best and the girls with their ribbons, and they all sang as Sam Bamford, who knew so well how to write their songs, had told them to.

And as the miles went by, the procession swelled as here and there an odd enthusiast, and from side-roads regular marching bands, linked on, and the dust rose up from thousands of marching feet and dimmed the laurels in Bamford's hat.

"And we were only the beginning of it," the Old Warrior would say. "Thousands and thousands of 'em, marching with their bands and banners down all the roads into Manchester. I never saw so many people in all my life. Children, too, dancing along as they always will when there's music and a march. You couldn't move in Mosley Street – not if you wanted to move backwards, that is. You had to go on now, and Emma was tired and hanging on to my arm, and I ended up by fair carrying her into St. Peter's field."

Young Shawcross could not remember how often he had heard the tale. But whenever his mind reconstructed the scene, as in later years it often did, as it was always to recapture the thrill of seeing the old man, his eye shining wildly, leap to his feet and stand trembling upon the hearth, his gaze fixed upon the sabre. "Why did I do it? God damn and blast my body and soul, why did I do it?"

He was such a shambling, done-for simulacrum of a man that the swift torrent of fury tearing through him and shaking him like a reed seemed to come not from within him but from the dead, well-nigh forgotten years when all those thousands lived and moved who now were gone like Emma who died that day.

The Old Warrior sank down with trembling limbs upon the worn-out leather chair. It was always Gordon Stansfield who arranged the cushions behind his back, pushed nearer to his hand the table on which stood his nightly drink of hot toddy. He would moisten his lips and go on with the story.

There they were, then, those thousands upon thousands of Lancashire working folk, men, women, and children, milling and shouting in the field that still stood open in the heart of the town.

A holiday crowd for the most part, some of them intent, but not too seriously, on hearing what the speakers would have to say about this improbable question of their lives being made a little more bearable; and a few blackly set on a desperate venture. The bands brayed, the people shouted and cheered in front of the wagons from which they were to be addressed, and the hot August sun burned down.

"There were two lovely white horses," old Etchells would say. "We squeezed back to let them go by, and they had to go so slow that Emma patted the one nearest to us. It was Orator Hunt going up to the platform in his carriage, and he had a woman with him, all in white, with a red cap on her head. It looked very pretty."

Ah, poor Warrior! The Cap of Liberty, and one or two such symbols – see that banner with the skull and crossbones! – did not look pretty to the magistrates safely secluded in a room above the heated cheering crowd. There was on the old man's face a look of pain and astonishment, as though a lifetime had not wiped out the emotions of that dark moment.

"We didn't know!" he cried: "We never guessed!" But they knew then, with the grey rounded rumps of the horses pushing among them, with the sabres rising and falling.

"There were so many of us, we couldn't move, and they came at us like mad. I thought at first they were just trying to clear us out, till I heard a woman shriek and saw the blood rush out of her mouth as she opened it. Even with that, her mouth spouting red, she managed to shout: 'Dragoons! Dragoons! Get Annie out of it!' and then she fell and they went over her.

"My God, the shrieks and yells! They came from all round us, and they came from the ground under our feet where poor devils had fallen and were being trampled by men and horses. I wasn't afraid…"

The Old Warrior's eyes caught a hint of fire as he looked round the small circle of his hearers in the warm Ancoats kitchen. "No, my friends, I was not afraid. I used to wonder sometimes what I should feel if I found myself in a great danger, and now I knew. I was angry, not excited, but angry with a cold furious anger. I said to Emma: 'Get behind me, luv. I'll shove a way out for you,' and I was ready to smash and kill anyone who stopped me. 'Keep hold of my coat, luv,' I said, 'an' then I'll know you're there,' and I pushed on with my big oak stick in my hand.

"I pushed through everyone: bleeding men, and women with their clothes torn off them, and whimpering children, and wounded people down on their knees or flat on the ground. I wasn't thinking about any of them. It was hot, and the sweat was pouring into my eyes, and I was thinking: 'A soldier! By Christ! Let me meet a soldier!'

"And there he was coming at us. The crowd had loosened. You could hear their wailing spreading out and away, and there was a clear space, and this soldier coming across it on a grey horse. I saw his empty scabbard clicking at his side, and the sabre red with blood in his hand, and I rushed to meet him shouting: 'God damn you, you bastard! You're a poor man like us. What are you doing? What are you doing?'

"I waved my stick, and I could hear the leather creaking in the saddle and see the shine of his lovely boots. And then, when I was on him, his horse reared up, and I could see its front hoofs dangling over my head with the shoes gleaming, and the big veins in its belly. I struck upwards with my stick and hit the beast in the belly, and then Emma shrieked and pulled me backwards. I slipped in some blood and fell, and when the hoofs came pounding down I thought I was done for. But they missed me, and I lay there for a second with the dark arch of the horse over me, and then I saw the sabre sweeping past the side of the arch and a spurt of blood hit me in the face. Then the horse was gone, and there was Emma, lying on the ground."

The old man's voice trembled. His hands trembled on the arms of the chair. "She was dead. The blood was spurting out of her neck."

He didn't speak for a moment, then he said simply: "He had cut through her hair at the side of her head, the bit she had tied the ribbon on. I picked it up and put it in my pocket. There was nothing I could do for her then. I went to find the soldier."

He found him spurring his horse into a desperate mass of fustian and corduroy, gingham and shawls and ribbon, found him with his arm again uplifted to strike. "I whirled my staff – good solid oak it was – and you could hear his elbow crack like a broken stick when I hit it. My anger was not cold any longer. God alone saved me from murdering the man. I was red and blind. The sabre fell on the field, and I picked it up, dropping the stick from my hand. I swung it round my head and aimed at the middle of him with a blow that would have cut him in two. He dug his spurs into his horse, and the beast gave a sideways leap that ended my blow in the empty air. Then the soldier pulled him round and fled with one arm dangling at his side as though it were tied on with string.

"I was finished. All of a sudden I was done for, no more fight left in me. I felt weak and wretched, and saw that the field was nearly empty, except for the groaning people lying on the ground. I went back to look for Emma, but I couldn't find her anywhere, and it wasn't till I was wandering down Mosley Street that I realized I was still carrying the sabre. A man went hurrying by me. 'Drop it, chum; throw it away,' he said. 'If they cop you with that, you're done.' And then I saw that I had the sabre in my hand.

"It was dangerous to keep it. Thousands of panic-stricken people were hurrying now down all the streets that led away from St. Peter's Field. They were hurrying to hide themselves, as though they, God help us, were the sinners who had committed some crime. The dragoons were harrying here and there, still shouting and striking, and the police were everywhere.

"But I knew I wanted to keep that sabre. I didn't know rightly what Sam Bamford meant about bread and liberty, and goodness knows whether I should have understood what Orator Hunt was talking about if they had let him talk. But I knew that this sabre had something to do with it. I knew that all us simple thousands, slashed and trampled by the soldiers, had something to do with it. Thoughts were beginning to trouble my head as I stumbled through the streets, and the sabre was the symbol of all that was worrying me: Emma dead, and me, that had never done anything but work hard for a small wage, chased through the sunshine by the police and the dragoons.

"So I slipped into my brother's little barber shop in Oldham Street, and we hid the sabre there. And there it stayed for many a day."

The Old Warrior gazed, almost with affection, at the curved, shining length of steel. "A symbol," he said. "Not much now to me." He shook his head and his beard trembled. "And not much to you," he said, looking with affection out of his watery eyes at Gordon Stansfield, kindly and placid on the other side of the hearth. "No, not much to you, you man of peace."

Then he turned his old head slowly toward young John Hamer Shawcross, sitting spellbound beside the lamp. "But what about him, eh?" he asked. "What about this young shaver? You've got a long way to go, young feller. You'll see things – many strange things. A symbol might help you to sort 'em out. Gordon there is a man of God." There was a hint of rarely permitted raillery in the Old Warrior's voice. "He will tell you: 'They that take the sword shall perish by the sword.' Well, there's a sword from the field of Peterloo. Think on, lad."

And now the tale would be told no more. The Old Warrior was in his coffin upstairs, and little John Shawcross stood in the parlour, with his nose against the windowpane, watching for the arrival of the hearse. He always felt proud that he lived in Broadbent Street, because Broadbent Street was different from any other street he had seen. On one side were the houses, on the other a wall, breast-high, behind which oozed the slow waters of a canal with the high soot-caked brick front of a factory rising beyond it. Young Shawcross, who liked browsing among the few books that Gordon Stansfield possessed, had once come upon a picture of Venice, with fretted balconies, flower-hung, breaking the façades of old palaces dreaming above the water; and often of a winter night, when the raw, damp air of Ancoats was favourable to illusion, and a light fell here and there with a diffused blur upon the water, he would imagine that Broadbent Street was as near to Venice as makes no difference, especially if you could shut your eyes to everything else and concentrate upon the flow of the water under the smooth round arch of the humpbacked bridge away toward the end of the street.

The coping of the wall that divided street from canal was a favourite place for the boys of Broadbent Street and the district round about to sit and talk; and standing now at the window, John saw that Arnold Ryerson and Tom Hannaway were there, looking with intense interest at a place so romantic as to contain a corpse.

Although John's nose was to the windowpane, he could not see much, because the blind was down. He could see only the narrow strip of territory revealed by drawing the blind slightly to one side. He wished he might pull the blind up, so that Tom Hannaway and Arnold Ryerson should see him properly. He was wearing a new black suit, and he hoped that his face was pale and interesting with grief. He felt no grief at all; but that was no reason why he should not hope to appear grief-stricken.

He was a thin, undersized boy, with a face that was almost white.

His forehead was beautiful – smooth and splendidly proportioned – with black curling hair falling slantwise across it, and large eyes, so dark as almost to be black, shining below the thick straight brows. Small as he was, his appearance was further diminished by the rounded stoop of his shoulders. He looked almost humpbacked, and the boys called him Charley, because he had a Charley on his back. He hated the nickname the more because he was too weak to fight, and he didn't see why a back like his should excite derision. In his own mind it was held to be interesting. He often looked at himself in the glass, and if he had weighed up in one word the dark eyes, and the broad brow brushed by its wing of hair, and the thin stooping figure, he would have called it interesting.

He pulled the blind a little aside and looked again into the street. A few women were leaning now against the wall on which the boys sat. They made quite an audience. Gordon Stansfield, who was upstairs in the back room, sitting by the coffin, had told him to stay where he was till the hearse came; but he opened the room door, went out into the passage, and thence by the front door into the street.

He did not look at the people on the other side of the way. He began to pace with a slightly dragging gait up and down in front of the house, his face composed into the accents of sorrow. He noticed with satisfaction that all the blinds along the street were down, so far as he could see. He would have liked tan-bark to be strewed in the road. That gave a real note of solemnity. He had seen it outside houses where someone was sick within, and had more than once paused to notice the satisfying parenthesis of silence that came when the lumbering lorries, drawn by heavy horses, slipped instantly from their thundering progress on the road to the softness of the tan, and then out to their thundering again. But tan was used only when someone was suffering a long illness. The Old Warrior had given no trouble. He had taken up his toddy one night, dropped the glass as it was touching his lips, and slid down from his easy chair swiftly into his last darkness.

Aware of the eyes watching him with the sympathy that goes out always to the bereaved, John Shawcross paused for a moment to gaze profoundly at the pavement, then raising his head and, with a swift sweeping gesture that was to endure for a lifetime, putting back the hair from his forehead, he saw the two black horses drawing the hearse round the corner of the street.

*

For a moment the boy was filled with elation at the thought of riding behind two such horses. They were magnificent creatures, black as coal, with red distended nostrils from which they blew clouds of breath that hung palpably on the heavy winter air. Their steel bits, polished to the brightness of silver, were frothy with spume. It would be grand if Hannaway and Ryerson could see him riding behind that noble pair. But a moment's reflection showed him that all this might of rumps and shaggy fetlocks and arching necks would be harnessed to nothing more considerable than the boxed corpse of the Old Warrior. There, within the glass, were the silver rails between which the coffin would be pushed home, so that it might be borne, as if in a shop-window on wheels, to the cemetery. This insignificant cab, drawn by one horse of ignoble proportions and whose very colour was not decidedly black: that would be the vehicle destined for him and Gordon Stansfield.

All the inhabitants of Broadbent Street who happened to be at home were now either standing at their doors or leaning against the canal wall. Very conscious of them watching him, the boy looked at the approaching hearse with a melancholy eye, and when it had come to a stand at the front door, he went into the passage and called up-stairs: "They're here."

The passage was so narrow that a hat-stand which usually stood there had been pushed into the front room to make a way for the coffin. Two of the undertaker's men carried it out easily: the Old War-rior, at nearly eighty, had not much substance left over from the young giant who, at twenty, had marched to Peterloo. Gordon Stansfield and his wife came down behind the coffin. Both were wearing black, and Gordon carried a silk hat in his hand. He was accustomed to wear it on Sundays when he went forth to his labours as a Wesleyan local preacher; but now it had an unusual air, derived from a band of heavy black crepe. A band of the same material had been sewn by Mrs. Stans-field round the left sleeve of John's overcoat.

Ellen took Gordon's face between her two hands and looked at him with eyes in which love and solicitude were mingled. They had been married for ten years, and she was to him mother and wife. "Look after yourself, lad," she said. "It'll be cold up there." She twisted a warm muffler round his neck. "I'll have everything straight by the time you get back."

It was then that Gordon brought the small wreath of yellow chrysanthemums from the front room and laid it on the coffin. There was a card tied to it with a broad mauve ribbon: "Last love, from Gordon, Ellen, and John." It looked a forlorn little tribute lying there in the crystal and silver box; and perhaps it was this that led Mrs. Hannaway to make her impulsive gesture. She knew, as everyone in the street knew, that the old man's sabre was kept over the fireplace in the kitchen; and she was always the one who could be relied on in Broadbent Street to do spontaneously a thing that the popular mind would approve. And so, starting forward now from the canal wall where she had been leaning beside her son Tom, with her hands wrapped in her apron, she shouted: "Will you hould on now a minute! 'Tis a poor bit of a funeral the poor old sowl is gettin', with one cab and a few flowers that'd trim a doll's hat. Wasn't he a hero wanst, an' he wrestling swords out of the hands of wild dragoons?" She rushed into the house, pushing past Ellen Stansfield, who stood in the doorway, and soon was out again carrying the sabre in her hand. She put it into the hearse on top of the wreath. "There, my Old Warrior!" she cried. "I've heard ye myself tell your grand story, and that'll help ye to prove it to St. Peter."

Then she went back to lean on the wall, and she crossed herself as the small procession started, and the boys and the few men came forward from their lounging or sitting, and stood upright, and took off their caps. John Shawcross noticed all this, looking out of the window of the cab, and he turned it over with satisfaction on his mind's palate. It was nice to see people stand suddenly upright and take off their hats as he went by, though even the child knew that the tribute was half for death itself and half for Gordon Stansfield, whom everyone in the street looked on with affection and respect.

The cab was an old four-wheeler, smelling of mildew and mouldy leather. Gordon, who had a mortal fear of cold, pulled up the window, leaned back, and took John's hand in his. He did not speak as they went at a slow trot through the lugubrious Manchester streets, with the grey sky pressing down upon them, and no tree, no open space, greeting the eye anywhere. Brick, stone, windows, chimneys, pallid people pausing on the pavements to stare at the black horses and the yellow flowers and the unaccustomed note that the sabre gave to a spectacle not otherwise unfamiliar.

"What's a symbol, Father?" the boy asked suddenly. Gordon had always been Father to him, and the Old Warrior Grandfather, though in law neither was anything of the sort. "What did Grandfather mean when he said his sword was a symbol?"

"A symbol," Gordon patiently explained, "is a material thing to remind us of some condition. A royal crown is a symbol that the man who wears it has the condition of kingship. This ring," he said, extending his left hand, seamed with work, blunt-nailed, "is a symbol that your mother and I are in the condition of marriage. I suppose what your grandfather meant when he called that sabre a symbol was that it represented a condition of warfare existing between two sets of men."

"What sets of men?" the boy asked.

"Well," said Gordon, who was ever, as the Old Warrior had called him, a man of peace, "I suppose your grandfather would have said between men like him and men like those who turned the soldiers on the people at Peterloo."

The boy said no more. The cab windows by now were misted over with condensed breath. He could hardly see through them, and he was content to sit there holding Gordon Stansfield's hand in the comfortable, stuffy obscurity. It was a hard, knotted hand, but there had never been a time, so far as John Shawcross could remember, when he hadn't liked to hold it and feel comfort flowing into him from it.

Suddenly Gordon said: "There's the bell," and above the sound of the horses' trotting feet the boy heard the long leaden note dropped into the leaden murk of the afternoon. The trotting of the horses stopped; they had fallen into a walk; and, sponging down the window with the sleeve of his overcoat, John saw that they were passing up a gravelled roadway. As far as his eyes could see, the gravestones stood up in the black earth blanketed over with sooty winter grass. Some of the stones gleamed white in the grey melancholy of the afternoon; some were as soiled as the earth itself, open there to the slow perpetual downward drift of mill-smoke.

The sound of the bell continued to drop at long intervals upon the disheartening scene, and when presently the cab came to a standstill, and the driver, holding his crape-enveloped hat in his hand, opened the door, the boy stepped from the security and isolation he had enjoyed with Gordon into a world that seemed suddenly inimical and immense.

The hearse and the cab had halted in front of a chapel, soiled, like everything the eye rested upon, with thick black accretions, and standing there on ground that rose a little, John could see the melancholy funereal landscape, dotted with recumbent stones, and upright crosses, and angelic monuments, reaching through the dun afternoon to the surrounding impingement of the town: line upon line of smoking chimneys and mean roofs, with a tall mill-stack soaring here and there into the sky which now was darkening before the onrush of a premature night.

Already the coffin was out of the hearse. Its few flowers made a little yellow gleam that seemed no more effective than a candlelight to disperse the immense darkness of the cemetery. Balanced on four shoulders, the coffin was moving ahead, following a minister who had been waiting under the porch of the chapel, and who now went forward with long swinging strides, as though anxious to have an unpleasant business over and done with. Gordon took off his hat, and he and the boy, hand in hand, followed the coffin. A little wind had arisen, enough to catch the words flying out of the minister's mouth and blow them like distracted birds about that desolate and stricken field.

There was not far to go. Soon they left the gravel path and trod upon the wet, black grass, threading deviously in and out of mounds and monuments, and so came to a new gash in the earth, piled round with yellow sticky clay. John was not aware of what the minister was saying. Gripping Gordon Stansfield's hand with an intensity of emotion, he was aware only of that deep, narrow hole, and of the men taking the flowers and the sabre and laying them to one side before they passed ropes under the coffin and stood there with the box that contained the Old Warrior held back from the abyss only by those cords that were stained with clay like the hands that held them. Then the ropes began to slip through the hands and he could hear the rasping sound of them, and presently saw the tension on them slacken. He wanted to step forward and gaze down into that hole in the ground, but he dared not. Instead, he let go Gordon's hand and turned his back on the spectacle and looked across the grim prospect to the sky that the night was now invading with swift strides. He did not turn even when he heard the first thud of the clay upon the coffin; he did not turn at all. He stood there till Gordon took him by the hand again and began to lead him away. Then he saw the sabre lying on the clay, and he picked it up. It made him think of the Old Warrior not as he now was, not even as he had been in his last years, sagging into his sagging chair by the kitchen fire, but as he had been on that morning of which his great story told. He looked up into Gordon's face and asked: "What was the good of it?"

"The good of what?" said Gordon.

"All his fighting."

A sad smile played about Gordon's kind mouth. "Well, between you and me, he didn't do so much fighting."

"But that day. Was it any good?"

And now that it was so long over, and this last tardy survivor passed beyond the possibility to recall it, one might indeed ask: Was it any good?

Gordon looked at the darkened sky, drew his muffler closer as the wind rose to a keener note, and shuddered a little. "Who can say?" he asked. He looked at the sabre in the boy's hand. "Are you taking that thing with you?"

"I'd like to, please."

"Very well, then."

When they got back to the chapel, the hearse was already gone. Of such meagre pomp as had attended the Old Warrior's departure from the sight and knowledge of men nothing now remained but the four-wheeler cab whose solitary horse was dejectedly waiting for the last lap of his working day. The driver, now that the funeral was over, and there was no solemnity of a corpse to put cramps upon his demeanour, did not get down from the box or mute his voice. "'Op in," he said cheerily. "We'll soon 'ave you 'ome."

As though he were as anxious as the horse to have done with the miserable business of his day, he laid his lash along the creature's side when the cemetery gates were left behind, and John's spirits rose with youth's fortunate resilience as they went at a spanking pace through streets now almost completely in the grip of night. The cab windows were fast shut again, the warm reassuring presence of Gordon seemed once more to wrap him about; the sabre lay across his knees. He kept the window clear with his coat sleeve, so that he might see the lamps shining behind fanlights and glittering on the tempting shows of corner shops; and, more speedily than they had made the outward journey, they were home again, and Mother was standing at the front door with the passage lighted behind her and the hat-rack against the wall once more. There was a light in the parlour window, too: an unusual sight.

Again the driver did not get down. Gordon and John let themselves out of the cab, and as soon as they were on the pavement the man whipped up his horse and shouted "Good night." They stood there watching the bunched-up figure, with the big cape swelling monstrously round it, caught by the wind which now had an audible voice and was snarling in the street. Presently the cab turned into Great Ancoats Street, and Ellen, who had joined them on the pavement, said: "Well, that's the end of that. Come on in."

Ellen was having no truck with grief. So long as the Old Warrior was alive she had looked after him, because it was Gordon's wish that she should do so. Now that he was gone, she would make no pretence of undue regret; nor, if she could help it, would Gordon be plagued by recollection. "Come on in," she repeated briskly; and then caught sight of the sabre in John's hand.

"Whatever made you bring that thing back with you?" she demanded. "I thought we'd seen the last of that."

"I like it," said the boy. "It's a symbol, and Father says I can keep it."

"Well, don't keep it where I'll have it under my eyes all day long," Ellen commanded him. "Keep it upstairs in your bedroom."

The boy pushed the sabre for the time being on the floor behind the hat-rack. Ellen unwound the muffler from Gordon's neck, helped him off with his coat, and led him into the front room. "I thought we'd have tea in here for once," she said. "It's more cheerful. You must be fair clemmed and yon cemetery's a cold place at best o' times. Hark at wind. It's getting up proper."

A gust shook the window and the flame in the lamp jumped. Ellen looked up from her kneeling position at Gordon's feet. She was taking off his boots, yellow with the cemetery clay, and putting on his warm slippers. "John," she said, "go and get sausages from kitchen."

The sausages were long thin bags made of stockings sewn together and stuffed with sand. John knew their use. He placed one on the ground inside the front door, then, coming into the front room and shutting the door behind him, he placed another in front of that, thus sealing up the crack through which a draught might blow into the room. The third he laid along the window where its two halves met.

He did this quickly, because he feared to look from a lighter room out into darkness. You were all lit up: anything out there might see you. He let the red serge curtains swing hastily down, and turned gladly to the room, to the firelight, to the lamp, with its white opaque globe, standing in the middle of the table spread for a meal.

Gordon and Ellen were already seated, their heads bowed, and as soon as John had scrambled to his chair he bowed his head too. "These mercies bless," said Gordon, "and grant that we may feast in Paradise with Thee."

"Amen," said Ellen. "Pass me your plate."

She lifted the cover of the dish before her and laid upon the plate a thick rasher of ham grilled to a golden brown. On top of that she placed a piece of bread that had been crisply fried in the fat. "If you get that into you, you won't hurt," she said, and filled Gordon's teacup.

Then she served John, and finally herself. The little room, filled with quiet lamplight, with the fire whispering and rustling in the grate, with the storm, now full-throated, howling and sobbing without, seemed islanded and inaccessible in its happiness, its simple undemanding contentment. To the boy, with the poignant memory of the cemetery, and the passing bell, and the wind-blown incomprehensible words of the minister, still too fresh upon his mind, it seemed perpetual and secure, among the fundamental things of life that nothing could change or destroy.

There was not much about it. It was a simple little room with red serge curtains and red serge, fringed with balls, looped from the mantleshelf, a few family photographs on the walls, and the fireplace differentiated from the kitchen fireplace only by this: that there the fender and fire-irons were of gleaming steel, here of gleaming brass. A bamboo tripod stood before the window, with a hart's-tongue fern in its green glazed pot; and a rag-carpet, into which Ellen had put months of her spare time, was on the floor. But always for John Shawcross the firelight and the lamplight, in recollection, would have here a special quality, never captured elsewhere, a quality that he could not have defined but which was associated in his mind with a remark Gordon once made: "I feel, Ellen, that ours is a Bethany household."

He was packed off to bed soon after the meal was over. "Good night, son, don't forget your prayers," said Gordon. "And thank you for coming with me today."

Ellen took him upstairs. He carried the Old Warrior's sabre with him. He was tired now, and it trailed, clanking against the cold, oil-clothed steps. "You see," said Ellen. "I didn't waste much time while you were away."

The big bed that had housed the Old Warrior was gone. John's little pallet had the whole space to itself. "This'll be your room now. Do you like it?"

He didn't. But he wouldn't say so. For the first time he realized that he would be alone. The old man's groanings and snorings and mut-terings in his sleep had sometimes been frightening, but it was always a human sort of fright that you could take hold of and deal with. This loneliness in the bleak room, so different from the warm room down-stairs, was another matter. He glanced furtively to the window, saw with satisfaction that the curtains were tight drawn. "Yes," he said firmly. "I like it."

Ellen put the candle on the chest of drawers, and the draught from the open door sent the light dancing and her shadow flickering hugely across the ceiling. "Very well," she said. "Say your prayers now."

He knelt by the pallet, and she waited till he had done, and then waited till he was undressed, robed in his long nightshirt, and in bed. She tucked in the blankets and kissed him. "Good night."

Then she and the candle went. The door was shut. For the first time, he was alone in the dark. It was long before he went to sleep. He could hear the comfortable rumble of voices coming up from below, overcome now and then by a fiercer lamentation of the wind. Thoughts of the Old Warrior obsessed him, and of the sabre which he had thrust under the bed. To keep his mind from fear, he resolved to think steadily of the old man's fight and to repeat over and over again: "Peterloo–Peterloo–Peterloo." And again and again the wind hammered at the window, hammered at his thoughts, till it seemed to him to have the voice of a wolf-pack hunting hungrily through the night. "Loo-oo! Loo-oo! Peterloo-oo!"

Chapter Two

"Ah, my friends, the lives of the poor! The basis of patience and misery on which all rests! Come back with me to the little grey street I knew. Listen with me in the cold hour before the winter's dawn. Down the empty street comes the clatter of clogs – one pair of clogs, breaking the silence on which the stars are still shining. The knocker-up is on his way. He pauses at house after house, calling the poor from the sleep into which they have sunk wearied with labour. Up, up! No rest! The day is not yet come, but you must be up and doing for your task-masters. Rouse yourselves! Come out into the cold streets; hurry, hurry! Already the lights are springing up in the mills. Already the angry hum of machines is heard. You are their slaves. Come, now, come!

"And out they come: the old men bowed beneath the yoke that the years have made habitual; the old women with their shawls about their heads wrapping them against the cold of the morning; the young men and women whose lives are all before them, all dedicated, though they know it not, to profits and percentages; the little children, blinking sleepily, the dreams of the night still bemusing their minds, dreams of an ease and happiness they will never know.

"Ah, my friends, it is those children I see! In imagination, the sound of my little clogs is joined with the chorus of theirs, clattering through the cold of the Manchester morning..."

The Rt. Hon. Hamer Shawcross threw up his head, pushed back the snow-white hair, and almost saw himself, a boy, sallying forth into Broadbent Street, a wage-slave twelve years old. To his audience there was no doubt about it. They did not know the dexterity of self-deception which had just managed to throw in those words "in imagination." They gazed at the venerable figure, the man who was known to have come so far, and they pictured the hurrying sound of his clogs, running, running, to be there before the mill-gates closed.

But it wasn't quite like that.

*

It was not often that little John Shawcross heard old Jimmie Spit-and-Wink, the knocker-up. When he did, he did not hear the clatter of Jimmie's clogs breaking the silence in which the stars still shone, because Jimmie did not wear clogs. Years before, he was standing upon a lorry, and a heavy bolt of cloth, dropped from a warehouse landing several floors above him, missed the usual precision of its throw, and smashed his leg. The leg went, and Jimmie's job went, and his nerves went, leaving him with the melancholy affliction that gave him his nickname. The whole side of his face would jerk his eye into a wink, and, as if by reflex action, he would then automatically spit.

They gave him a wooden leg, and on his other foot he wore a big, hobnailed boot, not a clog. For as long as most people could remember, he had been knocker-up, spitting and winking through the morning with none to see him, carrying his little bunch of wires upon a pole, and playing with this a tattoo upon the windows of his clientele.

There was no reason at all why John Shawcross should hear old Jimmie Spit-and-Wink, because he did not rise till eight. But he heard him on the morning after the Old Warrior's funeral. He had slept badly. The unaccustomed loneliness, the howling of the storm, the excitement of the day he had been through: all this brought him again and again from the edge of sleep to utter wakefulness; and in one of those waking intervals he heard the dull thud of Jimmie Spit-and-Wink's leather-shod wooden leg and the brisk clatter of his hobnails alternating down the street.

The wind had cried itself to sleep. The morning was black, cold, and still. In the stillness the rattle of Jimmie's wires on the windows could be heard, and the shrill sound of the witticisms which cheered himself and his victims.

"Come on theer, Mrs. Hannaway. Buzzer'll be goin' afore thee's got thi corsets on. Never mind *what* thee's doin'. There's bairns enough in t'world already."

Then off he went, *thud-clatter, thud-clatter*, down the empty street, punctuating the darkness with that raucous clearing of the throat that preceded expectoration.

The boy listened till the street was quiet; but he could not sleep again. He knew the quiet would not last, and soon a solitary pair of clogs went clanging by; then two in unison, leisurely, with time to spare. Soon the iron music was beating itself ceaselessly out of the pavement, with but little accompaniment of talk. Occasionally a snatch of conversation, an adjuration to hurry, a child's whimper, would reach the boy to whom all this stir and urgency out there in the dark and cold came as something that made him, instinctively as an animal in a burrow, cower closer into warmth and comfort.

The song of the clogs increased in tempo as in volume. Soon there was no talk at all, only the purposeful beat of iron on stone, quicker and quicker, and now at last passing away, save for a few laggards sprinting hell-for-leather. Then all other sounds were swallowed up in the wail that came from the throat of the steam buzzer. It was a vast, impersonal, indecent noise, swelling up and dying, swelling again till it filled all the little streets with its ravening howl, and at last fading out in a long-drawn steamy sob. To the boy, crouching in his bed, listening in the darkness, it seemed like the sound of something hungry and inimical that had swallowed up all the life and energy whose pulse had been beating noisily through the street. It was six o'clock, dark still, and now the quietness flowed back.

If the Old Warrior were here, and if he were awake, this would have been a good time to ask him questions. The old man had been a light sleeper. On those rare days when the boy woke early, he would often hear him tossing and mumbling in his bed, and he would ask him things because he knew his questions would get no further. By breakfast-time, all that they had talked about seemed to be wiped from the old man's mind, which now dwelt more readily in the distant past than in the last half-hour.

"Grandfather, what's a bastard?" There was no light at all in the room, but he could hear the Old Warrior tossing and chuckling.

"Eh, that's a rum 'un, lad, that's a rum 'un. What do you know about bastards?"

"Tom Hannaway says I'm one. He says his mother told him."

"Well, it's a mother's question rightly, boy. You'd better ask thine."

And so he had done, when Gordon Stansfield was present, and his mother had laid her arms along the kitchen table and cried and cried. And Gordon had said: "Now, Ellen, now. Take it easy, lass. Take it easy. That's all finished and done with."

Gordon had stroked her hair, and when she had at last raised her face, streaked with tears, he had said: "Now let's see a smile. Come on now. A smile's the medicine."

Then Ellen had smiled, a wan and piteous smile that made the boy want to cry in his turn. Gordon sat her in the Old Warrior's comfortable wreck of a chair and put a cup of tea on the old man's toddy-table.

"There!" he said. "John's as much my son as yours. You know that, don't you? Anything I could have done for a boy of my own will be done for John. No mill," he added with his engaging smile. "No mill for John. We'll try and do something better."

John listened to the quietness that had swallowed up the hurry of iron feet. "No mill for John." That was what Gordon had promised, and he knew that what Gordon promised was done.

At seven o'clock he heard his mother stirring in the bedroom across the little landing. His own room by now was full of wan light. He looked, over the top of the blankets, at its unaccustomed spaciousness. He would never live in a smaller room; but now; with old Etchells's bed gone, it seemed enormous. He got out of bed, took the sabre from beneath it, and, standing on the rug, held it at arm's length. It was too heavy for his puny arm. He swung it tentatively, but found it an awkward thing to master. He tried a whistling swipe through the air, but it was more than he could do to stand still beneath the impetus. The swing of the sabre carried him with it, making him stagger.

Suddenly he realized that this piece of steel had killed a woman. It had cut through flesh and bone, letting out the life of a girl in gingham, named Emma. Perhaps of others. Often as he had heard the Old Warrior tell his tale, he had never before so completely and irrevocably identified the sword with the deed. He walked to the window, pushed back the curtain, and stood with the cold of the oilcloth striking through the soles of his feet. The day was as drab as unpolished pewter; the light fell through the window without joy or exhilaration, and the sabre took on the dull sheen of a tarn in winter. It looked sullen and unquickened. The boy scrutinized it minutely, looking for stains. Week after week he had polished it; he knew there was no stain from haft to point; but his new realization of the sabre as a thing of death drew his gaze inch by inch along its length. Presently he put it under the bed again.

He was thoroughly awakened now. He could hear his mother

raking out the kitchen grate and Gordon preparing to follow her downstairs. He put on the overcoat which was both dressing-gown and quilt and crept to the chest of drawers. The two small drawers at the top had housed a few possessions of the Old Warrior. John saw that his mother's clearing-up of the day before had not got as far as this. The old man's things were still there, a pitifully small accumulation for so long a pilgrimage. The boy turned them over curiously. There was a volume of the poems of Sam Bamford, and a Bible, a few clean handkerchiefs, heavy grey worsted socks, a box containing a few English coppers and some foreign coins. There was another box full of seashore shells, and a bigger one containing simple tools: hammer and chisels and screw-driver. Beneath this was a little package, carefully tied with string. The knot was covered by a small red blob of sealing-wax, like a holly berry. On the package was written in a beautiful flowing hand the one word "Peterloo."

The boy closed the drawers and stood for a moment with the package in his hand. He got back into his bed and, sitting up with the overcoat on his shoulders, weighed it thoughtfully on his palm. It was very light. Its contents might be nothing more than a few feathers.

He tried then to break the string, but could not. It was cobbler's waxed thread. He leaned out of bed and under it, and rubbed the thread along the edge of the sabre. The paper came off in such stiff folds that clearly it had been undisturbed for years. Inside the paper was a small cardboard box, such as might have contained cheap stationery. Inside that was tissue paper, and, impatient now, John pulled it carelessly out of the box, and found himself looking at a corkscrew curl of dark brown hair, tangled round a red ribbon.

He knew what it was, but he looked intently to make sure. He could hear the Old Warrior saying of that berserk dragoon: "He had cut through her hair at the side of her head, the bit she had tied the ribbon on. I picked it up and put it in my pocket." He looked closely, allowing the curl to fall round his finger with the grace of a tendril. There were dark brown blotches on the red ribbon.

Then swiftly, so as not to be caught in the deed, he put the hair and ribbon back in the box, and the tissue paper on top of it. He wrapped it in its old paper, and, leaping out of bed, thrust it beneath the clothes in the chest's long bottom drawer. That was his own. No one would find it there. He did not want his mother, in a frenzy of "redding up," to make away with so impressive a relic. He would tell no one about it. He would keep for himself Emma's curl that had not grown old and grey, and the red ribbon with the bloodstains on it.

He heard the front door bang. It must be ten to eight. Always at ten to eight Gordon left the house. It would take him ten minutes to walk to Birley Artingstall's shop in Great Ancoats Street. Even if Gordon had not worked there, John would have liked Birley Artingstall's shop. The smell of new leather that came from it filled all the street, and the windows were decorated with brass and leather in every possible combination. Leather bags with brass locks, leather dog-collars with brass studs, leather horse-collars with all sorts of brass dingle-dangles polished up to the nines. Birley Artingstall himself could usually be glimpsed within, decorated as resplendently as a piece of harness in the window.

Over the window were the words: BIRLEY ARTINGSTALL, LEATHER; and when John had first learned to read, he thought that this was a piece of information intended to leave no one in any doubt as to what Birley Artingstall was made of. There was some reason for the child's misconception, for Birley Artingstall was a man of most leathery aspect. His face was of the lean and cadaverous sort traditionally associated with Vikings: long-jawed, hollow-cheeked, decorated with a yellow pendulous moustache and thatched with unkempt corn-gold hair that strayed down into his bright blue eyes. His skin was mahogany-coloured leather, and he always wore a leather apron that once had been a lovely red and now was scored with use and faded to the undistinguished brown of a blood-pudding.

This leathery man, who loved to feel leather and to see leather married to curiously wrought pieces of useful or decorative brass, was himself decorated with a tie-pin, ear-rings which were tiny but impressive hoops of gold reputed to be a help to weak sight, with many rings, none of which bore a stone, and with a watch-chain on which shields, coins, and emblems hung across his concave stomach as plentifully as washing on a Monday morning line. But you saw the chain only when the apron was off, and that hardly happened except on a Sunday when Birley Artingstall might be found at the Emmott Street Wesleyan Chapel, enduring everything patiently – anthem and hymns, sermon and announcements and collection – waiting for the prayer-meeting which followed the Sunday evening service. It was for the moment when the minister would say: "Perhaps Brother Birley Artingstall will lead us to the mercy seat" that Birley lived. The tall drooping length of him would stand, one hand grasping the end of his pew, the other clenching and unclenching spasmodically, and out of him would pour petitions that once had had the virtue of extempore utterance but now were polished and rehearsed litanies. His voice began with cool and reasonable suggestions to a Deity not beyond the reach of common sense, and gathered in a few dutiful "Amens." Stage by stage it reached at last a thunderous utterance which culminated invariably in a command to the Lord to come quickly and "sway the sceptre of universal dominion." The fervent "Hallelujahs!" that fell like bouquets round Birley Artingstall as he sat down made all but the most obdurate quick to follow him. He was always pathetically anxious and restless, once the prayer-meeting had broken up, until someone had said to him: "You led us tonight with great acceptance." Then he would go happily home to the rooms over the leather shop where he led a bachelor existence, looking after his own simple wants.

On what had once been the garden, or yard, behind the shop there now stood the large shed which was the workroom. Here Gordon Stansfield had begun to work when he was a boy in the days of Birley Artingstall's father. He and Birley had grown up together; they liked one another; and Gordon's was a rather more privileged position than that of the other worker who shared the big shed with him. For one thing, he too was an Emmott Street man, and it often happened that after some special service he and Birley Artingstall would find much to discuss concerning the choir and the sermon and the satisfactory or unsatisfactory amount of the offertory. So Birley always called it, though Gordon used the simple word collection. "Remember, Birley," he would say, "First Corinthians, sixteen, one: 'Now concerning the collection for the saints.'"

They were very happy together.

As soon as he heard the front door bang, John dressed quickly, ran downstairs to the scullery, washed his face and hands in a tin bowl under the tap, and went into the kitchen. He always breakfasted alone. His mother ate with Gordon and then prepared the boy's breakfast. They wanted him to get as much sleep as possible, because he was not strong.

Neither Ellen nor Gordon ever spoke of the first two years of John's life: the years when the seeds of weakness were planted in him, when he had wanted food and care and love. He had had all that for so long now, his life had been so set about with sheltering wings, that he could remember, as older people remember a cataclysm, the day when his mother struck him.

It was two years ago. He was a child of ten. The day was raw, damp, midwinter foggy, and Gordon had gone to work coughing. He had been looking for some time pinched and pale, and Ellen stood, as she often stood, at the street door, watching him walk away down Broadbent Street. She turned back into the house, anxious and foreboding, as she always was when Gordon was ailing. It was a Saturday, and so the child was about the house. At eleven o'clock Ellen made a jug of cocoa, put it in a basket stuffed round with straw to steady it, and told John to take it to his father at Birley Artingstall's. Gordon did not bother as a rule with eleven o'clock drinks; this would show that she was thinking of him.

The child rebelled. He was busy with something that seemed important to his infant mind; and he said: "Don't bother me, Mother."

Ellen looked at him in surprise. "Take this to your father, at once! Do you hear me?"

"Yes, I hear you. But why should I be bothered?"

"Bothered? Is it a bother to do a little thing for your father?"

"Yes," said the child.

She struck him, a smarting blow, flat-handed across the face. He did not cry, but recoiled with a look of astonishment and mental pain. Ellen, surprised at the intensity of her own emotion, snatched up the basket. "Stay there," she said. "Don't leave the house. I'll take it myself. It's no bother to me."

She switched a shawl round her head and shoulders and went out into the street. The fog was thicker. She could hardly see a house-length in front of her, and memory came about her sharp as pain.

It had been like this, eight years before, except that then it was night. The fog had seemed friendly to her desperate intention. On the preceding Monday morning she had arrived at her new place. It had been difficult to get, because of the child. She wore, without title, a wedding ring and she said her husband was dead. It was pointed out to her that a child about the house was inconvenient. Sitting on the extreme edge of a chair, nervously twisting her fingers together, she faced the façade of black satin, decorated with a gold chain, on which the firelight flickered. She raised her eyes to the heavy face and agreed that of course it must be inconvenient.

"Especially here, where all our children are out in the world long ago. We don't want to start crying at nights all over again."

Oh, but the baby was a good baby. It did not cry at nights, and if someone did not give her work, what could she do?

The rigid figure, set about with shining mahogany, gilt frames, and waxy fruits, stirred a little and said: "Very well. But in such circumstances, you could hardly expect wages."

Ellen gave a little cry of dismay, and the voice went on: "After all, in return for what you do, you will have food and a roof over your head. And a child about the house is *most* inconvenient."

There was nothing she could do about it – nothing at all: such people had you trapped. For two years she had been chivvied from place to place, never anywhere for long. The child was her undoing. Sooner or later, its story followed her, and with righteous outcries she was thrust forth. One would think there had never been a bastard in the world before; one would think the pale, undeveloped little wretch was monstrous or contagious.

Now she was using this pitiful subterfuge of the wedding ring; and even at that she was asked to work without wages. She looked up at the harshly brushed-back hair, the black brows and beady little eyes. She nodded mutely. There was nothing else to do.

"Very well then, Shawcross. You can begin on Monday. Don't come on Sunday night. We shall be at church, and after church my husband likes to meditate."

So on Monday she put her few things into her yellow-varnished tin trunk, roped it, and paid a boy sixpence to help her to carry it to the new place. She left it in the attic, ventilated only by a skylight, that was to be her bedroom; then went back for the child and carried him.

Her new mistress opened the door. "This is my baby," Ellen said with a shyness that a word could have blown to pride. The woman said: "The less I see of the baby, Shawcross, the better we shall get on. When you are ready I'll show you the run of things." With that, she went to her own part of the house.

Ellen took the child up to the attic, turned her things out of the tin trunk, and made up his bed in it. She had a horror that the lid would fall; that some day she would come to her room and find him smothered. So here, as she had done elsewhere, she tied a string from the lock of the trunk to a nail in the wall above it, and then hurried down to see what might be wanted of her.

Everything was wanted of her – everything from morning to night. From the kitchen below ground to the attics up in the air, everywhere was her province. She shopped and she cooked, she swept and she dusted, she scrubbed the steps leading up from the long bleak street, and she waited at table. Never had she had such a place, and at night she would creep to her attic exhausted in body and mind.

On the Saturday night she went up at eleven o'clock. She had just lighted her candle when a knock resounded through the house. Well, she was done for the day. Let them knock. Then the voice of her employer was heard, calling up the stairs: "Shawcross, the door!"

With death in her heart, Ellen wearily pulled on again the skirt that she had taken off. She answered the door and went back to her room. The small happening, coming on top of so much, had unnerved her. There was no end to it – no end at all. She carelessly pushed aside the chair on which the candle had been set down and threw herself, dressed as she was, on to the bed.

She lay there with her eyes closed, a prey to desperate thoughts, when a sudden metallic clang brought her upright. The candle-flame had caught a loose-hanging end of string. The flame had run up this to the knot on the wall, and the child was shut up in the box.

Ellen leapt off the bed and ran to raise the lid. Then she stopped, wild-eyed, gazing at the yellow varnish. She knew that the longer she stopped the harder it would be to lift the lid, and deliberately she made herself stop, a prey to dreadful temptations. She had gone to sleep exhausted…she had forgotten to blow out the candle…No, she had heard nothing. "Didn't I tell you – I was exhausted – exhausted, I say!"

Her mind was fearfully rehearsing, as she stood there with her hands grasped about her brow, gazing at what might soon be the coffin of her child. An imperious rapping at the locked door brought her, like a blow, to her senses. "Shawcross! Come downstairs at once!"

She tied up the lid again, blew out the candle with a shudder at her thoughts, and went down the flight of bare-boarded stairs, down the next flight of oilcloth-covered stairs, and down the last flight of carpeted stairs. She went into the room full of mahogany and wax and gilt. Her employer's husband said: "I'd better leave this to you, Agnes," and, without looking at Ellen, went out of the room.

The implacable black façade swelled and heaved silently for a moment; then the woman spat out: "Take off that ring, you liar, you whore!"

So it had come again; it always followed her; but never before had it burst upon her so venomously as this. She strove to be calm, to take it as she had taken it often enough; but this time she could not: she fell to her knees, buried her face in a chair, and wept.

Never had she imagined that such hurtful things could be said. It seemed as though the woman for years had brooded on indecency, damming up in her privy breast a flood of detail that she now unloosed with gloating on Ellen's head. Once, the girl rose and essayed to leave the room, her hands stopping her ears, but the woman seized her by the arm, forced her to her knees again, and hissed: "No! you shall stay! You shall hear me out and know how your filth stinks in a decent woman's nostrils."

When it was ended, Ellen crept up to her attic and flung herself again upon the bed. She did not undress that night, and she did not sleep. She lay as though her body and soul had been flayed, with the woman's words swilling endlessly back and forth through her mind, a filthy tide. She began to believe it was true, that she was fit for nothing but to be cast out.

The next day she was kept at work as hard as ever. She cooked the Sunday dinner, and she gave an extra Sunday polish to the master's boots. She did these things with a strange resignation, that was almost peace, about her heart, because she believed that she would never do them again.

At six o'clock the pair were dressed for church. "By the time we are back, be out of this house," said the woman. "I do not want to see you when I come out of God's presence."

Ten minutes later, Ellen followed them into the street. She left everything: her old tin trunk and her child; that was all she had, and she felt she would not want these things any more.

The fog was thick. As she breathed it, the cold of death seemed to pass into her body. At her table in the basement kitchen, she had sat with each meal of the day before her, but she had eaten nothing, and so she felt hollow, and the fog now seemed to fill her. She was like a foggy wraith herself, without human volition, following a blind instinctive command to have done with a world that, for her, had been without hope, without mercy.

The air was full just here of the vibration of church bells, and presently she passed the church, by day a black unprepossessing lump, but now endowed with the wistful configurations of fairyland. It was as insubstantial as a dream, its fabric non-existent, its outlines suggested only by the blur of gold that was the lighted doorway and the paler yellow luminosities that, here and there, the windows laid upon the darkness. A shudder of organ music inhabited the unseen space between these luminous landmarks, and, as Ellen went by human voices broke forth suddenly in a hymn.

She had wrapped a shawl about her head and shoulders, and now, holding this close about her breast with one trembling hand, she paused for a moment, listening to the voices:

The God of Abram praise.

This was the church her employers attended. She did not stay for long, but faded into the mist that soon wiped out the romantic apparition and the luring voices.

Ellen knew where she wanted to get to, but soon she became puzzled by her failure to get there. The darkness was absolute except where street lamps were like pale flowers blooming without stalks, high up, achieving a useless poetry that defeated the plain prose purpose for which they were intended. She could not read the names of the streets; she had turned and twisted toward the direction in which she knew that the canal lay; but now, chilled and shivering, she found herself completely lost. She could neither find what she sought nor make her way back whence she had come.

Now she was filled with desperation. She walked without direction, trusting to chance to guide her. The air was so dense that it felt as though you could take it substantially into your hands and wring the moisture from it. The fringes of her shawl and the lashes of her eyes were dewed, and the dew was cold. So cold that she felt now that she need not seek death; death would take her, there in the street, where her footsteps were fumbling in what felt to her like the last extremity.

When at last she saw again a light, she was ready to give up, ready to throw herself upon any promise of mercy.

What she had come to was a small street-corner chapel. She pushed open the door and staggered within, unaware of the incongruity of her intrusion at the very end of the service. She slumped down upon a back seat, and the warmth, reviving her a little, permitted her to see what a mean interior this was, and how small was the congregation dotted here and there: fifteen or twenty people – not more. A few oil lamps made all the light there was, and they burned each in its own pale aura, for the fog had penetrated here. The people turned and stared at her, but she was beyond caring.

The man in the pulpit was not a parson. He looked like a work-ingman, and his homely enunciation as he gave out the last hymn confirmed her guess that she had strayed into a Wesleyan chapel served by a lay preacher. She tried to stand with the rest as the hymn was sung, but her legs failed her, and she was too exhausted and indif-ferent to be annoyed by the glances that fell upon her as the little congregation went past her into the raw night when the Benediction had been said. She rested her arms upon the bench in front of her, laid her head upon them, and presently was aware of a hand upon her shoulder.

She looked up warily. It was the preacher, and the woman who had played the harmonium was standing by him. "You seem done up, lass," he said. "Tell us what's the matter."

There was something in Gordon Stansfield's tone that the weary and unhappy could not resist. It seemed to wake Ellen from the stupor of grief into which she had fallen, but to wake her to a half-crazed state in which she did not yet discriminate thought from action. "My baby!" she cried, not knowing clearly whether she had killed it.

The chapel-keeper was putting out the lamps. Gordon and his sister took each an arm and led Ellen through the fog to the house in Broad-bent Street. They lived alone there. The fire, which had been damped down, was stirred to a blaze, the lamp was lit, food was placed upon the table. Not till she was warm, not till she had eaten, did Gordon say again: "Now, lass."

And this time she was able to tell them, and when the recital was over he said nothing but snatched up a shawl and went out of the house. Three-quarters of an hour later he was back, and Millie Stansfield, who had guessed his errand, had warm bread and milk waiting for the child whose pale face was peeping from the shawl upon his arm.

Ellen was too bemused by the events of the night to notice the flush in Millie's cheek, the cough that tore her, as she took this strange girl to her own bed. Thence Ellen soon moved to other work, untroubled by the problem of the child, for the child stayed with Millie and Gordon till Millie went out a few months later to whatever reward there may be for those who tend the widows and fatherless.

On all these things Ellen was pondering as she walked through foggy Broadbent Street carrying a jug of cocoa to Gordon. She could hardly see across Great Ancoats Street, but, trusting to her ear, made the plunge and came to Birley Artingstall's shop that was a joyous golden smudge of light in the gloom.

"Some cocoa for Gordon," she said to Birley.

"Take it through, lass, take it through," Birley said. "Cocoa's good, but a sight of you'll do Gordon more good than cocoa on a day like this."

There was no fog in Broadbent Street on the day after the Old Warrior's funeral. The wind of the night before had swept the air clean.

As John sat at his breakfast, Ellen, unseen, considered him critically. He was never ill, but he never looked strong. The veins on his forehead and wrists were startlingly blue, his complexion was pale and transparent. He had a face whose fragility kept her palpitating with anxieties that were never justified.

Now, when he got down from his chair, she said: "Stand up straight. Don't drag your leg like that. What's the matter with your leg? Does it hurt you?"

"No," the child said. "My leg's all right. I'm not dragging it."

He did not know that he was doing it. It was a habit he had got into some time before. He had read of some hero or other whose wound caused him ever after to walk with a "dragging gait." He lived in a world of heroes. He could not yet share their wounds – that would come. But he could, and did, adopt some of their peculiarities; and these hardened into what an onlooker thought were mere bad habits.

He put on his coat and his cap. "Where are you going to?" Ellen demanded.

"The croft."

"Well, mind you stay at the croft. Don't go wandering away. And be back in time for your dinner."

The sun was showing when he went out into Broadbent Street: a ruddy, smoky sun that was all glow and no warmth. Its reflection lay in the sluggish water of the canal. He threw in a stone, making the reflection dance and shiver and spread out in circles of trembling colour. He walked on, and found a piece of orange-peel lying in a puddle. He put his heel upon it and squeezed, and the puddle became magic with veils of green and red and purple and yellow stretched upon its surface, coiling and fusing interminably. That, too, pleased him.

The croft was a small space of hard-beaten open land. Away from the street, a back-yard wall was its limit; on either hand were the raw ends of houses that looked as though someone had intended to finish them off some day and had forgotten all about it. The fourth side was open to the street. The croft was not a piece of land that had, by hazard, not been built on. It was a piece of industrial history. It had once been used for the bleaching of cloth – long ago, when cloth was bleached out of doors. Now, hammered hard as cement by the feet of a few generations, it was adopted by the children as a playground.

Tom Hannaway and Arnold Ryerson were already there. Tom, with his wide humorous face, his thick black curls on which, even in winter, he never wore a cap, was busy with coloured chalks freshening the notice which he had inscribed some time before on the backyard wall. The letters were immense. No passing eye could miss them.

T. HANNAWAY – MERCHUNT
Bring your Rags, Bones, Bottles, Jars to this Pitch.
Hannaway is here each Saturday
10 to 11 a.m. Finest Rats in
exchange, personaly bred by Thomas
Hannaway, whose decision is final.
Old Iron, Lead Piping, Anything.

Arnold Ryerson, as fair as Tom Hannaway was dark, with a sensible unsmiling face, stood by with his hands in his pockets as Tom framed this announcement in arresting arabesques of red and green and blue. Tom was the youngest of many Hannaways. It was unlikely that there would be any further use for the dilapidated perambulator which he had wheeled onto the croft. John stole up silently behind the other two and lifted the apron of American cloth which covered the pram. A scuffling and squeaking bespoke the presence of the rats. They were in the well that pushed down through the floor of the perambulator – the well in which many small Hannaway feet had pounded. Now scaly tails swirled there and the minute toes of the rats scratched, and pink noses were stuck up through the mesh of wire-netting that was weighted down over the well.

John watched the rats with mingled delight and repulsion. He would have loved to have one, but Ellen's decree had been uncompromising. "No vermin in this house, my boy – especially vermin from the Hannaways! The Lord only knows what you might bring home on rats from that place!"

The well seemed full of the creatures – all white, with eyes like rubies. He tried to count them – there must be a dozen at least. They were clambering over one another, squeaking frantically.

Tom Hannaway completed his work, stood away and regarded it with an artist's eye, added a touch of yellow, and then produced a couple of small cheese-dice from his pocket. He dropped them through the wire-netting.

"Well, Charley," he grinned, "you having a rat today?"

John straightened his back. "I can't," he said. "I'm not allowed."

Tom's impudent grin widened. "Allowed!" he scoffed. "I'm not allowed to do anything. I'm not allowed to have this pram. I'm not allowed to chalk on the walls. I'm not allowed to go near Darkie Cheap. Allowed! You just got to do things – not wait till you're allowed to do 'em."

"That's all very well," said Arnold Ryerson in his grave way. "When they don't allow me to do things, I reason with 'em. My father said I was never to come on the croft, so I just asked him why not. And then I proved to him that he was wrong about it, so he said I could go. You want to get things changed like that – not just fly off and do what you like."

Tom Hannaway's white teeth flashed between his fleshy red lips as he said: "Take's too long, Arnold. And I'd like to see you reasoning with my old woman. She reasons with a smack in the mouth, and all you've got to do is dodge it."

Tom and Arnold were of the same age – fourteen. They would soon be leaving school. Tom was burly for his years, heavily built as a young bull, and Arnold was tall and slight. They both regarded twelve-year-old John Shawcross with tolerance. He was always hanging round them, and they put up with him.

Tom Hannaway's trade by barter was soon in full swing. This was his fourth Saturday morning on the pitch at the croft, and the fame of his white rats had had time to spread. It had spread so far that his original stock was all but exhausted, and there was no longer any truth in the claim that the rats were "personaly bred." That had been true enough at first; and now that he was buying the rats he saw no reason to alter the wording of his announcement. It looked well, and he had the commercial wisdom to let well alone.

With a shock, John saw approaching him across the croft the head of the brass-knobbed bedstead on which the Old Warrior had slept. It was carried by two small boys, one holding each end, and even so both were staggering beneath its antiquated weight. John knew that his mother had given the bedstead away. Now he saw how the gift had been appreciated.

"Lean it against the wall," Tom commanded the panting youngsters. He looked at it with a despising eye. "Junk," he said. "Rubbish! Not worth carting away. What d'you think that thing's worth?"

"Two rats, please," piped the bolder of the two children, and the younger nodded vigorously and produced from his pocket a canvas bag in which he proposed to take home the fruits of his deal. "We've got a cage for 'em," he volunteered, "with a treadmill."

Tom Hannaway looked at John and Arnold Ryerson. "Two rats!" he said. "Did you hear that, boys? Two rats! They'd ruin a man. Two rats for half a rotten bedstead that's not worth taking to the marine store dealer. Can you kids read?"

The boys looked at him with pinched little faces. They nodded.

"Well, read that," said Tom Hannaway, "'whose decision is final.' My decision is one rat. Give us the bag."

He put the rat into the bag. "That's a buck. Bring me the other half of the bed, and you can have a doe. See?"

Again the youngsters nodded mutely. "Well, then, get along now." They trotted away, one of them holding the squirming bag. Tom turned then to the bedstead leaning against the wall. A broad grin of satisfaction widened on his face. "There's a bargain!" he exclaimed. "That'll fetch eighteenpence if it fetches a penny."

"You diddled 'em," said Arnold Ryerson. He left it at that, but there was no mistaking the condemnation in his tone.

"Of course I diddled 'em," Hannaway answered. "What are customers for? And d'you think I'll give 'em a doe if they come again? I will not then. It was a buck this time and it will be a buck next time. And if anyone gets a doe this time he'll get a doe next time. There's not going to be any competition around here."

By the time the rats were all disposed of, there was a miscellaneous litter on the ground at Tom Hannaway's feet: wornout coats and trousers, rags that had never been any garment that could be named, odds and ends of brass and lead and iron, jam jars, bones, bottles and bundles of newspapers. He continued to be high-handed. Some of the customers went empty away. "What! A rat that I've spent days and weeks personally breeding for an old coat like that? You leave it, and bring something next week. Then we'll see."

Now that the perambulator was empty of rats, Tom piled in his booty. The bed end, resting precariously across the top, threatened either to flatten or capsize the crazy little vehicle. "You coming to Darkie Cheap's?" Tom asked.

Arnold Ryerson shook his head. "Going home to read," he said briefly, and went.

"Reading! You're always reading!" Tom shouted after him. Arnold did not answer. In a moment he had turned the corner by the raw house end and disappeared.

"You come, kid," Tom said, for he wanted someone's hand to steady the bedstead on the perambulator while he pushed. "Hold onto that. Don't let it wobble."

John was delighted. Never before had Tom Hannaway invited his company. He took hold of the bedstead with his puny hand – the bedstead whose monstrous brass knobs had for so long been so familiar, which did not prevent it from having, out here in the street, under the light of this red wintry sun, an alien air.

They went trundling on through the glum unbeautiful thoroughfares, and suddenly Tom said surprisingly: "D'you know what I'm going to have some day? A racehorse!"

He stopped pushing, spat on his hands, and rubbed them up and down the legs of his trousers as he considered the effect of his announcement on young John Shawcross.

"Where will you keep it?" John asked, his mind occupied with an incongruous image of a polished, slim-legged horse confined in a Broadbent Street back yard.

"Where d'you think? In my racing stables," Tom answered. "Come on. Don't let it wobble."

Darkie Cheap's rag and bone business proclaimed itself while they were still a long way off. Its rotten odour permeated all the short street in which it was situated. It was in a large shed, whose only light came from the double doors that stood open. John, who had never been there before, looked round him curiously. At the end, and on both sides, the wall space was divided by hanging sacks into many small cubicles, and each cubicle was cluttered with a different sort of junk: one with bones that smelled abominably, one with old clothes, one with old iron, another with lead, another with brass. There seemed no end to the variety of rubbish that Darkie Cheap had accumulated here in this tall, dark building, floored with earth and festooned with cobwebs. In the middle of such floor space as the cubicles left uncovered stood an immense iron weighing machine.

John stood there, still holding onto the bedstead, till, his eyes at last accustomed to the gloom, he perceived Darkie Cheap himself. This was the more difficult to do because Cheap really was a darkie; you first became aware, in this his chosen habitat, of the whites of his eyes. John had often seen Darkie Cheap about the streets: an old, wrinkled Negro with curly grey hair, harmless enough; but here in his dark lair, amid the filth and the stench, he took on the proportions of an ogre moving with evil stealth among the clothes and bones of his victims.

The boy's thin hand tightened its grip upon the bedstead; but Tom Hannaway was not afraid. "How much for this lot?" he demanded with noisy assurance.

Then the comedy that had been enacted on the croft was gone through again with a change of characters. Tom, who had looked down his nose at everything he had acquired, now praised extravagantly the goods he had come to sell. But Darkie Cheap was not impressed by bravado. He quietly sorted out everything: rags, brass, iron, bones, each into a separate pile. The knobs were unscrewed from the bedstead in spite of Tom's hot protest that they were part of an article that should sell on its own merits, which, he pointed out, were considerable. Darkie Cheap said nothing. His bony pink-palmed hands threw the knobs among the brass, the rest among the iron. Then each lot was weighed: iron with iron, brass with brass, bone with bone. When this was done, he, announced his price, and there was nothing for Tom Hannaway to do but take it.

"That makes twenty-five and ninepence," he confided to John as they set out together for Broadbent Street.

"How much does a racehorse cost?" John inquired.

Tom let out a howl of laughter. "You don't think I'm saving up for a racehorse now, do you? Lord, kid! A racehorse costs hundreds and hundreds. There'll be a lot to do before I get my racehorse. I'll have to get where the money is. That's the first thing to do: get where the money is."

They had reached the Hannaway house, noisy with Mrs. Hannaway's voice upraised in song and with the howling of many children. Tom stood for a moment at the door, looking up at the round red sun, smothered in a smoky aura, as though he wished its disk were gold and that he could pluck it there and then out of the sky.

Gordon Stansfield came home, as he always did, to the midday dinner, but, as this was Saturday, he did not go back to Birley Artingstall's. He said: "Get your cap, John. Let's take a walk to town."

He did not ask Ellen to go with them, because he knew that she would not. It would take a lot to shift Ellen out of her house, but she was glad to see John out of it occasionally. Gordon knew that, and took the boy out whenever he could, so that Ellen might be alone.

So John set out with this placid commonplace man to whom he owed so much. Gordon had changed from his working clothes into a suit of stiff-looking brown cloth, with a collar that stood up all round his neck. A black cravat was bound about the collar, finished with a big bow. From a buttonhole high up in his waistcoat a silver chain dropped down to the silver watch in his pocket. His boots were fastened at the sides with buttons. But you didn't see much of this, because he wore a heavy overcoat, rather tight-waisted and flowing out into almost the fullness of a skirt. You saw, though, the hard squarish bowler that he wore on his head. No stranger would have looked twice at Gordon as he walked down Broadbent Street, one hand holding John's, the other rhythmically thudding to the ground a holly stick with a silver shield engraved with his initials. No stranger would have looked twice at the face that would have seemed thinner without its greying mutton-chop whiskers, at the kind brown eyes and the undistinguished nose and mouth. But Ellen stood at the door and watched till the pair had turned to the right into Great Ancoats Street.

It was no great distance to town. They went through Oldham Street where, on that tragic day of high summer so long ago, the Old Warrior had hidden the sabre in his brother's barber shop. Now, grand new shops were there, and when they came out into Piccadilly John thought he had never seen so much exciting life crowded together into one place. Hansom cabs dashed by and four-wheelers went more soberly. There were horse-drawn omnibuses, and splendid private carriages, and horsemen jogging quietly along till release from the press should permit them to go more gaily.

Gordon was a persistent walker. He did not dawdle to allow John to look into shop-windows. He went forward at his steady pace across Piccadilly into Mosley Street, and through Mosley Street to the Free Trade Hall. It was only when he got there that he at last paused, on the other side of the street, and looked across at the heavy solemn building that stood on the spot where the dragoons had ridden down the people.

"That's where it was, John," he said, thinking of the old man whom, yesterday, they had laid in the grave. "That's where your grandfather picked up his sabre. But it was morning, with the sun shining, and there was green grass where you see that big building now."

And that's where Emma was killed, the child was thinking. *That's where the soldier cut off her hair with the ribbon on it.*

He did not tell Gordon about the hair and the ribbon. To withhold this small piece of knowledge even from Gordon made it secretly and excitingly his.

The daylight was draining out of the sky and the air was keen as they turned and made their way to Albert Square. The gas-lamps were lit and shining fitfully on the white façade of the Town Hall. They stood right back across the square to look at it soaring up into the night, its towers and pinnacles dark perpendicular smudges on the greater darkness of the sky. They had often come to watch it rising there at the heart of the city, with all its ropes and cranes and pulleys and scaffoldings, its workmen scaling the raw and dizzy cliffs of masonry, its noise of hammers, saws, and chisels. And now it was finished, a virgin building, so soon to be befouled by the smoke and fume of the very prosperity that had called it into being. With childlike awe, Gordon walked round it, occasionally smiting his stick against the mighty ashlar of its base. With satisfaction he noted by his big silver watch that he needed nearly ten minutes to make the circuit.

Then on they went by Cross Street to the Shambles, leaving the last strident note of progress and finding themselves among the little crooked streets and leaning inns and houses that clustered where Manchester from the beginning had clustered, whether Roman camp or Saxon village, alongside the Irwell stream.

Here were cosier streets than those they had till now been treading: streets whose shops had windows bulging outward, patterned with many tiny panes; whose public houses had a friendly look, red-curtained, and a friendly sound as laughter and applause bespoke a sing-song; whose life seemed as much underground as above it. It was underground that Gordon now plunged, down a flight of rickety wooden stairs, into a catacomb of books.

John had been there before and knew what to expect. A call upon the second-hand bookseller was never omitted from a visit to Manchester. It seemed to the child that you could lose yourself in the place. You turned right and you turned left, and whichever way you turned you could turn again and still find yourself confronting a vista of books rising on either hand from floor to ceiling. In each of these corridors a gas light burned, enclosed in wire; and the smell, compounded of decaying paper and leather, gas-heated air and some aboriginal earthy odour, was one that he was never to forget.

Somewhere, at some time, if you went on exploring long enough, you would come upon Mr. Suddaby, a dusty old spider at the heart of his amazing web. Perhaps you would come upon him in his own special nook, where a fire burned, though by what tortuous means its smoke was conveyed to the outer air it was difficult to imagine. As likely as not, he would have a meal, sent in from a neighbouring eating house, on the table before him, and, with his carpet-slippered feet extended to the fire, he would be dividing his attention between that and the *Manchester Guardian,* propped against an ale bottle. He was an old man made of parchment, with a white moustache and little pointed beard that somehow emphasized the ironic cast of his yellowish face. He wore a black velvet skull-cap from beneath whose edge an outflow of white curly hair escaped; and a coat and waistcoat of black velvet, stained and dusty and not without historical reference to the meals he might so frequently be found consuming.

If you did not find him there in his own particular and domestic niche, which was shared by Sheba, his snow-white Persian cat, emerald-eyed, you might find him sitting on the top step of a ladder in one of his own bookish aisles, reading one of his own volumes; or, with his hands behind his back and his eyes sunk apparently in contemplation of his carpet slippers, he would be found fixed in thought, moveless and soundless.

Tonight he was doing none of these things. He was talking in his low-pitched voice, which seemed concerned always not to awaken the echoes of his own catacombs, to a boy whom John saw at once to be Arnold Ryerson. Arnold was looking red and embarrassed, and Mr. Suddaby was looking at once grave and mischievous.

"Here's a serious case, Mr. Stansfield," he said, recognizing his old customer. "I've caught a Tartar, a lawyer, a great argufier. We've had it out all ways, this boy and I, and now I'll turn the case over to you. What you say, I shall accept. This boy discovered a sixpenny book – namely, this battered copy of the *Idylls of the King* – in the tuppenny box. He argues that a book in a tuppenny box costs tuppence; and I maintain that a sixpenny book costs sixpence, wherever it may have fallen by accident. What do you say?"

Gordon tucked his holly stick under his arm, took the book, and allowed the pages to flicker through his fingers. Presently, he read, half aloud:

"Then from the dawn it seemed there came, but faint
As from beyond the limit of the world,
Like the last echo born of a great cry,
Sounds, as if some fair city were one voice
Around a king returning from his wars."

Gordon's murmuring voice ceased, and in the silence the four of them could hear the gas flame singing like a gnat. Then Arnold Ryerson, his face lit up, said: "You like it, too, Mr. Stansfield?"

Gordon nodded; and Mr. Suddaby, without the book, continued the quotation:

"Thereat once more he moved about and clomb
Ev'n to the highest he could climb, and saw,
Straining his eyes beneath an arch of hand,
Or thought he saw, the speck that bare the King,
Down that long water opening on the deep
Somewhere far off, pass on and on, and go
From less to less and vanish into light.
And the new sun rose, bringing the new year.

"I don't know what's coming over boys in these days," said Mr. Suddaby severely. "They want that sort of thing for tuppence – immortal verse for tuppence. What d'you say, Mr. Stansfield?"

"I've only got tuppence," Arnold Ryerson intervened.

"Pay your tuppence," said Gordon, "and I'll pay fourpence. Then everyone will be satisfied."

"No, no!" said old Suddaby, lifting his skull-cap with three fingers and scratching his head with the little one. "If there's generosity about, I can be as generous as the next man. We'll all pay tuppence each."

Suddenly John piped up: "Arnold, let me pay a penny."

At that Suddaby's face creased in an ironic grin. "Nay! Damn it all," he said. "This is becoming preposterous. Take the book, boy, and have done with it." And he thrust the *Idylls* into Arnold's hands.

Five minutes later Gordon was walking home with the boys. For himself, he had bought Hugh Miller's *Old Red Sandstone* and for John a coverless copy of *The Pilgrim's Progress*.

No one was ever asked into the Stansfields' house on a Saturday night. When Gordon and John returned, high tea was ready in the kitchen, and John well knew the unvarying routine that would follow. This was Gordon's sermon-writing night. As a local preacher, he was not called on every Sunday, but every Saturday he worked on a sermon.

He and Ellen washed up in the scullery; then Ellen put the red cloth on to the kitchen table and brought out from a dresser drawer the blotting-pad, the inkpot and pen, the half-sheets of note-paper which were the size Gordon liked for writing on. She placed a Bible, Cruden's *Concordance* and the Methodist Hymn-Book alongside the blotting-pad. She pulled out the wooden chair, ready for him to sit down. This was the total extent of Ellen's secretarial work in any week, and not for anything would she have abrogated one gesture of it. Then she sat down with a basket of mending at her side, and put a silence-commanding finger to her lips as she looked at John, sitting with his new book in the Old Warrior's chair on the other side of the purring fire.

The boy snuggled into the chair, aware of the keen cold without and of the warm silence within, a silence broken only by the steady scratching of Gordon's pen, the tinkle of ash into the grate, the tiny rasping of a woollen sock over his mother's rough-skinned hands.

As the hands of the clock touched nine, he did not need to be spoken to: he rose quietly, and Ellen rose, too, ready to steal out of the room with him, no word spoken, no good night said. But that night, for a wonder, as the boy got up, Gordon laid down his pen, removed the steel-rimmed spectacles from his nose, and smiled at him. "Good night, John," he said. "Yon Arnold Ryerson's a nice lad. See as much of him as you can."

Chapter Three

When John Shawcross was fourteen years old, he signed his name for the first time J. Hamer Shawcross. It was not till later that he omitted the J.

He had followed Gordon's advice and was seeing much of Arnold Ryerson. His little piping offer of a penny toward the *Idylls of the King* had tickled the fancy of the elder boy, who began, whenever he met John, to talk to him with a grave, humorous condescension, and this attitude soon gave way to one of unconditional friendship. Arnold was walking home from school one evening during the week after that encounter in Mr. Suddaby's, puzzling his honest head over a poser in arithmetic. It was dark, and he paused under a street lamp with the text-book open in his hand. John Shawcross, walking home by himself, found him there and said: "Can I help you, Arnold?"

He had never before called this bigger boy Arnold, and a surge both of shyness and of pride went through him as he uttered the name. Arnold was taken aback, and looked at the youngster, not knowing whether to reprove his cheek, to burst out laughing, or to accept his offer. John's embarrassment deepened under the stare. He pulled off his cap and nervously swept his hand through his hair that drooped upon his forehead. "I think I could," he said.

"It wouldn't be fair," Arnold answered. "Even supposing you could do it. I'm expected to do these sums myself."

John brightened under the friendlier tone. "Perhaps I could show you the idea," he said. "You come round to our house tonight."

Arnold said that he would, and John ran home strangely excited. He felt sure that he could help. He did not know what problem was worrying Arnold, but he had seen that the book was an arithmetic primer, and he knew that he was good at arithmetic. He liked it. He was far ahead of anyone in his class. Voluntarily, he had been doing advanced sums for a long time. His heart warmed with the thought of showing off his knowledge to a boy two classes ahead of himself, a boy who would soon be leaving school altogether.

But there was more in it than that. He had no friend. He had often enough been proud of this. He had read of heroes whose lives were lonely because of their greatness. No one understood them because there was no one of their stature; and so he walked with a dragging gait, and was lonely and misunderstood, and enjoyed it. For the first time, he had asked someone to "come to our house."

"Ah, my friends! Standing here once more, on the platform of this historic hall, at the heart of this great city which has so signally honoured me today, what memories crowd about me! What memories of loneliness and secret struggle! None so lonely as the poor child is lonely. To whom shall he tell his hopes? Into what ear shall he pour the urgency of awakening aspiration?

"It is not my intention to recall to this too indulgent audience the state of utter friendlessness which I knew not far from the spot where now the warmth of your presence makes all that happened then seem but an evil dream. I would only say to any who is here tonight, young, friendless, aspiring, lonely: 'Have courage! The way may be long but it winds upward. Have faith. The night may be dark but it brightens toward a dawn.' I, too, have cried: 'Oh, for a friend!' and known no answer." (The Rt. Hon. Hamer Shawcross, P.C., M.P., at the Free Trade Hall, Manchester, on the evening of the day when he received the freedom of the city, December 1934.)

From the beginning, Arnold Ryerson was all that a man could ask of a friend.

"Something new, isn't it?" Ellen asked when John poured out in one excited breath, as soon as he was over the doorstep: "Mother, I've asked Arnold Ryerson to come round tonight."

"Oh, you have, have you? And what d'you think your father's going to do with a lot of chattering boys around him?"

John remembered in time. "It's Father's class night," he said. "I thought of that. And Father told me to see as much as I could of Arnold."

"Seeing's one thing," said Ellen. "Asking him here's another. Well, go and wash yourself."

When Gordon came home and they were all seated at the table, she said: "My lord here's branching out – asking people to the house, if you please."

"It's Arnold Ryerson," said John. "We want to do sums together."

Gordon looked at John and at Ellen and at the well-provisioned table that was spread with ham and tongue, cake and jam, bread and butter. "It's a pity you didn't ask him to eat with us," he said. "That lad doesn't get too much to eat."

"If you want people to eat with you," said Ellen, "you must ask the fat 'uns. Them as haven't got enough are backward to admit it."

Gordon sighed. "There are too many of those Ryersons."

"Six children," said Ellen. "I don't know where they all sleep."

Gordon took a drink of tea. "There's room enough here. I shall be out tonight; but whether I'm out or in, there's room enough. If the lad's anxious to work, he won't find much room or much peace in that house. Let him come here."

"Well, they won't worry me," said Ellen. "I'll only want a corner of the table for my ironing."

Gordon looked at her with a smile that meant he had a plan. "No, they won't worry you, lass," he said. "They won't be near you."

"Nay, they can't go in the parlour and catch their deaths. There's no fire there."

"It's possible to light a fire," said Gordon, "but not in the parlour. No. Listen. Do you know what I always longed for when I was a boy, and never could get? A room of my own!"

"There's no room in this house going begging. Two up and two down don't leave much to spare."

"There's John's bedroom. There's nothing in it now but his little bed and a chest of drawers. I'd like him to turn it into a study."

Gordon brought out the last word diffidently. A study was an unusual thing to talk about; but it was a thing he had been thinking about. It was something wrapped up rather obscurely with all the intentions he had cherished for the child ever since his decree: No mill for John.

He looked rather anxiously at Ellen and the child. "You know," he said. "Nothing terrible. Nothing drastic. Just a place where he can keep his books as he gets them, and read them; and perhaps some day he'll want to write something."

"Well," Ellen burst out, "if the kitchen's good enough for you to write in—"

"Ah, yes – me. That's all right," said Gordon modestly. "My little bits of sermons and so forth – that's one thing. But I'd like to think of John working away up there. We could fit in a little writing-table and a bookcase, and that old chair could go up." He waved towards the Old Warrior's relic. "That would be cosy alongside the fire."

"Fire!"

It was the first word John had interposed into the conversation, the first idea to set his mind alight. A fire in his bedroom! This was revolutionary. Immediately, all that Gordon had been saying took new shape. He had been envisaging a cold, cheerless room, himself banished there, sitting in a chair with an overcoat over his shoulders to keep him warm. But now the light spread out from this one word Gordon had spoken. It fell on the hypothetical books; it warmed the chair and glinted on the not-yet-acquired writing table. It turned exile in Siberia to a home of one's own.

"Can we have a fire tonight when Arnold comes?" he asked excitedly.

"Why not?" said Gordon. "Thank God, we're not so poor that we can't manage that. I'll see to it now." He wiped his mouth on his handkerchief, the signal that his meal was ended, and Ellen and John bowed their heads. "Bless these mercies to our use and Thy service, for Christ's sake. Amen."

Ellen was up before him. "Nay!" she cried, lapsing into the dialect that she tried hard to overcome. "Tha'll not lay t'fire. If we're to have this nonsense, tha can leave it to me. Though what'll happen when Ah lay match to t'sticks, Ah don't know. That chimney's not been swep' sin' Ah don't know when. Full o' crows' nests or summat, Ah shouldn't wonder."

"It's a long time, lass, since crows nested in Ancoats," Gordon reminded her.

"Aye, but it's longer sin' that chimney were swep'."

She bustled off upon the job, and John cried: "Can we take the chair up now, Father?"

"Of course we can," said Gordon. "You take the cushions. I'll take the rest."

It was almost as difficult to take the Old Warrior's chair up the narrow stairs as it had been to bring his body down them. But before

Gordon set out to conduct his weekly Methodist class meeting, all was done that could be done at that time. Ellen's fears were groundless: the fire drew well, though the grate was a pitifully small one that held little more than a handful of coal. But there it was, glowing, a wonderful transformer. The solitary chair was before it. As yet there was nothing to justify the word "study." A lamp burned on the chest of drawers.

When the job was done, Ellen, practically, went down to her washing-up. John stood with his back to the fire, entranced, excitedly sweeping the hair off his forehead. Gordon looked about him with a slow, tranquil satisfaction. He felt that he was nearer to something that had been in his heart – he hardly knew what, but something important, and something that had been entrusted to him alone.

When Arnold Ryerson arrived, Ellen answered the door. "You'd better go upstairs," she said. "The room's on t'left. Nice goings-on."

Arnold hung his cap on a peg in the passage and went upstairs, mystified. Gordon shook his hand. "Well, lad," he said, "I'm glad you've come. I hope you'll come again. Come a lot. Come whenever you want to. Well, now, I've got to go. I'll leave you and John to get on with your work."

But he did not go. He hesitated and fidgeted in the doorway, then came back into the room. "I think I'd like to say a word of prayer," he said simply.

John felt the blood rush into his cheeks. He looked at Arnold Ryerson aghast. For the first time Gordon's religion had cut into a personal relationship, and the child felt shaken. Arnold Ryerson said quietly: "Yes, Mr. Stansfield," and without invitation knelt on the meagre rug before the meagre fire. Then John knelt, too, and Gordon Stansfield knelt between the two boys.

"O Christ," he said, "who in Thy earthly pilgrimage didst know and take comfort from the friendship of simple men, grant to these boys that they may be friends to one another, to cherish and sustain one another in all the tribulations that life may bring. And grant that out of this moment, in this humble room, some thing may grow and increase to Thy glory and to Thy knowledge among men."

John did not speak. Arnold Ryerson said in a firm voice: "Amen."

When Gordon was gone, John said: "Sit down, Arnold," and waved his hand toward the chair newly arrived in his room.

Arnold sat down. "This is very nice," he said. "You're lucky, John, to have a room like this."

"It is my study," John said proudly. "I am to have a bookcase and a writing-table." He sat on the rug at Arnold's feet. "I must get a couple of sausages," he said, "for the door and window."

Arnold looked about him slowly, as though daunted by magnificence. "I've never known anybody before with a room all to himself." He sighed. "It's terrible in our house if you want to read or do any homework. There's nowhere at all."

"Why don't you use the parlour?" John asked. The front room downstairs was always the parlour in Broadbent Street.

"Because my three sisters sleep in it," Arnold said simply, "and we three boys sleep in the back room upstairs. That only leaves the other bedroom, where my father and mother sleep, and the kitchen. There's always something going on in the kitchen – washing or ironing or bathing or arguing."

"Well, you come here whenever you want to," John said. "My father means that."

Arnold eyed the stingy little grate. "It's going to cost you a lot in coal."

"Oh, we can afford it," John answered grandly.

They did not do much work that night. John had a look at Arnold's arithmetic book, solved his problem, and explained the principle. Then they gave up all pretence of doing anything but enjoy the unexpected position they found themselves in. They walked about the room – although there were no more than a few paces to walk – and they discussed its furnishing as if the equipment of a cathedral were in question.

"You let me furnish this," said Arnold. "I know how to do it. I'm used to doing things on the cheap"; and furnish it he did. He came round the next night with a few planks, a saw, a hammer, and nails.

There was a recess on either side of the outjutting chimney breast. In one Arnold fixed up the bookcase. He nailed pieces of lath to two of his planks and stood these on the skirting-board in the recess. Then he cut his other planks to make shelves. He cut them infinitesimally too long, so that they had to be jammed down hard to rest on the lath supports. This pressure kept the side pieces upright and the whole taut. In the other recess, the "writing-table" was made in the same way. There were two lower shelves for books, and the third shelf, at writing height, was two planks wide instead of one. That made the writing-table.

When all this was done, Arnold conscientiously swept up the sawdust with the hearth-brush and threw it on the fire. Then he took from his pocket the arithmetic primer and the *Idylls of the King*. He put them solemnly on one of the shelves. Even in so small and haphazard a bookcase they looked lonely; but the two boys regarded them with satisfaction, almost with wonder. There was no doubt that this simple carpentry, adorning either side of the fireplace, made a great difference to the look of the room. They called downstairs to Gordon and Ellen to come up and look.

"That's fine," said Gordon. "We shall have to see Mr. Suddaby on Saturday and start filling these shelves. And we needn't wait till then. Let's see what we've got downstairs for a beginning."

The boys didn't go with him. They hovered about the work, touching it now and then, and again standing off from it and regarding it, rapt.

Ellen came back first. She brought a kitchen chair and placed it in front of the writing-shelf. "That'd better stay there," she said. "Happen I'll make a cushion for it."

Gordon brought half a dozen books – a strange lot: *Birds of the Bible, Wuthering Heights, Barnaby Rudge*, some bound volumes of the *Cornhill Magazine*, and a volume of John Wesley's sermons. Before putting the sermons on the shelf, he looked here and there through the pages. "If either of you lads ever takes to local preaching," he said, "you'll want this. You've got to be well up in some of these sermons, you know, before they'll accept you."

He looked at them expectantly, as though he would have welcomed a fervent response then and there, but they had no thoughts for anything save the wonders which were being enacted before them. "Well, think on," Gordon said; and then he added to the collection the last book he had brought up – Southey's *Life of Wesley*.

When they were left alone once more, John took two of the longest nails Arnold had brought, stood on the kitchen chair, and drove them into the wall over the fireplace. He took the Old Warrior's sabre from under the bed and hung it proudly as for so long it had hung in the kitchen downstairs. Then he remembered that among the Old Warrior's possessions in the chest of drawers there were two books. He took them out and added them to the collection on the shelves: the poems of Sam Bamford and the Bible.

"I don't think we can do anything else tonight, Arnold," he said; and at the same time Gordon's voice was heard, calling Arnold down to drink a cup of cocoa before going home.

The next day, as soon as the child was gone to school, Ellen went out, bought a penny bottle of ink, some pens, pencils, sheets of blotting paper. When she got home, she made up the rag cushion for the kitchen chair. She dug out two old tin candlesticks and put candles in them, and having furnished the writing-shelf she placed these upon it.

There seemed to be a conspiracy to do things in John's room. Arnold arrived that night with a jam-pot, a brush, and some crystals of permanganate of potash. Soon all the shelves were stained. Gordon had put a glue-pot on the fire during his evening meal. When he had eaten he took the pot upstairs, and then produced a fine piece of thin red leather, just the size to cover the writing shelf. He had tooled a gold design into the edge, and he applied the skin to the wood with a craftsman's loving care.

This was not all. He had brought strips of scalloped leather, also beaten with a design, and little brass nails with finely-wrought heads to fasten the strips to the edges of the bookshelves. When all was done the writing-shelf and the bookshelves looked very different from the raw job of the night before.

"You've got Birley Artingstall to thank for that," Gordon said. "I told him what we were doing, and he said he'd like to do a bit towards it."

So the first "study" that Hamer Shawcross ever knew came into being. Gordon and Ellen, Arnold Ryerson and Birley Artingstall: these had a hand in it. Hamer Shawcross alone did nothing but accept the good will and the good work of them all; and there he stood, pushing back his long shining hair, full of pride, looking at the shelves and the books and the curved cold symbol gleaming on the wall.

The walk to Manchester, the call on Mr. Suddaby, and the buying of a book or two had long been a Saturday ritual with Gordon and John. Now Arnold Ryerson began to join them. Arnold, at nearly fourteen, was unusually tall for his age: he was almost as tall as Gordon Stansfield. John was small. If you had seen these three from the back, going along Great Ancoats Street on some cold winter afternoon, you would have thought you were looking at two brothers, taking out a son and nephew. They strode along with John always in the middle, sometimes holding Gordon's hand, but never Arnold's. Small as he was, he never felt that Arnold was a superior or protector. Through that small matter of arithmetic, he had established an ascendancy. Arnold seemed to recognize it, and occasionally even acknowledged it, taking John's advice about the books to be bought at Suddaby's. In the catacombs, Gordon left them alone. He went his own way, looking for books that would give him things to point his sermons; and the two boys went theirs, whispering, rustling over the pages, looking at pictures. More often than not, the final choice for them would be made by Mr. Suddaby. He had come to expect them, and he would have a few books put by. It was thanks to him that they bought no rubbish.

When they got back to Broadbent Street, Arnold stayed to high tea, and then, Ellen having prepared the table for Gordon's sermon-writing, the boys would go upstairs, put a match to the fire, and sit down to their new books. Little enough use was made of the writing-shelf, but there was now a second easy chair. All through that winter they read and read, saying little, but growing toward one another, so that each would have felt a sense of loss if anything should have chanced to put an end to this happy and harmonious state of affairs.

Of course, it had to end. It ended with brutal violence. All through that winter, when John was twelve and Arnold Ryerson was fourteen, they spent three or four evenings together every week, with the lamp-flame singing quietly on the table between them, sometimes with the wind and the rain beating on the window, sometimes with the silence of great cold without, and once or twice with snow falling, so that they pulled aside the curtains and watched the dithering whiteness whirling down out of the black void of the night.

John would not now casually say "Good night," pick up the sausage from in front of the door, and unceremoniously watch Arnold go. He would go with him, stand about the kitchen as Arnold drank the cup of cocoa that Ellen always provided, then help him into his coat and see him out. His mind, by the end of the winter, was stored with memories: of Arnold rushing pell-mell through the rain; of Arnold standing still outside the door, lifting his face up till the snowflakes fell upon it and the light of the street lamp illumined it; of Arnold entranced by a night when there had never been so many stars. The sky was pricked full of them, sparkling icily, and he had run across

the road with Arnold and leaned on the canal parapet and looked
down to see the water of the canal shining like black velvet tricked
out with diamonds.

And now he no longer felt lonely in the little pallet bed tucked
unobtrusively into a corner of the room as he had felt when first the
Old Warrior went away and the big bed disappeared. He slept with
a glow still warm in the grate and the warmth of Arnold's presence
seeming still to irradiate the room.

It was not so good when the summer came. The mean streets of
Ancoats stewed in the heat. The room was stuffy, and, without the
lure of a fire and drawn curtains, it lost its romance. They did not
use it so much, but every Saturday they went with Gordon Stansfield
to Manchester.

On a Saturday toward the end of that July they were walking home
at five o'clock when Tom Hannaway, breathless with running, met
them. "Hurry up, Arnold! Hurry up! Your father's dying!" he shouted,
and, hooking his hand into Arnold's elbow, he snatched him from the
other two and whirled him away. John and Gordon quickened their
pace, and when they got to Broadbent Street there was a little crowd
leaning on the canal wall outside the Ryerson house, looking open-
mouthed at the doctor's gleaming victoria and polished horse that
made John think of Tom Hannaway's racehorse, and at the coachman
sitting up aloft.

The doctor came out, top-hatted for all the sultry warmth of the
day, just as John and Gordon reached the house. Gordon knew him
– one of the Emmott Street upper ten who never stayed behind to the
prayer-meetings – and asked for news. The doctor shook his head.
"He's finished."

A little gasp went through the crowd, some of whom had seen
Mr. Ryerson go out not an hour before. And now he was finished. And
all those children! There was a small boy who had seen it happen, and
he kept on telling his story again and again. "I seen Mr. Ryerson walking down the street and he met Mr. Hannaway and said 'Hallo, Mike!'
an' then he fell down dead."

Gordon thought of the florid Ryerson, so different from his thin,
diffident son: bloated, self-confident, with the face full of purple veins.
He had driven a dray, and sometimes, watching him haul on the reins
to bring his two great horses to a standstill, you would think he would

go off in apoplexy there and then. And now that sultry day, that excessive touch of sun, had done it; and there was Mrs. Ryerson, as the neighbours pityingly said, with all those children.

When they had finished their high tea, Ellen began to prepare the table for Gordon to write. "Not tonight, lass," he said. "Don't bother. I'm not preaching tomorrow, and that can wait. I'm going along to see Birley. He might know of something for Arnold. You can come along with me, John."

The shop was shut, and Gordon banged the polished brass knocker on the door that led to Birley Artingstall's private apartments. John had never been through that door before. When it was opened he found that it gave straight upon a stairway, up which Birley preceded them. He led them to his sitting-room at the rear, looking upon nothing but back yards and walls and chimney-pots. It was a very warm evening and the window was pushed up. John went straight to it and gazed at the uninspiring prospect.

"The abomination of desolation, eh, lad?" said Birley. "Aye, it's pretty bad in the summer, pretty bad. You must bring him round on some winter night, Gordon. That's the time, my boy, to see an old bachelor making himself comfortable. Have you got any imagination? "

John gazed at all the seals and medals dingle-dangling on the chain that adorned the old man's lean belly, and raised his glance to the fair drooping moustaches and the bright, boring blue eyes. He did not answer.

"He's got plenty," said Gordon. "As much as most."

"Well, just imagine this room on a winter night, my boy, with that dull-looking grate full of a cheerful fire, and the curtains drawn, and me in that chair with that lamp on a table at my elbow. Imagine a pot of nice hot tea, and this pipe in my mouth, and John Wesley's *Journal* to read. Have you read it?"

The child shook his head. "Read it," said Birley Artingstall, pointing a bony finger at him. "The times I've had with John Wesley! Up first thing in the morning, onto a horse, and off we go! Through rain and snow and wind; over the moors and the hills, preaching, being stoned, gathering in the souls of men! And all without leaving Ancoats. All without leaving this fireside. Ah, this is a precious spot to me! Come some winter night."

Leather and John Wesley seemed to be the dominant things in the room. As Birley and Gordon discussed the case of Arnold Ryerson, John prowled about. On the mantelpiece was a white bust of Wesley with curls of hair falling down to his shoulders and a parson's bands under his chin, and over it hung a large steel engraving of the itinerant saint still at last, lying on his death-bed, surrounded by disciples. Among them, an old gentleman was holding an ear-trumpet composedly to his ear, in the apparent hope of catching some last salutary words. Standing by him was a child, who looked younger than John himself, staring at the mounds made under the bedclothes by the dying man's feet. The *Journal* and the *Sermons*, and many volumes of the *Minutes of Conference*, as well as Southey's *Life of Wesley*, were in the bookcase, and over the bookcase, set in a surround of white pasteboard and framed, was a small printed card, which John did not know was Birley Artingstall's first "quarterly ticket," attesting his membership of the Wesleyan Church.

The leather interested the boy more than the Methodism. Birley's trade was also his private joy, and he had surrounded himself with fine craftsmanship of his own devising. All his chairs were splendidly upholstered, and all his books had been taken from their original bindings and bound anew. They were a lovely sight, with the gold lettering shining on blue, green, red, and brown leather. Even the prosaic *Minutes of Conference* had been transformed, and a long row of them shone in their splendid bindings as though they were works of exalted imagination.

There were boxes of leather, a pen-tray of leather, a stationery-rack of leather, and upon the panels of the door Birley had applied skins tooled and gilded into charming patterns.

With half an eye as he talked with Gordon, he saw the child's interest, and when the discussion was ended and Gordon rose, Birley said: "You come in the winter, my boy. Then you'll see how all these things should look. And take this now. There's a lovely thing for you. You won't pick up a thing like that every day. You take that home now, and when you look at it, just think: 'I must go and see that old chap in the winter.' Remind him, Gordon."

All the way home John hugged the beautiful leather box, rubbing his fingers over its embossed configurations, looking with satisfaction at its gilded embellishment. He knew what he was going to do with it.

He was going to make a casket of it to contain a brown curl and a piece of stained red ribbon.

In that immense and still new Town Hall that John and Gordon had recently circumnavigated Alderman Hawley Artingstall found a casket for his own magnificence. Up the finely twisting main staircase, onto the great landing whose floor was sown with a mosaic of bees – symbolic, he reflected, of wise men gathering their honey – along echoing corridor after corridor he would go, peeping into committee-rooms and Mayor's parlour, council chamber and great hall embellished with Ford Madox Brown frescoes; and never did he get over the wonder of having at last a setting so appropriate to his own grandeur.

Watching him standing there looking down from a tall pointed window upon the people walking languidly in the heat across Albert Square, you would never have guessed that he was the brother of that blond and bony Viking Birley Artingstall. Hawley was puffed out in the face and the belly and the pride. He had a habit of puffing out his cheeks and puffing out his big moustache and, when he spoke in public, as he loved to do, of puffing out his words. He had never succeeded, as Birley had, in overcoming his Lancashire speech, and as he had not been able to cure it, he intensified it, and carried it off as a matter of pride. "Nay, Ah'm jannock. What Ah says Ah means. Ah'm not soft in t'speech or in t'brain, like some."

He had always hated the leather shop that his father had founded. He had always hated Ancoats with its dirt and misery; and when, a young man in his twenties, he had started his draper's shop in Oldham Street, he couldn't understand why Birley declined to join him. Looking back on it all, he thought Birley was daft, sticking there over a shop in a noisy, soot-smothered region, with no one to look after him, and no one to talk to at nights.

"Birley Artingstall, Leather." Hawley smiled sometimes at the quaint inscription. As for him, he needed neither a Christian name nor a word to describe his trade. "Artingstall's." That was all it said over his shop at the beginning, and he had taken care that Artingstall's stood for something. And then there were two shops, three, and now four, with "Artingstall's" right across the whole lot of 'em; and if anyone in Manchester said "I got it at Artingstall's," you didn't need to ask where that was.

Hawley made money and married money. He had lived over his own shop, and now goodness knows how many assistants were living over them all. As for Hawley, he had moved out to Fallowfield, to a fine stucco-fronted house with lime trees in the garden – so many lime trees that on a warm June day the scent of the flowers came into the house. No wonder it was called The Limes. You wouldn't believe, out at The Limes, that this was the same city which comprised Hulme and Ancoats. In the springtime Hawley's garden was full of flowering trees – lilacs and laburnum, cherry and hawthorn – a dazzling spectacle under a sky which could be kind and blue. Walking there and thinking of Birley, he couldn't make the chap out. Why, the whole Ancoats' outfit could be put here in Hawley's stables, and Birley's living quarters weren't half so good as those which Briggs and Haworth, his groom and coachman, had in the loft over the horses.

Very delightful it was on one of those mornings of early spring to sit in the phaeton behind Haworth's broad back and spin through the streets to Artingstall's. He entered the building on the dot of nine, a paragon of punctuality, and it pleased him to see men set their watches by the passing of what some of his friends called with affectionate raillery the Artingstall diligence.

Hawley had long since given up his Methodist allegiance. The Church of England was an altogether more respectable shrine for the devotions of one who, already an alderman, would infallibly be Mayor and not inconceivably a knight. And so, driving on Sunday morning in a capacious two-horse equipage toward his customary worship at the Cathedral, Hawley, with these pleasant dreams in his head, would turn his puffy face to the thin hatchet-face beneath the lilac parasol beside him, reflecting that Lillian at least would know how to carry it off. Ann? He glanced at the girl riding with her back to the coachman and a doubt clouded his mind and his countenance. Irresponsible. That was the word that always thrust at him when he thought of Ann. All that he had done for her – all that he had given her – and she seemed to value it at two pins. Where did she get it from? Reluctantly he admitted that she was too much like that damn fool Birley.

Eight to eight were the office hours at Artingstall's, but Arnold Ryerson at least did not have the mortification of then "sleeping in." That was the fate of the elder men and girls, but Arnold, engaged after one of the rare colloquies between Birley and Hawley, was too inconsiderable a cipher in the Artingstall machine. He did not have to be subjected to Artingstall beds and food and general domesticity. He was a mere sweeper of floors, duster of chairs, runner of errands, and when on the morning of Arnold's first appearance Hawley breezed with a blowing out of the moustaches into the shop, he did not even know who this tall thin boy was, holding open a door for him with awe. Errand boys came and went. There was no reason why he should associate this one with that talk he had had with Birley.

Gordon Stansfield, pleased that Arnold had found work, was unhappy because John was now deprived of friendship. By the time Arnold had walked from Artingstall's to Broadbent Street and eaten his supper, it was nine o'clock, John's bedtime. Gordon thought the matter over, and was ready when Birley raised the question of Arnold.

"How's that lad of Mrs. Ryerson's getting on, Gordon?" he asked one day when August was ending and the workroom was insufferably hot, choked with the smell of tanned hides.

"He'll be all right," Gordon said confidently. "He's the sort of lad who'll make something of his life, give him a start. But I wish he and John could see a bit more of one another. The boy says nowt, but he misses Arnold."

"There's Sunday," said Birley. "Take 'em along to Emmott Street."

"Aye, there's that," Gordon admitted. "But I was thinking of getting 'em both to join my class. That's seven-thirty on Thursday nights."

Birley was doing some fine sewing. He looked quizzically at Gordon over the steel spectacles he used for close work. "And what will my lord the alderman say to that?" he asked.

"Well, Birley. I was hoping that would be where you'd come in."

"Look here, lad," said Birley. "An alderman in the family, especially an alderman married to one of them sour-faced Sugden lasses, is a bit of a responsibility. D'you know that when I go to The Limes I knock my forehead on the doorstep, crawl on my hands and knees into the parlour, and lie full length till all the family've wiped their boots on me? Well, not all of 'em. Not Ann."

"You're piling it on, Birley."

"Maybe I am. But it's more or less like that. Me a Wesleyan, too. That doesn't help. And now you want some of Artingstall's precious time off, just so that an errand lad can go to a Methodist class meeting.

Time's money, Gordon, time's money, especially at Artingstall's." He took up his work again. "Ah, well. I'll see him at the shop. I'll miss Lillian that way. Lillian! One look from that lass is enough to turn her own brass rusty."

"She's got plenty, I hear," said Gordon with a rare touch of wistfulness.

"Rolling in it, lad, rolling in it. All the same, she's the sort that puts a man off marriage. But there's no sense even in that, because look at Ann. Mr. Alderman and Mrs. Vinegar, and the result is Ann. Eh, it's a rum do. There's no sense in life anywhere, look at it how you will."

"Nay, you're wrong there, Birley," Gordon reproved him gravely. "I haven't seen this lass, but p'r'aps it's she that makes the sense. Sounds like it from what you say."

Hawley was annoyed at receiving a second petition on behalf of an errand boy. His interview with Birley ended on a note of temper. "Eh, well! Have it any damned way you like," he said, and with that ungracious permission Birley was content.

And so, on the following Thursday, a scrubbed Arnold, with hair down-plastered by water, and attesting his wage-earning status by wearing a pair of his late father's trousers miraculously brought to an approximate fit by Mrs. Ryerson – this Arnold, his face shining with joy at renewing an old intimacy, presented himself at the Stansfield door in Broadbent Street.

John, too, had been scrubbed and purified like a sacrifice. Ellen had never become a "class member" and so, though she attended services at Emmott Street, she was not a member of the Methodist Church. But she knew with what seriousness Gordon regarded this night's proceedings, and while he was assembling the class register and his Bible and hymn-book, she slipped a penny into each boy's hand.

"What's it for?" John asked in a whisper. "Do we have to pay to go in?"

"You'll see," said Ellen. "Put it in your pocket."

Gordon was silent and grave as he walked between the two boys through the sultry streets. They caught his solemnity, and when they passed Tom Hannaway trundling his perambulator in the direction of Darkie Cheap's, they nodded and said nothing.

It did not take them long to reach the Emmott Street chapel. Railings, as formidable as a prison's, shut it in, a blackened fortress, fashioned all of stone on which for years the clouds had wept sooty tears, so that, from the basement disappearing into the earth behind the railings to the sharp apex of the spire lifted upon a sky flushed now with pink, all was black and funereal as crape. Within the railings there was nothing green. The path to the front door went through sour-looking earth as hard as though no spade had turned it since "Emmott Street," as its devotees called it, was built. And indeed there would have been no point in turning that sterile and poisonous soil. A few elders had their roots in it. In the spring they fluttered green leaves for a few hopeful weeks; then the noxious airs of Ancoats blasted them as surely as frosts would have done, and for eleven more months they existed in twiggy desolation, recruiting their forces to perform again the puny and pointless miracle.

Gordon Stansfield and the boys did not go up to the front door, an affair of stout oak, nail-studded, which now was locked. They diverged to the left, along a path which fell downward toward a basement door. Here, in the great dimly lighted space beneath the chapel, there was a hall for those jollifications that could not be conducted on the more sacred ground floor. Opening off the hall were a number of rooms, and as the three hastened to their own objective the sound of hymn-singing came from one of these rooms, having in the cheerless half-light the eerie suggestion of timid Christians quavering in the catacombs.

There was no one in the small room to which they presently came. One window of opaque glass lighted the place and opened onto a wall divided from the room by nothing but a yard-wide path, so that the place was both dark and stuffy. Gordon stood on a chair and threw up the lower sash of the window. Then he lit the solitary gas-burner. The blue flame, uncovered by any sort of guard, sang with a high tiny whine.

"No one here," said Gordon. "Good! I like to be first. I like to greet them as they come in."

At the end of the room away from the window was a table with a wooden armchair behind it and on it a cloth of red rep. Whoever sat in the chair would look across the table at an array of straight-backed uncomfortable cane-bottomed chairs. Gordon placed his register, his hymn-book and Bible on the table in front of the armchair, and then took his stand at the door.

The boys sat side by side in the front row of chairs, not looking at one another, feeling awkward and self-conscious.

One by one, Gordon's class members assembled. They were all poor people. It was a gibe of Birley Artingstall's that Wesleyan "classes" were like that. "They're all graded, Gordon. You've got the nothing-a-weeks. Someone else has the pound-a-weeks, and so they go on. Anyone with more than five pounds a week doesn't bother to attend class at all, unless he happens to be a class leader."

Clogs thudded on the resonant uncovered floors. Shawls were draped over heads and held with one hand across the breast. Summer and winter these women wore their shawls. They were nearly all women – about a dozen of them: washerwomen and weavers and harassed-looking mothers who had left their babies at home in the charge of elder children. There were only two men, and one of them was Darkie Cheap. He must have disposed quickly of Tom Hannaway.

For each one Gordon had a hand-clasp and a cheerful appropriate word. When they were all in, he took his place behind the table and asked them to sing a hymn. He read the first verse:

> "What shall we offer our good Lord,
>   Poor nothings! for His boundless grace?
> Fain would we His great name record,
>   And worthily set forth His praise."

The little congregation sang with gusto. The tune was easy, popular, harmonious. Gordon had a thin but true tenor voice. Darkie Cheap and the other man achieved something adequate in the bass, and the women sang with the soulful fervour of the poor who find consolation in rich promises.

> "Stand in the temple of our God
>   As pillars, and go out no more."

they concluded, and then there was a scraping of clog-irons on the boards as they got awkwardly down on their stiff knees. John did not shut his eyes. Through the bars at the back of his chair he stared at one of those pictures that remained printed for ever on his photographic mind. A head bowed down, cowled in a coarse shawl, a back bent in worship that for so many years had been bent by labour, a pair of rough woollen stockings and clog-irons shining like a horse's shoes.

He glanced sideways and saw that Arnold Ryerson had laid his arms along the chair-seat and buried his face in them. He could not do this. He was alert and interested. He heard Gordon begin to pray, quietly and simply, with none of the emotional fervour to which Birley Artingstall could screw himself up. Gordon's prayers were conditioned by the circumstances of the people kneeling with him. He knew them all and knew their needs, and he sincerely believed that he was laying those needs before someone who listened from a mercy seat. Still on their knees, they repeated the Lord's Prayer together, and then they stood and sang another hymn.

"Now," said Gordon, "we are met to testify to the power of God in our lives. There are two new members in this class tonight, and they should know that John Wesley himself founded the class meeting as the very bedrock of his church. He founded it as a place where little companies of those who love the Lord could come together to comfort and sustain one another. It is a place for personal confessions and personal testimony. It is not a place for sermons or long addresses, and so I shall not make either. I shall lay before you and before God my own desire, which is that the two lads who are here tonight may receive of God's blessing full measure, pressed down, and running over. I ask your prayers for them, that this means of grace may work in their hearts like a leaven; and I ask your prayers for myself, that I may be a worthy shepherd. Now, if any brother or sister has any confession to make, or any need of our prayers, or any testimony to give, let us hear it."

It was evidently a well-understood routine. Gordon's eye rested on the first woman in the back row of seats. She stumbled to her feet and recited in a gabble: "Thank the Lord, Mr. Stansfield, and forget not all His benefits. I've felt the benefit of my religion all through this past week. I've needed the help of God, and I've had it."

She sat back, greatly relieved, into her chair, and Gordon said: "Amen, sister, amen. Praise God for that." Then his eyes passed on to the next woman. She was mute. She slowly shook her head to and fro, as though suffering from some affliction that prevented her from keeping it still. The next woman praised God that her husband had found work. She had prayed for it long and ardently. "Let me have your prayers," she said, "that he will bring the money home."

So it went. Some were silent; some uttered a few naive words; and John began to apprehend that his turn would come. A sweat broke out in his palm. He no longer heard what the people behind him were muttering or gabbling. He felt as panic-stricken as he sometimes did at school when the master, stick in hand, was questioning round the class. He glanced at Gordon, listening with a rapt expression to these poor people, an expression charged with pity, too, as though he wished he were God, so that he might himself bring some comfort to their lives. But Gordon was not looking at him: there was no help there.

And then deliverance came. It was Arnold's turn, and Gordon did not turn his eyes upon him. Instead, he took up the register. He called his own name first and laid a penny upon the book. One by one as their names were called most of the members came up to the table and laid down a penny. But some had no penny to lay down, and Gordon laid it down instead. There were no arrears of "class-money" in his class.

"Arnold Ryerson." Gordon wrote the name in the book as he called it. Arnold went forward with the penny that Ellen had provided.

"John–Hamer–Shawcross." Gordon split the name up, his voice dwelling lovingly on each part of it as he wrote. He looked up at John, and on his face was a smile so radiant that the boy, arrested on the other side of the table, for a moment did not stir. He stood there with the penny clutched in his moist palm. It seemed as though no one were present but him and Gordon, and as though between them were passing currents of love and understanding beyond belief. The meeting had perplexed him. It had seemed to him dreary and wearying. There had been nothing to explain the joy he had often seen in Gordon's face as he set out to go to "class." And now there that joy was again, in a measure that seemed almost physically to embrace him. He did not know that Gordon felt in that moment as though he were literally bringing the boy to God. John came to with a start. He opened his hand to drop the penny. Sweat stuck it to the palm. He shook it off and walked back to join with the others in the closing hymn. Most of those present thought it a strange hymn for a class meeting. How could they guess that Gordon had chosen it with care?

Jesus, who calledst little ones to Thee,
    To Thee I come;
take my hand in Thine, and speak to me,
    And lead me home;
Lest from the path of life my feet should stray,
And Satan, prowling, make Thy lamb his prey.

How could they know that Gordon's thoughts were ten years back, on a night of fog and bitter cold through which he had run with the child's head resting on his arm, to find Millie comforting Ellen and to see Ellen's face light again with the hope that had seemed to be gone for ever?

Mrs. Ryerson was not sorry to find Gordon Stansfield taking an interest in her son. With her husband dead, she had plenty to do. There were five other children, all younger than Arnold, all still at school; and as soon as they were packed off in the morning, she would set out, wearing an old cap and with her charwoman's apron in a roll under her arm, to lay into the scrubbing of other people's floors or the washing of other people's clothes. So far as she could, she took work which would permit her to return to Broadbent Street at noon, so that she might give the children their dinner, but that was not always possible, and then the young Ryersons would be sent off to school each with a packet of bread and lard or bread and dripping. On those days, whether it were wet or fine, they would have to "make out" for themselves, as Mrs. Ryerson put it, and when they had munched their food and had a drink of water from the school tap, they would play in the Ancoats streets till classes began again at two o'clock.

Arnold was a good boy. He did all he could to make life easier for his mother. He soon developed the habit of leaping from bed when he heard the *clash-thump* of Jimmie Spit-and-Wink going down the street. He found it no hardship on these summer mornings. He would go straight out through the front door and cross the road to lean on the canal parapet, drinking in the air which was sweet and cool, washed by the darkness of the night. He felt already grown up, liberated and responsible. There was no one to say "What are you doing out of bed?" Once the clang and clatter of the clogs had ceased, once the mill buzzer had given its fearful call and fallen to silence, Broadbent Street, flanked by the sleeping houses on the one side and the still water on the other, seemed beatific. The boy breathed deeply, and dreamed: not of leaving this jungle of stone so deceptively tolerable now that its denizens were quiet and its fetid airs were unawakened, but simply of being able to live in it unafraid, untroubled by the petty shifts and stratagems of the poor. If he could so arrange that his mother did not have to go to work, then he would feel he had achieved something.

At half-past six he went in, raked out the ashes from the kitchen grate and lit the fire. Then he laid the table for seven breakfasts and prepared two – for himself and his mother. At seven o'clock he went up and called her softly. He had ready for her in the scullery sink a tin bowl of hot water. She washed herself, and came into the kitchen for breakfast.

It did not take them half an hour, or anything like it, to eat what there was, but they did not get up from the table till half-past seven. They talked, their voices quieted by the still quiet sense of the morning and the thought of the children sleeping above. Arnold told her of the grandeurs of Artingstall's – an establishment she had never entered: of how Alderman Hawley Artingstall arrived on the stroke of nine, leaping from his phaeton and going with a sort of urgent waddle, looking neither to right nor left, to his private office; of the wonders of silks and carpets, of armchairs so downy that you could sink into them as if you were sitting in a billow of feathers, of gorgeous clothes and sumptuous blankets.

"One of these days," said Arnold, with his shy smile, "I'll buy you a blanket just like those."

"Go on with you," said Mrs. Ryerson, who did not believe in miracles. "You'll be getting me a carriage and pair next."

"Well, don't forget the donkey," said Arnold. The donkey was their private half-serious joke. He had promised her that some day she should have a gig and a donkey to pull it.

"Aye, I'll have a donkey when pigs have wings," said Mrs. Ryerson. "Off you go now."

It was half-past seven. Arnold set off for Artingstall's, and Mrs. Ryerson began to prepare breakfast for the five children. She was a tiny woman, shorter than Arnold, still only in her middle thirties, but there were anxious lines in her face and her hair was turning grey. Her hands were as rough as nutmeg-graters.

*

When Arnold went to work at Artingstall's he was paid five shillings a week. That was exactly the rent of the house in Broadbent Street. Two years later, when he was sixteen, the Ryersons felt that their fortunes were most happily changed. Arnold was earning seven and sixpence. He kept sixpence a week for himself, and now was able to contribute two shillings to the household expenses as well as pay the rent. This was not all. For a year, the oldest of the Ryerson girls had been in domestic service, living in, no charge at all on the exchequer, and sending home half a crown a week. Now the second girl had gone to work and was sending home one and sixpence. Here was indeed a leap up the ladder: only five to clothe and feed, and six shillings coming in after the rent was paid, in addition to what Mrs. Ryerson could earn herself!

Pay-day at Artingstall's was on Friday; and on a Saturday morning in December Arnold set out for work with sixpence in his pocket. It was the first sixpence he had kept of all the money he had earned. He knew what he was going to do with it. It had been a bitter night. He had been aware of clinging for warmth, all night long, to the brother who shared his bed. The frost persisted, and the ruts were frozen in Great Ancoats Street. He found it exhilarating: the horses going by striking their hoofs metallically upon the icy road and blowing great clouds of steam that hung upon the air after they had passed; the men hurrying to the city, muffled in overcoats and scarves; the red round sun rising slowly above the grey roofs crenellated with chimney-pots, and staring through a plum-coloured haze that prevented the fall of any shadow.

His job was now a little more responsible than dusting and sweeping and running errands. He was allowed to lay an occasional hand on the precious merchandise, to remove the cloths that swathed the goods at night, and once or twice he had even penetrated the holy place where, upon a mossy carpet, before a glowing fire, stood the desk of Hawley Artingstall, so placed that, sitting at it, one could take in the comforting vision of Alderman Hawley Artingstall, painted in full municipal canonicals, hanging in a gilded frame upon the wall. Arnold did not know it, but the artist had painted the picture twice, the second one at a reduced fee for the embellishment of the dining-room at The Limes.

But though these more important functions were now his, he still, when nine o'clock was near, posted himself at the main entrance in order to open the door for the alderman.

Mr. Tattersall the Manager – you never spoke of Mr. Tattersall but always of Mr. Tattersall the Manager – had been fussing here and there since eight o'clock, requiring the boy's presence continually at his heels, and it was already nine o'clock when Arnold began to sprint across the floor of the carpet department. He took the stairs in flying fashion to the next floor, dodged through its array of furniture, and sped down to the ground floor, glittering with seasonable things, hung with holly, draped with cotton-wool that scintillated under a powder of mica, festooned with coloured paper chains, glass baubles, and Chinese lanterns. Leaping like a hart through this festive and unaccustomed scene, he perceived that he was already too late. The alderman was within the door, which he had been compelled to push with his own august hand, and he was now holding it open for someone to follow him.

Not once in the more than two years he had been in the place had Arnold failed to be at the door. No one had told him to perform this service, but repetition had made it a ritual act, expected by both him and Hawley. So now, wishing to retrieve something, he did not check the rush which had brought him to the spot. He grabbed at the door, hoping at all events to show his morning courtesy to whoever it was that followed the alderman. The gesture went astray. Neither he nor his employer held the door firmly. They muffed it between them, and the heavy contraption of mahogany and plate glass swung back unexpectedly and hit the girl almost off her feet. Both her hands were in a muff of black astrakhan. Arnold never forgot that gesture, the first he ever saw her make: the hands in the muff flying up to her face to ward off the swinging door, and then, when all was well, lowering themselves a little, hiding all the face except the eyes, which, between astrakhan hat and astrakhan muff, suddenly smiled. Arnold smiled, too – the eyes were at once so inviting and forgiving; but Hawley brought him to his senses with a snarl. "Open t'door, you clumsy fool."

He stood glowering at Arnold after the girl was in the shop, and then glowered down at his own boots. Arnold's eyes followed his gaze and saw that he had indeed been clumsy. He had stepped upon the alderman's boots and scraped their burnished surface.

Suddenly the girl said: "Thank you." The unexpected words brought his eyes to her face again. Curling hair that was white almost as lint escaped from under the hat. The face was heart-shaped, with prominent cheek-bones, and the eyes were grey. So much he saw before Hawley barked: "What's there to thank him for?"

"Why, Father, for opening the door."

"Opening t'door!" Hawley snorted. "Wellnigh killed thee wi' t'blasted thing. Coom on."

She smiled again, as if to say: "Forgive him, won't you?" as she turned to follow her father to his office.

At ten o'clock Arnold saw her go. She looked a tiny thing, walking out alone from the office, all wrapped up with that hat and that muff and a big coat and furred boots. She looked no older than his own sister, who was younger than himself. She did not see him, and he had no chance to open the door. Mr. Tattersall the Manager was across the floor in a few lithe strides, bowing and showing his white teeth in a smile. Arnold saw the coachman leap down from the box of a victoria and arrange rugs round the girl as she sat beside an upright, stringy woman. Mr. Tattersall the Manager had bowed the girl right across the pavement. He stood there, bending his head and washing his hands till the victoria moved off. The girl took one hand out of her muff and fluttered it to him. The woman did not notice him. Some celestial drill-sergeant seemed to be saying to her: "Eyes front!"

When he left the shop at eight o'clock Arnold hurried through the biting air to Mr. Suddaby's. The catacombs were cold. The gas-jets had the wan look of spirits materializing in that graveyard of authorship. Arnold, with sixpence in his pocket, had come to look for a birthday present for John Shawcross. In a day or two, John would be fourteen.

His wanderings brought him at last to the alcove where Mr. Suddaby had his fire and his white Persian cat and his table. Arnold began to retreat again as the sound of voices told him that Mr. Suddaby was not alone. But the old man had seen him, and called him, "Nay, my young student, come here a moment."

The boy went shyly nearer. "Sit down and have a cup of tea," Mr. Suddaby said unexpectedly. "And before you do that, shake hands with Mr. Engels. Friedrich, this boy's name is Arnold Ryerson. He's a member of the oppressed proletariat."

Arnold had no idea what Mr. Suddaby was talking about. He sat on a wooden chair, and Mr. Suddaby poured some tea from the pot on the table. Mr. Engels, stretched out in a basket chair by the fire, had a cup on his knee. His face was heavily bearded; his clothes were of stout, excellent broadcloth. There was no smile in his eyes to answer the smile in Mr. Suddaby's.

"It is a bit of luck for you," said Mr. Suddaby, "that you came in tonight. I don't suppose Mr. Engels will ever be in Manchester again."

"No, Charles," said Engels. "I came to see you and a few other friends for the last time. That is all. When I go, I shall never look on this hell on earth again."

"You see, my boy," said Suddaby, "what Mr. Engels thinks of your native city. Hell on earth. He lived in it for a long time, and in those days we did a few things together – eh, Friedrich?"

Engels stared at the fire; one hand, hanging down, absently stroked the head of Sheba the cat. He did not answer.

"We were young men, my boy, and we believed in heaven on earth. I suppose Mr. Engels still does."

He looked toward the man slumped in the chair, but again Engels made no sign.

"As for me – well, you see, I'm just an old bookseller, with a cat that doesn't give a damn for me or anybody else, and a lot of memories. I *remember* it all, Friedrich, but the light's gone out of it for me. I remember all the talk and laughter, all the work and the meetings, and Mary Burns, and Lizzy."

Engels got up with sudden passion, his foot kicking the cat which sprang away hissing. "Do not mention them!" he cried. "They are dead, you are dead, all are dead."

Suddaby left him standing there, his elbow leaning on the mantelpiece, and drew the boy away into the bays of books. "Never forget," he said, "never forget that you met Friedrich Engels, who earned the bread and butter for Karl Marx and paid his rent, so that the world could be a better place. At least, that's what I thought. Now, I don't know. I'm not sure. The light's gone out of it, and Friedrich thinks I'm dead. Perhaps I am. Perhaps I am."

John's birthday that year fell on the day of the weekly class meeting. Gordon Stansfield arranged with a substitute to take the class. Only something remarkable would have caused him to do that, and there was, to Gordon, something remarkable about this birthday. John was fourteen. At fourteen schooldays ended. A boy became a wage-earner. It was a coming-of-age occasion, a coming of working-age; and Birley Artingstall and Arnold Ryerson had been asked to come and eat the birthday meal at six o'clock.

John did not go to school that day. The Christmas holidays would soon be beginning, and, anyway, he was now within the law in staying away. The day was both raw and cold – one of those days when Ellen wrapped Gordon's scarf well round his neck, fidgeted if he gave the smallest cough, and, as she watched him go along Broadbent Street, worried herself with recollections of that fatal affliction which so speedily had carried off his sister Millie.

Coming back into the house, she looked at the boy. He had grown a lot in the last two years. He was lanky: wrists, ankles, and neck all seemed to be too thin, all started out of his clothes in a way the eye couldn't overlook. His face, too, was thin, whiter than it should be; and this was emphasized by the burning lustre of his eyes and by that dark cascade of hair tumbling over the steep white brow. She was sometimes startled by her glimpses of him, and she was startled now. Never before had her mind been driven back so sharply upon what she wanted to forget: that other face, white, too, with desire, and, she could now believe, with terror of what was about to happen, because he was not a bad boy. He had been gentle and persuasive.

The kitchen was dim in the December morning, and as John stood there so thin and white in the doorway, she remembered that that was just how that other had stood, at once commanding and pleading. She had told him to go away; all the house was asleep – such a grand house, the grandest house she had ever worked in, a great park in Cheshire. There was a whole party of these young people – aristocrats all of them – she could hardly tell one from another, they seemed so alike with their thin bony faces and long hands and strange voices. But she had noticed this one as he lounged in the hall, his booted legs stretched out to the blazing logs. They had all come in from riding, and she took a tray, and when she reached him he continued to stare absently into the fire. He looked up with a sudden start. He did not smile, but his eyes held hers. Something struck like a spark between them, and when he took his drink his hand trembled. And then there he was, with all the house asleep, white, panting a little, urgent.

The next day they all went riding again. He looked flushed and boyishly triumphant. He was brought home on a hurdle, covered with a horse blanket. A little later, the horse that had rolled the life out of him was shot where it lay, its own back broken, behind a hedge. The hedge was not far from the house. She heard the shot. It seemed to go through her heart.

She said to John: "Go upstairs and light your fire. It's not a fit day to be out in." She couldn't stand seeing him there at a loose end, like a ghost without a job even of haunting to do. At times he seemed so detached from her, so independent, so little hers. She thought with comfort of Gordon's utter devotion. He at least was all hers. There had never been much occasion for letters between them, but she treasured a few signed: "All yours, Gordon." That was it.

"Well, if you want me, you'll know where to find me," John said. "If there's anything at all that I can do—?"

He turned at the door to give her a smile that was enchanting. But she was beginning to find out that he would not smile if she took him at his word and asked him to do something disagreeable.

In the bedroom he put a match to the fire and watched the woolly smoke go up the chimney in sluggish yellow plaits, then clear as a flame burst through. The sabre was bright above the mantelpiece. He still cleaned it every Saturday. The bookshelves were now well filled. Thanks to Mr. Suddaby, there was nothing second-rate upon them. They had disturbed the boy's mind with dreams of vague magnificence. Marco Polo's *Travels*, Prescott's *Conquest of Peru*, Hakluyt's *Voyages*: he was familiar with all these, with their fantasies and cruelties and heroisms. He had read Sir Thomas More's *Utopia*, and old Suddaby had fed him with much romance, too. There upon the shelves were novels by Scott and Hawthorne, Fenimore Cooper and Fielding, Goldsmith, Smollett, and Swift. The gentler writers had their place. Lamb's *Essays of Ella* and Holmes's *Autocrat* were among them. There was much to thank the old man for, unobtrusively feeding his peerless sixpennorths to an appetite ready for anything.

No doubt about it: as he entered upon his fifteenth year, John Hamer Shawcross had had his eyes opened in many directions; but the direction he most liked to follow was that in which some brilliant individual went out against great odds, and fought, and conquered, and was honoured. Many of whom he read conquered indeed, but died unhonoured and obscure. That was not his idea of a good ending to a tale.

He sat down in the chair that had belonged to the Old Warrior, enjoying his unaccustomed freedom. He knew that now he would have to work. What he would do he did not know. Gordon had said there would be no mill for him, and that was as far as it had gone. His own desires were both vague and grandiose. He thought of Tom Hannaway, who was going to own a racehorse. Poor Tom! He was working for Darkie Cheap, pushing a barrow about the streets, shouting "Any old rags, bones, bottles, jars! Any old iron!" Tom was sixteen, the same age as Arnold Ryerson. The racehorse seemed a long way off.

Something that had nothing to do with this: nothing to do with Tom Hannaway and Darkie Cheap, nothing to do with Broadbent Street and the early morning stampede of clogs and the moaning of the mill-buzzer: that was as far as he got in his meditations that morning when he was fourteen years old.

John's birthday party was simply the customary six o'clock high tea with a few frills on. It was held in the front room instead of the kitchen, and it gained a festal air because the Christmas decorations were already up. Sprigs of holly, with scarlet berries vivid against the dark green leaves, were stuck behind the pictures. Paper chains with many-coloured links began in each corner of the room, dropped in loops, and were all four caught up and fastened together into the middle of the ceiling. From the point where they met a Chinese lantern hung down, and at five minutes to six Ellen lit the candle in it and the lamp on the sideboard. The fire had been going all day to chase the chill out of the unused room.

It all looked very gay to Arnold Ryerson, who had hurried straight from Artingstall's, and the food upon the table made his mouth water. He was a growing, hungry boy, and though the Ryerson establishment a few doors down the street was faring better than had recently seemed likely, still, this display of an uncut ham, of jars of pickles, of bread and butter, cake and jam, with apples, oranges and nuts piled in a bowl in the centre, seemed to him a high spot both of elegance and of opulence.

Ellen came in from the kitchen with an immense teapot, and

Gordon followed her, carrying a kettle which he placed upon the fire. John came then, feeling self-conscious as the cause of these unaccustomed splendours.

"Where's Birley Artingstall?" Ellen asked. "That chap'd be late for his own funeral. You'd better start cutting the ham."

"Nay," Gordon protested, "give him a chance. I wouldn't like Birley to think I was giving him a hint."

So for five minutes they stood awkwardly about the room in the narrow space round the table, looking, all four of them, with childlike pleasure at the glowing lantern and the decorations, and the ruddy light that fell upon the white drooping end of the tablecloth from the flames dancing round the singing kettle. Then Birley's resolute knock was heard, and John, who was nearest to the door, hurried into the passage. A lamp was burning there, and as he opened the door its light showed him that Birley was not alone. A girl had her arm linked in his, a girl of whom John could see little but two bright eyes shining under the dark arch of a bonnet that was tied beneath the chin with a bow of wide ribbon.

"Many happy returns!" Birley cried. "I've brought a visitor. Come in, Ann, my dear."

Birley bustled into the passage, which was hardly wide enough to contain the three of them.

"I'm afraid I'm unexpected," the girl said, and John didn't know what to answer. His reading didn't help here. He felt awkward and foolish. She smiled, hoping to put him at ease, but he couldn't smile back. He had hardly exchanged a word with a girl in his life.

Birley raised his voice and shouted. "Mrs. Stansfield, I've brought a visitor," and Gordon and Ellen came out into the passage.

"I don't think you've met my niece, Ann," Birley said. "It's not often she calls on me, and when she does it's always at the worst possible time."

Ann Artingstall shook hands with them. Ellen said: "Let me take your hat," and Gordon said: "You're welcome, miss. Come into the front room."

"Yes, go in," said Ellen. "I'll get another plate."

You would not have thought, on seeing Ann Artingstall, that she was the one to whom all this was a great adventure. Never in her life before had she been in such a house as this one in Broadbent Street.

She was here now by the merest fluke and misadventure. Her father had promised to go home early that evening, and when she had done her shopping in the town she had called at Artingstall's. But Hawley wasn't ready, and didn't think he would be ready for an hour or two.

"Then I'll go And see Uncle Birley," said Ann. "I haven't seen him for months."

Hawley grumbled. He disliked the Ancoats he had sprung from. He disliked the affection for Birley which Ann never thought of concealing.

"Ah don't know what you want down in them low parts," he said. "If you want to see Birley ask him out to t'Limes."

"He's never at his best at The Limes," said Ann with truth. "I like him better in his own little room."

Grudgingly, Hawley conducted her to the door. "Take Miss Ann to Mr. Birley Artingstall's," he said to Haworth, who was sitting up on the box of the victoria, "and don't come away till you see she's met him."

He himself wrapped the rugs round her. "Stay there," he said, "till I come for you. That'll be about eight." He watched the carriage drive off through the murky night as anxiously as though Ann were being driven to an encounter with cannibals.

Haworth did as he had been told. Indeed, there had been no need to tell him. The black, forbidding length of Great Ancoats Street, with its poor shops and poorer houses, its few lights and ill-dressed passers-by, commended itself as little to him as to Hawley Artingstall. Not for anything would his well-trained rectitude have left Miss Ann alone there. He waited till Birley had come to the door, till Ann had entered, till the door was shut again, before driving slowly back to town.

Birley was already dressed for going out when Ann arrived. "Well, lass," he said, "you've come at a rum time. I'm just off to a birthday party. You'd better come with me."

"I'd love to," Ann said, and off they went, disposing thus simply of a situation which Hawley would have viewed with horror.

And there they were. There was Ann Artingstall, who was fifteen and who had no idea what the lives of the poor were like, entering the Stansfields' front room and deciding with one glance of her dancing eyes that they might be worse. "How lovely!" she cried, pausing in the doorway and taking in the ample table, the glowing fire, the decorations. And, more than this, she took in the sense of happiness and good will that seemed to abide in the house as a positive and palpable presence.

Then she came farther into the room, and there was Arnold Ryerson, gazing at her open-mouthed, as taken aback as if Hawley himself had suddenly appeared at John's party.

"But I know you!" Ann cried.

"Yes, miss," said Arnold. "I work at Artingstall's."

"Of course! You're the boy who stepped on Father's foot and nearly hit me down with the door."

She laughed so merrily at the recollection that Arnold joined in; and then Ellen came in with the necessary extra things, and Gordon brought in a kitchen chair, and there was a lot of pushing end rearranging round the table. Birley and Ann sat on one side, facing the two boys, and Gordon and Ellen were at either end.

Everything about the occasion was amusing to Ann. The solemnity with which Gordon said grace before laying into the ham was amusing; the mere fact of eating such a meal at such a time was amusing, for Alderman Hawley Artingstall was accustomed to dine at eight, when he got home from the shop, and since her fifteenth birthday Ann had been expected to join him. The grave way in which the two boys stared at her was amusing, too. Try as she would, she could not evoke more than the most transient smile from either. She thought the smaller of the two, whose birthday this was, was nice-looking, with his thin face and big dark eyes and tumbling hair that he swept nervously off his forehead every time she spoke to him.

"We'd better leave t'washing up," said Ellen when the meal was ended.

"Aye, leave it. I'll give you a hand later," Gordon said. "I expect you're dying to see your presents, eh, John?"

They were already rising from the table as Gordon hurried through the thanksgiving that even himself had almost forgotten. "Come upstairs," he said.

They went up in single file. There was no room for two abreast. John, who was last, gave a cry of delight when he came into the room. A little kneehole desk had been smuggled across from Gordon's room on the other side of the landing, where it had been concealed for some days.

"From me and your mother," Gordon said. "It's only second-hand,

and cheap at that," he added apologetically and with his customary grave honesty: "but I've patched it up and it doesn't look bad."

John could not resist sitting down at it there and then. He looked round the room, and could hardly believe that it was the same room which two years ago he had shared with the Old Warrior. Then, it had never to his knowledge known a fire. It was overcrowded by the big bed; it was bleak and gloomy and often frightening. Now it was as cosy a little room as you could desire. He looked across the desk at the five people facing him, and suddenly laughed.

"I feel so important," he said. "You're all standing up, and I'm sitting down."

"I hope you'll sit down there a lot," Gordon said. "I thought that would be a good place for you to write your sermons."

"Sermons?" the boy asked, surprised.

"Well," said Gordon, "I hope you'll take to local preaching some day. Perhaps even the ministry – eh, Birley? The Reverend J. Hamer Shawcross. Who knows?"

"Aye," said Birley. "Who knows? Perhaps the Lord will lead his thoughts that way."

J. Hamer Shawcross. The boy liked the sound of it and repeated it to himself: "J. Hamer Shawcross."

Birley produced a book. "I hope you haven't missed this," he said. "Gordon borrowed it from your shelves."

It was the volume of Sam Bamford's poems that had belonged to the Old Warrior. Birley had bound it handsomely in red morocco as his gift. Arnold shyly produced a sixpenny copy of *Marmion*.

"And what about me?" Ann cried. "I've eaten your lovely meal and I've got nothing to give for a present."

"You'd better give him your hair ribbon," Birley joked. Ann took it seriously. "I will," she said, and untied the ribbon impulsively from her hair. She took up the book that Birley had bound and flattened the ribbon out between the pages. "There!" she said. "A book-marker."

John opened the book. "I should like you all to sign your names," he said suddenly. "Then I'll always remember who came on my fourteenth birthday."

He got up from the chair, and one by one they sat in it and signed: Ellen in a sprawling illiterate hand, Gordon more neatly, Birley with fanciful copperplate twists and twirls. Arnold Ryerson signed next, and after him Ann Artingstall. Finally the boy wrote: "J. Hamer Shaw-cross." It exists today, that book with Ann's name written between the names of Arnold Ryerson and Hamer Shawcross, Against the names, thus first brought into conjunction, is the date December 20, 1879, which was a bleak night there in the mean Ancoats street.

Chapter Four

If Mrs. Ryerson had not had so tiring a day many things might have turned out differently in the lives of Arnold and Ann. On the other hand, some other compulsions might have driven their lives in the same direction. Be that as it may, it is a historical fact that the utter weariness of this poor woman caused a change of direction to come.

That day of young Hamer Shawcross's birthday was not substantially different from her other days. When Arnold was gone to work, she saw the three young children off to school. Cold as it was, it was one of those days when they took their meagre midday meal with them. Mrs. Ryerson would be busy morning and afternoon and would have no time to attend to them.

She spent the morning in one of those heartbreaking houses that Ellen Stansfield knew in the days when she was Ellen Shawcross. Mrs. Ryerson began in the basement with the week's wash. It was dreadfully cold when she got there. Even when the fire was lit under the copper, the week's chill clung to the stone-floored room, half buried in the earth, with one small window, on a level with her eyes, looking out upon nothing but a forlorn back yard given over to a few fowls pecking disconsolately behind their wire fence.

Soon the white billows of steam were filling the basement, and in that atmosphere she scrubbed and rinsed and wrung.

She wasn't complaining. It was a job she knew inside out. She did it automatically and thoroughly, gazing out into the back yard and thinking how much easier life had been since her husband's death. More certain, anyway, if not easier. The children were good and brought home their wages, which is more than Ryerson had done as often as not.

So the tiny indomitable woman wrought gamely at her job, pausing now and then to rub her face with the dry upper part of her arm, and thanking goodness that since she had had to come out to work there had been no lack of work to do.

When the washing was done she ascended to the kitchen of the house, where she was given her dinner. It was a good dinner, and this was what she called a good job. After dinner she had to "run through" the house, which meant a great deal of dusting and then a great deal of work on her knees, scrubbing deal floors and polishing oilcloth. The steel fireside fittings of the kitchen and the brass fittings in dining-room and drawing-room had to be done, and then she was at liberty to go. So the lady of the house was able to assure her husband and her friends that she was a good economist. "I do without a maid. Just a woman in once a week."

Mrs. Ryerson was not able to go home. It was three o'clock, and she hurried off to Great Ancoats Street where there was a shop that she had been engaged to clean. It had been empty for a long time and had now been let. Her job was to scrub down all the shelves and the counter and to clean and scrub the floor.

She had brought with her from Broadbent Street a bucket and scrubbing-brush and a piece of yellow soap, and she had the key of the shop in a pocket concealed somewhere within her skirt. She didn't like the look of the floor. Where the oilcloth had been taken up, fragments still adhered, some of them fastened down with tacks, and, being a thorough and conscientious worker, she knew that she would have to remove all this rubbish before she began to scrub. She decided to leave this to the last.

There was no hot water laid on. In a small room behind the shop there was a cold-water tap and a fireplace full of rubbish. Some wooden packing-cases lay about, and she smashed these up with her foot, set light to them, and put her bucket across the hobs. She had to make do with tepid water, and by the time she was ready to tackle the floor, darkness was coming on. "Tackle" was her word, a favourite word, suggestive of her attitude to her work: something to be rather aggressively fallen upon and downed.

Tackling the floor was no joke. The gas had been turned off in the shop. A lamplighter came along the street with a small smoky flambeau on his shoulder and lit a street lamp outside. The light fell in faint yellow squares upon that lamentable patchy floor, all odds and ends of oilcloth and nail-heads. She could not see well enough to get those pieces off, and anyway she had no tool to deal with the nails. By the ghostly light of the street lamp she slumped down upon the piece of sacking she used for a kneeling-mat and fell to.

She was very tired. Her knees creaked a little as she bent them and vexed her with a slight insistent pain. She was beginning to feel hungry, and more than once she knelt upright, easing the stiff ache out of her back, and she thought that a cup of tea would be very nice, especially if someone else prepared it for her. But there was no question of that. Her scrubbing water was almost cold. The packing-cases had flared to death quickly, and she must make do with the water as it was. Her greying hair began to fall down into her eyes from under the cap which she wore, but she went on painstakingly working over the floor washed with the yellowish light of the lamp and quartered by the shadows of the window-frame. Across these quarterings upon the floor there moved, too, the occasional shadow of a passer-by, giving the sense that she was working within a prison of impalpable bars. But such thoughts never entered her mind, which was entirely practical.

The day would have ended much like any other day if suddenly a sharp stab of agony had not made her cry aloud. She dropped her scrubbing-brush, shook her right hand vigorously, and saw the blood-drops shoot out and fall upon the floor. A nail, half buried in a plank, had entered her hand near the wrist and torn across the ball of the thumb.

She got to her feet and walked to the window, so that the light of the lamp should fall upon the injury. There was no more pain after the first fierce pang. She took out her handkerchief, which was too small to bind between index-finger and thumb, down across the wound, and round her wrist. So she used it merely as a pad, tearing the strings off her coarse apron to bind it with, pulling the knot firm with her left hand and her teeth.

Then, since work was work, she went on with the scrubbing, dipping her hand into the filthy water and getting what grip she could upon the brush with four fingers. When she had chased the dirt out of the last corner as well as the light and her condition would allow, she emptied her bucket into the sink in the room behind the shop, rinsed it out carefully, washed out her floor-cloth and scrubbing-brush, put these, with the remainder of the yellow soap, into the bucket, and was ready to go. She was precise and particular in all these matters, and only when the shop door was shut and locked behind her, and she out in the sudden bitter air of the street, did she stagger a little, overcome by tiredness, cold, hunger, and the shock of her pain. But it soon passed, and, dangling her bucket, she made for Broadbent Street.

The Ryerson children – two boys and a girl – had been back from school for some time. They had chalked a hop-scotch on the pavement outside the house, and were leaping nimbly about in order to keep warm in the raw evening air. Catching sight of their mother, they abandoned the game and ran down the street to meet her, shouting that they were hungry and wanted their tea.

She was as hungry as they were, and a good deal more tired, but she could not sit down. There was a lamp to light, a fire to lay, the food to cut up. It all took her a long time. The wound in her hand throbbed; she could not be as neat and swift as usual. It was past six o'clock when the meal was finished, and she at once put the two younger children to bed. They went with protesting screams. It was earlier than their usual time, but she was too worn out to have them near her. Had it been summertime, they could have played in the street; as it was, bed was the only thing.

She came downstairs exhausted by the contest with the children. At last she could rest for a moment. She sat in her rocking-chair by the fire and listened to the sounds coming from the scullery, where her son Francis was washing up. There was no need to ask Francis to do things. He was like Arnold. Indeed, all her children, she reflected with thankfulness, were good and dependable.

"Francis," she said, "I scratched my hand on a nail today. It's fair giving me jip."

Francis came into the kitchen and hung the drying-up cloth on a line before the fire. "Let me have a look at it," he said.

He untied the coarse apron string, revealing the filthy ball of handkerchief over the wound. Congealing blood had caused it to stick. Francis poured some warm water into a bowl and soaked the handkerchief off. He did it with great tenderness. Suddenly he looked at his mother and smiled. "I'd like to be a doctor," he said.

Mrs. Ryerson sighed. All her children seemed to want impossible things. "It looks nasty," Francis said, gravely examining the long red gash that was still oozing slowly. "You go along to the chemist at once and get him to put something on it and bind it up properly. I'll look after the house."

"What about the mangling?" Mrs. Ryerson asked. "I must run that stuff through tonight. It'll be called for first thing in the morning."

"I can do it," said Francis. "You go to the chemist."

Mrs. Ryerson leapt up. "Come on," she said. "We'll tackle it together. You turn, and I'll pass the things through. Let's get it over with, and then I'll go to the chemist."

Francis carried the bundle of folded clothing out to the scullery. He seized the handle of the mangle and began to turn as his mother fed the things to the rollers. She wasn't as rested as she thought, and her right hand felt terribly awkward. She fumbled to get straight a fold that was going in badly, and suddenly screamed: "Back! Oh, Francis, Francis!"

The child himself nearly fainted, so unnerved he was by such a cry as he had never before heard his mother utter, and by the swift realization of what happened. He whirled the handle into reverse. Mrs. Ryerson stared stupidly for a moment at the mangled ends of her fingers, and then she said urgently: "Fetch Arnold! Quick! Fetch Arnold! He's at Mr. Stansfield's."

The boy rushed out of the house. Mrs. Ryerson made her way to her rocking-chair, and as she felt her senses almost leaving her before the onset of her pain, she heard the two youngest children pattering barefoot down the bare stairs to see what had caused that agonized cry.

"We'd better be going, Uncle Birley," Ann said. "Father will be calling for me at eight, and it's nearly that now." She turned to Ellen. "Thank you, Mrs. Stansfield. It's been a lovely evening."

She was in the little passage, with her hat and coat on, and John had opened the door, when Francis Ryerson came leaping along the street. He rushed unceremoniously into the passage and yelled:

"Arnold! Arnold! Come home quick! Mother's crushed her fingers in the mangle."

Arnold rushed from the parlour, his face ashen. He did not say good-bye to anybody. He did not stop for coat or hat. Within a few seconds of Francis's cry the two brothers were tearing down the street.

"That poor woman!" said Birley. "That poor woman! I must go along."

"I'll come with you," said Ellen. She snatched her shawl off a hook, cowled her head with one dexterous movement, and followed Birley down Broadbent Street. Without a word, Ann went after them.

"There's nothing we can do, John. We'd only be in the way," Gordon said. "Your mother will see to this."

Ann overtook Birley and Ellen as they were entering the Ryerson house. She went in with them, and saw at once that she had been mistaken in thinking that Gordon Stansfield's was a poor man's house. This was different: this was a poor house: one step over the threshold told her. Her feet echoed on bare boards; there was not even oilcloth down in the passage; and when she came into the kitchen she saw such a room as she had never looked on before. There were no curtains to the window, only a linen blind that had not been pulled down. The light was from a lamp hooked to the wall: a lamp that had no shade and whose feeble ray was hardly helped by the tin reflector behind the chimney. The room was clean and threadbare – pitiably threadbare – no covering to the floor, no cloth upon the deal table. The fire was low and dispirited.

Mrs. Ryerson was rocking in her chair, and the two young children whom she had put to bed not long before were sitting in their nightclothes, howling at the tops of their voices. They knew Ellen, and her advent made them redouble their cries; but when Ann appeared, emerging suddenly from behind Birley Artingstall, their uproar began to diminish. They sensed in Ann a woman different from the women they knew. They stared at the hair which was lint-white yet lustrous with brushing, at the fresh face, the new clothes, the shining shoes. Their mouths opened, their eyes widened, their cries stopped.

Ellen had dropped to her knees at Mrs. Ryerson's side and taken the wounded hand into her lap. She and Birley looked at the crushed fingers and Ann saw their faces wince. There was nothing she could do for Mrs. Ryerson, so she turned to the children. They at least could be got out of the way. She put an arm round each thin pair of shoulders and smiled into the two wondering faces that lifted to hers. "What about getting back to bed now?" she said. "Come along. I'll put you."

They were such wraithy mites that they could all go upstairs side by side. The youngsters pressed in against her legs and did not seem anxious to ease away from the pressure of her guardian arms. The staircase was dark, and when she reached the small landing at the top she said: "Which room?"

"One in each," the youngest child said. "I'll put your hand on the candle." He took her hand in cold fingers and directed it to a small table pushed back against the landing wall. She felt the matches, struck one, and lit the candle in a blue japanned candlestick. On each side of the landing was a door. She opened the one to the right, and one of the children at once rushed from her, leapt into bed, and pulled the clothes up to her chin. Ann followed, and looked about among the wavering shadows. It was the smallest, meanest bedroom she had ever seen, carpetless like every room in the house, and, like them, scrubbed, spotless, and somehow for that very reason the more pitiable. The child in the bed looked at her with the bright eyes of a small animal. "Who are you?" she said. "What's your name?" Being back in bed seemed to give her courage.

"Oh, I'm just a girl," said Ann. "Just a girl, and her name is Ann."

"And she crept under the frying-pan," said the child, giggling now, her mother forgotten.

The little boy, the youngest Ryerson, seemed to think himself overlooked. He tugged timorously at Ann's skirt. "Put me to bed, please," he said very politely.

Ann tucked in the clothes round the little girl, who said: "My mother shares this bed," wished her good night, and then took the boy to the room across the landing. "I sleep at the foot," he said importantly.

She did not understand what he meant, so he took her hand and led her to the bed. "Here," he said, patting the pillow. "I stick my legs up between Arnold and Francis."

Then she saw that there were pillows at each end of the bed. "Oh, I see," she said; "three of you sleep together."

"Yes," the child answered. "Sometimes they kick my neck, but I can only kick their knees."

She had never heard of such an arrangement before, and it seemed to her remarkable, and, like everything in that house, pitiable, but she let him think that she knew all about these things. She tucked him in, allowed him at his request to blow out the candle, and by the light of a match tiptoed to the landing. There she left the candle, and went down to the kitchen. Arnold Ryerson was alone, sitting in his mother's chair, rocking gently to and fro. For a while he did not see her. She had time to observe the grave preoccupation of his face, the untimely shadow of care that darkened it. His bony hands were gripped so tight upon the chair-arms that the knuckles stood out whitely. When at last he saw her, he got up from the chair. "No," she said. "Sit down." But he insisted on her taking the chair. "When Mother gets back," he said, "she'll like a cup of tea. I've got the kettle on. I'll make one now for us. I'm ready for it."

With the air of one accustomed to such small household tasks, he quickly assembled the cups and saucers, the teapot, milk and sugar upon the table. And still he had no idea that this, to Ann Artingstall, was an adventure into the incredible, the fantastic. Looking about the room, at the tin clock on the mantelpiece, at the thick, chipped cups and saucers on the table, at the uncurtained window, and at the wallpaper hanging in loops in the corners, she suddenly burst out: "I always have tea brought by the parlourmaid on a silver tray!"

Arnold's face at once reddened and hardened. He thought she was condemning his impertinence in offering tea in that room. He put down the milk-jug with a little trembling clatter. "I'm sorry," he said stiffly.

She saw at once that she had hurt him. He showed it so quickly, like a child. She leapt from the chair and impulsively laid a hand on his arm. "Please!" she pleaded. "Don't you see! I was talking almost to myself. I was thinking of – well, the way I live, and then – well, the way other people have to live. It's terrible. I wasn't condemning anybody. I had no idea people could be so poor. That's all, really."

"Poor!" said Arnold. "D'you call us poor?"

He gave a scornful laugh, and she looked at him, mystified. If this was not poverty, what was? she wondered.

"If you want to see poor people," Arnold went on, "I'll show you some, one of these days. People without clothes, without food, without beds. Good Lord, no. Don't think we're poor. We've got a roof and food and clothes and a fire to sit by. And everybody ought to have that. Have you read Robert Owen?"

Ann had not read Robert Owen. She had never heard of Robert Owen. Arnold poured out the tea, and as they sat there by the small dying fire he opened his mind. Even to Hamer Shawcross he had never talked as he talked to Ann Artingstall that night. "So that's it. That's what I'm going to do with myself," he said earnestly. "I'm going to fight against poverty." He stood up and looked at her defiantly. "I'm a radical!" he said, expecting her to recoil as though he had announced that he held credentials from Hell. "Liberty. Fraternity. Equality. That's what we want, and that's what we're going to have."

"And to think that I don't even know your name!" said Ann inconsequently. "But that's like Uncle Birley."

"Ryerson–Arnold Ryerson. And look–you *must* read Robert Owen. Let me lend you one of his books."

"I should like to," said Ann, and Arnold opened the dresser drawer and fumbled among the books piled in there anyhow. "That's it – A New View of Society. You read that, and tell me if you don't think it's good."

"Right," Ann answered. "But how am I to tell you?" she asked practically. "We may never see one another again." His face darkened, and she added quickly: "But I expect we shall. Perhaps we'll meet at Uncle Birley's."

For a time they were silent; she sitting in the chair and he standing before the fire, looking down at her strange hair and firm little chin. He was pleased with her for having had the quick sense to take the children out of the way, and he was surprised that she had been so easy to talk to. After all, he had seen her get into her father's victoria. He had seen Mr. Tattersall the Manager bowing and scraping to her as if to a princess. He could not forget the incredible gulf that lay between them. And yet, there it was: she had talked to him as if they had been friends for years. She was sitting there now, nursing Robert Owen's book, with the lamplight shining on her hair, as if to sit in the Broadbent Street kitchen were a usual, an accustomed thing.

Suddenly he said: "Miss Artingstall, sometimes, when something good has happened to me, I say to myself: 'I'll never forget this morning' or 'this night' or whatever it happens to be. Like that, I make it stick in my mind and I never do forget it. Do you ever do that?"

She shook her head. "Oh, of course, I often say 'I'll never forget it,' but I usually do."

"You won't if you do it the way I mean," said Arnold. "You really fasten your mind on it and say 'I *won't* forget!' "

"What sort of things? When did you last say that?"

"Well, not long ago I was in a bookshop, and there was a man there named Engels. Mr. Suddaby who owns the shop said: "Never forget that you met Friedrich Engels.' He seemed to think it was important, so I shut my eyes and said: 'I won't forget Mr. Engels. I won't. I won't.' And I know I won't."

"And you don't want to forget tonight, is that it?" Ann asked smiling.

"Yes, that's it," Arnold answered earnestly. "I'm saying now: 'I'll never forget this night!' Will you say it?"

She laughed, tossing her fair hair in negation. "No, no!" she said. "I don't think that sort of thing's any good to me. Perhaps I'll forget. Perhaps I'll remember."

*

She remembered. Alderman Hawley Artingstall saw to that. At eight
o'clock the victoria stopped outside Birley's door, and Hawley, crossing the pavement, looked with frowning distaste upon the street in
which he had run wild when a boy. He hammered authoritatively with
the knocker – a violent rap designed to let all within know that he was
one who brooked no delay. But there was delay. A second and a third
rap brought no response but the echoes that rolled down Birley's stair.

Hawley said sharply to Haworth: "You left Miss Ann here?"

"Yes, sir. Mr. Birley came down, and she went in with him."

Hawley stepped back and looked up at the unlighted windows.

"What the devil are we to do?" he demanded. "Where can she have
got to?" He pulled out his heavy gold watch. It was ten minutes past
eight. He looked up and down the street, which offered a cold and
almost empty prospect. The only moving thing in sight was a four-
wheeled cab, bowling slowly toward him, its lantern throwing a blur
of yellow light upon the haunches of the woebegone hack. Hawley
turned back, tried one more thunderous assault upon the door, and
in the silence which fell when the knocking ceased he heard his own
name called. "Hey, Hawley!"

He swung round. The four-wheeler had come to a standstill. Birley
was leaning out of the window, his lantern jaws grinning. "Sorry I
can't stop," he said. "'Pon my soul, I forgot all about you. There's
been a bit of an upset. I had to take a woman to the doctor, and now
the doctor says I've got to take her on to the Infirmary. She's here in
the cab."

Hawley did not care one rap who was there in the cab. "Where's
Ann, you fool!" he demanded truculently.

"She's quite safe," Birley said cheerfully. "I left her in Broadbent
Street. You go along and pick her up." He gave the number, withdrew
his head, and pulled up the cab window. The old horse shivered and
jog-trotted off along the freezing road.

Hawley cursed openly. Broadbent Street! He knew it only too well.
He had enjoyed running along the canal wall. He had fallen off it into
the water and had his backside tanned for consolation. It wasn't the
sort of place that, even in his young days, an Artingstall child was supposed to play in. And that was where that irresponsible fool had left
Ann! And how had Ann got there, anyway? What was she thinking of

to go to such a place, Birley or no Birley? A black anger made him for a moment almost blind. He gave the street number to Haworth and got into the carriage.

It took him no longer than three minutes to reach the Ryersons' door, but in that little time a multitude of emotions had churned and ploughed his undisciplined mind. He had passed Ann in review, judging her in the light of her mother's gentility and his own aspirations, and had found her wanting. She wouldn't do what other girls did. She had complained openly that her life was silly and empty. Those were her very words: silly and empty. "Can't I *do* something? Can't I be *trained* for something? I'd like to earn my living." There she was, with everything life could offer a girl – good money being paid for a music-master, for dancing-lessons, for any reasonable thing she wanted, and in a few years there would be all the men she could want to pick from. The right sort of men, too. But no – "Couldn't I be a nurse? What about Florence Nightingale?" His only child!

Hawley was bursting when the victoria drew up. The street door was open. He didn't knock. He stormed into the passage, toward a thread of light that he saw lying under a door. With no more ceremony than one imperious rap, he flung the door open.

Ann simply could not believe that her world had changed so astoundingly. She sat at her bedroom window and gazed out into the garden of The Limes, now leafless and desolate. Beyond the garden wall lay the Wilmslow Road, and from time to time she could see the heads and shoulders of coachmen or of riders upon horses go by, the ones with a forward gliding, the others jog-jogging up and down. They looked as free as the air; and hidden by the wall, unseen by her but not for that the less clearly imagined, were foot-passengers going and coming as they pleased. The afternoon light was fading. Rooks went slowly, a deeper black, across the dark sky, and all these things – the men and the horses and the birds – made her imprisonment the more odious. Now she saw tit-tupping past the garden wall a black hat adorned with a stylish green feather. It was one of the girls from next door, riding slowly home to tea. Ann's agonized imagination ran riot with the fire-light and the muffins, the steaming teapot and the friendly chatter. It was more than she could bear. She pulled down the blind, ran to her bed, threw herself upon it, and began to cry again.

It was humiliation more than anything else that made her cry. Her thoughts kept engaging like cogs into this or that part of the dreadful things that had happened to her. At each engagement a shiver of misery would go through her. She *could* not believe that her father and mother had said such things.

Hawley had been utterly quiet on the way home. He had walked into the kitchen at the Ryersons', given one horrified look about him, and then barked to Arnold: "Don't let me see *you* at my place again! This is how tha takes time off for t'Wesleyan class, is it?" Then, without a word to Ann, he took her by the arm, led her to the doer, and put her into the carriage. He sat at her side, stiff with hostility, not speaking, but clearly bottling up an explosion that promised to be terrific.

When they reached The Limes he could hardly wait for the victoria to come to a standstill after it had swept up the circular drive and reached the big covered porch in which a gas-lamp was burning. He leapt out before Haworth was down from his seat, took her arm again as though he were her jailer, and held her while fumbling his key into the lock. He marched her in, and there was Mrs. Artingstall, impatience written in every peaked inch of her face, exclaiming as soon as she saw them: "You're late, Hawley! Dinner'll be ruined."

He flung his tall silk hat onto a table. "Dinner can wait," he said. "You go in theer!" He pushed Ann toward the door of the drawing-room. "And tha can go, too, Lillian," he added to his wife.

"Why, whatever's the matter, Hawley? What has Ann been doing?"

"She's disgraced us," he said. "That's all – disgraced us – dragged us in t'dirt. Ah've told thee," he went on, pushing behind her into the drawing-room, his voice becoming broader and broader. "Ah've told thee to control yon girl, and see what it's coom to now."

He shut the door behind him, advanced to the hearth, and stood there upon the white bearskin, his puffy little face swollen with anger, his round paunch pushed aggressively forward behind the golden decoration of its watch-chain. The fire gleamed between his slightly bowed legs.

Ann never forgot it all. To her dying day she could, if she wished to, call up the memory of the figured yellow brocade that made deep scallops from the edge of the mantelpiece, the tall curtains of the same material draping the window, the pleated yellow silk behind the fretwork front of the piano, the spindly tables that stood here and there and the chairs and sofas whose fluted woodwork was painted white with gold marks down the fluting. All this she could always remember, but especially the central figure of the drama, her father, posed like a figure of doom, no less frightening for being, in retrospect, ridiculous. He was arranged almost as in a stage setting; with the wings of the brocade drooping behind his shoulders, on either side of his head a round opaque white globe in which a tongue of gas chuckled quietly, behind his head a Marcus Stone picture of a lover languishing upon a mouldering and doubtless ancestral terrace.

Suddenly he barked at her: "What's that in thi hand?"

Only then did she realize that all through the last disturbing half-hour she had been clutching the book that Arnold had lent her. "It's a book," she said.

"Don't be damn soft," he burst out with a rudeness that was unaccustomed where she was concerned. "Ah can see it's a book. What book is it, and wheer did tha get it?"

"Arnold Ryerson lent it to me," she said.

"Who is Arnold Ryerson?" Mrs. Artingstall demanded, her sharp nose sniffing at the mention of a man's name.

Hawley snatched the book from Ann's hand. "Arnold Ryerson," he said, "is a little tyke who earns about tuppence a week in my shop."

"That's your fault, not his."

There was silence. Mrs. Artingstall looked aghast at her daughter.

The red of Hawley's face deepened slowly to purple. Ann herself could hardly believe that her own mouth had uttered the words. Now that they were out, they seemed appalling, rebellious, undutiful.

Hawley and Lillian spoke almost simultaneously. "Ann!" said Lillian. "To speak to your father like that!" And Hawley: "So! You not only disobey my orders, leave your uncle's house, and go to a place where you had no right to be, but now you presume to tell me how to run my business! And you bring this home with you – *A New View of Society!* Radical trash!"

"Radical?" cried Lillian, deeply perturbed.

"Yes, radical. Ah give her permission to call on Birley, and t'damned fool not only takes her in t'slums but leaves her there. When Ah coom, there she is – alone in t'kitchen of a slum house wi' that young Ryerson that runs errands in t'shop. What dosta think o' that? There's a daughter!"

"Alone?" said Mrs. Artingstall.

"Aye, alone. God knows what might have happened to her. In a dirty little room wi'out a cloth on t'table. There she was, suppin' tea wi' that young tyke, and scarcely a scrap o' fire in t'grate."

Again Ann found her tongue, and this time she did not regret it. She spoke up boldly out of her heart. "It's not the Ryersons' fault if they're poor, is it? Don't you think they'd have tablecloths and better fires if they could? They're nice people, and they work hard, and Mrs. Ryerson crushed her fingers in the mangle. That's why I was there."

"So! You're learning about life! You're seeing things. You're getting a new view of society." He flung the book behind him into the fire. "And you're learning to teach your father how to run his affairs."

"*I want* to learn things," Ann said. "I didn't do anything wrong. Why shouldn't I know poor people as well as rich ones?"

Hawley reached out a pudgy hand, took her by the shoulder, and pulled her upright. "So long as you're living under this roof," he said, "you'll know the people that Ah want you to know an' you'll do the things that Ah want you to do. T'classes don't mix. Theer's rich an' poor, an' they'd better keep apart. A lot o' good has come to that lad through you tonight. He's lost his job. That's the outcome o' your kind actions."

"It's not!" she cried. "It's not. It's the outcome of your cruelty. There was no reason at all for you to dismiss him. They need the money. They need a lot more money than they've got."

"So now I'm cruel!" Hawley shouted. "I work my fingers to the bone," he stormed, clenching his flabby fist, "to give thee an' thi mother every comfort, an' I'm a cruel tyrant! You'll take that back, my girl; you'll promise never to do again what you've done tonight; and you'll apologize for all the sorrow you've caused me and thi mother, before you eat your dinner."

"I don't want my dinner," said Ann.

"Before you leave this room, then, you ungrateful, headstrong girl."

She stood before him silent, her heart beating with furious anger. "Come along now, Ann," said her mother. "I know you've only been foolish and that most of the fault was your Uncle Birley's. Just apologize to your father and promise to be a good girl."

"I shall *not* apologize." Ann broke suddenly into sobs. "And I like Uncle Birley better than Father."

"Take her to bed!" Hawley commanded, and when Lillian had done so, he followed up the stairs, locked the door, and put the key into his pocket.

"Oh, dear! Dinner'll be ruined," Lillian lamented as they went down again. She seemed not greatly troubled by what had happened. Hawley, who had a deeper understanding of his daughter's character, was accordingly more deeply disturbed. "Damn dinner!" he snarled. "Ah'm going out."

If he had examined his heart closely, he would have acknowledged a feeling of defeat.

One of the troubles with Hawley was that he did not examine anything. Like a bull at a gate, he had gone head down for whatever he wanted, and he had always found that the method succeeded. What was crushed underfoot in the process did not matter to him. By this brutal directness he had achieved his business success and civic eminence; by it, too, he had carried off old Sir James Sugden's nose-in-the-air daughter Lillian; and he had had no doubt that the same methods would succeed with Ann.

But Ann, with her strange colouring, her resolute little jut of chin, her growing dissatisfaction with a world that seemed to Hawley well-nigh perfect, was no Sugden, and as certainly she was not much of an Artingstall. He could recall the lineaments of his mother, who died when he was in his early teens: a woman whom old Artingstall, the founder of the leather business, had met up on the north-east coast, where her father was a pilot. She was named Rika Petersen. That was where Ann came from, just as Birley did. But wherever Ann came from, he'd be damned, he told himself, as he sat morosely in a great leather chair in his club, if he'd let her have her way with him. He prided himself on knowing both the world and his way about in it. That was more than Ann did. In a few years, when she'd come to her senses and settled down; she'd thank him for having been the firm, intelligent father she had needed.

Comforted by these reflections, and by the porterhouse steak which he had consumed with a quart of ale, he leaned back in the chair, stretched out his stubby little legs as far as they would go toward the fire, and enjoyed his cigar in peace. He liked the club, with its rich red Turkey carpets, the dark oil-paintings of important-looking politicians on the walls, its stuffy opulence and dignified sleepy calm. An evening there occasionally was grateful, especially when Lillian's nose looked longer and thinner than usual.

When he went out into the street, a thin cold drizzle was falling. There was no cab in sight, but he knew there would be one round the corner on the rank in St. Ann's Square. He called to a boy who was lounging near the club door, evidently in the expectation of such errands. "Hi! Boy! Get me a cab." Then he withdrew into the shelter of the club portico. Ann and her poor people! That was what poor people were for. *Hi! Fetch! Carry!* He was smiling to himself when he noticed that the boy was by his side. "Eh? Where's that cab?"

The boy's hair was a mass of wet, tangled black curls. His eyes, as black as his hair, were lit with an impudent light. "I haven't fetched it yet," he said. "What are you paying me?"

Hawley stared at him in amazement. "Well," said the boy, unabashed, "do *you* take on a job before you know what you're going to get?"

The alderman burst into a guffaw. "Nay!" he cried. "Ah'm damned if Ah do! Tha's t'reight sort, lad. It's worth sixpence to meet thee."

"Pay it, then," said Tom Hannaway, holding out his hand.

"Nay, lad – no cab, no tanner. Get along wi' thee now and don't try my patience."

The dignified alderman was coming uppermost, and Tom Hannaway ran off into the drizzle, whistling shrilly with two fingers placed between his lips.

That's the sort of lad we want at Artingstall's, Hawley reflected; not a damned Methodist class-meeting tyke; and when Tom Hannaway returned, running alongside the shambling rain-polished horse, he said: "D'you want a job, my lad?"

"What sort of job?"

"Errand boy at Artingstall's."

"Nay, keep it," Tom Hannaway said with uncompromising directness, "I'll be no errand boy for you or anyone else."

Hawley flushed with displeasure. "What are you now, then? Son and heir of Lord Muck?" he asked with heavy sarcasm.

"I push a barrow for a rag-and-bone man," said Tom.

"That's a fine job, Ah must say! Is it so much better than what Ah'm offering?"

"It is an' all," said Tom. "It'd be a long time before I could buy Artingstall's, but it won't be long before I buy the rag-and-bone yard."

Hawley smiled again, amused by the boy's confidence. He handed him his sixpence. "Perhaps you'll buy Artingstall's some day," he said.

"I shouldn't wonder. Stranger things have happened."

The money in his palm, Tom shot away and disappeared round the misty corner. Hawley stood for some moments looking at the place where the boy had been. He thought of Ann; he thought of this handsome, cheeky youngster. "Well, the children are teaching us something," he reflected as he climbed into the little mouldy cage that bowled him home to Fallowfield.

Ann continued to teach him. The next morning he unlocked her bedroom door and advanced into the room with the air of one ready to bestow forgiveness and expecting it to be gladly received. The curtains were across the windows; the room was in twilight. Ann lay with her back toward him, nothing but a mound under the bed clothes and a shock of bleached, disordered hair.

"Come, come! Not up yet, lass?" he cried gaily. "Can't you smell the kidneys and t' coffee?"

There was no movement, no word, from the bed.

"Ann, are you awake, lass?" He laid a hand on her shoulder and shook her gently. "Come, lass," he said. "Tell thi old dad tha's been a little fool and that tha'rt sorry."

Ann wriggled her body from under his hand. Her muffled voice came from beneath the bedclothes. "Go away."

Hawley thought of the Artingstall diligence by which men set their watches. He had never been late. He was not going to be late this morning. "Ah'll tell 'em to send summat up, lass," he said, "and Ah'll see thee at dinner." He patted her shoulder. He was half-way across the room when, like a jack-in-the-box whose spring has been released, Ann sat bolt upright in bed. He turned and looked at her, sitting there straight as a young tree, one hand pressed hard down on the bed on either side of her, her hair flowing like shining white silk down to her waist. It had drooped across her eyes which glared at him through the lovely mesh. Her nightdress had fallen open and he could see her young breasts, rosy-tipped, firm and round. She was unconscious of her exquisite appearance. He thought: "My God! She's a woman, and she hates me."

She sat there for a moment like a venomous little statue; then she said: "I don't want anything sent up, thank you, and I shall not see you at dinner." With one gesture she enveloped herself in the bed clothes and lay huddled with her back to him again.

"Ah must go," he said weakly. "Ah'll send thi mother up to thee."

Lillian did not hurry. Hurry, fuss, excitement, would never have permitted her to preserve the thin, languid, genteel air which she opposed to circumstances. To Hawley's cluckings and flutterings at breakfast-time she replied that he could go to town, put Ann out of his head, and leave things to her. Calmly, when he was gone, she prepared a tray with her own hands, calmly she carried it upstairs. She tapped at the door, and asked in her sweetest voice: "May I come in, Ann?"

"You can try," Ann answered.

Lillian tried, and found that the door was locked. But this time it was locked on the inside. Lillian's calm did not fail her. "Ann, you foolish child, what joke is this?" she asked equably.

There was no answer. Lillian put the tray down on a table near the door and gently rattled the knob. She dared not make much noise. She both despised and feared her servants. She flushed at the thought that one might come by at any moment and find her pleading with her own daughter to open the door.

She took the tray down to the kitchen and said that Miss Ann was unwell: she did not want any breakfast. Then she set her cold brain to work. She had told Hawley that all would be well when he came home. She was going to keep her word. She decided that Ann would have to come out of her room sooner or later, and so she betook herself to her bedroom, sat with the door open a crack, and waited as unexcited and implacable as the Sphinx. She waited for two hours. Then Ann left her room and Lillian tiptoed into it. When the girl returned, her mother was sitting on the bed, Ann was still wearing her nightdress and a blue silk dressing-gown and fluffy bedroom slippers. Hawley had seen in her a woman; Lillian thought her an absurdly defenceless-looking child.

"Well?" said Lillian. "When is this nonsense going to stop? You have missed a dancing-lesson this morning, and this afternoon you have your music."

Ann did not answer that. "Do you think I did wrong yesterday, Mother?" she asked.

"There was so much fuss and talk, I hardly know what you *did* do," Lillian answered.

"Well, let me tell you, because I want to *know*," the child answered.

"All right, then. Come and sit here by me." Lillian moved up on the bed, and Ann knew that if she sat down an arm would be round her. Instinctively, she did not want that. She had come to a crisis with these grown-ups. She was prompted to keep emotion out of it. She pulled the dressing-gown tighter round her.

"I would never have left Uncle Birley's," she said, "if he hadn't had an engagement. He'd promised to go to a boy's birthday party, and he took me along with him."

"He ought to have had more sense. That man always was a fool. He could have cancelled it."

Ann shook herself impatiently. "Anyway, he didn't, and we went, and everyone there was very nice. One of the boys was from Father's shop, but I couldn't have known that, could I?"

"You could have cleared out when you did."

"And then we heard that the boy's mother had hurt herself with the mangle, so some of us went to see what was the matter. It was a terribly poor house. I've never seen such a poor house, and I put the children to bed."

"You what!" Lillian's calm was beginning to fail her.

"Someone had to, and that poor woman couldn't. You visit the poor yourself, don't you, Mother?"

"Visiting the poor the way I do it is one thing," said Lillian stiffly; "they know their place with me. What you've been up to, I imagine, is another matter."

"Well, you'd better let me finish telling you. When I came down after putting them to bed, Uncle Birley and Mrs. Stansfield – that's where I'd been to the party – had taken Mrs. Ryerson to the doctor. I had to wait till Uncle Birley came back, so Arnold Ryerson made me some tea."

"And you were alone there with that boy in that house!"

"Yes. We drank tea, and he told me about books he'd been reading."

Lillian sprang up impatiently from the bed. "I don't want to hear any more," she said sharply. "I think your conduct was infamous and disgraceful. How long were you there with that little guttersnipe before your father caught you? I expect this – this Arnold Ryerson, as you call him, enjoyed the little interview."

Ann was no fool. She was aware of all the unsaid things that wavered behind her mother's words. Her own cheeks suddenly flamed. "Do you think we were being indecent?" she asked.

The word knocked Lillian off her perch. She hated to see her own insinuations crystallized. She seized the child by the shoulder and shook her violently. "How dare you use that word to me?" she demanded. "Have done with all this nonsense. Come downstairs and eat some food, and when your father comes in tonight see that you apologize for your abominable conduct."

"So you think what I did was wrong?" Ann persisted.

"I only hope it will never reach the ears of your friends."

"Well, I don't think it was wrong. I think you are wrong and Father is wrong, and Uncle Birley is right and I am right. And I should do it again."

Lillian could not believe her ears. Never before had Ann spoken to her like that. All that was primitive under her veneer suddenly flamed to life. "Now, my girl," she said, "this is something your father can't do to you, so I'll do it for him."

She swept out an arm, taking Ann completely by surprise, and bent the girl face down across her knee. She pushed back dressing-gown and nightdress, exposing the bare flesh, and slapped till she was herself breathless with exertion and excitement. Then she thrust Ann away, and the girl rolled to the floor at her feet. Rising, with her knees trembling, Lillian looked down at the hair spread along the bedside rug and at the still exposed and smarting flesh. Hardly able to articulate in her excitement, she said: "I was older than you the last time that happened to me, and, what's more, my father did it. It cured me of my tantrums. Now get up. Get up! Do you hear?"

She was shouting now. Ann lay still for a moment. Then she got slowly to her feet. She was not crying. Her face was bloodless and her eyes burned. She shook down her clothes, pulled her dressing-gown about her, and said: "You beast! You filthy beast! I've finished with you." She walked to the window and stood there with her back to the room till she heard her mother go. Then she got into bed and stared stonily at the ceiling. She knew that the door was unlocked, but she remained in her room all day, hungry and rebellious.

Lillian was surprised when she got downstairs to find that her knees were still trembling. Her heart, too, was pounding. She could feel it quite clearly knocking against her ribs. She stood for some time holding onto the brocade-swathed mantelpiece in the drawing-room, hoping that the unpleasant oppressive feeling in her breast would pass. It did not. She became alarmed, and lay down on the sofa. Gradually the hammering died away. Even when it was nearly gone, the ear pressed into a cushion could hear with disconcerting clearness the suck and pump of blood. When Hawley returned at night, she did not tell him that she had thrashed the child. She said that Ann had argued so furiously with her that she had been quite ill. "My heart was in a terrible state." It was this which caused Hawley to say later that Ann had been the death of her mother. But that was a year ahead. Now, on that December evening, Lillian said: "I can't bear having her about the house while she's like this. I've written and asked Elizabeth to take her over Christmas."

Elizabeth Lightowler replied promptly that she would be delighted to have Ann as long as she cared to stay.

Chapter Five

Lizzie was the youngest of the Sugdens. She was fifteen years younger than Lillian. Her father and mother both died when she was in her middle teens, and so it happened that, of all the Sugden girls, she was the only one who chose a husband for herself. The other sisters felt that it was rather a scandalous affair. Lizzie met Arthur Lightowler during a holiday at Scarborough. There was no introduction; no family acquaintance; it was a "pick-up" – that was the only word for it. Lightowler saw the girl, liked the look of her, raised his straw boater, and said: "Good afternoon." Lizzie liked the bronzed tall youngster, returned his greeting; and they were married three months later.

None of the sisters could deny that the marriage was a smashing success. Arthur was not an adventurer, as Lillian had at first suggested. He was a junior partner in a prosperous Bradford wool firm; and if Lizzie was not as lucky financially as some of the others had been, at any rate she was in clover compared with most folk; and she had something that none of her sisters had succeeded in finding: a perfect marriage.

If Arthur Lightowler was not a financial adventurer, he was an adventurer in every other way. He dragged Lizzie off to the Lake District for the honeymoon and made her climb what seemed to her dizzying vertical rock-faces. Arthur laughed, and said it was a little practice for the Alps. In the evenings he read poetry to her, and during the first winter of their marriage he playfully upbraided her with her ignorance and set her going on languages. She protested that she could at least play the piano. He laughed again, and said: "D'you call that playing? Listen to this."

She had not known he could play. She was amazed, and under his guidance she found teachers who taught her to play, too, though she never played as well as he did.

"You women are so *uneducated*," Arthur teased her. "It's not your fault. It's the damn fool way you're brought up. But you wait. Your turn will come. It's in the air."

He taught her what a joyous and happy thing education was. He took her abroad twice a year; in ten years he made her a well-read woman. She spoke French and German, she played well, and Arthur joked: "Well, you've got a living at your fingertips now. When I'm gone, you can become a schoolma'am." And then he was gone, as suddenly and boisterously as he had done everything. She remembered watching the lanterns flickering up the path, and the white shoulders of the mountains shining under the moon. It seemed an easy job that he and a few guides had undertaken: to bring down a man who was lying up there with a broken leg. She never saw him again. The avalanche that tore out of the night carried the whole party into a crevasse and buried them there. She was thirty then. Now she had been running her school for five years.

During the ten years of her marriage Lizzie saw little of Lillian, nor did she wish to see more. She was a woman of the world in a way that Lillian would never be, and so she had the dexterity and address to keep their relationship on an easy basis, but she had no desire to come back to Manchester and lead the sort of life that Lillian, with an elder sister's solicitude and a born interferer's persistence, thought would be best for her. A Sugden girl running a school was a shock to Lillian at first; but she came to realize that it was not a usual school: there were few girls, and they were all from families who belonged to the commercial and industrial aristocracy. And so, when the crisis arose with Ann, Lillian had no misgiving about sending the girl to her aunt, especially as this was the Christmas season and there would be no pupils at the school.

Hawley prided himself on his hardiness, but the morning of December 24 was so bitterly cold that he told Haworth he would not use the victoria. The closed carriage was brought round to the door. In the hall Lillian pecked Ann's cheek frostily. "You've spoiled Christmas for us," she said; and added with the look of a Christian martyr: "I hope you have a very happy one with your aunt Elizabeth."

Ann submitted to the kiss but did not return it. She stepped into the carriage; Hawley followed; and when her box had been hoisted to the roof they started. By the time they reached Victoria Station it had begun to snow – so heavily that the horse's hoof-beats fell muffled upon the road.

Ann's spirits rose as soon as they were in the station. The morning was so dark that gas-lamps were lit everywhere. Down below, all was colour and movement. The bookstalls were enchanting splashes of red and blue and yellow and crimson; the jackets of the shoe-blacks glowed; piles of luggage trundled by on barrows. Up above, the roof was a dusky violet firmament; and far away, beyond the proscenium arch at the end of the platform, she could see the snow drifting down in a white flurry. She took her father's arm impulsively and hugged it. "Tha's glad to be going," he said with gruff affectionate disapproval.

He was wrapped in a great plaid ulster with a deer-stalker upon his head; and she in a sleek sealskin coat with a hat and muff of the same material. A porter staggered before them with Ann's trunk on his shoulder.

They travelled first-class, and had the compartment to themselves. Hawley was in a cross and disappointed mood. He didn't talk much, but sat back in a corner reading the *Manchester Guardian*. Ann, who had never made this journey before, was not sorry to be left alone to stare out of the window. It was not at first an exhilarating prospect. The slummy purlieus of the great city, even kindly disguised as they now were by the snow, could not but look their hideous selves; and soon they gave way to the not more inspiring plain in whose midst Manchester sits like a sordid egg in a frying-pan. Flat, featureless, depressing, the country spread out on either hand, punctuated here and there by the huge rectangularity of a mill, lifting into the falling snow its tall smoke-plumed chimneys over row upon row of windows lighted in the dark morning one above another like the portholes of a great ship at midnight.

Ann was looking forward, facing the way the train was going, and the snow hid the hills from her till the train was almost upon them. "Hills!" she cried, clapping her hands; for, to a Manchester-bred girl, hills were something to shout about.

Hawley put down his paper. "That's t'Pennine Chain," he said. "Aye, we're going through Todmorden. We'll soon be in t'tunnel, and when we get to t'other end we'll be in Yorkshire."

The engine suddenly shrieked, the train was precipitated into blackness, and even through the closed windows a foul and sulphurous reek permeated the carriage. "Ah think this is t'filthiest tunnel in t'world," Hawley announced, a mere voice speaking out of the circumambient obscurity. "It's a pretty long 'un, too. Right through t'mountains. Theer!" as the windows became faintly luminous, slowly brighter, and then fog-steamed and opaque but clearly apparent. "Yorkshire! "

Yorkshire was a surprise to Ann after the grey monotony of the Lancashire plain. She was glad that Hawley had returned to his paper; she looked out fascinated upon a different world. As if to emphasize the difference, even the weather had changed on this side of the great watershed. It had been snowing and the country was white, but now there were breaks in the clouds, patches of pale wintry blue, and here and there even a hint of sunlight falling upon the tumultuous landscape. Hills, shaggily fleeced with snow-laden trees, rose on either hand, narrowing down the view, but exchanging for the austerity of Lancashire a variety, an unexpectedness, a charm that yet was not soft but bold and striking and individual. She spoke aloud: "I'm going to like Yorkshire!"

Hawley put down his paper again and blew upon his cold fingers. "Ah hope so," he said. "Yorkshire's not Lancashire, but it's all reight so far as it goes."

The journey to Bradford took an hour and a half. As they approached the city the charm of Yorkshire faded. Slummy-looking townships and hamlets; a nauseous, reeking tunnel, and they steamed slowly into a station that seemed to Ann small and unimpressive after Manchester's Victoria.

Elizabeth Lightowler was waiting beyond the barrier – barely beyond it, for both her hands were resting upon it, and she was heaving up her small body and glancing with the bright intentness of a bird along the platform. She was the smallest as well as the youngest of the Sugden girls. At a casual glance, you might have called her the oldest, for, at thirty-five, she had a head of beautiful white hair. She was a living proof of the old superstition that hair can go white in a night; it happened to Lizzie Lightowler the night she knew beyond question that the lantern-shine moving up the mountain-path was the last she would ever see of her husband. It was hair that curled naturally and beautifully; she had cut it short, and the lovely bunch of it on her neck was her most characteristic feature. You soon saw that she wasn't old. Her face was round and unlined; her eyes were dark and bright, sparkling with intelligence; and her whole slight body had about it something vital and indomitable that gave Lizzie Lightowler an importance beyond her few inches.

She came forward now and took Ann in a warm embrace. "Well, my dear child," she said, "how you have grown! I shouldn't have known you."

And certainly Ann would hardly have known Aunt Elizabeth. Nearly five years had passed since she last saw her. The girl of fifteen, verging on young womanhood, did not retain very clear impressions from the time when she was ten.

"I hope you're going to stay to lunch, Hawley," said Lizzie, who hadn't kissed her brother-in-law.

Ann felt that Lizzie Lightowler looked almost relieved when Hawley said: "Nay, lass. Ah'll get a bite at the hotel. Ah must be handy for t'next train back. There's plenty to do at t'shop, what with Christmas an' all. Lillian sends her love."

"Thank you," said Lizzie dutifully. "And do give her mine. Now, Ann, let's be going. This is a draughty place to stand about in."

Hawley walked with them out to the station approach, where Lizzie had a four-wheeler cab waiting. He kissed Ann, tipped the porter who had brought out her luggage, and rather furtively – as though he feared that even at that distance Lillian might be watching him – he slipped her two golden sovereigns. "Theer, lass," he said. "Be a good girl and write often to thi mother. A merry Christmas. And to you, Lizzie."

They watched him disappear into the station hotel; then the cabby whipped up his horse, and off they went through the snowy streets. They were streets nothing like so long and imposing as Manchester's, but they looked attractive under the snow, and the shop-windows were bright with Christmas goods, and, above all, Ann was uplifted by a sense of freedom, of adventure, that seemed to heighten all her faculties and sharpen all her perceptions. The horse went slowly up the stiff slippery climb of Darley Street, and when he reached the top and mended his pace along the level of Manningham Lane, she saw that all the streets that came into it on the left flowed down toward them, and all the streets that went off it on the right flowed down away from them. Manningham Lane was carved out of a hillside. Down in the valley to which those right-hand streets flowed she could see the steam of passing trains; and beyond the valley bottom she saw the land rising steeply to a great hill, thickly built over with houses and mills.

Lizzie Lightowler divined her thoughts. "None of your Manchester about this, my dear," she said. "This is a good town for goats. You'll find you can't go far without going uphill or down."

Aunt Lizzie's house, Ann knew, was in Ackroyd Park. It was the house Arthur Lightowler had taken when they married. There Lizzie had remained and opened her school. Ackroyd Park, it appeared, was one of those right-hand turnings, dropping downhill off Manningham Lane toward the valley bottom. Like everything along the Lane, which did not seem to contain a single brick – nothing but buildings of hewn stone, darkened by the city's smoke – Ackroyd Park looked built to last for ever. Vast iron gates were at its entrance, hung between stone pillars on which the name Ackroyd Park was deeply carved. It was no park, but a wide road with spacious stone houses on either hand. Each stood in its own ground. All alike had the forbidding granitic integrity of fortresses. There was sufficient ground about Aunt Lizzie's house for the cab to go through the gate, pass round a small circular shrubbery of rhododendrons, and come to a stop before a front door which Ann perceived, when she alighted, was hidden from the observation of all neighbours. The imposing gates at the entrance to the Park, Aunt Lizzie's own private gate and garden, combined to give the house a feeling of being islanded and secure that Ann found very much to her taste.

"Who built these houses and why," said Aunt Lizzie, "I don't know. We've got a big garden and, as you see, even stables; but this place must always have been in the muck as soon as Bradford was Bradford. There's far more dirt here than you ever see at Fallowfield. But there it is. My husband liked the place, and so do I. Come in. Marsden, pay the cabby and bring in the box."

Marsden was an old man with white hair, rheumy eyes, and a little silky moustache that would have been white if tobacco juice had not stained it a dirty yellow. He looked at the trunk and said: "I'll do my best, Mrs. Lightowler."

"That's fine," said Aunt Lizzie. "Take it up to Miss Artingstall's room. Mrs. Marsden knows where that is. You come with me, Ann."

These Bradford merchants knew how to make themselves

comfortable. The hall was not big, but there was a fireplace in it and a fire was burning there. It was a proper little room, with a couple of easy chairs and a well-filled bookcase on either side of the fire. Ann noted it with satisfaction as she followed her aunt up the wide staircase, carpeted in crimson, with mahogany handrails that were as richly dark and polished as Haworth liked his horses' flanks to be. From the landing a corridor ran toward the back of the house. Lizzie opened a door at the end of the corridor and said: "Come in here, my dear. Let's make ourselves comfortable."

Ann gave an exclamation of delight. She thought it a lovely room with its olive-green woodwork and its simple olive-green fireplace, its biscuit-coloured walls, along one of which, breast-high, ran bookcases. The carpet and the curtains were fawn-coloured. There were no pictures, and, save for one piece of porcelain, which Ann did not know was a Ming horse, on the mantelpiece, there was nothing to represent that miscellaneous class of dirt-gatherers which Lillian referred to generically as "ornaments." Ann walked to the window and looked out on the large back garden, white now, and terminated by a dozen Lombardy poplars whose graceful vertical lines were brushed upon the snow-white face of the hill that rose across the valley.

She turned back to the room, which was rather dusky and for that reason the more inviting in the firelight twinkling on the brass fender and the surfaces of the writing-table, which made up, with two wicker chairs and a small folding table, all the furniture in the room.

"I can see you like it," said Aunt Lizzie, whose small resolute figure was posed in front of the fire.

"I love it," Ann confessed whole-heartedly. "I feel so happy – so safe – here with you."

Aunt Lizzie did not encourage emotion. "I hope you don't expect a big lunch," she said. "I rarely have more than tea and toast. Here it comes. You can make the toast."

She pulled forward the folding table and placed it between the wicker chairs in front of the fire. "Thank you, Mrs. Marsden," she said, as the housekeeper brought in a tray. "Did Mr. Marsden get that box up to Miss Artingstall's room?"

"He just about managed it," Mrs. Marsden conceded.

"Good. Now take Miss Artingstall's hat and coat along there. Thank you. There's a toasting-fork by the fire, Ann."

It was not for nothing that Lizzie Lightowler had managed in five years to make for herself an enviable position. There was no need at all for her to teach. She had money of her own and her husband had left her money. But she wanted to do something, and the training of young girls, once she had decided to try it, soon justified itself as an enterprise for which she was exquisitely adapted. Her house was not a school in the usual sense of the word. She took no girl who was younger than fifteen, and though there was a certain amount of formal schooling for those who wanted to improve their English, French, German, or piano-playing, her real intention was to introduce the girls to life as it is lived in an industrial city.

Mrs. Lightowler and her handful of girls could be found in the public gallery when the City Council met, at political meetings, police courts and the Assizes in neighbouring Leeds. They went to the art galleries, and to concerts, to theatres, and to dances, to mills and factories, workhouses, inquests, and prisons. Some of the girls stayed with her for a year, some for two. Few went away without a poise, a knowledge of the commonplaces of life, and a first-hand experience of wide social contacts that could not have been gained in the cloistered life of a "finishing" school. She never had more than six girls at a time. They came to her from all over the north of England, and her method had been so successfully its own advertisement that there were now more applicants for admission to the school than she could accept.

It did not take such a woman long to read between the lines of a domestic situation. When Lillian had suddenly written to suggest Ann's visit, giving slender and unconvincing reasons for sending the girl out of the house on the very eve of Christmas, Lizzie divined a domestic crisis of the first magnitude. There, in the quiet of her little sitting-room, with the firelight shining on her books and on her own white and deceptively venerable hair, she waited for Ann to make the first move of confidence. She was very quick at seizing such moments, and she saw her chance when the girl said: "I liked that, Aunt Elizabeth – having a little meal without fuss."

"I like it myself," said Lizzie. "When the girls are on holiday, I always have this meal up here by myself. When they're about, they come up one by one. There are six of them. They have one day a week each, and I have Sunday to myself."

"That's a good idea," Ann said. "It feels such a lovely room to talk in, and I should think your girls must like having a chance to talk to you with no one else about."

Lizzie smiled. "Between ourselves, that was the idea. I've never said so to any of them; but I find it works that way and that there's usually something they want to get off their minds. Making the toast seems to help them."

Ann glanced at the little clock on the writing-table. "How long do you give them?" she asked.

The smile on Lizzie's face widened. "How long will it take you?"

Aunt Lizzie let the girl run on. She knelt on the hearth-rug and spread her hands to the fire, and Ann, lying back in one of the wicker chairs, looked at the light shining through the dandelion-clock of her hair. She could not see her aunt's face, but caught her occasionally murmured word of encouragement or understanding. She appealed to her again and again: "Do you think I was right, Aunt Elizabeth?"

"Aunt Lizzie, please," she said, half turning her face over her shoulder. "Do you remember my husband?"

"Not very well," said Ann.

"He used to say to me: 'Ah, proud Elizabeth, I'll make a Lizzie of you yet.' And so he did; and I like to be called Lizzie, though Lizzie Lightowler sounds a horrible name to me."

"Well, Aunt Lizzie, do you think I was right?"

"I cannot see any right or wrong in it," said Lizzie. "There you were with your Uncle Birley at this Shawcross house, and then there you were without him at the other house. You had nothing to do with it either way, had you?"

"No, but I liked it. I thought it was exciting."

Aunt Lizzie would commit herself to no opinion about rights and wrongs. She contented herself with saying: "I understand exactly how you felt about it, my dear, and if I had been you, I should no doubt have felt the same."

Ann was comforted when she heard that, and when Lizzie added: "As to the Ryerson boy, we must see if something can't be done about him," she felt happier than she had been for days past.

Ann was accustomed in those days to say her prayers, morning and night. She had gone out with her Aunt Lizzie after dinner, trudging the hilly streets with the snow crackling underfoot, inspecting the big covered market, full of naphtha flares and sizzling gas-light, gay on this Christmas Eve with seasonable meat and poultry, fruit and berried greenery; and then they had gone home and Lizzie had taken her up to her attic bedroom. It was a long, narrow room under the roof, with a dormer window looking toward the hills of Idle. When her aunt was gone down, the girl did not undress for a long time. She stood before the window, delighted with what she saw. From her window on the Manchester plain she could see nothing but the few circumjacent yards of grass and trees. Now her eye feasted itself upon a prospect which suggested that all the constellations had fallen to earth. Chains and festoons of light, miles distant, looped and dipped upon the faces of the hills that were all a cold grey glimmer of snow; and besprinkled among these ordered galaxies were scores, hundreds, of little individual rebel lights burning with various brilliance like the uncharted star-dust of the heavens.

Ann found it an uplifting and liberating spectacle. Thinking of her last few miserable days, she felt almost literally unchained. She turned back to the narrow white room that had no fireplace and only a candle for light. She set the candle before the mirror on the dressing-table and for a long time brushed at her shining hair. Then she got down on her knees. Her childish jumble of requests to God contained two items: "God bless Mother." "Please God, let me stay here with Aunt Lizzie for a long time."

If Lillian Artingstall had been "blessed" in the simple literal sense that Ann had in mind, which would doubtless have meant kept in good health and enjoyment of her fortunate station, then it is not likely that Ann would have remained in Bradford for the long visit which she very much wanted. Providence, to give Ann that boon, had to do something about Lillian; and something had already been done. Little Ann could not know it, but while she was on her knees the woman upon whom she invoked blessings was on her back.

Hawley did not get home to his dinner that night. He was one of those individualists who believe that even a machine which they have themselves wound up perfectly cannot run without them. It was Christmas Eve, a gladsome season indeed, but also one which Artingstall's might expect to be profitable. The shops would be open late, and Hawley would want to see them working at their greatest efficiency to the last moment. He journeyed back, fuming at the time lost on this little fool daughter, but by eight o'clock the nerves of Mr. Tattersall the Manager were relaxing. Hawley's face was registering pleasure at the way things were going.

Lillian dined alone, without enjoyment. She had had to explain as best she could that Ann would not, after all, be able to accept this invitation and that. She knew that servants had heard her shouting as she thrashed the child, and that they were aware that Ann's departure indicated a family crisis. Her self-esteem was dependent on the opinion of other people; and, unsupported by Hawley, she could hardly bear to sit there with two servants fluttering in and out of the room. She retreated toward the drawing-room as early as possible, horribly aware that it was a retreat.

She was crossing the hall when a maid in the room behind her dropped a tray. It was the sort of thing that normally would have caused her to tighten her thin lips and march ahead with added dignity. One simply did not comment on the clumsiness of such louts. But now she turned back swiftly, pushed open the dining-room door, and saw the two girls grinning at one another. One was swinging the tray in her hand in a way which made Lillian think it had not been dropped at all: it had been deliberately gonged against a corner of the sideboard. "I hope that startled some of the starch out of the frosty old bitch," the girl said. As the words left her mouth she saw Lillian. Lillian would have retreated if she had not been seen. Now she had to do something. "Get out," she said. "Go and pack your things and get out."

The girl put the tray on the table and looked at her defiantly.

"You can't put me out on the street like that, you can't," she said. "Not without notice."

"Never mind notice. You'll have a week's money."

"An' how d'you think I'm going to get home to Blackburn at this time o' night? An' tomorrow Christmas Day."

"That's your affair. Get out," said Lillian. "I'll have your money ready when you come down."

"How am I going to get to Blackburn? Walk it?"

"You can run it if you like," said Lillian, and instantly regretted the idiotic words. They were the sort of cheap retort the girl would herself have used. That she had been trapped into them suddenly made her hate the girl, standing there, arms akimbo, staring at her insolently.

For the second time within a few days Lillian learned that hate is physically dangerous. Her heart was patting playfully against her ribs, gently, warningly. The girl sensed the deepening venom of her mood, and reacted swiftly.

"Oh, I can run it, can I?" she demanded shrilly. "That's funny, isn't it? That's your idea of a joke. Well, this was my first job as a slavey, and it'll be my last. Why any Lancashire girl is such a bloody fool as to leave a good job in a mill, I don't know. Well, this child's learned her lesson." She tore the absurd little goffered cap from her hair and untied her apron. She threw them at Lillian's feet. "Take 'em," she shouted. "Thank God, I'll have a shawl on my head an' clogs on my feet next week. No more slaving for the likes of you, a stuck-up bitch who can't manage her own kid."

Lillian could feel a mad stampede of vituperative words surging from her mind, crying for utterance. A lifetime's training made her fight them back. But the struggle was terrible, and now her heart was pounding. In her temples, in her throat, she could feel the blood working like a loud rhythmic piston. Suddenly she clutched at the table by which she was trying to stand with an erect patrician dignity. Then she was on her back on the carpet.

The girls were frightened out of their wits. They called the cook-housekeeper who sent one of them for the doctor and with the help of the other put Mrs. Artingstall to bed. The doctor was still there when Hawley got home. They were old friends. They had a drink together in the drawing-room. The doctor was solicitous, non-committal. "I didn't know Lillian had a heart like that."

"Like what?" Hawley asked brutally.

"Well – tricky – letting her down like that, you know. We'll have to watch it, Hawley, my boy. Avoid excitement. Could you get her away for a holiday?"

"It's as bad as that?"

"Well—" He finished his whisky and Hawley accompanied him to the front door. "Don't worry, Hawley, my boy. And a merry Christmas."

Ann away – Lillian ill; Hawley thought he had never had less reason to expect a Christmas to be merry. He stood before the dining-room fire, his arms resting along the mantelpiece, his head laid upon them. He kicked savagely at a lump of coal. "Blast that Birley!" he said. He did not go up again to see Lillian. He hated the look of her when she was unwell.

*

The Sugden girls made use of one another shamelessly. A refractory child was always packed off to Lizzie. Anyone in need of a holiday descended on Clara. Clara was the only one of them who had married money in the absolute sense that the owner of it didn't want to work any more and didn't need to work any more. Joe Blamires had a lovely house and exhibition gardens at St. Anne's on the Lancashire seacoast. The region was as flat as a board; the climate was mild; there were Joe's gardens to walk in, and Joe liked nothing better than to walk in them and, pipe in mouth, explain that all this – waving his plump arms about him – had been created out of Nothing. In fact, it had been created out of Joe Blamires's money, spent by a Scotch head gardener with four assistants.

This clearly was the place for Lillian with her troublesome heart; and thither she went early in the new year. Hawley had suggested that Ann should accompany her: Clara was accommodating and had no children of her own; but Lillian's opposition was so firm that it surprised him. Lillian had not forgotten that Ann had said: "You filthy beast! I've finished with you." Even to recall that moment imaginatively caused uncomfortable tremors. She felt that she didn't want to see Ann for a long time.

Then Hawley suggested that the child should come home; but again Lillian opposed him. "And be on her own all day long? How do you know what she'll be up to?" A child alone would always, in Lillian's view, be up to something. "You'd better leave her where she is, if Elizabeth will keep her."

Lillian wrote a long letter to Lizzie. She had not, she said, explained before that Ann's sudden departure from home was caused by bad conduct, and, as if that were not enough, by most insolent behaviour to her parents when the conduct was condemned. Lillian explained all about it at great length, but she did not mention the thrashing or the words that Ann had used when the thrashing was over. She said that the affair had distressed her so deeply that her health had suffered, and would Elizabeth be so kind as to keep Ann in Bradford until it would be convenient to have her home again.

During the last five years Lizzie Lightowler had learned a lot about girls. During the last few days she had learned a lot about Ann, and this, combined with what she knew about Lillian, caused her to crumple the letter with an impatient grunt and throw it into the fire. She was alone in her little sitting-room and, what is more, she was lonely in it. Since Ann had come, she had had one or two pangs of loneliness. She had thought she was done with that sort of thing. She prided herself on being a self-sufficient woman. But she hated the thought that the eager lovable child would soon be leaving her. And now Lillian wanted her to stay. But not on those terms, Lizzie grunted to herself. She crossed to her writing-table and sat down.

"Dear Lillian: I am sorry to hear that your health is not good, and I am sure that a visit to Clara and Joe will be beneficial. Give them my love. Ann is happy here, and if you would like her to stay I shall be delighted to have her. But, as you know, this is a school, and soon the pupils will be coming back after the holiday. I shall not be able to give Ann the attention she should have unless she, too, becomes a pupil and so gets counted in with all the others. You ought to know, also, that I never accept a girl for less than twelve months. If you could consent to Ann's remaining with me for that length of time, I am sure that both she and I would be delighted. I enclose a copy of the school prospectus, which shows you the fees. My love to Hawley and yourself. Lizzie."

"She hates the name Lizzie," she grinned to herself, "and she'll hate the idea of fees even more." But it was a good gamble on getting Ann for a year. Lizzie felt she could do something with the girl in that time.

Lillian's nose went even thinner than usual. "I should have thought Ann was an *educated* girl," she said with a sniff.

Hawley's face deepened its purple. "Payin' to stay wi' 'er aunt!" he cried. "Ba goom, Ah will say you Sugden lasses take after yer father. Ah used to expect 'im to 'and me a check after dinner every time Ah was there courtin' you."

Lillian sat up in bed, where she had remained since Christmas Eve, though now she felt well. She handed him the prospectus. "The fees seem reasonable enough," she said. "I see they're payable by the term in advance. You'd better send her a cheque."

The Artingstall diligence was waiting at the porch. Hawley glanced at his watch and saw that he had no time for argument. He blew gustily out of the room. "Payin' to stay wi' 'er aunt!" He couldn't get over it.

*

"Isn't that wonderful!" said Ann. "I didn't know there was such coun-try in England."

Lizzie looked with satisfaction at the girl's cheeks reddened by the frosty wind and at her shining eyes. "Yes," she said. "It's a good walk. I often do it."

They had set out after lunch and walked along Manningham Lane to Shipley. Then they had dropped down a steep street to the valley bottom and climbed up the other side to the village of Baildon. The snow was crisp underfoot as they passed through the one street of the snug place, with the old stocks still there outside the Malt Shovel Inn, though many years must have passed since a malefactor languished in them.

The village street petered out into a moorland track. Across the snowy undulations of the land, whereon the rough unmortared walls drew their crazy zigzags, and over which the sky was a milky blue, they could see the village of Hawksworth among bare winter boughs. A shoulder of hill thrust up behind it.

"When you climb that hill you're on Ilkley Moor," Lizzie said point-ing. "We'll do it some day."

They walked to Hawskworth, and then they turned to the left and followed the road that kept under the shoulder of the hill. It was lovely here, Ann thought, with the snowy hill running up so steeply on their right, its crest cutting a long glittering white line upon the blue of the sky. There was a wind in their faces, sharp and exhilarating, and, look-ing sideways at Lizzie, stepping out briskly with her white hair shining and a stout ash stick in her hand, the girl laughed suddenly for sheer joy and cried: "I hope we get tea soon."

Lizzie's stick pointed ahead to the only building now in sight. "That's Dick Hudson's. We'll be all right there."

"Who's Dick Hudson?"

"Goodness knows who he is. That's the name of the pub."

The pub stood under weather-battered trees. The road they were on flowed past it into the now quickly falling dark. Another road forked off to the left, and to the right a rough path climbed the hill. "That's the way we'll take when we go to Ilkley Moor," Aunt Lizzie said. "Now look at that. Isn't that encouraging?" She pointed with her stick to the smoke drifting up from Dick Hudson's chimneys.

In a moment they were sitting before the fire from which the smoke was ascending, in a room with a lighted hanging lamp, and drawn red curtains, and solid furniture of oak and elm.

"Now you'll see what a Yorkshire moorland pub understands by afternoon tea," Lizzie laughed.

Ann, with her winter-sharpened appetite, fell upon the inch-thick fried ham, golden-brown, and the eggs that came with it beneath a great metal cover. Lizzie cut at the loaf, poured the tea, and passed the butter.

"How does this suit Your Royal Daintiness?" she asked.

Ann, unashamed in her gusto, wiped grease from her chin with her handkerchief. "Not a crumb too much," she said.

"I shall never forget this," Ann thought; and then wondered where she had lately heard those words. Yes – that poor Ryerson boy, sitting in his miserable kitchen, telling her so earnestly that he would never forget her visit, as though she were a fairy princess or something. She had laughed at his grave persistence; "but all the same," she thought, "I *shan't* forget this."

This first moorland walk at night, in the darkness that had come on while they were in the inn. This grey mysterious shroud stretched over the dead earth, and the few trees clawing up and looking so ancient and cold and threadbare. This silence, broken only by the steady reliable tramp of Lizzie's feet and the tap-tap of her stick on the ground that the frost was stiffening again. And then the lights, scattered at first, winking out from lonely cottages, gradually thickening into clusters, and at last, as they approached the town again, suddenly leaping upon the sight in those myriad constellations that she was always to think of as one of the glories of Bradford. She said to herself: "A city that is set on a hill cannot be hid."

They were back on the hard prosaic pavements of Manningham Lane. She was tired, but she felt her cheeks glowing and her heart glowing, too. Why am I so happy? she wondered. Suddenly it struck her that she had never been so happy as this before – that perhaps she had not at all before this known what it was to be happy. As they passed between the heavy iron gates of Ackroyd Park she took Aunt Lizzie's arm and pressed it against her side, and when they came to the house she ran eagerly up the short curving drive and pulled the bell impatiently.

*

They had dinner in the dining-room. It was the only meal they took there – "but I have breakfast here, too, with the girls when they're about," Lizzie explained.

Ann was always glad to escape to the little room upstairs, but the dining-room was cheerful enough. Over the fireplace was an enlarged photograph of the Matterhorn. It was the only thing Lizzie kept to remind her of Arthur, and it wasn't necessary. She could afford now to laugh at her own loss. "Of course," she said, "I might have been like Queen Victoria and kept his climbing boots in the hall and an alpenstock in the umbrella-stand and used one of his ropes for a clothes-line. I don't think it would have done me any good. But I do like to see that picture. I never climbed a mountain myself. I did nothing but scramble about on little hills. He was so much better than I am at everything. Now let's go upstairs." She picked up the letters that had come by the evening post and that old Marsden had laid on the table. "That's your father's writing, isn't it?"

Ann nodded. Lizzie watched her closely and saw the disappointment clouding her face. "I expect he wants me to go back already," the child said.

"Well; maybe, and maybe not. Come along. We'll open it upstairs."

They sat on either side of the fire. Lizzie opened the letter. As soon as she saw the cheque she knew it was all right. "We've saved him!" she cried. "We've saved the little Ryerson boy! You've got to go home in the morning to get fitted up with the clothes you need, and then you're coming to live with me for a year – all, bar the holidays. Does that please you?"

She explained what she had done, and Ann listened with shining eyes. "It's wonderful!" she said. "That walk today, with the marvellous ham for tea, and now a year of you! But what's it got to do with the Ryerson boy?"

"You don't know anything about poor people, do you?"

Ann shook her head.

"Well, I do; and so will you before I've done with you. They're bound hand and foot. Supposing I got this boy a job here in Bradford, which I intend to do. What would happen?"

Ann shook her head again.

"I'd just be crippling the whole family. Poor people can't live unless they hang together. He's too young to earn enough to keep himself, and his mother couldn't get along because he'd have nothing to send her."

"He's got nothing to give her now," Ann whispered, recalling Mrs. Ryerson's suffering face and Arnold's white look of consternation when Hawley railed at him.

"But he's going to have something," said Lizzie. "That's the joke. The man that sacked him is going to keep him. D'you think I'd take a penny for keeping you? Not a ha'penny, my dear, however long you stay. No. This young Arnold can come and work in Bradford. Your father will make up his wages to what he needs to live on and he'll also provide something for Mrs. Ryerson. Don't you think that's good justice? And don't you think good justice can also be a good joke?"

"It's a beautiful idea," said Ann. "Thank you, Aunt Lizzie. Thank you very much."

"Beautiful? I should say it is. It's the loveliest idea I've ever had." She lay back in her chair and laughed. "If you breathe a word to your father or mother, I'll skin you alive."

Chapter Six

"Ah, my friends! Think of the poor whose lives, from the cradle to the grave, are blown this way and that by chance as dead leaves are blown by the wind. They cannot plan their lives. They cannot say: 'John, of course, will inherit the estate, George will go into the Army, and Henry into the Church.' No; they must take what offers. They must grasp at spectral chances. They must pick up the crumbs that fall from life's rich table. And yet, all these lives, each so casual, drifting as tramps drift from one cold charity to another, all these lives, none of which can safely formulate its own plan – all these lives, I say, coalesce into that solid basis which is the very foundation on which the state rests, the inexhaustible arsenal from which alone we can draw the defence of the national being. Think, my friends, of the poor. I could tell a tale of one poor boy, weak and lonely, thrown to the wolves of chance, whom yet the wolves miraculously did not destroy but suckled, as the fabulous Roman children were suckled on the Seven Hills." (The Rt. Hon. Hamer Shawcross, P.C., M.P., who liked a classical allusion. Ætat. 68.)

Hamer, at the age of fourteen, having done with school, was weak enough, but hardly lonely. Gordon Stansfield, Ellen, and Birley Arting-stall were standing by, and the two men were resolved that Hamer's fate was to be a Wesleyan parson. The wolves of chance to whom Hamer was thrown were not so very fierce. Indeed, getting behind the rhetoric of this fine-looking old man – white hair, elegant morning clothes, and the dusky red carnation which in his later years he always wore – getting behind all that, one found that there was only one wolf and that he appeared in the unfrightening guise of Mr. Suddaby.

Down there in his cavern at the heart of old Manchester, under the shadow of t'Owd Church, soon to be grandiloquently called the Cathedral, t'Owd Church that had stood beside the Irwell since

Saxon days and whose steeple-rocking bells were the only things that disturbed the subterranean calm of his life, this old troglodyte of a bookseller turned his thoughts more and more toward the past. Drowsing beside the fire, with Sheba the white Persian cat drowsing upon the mat beside him, he thought of the time when he and Friedrich Engels had been young together, and together had codified all the data of misery and hunger that Manchester so abundantly afforded. How they had corresponded! In Leeds, London, Liverpool – in all the big industrial cities – there had been rebels, prophets of Utopia, revolutionaries, who saw in every strike, in every brush with the police, the signal that was going to topple to ruins a world that needed remaking. With all these they corresponded.

Whenever the bells of t'Owd Church came dinning down into his ears he would think, but now only with a drowsy and not excited reminiscence, of standing in Albert Square with Engels as the bells danged in another year. Mary Burns was there, the working girl with whom Engels lived so happily, and her sister Lizzy; and as the bells clamoured they all four went walking up Oxford Street toward All Saints, talking excitedly of the things that filled their minds.

"Another year gone!" Engels shouted. "Another year begun. Charles, perhaps this dead and damned and rotten old year is the last year men will know in poverty and squalor. Perhaps this year that is now ten minutes old will be the Year One of truth and justice. Anything may set it going, Charles – anything in such a putrid world as this. It's like a rotten old shed. How it will blaze!"

And Mr. Suddaby – young Charles Suddaby, aged thirty – grasped Engels by the arm and cried: "Let's drink to it, Friedrich – to the time all the poor devils of Hulme and Ancoats deserve to have!"

Midnight though it was, there was a bar open, and Charles Suddaby pulled the half-hearted Engels through its brass-bound swing doors. Dreaming over the memory, the old man could still see the white curve of Lizzy Burns's throat as her shawled head leaned back and her hand held a glass to her lips. And Engels, with his beard and his solid broadcloth clothes, had a glass of ale, too, in his hand, standing there in the greeny-yellow gas-light upon the sawdust pocked with spittle. He looked uncomfortable among the labourers and artisans in their coarse clothes and clogs, filling the air with the fume of cheap tobacco smoked in clay.

Young Charles raised his glass of beer and cried: "To the slaves of Hulme and Ancoats! Freedom! This very year! Freedom!"

And then they were in the thick of an uproar. A burly chap, not too boozed to hear the word "slaves," knocked the glass out of Suddaby's hand. Mary Burns took Engels's sleeve and said: "Get out!' Get out quick!" But Engels wanted to stay and argue. He always wanted to argue. "Aren't you slaves?" he asked. "Put it to the test of reason."

Poor Engels was so utterly reasonable. When the crowd had chased the four of them from the pub and they were walking again along the street, he said: "But despite everything, Charles, despite the slaves who hate the name of slavery but not the thing, it will come. Perhaps this year. I have heard from Karl Marx today. He says..."

And all the way to the lodgings, he told Charles what Karl Marx had said. But it didn't come that year; it hadn't come at all; and now Lizzy Burns whose throat had shone so white that night was dead, and so was Mary; and Engels had called merely to say that he would call no more. The bells rang on, and the old man dreamed away his memories. Lately, he had been feeling very old indeed. Once he was in his chair he didn't want to get out of it. It was time he had someone to help him, even to look after him. He remembered that Gordon Stansfield had said his stepson was just leaving school. Not a bad boy.

So this was the grisly wolf to whom life threw Hamer Shawcross. When the venerable cabinet minister said that the wolf suckled him, it was no more than the truth. Suddaby had never married. Lizzy Burns, so full of Irish wit and vivacity, though she could neither read nor write, shone in his memory more brightly than any other woman. She had gone off to London with Engels when her sister Mary died. They had taken a house in Regent's Park Road so as to be near Karl Marx. And now she was dead. Engels had married her on her deathbed. Well, Suddaby reflected, Engels had given her a better time than he could have done. She had travelled; she had met the great ones; while he, to whom even she now seemed no more than one flicker in the hot rebellious flame of his youth, had done nothing but burrow deeper and deeper into his catacombs.

Not a bad boy, the old man reflected. He sat by the fire, his thin, ivory-coloured hands resting on the knob of his ebony stick, his chin in his hands. He watched the boy as now and then he came into view, emerging from one of the aisles of books. A serious-looking child, anxious-looking, too, with the blue veins in the temples, the dark hair waving off the broad white brow. He had told him to look round, to get the hang of things, find out where the stuff was kept. And now there he was, hopping through the aisles that were labelled Poetry, Drama, Religion, Belles Lettres, Biography, History, Travel, Social Science, and all the rest. Ha! and now here he was, bearing down towards the warm fireside bay, his hand thrusting back his hair. This meant a question.

"Please, sir, what exactly is Social Science?"

With the end of his stick old Suddaby rolled Sheba over on to her back and delicately scratched her belly. Then, lifting his skull-cap, he scratched his own white hair.

"Social Science, eh? Where do you live?"

"Broadbent Street, sir."

"Yes, Broadbent Street. I remember. How much a week does your father pay in rent?"

"I don't know, sir."

"Just call me Mr. Suddaby. And what shall I call you?"

"My name's Hamer, sir – Mr. Suddaby."

"I had thought I had heard Mr. Stansfield calling you John?"

"John Hamer Shawcross is my name. I prefer Hamer."

The old man cocked a sharp eye at him sideways, then went on tickling the complaisant cat.

"I see. Very well, Hamer. If I'm not mistaken, your father, and everybody else in Broadbent Street, pays five shillings a week. You see, there was a time when I used to collect information of that sort all over Manchester. Well, whom does he pay it to?"

"Mr. Richardson. He calls every Monday morning, and the money's always ready under the clock."

"Ah, now you're wrong, Hamer. The money is not paid to Mr. Richardson. Mr. Richardson merely collects it. Have you ever heard of Lord Lostwithiel?"

"No, Mr. Suddaby. But there's a public-house called the Lostwithiel Arms not far from our street-right opposite another called the Liskeard Arms."

"Excellent, Hamer. Now we're getting on with our lesson in Social

Science. The Lostwithiel Arms is named after Lord Lostwithiel, who is no less a person than an earl. The Liskeard Arms is named after his son and heir, Lord Liskeard, who is no less a person than a viscount, and these two public-houses are named after these two gentlemen because Lord Lostwithiel owns the land they stand on, as well as the land your house stands on, as well as many miles of land in that region. Your rent is paid to Mr. Richardson, who pays it to Lord Lostwithiel's agent, who pays it to Lord Lostwithiel, who has never seen Broadbent Street in all his born days and never drunk a pint in the Lostwithiel Arms. Lord Lostwithiel has very large estates in Yorkshire, where he shoots grouse and gets the Prince of Wales to help him to do it, and a house in Belgrave Square in London. Social Science, my dear Hamer, is the study of the why and wherefore of interesting things like that."

"Why we pay our rent to a lord?"

"To be going on with, put it that way: why Gordon Stansfield helps to keep Lord Lostwithiel on the fat of the land."

Hamer pushed up his hair and grinned. "That'd take a bit of thinking out, Mr. Suddaby."

"Yes, John – I beg your pardon – Hamer. That'd take a bit of thinking out. And while you're thinking it out, take that feather brush and start dusting Social Science. It's a dusty subject."

The boy went on with his work. The old man watched him, musing. That was attractive – the way his face lighted up when he grinned. Very attractive indeed. It could be a dangerous face when it was a bit older – that habitual gravity, almost sadness, that could suddenly dissolve in laughter.

It was said of Hamer Shawcross that he was the best-read man in the Labour Party and that his platform manner was that of a revivalist parson. Both these statements were true. The influences that shaped him that way were at work between his fourteenth and eighteenth years. There was a third thing about him, of which women were more aware than men. He had a body of great strength and beauty. Even towards the end, he was supple and erect, six feet high, with no stoop to the shoulders, and the easy assured carriage of a good actor. It was towards the end of his life that Sir Thomas Hannaway stopped him in Palace Yard, slapped him on the shoulder, and, with small shy eyes twinkling in the fat creases of his red face, said: "Eh! You're still a gradely lad, Hamer. You've got me to thank for that, you know. Remember the punch-ball in the old bone-yard?"

Hamer Shawcross did not like being reminded of the old bone-yard. "Yes, I do, indeed, Sir Thomas," he said, rather sourly.

"Tom, to you, I hope."

"Very well, Tom if you wish, Sir Thomas."

The tall, immaculate figure hurried away. Sir Thomas looked after him and shook his head, puzzled. Hamer had been more than a bit stand-offish when he was a member of the Labour Government. But now that he was an adherent of a National Government, and Sir Thomas was sitting as a National Conservative member, that ought to make a difference. They were both in the same boat. Well – not exactly. Sir Thomas saw the minister's tall body double dexterously as he entered a waiting car. Thomas was a connoisseur of luxurious things. He knew that car. "Lostwithiel's, or I'll be damned," he muttered. No; he was not in that boat. Poor vulgar Thomas would have liked to be. But he wasn't, though his horse Darkie Cheap had beaten Lostwithiel's Feu de Joie in the Derby.

Sir Thomas Hannaway was certain that he would win the Derby with Darkie Cheap, because Darkie Cheap was a lucky name for him. It was associated with his first successful business deal. He was just seventeen years old when he acquired Darkie Cheap's bone-yard.

There was only one thing that young Tom Hannaway wanted to know, and that was where the old man sold the rubbish that found its way into his hands. It was incredible that anyone would want to buy it: old iron, bones, bottles. But someone did; and when Tom knew where his outflow pipe from the business was, he set himself to dam the inflow.

Darkie was getting old. He couldn't move around as he used to. He depended on Tom to do the collecting for him. It was a touch-and-go business that at best gave the old man a bare living. Tom was present one Monday morning when Mr. Richardson called for the rent of the bone-yard. Darkie was abject and apologetic. He hadn't the money. "This is the third week," Mr. Richardson said sternly. "The office won't let it go on much longer."

("Note that, my dear Hamer," said Mr. Suddaby, when he heard of the affair. "The office is the secular arm of the Earl of Lostwithiel. The Earl must have even the marrow out of the bones that the poor have done with.")

Tom Hannaway set out with his handcart that morning, whistling gaily. Now was his moment. He went his usual rounds, and to half the people who brought their old junk out to him he said: "Store it up. There's not much demand this week." He used the word grandiloquently, like an economist who understands the laws governing these matters. Not much demand for Ancoats' rags and bones! He smiled, baring his white even teeth. The women liked him. "Whatever you do, don't throw your stuff away. It'll all be wanted later."

He continued to play this game, putting off more and more customers, till only a trickle of goods was coming into the bone-yard. A month later the news went round: "The bums are in on Darkie Cheap."

There was the customary rush to gaze with commiseration upon a misfortune that hung over everyone's head and now had fallen on Darkie. Foul catcalls were showered on the hated bum-bailiffs who were in process of seizing the few wretched things that might be sold. There were the handcart and the scales and other odds and ends. Darkie Cheap himself was there in the depths of his malodorous fastness, the whites of his eyes calling for a sympathy that would have declared itself in an attack on the bailiffs if Mr. Richardson had not been standing by. Too many of the onlookers were themselves in Mr. Richardson's bad books, so they held their hands.

Tom Hannaway came bustling through the crowd, pushing and thrusting the people aside, with his elbows, with his palms, his face alight with indignation, his black curls awry. "It's a shame, Mr. Richardson. It's a bloody shame!" he shouted. "If the man can't pay, he can't. And my job goes, too, if he goes. What about that? What about throwing innocent people out of work?"

"That's reight, Tom Hannaway. That's fair enough. Tell t'owd swine off," the people began to mutter; but Mr. Richardson looked at him with amusement and contempt. "You've only got to put down the rent he owes and back goes his stuff," he said.

Tom Hannaway put his hand into his pocket. There was a gasp of surprise when the chink of money was heard. "How much?" he demanded truculently.

Darkie Cheap had come trembling to the front of the yard. He held out his hands, the pink palms upwards. "Tom! You can't afford it. It's too much."

"How much?" Tom repeated, dribbling the money through his fingers. Mr. Richardson named the sum.

"Give me your rent-book, Darkie. Let me confirm that," Tom said importantly. "I don't trust this chap."

Darkie produced the book. Everyone crowded round, but silently, awed, as he studied it. Then he took money from his pocket, counted it carefully, and handed it with the book to Mr. Richardson. "Sign for it," he said. "And there's sixpence change."

Darkie Cheap broke out into wails of gratitude. "Oh, Tom, Tom!" he cried, hugging the youngster. "You've saved me."

"He's paid your rent, that's all," said Mr. Richardson. "And so we can't seize these things." He motioned to the bailiffs. "Take 'em back to the yard. And you," he said to Darkie Cheap, "get 'em out before the week's over. I'm giving you a week's notice to quit – understand? You're an unsatisfactory tenant."

Tom Hannaway burst out into fresh indignation. "Well of all the—! You can't do that, Mr. Richardson. You can't take my money and then clear the old man out."

"Can't I! You try and contest it."

Nobody did. Tom bought Darkie Cheap's equipment at a dirt-cheap price. This, with the rent, cleared him out, but he had the bone-yard, his first business concern. For he was the next tenant when Darkie Cheap vanished no one knew whither. Tom had known he would be the next tenant. He had arranged it with Mr. Richardson. His experience with Mr. Richardson was to him the most amazing part of the whole business. He had been trembling with fright when he suggested to Mr. Richardson that it would be worth his while to make Darkie quit. Tom Hannaway never again trembled when he had to suggest corruption. Mr. Richardson's conduct had been a valuable lesson to him. An extra shilling a week on the rent (which of course would not go on the rent-book) was all it cost Tom to have Darkie Cheap turned out. His gallant conduct in trying to save Darkie increased his already great popularity. The stuff he had caused to be hoarded was there to be picked up, and what with that, and short weight, and one or two other little tricks, he was soon able to recover all he had spent. He had noted, too, the fear of Mr. Richardson that held the crowd. He knew this was because many of them owed rent. Well, Tom thought, as he made his rounds, it would be easy, once he had a bit of free money again, to advance it to some of these rent-owing women who liked him so much. He had heard there was good interest to be made that way. Tom was already financier enough to know that not money, but interest on money, was the goal. He took lodgings, a shabby bed-sitting-room, as soon as the boneyard was his. Another thing he knew was that he was going to be on his own. There were too many Hannaways. He didn't consider that he owed them anything. They could be a weight round a rising man's neck.

On a Saturday night in February of 1880, when Hamer Shawcross was advanced a few months into his fifteenth year, he watched Ellen perform her secretarial ritual as she had done on every Saturday night as long as he could remember. Gordon Stansfield sat down to his table, dipped pen in ink, but, instead of beginning to write, looked up suddenly at the boy who was about to leave for his own room upstairs.

"What are you doing up there tonight, John?" he asked.

"Oh, I shall read."

"Good. D'you know, when I was your age I couldn't read. I was nearly twenty before I could get on with a book."

Ellen, who had her fingers outspread in the foot of a stocking wherein she sought the thin spots, looked up from her chair by the fire. "I doubt if he knows how lucky he is," she said. "I don't suppose there's another boy in Ancoats with a father like you and a room of his own to read in."

"I wish every boy could have such things," said Gordon simply. "But what I wanted to say, John, was this: try a bit of writing some night. Don't let it all be reading. Try to express yourself. I find it very hard," he smiled. "I didn't begin early enough. I was over thirty before I preached my first sermon."

John was hesitating uneasily, on one leg after the other, anxious to escape. "Oh, sermons!" he said

Gordon laid down the pen which he had been twiddling nervously in his fingers. "Yes," he said. "Look at Mr. Spurgeon. He was little more than a boy when he was preaching to thousands. Charles Haddon Spurgeon. John Hamer Shawcross." He mused over the names. "Eh?" There was an affectionate challenge in his voice. John did not take it up.

"Well," said Gordon, "we can't all be Spurgeons, but we can all bring such gifts as we have to the Master. I was a poor babbler when I began to preach. You'll do better than that. Perhaps I shan't be here much longer, and I'd like to know that you'd made a beginning."

Ellen got up with brisk indignation, the Lancashire side of her tongue stirred to activity. "Eh, lad! Now tha's talkin' daft. Not 'ere much longer indeed! There's nothing ails thee, so get on wi' thi work and let child get on wi' 'is'n."

She was almost in tears beneath her asperity. She hated to think of illness coming to Gordon.

"Well," Gordon said, dismissing the matter, "get up to your room, lad. But think on, now. Do some writing, and don't let it be too long before I sit under you in a pulpit."

It was probably this injunction to write which caused the boy to begin, that very night, to keep a diary. He went on keeping it almost to the day of his death. Who could guess from this opening that the diary would, as the years rolled on, record the thoughts and deeds of one living at the very hub of history as its wheel was in maddest whirl? This is what he wrote that night. It gives a valuable light on his mind as it was at last emerging from childhood:

"My father, as I call Gordon Stansfield, though he is not my father, said tonight: 'John, why do you not write something?' I cannot tell him that I prefer to be called Hamer. But I try to get everyone else to call me Hamer, except people like Tom Hannaway and Arnold Ryerson, who have always called me John.

"My father said again tonight that he would like me to be a parson. I do not want to be a parson, but this is something I cannot tell him. He is very good to me, and I do not want to hurt his feelings. His friend, Mr. Birley Artingstall, also wants me to be a parson. They often mention it in an offhand way, though never very seriously, but I expect that will come. Last Sunday was the Chapel Anniversary, and there was a special preacher. The chapel was packed. People were sitting on the pulpit steps and on the platform place round the communion table, and chairs were brought in and put in the aisles. All this caused an atmosphere of great excitement, and when the preacher came in there was a sort of hush, as if everybody was all strung up and he could do what he liked with them. Then I wished I was the preacher. He preached a very good sermon. When he had finished the chapel was very hot, and everybody sang the last hymn with tremendous voices, and you could feel again how powerful the preacher was, because they were singing like that in consequence of the way he had preached to them. Then I wished again that I was the preacher, because it must be very fine to have a great congregation in the hollow of your hand.

"So I shall learn to be a preacher, though I do not want to be a parson. I shall become a local preacher, because that will give me a chance to learn how to speak to large congregations of people. I do not know what I want to do, except that whenever I hear a good preacher like last Sunday I feel it would be very good to have large numbers of people hanging on my words."

That was all he wrote as the first entry in his diary; but now that he had begun he kept it up. Indeed, that chance remark of Gordon Stansfield's, setting the boy on this course of self-expression and self-examination, must be considered of vital importance in Hamer Shawcross's career.

"I said in the first entry in this diary 'I do not know what I want to do.' Strangely enough, Mr. Suddaby, my employer, said to me this morning: 'What are you going to do with yourself, Hamer? You can't spend long in this place. There's no future in it for you.' I was glad to hear him call me Hamer. So far, he is the only person to do this. I told him I did not know what I was going to do with myself, and he said: 'Well, make up your mind and then stick to it.' He smiled, and added: 'If you want to take up one of the learned professions, there's enough stuff lying round you here to qualify you for anyone of them.'

"Mr. Suddaby is always calling my attention in this way to the books. There is not much for me to do in his shop, and he says it is a pity to waste time. He asked me what books I have at home, and I told him about Samuel Bamford's poems. He said: 'Poor Sam! To think he was once a Radical!' I asked him what he meant, and told him about the Old Warrior who had marched with Bamford to Peterloo, and about the sabre which I have in my room. He was interested to hear about the sabre and said: 'That's a grand relic, Hamer. Keep that,' but he didn't say much more about Samuel Bamford except: 'He became a mild old buffer, Hamer – like me. I introduced him to Engels, who was furious with both of us that day. He shook his fist and said: "I wish to God I could shatter your faith in law and order." He never did. I just became old and tired. Sam just became a bad poet who thought a poet was a respectable being who should set an example to his fellows. Oh, yes, Sam wrote awful things. I can still remember one of his poems.

It begins:

> How happy may we be, my love!
>   How happy may we be,
> If we our humble means improve,
>   My wife, my child, and me.

You see, he felt that if he could get a few more shillings a week in his pocket, all would be well. And he was once at Peterloo and went to gaol for it! Take warning from Sam, Hamer, and from me.'

"Mr. Suddaby went back to his chair by the fire, and started talking to his cat. He said: 'Sheba, you lazy old slut, I'll have to call you Bamford or Suddaby. You used to be a fighter, and now you do nothing but lie around and purr for more milk.'

"I have just looked up Bamford's poem in the book which Mr. Birley Artingstall bound in red leather for me. It is there all right, so I am sure the words above are correct.

"I thought about what my father said and what Mr. Suddaby said – that I ought to make up my mind what I want to be, but I cannot make up my mind. I told Mr. Suddaby this, last thing as I was leaving the shop, and he said: 'Well, to begin with, make up your body.' He took hold of my arm and felt it. 'There seems to be nothing wrong with you,' he said, 'but there's nothing *to* you. You ought to do something about that.' So I shall attend Tom Hannaway's gymnasium."

And that is what Sir Thomas Hannaway meant when, so many years later, he said to the Rt. Hon. Hamer Shawcross: "Remember the punch-ball in the old bone-yard?"

In the mornings Tom went the rounds with his barrow. In the afternoons he was in attendance to deal with callers. In the evenings the doors of the bone-yard were closed and the light of a street lamp fell upon them. Tom Hannaway could often be seen shinning up the lamp with two cloths in his hand – one wet, one dry. With these he would clean and polish the glass of the lamp. He wanted the full value of every ray. He understood that illumination was publicity. He was one of the first men to use neon lighting in Manchester. When he bought Artingstall's, he kept the name, recognizing the importance of its immemorial sound in Manchester ears, but he wreathed it in lighted tubes of red, blue, green and yellow, even as he had wreathed in coloured chalks his earliest business announcements on the wall of the croft.

Falling upon the closed doors of the bone-yard, the light of the spotless street lamp illuminated these chalked words:

Hannaway's Club
Entrance Threepence
Bars, Rings, Dumb-bells.
Boxing Instruction by
Professional
Threepence Extra.

The fitting-out of this place had cost Tom very little. The parallel bars were of his own manufacture. The rings fixed to the ends of ropes hanging down from the dim rafters had come in a lot of old junk. So had the dumb-bells and the two oil-burning hurricane lamps that cast a smoky light round the gaunt evil-smelling shed. Once or twice in his time Tom Hannaway had accepted a challenge to "step up" in a booth at the fair which occasionally took possession of the croft. The batterings he there received from broken-down old pugs were turned to good account, for those hammerings, he now made out, those brief and gory appearances in a public ring, constituted him a "professional" and justified the "threepence extra" for tuition.

On only one thing had he spent money, and he had spent it wisely. He had devised a badge with white cross-bones on a blue ground and the initials H.C., for Hannaway's Club. After twelve attendances at the Club, a boy was entitled to a free badge, and he was then initiated into the secret gesture of Club members, which was simply to lay the index-finger of the left hand along the forehead, with the knuckle out-wards. Soon there was a score of Ancoats boys wearing the badge and making this occult gesture, and making it proudly if to Tom Hann-away himself. Tom would return it with the grave punctiliousness of a field-marshal returning a private's salute. A badge not greatly dissimi-lar was supplied to, and proudly worn by, thousands of children who, years later, belonged to the Artingstall Kiddies' Klub. Qualification was by the purchase of a complete suit at the stores. From his earliest days you could teach Tom Hannaway nothing about sheep or about the importance of mumbo-jumbo in herding them.

*

There was a black winter cold over the town as Hamer made his way home. He was well clothed; there were good boots on his feet; but his teeth chattered as a north wind, edged like a knife, cut at him round a corner. "Go home by way of Stevenson Square," Mr. Suddaby said. "You'll see something interesting."

The Square was not far out of Hamer's way. The first interesting thing he saw was that fires were blazing in it, bursting out of the sides of punctured buckets, and filling the open space with thick tarry smoke that the rioting wind tore to shreds. Round the fires scores of wretched people were warming their hands. There was nothing new to Hamer in the sight of thin and badly-clothed folks, but about these, gathered there in the howling wind, in the open space round which tall black buildings rose, with the ruddy firelight dancing upon white bony faces and outstretched skinny hands, there was some macabre quality that instantly touched and held him. Old women with grey wisps of hair blown about their faces; old men clutching their rags around them and even so not hiding their all but nakedness; barefoot children with the elfin eerie faces of knowledge bitter and premature: no, he had never seen this. This was, after all, something new. These were not people acquainted with poverty but overwhelmed by it, crushed, hopeless, utterly defeated.

He saw that they all carried basins or saucepans or jam-jars. Presently, rumbling over the granite setts of the road, there came a horse-drawn lorry, and on the lorry was a boiler with a fire burning beneath it. As soon as it was sighted, every man, woman and child ran from the fires, brandishing their pots and pans, howling like animals whose time for feeding has come. In a confused, gesticulating mob, they surrounded the lorry, accompanying its progress, some running before it, behind it, on both sides of it, all waving their utensils aloft.

There were three men on the lorry, besides the driver. "Get back!" they shouted. "Get back. Some of those children will be run over. There's plenty for all of you. Get back!"

But the starving scarecrows would not listen. They hung on to the lorry with their hands. They tried to leap upon it. They clung to the horse's harness. They patted his nose and flanks.

The lorry came to a standstill in the space between the fires, little warmer in that snarling north wind than any other spot in the black square. The driver sprang down and threw a yellow blanket over the round sleek haunches of the horse. "Never mind t'bloody 'orse, mister! 'E's warmer'n we are. Let's 'ave t'soup!" someone shouted; and the whole tatterdemalion crew, rattling their pots upon the lorry, screeched: "Soup! Soup! Soup!"

The lid of the boiler was lifted. A white cloud billowed up into the air; the wind snatched upon a thick luscious aroma and threw it into the sniffing noses of the pack. A sound like a great sigh greeted it. "A-ah!"

The men upon the lorry compelled the crowd into a rude line. With a great iron ladle, one of them dished out the soup; another put into each out-thrust hand a hunk of bread. None, being served, lingered near the fires. All had, somewhere, holes and corners into which they could slink to eat their food. Mysteriously they disappeared into the dark streets leading to the square. The windy darkness swallowed them up.

Then all the soup was gone. A few old people, a few children, lingered disconsolately, no longer clamorous, no longer part of a yelping herd: nothing but hungry and deflated men and women and children. The men and women drifted away in ones and twos, carrying their empty pans, and soon were part of the darkness from which momentarily they had had the temerity to emerge. No one was left but two small children, a boy and a girl, both bare-legged, whitefaced, thin as reeds. They said nothing, but side by side went to one of the fires and stood there, the boy's left hand in the girl's right, each with a hand warming at the blaze. Then the men came down from the lorry and said: "We've got to take these fires away. We aren't allowed to leave 'em burning here."

They doused the flames with buckets of water brought from the lorry. An acrid stink arose where the good smell of soup had been. The men put the fire-buckets on to the lorry, unblanketed the horse, and drove away. The wind howled in the square. The children, with tin mugs fastened by string round their necks, stood there looking at the place where the fire had been, and still were standing there when Hamer Shawcross hurried towards his home.

In the morning, old Suddaby said: "Well, Hamer. Did you see anything interesting in the square?"

Hamer had slept badly. He had said nothing to Gordon Stansfield or to Ellen about the scene in Stevenson Square. But he couldn't get it out of his mind. For the first time in his life, he had encountered an experience that kept him awake, tossing in his bed, troubled in mind. The wind had persisted. It rattled the window; it howled "Loo! Loo!" as it had done on the night following the Old Warrior's burial. The flame of a street lamp, shaken by the wind, fell upon the sabre and shivered up and down its length in pale undulations. The weapon itself seemed to take on life, to stir and tremble upon the wall. It worried the boy so much that he got out of bed, and ran down his blind. Then he could not see the sabre any more, and he slept.

So when Mr. Suddaby asked him whether he had seen anything interesting in the square, he told him of this. The old man, leaning forward with both hands clasped on the head of his stick, said: "That's a pity, Hamer, that's a pity. It isn't everybody is entrusted with a Peterloo sabre. Don't run the blind down on it yet. Sam Bamford's dead, and so is your Old Warrior, and I'm as lazy as Sheba and a lot older. You must excuse me. But don't excuse yourself."

He smiled, half-serious, half-mocking, and shook open his *Manchester Guardian*.

"Read Tom Paine," old Suddaby said, "Read Rousseau, read Cobbett, read Voltaire. Read the Communist Manifesto. Engels had a lot to do with that." And Hamer read.

"Read your Bible," Gordon Stansfield said; and Birley Artingstall backed him up. "Read Wesley's sermons. Read Barnes on the Epistle to the Hebrews. Read Bunyan, Foxe's *Book of Martyrs, Holy Living and Dying*." And Hamer read.

"Get that punch right," Tom Hannaway said. "No! Cover up with your right. Now then; put something behind your left. Don't pat him, hit him. Put your body behind the clout. That'll do. Chuck it now. Running tomorrow?"

"Yes."

"Same time?"

"Yes – seven o'clock."

And at seven o'clock – spring was coming now, and there was light at seven and the air smelled good – Hamer found Tom Hannaway waiting in Broadbent Street, and off they went together, no word spoken. They were not stylishly dressed for the occasion: they had no running shorts or shoes, but what of that?

"Shut your mouth," Tom said. "Breathe through your nose. Pick your knees up. Head back. That's better. No need to force it. Take it steady."

Hard pavements, grim buildings all about them, no tree, no greenery of any sort, but a tender blue sky above and youth and ambition in their hearts. For Tom, an ambition already harsh, concrete, well-defined; for Hamer only a vague stirring, only this fever which has somehow awakened in his veins and that is now for ever unquenchable. To be someone. To do something. To hold people in the hollow of his hand. A full mind. A fit body. The tremulous and hardly-fledged desires fluttered through his mind as he lifted his knees and swung his arms and held back his head, breathing the spring air deeply, running through the stony streets of Ancoats. He didn't want any more to drag his leg and look interesting. He never thought now that the Broadbent Street canal had a hint of Venice. He knew it was dirty water and that he wanted to see the last of it; he knew that in the life he was going to lead he would want to be strong. He could see a tall figure – straight – dominant – imposing itself. *Ah, my friends...*

They were back at half-past seven, their chests heaving. "We've got to get it better than that," Tom said. "We've got to get back as fresh as we started."

"We'll do it."

"Ay, we'll do it. Same time tomorrow?"

"Yes."

He and Tom weighed themselves every week on the bone-yard scales. They were putting on weight. They were putting on breadth and height. They swung on the rings; they vaulted; they boxed; they ran. In the autumn, as Ellen and Gordon and Hamer were about to sit down to an evening meal, Ellen said: "You're as tall as your father."

"I'm taller," said Hamer.

They stood in their socks, laughing, against the kitchen door. Ellen scratched their height on the varnish. Hamer was by half-an-inch the taller. Gordon looked at the boy affectionately; then looked at Ellen. He would say nothing while the boy was there, but she knew he was thinking of that Sunday night when she had sat by this very fireside more dead than alive, and he was hurrying back through the fog with a wizened mite in his arms.

"Tom Hannaway's yard has done you some good, John," he said.

"I must say I didn't much like the idea of your going there, but it's certainly worked out all right."

"He needs something like that, with all that old reading," said Ellen. "I never knew such a boy."

Hamer grinned at her. "I'm only just beginning," he said. "I'm starting French when the winter comes."

Ellen had lifted the tea-cosy from the pot. She sat with the grotesque black and yellow woollen thing crushed in her hand and stared at him. "French?" she said; and Gordon who had bowed his head with the intent to say grace, raised his chin again. "Well, lad, that's a bit off the usual track isn't it?"

Hamer had got it all worked out; he was beginning to make his own decisions. He said he had been round to see Mr. Heddle, his old board-school teacher, and Mr. Heddle had agreed to give him an hour twice a week. "I can pay him out of my wages," Hamer said proudly.

"Ay, and I suppose you're the only boy for miles round here who's allowed to do what he likes with his wages?" said Ellen.

"Well," Gordon said, "that's all right. He's never yet done anything that isn't sensible."

The life he was leading now certainly gave him little opportunity to go astray. At seven every morning, whatever the weather, he was running with Tom Hannaway. After breakfast he went to the bookshop. He walked with his chin up, his arms swinging. Every step he took now belonged to this campaign he was waging to make his body fit. During the day he found little enough to do for Mr. Suddaby. He lit the fire, kept the books clean, and ran errands, but there were few days when he did not read for two or three hours in the shop. When he had eaten his midday sandwiches, he walked again till two o'clock – head up – deep breaths – quick march.

At six o'clock he took his evening meal with Gordon and Ellen. At half-past six he went upstairs to his room and wrote in his diary for half an hour. At seven he set off for Tom Hannaway's gymnasium where he swung, boxed and leapt till eight. Back in Broadbent Street, he went straight to his room and began to read. At nine Ellen brought him a mug of cocoa. At eleven he went to bed.

Out of this strict regimentation of his life he got a keen enjoyment. "Read Milton," Birley Artingstall said. Read this, read that. Someone was always at him. He always obeyed. He read Milton. He read:

> Fame is the spur that the clear spirit doth raise
> (That last infirmity of noble mind)
> To scorn delights and live laborious days.

He murmured the words over to himself. "To scorn delights…" He liked the sound of it, and it seemed to shed a ray on his condition. He loved the life he was leading; he loved every moment of it; but he hadn't any idea why he had arranged his life that way. He read the lines again. "Fame is the spur…" Fame…It buzzed in his head for days. He couldn't get rid of it.

There were two days in the week when he changed his routine: on Sundays and Thursdays. On Sundays, if Gordon were preaching somewhere, he would go with him; if not, he would attend service, morning and evening, at Emmott Street. He liked doing this. Sermons and hymn-singing began to stir him. He stayed behind to the prayer-meeting with Gordon, when Ellen had slipped away to get supper ready. He listened to the fervent supplications of Birley Artingstall. And during that autumn he remained for his first communion service. Little thimbles, hygienically filled for each communicant, were not in use at Emmott Street. Kneeling on the long red cushion that edged the communion rails, with Gordon on one side of him and Birley on the other, he took from the hands of Mr. Wilder the large cup from which everyone drank in turn. "This is My blood of the new Covenant," Mr. Wilder murmured. "Do this, as oft as ye shall drink it, in remembrance of Me."

Hamer surrendered the cup into a pair of long pale hands, and looked up into a long pale face. The Rev. Robert Wilder smiled down at him kneeling there, a smile which seemed to understand that this was a first communion, a smile quiet and comforting. He was a new minister. Hamer liked him. It was the persuasiveness of his sermon that had induced the boy to stay behind for the communion service.

An interesting thing about Hamer Shawcross's diary is the ease with which it is composed. The lines flow on without erasure. The first sign of hesitation is when he comes to put down his impression of Harriet Wilder.

"In the chapel porch, after service last night," the entry reads,

"Mr. Wilder was shaking hands with the people as they left. He is a very tall man with a pale face and a long black silky moustache that droops down like Mr. Artingstall's, only Mr. Artingstall's is reddish. Father said to Mr. Wilder: 'Will you come home and eat a bit of supper with us, Mr. Wilder?' Mr. Wilder said that he would. This is the first time the parson has been to supper with us on a Sunday night. As a rule, he goes off with one of the toffs, but Mr. Wilder, who has only just come to Emmott Street, looks the sort of man you could ask. He said: 'My girl Harriet is about here somewhere. I'll find her and tell her to slip home.' My father said it would be nice if she came, too, and so she did, as well as Mr. Birley Artingstall. All three of the men were wearing tall silk hats.

"My mother was surprised when we all trooped in. She had laid supper for three, and in the kitchen at that; and there were the three more than she had bargained for. She got into a terrible fluster, and started ordering my father to make a fire in the front room. She wanted to take off the cloth and carry everything in there. But Mr. Wilder said: 'Please let us stay where we are, Mrs. Stansfield. This is a beautiful cosy room,' and Mr. Birley Artingstall laughed and said: 'Eh, Ellen lass, it's a cut off the joint we've come for, not a seat in the stalls.'

"Miss Wilder then began to help my mother, and soon everything was ready. We had the beef that we had had for midday dinner served cold, with bread and butter and tea and pickles; and after that we had cake. It was all most enjoyable and friendly.

"After supper Miss Wilder borrowed an apron from my mother and helped her to wash up in the scullery. Mr. Wilder asked if he might light his pipe, and did so, and so did Mr. Artingstall. My father does not smoke. They all three started talking about the chapel and about Ancoats and how many people attend class meetings, and all that sort of thing, and I felt rather out of it till Miss Wilder came out of the scullery and sat in a chair alongside me at the table. We talked in quiet voices so as not to interrupt the others. She told me about the places she had lived in, because Wesleyan ministers are changed from town to town. She said she found Ancoats dreadful. She had just come from Chester where she and her father could get out easily into the Welsh mountains. I told her about my work and even about seeing the poor people getting their soup in Stevenson Square, which I have not told anyone else. She said she had always wanted to go to India as a medical missionary, but now she was going to stay with her father because her mother had died at Chester.

"Her name is Harriet. She is unattractive looking." Those four words are crossed out, and he tries again. "Some people might not think her attractive. Her face is thin and sharp and brown." Sharp is crossed out and "eager" written above it. "She is full of life and is about my age. When she is standing up she is fidgeting all the time." Here again he has failed to say exactly what he means, and it is clear that he wants to get Harriet Wilder down as he saw her. The whole of that last sentence goes, and he writes in its place: "She is tranquil to sit and talk to, but once on her feet she is alert and animated. They stayed till half-past ten."

Altogether, one gets the impression of a thin, dark girl, not conventionally good-looking, but with an alert intelligent face, perhaps, if Hamer had cared to risk the word, with an elfin touch. One gets the impression, too, that Harriet Wilder had impressed the boy pretty deeply.

The other night of the week when Hamer's rigorous programme went by the board was Thursday. That was class night. As the autumn deepened toward another winter, he did not abate his strenuous endeavours. Tom Hannaway would not turn up for the running now that the mornings were dark and blear. Hamer ran alone, through fog that hid the canal, through rain that pitted it, through wind and through exhilarating frosty mornings when even the air of Ancoats seemed a heavenly elixir, distilled by angels. And now, when he was back, his chest was not heaving. He was in control of himself. He could understand what Mr. Wilder was talking about when he preached on the text "They shall run and not be weary. They shall walk and not faint."

"Now that Tom Hannaway was no longer with him, he changed the route of the run. He went down George Street, where Mr. Wilder's house was. He never saw Harriet, but once or twice the gaslight was burning in the front bedroom, and that cheered him up, although he got no cheer from all the other planes of yellow light lying along the face of the street.

On a Wednesday morning, he came out, dressed, on to the landing, ready to set off as usual, when the sound of coughing made him pause for a moment. The door facing him on the other side of the landing opened, and Ellen appeared. She, too, was dressed, and carried a lighted candle. She closed the door behind her, and began to whisper in a quiet conspiratorial voice. "Don't go out this morning, John. Your father doesn't seem well."

Another burst of coughing came from the room. Ellen tiptoed down the stairs, the candle throwing grotesque shadows about her in the quiet house. Hamer followed. In the kitchen she said: "Light the fire and let's have an early breakfast. I've had no sleep. He's been restless and coughing all night."

Hamer lit the fire, but he did not feel disturbed. His mother was always like this if Gordon had a bit of a cough. "I'd better let Mr. Artingstall know he won't be coming today," he said.

"Yes, do," said Ellen.

Before going to work he went upstairs. Gordon was asleep now. He had never seen him in bed before. Gordon, with a night's grey stubble on his chin, with a flush on his thin cheeks and the lids of his closed eyes blue-veined transparencies, looked older, frailer, than he had ever imagined him to be. A pang of pity touched the boy, strong, upright, proud of his condition, and a pang of fear, too. Suddenly he wondered what he and Ellen would do if Gordon should die, and then, banishing the thought as monstrous, incredible, he walked slowly out of the room.

Ellen was packing his sandwiches when he got downstairs. "Don't bother with those," Hamer said. "I'll come home at midday. I'd like to see how he is." The words surprised him. They admitted an anxiety that he was trying to push into the back of his mind. To reassure himself, he added: "I'll run home, since I'm not running this morning."

He did, and surprised himself by the urgency of his running. This was not the steady lope of the mornings. He was pelting hell-for-leather, disturbed by the memory of Gordon's burning cheeks and shallow-rapid breath. Ellen was at the door, waiting for him to come. "He's better!" she shouted when the boy was still ten yards away. He knew then, by the great surge of joy that went through him, how fearful his heart had been. He flung his cap upon its hook and went straight upstairs. A fire had been lit in the bedroom. Gordon was sitting up in bed, wearing a pink woollen jacket of Ellen's over his nightshirt. His steel spectacles were on his nose, his Bible was in his hand; but he was not reading. He was gazing abstractedly, through the iron rails at the foot of the bed, at the fire. Even Hamer's entrance did not at once shake him out of his preoccupation. When he saw the boy, he took the spectacles off his nose, folded them and laid them on the Bible, and smiled. "Well," he said, "this is a nice thing – me sitting here dressed up like an old woman."

Hamer sat on the edge of the bed, uncomfortable. He looked out of the window. There was nothing to see but the black face of the mill which stood there with its feet in the canal. It was a dark, brooding day. The mill windows were lit. "I'm glad you're better, Father," he said.

"I think I'm a bit better. But I feel very tired, and I go hot all over, then cold. I won't be able to take the class tomorrow night." He hesitated for a moment, then said: "I should feel very happy if you would take it. It would be a – start."

Hamer swung himself off the bed and took the few paces which brought him to the window. He stood there looking down at the sullen water of the canal, and at Mrs. Hannaway, chasing her smallest son to school, and at Mrs. Ryerson, setting off with her customary brisk step, cap on head, roll of coarse apron under her arm, on her way to tackle something. He was disturbed by a deep emotion. He knew that Gordon was no better. Gordon had never before admitted that he would be unable to do something on the morrow. He had always said: "I'll be up all right in the morning." Hamer felt that he wanted to do something – anything – to please Gordon. He turned from the window. "All right," he said. "I'll take the class. I'll do my best."

"Good boy!" Gordon said. "Your mother will give you the register. And you'll find some pennies in a cup on the dresser. I always keep 'em there for the people who can't pay class money."

"What about a doctor?" Hamer asked.

"Doctor? For a chap with a bit of a chill on the chest? Oh, nooh, dear, no."

Suddenly he began to cough. It became very bad. He doubled up with the paroxysm, and Hamer saw sweat break out in little shining beads on his forehead. Ellen came running, and Hamer said: "I'd better go. I'm a bit late already. I'll eat my sandwiches as I walk."

He took the sandwiches with him, and when he was sure no one was watching him he dropped them into the canal. He felt that a mouthful would choke him. He began to run, and when he had turned the corner into Great Ancoats Street he saw Harriet Wilder walking ahead of him. Then he stopped running. He did not want her to think that he was running after her. But he went on at a good lick, so that he should overtake her nevertheless. When he came abreast, he said: "Good afternoon, Miss Wilder," and fumbled with his cap. He had not learned to make this gesture elegantly.

This was the first time he had spoken to Harriet since she had been to supper. She smiled at him frankly, the whole of her almost ugly but attractive and intelligent face lighting up. He was very glad to meet her. The misery in his heart lightened, and when she held out her thin brown bony hand he took it with gratitude for the warmth and sincerity of its clasp.

She was going into Market Street to do some shopping. They walked together as far as the steps leading down to Suddaby's cavern. He had told her by then all about Gordon's illness and his promise to take the class. He confessed to being nervous.

"Oh, you'll find it's nothing," Harriet said comfortingly. "I take a Sunday school class. There's nothing in it. Perhaps it helps the first time if there's a friend with you. Would you like me to come? I'm a member of Father's class, but I could come to yours for once."

"Would you?" he said, with a tremble of excitement. "They're all so old in that class. That's what frightens me."

She grinned, with a puckering of her little monkeyish face in which the golden-brown eyes were so bright. "How solemn you are," she said. "I thought so the other night."

And the idea that she had thought of him at all, whether as a solemn fellow or not, pleased him so much that a smile dawned in his eyes and spread to his mouth; and it was this smile that she remembered when he had waved his hand and dived down the cellar steps and she was going on through the grey afternoon towards Market Street.

It was strange to be walking on a Thursday night to Emmott Street by himself. It was strange to hear the class-money pennies chinking in his trousers pocket and to be aware of the words that he had prepared chinking through his mind. He had prepared them last night in his room, wrestling as with demons, pausing now and then to listen to Gordon's cough sounding from across the landing. Ellen was there, sitting by Gordon's bedside. She did not bring Hamer's cocoa at nine o'clock that night. He went without it. At ten o'clock she looked into his room and said: "I'm going to turn in myself now. Are you all right?"

Hamer got up to ease his stiff limbs. They talked in whispers. "Yes, Mother. I'm all right. Shall I go in and see him?"

"No; he's just fallen off."

"Why don't you get a doctor?"

"He doesn't need a doctor," she said, almost fiercely. "He wants rest and quiet. Besides, doctors cost money."

"I've saved up a bit," he said. "I can do without the French lessons."

She kissed him suddenly – a thing she did not often do – and she had not to stoop to kiss him. She kissed him on the cheek as they stood face to face. Then she went out, and there were tears in her eyes.

It was such a small house that presently he could hear the creaking of the bed as she got in beside Gordon. Gordon must have wakened, because there was a little more coughing and a quiet rumble of voices, and then silence, within the house and without. In the silence Hamer took up his pen again and went on writing the first of the millions of words he was to utter in public.

In the morning Ellen was almost gay. Once more she declared that Gordon was better. Her confidence cheered the boy so much that he went for his run as usual, and when he came back, shining with health, Gordon was sitting up in bed and able to smile at him. Hamer took his sandwiches to work; when he got home at night he was surprised to find Mrs. Ryerson in the kitchen. Each of the two middle fingers of her right hand now lacked its top joint, but she was nimble and handy.

"I've just been tackling a bit of fettling for your mother," she explained, as though she had not fettling enough to do for herself and those who employed her, "and your supper won't be two shakes. I've got t'kettle on and a bit o' summat in t'oven."

With her maimed hand she put back a wisp of greying hair that had strayed into her eyes, then, finger to lip, advanced her tough five foot of length towards him. "If you take my advice," she whispered, "you'll get t'doctor. Your mother carried on like mad when I suggested it. She will 'ave there's nowt wrong wi' 'im. But you get t'doctor, lad."

She bent to peep into the oven, and Hamer tiptoed upstairs, his heart full of foreboding. Gordon was not sitting up now. He did not sit up again. His head, in the narrow valley it had worn in the pillow, was moving restlessly from side to side. His eyes were closed, the silvery stubble was lengthening on his face. As Hamer stood looking down on the man he had always known as father, whose hand had seemed so comforting in the mouldy cab on that bleak day when they buried the Old Warrior, whose hand indeed had been so comforting and dependable all the days of his life, he knew suddenly of a certainty that Gordon's days were numbered. He said urgently: "I mustn't go out tonight, Mother. The class can look after itself."

Ellen, sitting in a wicker chair by the tiny fire, had not stirred when Hamer entered the room. Now she stood upright and cried: "He's better, I tell you! He's better – better!"

Gordon's head ceased to roll. The tired lids raised themselves from his eyes. "Aye, I'm all right," he said feebly.

Hamer knelt by the bed and took one of the short stubby hands that had gone very white and burned in his own. "I shall stay with you tonight," he said. "Let the class go hang."

"Nay, lad," said Gordon gently, "that's no way to talk. This is your start. I'll be awake when you get back. I'll want to know how you got on. Don't forget the pennies."

He closed his eyes again. Hamer stood up and watched him for a moment, saw the head begin once more its frightening roll, then went down to the kitchen. Mrs. Ryerson had a hot-pot waiting for him. "Well, lad?" she asked.

"I'm going for the doctor," he said. "Can you stay till he comes?"

"Aye, that I can," she said. "There's the washing-up to tackle yet an' a two-three little jobs besides. My two are in bed. They're all right. Francis'll look after 'em."

He had started off early and called at the doctor's, and there he was making his way through the murky evening to Emmott Street. He passed the stunted elderberries dripping black moisture in the chapel yard, went down the descending path to the door opening into the subterranean rooms. The chapel-keeper whose business it was to attend to fires and gaslights had done his work and gone. The classroom, now so familiar to him, with its bare plank floor, its whining gas, its welcome fire, did not look so reassuring as usual. No one had yet come. He placed his Bible and hymn-book and class-register on the table, and slipped beneath them a postcard on which he had written the points of the address he had composed the night before.

Then he stood still and listened. Down here under the chapel it was eerie. A distant footstep sounded hollowly on a wooden floor.

A door banged. A sound of feeble hymn-singing petered out and died. From a nearby room came the sound of a voice uplifted. It rose and fell; it swelled to impassioned supplication, diminished to soft entreaty; it went on and on. Birley Artingstall was before the Mercy Seat. Hamer stood there, lonely and unhappy, more than unhappy, utterly miserable and forsaken, thinking of the hot little bedroom in Broadbent Street, and Gordon's hot hand, and Gordon's head rolling, rolling, rolling, and Ellen despairing beneath her desperate defiance. He was on the point of seizing his hat and running, letting the class go hang, as he had said, when again the hollow sound of someone approaching broke the silence. Harriet Wilder came into the room.

He was not himself aware of the eagerness with which he started forward to greet her. He did not know that she had seen his face set in grim lugubrious lines, seen, too, those lines melt suddenly before the onset of happiness and relief. Anyone young, friendly and familiar would at that moment have wrought this transfiguration in him, but how was Harriet Wilder to know that?

He took her hand, and she spoke shyly. "The minister's class – that is, Father's class – meets in his house. I've never been down here. Isn't it grim and cold?"

In the distance Birley Artingstall's voice rumbled to silence like thunder muttering to extinction beyond the horizon. Then there was utter quiet, save for the gnat-whine of the gas, and in the grate the tiny flapping of the flames like little shining banners. They stood listening for a moment to the silence, still holding one another's hands. It was she at last who quietly took her hand from his and went to a chair in the front row. She knelt there, with her face right down on her hands that lay on the chair seat, and Hamer, who had gone to the armchair behind the table, could see that her brown hair was curly on the white nape of her neck. As she got up and dusted her knees two women came in, and presently all were there who might be expected. Hamer's first audience was made up of Harriet Wilder, five old women gnarled by a lifetime of rough occupation, and two men: one who might be seen any day sweeping up the refuse of Great Ancoats Street, and one who was a teetotal cooper, torn continuously by doubts whether God would forgive him for making barrels which he knew were destined for the liquor trade.

It was Gordon Stansfield's habit to remain seated in his chair and to discourse in his quiet, comfortable and rambling fashion for ten minutes or so. Hamer did not do this. When the moment came at which the class expected to hear the leader's few words, he pushed back his chair, stood with his left hand grasping the lapel of his coat, and with his right quietly manœuvred his notes into view. Then he announced a text: "To him that hath shall be given," and he proceeded to preach an austere doctrine of self-improvement. To him that hath the ability to read are opened all the continents of literature; to him that hath a body and the will to use it is given the satisfaction of feeling it develop into a strong and subtle instrument. As a concession to the religious nature of the occasion, he spoke of the hunger for God, of which, it may fairly be assumed, he then knew nothing, and said that to those who cultivated this appetite would be added blessings beyond what they could ask or think.

But, taking it by and large, the address was a survey, undertaken not without satisfaction, of his own achievements up to that moment. Had the sermonette survived and fallen later into the hands of his enemies, they might well have said: "Aye, it's the true Hamer touch. Ah, my friends, see what a good boy am I." But the address did not survive. The diary only notes: "I was surprised to find that I could speak without feeling nervous, and managed to bring in on the spur of the moment one or two things that I had not written down. Harriet Wilder listened attentively."

So did everyone else, if it comes to that. They were a polite and not very spirited little assembly, and if they drifted away into the dark Ancoats night feeling that the occasion had missed something that Gordon Stansfield never failed to impart, they doubtless felt also that the fault was theirs.

Harriet lingered behind. Hamer put on his overcoat, turned out the gas, and in the darkness they groped their way towards the door. "Where are you?" she said, and reached out her hand and took hold of his arm. She held on to it till they were in the passage which led to the forecourt of the chapel. At the end of the passage they could see through an open door the oblong slab of wan light that was part of night over Ancoats. She released his arm then, and they went out into the open air together. He was tingling to know what she thought of his address, but, as he would not run to overtake her in the street, neither would he ask her. So, with nothing said between them, they covered the short distance along which their ways coincided. Then she said: "Good night. I hope I'll hear you again. You were good."

His heart leapt up on hearing that. "Thank you," he said. "Good night." And only when her light step had pattered to extinction did he remember that she need not have come at all, and that he had not thanked her for coming.

She was to do so much for him, and little thanks she was to get for any of it.

Chapter Seven

If an announcement of Gordon Stansfield's death had appeared in the *Manchester Guardian*, it would have appeared on the same day as the announcement of Lillian Artingstall's. By the time Hamer got home from his first, and so painfully obscure, public appearance, Gordon was beyond recognizing him. Pneumonia carried him off the next day.

The newspaper announcement said that Lillian had died "suddenly, of a heart seizure," and that was true so far as it went. Hawley's cronies about the Town Hall nudged one another in the ribs, whispered in corners, and licked their chops over the stories that were going round.

The fact was that Hawley was tired of Lillian, of her airs, her gentility, her long cold nose. Damn it all, he sometimes thought to himself, it was like an icicle. He wouldn't have been surprised to see it melt away before his eyes, drop by drop. To marry a knight's daughter with a lot of money when he himself didn't amount to so much: that had been all right; that had given him a kick; but it was a long time since he had got any kick out of Lillian Sugden, and he was a big enough man now to do without her and what she had stood for.

Once she had disappeared to St. Annes, he didn't feel as bad as he had expected to. He missed Ann far more than he missed Lillian, but his work and his club made up for them both. He breakfasted at The Limes. The Artingstall diligence started with its accustomed punctuality, and then he remained in town all day, eating his lunch and dinner at the club, busy with his shops and with committee meetings at the Town Hall. This, he began to assure himself, was a happy life, the ideal life; he'd live more and more like this even when Lillian was back. Let her dribble her icicle into her own soup.

All very well; but Hawley was a gross animal with an animal's lusts; and Hilda Popplewell was still in his house. Hilda was the girl from Blackburn who had had her share in causing Lillian's illness.

The illness itself and the arrangements for her departure to St. Annes had made Lillian not so much overlook the case of Hilda Popplewell: she had decided to postpone it. She couldn't be bothered with Hilda at the moment. That could wait till she was back, strong.

Hilda was a big robust girl, full-breasted, with a throat like a pillar holding up a fine head crowned with a loose mass of auburn hair. She was a product of generations of artisans, proud of their skill. She had been a weaver herself. She thought it a come-down to be a servant in the Artingstall house, and so did all her relatives. They only half-guessed at the passionate and abortive affair that had driven the lusty wench to hide herself in Manchester.

Hilda would have returned to Blackburn soon enough, or gone to some other place where there was a market for her hereditary skill, if Lillian had not ordered her out of the house. It happened that Sir James Sugden was a Blackburn lad. Hilda's grandfather and he had been half-timers in a mill together, and Hilda had heard the old man chuckle over Sir James's grandeur. "Aye, Ah remember Jimmie Sugden wi' 'is shirt 'angin' out o' the backside of 'is pants, when 'e 'ad a shirt to wear." That was the sort of reminiscence that buzzed behind Hilda's broad calm brow when the peevish Lillian, daughter of this Jimmie Sugden, was distilling her frigid hauteur. It was a bad day for Lillian when she put this girl's back up, and then left her at The Limes with Hawley.

Hilda was accustomed to serve Hawley's breakfast. When she thought the time ripe to open her attack, she went into the breakfast-room with her ridiculous white cap loose, so that she could shake it off at any moment. She shook it so that it fell into Hawley's plate and lay there looking as stiff and formal as a gardenia. Hawley looked up, startled, to be aware of Hilda's fair skin and of the hot blood that was blushing below its surface.

"Eh, what's this? What's this?" he said, picking up the cap between his blunt fingers.

"I'm sorry, sir. It's my cap. I find it hard to make it stay on. My hair is so-so—"

"Tha's got plenty of it, onny road," said Hawley, looking at the coiled heavy masses.

Hilda took the cap from his hand. "I'll go and put it on again, sir," she said.

"Nay, don't bother wi' t'damned thing," said Hawley impatiently. "They always look daft, anyway. Thee stay an' pour out my coffee."

Hilda thought that was very good for a beginning. She was aware of Hawley's watching her furtively, and when he glanced at the clock and saw that he must rush for the carriage, he said: "Well, thanks, lass. Good mornin'," which was unusual.

Hilda went to bed early that night. She told the housekeeper that she had an appalling headache and shivers. She did not get up the next day. The approach of footsteps would set her body trembling with shivers which she could marvellously induce; and as soon as she was alone again she would pull from under her pillow Miss Brandon's *Lady Audley's Secret*. She finished the book the next day, and on the third day was back on duty in the breakfast-room.

"Tha's lookin' none too well, lass," said Hawley, regarding her critically; though Hilda had never looked better in her life. On leaving, he patted her big capable hand and said: "Take it easy. Don't overdo things."

Hilda was determined not to overdo things. She would do them very gently. It was not till a month later that she crept out of Hawley's bedroom at four o'clock one morning, her red hair streaming down about her big shapely buttocks, and felt her way up the dark narrow stair that led to her attic.

Hawley was like an old fool with a new toy. He couldn't have too much of his entrancing woman. Hilda gave him delights he had never known with Lillian. She was demanding; she flattered his virility; and it was fascinating to both of them to walk along the thin edge of danger. If Lillian had come home there and then the thing might have been nipped in the bud. But she did not come home. At Easter and in the summertime, when Lizzie Lightowler's school was closed, Ann joined her mother at St. Annes. Hawley went over, too, for a week in the summer, pleaded an accumulation of work, and returned to Hilda. He sent Hilda away, ostensibly to spend a week with her people in Blackburn. He left with Mr. Tattersall the Manager a couple of letters to be posted one at a time, with a few days' interval, to Lillian. There was no telephone in those days at Artingstall's. Then with a light heart Hawley set off to join Hilda in the Lake District. It was such a honeymoon as he had not before enjoyed. Hilda knew him inside out, as Lillian had never done. They were made of the same stuff.

*

Lillian decided to come home just before Christmas. She was feeling as well as she had ever felt in her life. She wanted to have the house ready for Ann. There was no reason why the child should go back to Bradford. Lillian began to pine for life as she had known it a year ago; her own home, her own husband, her own daughter.

She had forgotten Hilda Popplewell. The girl's burly figure and rude good looks were the first thing she saw in the hall when she came in from the carriage. Hawley was with her; he had met her at the station. She remembered this girl's impertinence, but now it seemed a thing she could not be bothered with. It was all so long ago. She would see if Hilda had developed better manners.

It was late in the afternoon. Lillian went straight towards the drawing-room door. "Bring some tea in here, Hilda. At once," she said, speaking over her shoulder.

She threw her hat and coat on to a chair, and sat near the fire, stretching her hands towards it. Hawley stood upright, his hands under his coat-tails, looking glum. He was aware that from this point forward his life was going to be complicated. He lacked subtlety and couldn't see his way.

There were a number of things which Hawley couldn't see. Lillian saw one of them at once. When Hilda came in with the tray, she gave a slight start. She stared at the girl hard. Now, indeed, she need not wait to see whether Hilda's manners had improved. Now she could strike back for that humiliating moment nearly a year ago. She was a woman without mercy. When Hilda had put down the tray, Lillian said, as coolly as though she were asking for a glass of water: "Hilda, this is not a lying-in hospital. You'd better go and have your baby somewhere else. When are you expecting it?"

She sat up very straight in her chair, a malicious smile breaking bleakly upon the arid gentility of her face. She waited to see the girl crumple up, fling herself at her feet, beg, howl. But Hilda only stood there, a hot flush mounting her cheeks, her hands instinctively folded upon her belly as though she would defend her child from this viper. She kept a level gaze directed upon Lillian, the daughter of little Jimmie Sugden, who had run round Blackburn with his shirttail hanging out.

Lillian's fingers drummed impatiently on the slender arms of her chair. "Well," she said. "You don't deny it, do you? When are you expecting it?"

Hilda's face broke suddenly into a radiant smile. "You'd better ask its father," she said. She jerked her head towards Hawley, turned on her heel, and left the room. She was not without humour. Ten minutes later, though she had not been summoned, she came back, bringing a jug. "I thought you might like some *more* hot water," she said.

She went out once more, carrying in her mind a picture of Lillian sitting there, tight-lipped, white, her eyes black and blazing, and of Hawley prowling up and down, up and down. "They look as if they haven't said a word to one another," she thought.

They hadn't. Presently, Lillian rose and went to her bedroom. Hawley stayed where he was, gazing at the fire. When Hilda came in to clear away the tea-things he looked at her as unhappily as a sick dog. "You've eaten nothing," she whispered. "Let me get you a fresh cup." He motioned her away, and an hour later went down to his club.

Lillian died that night, and she died farcically. When Hawley came home, sullen and morose, as though someone had done him a great wrong, she was in bed, wide awake. It was the large double bed that their respectability demanded. Lillian sat up when Hawley lit the gas. Her heart was at its old tricks again, thumping and jumping, starting and stopping. "Where are you sleeping tonight?" she asked.

"Ah'm sleeping where Ah's always slept – in that bed," said Hawley doggedly. He tugged off his tie, removed his collar, and laid it on the dressing-table. His coat and waistcoat were already over a chair. Somehow, he looked a lesser figure, with a bare shirtband round his neck and braces crossed on his back.

"You will *not* sleep here. You'll find a bed somewhere else," Lillian cried. She strove hard to control her voice. It wanted to rise to a scream. Her battle with it made her heart leap savagely. But Hawley was not aware of that. A little more drink than he was accustomed to take made him aware only of an immense self-pity, a determination not to be put upon. With exasperating calm, he sat down and removed his boots, that had buttons down the side, and his socks. Then he stood in his bare feet before the dressing-table and with a brush in each hand began to brush the little hair he had.

Watching his slow, deliberate movements, Lillian found each of her hands grasping the bedclothes with a rigid clutch. "Get out!" she said.

He turned towards the bed, slipped his thumbs under his braces, and jerked them off his shoulders. At that, Lillian leapt out of bed.

The sense of outrage that had been simmering in her brain all night boiled over. She could feel it in one swift rush almost literally blind her. A blackness fell upon her, then cleared. She was determined to get him out of the room. She seized the first thing that came to her hand, which was the dangling braces. She did not see that Hawley had by now undone his trouser buttons.

"If you don't get out, I'll pull you out," she said thickly. She heaved and heaved, trying to get him towards the door.

Hawley began to giggle. "Nay, lass, nay," he cried. "Don't be a fool. Tha's pullin' my trousers off." He slapped feebly at her hand.

"Strike me! Strike me!" she cried, and all of a sudden collapsed, holding onto the braces. For a moment, Hawley did not realize what had happened. He stood there, a ridiculous figure, with his trousers lying round his feet and long woollen pants swathing his bow legs. At last he realized that in this cruelly farcical fashion death had come for Sir James Sugden's genteel daughter.

It was a hard time for Hawley. You can't live with a woman for the best part of twenty years, even if she is a bitch like Lillian, without feeling wounds when she is torn away. Hawley got what consolation he could out of splendid obsequies. The procession which left The Limes for the cemetery was as lengthy as a Lord Mayor's show; and while the body was being committed to the grave a memorial service was being held in t'Owd Church. The bell tolling for that service had disturbed old Suddaby, lonely in his musty labyrinth, for Hamer was away, attending the funeral of Gordon Stansfield. Old Suddaby stuffed cotton-wool into his ears. He hated the sound of the passing bell. He was too old to hear it sentimentally.

The things said at the memorial service were reported in the *Manchester Guardian*, and Hawley, stiff and stocky in black, standing with his back to the dining-room fire, read them the next morning. Lillian's perfunctory slumming had somehow got translated into a godly life devoted to good works, and rotund ecclesiastical phrases presented her to the world as a sort of holy spirit, breathing upon Hawley and sustaining this pillar of Manchester's corporate being in its task of holding up the municipal edifice.

Hawley folded the paper open and laid it beside Ann's plate. He did not expect she or Lizzie Lightowler, who was staying in the house, would be down to breakfast before he left for the shop. He had decreed that the Artingstall diligence should set out at the usual time. He would act in a Roman fashion. There would be black boards across the shop windows, and he had instructed Mr. Tattersall the Manager to supply to each male employee a black tie and a crape arm-band out of stock.

He had done all this, and he certainly liked what the *Guardian* reported. But all the same, he was raw and uncomfortable. Birley, his own brother, had not attended the funeral. "There's another funeral on at the same time," Birley said, "the funeral of someone I respect."

Hawley raised his eyebrows. "There's no call to throw stones at Lillian now she's dead," he said severely.

"I'm throwing no stones, and I'm not going to throw posies either," said Birley. "What I'm telling you is the truth. There's this other funeral – a very unfashionable one – in Ancoats."

"You never liked Lillian," Hawley charged him flatly.

"Neither did you," said Birley, "not as I should want to like the woman I married, anyway."

They were standing in front of the Town Hall. Birley walked away, leaving Hawley to chew over these bitter words at leisure. He was chewing them over now, as he sat down to breakfast. Hilda came in, carrying the tray, and, to Hawley's surprise, Ann and Lizzie came into the room behind her. Ann took the tray from Hilda's hands. "You go," she said. "I can look after all this."

She put the tray on the table, and when Hilda had shut the door she said: "Really, that girl shouldn't carry great weights like this. She's going to have a baby."

Hawley started up in his chair, his face purpling. "Ann!" he said. "What are you talking about? How dare you say such things?"

"Sit down, Hawley. Don't be foolish," said Lizzie Lightowler. "Of course the girl's going to have a baby. It's as plain as the nose on your face."

Hawley sat down and looked at the two women. Women – yes. This year had made a wonderful difference to Ann. There she sat with that strange hair like white lustrous silk seeming the more startling against the black of her clothes. He would have liked to see some sign of grief on her face, but she had shown no grief at Lillian's death.

The girl had grown. She was inches taller; she was a little taller than

Hawley himself; and she had a tranquillity, a perfect grip on herself, that both startled and scared him. He knew that, if he had at any time had a hold over this daughter of his, he had none now. More than ever he saw her as neither Sugden nor Artingstall, but as belonging to that dimly-remembered woman who was his mother.

She poured out his coffee, gave him eggs and bacon from under the big metal cover. She served Lizzie, and then herself. When she sat down, she took up the newspaper, glanced at what Hawley had evidently intended her to see, and then, without reading, laid the paper aside.

"Yes," she said. "Something ought to be done about that girl. I saw her carrying a great bucket of water upstairs yesterday."

"She looks five or six months gone," said Lizzie.

Ann considered the matter. "Quite that, I should say."

Hawley looked up, his eyes smouldering like an angry bull's. "Ah don't like such talk," he said. "It's not decent."

"It's not decent," said Lizzie, "to have that girl carrying heavy things about. It's not decent, and it's not fair. I'm surprised Lillian didn't do something about it."

"Lillian!" The snort was out before Hawley realized its significance, its contempt, its utter loathing of Lillian. "She knew nothing about it," he said lamely.

"Some one must have known something about it," said Ann. Hawley got up from the table, trembling with wrath. "Don't bait me!" he cried. "Ah'll not have this sort o' thing talked about in my house."

"I'm not baiting you," Ann said coolly. "Do be reasonable, Father. Something's got to be done about the girl. Would you like Aunt Lizzie to speak to her?"

Hawley crashed his fist down on the mahogany. "Ah'll not have this interference," he cried. "Something's got to be done, has it? Something *is* going to be done. Ah'm goin' to marry 'Ilda."

He ended up on his broadest accent, his face an angry confusion of annoyance, resolution and sudden clean relief. He had seen his way, straight and honest, at last. He walked to the fireplace, and hauled the bell-pull. When Hilda came into the room, he said: "Tell 'Aworth t'carriage isn't goin' this mornin'. An' when tha's done that, coom back 'ere. Ah want to talk to thee."

He glared at Ann and Lizzie as though he hoped they would realize that only something cataclysmic could cancel the Artingstall diligence. Now, his glare seemed to say, you're going to see something! Now you're going to hear something!

Very late, the Artingstall diligence rolled towards town. Ann and Lizzie went into the drawing-room. "So that's that," said Lizzie. "What are you going to do about it?"

Before the two of them, Hawley had point-blank asked Hilda to marry him, and Hilda had said she would. Hilda would go away till her child was born, and the marriage would not take place for a year. It was quite a business conference, and Hilda seemed an intelligent business-like girl. Ann liked her, for both her vigour and candour, but at the same time, as Lizzie could see, she was deeply upset. It is not easy to put a bright face on adultery encountered for the first time, if the deceived person is your mother, buried yesterday.

Standing by the fireplace, Ann could feel her knees trembling. She sat down, and looked across at Lizzie. "It's just a year ago," she said, with a smile on the edge of tears, "that Mother put me over her knee and thrashed me, and Father as good as turned me out of the house for spending about twenty minutes talking to a poor boy. And now I'm to have a girl not much older than I am, of the same class as this boy, for my new mother. It doesn't seem to make sense."

This was the first Lizzie had heard of the thrashing. She said nothing about that, and let Ann run on. "I *like* Hilda. There's no nonsense about her. But I can't like the *relationship*. You see that, don't you? It's impossible. She can't be more than five years older than I am. As a friend, as a companion, I could get on with her; but as a mother, why—"

"I know what's worrying you," said Lizzie. "You can't stay here now. I agree with you. It would be an impossible situation, for you and Hilda. And you're wondering what you can do."

"What *can* I do? Father won't go on paying for me to stay with you any longer."

"And would you like that very much?"

"Like it? Dear Aunt Lizzie – if you knew how happy I've been for the last year!"

"So have I been, and why can't we go on being happy?"

Ann's woebegone face brightened. "That would be lovely! But he won't pay you. And how do we know he'll let me go, anyway? I'm his child. I'm still young. He can do as he pleases."

"As to pay, we shan't quarrel about that. Did you ever think what a lonely old thing I was, my dear, before you came? Not so much as a cat to purr round my feet. And as to Hawley's letting you go – well, I think he'll listen to Hilda if he won't listen to us. D'you think she'll want you about? Not on your life, my dear. I'm sure she likes you, and I'm sure she'd hate to have you for a daughter. If you'll disappear for half-an-hour, Hilda and I will soon come to see what needs to be done. And while you're in Manchester, why don't you visit that nice man Birley? I don't think your father can very well object now."

It was very necessary, Birley Artingstall thought, to cheer up these two young men. Arnold Ryerson had managed to get a few days' holiday for Christmas. He and John, Birley and Mr. Wilder, had all come back together from Gordon Stansfield's funeral, packed together in a four-wheeler cab. The two boys got out in front of Hamer's house, and before the cab drove on with Birley and the minister, Birley put his head out of the window and said: "Can you two come and see me tomorrow night? Seven o'clock?"

Arnold said: "Thank you, Mr. Artingstall," and Hamer, who was mute with misery, merely nodded. They stood watching the cab till it was out of sight, and Birley, keeping his head stuck out of the window, noted the difference that a year had wrought. Arnold no longer overtopped his friend: they were of a height, and Hamer carried himself better. He stood straight as a lamp-post, his head set proudly on his shoulders, alongside his pale companion.

Poor young chaps, Birley thought, as he prepared to receive them the next evening, they had a tough time ahead, the pair of them. He drew the curtains, mended the fire, and opened out his gate-legged table. He put on the table-cloth and laid three places. He enjoyed doing this. It was not often he had company. He surveyed the room with some complacency: the little white bust of Wesley, the engraving of the death of Wesley on the wall, the books in their gay leather covers. He allowed his thoughts to stray for a moment to his brother Hawley, to Hawley's sumptuous home, and to Hawley's dead wife. Well, he reflected, he wouldn't swap with Hawley, not anyhow, not with Lillian alive or with Lillian dead. This was his idea of a home: this quiet room, this old leather chair in which he could smoke his pipe and read and re-read John Wesley's Journal, and cogitate on an occasional stupendous twist to his prayer-meeting petitions. "Be still," Birley murmured to himself, "and know that I am God." Birley liked being still. That was the trouble with Hawley, always had been: big shops, rich women, corporation committees, magistrates' bench: anything except a minute in which he could listen to his own heart beating. "Teach us, O Heavenly Father," Birley tried over, "to listen always for Thee, whether Thou speakest with the still small voice or soundest the blast which shall herald Thy coming to sway the sceptre of universal dominion."

A thump of the knocker made him start. He pulled an old heavy watch out of his pocket. It could not be the boys: they were not due for half an hour. He turned up the gas at the head of his stairway and went down to the street door. Ann threw her arms round his neck and kissed him.

"Well, lass!" he exclaimed, holding her away from him and surveying her against the blear background of Great Ancoats Street. "You've grown out of all recognition. Come in. How did you get here?" He stood aside to give her a way to the stairs, then looked out again into the street, expecting to see Haworth disappearing with the victoria.

"I walked," Ann said, and added with a laugh: "But don't be afraid. There'll be no dreadful consequences this time. I called at the shop. Father knows all about it."

"And he let you come?" Birley asked with wonder, following her up the stairs.

Ann felt it was not her business to tell Birley what had happened that morning to change her relationship to her father. She merely said: "Yes; he let me come. I told him that no doubt you would take me to some civilized part of the town and see me into a cab."

"Aye, I'll do that, lass," said Birley. "Here, give me your hat and sit you down."

She took off her hat but did not sit down. Birley looked at her with admiration – so tall and fair and self-possessed. "I don't know what's come over you," he said. "A year ago – that's when you were here last – you were a slip of a thing, and now, well, I dunno—"

She laughed happily. "Just growing up, Uncle Birley – growing up, and learning all sorts of things, and meeting all sorts of people, and being happy for a year. That's all it is."

"Well, you'll make a fine eyeful for these two young men," said

Birley. "And that's a funny thing – I hadn't thought of that. A year ago you went to their party, and now here you are coming to mine, and the same two youngsters are just about due."

"What! Arnold Ryerson? But I see a lot of him in Bradford."

"Aye, he told me something about that. Well, I've asked him here tonight, and young John Shawcross-Hamer, as he fancies to call himself."

"That's the boy who had a birthday."

"That's the one, and you gave him your hair ribbon for a present."

Ann knitted her brows in an effort at recollection. "Did I? It's quite gone out of my mind. So much else happened that night. I don't remember a bit what he looks like."

"It'd be no use remembering, lass. He's changed as much as you. And you're both in the same boat. His stepfather died the same day as your mother. Now I'd better put another place for you. There they are. Wait here. I won't be a minute."

He ran happily down the stairs, seized the boys by the arm, and took them with him along the street. "Come on," he said. "Only three doors down. Mrs. Sibbles."

"What about her?" Arnold asked.

"She's cooking for me," said Birley. "All very well mucking along on my own, so long as I'm *on* my own. But this is a special occasion." He banged a knocker, pushed a door that was ajar, and yelled: "Mrs. Sibbles!"

"Come on in, Mr. Artingstall," a voice answered. "It's all packed and waiting."

The three pushed on down Mrs. Sibbles's passage and into Mrs. Sibbles's kitchen, which was filled with an appetizing smell. There was a large basket on the table. "That's t'steak and kidney pie," said Mrs. Sibbles, pointing to a white cloth wrapping at one end of the basket, "and that's veges. Ah've put 'em all in one dish. You'll 'ave to sort 'em out. An' 'ere in t'middle's Christmas puddin'. Boiled for twenty-four hours, that 'ave, in t'kitchen copper. An' 'ere's a bit of 'olly to stick in t'top."

They marched back to Birley's house with the basket. Birley shut the door and put the basket behind it. "Now, lads," he said, "we'll take one each, and make a procession of it."

He stuck the holly behind his ear, himself took the Christmas pudding, and commanded Arnold to take the vegetable dish and

Hamer the steak and kidney pie. He thumped heavily up the stairs to announce his presence, and shouted: "Open! Open!"

Ann stood behind the door. The boys did not see her until, following Birley with heavy rhythmic stampings, they had passed round the table and laid down their burdens. Then Arnold exclaimed: "Why, Miss Artingstall—!" and Birley, twiddling the sprig of holly in his fingers and watching that encounter, was aware that the boy's face lit up, and that Ann, though he had warned her whom to expect, advanced and took Arnold's hand with a sudden brightening of the glance, a slow deepening of colour.

"Now, sit down," he said. "You all know one another. You do remember my niece Ann, don't you, John?"

Hamer remembered the occasion rather than the girl. He remembered a number of people signing their names in a book, and he remembered a girl, with a sudden whim, giving him a hair-ribbon. He had put it in the box which contained the ribbon, tied round a curl, that the Old Warrior had carried away from the field of Peterloo. He had not opened the box since. He had not opened his memory of the girl. He would not have recognized this one. She seemed, standing there in black, so tall before Birley's fireplace, woman rather than girl. He shook hands with her nervously. He wasn't used to girls. Harriet Wilder was the only girl he knew.

Ann did not remember him. She remembered a pale thin boy. This boy was not pale and thin. His eyes were large and beautiful under his broad brow and Gordon's death had deepened the habitual gravity of his bearing. But he stood with his head up and his shoulders back, with an elasticity and resilience in the carriage of his body that made it impossible for her to think of the poor rough clothes he was wearing. She smiled at him, holding his hand for a moment. "No," she said. "I wouldn't have remembered you."

Birley put the Christmas pudding on the hearth, and piled an extra log upon a fire already sufficiently hospitable. "Now then, sit down, all of you," he commanded again. "But first of all, shove the sausage down to that door, John."

Hamer did so, and came to the table where the others were already seated. He stood with his hands resting on the back of his chair, and looked down into the three faces. "I wonder," he said, "whether you'd mind calling me Hamer?"

"Good Lord, lad, whatever for?" Birley demanded.

"Well," said Hamer, continuing to stand, and smiling down upon them all with an air of sweet reasonableness, "it *is* my name, you know."

"Aye, but no one's used it, so far as I know."

"Well, I'm starting a sort of new life now – on my own. It's just a fancy of mine – if you don't mind."

"Sit down," said Birley. "It's nowt worth arguing about while the pie gets cold. It's a queer idea, but perhaps there's something in it. Aye – Hamer Shawcross. It's not a bad name."

Hamer slid into his chair, as Birley took up a knife and plunged it into the brown crust of the pie. The rich steam rushed forth and Birley sniffed with gusto. Then he laid down the knife and looked reproachfully at Hamer. "Look at that now," he said. "You standing there speechifying: you've made me forget the Almighty."

But Birley was always equal to converse with the Almighty, and as the three young people bowed their heads, he covered his false step with his resonant opening words. "This savour of a sweet-smelling sacrifice, a God, which Thou has put it into our hearts to cause to ascend to Thee, comes from the devotion of these Thy humble servants who now beseech Thee to bless this food to our use, that we may strive among men to hasten the day which shall see the glory of Thy coming to wield the sceptre of universal dominion."

He raised his bony old Viking head and glanced round the table with a humorous twinkle in his eyes, as much as to say that he had got out of that pretty neatly. Then he took up the knife again and deftly removed the first segment of crust. His nostrils flared above the savour of the sweet-smelling sacrifice, and, looking almost beatified by his own hospitable happiness, he passed the plate down the table to where Ann sat with the vegetable dish before her.

"We must do this every Christmas, Uncle Birley," she cried, when they were all served and eating with unconcealed relish. "That is, if I happen to be in Manchester."

"You'll be in Manchester," said Arnold. "But shall I be? I may not always be able to get a Christmas holiday."

"Neither may I," Ann answered.

"But you're staying in Manchester, now – that – that—" Arnold stammered over the words – "now that your mother's dead."

Ann shook her head. "No, I'm going back with Aunt Lizzie," she said; and Birley saw again how Arnold's face could not tell a lie about the joy this affirmation brought him.

"How do you get on, lad, in Bradford?" he asked. "You've been there a year now, and we don't hear much about what you do."

"It's what he's *going* to do that matters," Ann broke in, and when Birley looked inquiringly at Arnold, the boy coloured and murmured: "Oh, that's just an idea of Mrs. Lightowler's. She's got in with a lot of people who meet and talk politics."

He left it at that, and Ann took up the story: "I don't know how Aunt Lizzie has the nerve to be under Father's roof. He'd die if he knew what a Radical she was."

Birley cocked a questioning eye, and she said: "She's one of those who believe that working people will have to have their own members in the House of Commons. Now they get elected as Liberals and try to do what they can. She thinks that's nonsense, and that they'll have to form their own party. She takes Arnold about with her to meetings of these people, and he's spoken once or twice."

"So have you," said Arnold; and the two laughed, as though caught in a conspiracy.

"Well, bless my soul," Birley cried. "I never heard the like. Working people have their own members? I've always voted Liberal. I think we're safe enough in Mr. Gladstone's hands. I can't take this seriously."

"Oh, it's serious enough," said Arnold quietly. "It'll come."

"Well, it's,...no topic for a Christmas dinner," Birley asserted, and Hamer said, surprisingly: "Perhaps it's a better topic where there are no Christmas dinners."

"Three of you, eh?" Birley looked comically threatening. "I hereby ban this topic," he cried, striking the haft of a knife sharply on the table. "Ann, side the plates, and bring on the pudding."

He poured the brandy, struck a match, and looked with childlike pleasure at the brown globe before him trembling with blue liquid fire. "Look at that!" he cried. "That's a pleasanter matter for Christmas consideration. And when we've eaten it, we'll sing some carols."

They did. They piled all the dishes on to the table in the kitchen and left them there. They sat round the fire, and Birley and Arnold Ryerson lit pipes – Arnold rather self-consciously. For a moment they were quiet. Birley had put out the gas; there was no light save the firelight that fell ruddily on their faces, no sound but the sound of the flames, wrenching themselves with little tearing noises from the gross contact with the coal. Death was raw and vivid in all their minds, and for two of them the future was grey with uncertainty; but, sitting there quietly together, they felt tranquil and content, understanding one another, liking one another, comforting one another. As though their silence had been a prayer, Birley suddenly broke it with a hearty "Amen!" Then he said: "Now, let's have the carols."

Carols, to Birley, were hymns. They sang hymn after hymn, and presently Birley said: "Now the grandest one of all – Number 133 – 'Let earth and heaven combine.' Charles Wesley. Ah! There was no one like Charles when it came to writing a hymn – not even John."

Birley didn't need a book in his hand to know that the hymn's number was 133. He could give you the number of any hymn in the Methodist Hymn Book or the chapter and verse of any Bible quotation. The hymn has a grand tune, and Birley led them energetically to the attack:

> Let earth and heaven combine,
>   Angels and men agree,
> To praise in songs divine
>   The incarnate deity:
> Our God contracted to a span,
> Incomprehensibly made man.

They sang it through to the end:

> Then shall His love be fully showed,
> And man shall then be lost in God.

Birley leaned back in his chair and laid on the table alongside him the pipe with which he had been conducting the singing. In the fire-shine his eyes were glistening. "That's it," he said. "That's it. You young people have all been talking about reforming this and reforming that. Well, it's all there in two lines. When men love one another, all the reforms will be over. There's no other way."

He got up and lit the gas. Arnold Ryerson rose, too. "I'm glad we sang those hymns," he said. "I don't agree with Robert Owen about religion or marriage. He didn't believe in either."

Arnold looked very young and naive, standing there making his solemn affirmation, with the unaccustomed pipe in his hand. Ann laughed at him merrily. "You and your Robert Owen!" she said. "It was Robert Owen, as much as anything, that got me sent into exile a year ago."

"Are you sorry?" Birley asked.

"No, indeed," she said. "The last year has been worth all the rest of my life put together." She put on her hat and coat and took up her muff. "Now, you must keep your promise, and see me safely into a cab."

Birley prepared to go with her. "You boys stay here," he said. "I'll not be long, and there'll be plenty to go on talking about when I get back."

The boys stood listening as the young eager footsteps and the old careful ones sounded together on the hollow stairs. They heard the door bang. Then Arnold, his face shining, turned to Hamer and asked with childlike enthusiasm: "What d'you think of her?"

Hamer grunted a non-committal answer and turned to rummage among Birley's few books. Arnold went into the kitchen. "Come along, Hamer," he shouted. "Let's tackle the old man's washing-up before he gets back."

Hamer did not want to do the washing-up, but he smiled at hearing that name for the first time on Arnold's lips. They took off their coats, rolled up their sleeves, and went to it.

In the street, Ann put her hand upon Birley's arm, and he patted it comfortingly. "Uncle Birley," she asked, "what do you make of that boy Hamer Shawcross?"

"Make of him? Why, my dear, it's difficult to make anything of him just yet. So far, he's hardly known that he's born, but now he's going to find out."

Chapter Eight

The Rt. Hon. Hamer Shawcross, P.C., M.P., with a dusky red carnation in the lapel of his evening coat, with the jewel of an Order glinting beneath the stiff white butterfly of his tie, his hair shining like burnished silver, accepted the soup from the waiter at the Lord Mayor's banquet. The Prime Minister, Mr. Ramsay MacDonald, sat a few places to his left; the Archbishop of Canterbury, with his harsh, hairless prelate's face, was to his right. It was turtle soup.

A flunky bowed at Hamer's shoulder and handed him a note. Many eyes watched him as he took the horn-rimmed spectacles from their case, adjusted them to the bridge of his handsome nose, and opened the twisted paper. What affair of state could not await the dinner's end?

Hamer read: "Turtle soup reminds me. Remember t'tortoises? T. H."

The minister's face flushed with annoyance: flushed as duskily red as the flower he wore. The man was hovering there as though perhaps there might be an answer. Hamer gave an impatient shake of the head, raised his eyes, and beheld Sir Thomas Hannaway grinning impudently from a distant table and raising a glass in greeting. Hamer did not respond. He turned to the turtle soup and his Archbishop.

When the boy got home that night from Birley Artingstall's party, he found his mother and Mrs. Ryerson sitting by the kitchen fire. There was a teapot on the table, and the fingers of both the women were busy. Ellen was darning; Mrs. Ryerson, her maimed fingers as active as whole ones, was knitting. She got up when Hamer came into the room, and said: "Well, you tell him, Ellen. Now I must go and get t'bread going."

She went, with that air she had of expending a good deal of energy even upon the business of leaving a room, and Hamer sat down in the chair she had vacated. Ellen was swathed from head to foot in heavy black, relieved only by the cameo brooch at her throat. "We've been having a talk," she said, "about what we're going to do."

She spoke in a low voice, keeping her head bowed over her work. She did not want him to see that her eyes were red. "We could go in with t'Ryersons," she added after a moment.

At first Hamer did not understand, then he flushed, getting to his feet and sweeping the hair back from his forehead. "You mean share their house?" he asked.

Ellen nodded. "Mrs. Ryerson and I could sleep in one bedroom and t'little 'uns in the other. You and Francis could have the front room downstairs. He's a nice lad."

Hamer looked at her incredulously. "No!" he said fiercely. "No!"

Ellen spoke patiently, as though she were not surprised that he found this hard to stomach. She rolled into a ball the pair of socks she had finished darning and stretched another sock across her fingers. "It's no good talking like that, lad," she said. "People like us don't save money. There's just enough to go on with from week to week, and now that your father's dead there's nothing but what you earn. He was getting thirty-five shillings a week. You're getting seven-and-sixpence. T'rent's five shillings. We can't eat and dress on half-a-crown. I'll have to go out and work as it is. But if we go in with t'Ryersons, we could save in all sorts o' ways."

It seemed logical, unanswerable; but again Hamer shouted: "No! I'm not going to give this up. It's our home."

"Aye, I know that, lad, but there's nowt comin' into it now."

At that, she began to cry quietly, and Hamer, who had not seen her cry till these last few days, stood with his back to the fire, his hands in his pockets, scowling to hide from her that his own eyes were smarting. Suddenly there came into his mind something Mr. Suddaby had said about Lord Lostwithiel, who had never seen Ancoats, living at ease on Ancoats rents. Even when Gordon had been paying the rent, the question seemed no more than academic; but now he realized that if this rent was to be paid it must be paid out of *his* earnings. "Why should we pay rent, anyway?" he burst out angrily.

Ellen dried her eyes and looked up at him in surprise. "Nay, now tha's talking daft, lad," she said. "Rent's rent, and it's got to be paid. Talk like that, an' Mr. Richardson'll soon 'ave thee on t'street."

"Well, we're staying here," he said firmly. "Do you understand that?

– staying here. Where my room is upstairs. Where your kitchen is. Where old Grandfather lived, and Father lived. It's ours, and we're going to keep it."

She liked to hear him talk in that way. He looked proud and resentful. She stood up, tumbling things from her lap on to the rug, and took his face between her hands and kissed him. He didn't seem to like it. He was not used to being kissed. He drew away like a sensitive animal that hates to be handled. At the door, he paused and said: "I'm going up to my room to think. I don't know what we'll do, but we're not going to share with the Ryersons."

"There's no fire in your room," she said. "We've got to think about coal now."

"I can do without fire," he said. "I can do without a lot of things. But we're not going to do without a place of our own."

When he was gone, Ellen picked up the things from the floor and went on with her darning. She felt sad and lonely. She wished he had stayed there and sat in the fireside corner where the Old Warrior had sat and where Gordon had sat. Why couldn't he do his thinking, such as it was, there instead of in a cold bedroom? She could feel his body stiffening away from her kisses. She did not hold him as she had held those two others. But she felt proud and glad when she thought of his handsome angry face. What was there about him that the Old Warrior had never had – that Gordon had never had? She made up the fire, and, unconsciously, she made it up very quietly, so that even so small a noise should not disturb him.

Mr. Richardson was a bachelor, living in two rooms in George Street, where Mr. Wilder's house was. He was not a companionable person: his job didn't lend itself to that; but he liked, especially in the wintertime, to look in at the Lostwithiel Arms on a Saturday night. He did this partly for business reasons. If he found a notorious rent-ower spending his money on booze, he would fix his eyes, hung beneath with blue heavy bags, upon the offender, and so force upon him a realization that this was an enormous offence: to be throwing down his neck, in burning spirits or frothy ale, the good money that was owing to "the office."

But this was secondary. Though not companionable, the man liked to be in company. He would talk to nobody, and few wanted to talk to him; but there he would sit, in the chair that was reserved for him on Saturday nights, his feet to the fire, his glass on the mahogany table, the gas in its round, white, opaque globe glowing above his head, the landlord attentive. The Lostwithiel Arms was not a "free" house. Not only did Lord Lostwithiel own the land it stood on; he was a dominant shareholder in the brewery company that ran the place; and so, to the landlord, Mr. Richardson was in a way Lord Lostwithiel's very vice-regent, to be treated with honour and deference. The explosions of drawn corks were almost, on these occasions, a salute of guns. Mr. Richardson's eye-pouches, his oiled quiff, his short spikes of moustache, the rigid collar that uplifted his chin, the yellow waistcoat sprigged with green and red flowers: all these things and the landlord's deference were a rampart about him as he sat observing the artisans in their rough clothes, their clogs, their mufflers, standing at the bar and spitting into the sand. That Tom Hannaway of all people, a whipper-snapper, a person who had never been in the bar before, should walk casually over, seat himself at Mr. Richardson's table, and engage him in conversation: this seemed to the landlord an outrage.

Tom Hannaway had come in and ordered himself half a pint of bitter. He sipped it as though he didn't like it. He was a popular fellow, and he stood a few drinks, and soon had his little circle happy. "'Ows trade, Tom? Tha seems t'ave brass to chuck about."

"Not so bad," said Tom, "not so bad. I make ends meet. Once I've paid the rent there's not much to worry about. But fifteen bob a week takes a bit o' finding."

A little consumptive mechanic swilled the dregs of his beer round and round in his glass, looked at them sadly, and said: "Fifteen bob? That's a bob more than Darkie Cheap ever paid."

"Maybe," said Tom. "But it's what I pay, all the same. Ask Joe Mathers there. Joe's taken my rent to Mr. Richardson for me more than once – haven't you, Joe? – when I've been out and Mr. Richardson hasn't been able to get at me."

Joe nodded. "That's true enough, Tom. Fifteen bob it was."

Then Tom, who from a dark doorway had watched Mr. Richardson enter the pub half an hour before, cried with surprise: "Why, there's Mr. Richardson himself! Isn't the rent of my bone-yard fifteen bob a week, Mr. Richardson?"

Mr. Richardson looked as if he did not want to discuss the matter, but he was seen to nod. It was then that Tom walked across from the bar to the nook by the fire and said: "Thank you for confirming that, Mr. Richardson."

The rent-collector, who usually remained till ten o'clock and then went home full of a gentle melancholy, rose to his feet and almost roughly put Tom aside. "Excuse me," he said. "I've got affairs to see to at home tonight." No one but Mr. Richardson heard Tom Hannaway say: "I'll be calling on you."

He called half an hour later. When they were alone in the dingy little room of the lodgings, Mr. Richardson snarled: "What do you want?"

Tom had not been invited to sit down. He did so, and waved his hand toward another chair, as though he were the host. He smiled, showed his strong young white teeth. "Mrs. Burnsall owes you a good deal of rent for that lock-up shop on the corner of Broadbent Street."

"That's my business, and I don't want you sticking your nose into it," said Mr. Richardson.

Tom ignored this. "I've been lending a few shillings to one or two people," he said frankly. "Mrs. Burnsall wanted to borrow two pounds. I couldn't let her have it. I want that shop. It's time I expanded my affairs."

Mr. Richardson, who had not taken a seat, stood with his back to the dull smouldering fire, looked down at the youth, and sneered. "Expand your affairs, eh? Affairs! Running a bone-yard and robbing the kids of their pennies for swinging on a few ropes. Hannaway's club!"

"Forty-five members," said Tom. "I could tell the forty-five of 'em that you're putting a bob a week rent in your pocket, and they could tell forty-five fathers and forty-five mothers. One of the fathers works in the Lostwithiel Estate Office."

Mr. Richardson's face took on a horrid mottled look. "You dirty little swine!" he said.

Tom smiled. "You heard the boys in the pub? There are witnesses that I've been paying you fifteen bob. My book only shows fourteen."

Mr. Richardson sat down and licked his lips. "I don't want to turn Mrs. Burnsall out," he said. "She's a widow."

Tom Hannaway's smile widened to an impudent knowing grin. "Of course you don't want to turn her out," he said, "but between you and me, old cock, she's tired of paying the rent that way. That's why she came to me."

Mr. Richardson leapt to his feet and stood over Tom, his face wild with anger. He raised his fist to strike, and the boy, not smiling now, said quietly: "Don't do that, Mr. Richardson!" Richardson sank again into his chair, put his elbows on his knees and his forehead in his hands.

It was Tom's turn to get up now. "That's better," he said. "Now listen to me. Are you listening?"

Mr. Richardson moved his head up and down. "Good," said Tom. "There are only two things to get into your skull. One is that I want that shop. I know what Mrs. Burnsall's been paying for it, and that's what I'll pay you. The other is this: the rent of the bone-yard is fourteen shillings a week – in your pocket as well as in the books."

Tom Hannaway had two more calls to make that night. First of all, he went to the widow Burnsall's. She was at this time in her early thirties, and Tom was just eighteen. He remembered how, the last time the fair had come to the croft and he had gone up to the boxing platform, stripped of everything but his trousers, he had seen Mrs. Burnsall at the front of the crowd, with the naphtha flares shining on her face. The crude light brought out the height of her cheekbones and sank her eyes into dark pits. Tom thought she was an exciting-looking woman, and she gazed frankly at his fine arms and white body and at the little dark curl beginning already to sprout on his chest. Tom was a plucky boxer, not a good one; but that night he managed to rattle his opponent, to send him down to the count more than once, before he was himself, bruised and bloody, knocked almost unconscious.

He put on his clothes, and was making his way to his lodgings. feeling sore and sorry, when Mrs. Burnsall overtook him, walking fast. They knew one another slightly, as inhabitants of the same region.

"That was a good fight," she said.

"But not good enough," Tom grinned.

"I never knew you had such arms," Mrs. Burnsall said, "till I saw you with your shirt off." She took hold of him by the upper arm and squeezed his biceps. "You're more of a man than a boy, already," she said.

At the touch of her hand on his arm, Tom felt a shiver go through him. He broke away down the first turning he came to, though it was not his way home. "Good night, Mrs. Burnsall," he said.

He had seen her once or twice since that, when he had been out with his truck, collecting junk. She had asked him to come into her house. He had not gone, but, gossiping on her doorstep, he had learned a lot about her. She was the only woman he knew who had money. She had married an old man of the most miserly habits. She was twenty-five then, and he died when she was thirty. A lifetime of the most igno-minious scrounging and scraping permitted him to leave less than a thousand pounds. Mrs. Burnsall had fifteen shillings a week income. It was just not enough to manage on. So she had tried running the lock-up greengrocer's shop, and now that was a failure.

Tom Hannaway was turning all these things over in his busy mind as he hurried through the night from Mr. Richardson's to the widow Burnsall's. The lock-up shop would not be a failure under *his* manage-ment, and what could be nicer for Mrs. Burnsall than to make up the few extra shillings she needed by taking him for a lodger?

It was the sort of house he was used to: two up and two down. But it was the most comfortable house he had ever been in. Polly Burnsall, surprised and delighted to see him, took him through to the kitchen. The steel of the fireplace and of the fender was shining like silver. The fire was bright. He had never before seen such a lamp as hung from the ceiling over the centre of the round table on which Polly's solitaire cards were set out. It had a shade of red silk, and there was an arrange-ment by which you could push it right up to the ceiling or lower it to the table. There were big coloured pictures on the walls: lovely inn-ocent children fondling St. Bernard dogs, red-coated British troops doing and dying against dastardly Indians who were having the nerve to try to hold India, languishing Greek maidens on terraces of marble veined with blue shining against an incredible sea. On each side of the fireplace was an easy chair, and the crockery was not packed out of sight in a cupboard but was ranged on a Welsh dresser and shone with cleanliness.

This was a sumptuousness which Tom had not expected; nor had he expected to find Polly Burnsall herself so spick and span, seeing that she could not have been long back from her disastrous failure of a shop. But her hair looked as if it had just been dressed; her high cheekbones were obviously fresh from soap and water, and her dress actually included a gold chain round the neck, passing to a watch tucked into her girdle.

Tom began to wonder whether the exciting things he had been dreaming about were not, after all, presumptuous and abominable. Polly put him into one of the easy chairs and asked if she should make him a cup of tea. He said "No," and plunged at once into his business.

"I wanted to warn you, Mrs. Burnsall. It's no business of mine, but old Richardson's been saying he's going to turn you out of the shop."

He waited for her comment on that, but there was none. She sat at the table, with her chin resting on the knuckles of her two hands, looking steadily at him with her dark piercing eyes. It was almost as though she were trying to hypnotize him. He stared for a moment at a couple of bangles which had fallen from her wrists down her bare shapely forearms; then he went on: "Well, I wanted to warn you, see, and help you, too. I know you can manage if you get a bit more money, and I wondered if you would like to take me for a lodger. I could pay you fifteen shillings a week."

Tom had settled in his mind on twelve and six, but something was working him up, and the fifteen shillings was out before he knew it.

She continued to gaze at him with black, inscrutable eyes, not moving her position. He did not know what emotion she was keeping under control, how passionately the woman who had married miser Burnsall desired this handsome, black-haired youth with the white skin and the red lips through which the teeth shone like hailstones when he smiled.

"Well," and he managed to grin uncomfortably, "d'you think I've got a cheek? Could you do it at the money?"

"When could you come?" she said, and he was surprised, then thrown into a wild joy, to hear that her voice was as strained as his own.

"Tomorrow night," he said.

In the passage she took his arm. "Come tonight," she whispered. "Stay now."

He shook himself clear, once again the confident Tom Hannaway, the man in control of the situation. "No. Sorry," he said in his bold clear tones. "I've got to run on and see a man about a bit of business."

This was the night on which Hamer and Arnold Ryerson had been to Birley Artingstall's party. Hamer had gone up to his bedroom, fireless for the first time since it had been also his study, as the diary notes:

"This small fact brings home to me more than anything else the change in our economic situation. Mr. Suddaby is paying me seven and six a week. I am nothing more than an errand boy. I cannot expect him to increase my wages, and yet more money somehow must be got. I have read an enormous amount in the last couple of years, but what is the use of all that to me now? How terribly the scales are weighted against the poor! Had I been the son of well-to-do people, all this reading would have been to my credit. It would have been said that I was doing well. But now it means only that I have been neglecting to acquire the mean accomplishments that would give me employment. I begin to see how men are *forced* to be servile. I shall not be one of them. I will, somehow, get a more profitable job, but, however hard that may cause me to work, I shall not drop one single endeavour toward the raising of my condition. I swore this last night on the Old Warrior's sabre. It caught my eye, hanging there on the wall, and more keenly than ever before I saw what the old man had meant when he called it a symbol. Hereafter, I shall never look at it without thinking of the unending battle between the rich and the poor. As this idea of swearing the oath came into my mind, I took down the sabre and was actually holding it above my head when Tom Hannaway came into the room."

Ellen had told Tom to go up. She was too dispirited to accompany him. "You'll find him in the room on the left of the landing," she said.

Tom, who had never been inside the house before, pushed open the bedroom door, to find himself confronted by Hamer, holding the sabre above his head and muttering. Tom recoiled upon the landing. "For God's sake!"

Hamer lowered the sabre till the point touched the ground. "Come in," he said. He did not explain what he had been doing. He might have explained to Arnold Ryerson. To Tom Hannaway – no. He hooked the sabre back to its nails. "Sit down."

Tom Hannaway slumped into a chair, took out a pipe, and, without asking permission, lit it. He looked round him in surprise. He had never seen a room like this before. It was unlike Mr. Richardson's dingy lodging; unlike Polly Burnsall's comfortable kitchen.

"This would be nice with a bit of fire in the grate," he said.

Hamer stood before the cold fireplace, his hands in his trousers pockets, and scowled. "Can't afford it."

"You want a job with more money attached to it," said Tom Hannaway. "I've come to offer you one."

It seemed incredible. It seemed only a day or two ago that they were both at school, and here was Tom Hannaway talking about giving him a job! Some boys would have laughed. Hamer didn't. He did not underestimate Tom Hannaway. He was perhaps the only person at this time, except Mr. Richardson, who had a feeling that Tom Hannaway was a personage, after his fashion.

"Tell me about it," he said briefly.

It was going to be harder than he had thought. Tom Hannaway left him in no doubt about that. "You'll have to be up early – at the market while the good stuff's there. It's not my business to tell Mrs, Burnsall why she's made a muck of it, but that's one reason: she'd never get up early enough. Come home with a few mangy lettuces and sticks of rhubarb. You won't do that – not if you want this job. You'll be in the markets at six, and you'll open up the shop at eight, and shut it at eight at night. And you'll keep accounts of what you spend in the market, and what you take in the shop, and we'll check 'em over every night, an' square that off with what's left in stock. And there'd better not be much of that, because this is perishable stuff. I don't want to see my money withering in the window."

"I could buy the stuff," Hamer said. "I don't see how I can make people buy it. They do or they don't."

"Hey! Hey! Don't start talking like that," Tom Hannaway shouted, belching out a cloud of smoke. "That's no way to talk when you've got something to sell. We'll make people buy. I've been thinking up a few ideas. Window-dressing, to begin with."

"I can't dress a window."

"Well, learn to, instead of filling your head with all this stuff." He waved his pipe comprehensively toward the books. "Then I'll tell all the club members. One night a week free for all whose mothers shop at Hannaway's. And you see that all *your* friends shop there, too. Then there could be a few special ideas. I thought of tortoises."

"Tortoises?"

"Yes. Why not? Kids love something like that. We give the mothers a book. I'd get a little stamp made, and you stamp the books for every shillingsworth of goods bought. When they get thirty stamps, they're given a tortoise for the kids. You could feed 'em on lettuce.

No difficulty about that. You want ideas." Again he waved his pipe with a vague magnificence as if limning unimaginable tracts of thought. "That's what got Mrs. Burnsall down. Too much bed and not enough brains."

"And what do I get?"

"Fifteen shillings a week to begin with."

"When do I start?"

"As soon as I've got the place ready. It needs a coat of paint. I couldn't stand a dingy place like that. I reckon it's the landlord's job to brighten it up. I'll see Mr. Richardson about that. I think he'll do it for me." Tom smiled quietly at some thought which Hamer could not share, got up, and knocked out his pipe in the cold grate. "You taking it?"

"Yes."

"Good lad. I thought you'd be looking for something, with the old man gone. I expect," he added, with a condescending look at the book-shelves, "it'll mean less of this, but still—"

"It'll mean nothing of the sort," said Hamer. "Not if I can help it."

In keeping track of Hamer's career, it is often necessary to check what he said in the years of his maturity against the record of the diary. At the very end, when he became Viscount Shawcross, one of the first of the Labour peers, he was inclined to magnify his tribulations, uncon-sciously perhaps. It has already been seen that he almost persuaded himself that he had been one of those children disturbed from their sleep by the rattle of Jimmy Spit-and-Wink's bundle of wires on the window. It has been seen how the "wolves" to whom fate threw him were nothing more savage than Mr. Suddaby. But the diary is a record made at the time, with no thought that in years to come it would see the light of day. It is, on the whole, a reliable document.

"Ah, my friends! Many of you here are here because of the self-sacrificing love and devotion of parents." (This was an address to the undergraduates of a Scottish university.) "Do not forget them. If the world goes well with you, recompense them, though they will think your triumphs are all the recompense they need. If it goes ill, remem-ber that anything you may be called upon to endure has already been endured by those who stinted themselves to furnish you with weap-ons which they themselves had not the opportunity to carry. I can speak – and I do it with humility – of a mother's love. I can speak of a poor home smitten by sudden calamity, of the loaf dwindling in the cupboard, the oil failing in the lamp, the fire sinking low upon the hearth, and hope burning low in the soul. Against that grey background I see shining the unquenchable flame of a mother's love. Work must be found, and she was there, seeking, seeking, seeking, till the spectre that haunts the lives of the poor – worklessness – was at last banished."

All this dying and dwindling and fading, all this seeking and seeking, suggests a long period of privation which did not, in fact, occur. The diary is clear:

"Now I'm a greengrocer! I suppose all the days will be more or less like this first one, so I shall write here what it has been like. Tom had already laid in at the shop a great deal of stuff that would not perish quickly – things like potatoes and carrots, turnips and parsnips, kippers, apples and oranges. I had not much idea what I should do when I got to the market. I was pushing the handcart along Great Ancoats Street at six in the morning – a wretched rainy morning, too – when a man driving a pony attached to a flat cart overtook me, and stopped. He asked if I was Hannaway's boy, and when I said 'Yes,' he said Tom had paid him a pound to help me with the buying for the first week. I must say there is nothing about this business that Tom Hannaway has not thought of and provided for. The shop looks beautiful with its new paint outside and its scrubbed shelves inside, and he has provided the tortoises he talked about the other night. He is the sort of young man who seems bound to succeed with everything he does, which is something I do not feel about Arnold Ryerson. though I like Arnold better than Tom.

"I think I shall soon learn this buying business. It went well enough with a little advice from the man, and when I got back Tom was at the shop, though I had not expected him. He had written a list of prices, so that I shouldn't sell anything too cheaply. He turned up again at half-past twelve, and told me to go home and get my dinner.

"We have sold a lot of stuff today, and my most interesting customer was Miss Harriet Wilder. She came with her father, of all people! She filled her string bag with stuff, but I think these purchases were only an excuse for coming to talk to me, though Miss Wilder says she will in future buy all her greengroceries from Hannaway's. But I could see that Mr. Wilder wanted to talk about how my mother and I were managing now that Father was dead. I said my mother was going to look for work. She didn't mind what it was, so long as we could keep our own house to ourselves. Mr. Wilder said the chapel caretaker, who is a very old man, was giving up the work and going to live with his married daughter at Oldham. He said it was usually a man's job, but if my mother would like to have it, he thought he could arrange it with the chapel committee. This was in the morning, and I told her about it when I went home to dinner. She went straight away to see Mr. Wilder, who then told her that he had already arranged with the committee for her to take the job if she cared to have it. This is a remarkable stroke of luck, because between us we shall earn nearly as much as Father earned, though we shall both have to work much harder than we ever did. But there it is. Thank God, we are out of the wood, without any miserable period of wondering how on earth we can make both ends meet."

He was at the market at six in the morning. By half-past seven, he had returned to the shop and put the stuff where it had to be. Also, if the window needed rearranging he saw to that. In the early days of his life as a greengrocer, Tom Hannaway had appeared on the pavement one morning at eight o'clock, examined the display critically, and then walked into the shop. He seized three or four lettuces out of the window and shook them angrily under Hamer's nose. "What d'you call that?" he demanded. "Shrivelled! Withered! Horrible!" He threw the lettuces out into the road, then went after them and brought them back. "No waste," he said. "Keep 'em for the tortoises, or if some kid comes in for rabbit-food sell 'em half-price. But don't let me see that sort of stuff in the windows again."

The next day Tom brought along a streamer, printed in gay colours: "The Dew sparkles on Hannaway Produce." He pasted it across the window, looked at it with his head on one side, and, coming back, indicated a water-can. "Live up to that motto," he said.

So now, by half-past seven, Hamer had looked to the window. Then he went home to breakfast. There was no early-morning running now, but the barrow-pushing opened out his shoulders, and he remembered to breathe deeply. Ellen could not get over her habit of looking at him solicitously. She could not forget the child with the dragging gait, the head that had seemed too big for the slender blue-veined neck. He knew what she was thinking. He got up one morning from the breakfast table, threw off his coat, rolled up his shirt-sleeves, and flexed his biceps. "Get hold of that," he said. Ellen pressed the hard muscle with her fingers which were now so rough and red with constant immersion in soda-water. "It seems all right," she smiled.

"Stop worrying," he said. "They won't get me down."

Mysterious hidden forces – "They" – were beginning to appear to his mind, forces associated in some vague fashion with the field of Peterloo, and the trampling, snorting, red-nostrilled horses of the Hussars, and with all that old Suddaby had been accustomed to talk about in his quiet hinting way. Associated, too, with the famished ragged horde clawing round the soup cauldron in Stevenson Square, and with a boy and a girl standing there hand in hand with tin mugs tied round their necks: hopeless, defeated, and unprotesting in their defeat. But They would not get down him, Hamer Shawcross.

By eight o'clock he was back at the shop and had opened for the day. Behind the shop was a tiny room, used as a store, with a window opening on to a back yard. When he was in there, no one could see him, for a curtain hung across the glass door that communicated with the shop. And no one could come into the shop without his knowing, because there was a bell that sounded when the shop door opened.

In this back room "They" met their adversary, wrestling through the hours. For there were long stretches of time with no customers, and then he would fling up the window, breathe deeply, and run standing. That is to say, he would throw back his head, lift up his knees – up, down-up, down – covering an imaginary mile; and then he would bend and twist and stretch, suppling his muscles and making his body do what he would. When all that was done, he would take from his pocket a primer he had got from Mr. Suddaby, and recite: *J'ai, tu as, il a.* There was not the time now, or the money, for those French lessons he had promised himself; but all the same, They were not going to get him down. *Nous avons, vous avez, ils ont.*

Back into the shop. No one about. With the fine-sprayed watering-can he put the dew on to Hannaway's produce. Tom would be here any minute, and Tom would expect to see the synthetic virginal freshness. Tom would have had a mechanical lark to sing over this happy garden had he been able to manage it.

Tom came, as he always did, at a quarter past one. Hamer wondered a little at the brightness of Tom's eye in these days, and his even more- than-usual confidence and grown-upness. Tom was only eighteen, but in those days he seemed suddenly to have leapt into an adult aptitude.

But what lay behind this was a speculation outside Hamer's range at that time. What he knew was that there was only three-quarters of an hour for dinner and that Tom's good humour would be gone if he were not relieved at two o'clock sharp.

In the afternoon, it was the same performance: greengrocery, running a standing mile, bending and doubling and twisting, *j'aurai, tu auras, il aura.*

It was not yet four when he lit up. By half-past three the shabby Ancoats street was full of a grey creeping dusk, chill with a faint misty miasma that seemed to arise from the canal in Broadbent Street and slide and seep down all the ill-lit dingy ways. Then the gaslight sputtered, and its yellow radiance fell on Hannaway's produce, again prudently and providently dew-scattered, and on the red apples and golden pyramids of oranges, and the tangerines wrapped in silver tissue, and the golden-brown flat kippers that once had been finny and stream-lined, and the oblong blocks of dates, compressed into so solid a compass that they looked as though enduring works of architecture might be achieved with them.

The lamplighter's clogs rang out into the darkness, as the pale shambling Prometheus, carrying at the end of a pole his eternal morsel of smoky flame, went from lamp to lamp, thrust up the small tin trap-door, and passed on, leaving behind him a long-spaced trail of feeble lights. Feeble indeed and ineffectual they seemed, blooming in the grim Ancoats night, throwing into prominence by their consumptive and spectral auras the brave glow and glitter of Hannaway's window. "Don't spare the gas. When it's dark, turn 'em all on, and keep 'em all on, all the time." So spake Thomas, juvenile master of publicity.

Out of the night, out of the dark lanes and ill-lit streets, justifying Tom's prescience, the children crept, pale moths attracted by the festive glare, pointing with skinny fingers at the dates that had swayed on camels across the insufferable light of the desert, and at the oranges that had glowed on trees in Spain, and at the cabbages and lettuces cunningly fresh and diamond-hung. They came, and hovered for a moment, and disappeared again, pallid and inscrutable goblins out there in the night, and Hamer saw their wan and glass-distorted features, and would not allow his mind to be distracted from its fierce and bitter concentration. *Nous aurons, vous aurez, ils auront.* They *should* not get him down.

Three and a half hours still to go, before, at half-past seven, Tom came to count the cash, check the stock, and take a general look round. Three and a half hours in which he remembered the old urgent promptings of Gordon Stansfield and Mr. Suddaby and Birley Artingstall: Read this! Read that!

Locke on *Human Understanding*, Grote on *Greece*, Gibbon on *The Decline and Fall of the Roman Empire*, Hakluyt, Prescott: they were all in the drawers and cupboards of an old sideboard that Polly Burnsall had left in the back room. Under the golden rain of Tom's extravagant gas-consumption, he brought his fields to ripening, reading with the same fierce and bitter concentration that he gave to *Avoir* and *Être*. He read leaning his elbow on the end of an upturned orange crate; and sometimes, rapt away into the world of his imagining, he would lift his eyes from the page, stare out into the black abysm of the night, peopled by shadows sliding from one plane of darkness to another, and, not seeing them, would see instead faces stretching back and back, down a long floor and up exalted galleries, and the orange crate would become a pulpit, a rostrum, and he the focal point of ten thousand watching eyes. Ah, my friends!

At eight o'clock Tom, whistling, hurried away to the ever more-deeply appreciated comforts that Polly Burnsall afforded; and Hamer, turning out the gas, locked up the shop and went home to his late "high tea." Sometimes Ellen was there to give it to him, but often now something demanded her presence at Emmott Street. Then he would look after himself; but, whether she was there or not, he would go straight up to his room at half-past eight and write in his diary till nine. From nine to ten he read fiction or poetry; at ten he put on his hat and coat, and, with an ash stick in his hand, walked the streets till eleven. Then he went home and to bed. That was his day. And for a long time that was every day.

When the summer came, it was different. He didn't need to listen for old Jimmy Spit-and-Wink. He was up, with the sun shining in at his window, at half-past five, and, pushing his handcart, he went down Broadbent Street with the clog-clattering horde rushing to reach the mill before the direful wailing of the buzzer died away. But no mill-gate closed behind him. He was there on the road, pushing his cart, with the sweet morning air about him and the sky stretched above the chimney-pots like taut milky-blue silk. No mill for John! So much Gordon had promised – poor Gordon who had been able, after all, to do so little of what he would have liked to do. No mill. But what instead?

Hamer didn't know. He knew only that he was being driven, and that he responded gladly to the goad. He could not imagine anything finer than the grinding slogging life he was leading now, though he would have liked to live in different conditions. But give up a moment of there ardours and endurances? Not on your life!

Even at six in the morning there was no dew on Great Ancoats Street, no lark singing overhead. But at least, in those days, there was no stink of motor traffic, and, as he plodded along among the horse-drawn wagons and the handcarts like his own, all churning up the grey dust of the road, he felt strong and happy, contented for the moment with his striving discontented life.

What on earth possessed him to buy the wallflowers? If there was one thing that didn't sell in Ancoats, it was flowers. They had come in from Cheshire; they were piled all over the stall of a little woman with cheeks as rosy as a pippin. Hamer had often seen her there before. The stall said her name was Margaret Billington. She dealt in nothing but flowers, and so he had had no dealings with her. But the scent of the wallflowers was so sweet and penetrating that it prevailed over the indefinable market smell that by now he knew so well: a smell compounded of wholesome things on the stalls and squashed pulpy things on the floor and horse-droppings and human sweat. The wallflowers were shining with authentic dew, and their ruddy-brown petals had a smooth velvet nap and made him think suddenly of the colour of Harriet Wilder's eyes. Well, Tom could hardly be severe with him for investing in a dozen bunches. They cost him a penny a bunch, and he would price them twopence.

Mrs. Billington wrapped the stalks in paper, leaving the dewy petals uncovered. "The butterfly goes with them," she said.

And there the butterfly was, though Hamer had not noticed it before, for the ruddy-brown of its folded wings was the very colour of the flowers. No dew and no skylarks in Great Ancoats Street, but, here in the market, dew sparkling on the wallflowers like sequins on velvet, and a butterfly whose wings were now upraised and pressed close together above its long, thin body, now dropped down and outspread in a gorgeous patterning of peacock colours.

He took the bunch with fearful circumspection, almost holding his breath, feeling his hand tremble, overjoyed when the flowers, the last purchase of the morning, lay upon his handcart with the butterfly still pulsing its wings upon them.

Already, when he got once more into Great Ancoats Street, the balm was gone from the morning. The sun had strengthened and promised a day of heat sizzling down upon the little houses packed in narrow rows. What was there here, in this stony waste, for this butterfly, this fragile lotus-eater, this drinker of dew? As the handcart jolted along the road Hamer watched the creature, fascinated, and it became a question of pride that it should go with him all the way. "If it does, something good, something lovely, is going to happen. I don't know what. Something good, something lovely."

The butterfly stretched its wings, quivered, fluttered an inch or two into the air. Hamer's breath sharpened. Oh, what a silly game! Ah, now it's down again upon the wallflowers that are the colour of Harriet Wilder's eyes. He quickened his pace. Get back to the shop before it goes. Never, surely, has a butterfly with peacock's colours on its wings been seen in an Ancoats shop. When, indeed, was a butterfly last seen in Ancoats, anywhere in Ancoats? Were there gardens in Ancoats, where now, in this month of June, roses would be blooming and bees fumbling for honey, in those far-off days when the Old Warrior and his girl marched behind Sam Bamford with the green sprig in his hat? Perhaps not even then.

So stay, butterfly. Surely you are a symbol of something wonderful that is going to happen in Ancoats today.

Suddenly the butterfly made up its mind, rose from the flowers, and zigzagged above the roadway, falling this way and that, as though, on this breathless morning there were airs unfelt by any but itself, strong enough to send it careening down invisible troughs and surging up unseen crests like a little yacht on a bobbly sea.

Hamer watched it go, rise higher and higher, till it was a speck disappearing across a roof-ridge, and then, with a half-rueful laugh at his own nonsense, he turned to the serious business of pushing greengroceries back to the shop.

He passed into Broadbent Street, and his heart gave a sudden bound. He would not have thought it possible that so trivial a thing could give him such joy. The butterfly, opening and shutting its wings, was perched on the parapet of the oozy canal that nowadays reminded him so little of Venice.

Hamer brought the handcart to a standstill. There was no one to see him. Broadbent Street had not yet reached the time of its second stirring. He tiptoed toward the parapet, one hand reaching out in a scoop toward the butterfly. But it did not wait for him. It rose, and went with its dizzy, zany flight up the black face of the mill beyond the canal. This time, it did not disappear. It came back and fluttered tantalizingly out of his reach; then, in its drunken erratic fashion, it fell once more upon the wallflowers, as though all the time it had been searching for that one spot of colour and odour and dew in this unaccustomed wilderness. Now it stayed where it was. Even when Hamer picked up the flowers and carried them into the shop, it stayed where it was. He took them into the little back room, butterfly and all, put them in a jam-jar full of water, and shut the door. The butterfly that was the colour of the wallflowers; the wallflowers that were the colour of Harriet Wilder's eyes.

She came with her string bag at three in the afternoon. Ancoats was like an oven. Hamer stood at the shop door. As far as he could see, all the little house windows were up, but the cheap lace curtains hung down as rigid as board. The sky was a strip of brassy light burning above the canyon of the street. Women sat on the yellowstoned doorsteps, apathetic as cows in a summer field, and a few children tumbled in the gutters, stirring the dust and the dry rustling shreds of paper. In one side of the shop-window was an array of bottled lemonade, cheap and venomous-looking yellow stuff, one of Tom Hannaway's seasonal "lines."

"Well, Hamer."

He turned. Harriet had come from the other direction. She looked pale, wilted. She had been getting like that lately. The wild colour that had been in her cheeks when she came from Chester had been fading in the Ancoats murk, and this present spell of torrid heat made her droop like a tree whose root has been cut through.

"Hamer." She had taken to calling him that. He was growing, and his breadth was keeping pace with his height. He was beginning to look like a man, and a lot of people were beginning to call him Mr. Shawcross. But he preferred this. Hamer.

He followed her into the shop. She suddenly stood still, gazing at a piece of paper fastened by a drawing-pin to the side of an upended orange crate. It was the complete conjugation of the verb *Avoir*.

"Hallo! I didn't know you were doing French."

Hamer blushed. "I didn't intend you to know. I thought I'd taken that down." He unpinned the slip of paper and put it in his pocket.

To his surprise, she put her hand, which was no longer brown but as thin as ever, on his sleeve. "Don't do that," she said. There was a smile in her tired eyes.

"Don't do what?"

"Bottle it up. Let me talk to you. Shall I?"

He nodded.

"Good. You're bottling everything up. I've felt that for a long time. Your mother's told me about things you're doing: all the reading and writing. It's hard, all that sort of thing, when you keep it to yourself. There used to be Mr. Stansfield, and that boy Arnold Ryerson, and old Mr. Suddaby."

"You seem to know a lot about me!"

"It's your mother. She talks a lot about you. You must forgive her. She's very proud of you."

"Well, I do miss all those people – Gordon and Arnold and old Suddaby."

"I'm sure you do. Try and find someone else. Look at this French. Rather than let me know anything about it, you fold up the paper and tuck it away as though it were something to be ashamed of. Don't bottle things up. You see, I *know*. My father was like that. He was as poor as you are. He's told me how dreadful it used to be, studying without anyone to help, without an encouraging word. Now he's a great scholar."

At that Hamer looked up wistfully. That was something – a great scholar. That was not everything, but that certainly was something that he wanted to be.

"Is he?"

"Yes. Many Wesleyan parsons aren't," she added with a smile. "But he is. He'd like to know you. He complains that there's hardly a soul in his circuit with whom he can have a good crack about the things that interest him."

"I don't think he'd find me any great shakes."

"You don't believe that," Harriet said. Her hazel-brown eyes looked him frankly up and down. "No. You don't believe that. You've got an opinion of yourself, and," she went on hastily as he tried to break in, "you've got a right to it. I don't know how long you're going to be satisfied with this" – she looked round the stuffy little shop – "but it won't be any longer than you can help. Now, let me try you in *Avoir*."

He began to run through the tenses. He was nervous and confused. Now and then she had to prompt him; and when he had done she said: "Good! But you want someone to teach you the pronunciation. Let me do it."

His face lightened. "Will you – Harriet?"

"I'd love to. Come round on Sunday night after service and have supper with me and Father. We'll have a good talk and arrange things. Don't be afraid of him. His father was a bricklayer."

The talk had given back to her face something of its old animation, its ugly-monkey attractiveness. "I'll buy two bottles of that awful-looking stuff in the window," she said. "We'll drink to your stepping-out. Because you've got to, you know."

They did that, and, as there were no glasses, they drank from the bottles, and the horrible liquid gas made them belch companionably. Then Hamer said: "Come and see what I've got in here."

He opened the door of the back room, and there was the butterfly, beating its wings against the window. "Oh, the lovely thing!" Harriet cried. "Let it out! Let it out!" She threw up the window. The butterfly, dazed for a moment, fluttered dizzily in the air without, as though unable to apprehend its freedom. Then, zigzagging higher and higher, it disappeared into the torrid crash of the heat.

"There!" said Harriet. "Things like that should be given the use of their wings. Don't bottle them up."

Mr. Wilder was not the great scholar that Harriet imagined him to be, but he was an intelligent and well-read man. He had acquired enough Hebrew to rummage his way, if need be, through a passage of the Old Testament in its original tongue, enough Greek to make him at ease with the Greek New Testament. His Latin was better than his Greek or his Hebrew, because he had not learned it for any other reason than that he wanted to. He read his Latin authors for fun, and his French authors, too. Those were his four languages, and, for the rest, he was a man who loved good things in his own tongue. When his wife was living, he would often roll out a hundred majestic lines of Milton without pause or hitch, or a long passage from Shakespeare. These two, with Wordsworth, were his favourite poets; and the great prose writers, too, had taken such a hold on his imagination that, without having consciously learned them, he could recite the flowing periods of Browne and Addison, Bunyan, Swift and Jeremy Taylor.

Since the death of his wife in Chester, he had tended to shrink in upon himself. Here in this Ancoats circuit he had made no friends. His long pale face had grown longer and paler, and, when he was not engaged in circuit tasks which could not be put to one side, he sat in his study with his favourite books about him, now reading, now, with a book face downwards on his knee, abandoned to reverie and reminiscence.

It was perhaps as much for his sake as for Hamer's that Harriet brought the two together. Now the outline of Hamer's day began to change. After the evening meal, he would, as usual, go to his room and write in his diary, but after that, instead of settling down to read, he would, as often as not, go round to the Wilders'. Harriet coached him in his French, Mr. Wilder set him going on Latin, and night after night they sat there till eleven o'clock discussing some book that all three had agreed to read.

This was literally the first home that Hamer had gained access to in a familiar and continuous way. He had occasionally been in Birley Artingstall's bachelor room, but nowhere else. It did him good. Harriet always brought in coffee. The first night he was there, as she was leaving the room with the tray of empty cups, it was Mr. Wilder who jumped up to open the door. The second night, and for all nights thereafter, it was Hamer. He learned to be easy in the company of a woman; he learned to take his hat off without embarrassment, to stand when she entered a room, to see that she was provided with what she needed at supper. Mr. Wilder's manners had been formed in an old school; they were punctilious; and so were Hamer Shawcross's to the end. It was a surprise to many, in those early days when a Labour politician was a curiosity that might be expected to have the uncouth habits of a performing baboon – it was in those days a surprise to find that this man exceeded most people not only in the range of his knowledge and in the felicity of its presentation but also in his physical appearance and deportment. To see the Rt. Hon. Hamer Shawcross, or, a little later, Viscount Shawcross of Handforth, wearing his full evening fig and greeting a lady at a reception in the mansion of some famous Tory hostess – ah! the grand staircase, the flunkeys' plush, the chandeliers raining down their light on bare shoulders and proud tiara'd brows – that was a matter almost Arthurian in its grace and chivalry. *Tory* hostess? Ah, my friends, who would have thought it! What would the Old Warrior have said had he been able to project his vision into the future and see the small sharer of his Ancoats bedroom, the boy tossing on the pallet bed, casting his eye upon some debutante sprig of the nobility and thinking how sweet she would look alongside Charles? But Charles Shawcross is a long way off. This much, however, may be said: you, Harriet, with your wild elfin face and eyes the colour of wallflowers, you with that look of quick devotion which may be surprised in your glance now and then as you contemplate this emerging phenomenon of beauty and grace, you will not be Charles's mother.

And why Viscount Shawcross of Handforth? Why Handforth? Well, when you are an old man, not far off your seventieth year, even though your body be still upright and your white hair have a shining vitality, there come moments, especially if you are left alone in the evening, when the mind loses its grip on the present and wanders back and back.

So it was with the handsome and dignified Minister for the Co-ordination of Internal Affairs. For once in a while he had an evening to himself. He had dined alone at his house in Half Moon Street. He had told the servants that, whoever called, he was not at home. They told him afterward that a Mr. Ryerson had called. He was almost sorry that he had not seen him. It was so many years since they had had a talk together. But, after all, what had they to say to one another? And there was this question of the title to be settled.

He passed from the dining-room to the library; that well-stocked library that was the admiration and the envy of many people. It was cosily lighted, and the coal fire shone on the bottom rows of the books. He browsed about for a moment with a cigar between his lips, pulling out a volume here and there. Sam Bamford's poems. That went back a bit! That had belonged to the Old Warrior. Birley Artingstall had bound it in leather, and on a birthday night in Ancoats – the first time he had ever seen Ann – they had all signed their names in it. He turned back the cover: there they were – those names that had been signed more than fifty years ago – brown with age; Ann's name between his and Arnold Ryerson's, all three sprawling childishly.

In Ancoats. Well, you couldn't call yourself Viscount Shawcross of Ancoats. You might as well have a Duke of Wapping or a Marquis of Whitechapel. He dropped into a chair by the fire and allowed his rigid spine to relax for a moment. No, not Ancoats. Strange; he had never wanted to be John Shawcross, but Hamer Shawcross; and now the Hamer was going, too. He would be just Shawcross. The way they called servants. That's what they would have called his mother, before she married Gordon Stansfield. Here, Shawcross!

The memory of them all seemed to be flooding in on him tonight: Gordon and Ellen, Arnold Ryerson, and Ann, and Birley Artingstall. "Call myself Shawcross of Peterloo and have done with it," he smiled wryly.

That's what they had called him years ago, in the days of his earliest campaign, when he had carried the sabre with him, and flashed it at meetings – and nearly cut down Lostwithiel, by God! one day. He still had it. He had had a lovely box made for it, a craftsman's job if ever there was one, the lid inlaid with rare woods. At least, Lettice had had the box made – Lostwithiel's wife – and the sabre lay in it on a bed of royal blue. "Ah, so tha's finished wi' t'owd bacon-slicer? It's nobbut a curio these days?" That was Sir Thomas Hannaway, who cultivated, as carefully as others sought to eradicate it, a northern accent which he had never possessed in youth.

Well, it was from back there somewhere, from those old days and earliest associations, that his title would have to come. The coals tinkled in the grate, little flames flapped their banners, and through the quiet of the night he could hear the dull unceasing *bourdon* of the traffic in Piccadilly, beyond the end of the street.

Far away and long ago. That was a title of Hudson's. There seemed more grey than green in his old memories, more winter than summer, more streets than hedges.

"Hedges! I love hedges! I can't imagine England without hedges. D'you know, there used to be very few. There was a vast amount of open cultivation. You could stand on a hill in England then, and see miles of land with not a hedge on it. Then, I suppose, people began to be terribly fond of 'my little bit' and 'your little bit' and thousands of people had no little bits at all. So I ought to dislike hedges. But I love them."

Slowly, down the long dwindling perspective of the years, the country road, white with the dust their boots kicked up, came into clearer focus. There the hedges were; it was almost as though they were marching through snowdrifts, so thick was the May blossom. The ditches in the hedge-bottoms were damp and full of the young uprushing green of late spring. Ragged robin and campion, and the tall swaying gold of buttercups, and the gleaming white plaques of dog-daisies, filled those hedge-bottoms, and the white curved shoulders of the hedge-tops rested against a tremulous blue that was full of the melody of invisible larks.

"Oh, this is good!" Harriet cried. "This reminds me of Chester, and the days we had when Mother was alive and we walked into Wales. Let's do this often!"

Hamer shook his head. To ask him to take a whole day off in this wild and reckless fashion when there was so much to do, so much to do, was almost like asking him for a hundred pounds.

It was Whit-Monday. Everyone was on holiday. Manchester was dead. That was his excuse, and in those days he had to give himself a good excuse indeed when his nose came up from the grindstone.

All day long they walked. They walked under the silver-grey pillars of the beech trees; they pushed through hazel coppices and came upon little meres, scaring the coots and moorhens; they found a thrush's nest and looked with wonder on the blue, black-spotted eggs; they laughed at the leggy antics of the lambs. Harriet's wild colour came back; she was as gay as though out of some immense beneficence of her own she had conjured the day and its glories for his delight.

"Oh, you've earned it, you know! You've earned it all," she cried, as they settled down in a warm brown crackling nest of last year's bracken to eat their sandwiches. "I've never known anyone work like you. It's just ten months since you began coming to our house, and haven't you got on since that!"

"Ten months. Is it ten months?" He hadn't remembered, as Harriet had.

He lay back when they had eaten, and closed his eyes, and allowed the warm sunshine to play upon his face. She sat upright at his side, and looked at the broad forehead and the shock of hair tumbling across it, and at the long line of his mouth that could be so sulky and humorous and sensuous by turns. She would have loved to put the hair back from his forehead, or to lay her hand along his brow, or, she admitted to herself, trembling a little, to bend down suddenly and kiss the lids that were shut upon his eyes. But she didn't do any of those things. She pulled a stalk of grass, and nibbled the end of it, looking at Hamer stretched out there unmindful of her, more aware of the warmth of the sun than of her glance, more sensitive to the calling of the blackbirds than to the beating of her heart.

"What are you going to do?" she asked presently.

"Lie here," he said lazily, "and get baked right through to the backbone."

"No, no. I mean – you're not going to be satisfied much longer with the greengrocer's shop, are you?"

He sat up and shook his head vigorously. "Of course not. But I don't know what I shall do. I don't know what I *want* to do. But something will come along, and then I shall do it. The thing is, to be ready. That's what I'm doing – that's what I've been doing for a long time – getting ready. So long as I can run a mile and preach a sermon, I'm all right."

She smiled at this strange notion of equipment for a career. He smiled, too. "Well, you see what I mean – fit in body and mind."

Harriet said: "Oh, you don't need to be so fit in mind to preach a sermon."

"You do to preach my sort of sermon," he assured her earnestly. "Making 'em listen. Every man and woman hanging on your words."

"Well, you can run the mile already. When are you going to preach the sermon?"

"Next January."

She had not expected the answer to come so pat. "You seem to have it arranged."

"Oh, yes," he said. "I shall be seventeen in December. I thought I'd better wait till I was seventeen. But there's no harm in thinking about it now. I'll speak to your father and Birley Artingstall as soon as I have a chance. And now for that mile." He leapt to his feet. "Here! Bring these! Follow me!" He piled coat and waistcoat and hat unceremoniously into her arms, scrambled down the little slope that separated them from the road, and started off. Head up! Knees up! A good easy lope! Before she was on the road he was round a bend. She followed, cluttered with his belongings, as proudly as though she were a page bearing the accoutrements of a knight.

They had tea at Handforth. How was Harriet to know that, years hence, more than half a century hence, an old man, looking backwards through the long tunnel of his years, would see that day, and especially that hour in the garden, with an inexplicable hard brightness, all its details clear save one. Foraging among his memories, it came to him suddenly, not one of those days of which one says "I shall always remember this," but one of those days which, for no especial reason, mark themselves upon the mind, indelibly, for ever.

Handforth! He could see it all. He threw the stump of his cigar into the fire, burning down to a soft glow in the Adam fireplace that pleased his æsthetic taste so much. Yes. It was like turning on an old tune, finding in an album an old photograph. There was nothing remarkable about Handforth, a dullish village in the Cheshire plain; but he could recall the easing of his limbs as he sank, after much exercise, upon a bench in the garden. There were a few roses already abloom, though the time of roses was not fully come. The scent in the air was mainly lilac. It hung upon the senses like something palpable. Yes; Handforth and lilac-scent: the two were intermixed in his memory. There were beehives, too: some of white-painted wood and some of plaited straw. A woman brought them tea out of doors, under the lilac trees; and how they enjoyed it as the swifts hurtled by with their wild cries; the tea from a big brown earthenware pot, and the bread and butter and jam and the little fancy cakes. How they had enjoyed it, he and the girl who was with him. But that was where the memory broke down. Bright as a miniature in a gold frame the whole picture was, except for this one detail. He could not for the life of him recall the look of her face or the tone of her voice. Wilder – that was her name. Helen or Hilda Wilder, the daughter of a Wesleyan parson he had known before the wandering life of the circuits swallowed him up. He had never reappeared. As for the daughter... The old man put back the falling lock of white hair from his forehead, forced his mind to fish for this missing speck of the bright mosaic; but it was no use. And, after all, what women he had known! What changes he had seen! He could remember women swathed up in voluminous clothes, and women with leg-of-mutton sleeves puffing out their arms and bustles puffing out their sterns. He could remember that extraordinary time just after the war when they wore skirts above their knees. He had actually seen Ann like that, and Lady Oxford, too. Incredible. And now here they were going back pell-mell to the styles with which Victoria had charmed her Albert. Women! So many of them! How should he remember that girl at Handforth? But Handforth itself – that remained, glowing with light and beauty in those beginnings of his time when light and beauty were not common things. Well, then, he thought: Let it be Handforth; and, though he was not likely to forget such a decision, he drew a writing-pad on to his knee, took out his fountain-pen and wrote "Shawcross of Handforth."

He contemplated the signature with his head on one side. It looked well. He wondered whether to smoke another cigar or read a book. He decided against both, leaned his handsome old head back in the chair, and closed his eyes. It was not often life let him have a night to himself.

He was seventeen; and he was eighteen; just turned eighteen, and this was the last night of 1883. A lugubrious and lamentable night, with but another hour to live. Its old eyes were closing in a blear weeping mist that clung to the hairs of Hamer's overcoat as he hurried from the house in Broadbent Street.

He had run down from his room, with the notes of his address in his pocket. He looked into the kitchen where Ellen sat by the fire, bowed over the work in her lap with the immemorial and sacrificial stoop of poor women. She raised her head as the door opened, saw him standing there, tall, erect, already with something commanding in his very air and presence, and again a pang of remembering showed her a straight bright figure going out, and a cloth-veiled figure coming back supine upon a hurdle, and down nearly twenty years of time she heard again the brief decisive sound of the shot that stopped the agonized plunging of the horse. She withdrew her eyes from him, and the lamplight fell upon the grey lying in her hair like snow streaking shallow furrows in black land and upon the long needles glinting and clicking above the growing length of the muffler.

"You won't change your mind? You won't come?"

She shook her head and said: "I'll wait up for you." Perhaps she wouldn't have gone, anyway; but she couldn't go there; she couldn't go to this little chapel where, after a year's preaching here and there, he was going this night to conduct the watch-night service. She waited till the front door banged and quietness and loneliness were like presences in the room; then she put down the muffler in her lap, and folded her hands above the muffler, and stared into the fire. She couldn't go there, because that was the chapel where, blundering in her blind fashion through a night worse than this, she had come for the first time upon Gordon, talking in his comfortable voice that was a rumble charged with homely wisdom and goodness, though then she had been in no state to understand it.

She told herself she was wrong, she was wicked, to feel like this: that she couldn't listen to the boy talking in the places where Gordon had talked. Mr. Wilder was enthusiastic, said he had never known so young a preacher with so powerful a gift, and already people were filling the chapels to hear him. She had heard him herself and marvelled that this was her son. Yet in her heart was a doubt, that no one shared; and the easy brilliance, the challenging eye, the persuasive gestures and the rise and fall of the voice that could plead, condemn, exhort: these, though they might make her marvel, could not touch her heart, as Gordon's simple godliness had never failed to do.

She had no part or lot in the boy. Things had changed now at Hannaway's. Tom had prospered and opened three more greengrocer's shops. He had a man running the bone-yard for him. Hamer did all the buying for the shops and had the general supervision of them, while Tom himself went about with a gold watch-chain across his stomach and had walked right past his own mother without so much as a nod the day after she had suddenly leapt at Polly Burnsall and pulled her hair about her ears outside the Lostwithiel Arms.

Hamer didn't have to work so hard now. He had his evenings at home, and Ellen didn't see why he shouldn't do what Gordon had always done and read and write in the kitchen. Saturday night was for him now, as it had always been for Gordon, sermon-writing night; and her eyes burned now as she remembered, sitting there with the knitting in her lap and her hands folded upon the knitting in the quiet house, that Saturday night a month ago when, after supper, saying no word but with her heart painful in its beating, she had put the red cloth on the table beneath the lamp, and the paper and pens and inkstand; and beside these she had placed the Concordance and the Bible and the

Methodist Hymn-book, performing all that small significant ritual with which for so long she had associated some humble contribution of her own with Gordon's endeavours.

It was her mute invitation to the boy to give her some part, some trivial, menial contact with all this spread of new wings, this striking into new ether, that was about him, what with his French and his Latin, and all these books, overflowing now from his shelves and pell-mell upon the chairs and window-ledge and floor of his room – all that, and this power of speech that was drawing people to hear him talk.

He looked for a moment, as if uncomprehending, at what she had done, and at her, almost virginally blushing at the advance she had made, where she sat in a quick pretended absorption once more over the mending work in her hand; and then he said, with that swift, placating smile, putting back the hair from his forehead: "I work so much better upstairs, you know," and went, leaving her there abashed at the rebuff.

So, as the year oozed away its last wan and sickly hour, she thought of these things and knew she had no part or lot in him and that she would die in defence of one hair of his head.

Harriet Wilder met him, as she had arranged to do, at the corner of her street. He raised his hat and shook hands with her formally, because for a long time now he had forgotten that once wallflowers had made him think of the colour of her eyes. A street lamp cast a pallid light upon them, he trying to look grown-up, wearing an almost square bowler hat and a heavy ulster; she small and lithe, almost a foot below the height he had now reached, animated, full of chatter as a monkey.

She had taken to going with him wherever he was planned to preach, and more and more she knew, as Ellen knew, that she had no part or lot in him. She had pushed on all his enterprises; she and her father had given him all they had to give of time and knowledge and courtesy and approbation; and all this he had absorbed with an almost terrifying intensity.

That obsession to make a parson of him that had been upon Gordon Stansfield and Birley Artingstall was upon Mr. Wilder, too. He offered to start Hamer in Greek and Hebrew, and the boy said No. Some instinct told him the things he would want, and those were not among them.

He and Harriet moved out of the milky aura of the lamp. Their footsteps echoed in the deserted street. "Do you know any German?" he suddenly asked.

"No. Not a word."

"Does your father?"

"No."

He's coming to the end of us, she thought. We've got no more to give him.

The little chapel was lighted by oil lamps. It was very cold and full of creeping mist. There was no side entrance to the vestry. You had to walk the length of the big room and pass through a door at the side of the pulpit. As he passed swiftly down the room, Hamer's heart lifted to see that the little place was packed. He had been saying to himself all the evening: "If they come tonight, I'm all right – all right." On such a night, when a fireside would be snug; and to a watch-night service, which was never much of an attraction anyhow: they had come! He was aware, with a sideways flick of the eye, of men with their coat-collars about their ears, women with shawls about their shoulders, all breathing smokily in the cold damp air,

He came out of the rabbit-hutch that was called a vestry, ran up the two creaking steps to the platform on which a table stood, and paused for a moment, erect, shoulders back, surveying them; then passed his hand slowly through his hair as he spoke the first words. That was one of his tricks to the very end: that pause – Here I am: look at me – that gesture with the hand as though smoothing his thoughts into order behind his brow. It persisted when the brow had become loftier and lined and venerable, and the thoughts as misty and inchoate as the Ancoats fog which at this moment was dimming the lamps and chilling the people's bones.

He gave them their hymn in that voice which had a most clear and piercing quality, though he rarely needed to raise it:

The old year's long campaign is o'er;
    Behold a new begun!
Not yet is closed the holy war,
    Not yet the triumph won.

Then he spoke to them from the text: "Ye have not passed this way heretofore." It was a simple address, obvious as the daylight, as all his addresses then were; but it had the quality of his personality behind it. He was more and more, at this time, savouring his life as an adventure towards he knew not what. Few men could have sustained his emphatic belief in a great achievement lying ahead unless they had been upheld by some inkling of what the achievement was to be. But he had no intimation whatever of the lines his life was to follow. Every day was an unrelenting adventure, but an adventure in the dark, and an adventure full of unreasonable faith. And so he was able to impart to his audience something of this driving confidence in life, this challenge to lions in the path that proved to be only chained lions, this belief that though ye have not passed this way heretofore, ye *shall* pass, and come out safely on the other side. And if to this quality of almost pagan confidence he was forced to impute some religious tinge, to make some profession of faith that behind it all was a God of whom he was, in fact, not aware: well, that was in the nature of the case and of the circumstances in which he then found himself.

When the year had but a minute more to live, they all knelt in the clammy silence, going down upon the boards with a scuffle of heavy boots and clog-irons. "It seemed to me, standing above them" (so runs the diary, which throws the true light on the occasion) "that the year which was about to begin for all these people could hold nothing that the dying year had not held, and that was but a bare permission to live, and eat a little, and roughly clothe themselves. But when, presently, a jangle of discordant bells and a blast of hooters told us that the new year had come, they stumbled to their feet and looked at one another with the manifest belief on all their faces that in some way at which they could not guess this year *would* be different, though all experience should have taught them that it would do no more than bring them nearer to the grave."

But it was true. There was an added lilt to their voices, a fresh buoyancy to their manner, as they greeted the year:

Come, let us anew
Our journey pursue;
Roll round with the year,
And never stand still till the Master appear.

They sang it with gusto, and then stood chattering about the building, seizing one another's hands, and Hamer's hand, and Harriet's hand, and shouting "A happy New Year!"

A few desultory bells were still maintaining their clamour as Hamer and Harriet walked homeward. "It was a lovely address," she said, pausing at the corner of her street. She held out her hand. "Well, a happy New Year."

"And to you," he said. "Many happy New Years."

"It will be our last year in this circuit." she said. "We move on in the autumn."

"Good gracious!" said Hamer, "It's incredible how time passes."

She watched him till he was out of sight. He swung into Broadbent Street humming to himself: "Come, let us anew our journey pursue," and it was of no celestial journey that he was thinking. He could look back on the past year with satisfaction. The year ahead was a challenge, an allure, a beckoning. He smote the door vigorously with the knocker. Ellen, drowsing by the kitchen fire, started up at the sound and went to let him in.

If it had ever been your luck to see Lady Hannaway driving in a mustard-yellow Rolls Royce through Hyde Park, you would have been hard put to it to recognize Polly Burnsall. She was eighty when she died. Sir Thomas was then sixty-five. There didn't seem such discrepancy as when he married her. And "seem" is the right word. There had never been essential discrepancy. They had suited one another down to the ground from the beginning. Polly was another of Tom's lucky speculations, perhaps the luckiest of all. She was the first woman he had; she was the only woman he had; he was desolate when she died.

If that devout Catholic Mrs. Hannaway had not pulled Polly's hair round her ears and called her a Protestant bitch, Tom might not have married this woman who was to be his helpmeet and his stay. But the coarse insult in the face of all who knew her suddenly set to work in Polly's mind forces that Mrs. Hannaway had not reckoned with.

Her resolve to marry Tom was born in that moment. She was a strategist, as a woman in her position needed to be. There were two things to be done: one was to make herself and her home indispensable to Tom, something without which his life would be unthinkable;

the other was to wait till he wanted her money. She knew him well enough to be sure that that time would come.

Strenuously as Hamer Shawcross was working for he knew not what—"Ah, my friends, think of Saul, who went out to look for the asses and found a Kingdom" – so Tom Hannaway was working, no less strenuously, with every step clear, defined, before him. Polly Burnsall knew of the awful agitations of his spirit when twenty or fifty pounds were at stake. These, at that time, were for Tom moments as shattering and full of suspense as any he would know later when his adventurous and restless mind had tens of thousands trembling before the blowing of some financial wind. Indeed, they were more nerve-racking, because he was chancing his all. There was not then a comfortable reserve tied up beyond the reach of ill-fortune.

Taking the success or failure of a new greengrocer's shop with the enormous seriousness that Tom himself attached to it, Polly knew how to surround him at those times with the especial aura of her protection. She would take him off to town for a cheap meal in a restaurant, which was something new in his experience, then go on with him to a music-hall, and finally give his black tousled curls a resting-place on the bosom of which he never tired. "Forget it, Tommy. Just for tonight, forget it."

This was so good for Tom after the crowded squalor of his home, and so good for Polly after years of emotional penury when married to her miser, that the breach of years between them meant nothing. It would all have been different if Tom then, or soon after, had met a woman of his own age who attracted him; but it was Polly's luck that he didn't, and his own luck, too, if it comes to that.

The little shop with "Hannaway's" painted on the fascia remained next door to Artingstall's, like a coracle under the lee of a galleon, so long as Tom Hannaway was alive. He never had the name changed, even when Hannaway's and Artingstall's were one concern. The sentimental affection for the success of an early venture which caused him to call his Derby winner Darkie Cheap would not permit him to have the little shop altered.

There was a sentimental streak in Hamer Shawcross, too. It deepened as the years went on, so that, when he was a famous and venerable figure, he could stand before that little shop, during one of his rare visits to Manchester, and, pointing to the name "Hannaway's," say to his companion without a blush: "In that, I see the finger of God."

The diary puts it more prosaically. "So now that Tom Hannaway has decided to sink all his other ventures in order to buy this shop, I am at a loose end. The time has come when I must ask myself, as so many people have asked me: 'What are you going to do?' And still I do not know; but I feel the moment has now arrived when I must decide what I have been working for."

As soon as Tom Hannaway knew that Darkie Cheap was behindhand with his rent, he made up his mind that the place must be his. As soon as he knew that Polly Burnsall was not making her business pay, he resolved to take it over. So with the shops he acquired later. His mind was of that sort that does everything swiftly or not at all. Thus it was when he wanted the little draper's shop. He calculated what his green-grocery shops and the bone-yard would bring him if he parted with them, found it was nothing like enough and went straight home to Polly. "Polly, if you get hold of that bit of capital of yours, it'll do us some good. It's only bringing you in fifteen shillings a week, and it'll help to give us a first-rate little business."

But now the swift and instantaneous mind of Tom encountered a mind which could wait and wait. Polly had waited for some years, and now she knew that her moment had come. Tom had a week's option on the draper's shop. She would not decide; she could not decide; what if the business failed? At least now she had fifteen shillings a week between her and starvation; but where was a woman, with no status, no one to rely on, supposing this venture fell through? She kept Tom in a crisis of nerves for six-and-a-half days. She made imaginary visits to an imaginary lawyer who cautioned her, advised prudence.

"It *can't* fail. When did I *ever* fail?" That was Tom's sole contribution to the debate, with a thousand variations, throughout the week.

"But if it *does*? Where am I then? I've got no one. Who's going to bother with a woman getting on for forty and without a brass farthing to her name?"

"My God, Polly!" Tom shouted. "Don't I look after you? Do I think of you as a woman going on for forty? Well, then, blast your money, if that's how you feel about it. I'll go on selling cabbages. But I thought you'd want something better for me. I thought you'd want to see me out of this rotten slum and in the town by the time we married."

"Married?"

"Of course married. You don't think we're always going on like this, do you?"

"Well, then; what are you shouting about? If we're married, you can do what you like with the money. A married woman's property is her husband's. That's the law."

Tom looked at her flabbergasted. "Why the hell didn't you tell me that six days ago?" He snatched up his hat. "I'll go and see that man."

Though the finger of God was hardly apparent, save to prejudiced eyes, in the fascia of the little draper's shop which marked Tom Hannaway's transition from back-street trading to the limelight of a great shopping centre, yet some sort of providence was looking after Hamer Shawcross. Sir Thomas Hannaway himself expressed this once with the whispered remark, when the Minister of the Crown was hinting at incredible hardships in youth: "Y'know, he had a better time than most. Something always turned up to see him through."

This was true. The very day on which he ceased to work for Tom Hannaway brought him a letter from a Manchester solicitor, which said that, if he would call at the office, he would learn "something to his advantage in connexion with the estate of the late Charles Suddaby, Esquire."

He had not been near the old man for a long time. His daily work, his frantic studies, his sermon-writing and preaching, had kept him chained to Ancoats. Outside his work-time and preaching-time, he lived the life of a solitary. The Wilders were gone; he had not bothered to get on visiting terms with the new parson. He never went to town. Old Suddaby and his concerns seemed so remote that this, the first intimation of his death, stirred in the young man's mind hardly more than a formal regret and a strong curiosity about what he might hear "to his advantage."

It was with a feeling of exhilaration rather than of mourning that he set off along Great Ancoats Street. A day with no job to tie him by the leg was so rare that it was delightful; the weather was frosty, yet with a clear blue sky; and to sharpen all was this expectation of some piece of good fortune.

The lawyer's office, full of black japanned tin boxes and bundles of papers tied in red tape, was over a shop in St. Ann's Square. There was a fire burning in the grate, a carpet on the floor, and a picture of Queen Victoria over the fireplace, flanked, with splendid impartiality, by Disraeli on one side, looking like an Eastern necromancer, and Gladstone on the other, looking like the voice of God uttering Liberal doctrine. It was very cosy and reassuring.

Hamer sat in a chair by the fire as the solicitor read the will. There was small need to read it, but this man had written it himself and was not to be denied the joys of rolling out its involved and complicated inanities. When he had done that, he explained in two sentences what it meant. "So Mr. Suddaby leaves you twenty pounds and five hundred books, which you can choose yourself from the stock. Everything else goes to this Friedrich Engels, whoever he may be." Then he added: "Oh, and there's a letter. He left a letter for you. Here it is."

Hamer walked out of the office with twenty golden sovereigns, more money than he had ever handled before, jingling in his pocket. He had the key of the shop, he had Mr. Suddaby's letter; which he had not yet opened.

He had learned that only a week ago Mr. Suddaby was at work in his cellar, but already a sense of desolation and decay had begun to descend. The few shallow steps that led from the street level down to the door were littered with bitter winter dust, some broken bottles, tatters of blown paper. When he pushed open the door and inhaled the well-remembered smell, it seemed to him that there was now added to it some ingredient other than the perishing leather and mildewed paper and earthy damp that he knew of old. Then it had smelled like a cavern. Now it smelled like a tomb.

He shut and locked the door behind him, not wishing to be disturbed. He struck a match to light the gas, but already some zealous official had cut the gas off. He remembered where candles were kept, and found them. A feeble yellow flame trembled in the musty-smelling dark as he carried it towards the spot where Mr. Suddaby had been accustomed to sit. There, before the fireplace full of cold ash, was the rug on which Sheba the green-eyed cat had been used to drowse; there was the table, there the easy chair, with the old man's ebony stick leaning still against it, as though laid ready to a ghostly hand.

Hamer dropped some grease upon the table, feeling a little

compunction at so untidy an act, and stuck the foot of the candle into it. Then he sat down in Mr. Suddaby's chair, and, his own movements being still, he became aware of the cold silence shuddering through all the deserted aisles of the catacomb. He took the letter from his pocket, flattened it on the table under the wavering light of the candle, and began to read. Began and finished almost in a flash of the eye, for this was all the letter said: "Don't forget the sabre from Peterloo. Keep it shining."

The boy got up and began to pace the dark labyrinth. He took but a few paces from the candle, and the darkness swallowed him up. The ways were familiar and he needed no light. Up and down and in and out he walked, pondering old Suddaby's strange message. The sabre from Peterloo. It was no great distance from this cavern where he now walked, that bloody field on which the Old Warrior had seen his girl struck down, that field from which the frightened thousands had fled with the horses plunging among them and the blades whirling and falling.

What had it all to do with him? He turned a corner, and looked down the length of the cavern to where he could see the table and the candle upon it, far off, burning now with a small light, clear and steady. It scarcely illumined the old man's chair. You could almost imagine him sitting there, quiet and collected. "What does he want me to do? What do they all want me to do?" the boy asked himself.

He did not stay then to choose his books. In the thin winter sunshine without, and all through that day, his own question plagued him; and when, that night, he lay in bed, having drawn back the curtain from the window, he gazed at the sabre where the streetlamp's light lay upon it, and still it had nothing to say to him. It was but a serene and enigmatic curve of silver, except that now and then, when the lamp's light wavered, it trembled for a moment, charged with a life and meaning that he could not understand.

Part Two

Sabre in the Hand

Chapter Nine

The last thing Birley Artingstall did for Hamer Shawcross was to make a scabbard for the sabre. The old man called at the house in Broadbent Street on the night when the boy was going through his few possessions, deciding what to take, what to leave behind. Ellen could not speak to him. It was a hot summer evening, and from force of habit she was sitting by the kitchen fire. Birley put his head through the doorway and asked "Upstairs?" She nodded, and when he was gone she relapsed into misery.

She couldn't understand the boy. A few years ago, when Gordon died and she wanted to go in with the Ryersons, sharing a house, he was fiercely against it. Now that he had taken this whim to go off wandering, it seemed to him excellent. He brought it out as though it were a brand new idea of his own: "You could go in with the Ryersons."

Well, so she could, and so she would. But she didn't understand his way of living. She was not getting younger. She thought it was his place to stay at home and look after her. But she didn't say this. If he wanted to go, let him go.

Mrs. Ryerson came in with her eager bustling walk. "Well, Ellen! You don't want to sit there brooding. I've just put t'kettle on. Come an' 'ave a cup o' tea."

They went out of the stuffy kitchen, along the stuffy street, into another stuffy kitchen, and sat down companionably together.

The five hundred books that he had chosen from Mr. Suddaby's stock, and all the other books that he possessed, were crated and nailed down. They were to be left behind. Birley sat on one of the crates, took out his pipe and lit it. "So you don't reckon on doing much reading, Hamer?"

"None at all, if I can help it. I want to see the things that other people read about."

"Such as?"

"Venice, for one thing."

If the boy had said Heliopolis or Babylon, Birley could not have been more surprised. "Venice!" he cried. "What on earth d'you want to see Venice for?"

Hamer stood at the open window, looking down into the street that, for longer than he could remember, had been his home. He had come there when he was two. Now for six months he had been twenty. A few boys sat on the canal wall, their legs dangling. The black water had a faintly evil smell in the torrid night. The mill face rose beyond it, stony and forbidding. Hamer turned back towards old Birley, who was puffing contentedly, well pleased with Ancoats. "Because," he said, "I used to imagine that Venice was like that. I know now how daft that idea was; but my mind is full of other ideas – about places, about people – that are no doubt just as daft, but I don't know it. Well, I want to get rid of those illusions. I want to know about things as they are."

Birley took a long pull at his pipe. "Well," he said, " a ship's boy *may* have a chance to see all those things. And then again he may not."

Hamer smiled, as though there were more in his mind than he cared to divulge. He took down the sabre from its hooks on the wall. "I shall take this," he said.

It was then that the old man said he would make a scabbard. When it was finished, it was a fine piece of work: a curve of glistening brown hide studded with strips of brass into which all Birley's love went in deeply-cut scrolls and arabesques. He made a belt from which the scabbard could hang. Belt and scabbard went into the small wooden box which contained all that Hamer Shawcross took with him. Birley paid for the cab which took the boy and his mother to the station, and he travelled with them. By chance, Tom Hannaway, stout and prosperous looking, was walking the platform. When he heard of the adventure on which Hamer was bound, he roared with laughter. "Well, that beats all!" he shouted. "I taught you a perfectly good trade – money at your finger-tips – and you're off before the mast. Well, well: a rolling stone gathers no moss."

Hamer gave him the look that Sir Thomas was so well to know forty, fifty years later. "I'm not looking for moss," he said. "It grows in the shade, like toadstools."

Tom did not wait to see the train out. He bustled off importantly on some affairs of his own. When the train swung round the curve, Hamer, leaning out of the window, saw only his mother and the tall figure of the old Viking with one hand on her shoulder, the other waving a black hat. When he came back to the same station three years later, only Ellen met him. The fascia which said "Sweets and Tobacco" over the shop in Great Ancoats Street was already faded and weather-beaten, for "Birley Artingstall, Leather" had been dead for two years.

"Such a consideration may not seem material to the Right Honourable gentleman, but I know what I am talking about."

This was both insolent and true. It was not the way in which the Prime Minister was accustomed to being addressed by an unknown Member, on his legs in the House for the first time. But it made people look at the Member for the St. Swithin's division of Bradford, and the Member wanted to be looked at. He could stand being looked at: six feet two inches high, broad, brown, with an upturned moustache that he shaved off later in life. He was dressed as well as any man in the House. He never wore a cloth cap, as Keir Hardie did. He liked good clothes. But, though well-dressed, he was not conventionally dressed. He looked more like an artist than a politician. A bow of black silk was at his throat. In the streets he wore a black sombrero hat and never an overcoat. A flowing cape looked better. He carried his walking-stick like a rapier.

This was the new Member upon whom the House turned its regard as he declared insolently: "I know what I am talking about." It was a question of trade with the Argentine, and he knew more about trade with the Argentine than the Prime Minister would ever know. He had lived in the Argentine for six months, and though the Prime Minister, even had he lived in the Argentine for six months, might conceivably still have known nothing about the place, that was not conceivable with Hamer Shawcross. In six months, he added Spanish to his languages, read the local newspapers, talked to every Spaniard who would listen to him, and sucked them all as dry as he had sucked Mr. Wilder and Harriet.

It was his longest stay in one place during the three years of his wanderings. He had no intention of serving a long term as a ship's boy. He used the ship as he used everything else. It was to get him to some far-off spot whence he could start a course of uncharted vagabondage. He left the ship at the first port it touched, which was Buenos Aires. Mr. Suddaby's twenty pounds were sewn into the belt that Birley Artingstall had made. With this round his body and the sabre in his box, he got ashore on a dark night. He kept out of sight – lodging at an obscure inn, till the ship sailed.

The next day, he bought some decent clothes, and in the evening ventured out into the street. It was now that he acquired his taste for cloaks and sombreros. Perhaps he wished to be reminded of an experience that burned into his mind. At twenty years of age, he could indeed say "Much have I travelled in the realms of gold," but, when all is said and done, those bookish travels, those inward explorations, did not alter the harsh, binding fact that, save for an occasional journey into the surrounding countryside, he had never once set his foot outside the bricks and the acid soot and the summer stench and winter fog of Ancoats, where no bird sang, where no green thing grew, where a butterfly looked as exotic as a tiger.

On the voyage out, sick and sorry and overworked, always worried and sometimes frightened, he had no opportunity to savour that release which he had come to find.

He would never forget it: that night of bloomy dusk and incredible stars, the metallic crepitation of strange trees, the accent of a liquid foreign tongue singing a song to the accompaniment of plucked strings. The white dust rose about him as horses trotted by, drawing open carriages in which men and women lolled with a frank acceptance of sloth that was new to him. The warm luminosity of the street lamps made him think of the always-misty aura which, even at midsummer, seemed to hang about the lamps at home. Now he was *knowing*. "This is Buenos Aires. When people say Buenos Aires, I shall know."

He walked about aimlessly, full of content. Tomorrow he would have to look for work: tonight was his own. What work he would do he did not know. He thought that he could teach English or write the letters of some business house that had dealings with England, but before he could do either of those things he must learn some Spanish.

The diary is not a very humorous document, because Hamer Shawcross was not a humorous person; but even he could not resist the humour of this drunken Englishman who was shot through the door of a drinking-house and flapped upon him, as he writes, "like a great bat." The image is apt enough, for the man appears to have been wearing one of those cloaks that were to impress themselves so deeply on Hamer's imagination; and this was undulating hugely about him as he almost swam through the air, head first, propelled by a boot. His long white hands, the right grasping a silk hat, made one breast-stroke before he belly-flopped at Hamer's feet. He sat up, put the hat upon his head for no other reason than to raise it to this stranger who had stopped to look down upon him, then began to sing, in Spanish, that Dona Eulalia was a bitch and that he hated her white face and violet powder.

This was the first Englishman Hamer had met in Buenos Aires. He raised him up tenderly and stuck to him, because he thought the fellow might be useful. He took him to his lodgings, and arranged to call upon him the next day. He doubted whether the engagement would be remembered, because the man insisted that his name was Tommy Carlyle and that they were in Ecclefechan. He insisted, too, that Hamer was John Stuart Mill, the only man in Ecclefechan who knew the meaning of liberty.

As it happened, the man's name *was* Thomas Carlyle, which had long been a matter of annoyance to him; but he was not inclined to dwell upon it so much when sober as when drunk. He received Hamer amiably enough the next day, learned that he wanted work, and said he would introduce him to Dona Eulalia Cardenas. He was reserved on the subject of Dona Eulalia, merely remarking that he had had enough of her, that he had had enough of Buenos Aires, and that he was pushing off for New York on the first available boat. Dona Eulalia wanted someone to come in daily to read to her in English. The pay would just keep body and soul together; but that was all Hamer wanted. It was arranged that he should start the next day. Outside the lady's house Hamer said good-bye to Thomas Carlyle, who presented him with a copy of *Sartor Resartus*, autographed, and said he didn't know what he had let himself in for.

A sense of humour would have made it impossible for Hamer to continue with that crazy occupation. The widow Cardenas, with the white face and violet powder that had driven Thomas Carlyle mad, received him the next day in the cool courtyard of her house. All round it was a pergola, vine-covered, and hanging from the pergola here and there was a parrot in a cage. There must have been a dozen of them: white and green and sulphur and crimson. A little fountain tinkled, and the parrots screamed, and Dona Eulalia, her oozing bulk confined in a prison of lilac silk, reclined on orange cushions. She handed Hamer the book he was to read. It was *Jessica's First Prayer.*

He read for two hours, and at the end of the third day the book was finished. On the fourth day he began *The Basket of Flowers,* by the same author; and when that was done he began on *Jessica's First Prayer.* These were the Dona Eulalia's English library, not, it seemed, because of any difficulty in getting other books, but from choice. When Hamer suggested a change, she clasped together her pudgy hands emerging from a lather of lace and a tinkle of bangles, and said: "Ah, no! They are so beautiful!"

He began to understand why Thomas Carlyle had gone mad, taken to drink, and sung out his insults to the Dona Eulalia in the gutters. But it would take more than this to drive Hamer mad. He read on grimly. It was only two hours' work a day, and the old fool paid him enough to live on. Meanwhile, with the passionate energy that he could always apply to gaining knowledge, he picked up his Spanish from books, from the streets, from the newspapers. After all, he could wait, and it was an experience to be sitting there in that courtyard, with the vines and the fountain and the parrots, and the burning blue sky above him. This also was knowledge for a boy from grimy Ancoats. This also was something about which he could say: "I know what I am talking about."

It is not necessary to follow in any detail the wanderings of Hamer Shawcross during the next three years. The diary is not very helpful where this period is concerned. For example, under three consecutive dates you read "Lima." "San Francisco." "Samoa." Nothing else. But one thing becomes clear. After leaving the Argentine, he earned his living by working with his hands. There is only one recorded exception, and that is when he spent a month arranging in Sydney the books of a mutton millionaire who had bought the contents of an English nobleman's library. He seems gradually, and perhaps unconsciously, to have fallen into the intention of making this tour a study at first hand of working-men earning their living. He worked on boats and about docks, in mines and on railways. He sweated like a coolie in India and felled timber in Canada. In South Africa he worked in the diamond mines. Wherever he was, he read nothing but the newspapers of the country; and, whenever possible, he forced his way into any assemblies that were open to him, whether they approximated to parish councils, town councils, or meetings of Parliament.

An entry made in the diary in December 1888, when he was in Kimberley, is valuable to a study of his mind at this time.

"Carradus* was here again tonight, and for a wonder was talkative. He recalled his early days in Kimberley – not more than fifteen years ago. He told me that he had known Alfred Beit when Beit first came out here. I said to him that I supposed Beit had had to work like a slave to make his fortune. Carradus laughed and said: 'Beit work? You don't make fortunes like Beit's by working. Let me tell you about Beit, He came out here as a clerk for a Paris firm named Porges. I don't suppose they were paying him more than three hundred a year. He was always growsing about not being able to make ends meet. He wrote to his father in Hamburg and the old man screwed together a couple of thousand pounds and sent it out to him. Did Alfred buy diamonds? Not he! You can't imagine what this place was like in those days. People were flocking here in droves, diamond-mad. They were shouting for offices – houses. That's what Alfred gave 'em. He bought a bit of land and put up twelve shanties. D'you know what he got for them? Eighteen hundred pounds a month! Twenty-one thousand six hundred pounds a year for years and years – for at least a dozen years. At the end of that time, Alfred sold the land the shacks stood on, and now, boy, hold your breath and I'll tell you what he got for it. Two hundred and sixty thousand pounds. No. You don't *work* for a fortune if your name's Beit. You put your mouth tight on the nipple, and suck.'

"There was no more to be got out of Carradus except a groan later in the evening: 'God in Heaven! Why didn't my old man have a son like Alfred and two thousand to lend him!'

"I suppose Carradus's story is true enough, and it bears out what I have observed all over the world. It's not the worker or the inventor

---

* There is no reference anywhere else to Carradus. He appears to have been a man whose acquaintance Shawcross made in Kimberley. There is a photograph stuck into the diary at this point, showing Shawcross with a short beard sitting on a bench outside a shack with another man, under whom is written "Carradus." He is an older man than Shawcross, and looks of no distinction. Nothing is known of him.

who makes a fortune. It's the smart chap who nips in and gets a hold on the land and what's under it or on it. Old Astor in New York; the coal-royalty owners in England and Wales; Lord Lostwithiel with his Manchester slums; and half-a-dozen people with the richest slices of London. Who was paying Alfred Beit eighteen hundred pounds a month for twelve shacks? Why, thousands of people who produced the eighteen hundred pounds' worth of goods that Mr. Beit was at liberty to consume. They had to produce this before they could start producing anything for themselves. This was the first charge – Mr. Beit on their backs, because Mr. Beit had been a smart chap. All very elementary thinking, I know, and if I open my mouth about it, someone will say: How can it be altered? But I'm glad to have seen all this with my own eyes – to have talked to Carradus who knew Beit, and to have seen and worked among the Negroes who bring the wealth to Mr. Beit's feet like retrievers bringing bones. When you've seen things as I have, at least you know what you're talking about."

In the three-and-a-half years of his journeying, Hamer gratified only one sentimental desire: he saw Venice. He worked on a boat carrying a cargo from Cape Town to Genoa, and thence went at once to dispel the illusions of his childhood. All the time he had been away, he had lived thriftily; he had money to spend, and he remained in Venice for six weeks. He visited churches and picture-galleries, dawdled on the canals, and, characteristically, worried along with the newspapers and a dictionary till he could make something of the language. When the six weeks were up, he made his way on foot through Austria and Germany. At Hamburg he found a ship bound for Liverpool, and worked his passage home. In his diary, while he was on the ship, he wrote: "I don't know what made me tear myself out of Ancoats as I did. The impulse to do it came suddenly, and now that the adventure is over I am glad I did not resist. Whatever life may do to me now, I have had these three-and-a-half years. I can honestly say that I feel a different being from the one who set out."

He looked a different being. When Ellen met the train from Liverpool, she could hardly believe her eyes. This man of commanding height, with the bristling moustache, the square shoulders, the face which sun and wind had burned and weathered: this was something difficult to reconcile with the secret vision she had nurtured. For while he was away she had not remembered him as she had last seen him, much less imagined him as he would become, but with a fond aberration had permitted her mind to fall back upon memory of a small leg-dragging boy with a broad white forehead and a purple vein too prominently pulsing in his neck. She herself had shrunk a little, for she was then nearer sixty than fifty, and a swift consciousness possessed her that life had changed their positions. She had come out filled with solicitude and protectiveness, which one glance at her son made suddenly absurd; and this left her feeling strangely empty and bereft as though, at a stroke, one of the necessities of her existence had been swept from beneath her.

To Hamer, also, the meeting was not what he had pictured. All very well to write in his diary "I feel a different being." Somehow, one didn't expect other people to be different beings. The years had given him self-reliance. In most of the circumstances of life he could fend for himself. He had fought for work of every sort and got it. He had more than once physically fought and conquered with his hard bare fists. He had learned to throw himself unhesitatingly upon chance in strange lands whose customs and languages he did not know. He had come through all that; yet, during the brief railway journey between Liverpool and Manchester, he had been thinking of his mother in terms which now he saw to be untenable.

He had forgotten, or never realized, that she was so small a woman. In her infrequent letters, she had never told him that she had lost her work as chapel caretaker and that she was earning her living, as Mrs. Ryerson did, by such odd jobs as she could come upon. She had picked up a lot of Mrs. Ryerson's habits, including the habit of wearing an old cloth cap when out at work; and there she was now, having come straight from scrubbing some offices, with that cap aslant upon her grey untidy hair and a rolled coarse apron under her arm. She was so small and her eyes were so bright with emotion as she peeped up at him from under the peak of the cap that he remembered suddenly how the Old Warrior had always said that his girl used to stand on his foot and then get on tiptoe to kiss him. So would Ellen have to do now; and sure enough, when they had looked at one another for a moment, each feeling illusions fall away, she said: "Well, haven't you got a kiss for your old mother?"

He stooped then and kissed her; and, feeling the protector, and no more – never again – the protected, he said: "Let's get a cab."

It seemed to her an extravagant thing to do; but he insisted, and, with the windows down, they went clipper-clop through the mild and misty sunshine of the late autumn afternoon, into the little street which in that light, if ever, would have looked like a street in Venice, and didn't; and so arrived at the Ryersons' door. It came to Hamer with a shock that he no longer had a home of his own. All the time he had been away he had not once thought what it might mean to Ellen to have no home of her own.

Hamer slept that night on a bed made up on a couch in the Ryersons' front-room downstairs. Rather, he lay upon it, not sleeping. He had been accustomed to sleeping in strange places, but here he could not sleep. He felt as though no place he had been in had been so strange as this place which he should have known so well. The strangeness was in his heart, because once more he was confronted by the question which he had kept behind his back for three-and-a-half years. What to do?

Now it was a question that could be left unanswered no longer. In the first light of dawn he was up and dressed. He went out and sat on the canal wall, staring at the blank faces of the houses opposite, all with windows shut and blinds down, and at the pink suffusion gradually strengthening to daylight in the sky. He watched the street lamps put out and saw Jimmy Spit-and-Wink, incredibly old and decrepit, creep along the street and rattle at the windows. Soon came the rush of clogs with which he was so familiar, the savage bellowing of the mill buzzer, and then, once more, silence and solitude. No one had recognized him. Not a head had been turned towards the tall bronzed man lounging on the wall.

Suddenly he threw up his head and smelled the morning. Recollection flooded upon him, and, throwing his coat and waistcoat into the Ryerson passageway, he rolled up his shirt-sleeves, took a deep breath, and started to run. Automatically, he followed the mile route that he and Tom Hannaway had laid down. Nothing seemed changed, Brick, stone, soot, no green thing; long perspectives of identical small houses. He was breathing easily when he got back, to find Mrs. Ryerson on her knees yellow-stoning the entrance step of the house. "Good morning, Mrs. Ryerson," he said. "Let me do that."

The little grey woman got creakily to her feet and looked up at the tall smiling handsome man. Friendly, too, and charming. He knew how to be so. She wished for a moment that Arnold, pale and earnest, was like that; then loyally reminded herself that Arnie was all right. To most men making Hamer's offer she would merely have said: "Get on with you" and continued her work. But she felt flattered by the attention and said, making way for him: "You look as if you'd come into a fortune, Mr. Shawcross."

"I've just run a mile," he said, "and I'm not puffed. Feel." He took her small maimed hand, etched with fine lines of ineradicable dirt, tough as a parrot's foot, and laid it on his shirt over his heart. "Not a flutter," he laughed. "And d'you know what I decided to do while I was running?"

She shook her head.

"Go over to Bradford," he said, "and see Arnold."

He did not know that this was the answer to all his questions.

Chapter Ten

Old Marsden who, with his wife, looked after Lizzie Lightowler's house in Ackroyd Park, was glad when it ceased to be a school. Now that there were only Mrs. Lightowler and Miss Artingstall to look after, things were much easier. Indeed, he and his wife were in clover, though he still said, with a martyred look, "I'll do my best Mrs. Lightowler," when the smallest task was suggested to him.

One good safe grumble was these breakfasts. Why in the name of fortune Mrs. Lightowler should ask people to breakfast he couldn't understand. "Well, you see, people who come to breakfast have got to *go*," Lizzie patiently explained. "They've got work to do. If you have them to dinner, they sit around all night, and I don't want that."

Old Marsden accepted the explanation as reasonable till the next time he was told to make extra coffee and lay a third or fourth place. Then he would shake his head. "I'll do my best." That Mr. Ryerson was the worst offender. He was always being asked to breakfast. Might as well make it a regular thing. Marsden, his eyes shining with rheum, his little white silky moustache trembling, would never, as he threw open the door of the breakfast-room, announce Arnold in the usual way. On an October morning in 1889 he opened the door and used the formula his cunning had devised: "Mr. Ryerson *again*, mum." Then, seeing that Ann was alone in the room, he corrected himself: "Miss Ann, I should say."

"Come in, Arnold," Ann said. "Aunt Lizzie isn't coming down to breakfast. She's got a bit of a cold."

Sunlight, thinned by the city smoke, was striking through the wide window from whose seat Ann had risen. It shone on the lustrous white-gold of her hair, making it seem suddenly to radiate light. She was dressed in a material of filmy white, and there were red roses: among the silver and porcelain of the breakfast table. Arnold noticed all these things with a sudden joy at his heart. Aunt Lizzie was not coming down to breakfast!

*

This young man, at whose entrance Ann looked up with a welcoming affectionate smile, was as much a part of her daily life as her food and drink and Aunt Lizzie. He was at this time twenty-six years old, and she was twenty-five. That night when she had first met him in his mother's kitchen – the night when Mrs. Ryerson's hand was crushed, and Ann had put the children to bed, and then had come down and found Arnold staring into the kitchen fire – that night seemed incredibly remote, and, indeed, it was getting on for ten years ago. You would have thought it was twenty to look at Arnold! He was bent on being grown-up, and as the young of a later generation would seek at any cost to prolong and perpetuate their youth, so Arnold, like many of his contemporaries, sought to pass without intermission from boyhood to the gravity and responsibility of age.

His face, as he stood there by the breakfast table, was already almost heavy in its refusal to take life easily. His chin was the only part of it that had ever been shaved. Brown frizzy side-whiskers and a considerable moustache made it difficult to guess his age. The hair upon his forehead did not fall, as it did on Hamer's forehead, in a wide silky wing. It dropped in a gauche oiled quiff, which combined with his pale skin and blunt nose to give his face the look of an honest artisan's.

A high collar, sawing into his Adam's apple, kept his neck stiff. His clothes were of heavy dark grey broadcloth, and from the brassy chain which crossed his waistcoat-front a few medals hung. In the hall he had left a bowler hat and an ash stick. He looked altogether like a young engine driver wearing his Sunday clothes; but the softness and spotlessness of the hands destroyed this idea.

Arnold's hands had not always been spotless. He could – and often did – recall those early days in Bradford. Even now he could savour again the breath-taking sense of relief that came to him when Aunt Lizzie (as he now thought of her) first appeared in Broadbent Street. It was close upon Christmas time. He had no work. One barked command from Hawley Artingstall had thrown him into the pit. How often, urging men to combine and co-operate, he remembered that bitter moment! "They own you, body and soul. One word, and they put out the light for you. No clothes for your wife. No food for your children. I tell you, God Himself shouldn't have such power; and you allow it to remain in the hands of men who have never yet shown that they are any better than yourselves," It seemed strange to him that this bitter lesson should have come from Hawley Artingstall, dear old Birley's brother, Ann's father!

But there it was: he was without work, and his mother couldn't work. He remembered going down to town, resolved to call at Artingstall's and demand the few shillings that were his due. The windows were ablaze with gaslight, gay with coloured streamers and a glittering imitation of frost. A monster Father Christmas, redcoated, white-whiskered, benign and benevolent, stood in the middle of one of the windows, backed by a notice: "Artingstall's wish a Merry Christmas to One and All."

Little Arnold, shivering in a light snow that began to fall less attractively than the cotton-wool snow in the windows, gazed through the glass doors which he had been accustomed to swing open to admit Alderman Artingstall. He couldn't screw up his courage to enter. He could see Mr. Tattersall the Manager darting hither and thither, all-seeing and omnipresent, the tails of his frock-coat flying. He could not believe that he would be included among the one and all to whom Mr. Tattersall the Manager, on behalf of Artingstall's, would extend the compliments of the season. Young as he was, he had a sudden disillusioned insight into the false heartiness, the commercial cant, that the window represented. Thrusting his cold hands into his pockets, he ran home.

Birley Artingstall sent them round a Christmas dinner and a few shillings. They scraped along, as the poor do on one another's charity, till the new year came; and then one day there was the energetic woman with the white hair descended upon them in Broadbent Street, making proposals which seemed to have dropped from heaven. With the few goods he possessed packed in an old leather bag that Birley gave him, he accompanied Aunt Lizzie back to Bradford.

Even now, when the place was so familiar to him, it was not difficult to recapture the thrilling sense of being for the first time in a town that was not his own. A town full of strange contrasts. For example, there was Ackroyd Park where Aunt Lizzie lived, with its heavy, roomy houses built of solid stone, each standing in a considerable garden, in a road that ran downhill from Manningham Lane to the valley bottom. And parallel with it, running downhill in just the same way, was Thursley Road, for all its proximity a very different affair.

True, Thursley Road seemed a cut above Broadbent Street, because the front downstairs window of each house was a bow window, and the houses were divided from the pavement by gardens. But each garden was only a couple of yards long and nothing grew there. They looked like patches of battered soot, and down in the valley to which the road led the railway trains roared by, filling the air with noise and with white billowing steam upon which, when night came, the fire-boxes threw up a red glare travelling against the stationary lights of mills and warehouses and the winking street lamps that climbed the opposite hill.

It was in Thursley Road that Arnold was to live. It was there that Aunt Lizzie left him under the charge of Mrs. Muff, the landlady, who took him to his room on the first floor. It was an unexciting little room with a bed and a wicker chair, a small chest of drawers, and a wash-stand which could also be used as a writing table. Mrs. Muff was too used to lodgers to be moved by Arnold's coming. She told him he must take his meals in the kitchen, and that for the rest of the time when he was in the house she would expect him to keep to his own room. This was the room: cold, bleak, clean. The wash-stand was pushed against the fireplace in a way which said plainly enough that no fires were lighted here, and for illumination there was a candle in a red enamelled candle-stick on the chest of drawers. But Arnold was not daunted. When Mrs. Muff was gone, he put his few things away and then sat on the bed, tentatively heaving up and down. It was soft and springy. He smiled to himself. This would be the first time in his life, so far as he could remember, that he had had a bed all to himself. He pulled the chair up to the wash-stand, took some paper and a pencil out of his bag, and sat down to write to his mother. He had as much to tell her as if Bradford were a new continent and he its discoverer. Then he went out to post his letter and to wander up and down Manning-ham Lane, entranced by a town which showed you, whichever way you looked, a prodigality of lights, scattered upon the hills like jewels.

Mrs. Lightowler had said: "You'll have tomorrow to yourself till the evening, because I can't see Mr. Greenhalgh till eight o'clock. His office is in Piccadilly."

That sounded imposing, Piccadilly suggested to Arnold's mind a press of chariots and a coruscation of lights; but when the next evening came he discovered that in Bradford things might have London names without London manners. He and Mrs. Lightowler walked to Piccadilly. Piccadilly was in the heart of the town, but the heart of the town, at eight o'clock on a winter night, was all but dead; and once you side-stepped off one of the two main streets, you were in a region of rough uneven roads, paved with stone setts that the rumbling lorry traffic of the years had worn into grooves and ruts. Piccadilly was one of these roads. There was the name, or Arnold could not have believed it – the name picked out by a bracket-lamp fixed to a wall. The street ran downhill. It was so dark and narrow that the boy did not notice, that first time, that its façade was made up mainly of the great double-doors of warehouses. Not a light showed in the whole dark canyon except the one which had revealed the name and, away to the bottom of the street, a pale yellow glimmer above a doorway. When they reached this, Arnold saw that the glimmer was a gas-burner inside a little glass box on which was painted *Bradford Mercury*.

"This is it," said Mrs. Lightowler. She seemed to know the way well. He followed her up a steep narrow wooden stair, lit by an unshaded gas-burner, and when she reached the landing she banged on the floor with her umbrella and shouted: "Are you there, Henry?"

An enormous voice bellowed: "Aye, come on in, Lizzie!" and when Lizzie opened a door that faced her and took Arnold into the room, the owner of the voice said: "So this is the boy?"

Mr. Henry Greenhalgh got up from the only chair in the room, which stood before a table strewn wildly with newspapers, manuscripts and galley proofs. He motioned to Lizzie to sit down, and himself took up a stance on the hearthrug, dominating the room. Abundant brown hair streaked with grey, a beard that flowed down to his chest, a hand stuck into the overlap of a tightly-buttoned frock coat whose lapel carried the little blue ribbon of the teetotaller: these were the salient facts that struck the boy as he took first stock of Henry Greenhalgh, editor and proprietor of the *Bradford Mercury*.

Arnold looked at the fire flickering behind Mr. Greenhalgh's straddled legs, and at the portraits, which he did not know were those of Bright and Cobden, behind Mr. Greenhalgh's head, and he thought that this was a fine room: ramshackle and untidy, but full of warmth and somehow of feeling. Suddenly, as he stood there with a happy realization that he was not at all nervous with Mr. Greenhalgh, as he had always been with Mr. Hawley Artingstall, there was beneath their feet a rumble which swelled quickly to a roar. Mr. Greenhalgh, as though this were a signal he had been awaiting, shouted: "She's gone!" leapt to the umbrella-stand, took out an umbrella, and with one imperious gesture swept the table clean. Inkwell, gum-pot, blotting-pad, manuscripts, proofs: all fell in a fine flurry into an enormous basket, and when the desk was clear Mr. Greenhalgh threw the umbrella on top of everything else. "Long live Liberalism!" he shouted. "And thank God we're only a weekly. I couldn't do this every night; but once a week it's worth it."

At that moment, a boy wearing an apron impregnated with printer's ink, and with hands and face suggesting that he had recently used the apron as a towel, came into the room. A copy of the paper was squeezed against his body under his arm and he carried a tray which contained tea for three. He placed paper and tray on the cleared table, and, as though it were a task accustomed and understood, he began then to drag the basket out of the room. Mr. Greenhalgh, holding up a hand, caused him to halt. "Has Queen Victoria died tonight?" he demanded.

"Not that I know of, sir," said the boy.

"And what would I say if she had done?"

"I don't know, sir."

"Then it's time you did. I've told you week after week. I'd say: 'Thank God we're a weekly. We needn't do anything about it for seven days.' Now take away that basket and sort it out. Next week this boy will be doing it."

With a jerk of his thumb Mr. Greenhalgh indicated Arnold, and that was the only spoken word by which the boy understood that he was engaged. When they had drunk their tea, Mr. Greenhalgh said: "Mind you be a credit to Mrs. Lightowler, because she's a fine woman, and one of these days she's going to marry me. Isn't that so, Lizzie?"

"One of these days, Henry, pigs are going to fly," said Lizzie. "When do you want Arnold to start?"

"Arnold? Oh, the boy. It doesn't matter. We're only a weekly. Make it Monday morning. I'll tell the foreman printer."

Arnold did not know till years later that Aunt Lizzie had paid a premium to enable him to learn the craft of printing. By that time, it did not surprise him, for if Aunt Lizzie had come one morning on big white wings flapping down Thursley Road and had alighted on the sill of his window, he would almost have regarded it as being in the course of nature. At first he did not see much of her. She got her information about him from Henry Greenhalgh, who reported him to be a hard worker, painstaking and uninspired. Lizzie was not able to do much more for him, now that she had launched him. For one thing, at that time she still had her school. It was not till the Easter after his coming to Bradford, when all her pupils were gone home, that she invited him to lunch. There were only the three of them present: Lizzie, Ann and Arnold; and it was a most unremarkable occasion. Arnold as a guest was like Arnold as a printer: painstaking and uninspired. Lizzie did not know – for all her knowledge of the world, she could not guess – that this visit was an awful and awe-inspiring business for Arnold. He had occasionally gone in to the Shawcross's for a meal, and Birley Artingstall had asked him once or twice to share a rough-and-ready supper; but he had never sat down in a house like this of Lizzie Lightowler's, never encountered such a perplexity of cutlery and crockery. Ann's presence did not help him, for all her amiability. He could not forget that she was the daughter of Hawley Artingstall, that she was the girl who used to arrive at the shop in a victoria, causing Mr. Tattersall the Manager to leap about like a provincial official doing some small service for the Queen. And so Arnold was most horribly deferential, and Ann was most carefully kind, and Lizzie was bright and supervisory. She gave him some books to take home and read, and there seemed no more in it than if she had presented a lump of sugar to a good dog.

Once outside the house, Arnold was able to give way to the emotions that he had kept bottled up during the meal and the hour's painful conversation that had followed. He did not go back to Thursley Road, but turned in the other direction, walked along Manningham Lane as far as the park, and then climbed the streets behind it to the top of Heaton hill. All the way along the lane he had been conscious of the lilacs blooming in the gardens, and the daffodils making their brief brave fires among the sooty grass. Now, on the hill, the full glory of the day took him in charge. Leaning on a grey wall of unmortared stones, he looked down into the wide valley below him with its long straight road running from Keighley to Bradford – the way the Brontës would go, he reminded himself, when they came in from Haworth to see their brother Branwell. Beyond the valley bottom the land rose in rough craggy outcrops to the crests of Baildon Moor; and when he looked to his left he could see ridge upon ridge fading away into a blue distance that was the more enchanting because here and there it was punctuated by the tall interjection of a mill chimney, wearing a lazy plume. Over his head larks were singing. That was one thing about Bradford: you hadn't to go far from the middle of the town to hear larks, or for that matter to see magpies. Two went sweeping down the field before him, their long rudders steering dexterously in the fresh spring breeze.

It was a good place, was Bradford, Arnold thought. Because of these hills, it wasn't so cursed as Manchester. You could always climb somewhere and see something, and there always seemed to be a bit of wind to clear the smoke.

He climbed over the wall, carefully replacing a few of the loose stones that he had caused to tumble. All good Yorkshiremen learned to do that. He sat down in the sunshine, took some paper and a pencil from his pocket, and began to write to his mother. He wrote to her nearly every day. He began to tell her about the lunch, and about Ann Artingstall, but something said to him that his mother wouldn't want to hear about Ann Artingstall. So he crumpled the paper and put it into his pocket, and leaned on the wall in the warm sunshine, thinking of Ann's lustrous fair hair, and presently he was asleep, with the larks above him singing their way up aerie spiral staircases.

Once or twice in the years that followed the death of her mother Ann visited her father in Manchester, His new wife Hilda managed him dexterously. She had given him a son, and this unexpected child of his late middle-age permitted her to do almost as she liked with him. There was not a servant about the place who had been there when Hilda was herself a servant. She was too jealous for her status to permit that. Even Haworth was gone: Haworth who seemed to Ann to be associated with her very roots, and with her earliest memories of tom-boying in the stables and wandering in the gardens when the not very large walled enclosure of The Limes had been to her a varied continent of forest and plain, and Withington itself, its trees in those happy days unwithered by the blue miasma of petrol, seemed a remote Arcadia.

Haworth's going, above all things, made Ann feel that this was not any longer her place; and her young assertive step-mother and lusty little half-brother were dug in where she herself felt her roots exposed and withering. During her few visits, each more widely spaced from the last, Ann found herself longing for the moment of return to Bradford, thinking of the house in Ackroyd Park, with its sweeping view of industrialized but still magnificent hills, as her home. She knew that soon she would not want to come back to The Limes at all; it needed only some small explosion to blow her out of the place for ever.

A silly trivial quarrel with Hilda, a loyal memory of the vanished Haworth, sufficed. Hilda was expecting another child. On a day of high summer, when the road running past The Limes was quaking and dancing under a mirage of heat, Hilda said after lunch that she would go and lie down. Ann, who was careful to ask the mistress of the house for permission in all matters, said that if that was so, since Hilda would not want the carriage, she would like to drive out in the fresh air towards Knutsford.

Hilda gave permission, and half an hour later, though Ann did not know it, she was standing at a flung-up bedroom window, feeling irked by her heavy child-bearing condition and by the excessive heat of the day, and looking down enviously at the light slender girl who stepped out of the house dressed all in white: a white flounced muslin dress sweeping the golden gravel, a white flounced parasol held above her head.

Hilda succeeded well enough in concealing a dislike for Ann of which she was herself scarcely aware; but she could not forget that, though all the old servants had been cleared out of the house, here was one person who was well acquainted with what Hilda had sprung from. She was never quite comfortable while Ann was about the house.

The victoria drove round from the stables and pulled up at the little pillared porch. Haworth had always leapt down, with a word and a smile for her, and opened the door. It was merely because this had become so much a habit that she stood there now, waiting for the new man to do the same. (God knows, she said to herself afterwards, when laughing over the whole absurd affair, I am no snob.)

The man did not stir from the box, and though, had she once instinctively gone forward and opened the door for herself, she would have thought no more of the matter, the fact that she had waited hardened a resistance in her, and, tilting the parasol back upon her shoulder, she looked up at him, outlined there against the blue blare of the sky, and she said: "Well?"

"We're all ready, Miss. Get in," the man said.

The sky darkened for Ann. She thought of how, not so long ago, this trivial piece of nonsense could never have happened. She and Haworth would by now have been bowling along in perfect friendship, he calling back to her over his shoulder some comment on this or that which he pointed out with his whip. She looked again at the new coachman's face, saw that it was a dark face which created and resented its own servitude; and she said: "Thank you. You may go back."

She folded her parasol and walked into the house. She was standing in the dark cool hall, thoughtfully tapping the frail thing against her shoe, when she was aware of Hilda, storming down the stairs, lit with anger. Her face was white, and the heavy masses of her red hair were shaking loose about it.

"How dare you! How dare you!" Hilda shouted; and to Ann's surprise the girl took her by the shoulder with a heavy hand.

Ann shook herself free, and looked sideways and down fastidiously at the white fabric which Hilda's hand had soiled and crumpled. "Don't," she said. "Your hands are sweating."

At that, Hilda burned up. "Under my very nose," she shouted, "you insult my servants, and now you come in here and insult me. You expect to be danced attendance on. You expect people to jump about and open doors for you, bow your ladyship into the carriage. My God! You ought to train the horses, too, to go down on one knee like the horses in a circus. Well, you're not going to do that sort of thing here. You can take us as you find us – take us or leave us – the servants with the rest. You – so damned prim and proper I mustn't lay a hand on you. You'd sweat if you were going through what I am. And you will some day," she gloated. "You'll have the straight lines knocked out of you and a cushion under your pinny."

She looked at Ann's clean-built body with the old ill-shaped resentment suddenly defined as hatred. Ann said: "Hilda, please! You're exciting yourself about nothing at all. And it's so hot. Hadn't you better go and have your rest now?"

"Very concerned about me, aren't you?" Hilda mocked her. "Well, you needn't be." She slapped a hand on to her broad full breast.

"Sound!" she announced. "Sound as a bell. There's nothing wrong with *my* heart. You can't kill me like you killed your mother."

Ann was shocked. She laid down the parasol on a chair, took off the large picture hat, and stood there with it trailing at her side, looking incredulously at the heated woman who had made this accusation. "That's a terrible thing to say, Hilda," she said. "I wasn't even in the house when Mother died."

"When she died, perhaps not. Was that the beginning of it? Didn't you start her heart off bad with a row just like you're trying to have with me? Didn't you cheek her when she only did what a mother ought to do when you were carrying on with that boy in Ancoats?"

Ann's amazement was transmitted swiftly to anger. Her cheeks reddened and her eyes flamed. "Where have you been hearing all this trash?" she demanded.

Hilda recoiled a step or two backwards up the stairs as Ann advanced towards her. Then she stood her ground, holding the banister with one hand. "My husband – that's where," she said.

"Do you tell me that my father says I am responsible for the death of my mother?"

"Aye, that he does."

Ann said no more. Still trailing the hat, she ran up the stairs, pushing Hilda indignantly aside. She packed swiftly, changed into a travelling dress, and went out and called a hackney cab. She wired to Lizzie Lightowler that she would be home that night. Home was the right word now. She never again considered The Limes to be her home.

It was not till she was twenty-one that Ann learned that her mother had left her money. Lillian, for all the heart-tremors of her last year or so, never imagined that death was near her. Had she done so, she might have altered the will which she had made when all was smooth, and Ann was obedient, and Hawley had cast no eyes in unlawful directions. But the will was not altered; it gave to Ann at twenty-one, should her mother pre-decease her, the capital which Lillian herself on her marriage was dowered with by old Sir James Sugden. Sir James had never much liked Hawley Artingstall. "Yon's a bouncer, lass," he said to Lillian. "He's up now, but Ah wouldn't trust him not to be in t'gutter again any day. Tha'd better have a bit o' brass so tha can fend for thisen if it comes to t'worse," and Sir James tied up ten thousand pounds in a way that put it beyond the reach of Hawley's fingers. Sir James never knew that in the early days of her marriage, when Lillian was obsessed with the pushing, floridly-handsome youth who was her husband, she allowed him to use the greater part of the income from the money. To give Hawley his due, he used it in a way that Sir James himself would have approved: Lillian, in the long run, was the richer for it. But the capital sum Hawley could not touch; and on her twenty-first birthday Ann discovered that she had ten pounds a week to do as she liked with.

It was soon after this that Lizzie Lightowler gave up the school. She had all the companionship she needed in Ann; the girl had been receiving a small salary for helping with the pupils; now she needed this no longer; the house in Ackroyd Park became their joint home and their joint responsibility. In each of them there had developed with the years a profound interest in the stir of social currents that they sensed all about them. Few places gave them a better opportunity than Bradford did to keep in touch with what was becoming more and more the leading motive of life to each of them.

Mrs. Muff, Arnold's landlady, got along somehow. Arnold paid her twelve and sixpence a week; she did a little dressmaking; and she had a working daughter who had been christened Penelope and was called Pen. Arnold did not see much of Pen Muff. She seemed to him to be a spiritless creature as he watched her sliding in and out of the house. She was never at a kitchen meal when he was. He had noticed the unhealthy pallor of her face, her peering shortsighted eyes, her finger-ends cracked and sometimes bleeding. She worked, he knew from Mrs. Muff, in a paper-bag factory. All day long paste was congealing on her fingers.

To his surprise, he found her one winter morning sitting at the kitchen table with her mother when he went into breakfast. He sensed at once domestic trouble. Mrs. Muff looked flushed and angry, as though she had been scolding the girl. Pen looked more depressed than ever; her eyelids were red as if from recent weeping, but behind all this was something new: a dull obstinacy, mulish and intractable.

"Good morning, Mrs. Muff. Good morning, Pen," Arnold said uneasily; and added to the girl: "We don't often have the pleasure of seeing you at breakfast."

Pen did not answer. Mrs. Muff looked at the young man who had grown from a boy under her eyes. She had come to like him; he was a quiet undemonstrative chap, one you could trust. She suddenly blurted out a private matter, a thing she had never done before. "She ought to be ashamed of herself," she said harshly. "Chucking a good job over a shilling a week, a place where she's been for years and years—"

Pen raised her sulky eyes, but now, Arnold saw, they had a little fire in them. "Yes, years and years," she said. "Years and years of slavery. Eight in the morning till eight at night. D'you call that a life? I don't, anyway. And now to cut down our wages – just like that!" She snapped her fingers. "Not even giving us a reason. You must work for less. That's all we're told. As if we weren't getting little enough as it was. Well, I'm not going on with it. I'll find something else."

Colour had come into her face. She glared defiantly at her mother, who poured out Arnold's tea from the large earthenware pot with an air of martyrdom. "All right, my lady," she said. "You'll find that jobs are easier to lose than to get. Since you've made up your mind and are going to be about the house all day, you can go and make the beds."

Pen got up from the table, and Arnold suddenly halted her. "One minute," he said. "Why give up the job? Why don't you go back there and work among the girls – get them to organize themselves – join some union?"

Pen sat down again and stared at him with her pale weak blue eyes. "Organize?" she said. "You don't know 'em. They've got as much idea of organization or anything of that sort as my foot."

"I expect they're as good as you are, my girl," said Mrs. Muff.

"Oh, no, they're not," said Pen, with a confidence that surprised Arnold. "As a matter of fact, I *have* told them what fools they are. I have asked them to refuse to have their wages cut – to come out on strike. They don't even seem to know what I'm talking about."

"I should think not," Mrs. Muff sniffed. "Strike, indeed. A fat lot o' good strikes ever did for man or woman, Them as have got the money can hold out till you come crawling back, starving."

"All right, you'll see," said Pen darkly.

"Yes, I'll see the pair of us in the workhouse, you hare-brained senseless little fool."

Arnold said nothing more to Mrs. Muff. This was not a matter for her. But as he went on munching his breakfast a resolution was shaping in his mind – a resolution that warmed him with a fine sense of excitement and that surprised him by its vehemence. Some day – some day – he had been saying to himself for years, he was going to *do* something for working people. Ever since, as a boy, he had read Robert Owen this resolve had been growing in him. He had read much since then; and in his frigid little Thursley Road bedroom he had even tried to put his thoughts on to paper. What he had seen and heard at Mrs. Lightowler's during the last few years had helped him, too. His invitations to Ackroyd Park were still few and far between. He was, for the most part, silent and awkward there, but he could use his ears, and Lizzie Lightowler had a way of assembling good talkers, men and women displeased with things as they were foreigners, some of them. He remembered a man called Kropotkin, balancing a tea-cup as he predicted a new world in words of blazing sincerity.

It was all deeply moving to the dull-seeming, wordless young man. Old Mr. Suddaby's youth, he reflected, must have been full of talk like this. He remembered Mr. Suddaby introducing him to a bearded man in the cellar bookshop, and saying: "Never forget that you met Friedrich Engels." He had learned something about Engels since then; and he knew now that he never would forget him. He had learned a great many things; that Mrs. Lightowler and Miss Artingstall, for all their kindness, probably thought him as dull as he thought Pen Muff; that this business of *doing* something was not as easy as he had imagined. But sitting there, with a mouthful of bacon turning over on his tongue, he had the surprising conviction that the moment had come, that this trivial affair of Pen Muff's shilling a week was where he stepped off from.

Pen surprised him. When he went up to his room, there she was, not making the bed, as she had been told to do, but standing at the window, holding back the Nottingham lace curtain with one hand, and gazing slantwise down the road to where the engine-steam billowed over the railway in the valley.

She swung round on his entry, and, as though she had been awaiting him, poured out vehement words. "Do something!" she cried. "All very well for you to say do something – organize – do this, do that. What are you doing yourself? What's anybody doing about girls like us?"

"I didn't know you thought about these things, Pen," Arnold said. "As for what I'm doing myself, I'll tell you. I've got a day off today. I'm going down to your factory when the girls come out, and I'm going to talk to 'em. Eight o'clock, isn't it?"

Pen nodded. "You don't know 'em," she said. "They're no better than wild cats. They'll mob you. And what do you know about speaking?"

"I take a Sunday school class," Arnold said, blushing a little at the admission.

"Fat lot o' good that'll be. If you'd been in the Salvation Army, now, ranting on the street corners. That's what you want."

"I'll do my best," he said stoutly. "I've got to start some time. I've never told you, Pen – I've never told anybody. But that's what I want. I don't want to go on being a printer. I want to go in for political work – address meetings – get things better."

He had always thought her so pale, so callow, so colourless, as she dodged past him, going about her affairs in the house. Now she looked at him as though he were a child in arms. "Addressing meetings isn't likely to get things better," she said. "But still," as though not to discourage him, "go and talk to 'em if you feel like it. I'll come and stand by you."

"You will?"

Pen nodded, and Arnold felt a resurgence of the excitement that had filled him as he sat at breakfast. Something he could do – something real and definite at last – and now an ally!

"Make up that bed, will you?" said Pen. "I hate the job. And don't forget you'll want a soap-box." She slouched out of the room.

How well Arnold got to know his soap-box! But for all the hundreds of times he stood upon that humble pedestal, he never forgot the winter evening in Bradford when first he lugged it with him. A fine rain was falling as he made his way down to the lugubrious road that ran, side by side with the railway, through the valley. He had not gone far when Pen Muff joined him. Neither of them had spoken to Mrs. Muff of the adventure, and they had thought it wise not to leave the house together. Arnold was wearing a heavy overcoat and a bowler hat. The soap-box depended from one arm. A moment or two after he had heard the patter of Pen Muff's footsteps on the wet pavement behind him, he was surprised to find the other arm seized. Without a word,

Pen took it in hers, pressed it close against her side. It was the first
time in Arnold's life that a woman had taken his arm. He was discon-
certed and tongue-tied. Presently, as they passed through the lighted
area round a street-lamp, Pen looked into his face and said: "You don't
mind, Arnold?" He merely shook his head; he could not speak.

So they went on in silence, Pen seeming to get some satisfaction
from the contact, Arnold getting nothing but a deepening sense of
embarrassment; and soon they came to the place. The door of the paper-
bag factory opened straight on to the street. On the opposite side of
the street a lamp was burning. Arnold, relieved to have his arm free
at last, put his box under the lamp and stood upon it. He looked right
and left along the dark road, melancholy in the increasing rain. Not a
soul was in sight in either direction. The rainwater gurgled quietly into
the drains. In front of him, one or two windows of the factory burned
brightly. A foot below his face was Pen's, looking up at him intently.
He smiled down at her, feeling easy now that she had let him go.

"Well, here it is, Pen," he said. "My first public meeting. I've often
thought about it, but I never imagined it would be like this: a soap-box
under a street lamp on a wet night in Bradford."

Pen had a shawl over her head. A wisp of hair, escaped from under
it, lay upon her forehead, flattened by the rain. She looked as sallow
and unattractive as ever, but he felt he understood her better. He was
glad she was there. He was glad of an ally. Her pale blue eyes peered up
at him, and she smiled. "You've got some courage, Arnold," she said,
"and by heck! you'll need it. I know 'em. Hold on now. They're coming."

About fifty women were employed in the factory, from girls in
their earliest teens to ribald old grannies. Suddenly the door was flung
open, and clutching their shawls about them, they began to pour out
into the dark wet street. The light tap of leather, the staccato clatter
of clogirons, the loud raucous voices of a horde shouting with gladness in the moment of release, broke the stillness of the street. Arnold
felt his throat tighten and his tongue go dry. He had imagined people
standing about him, and had been prepared for that. He had not bargained for this swift stampede, this rush in both directions towards
home and supper. His audience was melting before his eyes, and he
didn't know what to do about it. Should he shout: "Ladies!" or did one
begin formally: "Ladies and gentlemen?"

As he dithered and the precious seconds fled, Pen Muff, with a rough elbow-thrust to the stomach, pushed him off the box and mounted it herself. "Hey! You! All of you!" she shouted in a clear penetrating voice. "Just a minute! It's Penny Muff talking. There's a chap 'ere as 'as got summat to say t'you. Just gather rahnd an' listen."

This was a robust vernacular speech that Pen never used when speaking to Arnold. He was both surprised and pleased. It certainly was the way to talk to them. He must try it himself. Pen gave way as he climbed on to the box. "Lasses!" he called. "One moment! I'll not keep you long on a night like this."

The women began to crowd round. A stout, coarse-looking old body, holding her shawl in a gnarled fist, shouted: "What's wrong wi' t'night? Tha's a good enough lookin' lad. Keep me as long as tha likes. What dosta say, girls? This is just the sort o' night for it."

The women pressed closer to Arnold, grinning and cackling at the ribald sally. "It's the sort of night when you want warmth and comfort," Arnold went on.

"Just what Ah'm sayin', lad. What abaht it?"

"Warmth, comfort, food, are the right of every one of you."

"Oh – food! He's nobbut talkin' about food, my dears. Let's push off."

"No, stay and listen to me," Arnold cried, one hand holding his overcoat collar tight about his neck where the rain was overflowing in a steady trickle from his bowler. "Stay and listen. How will you ever be sure of the three things you have a right to – food, clothes, shelter – if you tamely allow the bosses to cut down your wages whenever the fancy takes them?"

A sullen-looking woman at the back of the crowd called: "Don't listen to 'im, girls. This is Penny Muff's stuff. We've 'eared it all. Work isna good enough for t'stuck-up bitch. She's full o' fancy notions. Let 'er work like t'rest of us."

"I'm willing to work – as willing as any of you," Pen answered shrilly. "But Ah'm damned if Ah'll work for nowt."

Another voice broke in: "Tha doesn't need to work wi' a fancy man to look after thee. A grand-lookin' lad, too. Take off thi bowler, duckie. It's dribblin' t'water dahn thi neck."

"P'raps 'e needs coolin'."

The women milled closer, screeching with laughter. Arnold saw his meeting dissolving in the heat of a coarse jest or two, and made a desperate effort at recovery. He removed the bowler with a wide-flung dramatic gesture, spattering its contents into the nearest faces. "Women!" he appealed.

"Eh, don't thee spray me, young feller," a woman called. "Not 'ere, any'ow."

"Women!" Arnold appealed again amid the laughter. "Are you going to listen to me? I want to talk to you about your own good, your own rights, about common or garden justice. Are you going to listen?"

The sullen woman at the back had picked up a newspaper that lay soaking in the gutter. She squeezed it into a filthy soggy ball. "Ach, shut thi gob," she shouted, and hurled the missile. It smacked Arnold full in the mouth and sprayed out in a wet mess over his cheeks. He wiped fragments from his eyes, and when he could see clearly again, when he could look at the stretched mouths and grinning eyes and disordered hair, the young faces, the old faces, fantastic and nightmarish in the fluttering light of the lamp, he wondered whether the squashy blow had knocked the senses out of him, for pressing through the back of the crowd, as though coming to his aid on the box, he saw Lizzie Lightowler and Ann.

He made his last effort to impose himself on the meeting. "If you do not resist," he shouted, "if you do not take a firm stand now, your wages will come down and down—"

"So'll yer trousers," cackled the old hag who had started all the fun.

Arnold stopped. He knew that this time he had not paused; he had stopped, finally. He was defeated. He made a gesture of despair and got down from the box. Pen Muff immediately sprang upon it, furious with anger, and began to pelt back at them the stuff they could understand. "You pack of silly dirty-minded old bitches!" she yelled. "All you're fit for is to sweat your guts out and give away a bit more of your pay every time the bosses ask for it. Why should anybody try to help you? Why should anybody try to give you a better life, a more decent life? It'd be wasted on you. You wouldn't know what to do with it, you dirty trollops, you bosses' doormats!"

She had pulled off her shawl and clutched it frenziedly in one hand. Her coat had fallen open, and the rain was soaking her thin white muslin blouse. It caused some pink undergarment to show through, and the light of the lamp, shining down on her rain-glistened face, caused anger, humiliation, despair, to show through that.

She's never talked to them like this before, Arnold thought

suddenly. It's because of me. It's because of the way they treated me. Anyway, this is the end of it. They won't stand that.

He was right. The women surged forward in a furious stampede. The clogs struck with sharp angry notes on the stone setts of the road. Arnold saw, in a sudden wild chiaroscuro, faces change from laughter to masks of fury, hands change to clenched uplifted fists. He saw women stoop to pick up garbage to throw. The spatter fell slapping on the wall behind them, and on their faces and their clothes, as the milling horde closed about them. In the midst of the crowd he saw Lizzie Lightowler's white hair tossing like a mane. Her hat was gone. He saw Ann Artingstall in a wet raincoat, shining like a seal, her face white and resolute as she fought towards the box where he and Pen were now trying to beat off the attack. All the hands that clutched at them, that knocked off his hat, that pulled his hair, that struck at his face, that tried to tear the clothes from their bodies, were like Pen Muff's hands: cracked and sore and sometimes lightly bleeding. It was a nightmare to him for long afterwards: the assault of the bloody hands.

He and Pen were pressed back now to the wall. The soap-box had been splintered by the charging clogs. Women picked up the fragments and used them as weapons. The venomous woman who seemed to have some personal spleen against Pen was armed with a fragment of wood in whose end Arnold saw in a gleam of lamplight a long silver-shining nail. She struck at Pen's head and Arnold's forearm took the blow. He closed with the woman, wrestling to take the deadly weapon from her, and was aware that Ann and Lizzie were now at his side.

"Get out of it," Lizzie shouted. "Don't fight, you fool! Run! And take that girl with you. They're tearing her to pieces."

Arnold would have run had he been permitted to do so. But as he turned, looking for Pen, the spiked wood in his hand, the woman from whom he had wrested it bent swiftly, took off a clog, and smote him on the crown of the head with its iron sole.

That was the end of the fight, though Arnold did not know it. As he went down with a groan, consternation fell upon those Mænads. There was a moment's silence, then swiftly they fled, and when Arnold opened his eyes, dazed but little hurt, there was nothing but the quiet lamplight shining through the rain and the long perspective of the dreary, empty street.

Between his eyes and the lamp Arnold saw the silver aureole of Lizzie's hair. She helped him to his feet, and he stood for a moment, dizzily, unsteadily, supported by the lamp-post, Lizzie's hand round his shoulder. Then he saw Pen Muff, leaning against the wall, breathing heavily, her hair like wet seaweed about her scratched and bleeding face, her coat gone, her blouse lying in ribbons at her feet, her pink bodice torn down the middle. The rain was falling on Pen's bare breasts, pointing up defiant in the lamplight. "By heck!" she panted. "It was a good fight. I nearly gouged the eyes out of the bitch that downed you."

Arnold turned with embarrassment and distaste from her proud flaunted nudity. He looked for Ann. "Are you all right?" he asked.

Pen answered for her, surlily: "As right as rain. She came in when it was all over bar the shouting."

Pen Muff lay in a bath at Lizzie Lightowler's house. It was no great shakes as a bath by modern standards. It was made of iron, painted over with enamel, and the enamel was chipped and stained. The bath was enclosed in a frame faked to look like fine-grained wood. Varnished wall-paper, yellow with age, glistened with condensed steam in the light of an unshaded gas-burner that gave a greenish light. It was, look at it how you will, a repulsive little box of a room; and Pen, lying there at full length with the aches easing out of her limbs, with a hot sponge from time to time comforting her bruised scratched face, thought it sumptuous.

She sat up in the water, looking about her, looking at the pile of Ann's clothes lying on a chair for her to choose from. So this was luxury! So this was how that girl lived who was all over Arnold once the fight was done!

She sank back, giving herself up to the sensuousness of the moment. She had never, in all her twenty years, been in a bath before. She made do as well as she could with an old tin tub in front of the kitchen fire. And that girl could have a bath like this every day! Probably did. Looked as if she did. Pen thought of Ann's strange hair, shining like thick creamy silk, and of Ann's hands, white and cared-for. She raised her own hands out of the water, gazed at the cracked and roughened ends of her fingers, and then got up and dried herself with indignant vigour. She picked up clothes at random, and when she was dressed she crept to the head of the stairs. There was no one in sight. She went down cautiously. A murmur of voices came from the drawing room opening off the hall which was warmed by a fire and illumined by gas burning in a box-like contraption of stained glass. All very fine. All very grand and swish, Pen thought. She tiptoed to the front door, went through, and shut it softly behind her. The path led through laurels and rhododendrons, their wet leaves shining and dripping. The rain had stopped. She could smell the earth and see a star or two among the hurrying clouds overhead. She went swiftly up the acclivity of Ackroyd Park to the flat familiar promenade of Manningham Lane. She allowed herself to be caught up gladly in the life she knew.

Down in the road which ran through the valley was a little chapel hall. Lizzie Lightowler, with Ann to help her, ran a clinic there. Lizzie was up to the eyes in all sorts of activities which, she said, the government or the local authorities would one day take off her hands. She knew nothing about medicine, but she and Ann both knew a lot about hygiene and more about malnutrition. It wasn't difficult to tell a dirty baby or a starving one when you clapped eyes on it; and, for the rest, Lizzie was paying a young doctor to attend once a week.

The two women were returning from the clinic when they ran into Arnold and Pen Muff battling with the factory-hands. When it was over, and the four of them were walking to Ackroyd Park, with Pen's nudity concealed beneath Arnold's overcoat, little was said by any of them, but Lizzie and Ann were busy with an identical thought.

They had been discussing Arnold that morning at breakfast. It began with a theme that occupied their minds a good deal. They were both steeped in Socialist literature and conversation and correspondence. The needs of the people were bare before their eyes in that town compacted of mills and factories, warehouses, back-to-back dwellings climbing the steep streets, built in the riotous heyday of the industrial revolution when the housing of the "hands" was a matter of less thought than the kennelling of dogs. Nothing had ever been done about it. The impetus of the great industrial change-over from hand-loom weaving in the homes, with pure streams flowing by the doorstep, to factory production, and polluted rivers, and congregated thousands in dwellings that were ugly to begin with and now were squalid and filthy and insanitary: that impetus still rolled woolmaking Bradford along – the town of the golden fleece – pleasant to live in, as Lizzie said at breakfast that day, if you were fleecing and not being fleeced.

"And you see, my dear," said Lizzie, "I'm one of the fleecers, and so are you."

She looked at Ann across the shining things on the breakfast table, across the few flowers which, even in the depth of winter, had been bought at great price. With one comprehensive gesture she included the fire, screened off from her back by a framed square of plate glass, the carpet beneath her feet, the hangings of sage-green velvet that were pushed right back to admit the reluctant day. "What right have I to all this? Or what right have you?"

Ann knew the argument. Lizzie had burst it upon her soon after her twenty-first birthday, when she had become the inheritor of ten pounds a week. Ann had discovered that, because Lord Nelson had done his job more than a century ago, his descendants to that day were receiving a pension. She exclaimed at what she considered the enormity of this. "Where does the money come from?" she demanded, her new-born social instincts outraged.

Lizzie crushed her decisively. "From the same place as your ten pounds a week – out of the pockets of working people. All interest on money does – there's nowhere else for it to come from. The only difference is that Nelson did do something for his country, but I have yet to learn that Sir James Sugden did, though he was my father and your grandfather."

Ann stared at her aunt speechless. She was so full of young enthusiasm; she was continually making shattering discoveries like this, only to find how naïve they were, how long ago they had been made by other people, how easily they could be twisted against herself.

"Then," she stammered. "I'm a – a – mere social parasite?"

Lizzie laughed into her earnest crestfallen face. "Thanks for the 'mere,'" she said. "That saves us. Yes, I'm afraid we are both a sort of parasite, insofar as all our sustenance is provided, with no effort on our part, by other people; but I'm not going to allow you or anyone else to call me a 'mere' parasite, because I do use my body and my brains in returning what I get, as far as I can, to those who make it for me. Yes, there are plenty of 'mere' parasites to make the present system stink; but I'm not one of them."

Ann was cheered; she turned her aunt's answer over in her mind; and that morning when Lizzie demanded to know what right they had to all the comforts that surrounded them, she was not unduly depressed.

"One of the fleecers," Lizzie had said, and Ann took her up. "It will never be changed," she said, "unless the people change it for themselves."

Lizzie buttered her toast and smiled. "Treason, my dear, treason to your father and your grandfather. Alderman Hawley Artingstall is chairman of his divisional Conservative Association. Sir James Sugden was a pillar of the Liberal Party. Do you mean to tell me that neither of these historic parties can cure the ills you complain of? Remember, there is no other party in this country. When working men go to Parliament today, they go as Liberals. Is that wrong of them?"

Ann tossed her fair head. "They make me sick. They go to Westminster and wear top hats, forget where they came from, and ape their betters."

"Betters?"

"Oh, you know what I mean," the girl cried impatiently. "It makes me so angry I can't even speak logically. But I know, and you know, it's got to come soon. There must be people in the House to speak for labouring men and call themselves Labour men. There'll have to be a Labour Party."

Lizzie got up. "Forgive me, my dear, for jollying about it. You're right, of course. It's the natural and logical thing. But why are you so vehement about it this morning in particular?"

"Because I've been thinking about it all night. Why can't working men go to Parliament? Because they've got no money. You've got to serve the country for the honour of doing it, which means that only the rich can have the honour of the country at heart. Well, that's where my ten pounds a week comes in. A man could live on half that."

She looked at Lizzie as though expecting a rebuke for quixotry, and saw to her surprise that her aunt was overwhelmed. Lizzie's eyes suddenly brimmed. She came round the table and took Ann's face in both her hands and gazed for a long time into her eyes. Then, as if to hide a tear that began to trickle down her nose, she buried her face in the girl's hair. "My dear," she murmured. "What a lovely idea! Now if I did that sort of thing – well, I'm getting on. I've had my good time. But you are so young. It is giving up so much."

"You don't think it's a mad thing to do?"

"Mad? Dear Ann, I wish I had a mad daughter like you."

Lizzie held her off, half-laughing, half-crying; then cut short the emotional scene. "Well," she said, "the money's there; and now *cherchez l'homme.*"

It was then that they began to talk about Arnold Ryerson.

They could not believe that Arnold filled the bill. He was a disappointment to them both. So much was soon apparent. "I like him," said Lizzie. "He's a good young fellow. I'd trust him with my purse or reputation, but—"

"But not with your vote."

Lizzie laughed. "I haven't got a vote to trust him with, child. Nor have you. Remember, we're mere females. But I'm not sure Arnold is to be trusted with anyone's vote. It's no good having the root of the matter in you, as they say. You've got to be able to get it out of you if you're to be of any use at the sort of thing we have in mind. Arnold doesn't open his mouth."

Ann could not help looking upon Arnold as in some sort her protégé. After all, it was her adventure into Broadbent Street that had been the first cause of his coming to Bradford. She had gladly backed up all that her aunt had done for him. During his visits to Ackroyd Park she had done her best to draw him out, but she had never found him even as communicative as he had been on that night when first they met. She did not know that on his own ground, in his own kitchen, he was at ease as he never could be in a different social setting. He hadn't Hamer Shawcross's swift adaptability. He hadn't had enough of Ackroyd Park: that was all that was wrong with him.

Something of this began to filter into her mind as she and Lizzie discussed him. She said uneasily: "You know, Aunt Lizzie, we rather dumped him into the deep end to sink or swim, didn't we? I vote that we reserve judgment. We ought to see a lot more of him. Have you realized that we've tended almost to drop him entirely? It's nearly six months since he was last here."

Lizzie, too, felt a stir of self-reproach. When she set her hand to a job, it was not her way to leave it half-finished, and Arnold Ryerson was certainly a job she had set her hand to.

"Good gracious!" she said. "I hadn't realized that. I've got too many irons in the fire, that's what's the matter with me."

"We must have him here to dinner," said Ann.

"Pretty often," said Lizzie.

And then, coming home from the clinic that night, they had run into the fight under the street lamp. What it was all about they did not know until they and Arnold and Pen Muff were walking back to Ackroyd Park. Then Arnold said to Pen in a tone of bitter disappointment: "What can you do with people like that?" Pen said: "It's because they're like that that you must go on and on and on, doing and doing."

"It makes you wonder," said Arnold, miserable, with the rain soaking his coat, "whether they're worth saving."

Pen, with Arnold's overcoat grotesquely huddled about her, swishing the wet pavement at every step, fell into her vernacular. "Tha can wonder that, lad, as often as tha likes, so long as thee always answers Yes. People are all we've got to work with – all God Almighty's got to work with, come to that."

"That girl's a long time," said Lizzie. "Pop up and see if she's all right, Ann."

Ann came back and said that that girl had disappeared. Arnold apologized for Pen. "I can guess how she feels," he said; and at that Ann and Lizzie exchanged glances, for it was a light to them on how Arnold himself had probably felt in that house.

"We'll have some coffee taken upstairs," said Lizzie. "It's a more comfortable room than this for a talk."

And so for the first time Arnold found himself in what was the very *arcanum* of Lizzie's house: that room at the end of the passage on the first floor, with its green bookcases breast-high, its green fireplace and pale fawn carpet and curtains, and with the firelight falling on the brass fender and the shining mahogany of the writing table. Arnold sat on one side of the fireplace in a wicker chair, Lizzie on the other. Ann was cross-legged on the floor between them, pouring out the coffee. Arnold had been into the kitchen to shed his soaking coat and trousers and boots. He was now a comfortable-looking bundle in clothes borrowed from Mr. Marsden. Large carpet slippers flapped on his feet. Mr. Marsden's black dignified trousers swathed his legs, and Mr. Marsden's dressing-gown, whose pattern was a faded green, blue and yellow plaid, wrapped him about. He had never before worn a dressing-gown, and liked its easy comfort.

"I don't know whether you smoke, Arnold," said Lizzie Lightowler, "but if you do, you may."

Arnold produced a pipe and a tobacco-pouch made of red rubber. He was no longer self-conscious about his pipe, and now, as he blew a soothing cloud of smoke into the air, the familiar sedative, combined with the ease of his attire and the happy relaxation after the brief bitter encounter in the street, gave him an expansive unshackled feeling, and he began to talk as he had never talked to Ann and Lizzie before. He talked about the books he had been reading, and about his hopes of active work as a Socialist. "You see, I know it inside out – not the theory but the facts of the matter. I know how the poor live. I know what ought to be done, and when I hear people talk about things like 'the theory of rent' – well, I know what's behind the theory of rent, because I've seen my mother scrubbing floors to earn the five shillings a week for Mr. Richardson."

They let him run on. It was getting late, and he had changed back into his dried clothes, when Lizzie said: "Well, you must come and see us more often, Arnold. It's been a treat to have you tonight. The way you're framing, I shouldn't be surprised to see you an M.P. one of these days."

Arnold was standing under the stained-glass box that shielded the gas light in the hall. He threw back his head and laughed with unaffected surprise and merriment. "Me an M.P.? Never! No, I don't hope for that. Perhaps I can do a bit of good some other way. But an M.P.? I don't see it."

And he never did see it. Perhaps he would have seen it, and seen many other things, if Hamer Shawcross had not said to Mrs. Ryerson: "I'm going to Bradford to see Arnold." Though no one knew it at the time, this was one of fate's utterances, right out of the mouth of the oracle.

Between that night when Lizzie and Ann began to revise their opinion of Arnold, and the coming of Hamer Shawcross to Bradford, there was a long time. Once launched, Arnold Ryerson worked indefatigably for the cause he had for years pondered over, and, though he hardly realized it, he worked along lines that Lizzie and Ann laid down. The idea of a Labour Party devoted to the interests of Labour, as the Irish Party was devoted to the interests of Ireland, was not unfamiliar to him, but he had not, till now, considered it very seriously. Trade unionists were getting into Parliament, calling themselves Liberals, or, in extreme cases, adopting the tag "Lib-Lab," and Arnold, like plenty of others, thought this system could be made to work well enough. But this was not the gospel according to Ackroyd Park.

Arnold soon learned the new gospel and industriously preached it. He became a familiar figure wherever trouble broke out, a ready speaker of a solid reliable sort, lacking wit, humour or any touch of brilliance, but managing none the less to hold most audiences by virtue of a native integrity, a sense he conveyed of utter honesty and straightness of purpose.

By day he continued to work as a printer. Most evenings were his own, and he was to be found tramping as resolutely as some itinerant Methodist preacher to the outskirts of Bradford and to the villages round about it, wherever he could find a platform under a roof or a street corner for his soap-box. Soon he became sought after farther afield: in Leeds and Keighley, Halifax and Huddersfield, wherever the growing discord was heard as the industrial wheels roared and rumbled.

Where he went Pen Muff went, too. When he got back to Thursley Road on the night of what Ann Artingstall always called the Battle of the Amazons, Pen was still up, prowling restlessly in the kitchen. Mrs. Muff had gone to bed. As soon as Arnold's key was heard in the lock, the girl went into the passage – not rushing, but quietly, keeping herself in hand.

"I've got some tea ready for you," she said gruffly.

He had the sense not to tell her he had been drinking coffee all the evening. If it had been Hamer Shawcross, he would have said: "Tea! The very thing I'm dying for." Arnold said: "Thanks, Pen," hung his coat on a hook in the passage, and followed her into the kitchen. The kettle was boiling on the fire. She quickly made the tea and poured out two cups. She poured hers from the cup to the saucer, and, with the saucer at her lips, her eyes staring at him across the shallow shell, she asked: "Been with those women all night?"

He nodded, sipping the tea.

"Who are they?"

He told her, and she said: "There's more an' more of 'em knocking about these days – toffs trying to nose into working people's affairs. I don't trust 'em. What do they want to change the world for? Isn't it comfortable enough for 'em as it is?" She sucked in her tea noisily.

"Change the world? That's a big order, Pen," Arnold said. "Is that what you want to do?"

"Aye," she said. "Just that, to be going on with. Take your coat off and roll up that sleeve."

"Whatever for?"

"Didn't I see you take it on the arm when that bitch with the spike swiped at my head?"

"Get on with you. It's nothing."

"Let me see. I'll bet *they* never thought of looking at it."

"I don't suppose they saw it happen."

"A lot they'd have cared if they did. People with baths!"

"Don't be unfair."

"Don't you be daft, going round with people like that. Let's see the arm."

Arnold rolled up his sleeve. The cut had broken through the skin and torn up the flesh over the biceps for a few inches. It was still oozing a little blood. Pen cleaned it with almost-boiling water, poured witch-hazel on to it, tied it round with a clean handkerchief. "That ought to have been done long ago," she said. "Now get to bed."

The next evening Arnold was reading in his chilly bedroom when he heard the front door bang. A moment later there was a tap at his door and Pen looked in. "Come down to the kitchen," she said. "There's a bit of fire there. Mother won't be back for an hour."

He hesitated: "Come on," she said. "I won't eat you."

They sat by the kitchen fire, and Pen handed him a little newspaper called *The Miner*. "Ever see this?" she said.

He shook his head and smiled. "What have miners got to do with you, Pen?"

"It's time someone took your education in hand," she said. "Mines and paper-bag factories and wool mills are all one thing, and the sooner you realize it the better."

She let herself go on the solidarity of labour, and he listened with the patience which was one of his excellent qualities.

"This paper comes out every month," she said. "I'll pass it on to you. There's more sense in it than in anything else I know. Ever heard of Keir Hardie?"

Arnold said that the name was vaguely familiar to him.

"It'll be more than vaguely familiar to a lot of people before long," Pen assured him. "He's editor of *The Miner*."

He wanted to know how she got hold of the paper, and she said it came from her sister, who was married to a miner living at Cwmdulais, in the Rhondda Valley. "You'll like Nell," Pen assured him, as though, he noted in his quiet way, he were already a prospective member of the family. "And you'll like Ianto, too. Ianto Richards – that's Nell's husband. A hauler."

Pen made some tea, her one idea of hospitality; and as they drank she told of her sister Nell, soprano in a chapel choir, who had gone with the choir to an all-England contest at Sheffield. It was there that Ianto, a member of the Horeb Calvinistic Methodist choir from Cwmdulais, had met her. Nell, Pen said, was a fine girl, fair and red-headed, and Ianto was the smallest thing you ever saw, a little dark slip of a chap, with blue powder-marks bitten into his face. They had one boy, Dai; and though Dai was only a year old, he was already, it appeared to Pen, a miraculous creature of profound endowments. "But you'll meet 'em all, and see for yourself," she prophesied; and though Arnold thought this unlikely, as he returned to his room with the copy of *The Miner*, Pen was right and he was wrong. It was often to be so.

A year later Arnold left the house in Thursley Road. It had been a year of intensive work. That not dishonourable stigma which Henry Greenhalgh had applied to him – "painstaking and uninspired" – stuck like a burr. It was true of his public speaking and of his sturdy honest appearance. But he and Lizzie Lightowler and Ann Artingstall had learned where his strength lay. As an organizer he was superb. In the course of that year he organized two trade union branches where they had not existed before, kept them in vigorous being, did his daily work as a printer, and continued indomitably to blunder through innumerable public speeches.

It was, in many ways, the most important year of Arnold's life. It shaped him, definitely and finally. At least once a week he dined at Ackroyd Park. There, and in the course of his work, he met all sorts of people who understood and valued his sound modest talents. His awkwardness fell away. He had seen his limits, was working happily within them, and reaped the inevitable reward of ease and confidence.

It was a year of pride and misery for Pen Muff. Arnold guessed, what now became obviously true, that he had been to Pen an object of sentimental interest before the Battle of the Amazons gave them a solid matter in common. Pen felt that she had, because of her part in that affair, in some sort launched Arnold on his career. She took no pains to conceal her suspicion of Lizzie and Ann, who were able to do for that career so much more than she could do herself. It was because she was determined to accompany Arnold on his wanderings that she refused all work which would have kept her, as the paper-bag factory had done, at it till eight at night. She found employment at last as a waitress in the Kurdistan Café, a place of alcoves and cosy fires, set in the midst of the dark interlacing streets of warehouses, where the wool-merchants and brokers clove a way through their harassed mornings with the help of chess and dominoes. It was gentler, easier work than she had been accustomed to, and as well paid. She was through with it by six at night.

Arnold found her useful and devoted. "Pen, will you make a list of those new members, with their addresses?" "Pen, we ought to start some proper books for these subscriptions." "Pen, you might call and see if those hand-bills have been printed."

She did all he asked; and, without being asked, she read books and newspapers, marked passages that he ought to read, carried a bottle of cold tea to his meetings and saw that he had a drink when he had finished speaking. Pen and her cold tea – a painstaking and uninspiring drink – became a joke for miles round Bradford. "It's all he'll have while I'm looking after him," she declared uncompromisingly. "An' if some of you stuck to tea you'd be able to pay your union subs."

"Looking after him." Arnold knew it, and if you had asked him whether he liked it, he would have said Yes and No. Pen was a grand comrade; she knew he was aware of this, and that made the year for her a year of pride. But if it came to being looked after, he would have preferred to be looked after by Ann Artingstall. Pen knew that, too; and so the year was one of misery.

Before the year was out, they were an inseparable trinity at Ackroyd Park. To one another they had become Ann and Arnold and Aunt Lizzie. Ann and Lizzie still cherished the notion of building up a Member of Parliament. Arnold was shaping as they wanted him to shape, but nothing had been said to him about the scheme. Work in a common cause was the cement that held them together. Everything was businesslike and practical, and Arnold's feeling for Ann was still so much the beggar-boy's for the princess that it was a long time coming to the forefront of his consciousness. It did not obtrude upon him at all, save as an unrealized incentive to work, till an evening in the high summer of the year.

It was a lovely evening. He was to speak at a meeting in Bingley, and he and Pen walked the few miles to the place. They plodded along the torrid pavements of Manningham Lane, through the township of Shipley, and came out into what then was the attractive countryside round about Nab Wood and Cottingley. They lingered for a moment on the old grey stone bridge over the Aire, watching the swifts that hurled themselves to and fro with shrill cries upon the face of the water, then went on towards the sunset that had left the sky pulsing and luminous.

There was not much that was romantic in Arnold's make-up, but the sky and the water and the beech trees that stood isolated here and there, withdrawn into themselves and wearing the gravity of the twilight, touched him to a mood that he tritely expressed. "It seems a shame to drag people to a meeting on such a night as this, Pen."

Pen, with the tea-basket on her arm, said practically: "You won't drag many, lad, worse luck. And it's never too good a night to hear a bit of common sense. Mind you give it to 'em."

She was right. The drab little hall was sparsely peopled, and those who had come were apathetic. There were two speakers before Arnold Ryerson. They were harkened to without enthusiasm. There was not even opposition. There was only a cold politeness. Half-way through the address of the second speaker, a man in the audience reached for his cap and sneaked out with that furtive tiptoe unobtrusiveness which is more galling than the fiercest heckling. And, indeed, Arnold thought, his gaze fastened upon a square of window through which he could see the sky now turning a translucent green, why plague them on such a night? What was it all about if not the freedom to enjoy, among other things, nights like this? He thought of his mother, toiling in Ancoats – always a strong lever to his actions. What did he want for her? If she had been near, he would have taken care that she was out by the river, not in that stuffy hall.

The end beyond the means for once obsessed his imagination – the end for him, as well as for the cause he served. He was aware of a dissatisfaction, a lack, which this lovely night emphasized as an ache in his heart, and the consequence of this was that when his turn came to speak, he spoke with less spirit than usual, and also with less of the plain common sense that had so often served as a substitute for a lively manner.

The audience shuffled and was bored. Pen, sitting in the front row, watched with anguish the growing ineptitude of Arnold's performance, and presently, when he stammered and came for a moment to a standstill, gazing fixedly at the back of the hall, she swung round in that direction and saw that Ann Artingstall was standing by the door. Ann smiled at Arnold, a smile that was meant to be encouraging, but it finished him completely. For the first time in his life he saw her clear of all but her personal attributes. He saw her not as Hawley Artingstall's daughter, not as the rich girl who had shared a cup of tea with him in an Ancoats kitchen, not as anything at all except as Ann Artingstall, smiling at him from the doorway. A desirable woman. The most desirable woman he had ever known. She was, he felt, the answer to all his dissatisfaction, all his sense of lack. Never, so much as now, had he wished to be through quickly with the matter in hand.

And quickly enough indeed he got through with it, in a few tangled sentences, and the audience escaped with gladness into the cool of the now swiftly-falling night.

Arnold leapt down from the low platform, and Pen rose to meet him, glowering. "That was dreadful, Arnold," she said bluntly. "I've never heard you worse. I felt ashamed of you." The two local speakers, with hurried good nights, left them. "You'd better have your tea now," Pen added.

Ann came up the hall towards them, and Arnold turned to her eagerly, leaving Pen standing there with the tea bottle in her hand. "How on earth did you get here?" he asked.

"Hasn't she got a pair of legs, like any other girl?" Pen asked.

Ann laughed. "Good evening, Pen," she said. "Yes, I have got a pair of legs, and I can do twenty miles on them if I want to. But, as it happens, I didn't use them tonight." She took Arnold's lapel between her fingers. "I seem to have put you off your stroke."

"I was wool-gathering before you came," Arnold said. "I couldn't settle to it tonight. I know I was bad."

"I shouldn't have disturbed you. I should have waited till you came out. I knew you were talking here, and I looked in to ask if you'd like a lift home?"

It seemed that a friend of Aunt Lizzie's had driven out to Bingley to see some relatives. Ann had accompanied her. "Now they've persuaded her to stay the night, and she's sending her carriage back empty. There's plenty of room for all of us."

They had moved towards the door of the hall as they talked. Ann and Arnold walked side by side. Pen followed behind, glum and silent, the basket swinging in one hand, the other carrying the uncorked bottle of tea. "He's forgotten it," she thought. "He's forgotten it, and he's forgotten me. I'm not here. There's only her. Look at his face." She had never before seen him so lit up.

The carriage stood outside the dingy hall, with a caped coachman on the box, the shine of the lamps pallid in the lingering midsummer light. A few poor children stood by, looking admiringly at the brown glossy horse.

"Which way would you like to sit, Pen?" Ann asked, turning back on the pavement.

"I'm sitting no way," said Pen dourly. "I walked out and I can walk back."

"But—"

"But nothing. It looks a rum do to me – driving away from a Socialist meeting in a carriage. It was a rotten speech, but this is rottener."

She was right, and Arnold knew she was right. He would have given anything to hear Ann say: "Very well, then. Let's all walk." And deeply as he wanted her to say it, equally deeply he wanted her not to say it. If Pen would ride, he and Ann could walk; but if Pen insisted on walking, then he and Ann would ride. And the idea of Pen riding was, of course, ludicrous. He understood her well enough to know that. She stood back, close to the wall, looking almost tall in her anger, her sallow face a little flushed. "Go on," she said. "Get it over with. Don't let's stand arguing."

Ann stepped first into the victoria. Arnold followed and sat by her side. He could not look at Pen again. He stared straight ahead as the carriage started. They had gone hardly twenty paces when there was a sound like an exploding bomb. But they did not look back. Pen had hurled the tea bottle furiously to the ground.

*

There was now no light from the sun, nor was there a moon. That, a slip of a thing, had set hard behind the sun. But rivers of stars were flowing overhead, and the midsummer air was warm. The victoria rolled smoothly forward through a silence broken by nothing but the rhythmic impact of the horse's hoofs upon the road and the occasional jingle of metal and creak of leather as he tossed his head up and down.

All very delightful. Arnold should have been enjoying himself, especially as this was the first time he had ridden in a private carriage, and at his side was the woman who had suddenly broken upon his consciousness as the beloved.

He had often thought tenderly of Ann, but he had always uprooted such thoughts and thrust them away. They were incredible, impossible. But were they? Tonight he had asked himself that question, and once it had been admitted even as something that might be asked, everything was changed. To himself, at all events, he could now freely say that he loved Ann; and here was Ann riding at his side through a perfect summer night. He should have been exalted. He felt, instead, as miserable as sin.

The tiff with Pen Muff affected Ann's spirits, too. She and Lizzie liked the girl, and if they saw little of her, that was Pen's fault. She insisted on maintaining a distance. Ann was always aware that Pen was waiting to force attention to the difference in their status, to deride her as a parlour Socialist, and tonight she had found her chance with a vengeance. Ann's annoyance was not lessened by the reflection that fundamentally Pen was right. To take the carriage to the door of that poverty-stricken little hall was folly. She should have ridden home alone or walked with the others. This was so obvious that she wondered why she had been guilty of such foolishness, and she surprised herself with the conclusion that she had brought the carriage along because she had thought it would please Arnold Ryerson.

Small wonder that Ann and Arnold had nothing to say to one another. In silence they bowled through leafy Cottingley, and urban Shipley, and came to the familiar stretch of Manningham Lane. Each was aware of the other with an intensity not before experienced; but between them was the righteous little figure of Pen Muff, as straight if as narrow as a ruled line.

Where Manningham Lane ran into Ackroyd Park Arnold got out,

thanked Ann, and wished her good night. He strode off toward Thurs-ley Road, but no sooner had the victoria disappeared than he reversed his tracks and began to walk back toward Shipley. It was actually in Shipley, at eleven at night, that he saw Pen trudging doggedly toward him, basket over her arm.

"Well, Pen," he said, forcing his cheerfulness a little, "you see I've had the best of both worlds: a ride and a walk."

She did not return his smile, and they had walked some little way side by side before she said: "The best of both worlds, eh? You think you can have that, do you? You'd better be a Lib-Lab, or better still a Conservative working man. Though what the heck you'll have to conserve except an empty belly I don't know."

"Pen, please!" he pleaded. "Aren't you taking this all rather too ser-iously? Aren't you making a football out of a pill? What happened tonight was nothing – an accident – the sort of thing that'll never occur again."

She stopped dead under a high wall that hid a garden from the street. Trees lifted their branches over it, and the light of a street lamp, shining through the leaves, made a dappled pattern upon her white face. "You don't believe in things as I do," she said. "You couldn't have done it – you just couldn't – if – if…"

She couldn't go on. Arnold looked at her helplessly for a moment, then said: "Fanaticism won't get you anywhere."

At that she fairly blazed at him: "What else will, you fool? You rea-sonable men are all right to keep things going when they're set, but when they want changing what on earth can do the job except fanat-icism? What are saints and martyrs but fanatics? Now then, I want to walk home alone. Shall I give you a start or will you give me one?"

She didn't wait for his answer, but set off violently. He loitered till she was out of sight, then followed, feeling sick and desolate.

And this was why Arnold left the house in Thursley Road. It became intolerable. Pen said no more about the matter in dispute, but she said no more about anything. She became just what she had been before the fight with the factory girls. Arnold saw her slipping unobtrusively about the house, her whole personality, which their friendship had illuminated, dulled once more. There was no more to her than to a grey mouse, darting for its hole on the approach of danger. Except this: that when, once or twice, they came unavoidably face to face, her lifeless features held an infinity of reproach which made him feel as though he had murdered something.

Pen no longer helped him with his work, no longer accompanied him to meetings, no longer made a nuisance of herself at the Kurdistan Café by her anxiety to be away as soon as the clock struck six. June went out and July came in; and when August was wilting the leaves in Ackroyd Park, Arnold felt that he could put up with Thursley Road no longer. That skinny, sallow little ghost, disappearing through doors, vanishing behind curtains, sighing and glowering, made the place impossible.

He was helped in his decision to go by another decision which was made at this time. The heat of an August day was still exhaling from the pavements when he turned into Ackroyd Park to keep his weekly dinner appointment. The dinners were no longer a terror to him. He had ceased to be self-conscious about his printer's-ink-stained fingers and about glass and cutlery. Use and wont had done their work. He walked with happy expectation between the rhododendrons and laurels, that were sagging with dust and heat, and rang the bell. Old Marsden looked at him with no welcome. "Dinner's ready – and spoilin'," he complained, "but when *they'll* be down I don't know."

Then Lizzie's voice was heard, crying over the banister: "Arnold, come up here for a moment, will you?"

Arnold went up to the study at the back of the house. The window was flung open upon the poplars standing up like spears, with not a breath to bend them, and upon the view of the distant hills, cutting a line across the red smudge of the sunset. But the room, nevertheless, felt stuffy, and both Ann and Lizzie, who were sitting at work, looked hot and exhausted.

Lizzie threw down a pen, got up, and said: "Come, Ann. What isn't done must be left. We'll finish after dinner. There's no end to it, Arnold, once you start this game. Letters to the Pankhursts in Manchester, to Keir Hardie up there in Ayrshire, to secretaries and presidents of this and treasurers of that—"

Ann took up the litany: "To M.P.s and K.C.s, to Boards of Guardians and School Boards, to Trade Unions, Suffrage Societies and political fussers in general. What we need, you know, Aunt Lizzie, is a full-time secretary."

Lizzie, passing a distracted hand through the white mop of her hair, paused with a sudden intent in her eye. "We do!" she said emphatically. "Arnold, will you take it on?"

Arnold laughed with good-humoured scepticism, as he had done that day when Lizzie suggested he might become an M.P. "Me?" he said. "A fine secretary I'd make!"

"Good gracious, man," said Lizzie, "you can read, you can write. Perhaps we'll get you one of those typewriter things. You're up to the eyes in the same work that we are. Where could we find a better man?"

"We couldn't," said Ann. "Not anywhere. Arnold, you *must* do this."

Arnold knew that this appeal – this command, almost – had settled the matter. But it was a measure of his new ease in Ackroyd Park that he said he must think it over. Precious little thinking there was about it as he walked swiftly, exultantly, up the hill to Heaton when dinner was done. To see Ann every day, to work every day with Ann: no, this didn't call for deliberation. He leaned on his now familiar wall, looked at the few embers dying in the western sky and at the chains of light springing up in the valley at his feet and on the hills to which the valley climbed. He gave himself to dreaming. Surely there was in her voice and in her look an appeal that meant more than a wish to see him doing this job? Surely – surely—

Surely nothing, Arnold – not in this life.

But no voice said that to him as he strode elatedly down Manningham Lane toward Thursley Road. At the top of the road he paused, and looked objectively down its declivity. He did not often do that. He had lived in it for years, had come to take it for granted. But now, with the splendour of the hills he had been looking at still moving his imagination, he saw the street meanly: saw its dingy little close-packed houses, its miserable and sterile garden plots, all sliding down the hill through the sultry and oppressive night to the pandemonium of the railway in the bottom.

He decided suddenly to leave it. It was no better than Broadbent Street. Well, very little better. Anyway, it wasn't good enough. A new job, new lodgings, in some place where the air was fresh and the eye could range. And he would be free of Pen Muff, trailing her sorrow and disappointment like a grey web for ever between him and satisfaction.

He went on eagerly down the street and opened the door with his latchkey. There was no light in the narrow passage, and Pen was more than ever like an uneasy ghost as she loomed up and said in a shaky voice: "Here's *The Miner*, Arnold. You haven't seen the last few numbers."

"Oh, yes, I have," he lied. "They get it at Ackroyd Park."

He left her standing there, the paper in her hand, her eyes following him as he ran through the dusk up the stairs to his room. He had never lied to her before, and as he lay, without undressing, on the bed and inhaled the heat-oppressed darkness he didn't feel any better about Pen Muff. He thought of his mother and of how well she and Pen would have got on together. Suddenly he hated himself.

Lizzie and Ann, contributing equally, paid his salary of three pounds a week. He sent his mother one. He had two rooms in the little stone-grey street that can through Baildon village to the moors. Baildon is not a lovely village now, but it was a lovely village then, with its old Malt Shovel Inn, its ancient stocks, its church, its stone-built woollen mill. Climb where you will out of those West Riding valleys and you come to a moor on the top. Day by day, when he was done at Ackroyd Park, Arnold climbed steeply out of the valley in which Manningham Lane was ruled like a straight line, and there at the top was Baildon, the gateway to the moors. He had only to step out of the house where he lodged, turn to the left and walk a hundred yards, and the immortal landscape was before him, unchanged since it hardened out of chaos: the rough bent grass, the ling and heather, the peewits crying.

He was better for the tough daily walk to and from the town. He had not to be at Ackroyd Park till ten in the morning, unless he chose to come to breakfast at nine. The invitation stood open. He still spent many evenings tramping about on his missionary work, and now that Pen was not there to accompany him, Ann often came. Then he would climb the hill to that eyrie of a village where the clean air blew in through his window and where, as he sometimes did, he could before sleeping take a turn on the moorland road, a white glimmer twisting through the night under the immensity of the stars. Once or twice Ann had walked up there with him, and, saying nothing, they had stood close together and listened to the silence threaded with little sounds: the tinkling of hidden streams, the barking of a distant dog, the shutting of a cottage door. It was so quiet that when they saw a lighted pane fall to darkness they could almost hear it.

Once Arnold ventured to break the silence. They stood on the road, their faces turned toward the distant cluster of cottages called Hawksworth which they could see as nothing but a few points of light immobile upon the darkness. "What are you thinking about, Ann?" Arnold asked.

"Oh, the world and all that therein is. All the work we're doing – you and I and Aunt Lizzie and so many other people, and all the work there's still to do. And I was thinking of the night when Uncle Birley took me to that boy's birthday party..."

"Yes – Hamer Shawcross."

"...because that was the night when it all started for me. If Father hadn't found me in your kitchen I should never have been sent to Aunt Lizzie's. I should have been a nice miss, or even a nice married woman." She turned toward him in the darkness. "You were very solemn that night, Arnold."

"Was I?"

"Yes. You seemed to want me to swear some sort of oath that I'd never forget it. Ah, well. I haven't forgotten it, anyway."

They turned back toward the village, and he walked with her through it and to the brow of the hill whence they could look down on the lights shining in Shipley. "Don't come any farther," she said. "I shall be all right. I'll get a train at Shipley, and that'll see me in Manningham in no time."

They did what they rarely did: they shook hands at parting. "It's good work, Arnold," she said, "and I'm glad I'm doing it with you."

He watched till she disappeared into the darkness, then walked rapidly back through the village. Late though it was, he did not go into the house, but went again out on to the moor. He sat upon a boulder with his feet in the ling, lit his pipe and gazed into the darkness where now there were no lights showing anywhere. Surely, surely...Once more his mind was off in pursuit of his inclination. "I'm glad I'm doing it with you."

Surely there was more in that than the words' cold meaning. Surely in the tone of the voice, in the way she had let the words fall and then hurried into the darkness...

He smoked the pipe through, then knocked out the dottle against the boulder and stood up. He spoke her name aloud in the silence, as though it were part of the beauty, the healing, about him. "Ann," he said. It sounded like no other word he had ever spoken. He said it again: "Ann...Ann."

This, then, was the young man Arnold Ryerson, so grave in demeanour, so stiffly and formally dressed, so much in appearance like a decent mechanic, who, on an October morning in 1889 felt his heart lift when he entered the breakfast room at Ackroyd Park and Ann said: "Aunt Lizzie isn't coming down to breakfast."

He had screwed up his courage to say so much to Ann, and that was why, first of all, he had better say something non-committal, something negligible. "Oh, Ann," he said, "you remember that boy Hamer Shawcross? I got a letter from him this morning. He's been trotting about the world for years, and now he's back. He's coming over to pay me a visit."

Chapter Eleven

Lizzie Lightowler, unaware that Fate, or Luck, or Providence, or what you will, was about to speak through her mouth, sat up in bed, reading the *Yorkshire Post*. She was not ill; the indomitable creature could not be ill; but she was tired. A hint of a cold gave her an excuse for having breakfast in bed. But she couldn't keep her mind off the affairs of the day; and now, the breakfast tray pushed to one side, she was reading the paper. Suddenly she hauled on the crimson rope suspended above the bed, and a bell jangled in the kitchen. Mrs. Marsden slippered leisurely up to the bedroom. "I want to see Miss Ann – at once," said Lizzie.

"Excuse me, Arnold," Ann said, when the message reached her. "Finish by yourself. I've had all I want." She ran out of the room.

Arnold, too, had had all he wanted. He pushed aside his plate impatiently, went to the window and glowered at the chrysanthemums and Michaelmas daisies blooming against the wall of the disused stable. He glowered, and he also felt hot and uncomfortable, because he believed Ann had run away as though with relief. He had not said a word of all the words he had wanted to say. When it came to the touch, they had stuck in his gullet. But he would have said them, he told himself, beating his fists moodily against his thighs. And Ann, he was sure, had known what was coming. You can always tell, he thought, when someone knows. There had been something between them, passing from his own tongue-tied awkward dumbness to her unusual vivacity – a vivacity which seemed like a lively defence, a warding off. Yes; he was sure she had known what he was going to say. Then there had come that message from Aunt Lizzie, and Ann had fairly bolted from the room.

He returned to the table and gloomily swigged the half cup of coffee he had left there. Then Ann came back. "Arnold," she said, "Aunt Lizzie would like to see you. Henry Thornton's dead."

He followed her up the stairs, and Lizzie called: "Come in, Arnold. You're not afraid to see an old woman in bed, I hope?"

He did not know what was in her mind as she looked, with a scrutiny unusually keen, at this careful steady young man in broadcloth, with the heavy watch-chain, the responsible side-whiskers, entering the room. Her white bobbed hair shone against the dark of the mahogany bed-head. A shawl was round her shoulders. She looked as if she were enjoying her vacation. She gave a half-sigh as her examination of Arnold ended, took the spectacles from her nose and tapped them on the *Yorkshire Post.*

"Well," she said. "Ann has told you, I suppose. It has pleased God to remove the Conservative Member for the St. Swithin's Division."

She waved Arnold to a chair and threw the paper across to him, folded open at the column which said that Henry Thornton, who had represented the St. Swithin's Division time out of mind, had died suddenly in a hansom cab in Pall Mall, London, on his way home from a banquet.

"Overeating," said Lizzie heartlessly. "I always thought that would be the end of him. You couldn't have slipped a knife between his collar and his neck."

"I never saw him," said Arnold.

"I don't suppose you did. He didn't trouble his constituents much. He was at dinner here once when my husband was alive. I couldn't stand him. But that's beside the point. The point is that there'll be an election in the St. Swithin's Division."

"The Liberals have got a prospective candidate – Crossley Hanson," said Arnold, the efficient secretary. "They've been nursing the constituency for years."

"Nursing is the word," Lizzie replied. "Giving it the usual soft pap. What about a bit of solid Labour food for a change?"

"You mean a Labour candidate?" Arnold asked.

"Why not?" Lizzie shot at him.

"They're few and far between, the right sort of people."

"Well – there's you."

So that's it, thought Arnold. That explained the twitter of excitement with which Ann had called him to the room. They had talked this over, and then sent for him. When Aunt Lizzie, long before, had mentioned Parliament in a casual, joking way, the idea had been too remote to take seriously. But here was something practical, immediate. He felt the sweat break out on his body and on the palms of the hands gripping the chair. Parliament was august, incredible. Working men simply did not go there. He knew that theoretically they should. Oh, yes; he himself had preached from his soap-box passionately enough on the representation of the people by the people.

"But – Parliament!" he gasped. "Me!"

"Don't let that worry you," Lizzie said robustly. "You won't get in. But we'll burst into the constituency. We'll make a noise. We'll get a footing there. Then we'll stay on and, to use the lovely word, we'll nurse it. It's only a matter of time. Good heavens! St. Swithin's! I should think ninety voters in a hundred there are working men."

"And hide-bound Tories at that," Ann put in morosely.

"Well, what of it?" Lizzie truculently demanded. "If God can turn apes into men He can turn Tories into Socialists. He just wants time. And now, Arnold, what about this – this – Shawcross boy? Ann says he's coming to see you. Who is he? What's he like? Have I ever met him?"

They began to tell her about Hamer Shawcross. Arnold said he supposed he'd have to put him up in the hut.

The hut was a rare concession from prosaic Arnold to romance. When you had passed through the homely little main street of Baildon out on to the moor, you saw, away to your left, a few rough fields that had been won from the ling and heather. You will see many such in the moorland parts of Yorkshire. The people thereabouts call them intakes.

Crossing the intervening strip of moor one afternoon that autumn, Arnold sat on the wall of the intake – a wall of time – blackened stones, piled and unmortared. Where he sat was the angle of the intake wall, and presently he slipped over it and sat down there with the wall at his back, the green field stretching before him, the blue sky above.

His years in Ancoats, followed by the years in dreary Thursley Road, gave him a heightened sense of the value of the freedom in which he now lived. But even the house on the road to the moor irked him at times. He was not alone there, and he wanted to be alone. The intake was roughly farmed by the husband of the woman with whom he lodged, and from him Arnold got permission to build his hut in the angle of the field.

A great many people got to know of that hut. "Ah, my friends" – this was Hamer Shawcross, M.P., on the housing question – "I have seen you herded in your slums, and what is more I have lived in them with you. I have looked at the houses of the poor with these very eyes of mine in every quarter of the globe. Festering in the heat of the tropics, freezing in the cold and damp of less congenial climes, the poor are shoved away to make what shift they can. At the very moment when I myself was entering upon that Parliamentary struggle for the betterment of the conditions of the people, a struggle into which, as you who know me realize, I have put, and shall put, every ounce of my strength and virtue (cheers) – at that very moment I was condemned to live in a shack, a hovel, with rude winds whistling in at the door, but, thank God, with the clean free sky above me, speaking with the immortal encouragement of the stars."

He could do that sort of thing. No one was quite sure what the last phrase meant, but Hamer Shawcross, riding hell-for-leather on his oratorical mount, didn't give people a chance to think what he meant. He was a very great politician. No doubt that was how, years later, Arnold's simple hut did present itself to his mind; but that was not how it presented itself to Arnold. He was proud of it. He and his landlord built it between them out of odds and ends of timber. They covered the outside with waterproof felt. They put in an old stove whose right-angled chimney-pipe went through a sheet of asbestos which they fixed for safety to the wall, high up. They thought it was a good job, and certainly it was comfortable enough. Let it be celebrated, for it had its part in the history of the Labour Party.

Arnold was entranced when the work was done. He embellished the place. He took an old ladder-back armchair into it, and a table to write at. He rigged a few shelves for books, hung a paraffin lamp from the ceiling, and made sacks do for carpets. Wire netting stretched over a wooden frame and covered by a palliasse served for a bed on those frequent occasions when he had sat there reading till late at night and did not wish to walk back to the house. Out on the moor he had cut peat and had a stack of it against his wall.

It was half fun, a hermit lark; half seriousness, because he did get something out of his solitude. The quiet deeps in the inarticulate fellow were moved and satisfied when he came out at midnight, leaned on the wall, and in the utter silence looked across the moor, stark and elemental under the night. He could never, for the life of him, say any such thing as that the night spoke to him with the immortal encouragement of the stars. He merely felt, puffing stolidly at the last pipe, that this was a good life. Then he turned in, happy, to his palliasse.

"What about this Shawcross boy?" Aunt Lizzie had asked; and Ann, as she walked down to the Exchange Station with Arnold to meet the train from Manchester, had not moved in imagination beyond the point where Shawcross was indeed a boy. She remembered, though not clearly, the birthday party. She remembered sitting down with Birley Artingstall and Arnold and this boy Hamer Shawcross to a Christmas dinner. There was nothing about any of it to prepare her for what she met. Years afterwards, out of the emotional dazzle and confusion of the moment, there was only one thing that she could clearly recapture, and it seemed an incongruous thing. They were all three walking through the echoing subway that led from the station, when Arnold, in his trite way, babbled concerning Hamer's travels: "Well, I suppose, as Pope says, the proper study of mankind is man." And this extraordinary being who had somehow intruded on and smashed in a moment all her preconceptions, this swarthy, moustached giant with the piercing eyes and the ringing voice, who was overtopping them as he strode along with a big wooden box swung up as lightly as a matchbox on his shoulder, gave a great laugh as he slapped Arnold on the back and said: "True, little one; but Pierre Charron said it rather more than a hundred years before Pope."

And yet, she sometimes wondered, was it incongruous? It was so much a part of Hamer, this ability to confound and dazzle by fishing up a piece of knowledge that not one man in a thousand would have. She herself had never heard of Pierre Charron, but then, she asked herself, laughing rather ruefully, who had, except this being who seemed born to sweep women off their feet?

They were going up the steep hill which is Darley Street, and Ann had a feeling that she was having to put her best foot forward in order to keep up with Hamer Shawcross. Uphill, and with a box on his shoulder, but he seemed the quickest of the three. She walked between the two men. Hamer was taller than she was; Arnold was shorter by an inch or so. "It's a long time since I ran a mile every morning," Hamer suddenly said. "This air makes me want to do it. It's good." He breathed deeply. "Better than Manchester air."

"You'd better not run a mile with that box," Arnold warned him.

"It's nothing," said Hamer. "Try it." He put the box down on the pavement and Arnold swung it up to his shoulder, but with difficulty.

"I wouldn't like to carry that far," he said. "What on earth have you got in it?"

Hamer answered, swinging the box back on his shoulder: "A cake for you from your mother. And also all my wordly goods, except my books. I've come for a long stay."

"It's lucky I can put you up," said Arnold. "But Baildon's a goodish way out, you know."

"I do know. We'll take the train to Shipley, then walk up the hill. I can manage that."

"How did you know there was a train to Shipley and a hill to walk up? You've never been here before."

"I am in the habit of consulting maps. Maps, globes, encyclopedias, dictionaries, concordances: learn to use these things, little one. They will serve you well."

Arnold winced. *Little one.* That was the second time. Ann was aware of the almost imperceptible sudden shrinking-in of Arnold upon himself. She was aware, too, of the instantaneous apprehension by Hamer that he had hurt his friend. Hamer stopped and put the box down on the pavement. She thought for a moment he was going to take Arnold's hand and apologize. He did nothing of the sort. He said: "Arnold, this box is more than I bargained for, after all. Could you take a turn?"

Arnold picked up the box and hoisted it to his shoulder – this time apparently without difficulty. "It's not so heavy as all that," he said, and they went on gaily. The box against his face prevented Arnold from seeing the other two. Hamer looked down and sideways at Ann with a conspiring smile, a smile which took her right into his confidence and seemed to say: "I managed that pretty well, didn't I?" And Ann thought to herself: Yes, you did. I can see that you're the sort of man who can manage most things pretty well.

When they had gone a little farther on, Hamer asked: "Why are we coming so hopelessly out of our way? We should have got the train to Shipley in Forster Square." He seemed to have the map of Bradford in his head.

Arnold answered from behind the box: "We can pick up the train at

Manningham. I thought we'd see Miss Artingstall home. The station's not a stone's-throw from her house."

Hamer gave her another smile. So that's it. He'd allow me to lug that box uphill, and now he'll go on lugging it himself, because thereby he gets an extra twenty minutes of this girl's company.

"If we had got in at Forster Square Miss Artingstall could have got out at her station," he said, hoping to see her blush, and being rewarded. A train ride doesn't take so long as a walk.

"It was thoughtless of me," said Ann. Thoughtless was the word. She had been without thought, carried along in the trail of this vivid being who had so unexpectedly answered to the name of "the boy Shawcross." They were turning into Ackroyd Park when she took possession of herself. She suddenly laughed aloud at the absurdity of their proceedings. Why hadn't they taken the train? Or, if not the train, a cab? Or, if they had to walk, why hadn't they left the box and called for it later?

"Really, Arnold," she said, "we've been acting like a couple of mad creatures."

Arnold put down the box and looked as if he hardly saw why, and Hamer said: "I've carried that box miles. Don't let it worry you."

"Well, at all events," said Ann, "now that we *are* here, let's see if old Marsden'll do his best to find us some tea. There are dozens of trains to Shipley. You're not in a hurry, are you?"

"I am not," said Hamer. He picked up the box once more and followed Ann along the path that twisted through the rhododendrons.

Many years later: how many years it was! "Oh, the years, the years!" thought Lizzie: Mrs. Lightowler found herself at a great reception with which Sir Thomas Hannaway was warming his house in Eaton Square. She saw the tall form of Hamer Shawcross, the hale red face, the white hair, going up the stairs before her. When she herself was up, she heard Lady Hannaway – and what a miracle of preservation that woman was! – say to her husband: "I always feel proud, Tommy, that we knew him in Ancoats. It's marvellous to think that he sprang from the people."

Sir Thomas patted Polly's stout arm. "Yes, my dear. And while he was about it, he took care to spring a good long way from 'em."

Lizzie shook hands with her host and hostess, and hurried on, blushing hotly. There was a great deal at that time that she felt she could never forgive Hamer Shawcross. And yet there was so much that she would forgive him seventy times seven. The years, she reflected, as she passed through the boil and bubble of the senseless occasion, were full of him: the years of the country and her own years. Nothing could ever alter that. Let them say what they liked about him: he was a great figure. He filled a place that men would see to be empty when he was gone. There were not many people of whom you could say that.

From the beginning she had loved him, in the way that a woman already heading toward middle-age may love a young man; and from the beginning she had believed in his star and followed it.

He was easily, she thought, the finest-looking man in the room, and Lady Lostwithiel seemed to think so, too. She did not imagine that Lady Lostwithiel would have graced Tom Hannaway's jamboree if she had not known that Hamer would be there. But handsome as he looked, with that Order which he liked to wear sparkling on his shirt front and the dusky red carnation at his buttonhole, this present apparition could not eclipse her memory of the old house in Ackroyd Park and the young Phoebus who had appeared there with Ann and Arnold Ryerson.

Lizzie found herself a seat under the ostentatious palms that Tom Hannaway had got in from some nurseryman. They tickled her neck, but at least they gave her privacy; and she thought of Arnold, who had been so grave and middle-aged-looking that far-off night; so grave still, rather stout and flabby, with heavy purple bags under his eyes, dreaming of nothing but his miners, working for nothing but his miners, whose case seemed so hopelessly doomed and damned. He insisted – it was the sort of honest, useless, dogged gesture he would make – on being with a squad of them singing about the London streets. She had seen him, and Pen with him, too, trudging the Strand, wailing those dolorous, heart-breaking hymns of the Welsh. Her bus had stopped, and the tune floated up – Jesus, Lover of my soul – and there was Arnold holding his blind Pen by the hand, carefully keeping himself on the side of the traffic. She had wanted to run down and throw her arms round them and cry "Oh, my dears! my dears!" but the bus jerked forward, pouring its blue exhaust into the foggy London air, drowning the sad singing; and, anyway, what was the use? One was old, and it was all so long ago.

A famous voice said: "Well, Liz!" and she was all excitement, dropping her bag, stumbling to her feet. Why did one always get up when one talked to him? she wondered. She was an old fool. He bewitched her: shining jewel and dark red flower.

"Lettice, I think you've met Mrs. Lightowler?"

Longer ago than you think, Lizzie thought. When Arnold was fighting St. Swithin's.

"She goes back a long way, don't you, Liz?" said the beautiful voice. He put an arm round her waist and gave her a little squeeze; then he passed on, and she sat down again, thinking that it was a very long way back indeed, and wondering whether he remembered the first thing she had ever said to him.

"Why! I thought you were a boy – something about fourteen, with short trousers and a Lancashire accent."

He didn't smile. He looked hurt. She was soon to learn how touchy he was. He said, with the arrogance that was to develop in him so deeply: "I, too, used to come to conclusions without evidence. There was a street in Manchester that I used to think was like a street in Venice. Now I know that it isn't. I have spent nearly four years travelling the world in order to clear my mind of illusions. And if I have a Lancashire accent, I impart it to four languages in addition to my own."

All this without a smile – quite an oration. Lizzie smiled to herself, but did not allow it to appear. "Oh, Liz," she thought, "you *have* touched raw withers. Sooth him! Sooth him!"

"Oh, dear," she said, "you make me envious. When my husband was alive we travelled a lot, but now I hardly ever get out of England. Do come in now and sit down. It'll be a treat to hear something of what you've been doing and seeing. But first of all, let us have tea."

They went into the drawing-room, where a fire had been lit, and Marsden brought in the tea. Arnold Ryerson said: "I think, you know, Aunt Lizzie, Hamer and I ought to go as soon as we've had tea. It'll take some time to get up to Baildon and settle him in, and then I've got that meeting at Keighley tonight. You're coming, Ann, aren't you?"

The colour rose in Ann's cheeks. "I'd forgotten, Arnold," she said; and, indeed, she had forgotten everything during the last hour. The prospect of seeing Hamer Shawcross depart as soon as he had swallowed a cup of tea, and then of going to Keighley to meet Arnold, seemed suddenly disagreeable. Lizzie was watching the girl closely. "You'd better excuse Ann tonight, Arnold – will you?" she said; and to Hamer's surprise she added: "And you'd better excuse Mr. Shawcross, too. There's no reason at all why he shouldn't stay here tonight and go to Baildon comfortably in the morning. You take the morning off and wait there till he comes. Let me be selfish and have him here tonight for a good long talk."

Arnold looked at the three of them: Lizzie with that authoritative way of hers, that way of settling things for other people; Ann, who was usually so calm and self-possessed, now flushed and confused; Hamer Shawcross standing there with a cup of tea in one hand, the other pushing back the hair from his forehead and looking as if he were weighing up a situation which he knew to be difficult and unusual; and he felt somehow that they were leagued together, leagued against him, that he was outside. There was no need for him to go. He could have stayed for a couple of hours and then caught a train to Keighley; but now he didn't want to stay for a moment longer than he could help. He had not felt so desolate since the day when he stood in the snow outside Artingstall's window and wondered whether he dared to go in and ask for his wages. He swallowed his tea, and said with a desperate effort at brightness: "Well, I must go. I've left my notes in the hut, and there are one or two things I want to look up. I'll look out for you in the morning, Hamer. Good afternoon, Ann. I hope your cold will be well soon, Aunt Lizzie."

As if in contrition, Ann went with him as far as the front door. "Hamer's a bit of a surprise to me," he said. "He's – developed." He added anxiously: "What d'you think of him?"

"Oh, my dear," said Ann, "how can I think anything of a man I've only known for half-an-hour?" and she ran back to the drawing-room with the confusion wiped from her face and her eyes shining.

What were you to make of such a man? Neither she nor Aunt Lizzie had ever come across such energy and force. Before they had finished tea Lizzie had told him of the intention to run a Labour candidate in the St. Swithin's division.

"When are you telling the electors?" he asked. "You should do it tonight."

Lizzie looked up, surprised. "What! With old Thornton not yet in his coffin?"

Hamer put down his cup, stood up before the fire, looking to the seated women immensely tall, and demanded: "What's that got to do with it? Look. The Tories have got all the advantage of having held the seat for years. The Liberals, you say, have a well-oiled organization. You've got nothing. You've got to start from the beginning. Make the beginning now – this very minute."

"What on earth can we do now – this very minute?" Lizzie asked, more amused than impressed. She did not imagine he would have anything practical to offer.

"With your permission we can do this. I will go to town at once and find out who represents the *Yorkshire Post*. That's the paper we want – it's a daily – and we want the news in in the morning. Where is a good open-air pitch in this – this St. Swithin's Division?"

Lizzie began to sit up, and so did Ann. "There's Four Lane Ends," said Ann. "There are always a lot of people about there – and three public-houses."

"You should have a meeting there tonight," said Hamer. "Tell the people that for the first time in the history of the division there is going to be a Labour candidate – and an independent Labour candidate at that, who will vote Labour and nothing but Labour."

"And who's going to address this meeting?"

"I am."

There was silence in the room, save for the purring of the fire. The daylight was nearly gone. Looking back at the moment, Lizzie could always persuade herself that she recognized at once its fateful quality. "I am." There was something as proud as Lucifer in the declaration, something which carried its own conviction. He stood there as straight as a blade, and the firelight shone past him, threw his immense shadow on the wall, and lit up the face of Ann, looking up at him with wonder and delight.

Suddenly Lizzie thought to herself: "Poor Arnold!" and aloud she said: "You carry a woman away!"

"Don't you want to be carried away?" he asked. "Well, do you agree? Shall I go and tell the *Yorkshire Post* man that an important announcement about the St. Swithin's Division will be made at eight o'clock at Four Lane Ends? They'll report it. A Labour candidate is news all right."

At last Lizzie smiled. "Go ahead," she said. "I can't resist you. But will you have time to make notes for a speech?"

"Notes? I shan't need notes."

"What will you talk about?"

He walked out into the hall where his box lay, hastily undid the straps, and came back carrying a leather scabbard attached to a belt. He drew out a sabre whose cold steel flashed in the firelight. "This," he said. "This is the text and the sermon both. I shall talk about this."

"But your cold, Aunt Lizzie! Do you think you ought to go?"

"Don't be a fool, child. You must have seen that I was only pretending. And anyway, what cold could stand against a man like that?"

They were upstairs, putting on their coats. "He certainly is the most extraordinary person," said Ann. "I've never met anyone like him before.

"If I'm any judge, it'll be a long time before you meet anyone like him again."

"I wonder how he speaks? It's no joke addressing an open-air meeting. It can be horrible."

"I don't think you need worry."

"Most speakers make politics so dull."

But this one didn't. "Men of Bradford, I want to talk to you about a murder. I want to appeal to you to help me to deliver criminals to justice."

It was a startling opening. He had borrowed a large box from a shop near by, and he stood upon it where the four roads met. His great height could not be overlooked. A few people gathered round, but he did not begin until there were more than a few. He did not despise mountebank tricks. He drew the sabre from its scabbard, whirled it round his head, and then stood patiently till this unusual exhibition had collected all who were within sight. Then he began: "I want to talk to you about a murder. I want to appeal to you to help me to deliver criminals to justice. In 1819 this sabre cut down a young and innocent woman. It was a lovely June day. Bands were playing, flags were flying, the people of your neighbouring town of Manchester were making holiday."

He told the story of Peterloo. Ann and Lizzie, standing by the box, were like children fascinated by the power of a born story-teller. They were so absorbed, listening to a voice whose range of emotion was to make it famous, that they scarcely noticed the crowd as enthralled as themselves. They saw the girl Emma setting off with her tall young lover, they heard the horrid hiss of steel through the air, they saw the man who was to be the Old Warrior walking distraught from St. Peter's field with the blood-stained ribbon in his pocket and the sabre in his hand. Never, never, thought Ann, had she known an open-air meeting so quiet, so breathlessly hanging upon a speaker's words.

"Ah, my friends, that was murder most foul, but it was murder in daylight, murder aboveboard. Still – this day – in your midst – the same crime is covertly committed. Not with the sword but with subtler weapons. Want and misery are turned loose upon you as the dragoons were turned loose that shameful day. Your life is sapped from you inch by inch instead of in one clean stroke, and those who should be your shepherds, securing for you your share of the rich pastures that clothe the world – these men are keeping you in subjection to those who swig the wine of life and leave you the rinsings of the cup.

"One of these fat shepherds lies dead in London. My heart does not bleed. No, my friends, it rejoices, because now there comes to you the chance to choose again. This time, choose wisely. You are to have what you never have had before, the opportunity to send to Parliament a man of your own class, with hands as hard as yours…"

The *Yorkshire Post* man approached him as he stepped down from the box. "I didn't get your name."

"Shawcross – Hamer Shawcross. I am known as Shawcross of Peterloo."

The three walked back to Ackroyd Park. "Have you often spoken about Peterloo?" Lizzie asked.

"Never before in my life."

"Then where did you get the nickname from?"

"I didn't get it from anywhere. I just thought of it. A nickname helps. I hope it will get into the *Yorkshire Post*. Then you can put it on all the bills."

"We haven't come to bills yet," said Ann.

"No. But we must deal with that tonight." "Tonight!" Lizzie cried. "It's ten o'clock."

"You must get something into the printer's hands first thing in the morning," said Hamer. "I can distribute them in the constituency in the evening."

They turned out of Manningham Lane and walked down toward the house. "It looks as though Arnold is going to wake up and find the election won," said Ann.

"Not a bit of it," said Hamer. "But I want the Liberals and Tories to wake up and find we're there."

They went up to the study on the first floor. Lizzie began to make tea, but Hamer did not wait for tea. "Do you mind if I rough something out?" he said, and sat down at the writing-table.

Presently Ann put a cup of tea at his elbow. He went on writing, drank the tea at one gulp when it was cold, and said: "How's this?" He began to read:

"There's an old Yorkshire saying 'If tha does owt for nowt, do it for thisen.' You Yorkshiremen of the St. Swithin's Division of Bradford have been doing something for nowt for a long time, and you haven't been doing it for yourselves. You've got votes and you've been giving them away for nothing to Liberals and Tories. It has not been your fault. You have had to choose between two evils. If you do it again, it *will* be your fault, because you are going to have a chance to vote for a man of your own class who will go to Parliament to work for your class. You will be told that this is a bad thing to do: no man should think of class: he should think of his country.

"What is your country? Is it the land? Who owns the land? Liberals and Tories.

"Is it the coal and iron under the land? Who owns that? Liberals and Tories.

"Is it the houses on the land? Who gets the rent for them? Liberals and Tories.

"Is it the money in the banks? Who gets the interest on it? Liberals and Tories.

"Is it the jobs by which men live? Who owns the mills and factories, the warehouses and workshops, the ships, forges, railways and mines wherein the jobs are done? Liberals and Tories.

"What then is this country that you are told to consider *your* country? What part of it did you inherit from your father? What part of it will you bequeath to your son? You did not inherit even the certainty of being permitted to earn a living. The bosses who make up what are called the two great historic parties could turn you out with a snap of the fingers. You may be able to bequeath this certainty to your son if you support a man who goes to Parliament with the intention of fighting for the working class.

"Men of the St. Swithin's Division! Labour is in the field. The name of YOUR candidate will be announced in due course.

> "Shake your chains to earth like dew.
> You are many; they are few."

The committee of three approved this pronouncement. It was eleven o'clock. Lizzie rose. "I think now—" she began.

"One moment," said Hamer. "We musn't let the grass grow under our feet." He paced up and down, a hand in his hair.

Lizzie sank back into her chair with a laugh. "I thought we'd trodden the earth threadbare," she said.

"Not a bit of it. Now let's make notes of things to be done. If you want speaking in halls, book your halls at once. As soon as the opposition wakes up, they'll try to spike you."

"That's true enough," said Lizzie. "Ann, make a note of that."

"And you'll want committee rooms. Book them tomorrow." Ann made a note.

"Speakers. Get hold of all the local talent, and some that's not so local. Write to them at once, or you'll find they're booked up. You ought to get that man Keir Hardie down from Scotland."

"I think we could," said Lizzie. "We'll try. Anything else?"

"Workers. We'll want dozens – scores if we can get them. Put down any names you can think of to begin with."

Ann put down a few names. Among them was the name of Pen Muff. Then at last Hamer got up. "I think we could go to bed now," he said.

Lizzie twinkled. "May we?" she said. She was liking this starry dynamo immensely.

Ann came down to breakfast early. It was a glorious day. She threw up the windows to let its autumnal astringency flow into her lungs. She was exhilarated, filled with excitement at the many things to be done. She had slept well, but sleep had not banished the sense of urgency that Hamer Shawcross had instilled into her last night. He was like this day, she thought, as she breathed deeply of the air that was faintly frosted. It was a day that made you want to stir yourself, face up to something, defeat something.

Old Marsden came in with the coffee-pot. "Is Mr. Shawcross up yet?" she asked.

"Up!" the old man grumbled. "He was up before I was. When I came down, there he was stuffing things into that box of his. I give him a cup o' tea, and off he went. He left this note."

She took the note to the window. "Dear Miss Artingstall – I think I'd better be off to see Arnold. He knows nothing of what we've done, and I want to galvanize him. My thanks and apologies to your aunt. Remember, all we decided to do is urgent and important. Shawcross of Peterloo."

She was disappointed. But what did you expect, you fool? she asked herself. And yet, the note seemed a part of the man. Galvanize…urgent…important. The three words were like fragments of his personality left behind. And, after all, the note *was* addressed to her, not to Aunt Lizzie. She folded it, and laid it beside her plate. Later on, when Lizzie had read it, smiling – "Can't you see him striding past the Malt Shovel with that box on his shoulder?" – she put it away in her writing-table.

On the way up to Baildon, Hamer bought a copy of the *Yorkshire Post*. This would let Arnold see how people had been working for him while he slept! The two young men breakfasted together in Arnold's room looking upon the village street. No sooner was the first mouthful of tea drunk than Hamer opened the paper. He would not have been surprised to see "Shawcross of Peterloo" at the head of a column. He saw nothing of the sort. He saw a column sedately headed "The Late Mr. Henry Thornton, M.P." First of all there was a "Tribute from a fellow Member" half a column long. Then there was this announcement: "It is not improbable that, when the question of a successor to the late Member arises, the St. Swithin's Divisional Conservative Association will consider the name of Viscount Liskeard, the heir to the Earl of Lostwithiel."

Tucked away in ignominious obscurity below this was a further paragraph. "An open-air speaker named Hamer Shawcross announced in the constituency last night that a Labour candidate would be put into the field, pledged to independence of either the Conservative or the Liberal party. There has never been any Labour organization in St. Swithin's, and it is not known who would provide the funds for such a candidature, or whether Mr. Shawcross had any warrant for the announcement he made."

Hamer swallowed his disappointment. All that lovely stuff about Peterloo! Not a word of it. Not even a mention of the nickname he had invented for himself. "Well, Arnold," he said, "you're going to lose this election. They're putting up one of the nobs – Lord Liskeard. The British working-man loves being represented by a lord."

"Liskeard?" said Arnold. "That's Lostwithiel's son."

"Right!" Hamer answered. "And you and I know something about Lostwithiel. Remember old Suddaby?"

"I do. He introduced me once to Friedrich Engels."

"He did more than that for me. He introduced me to thinking. He taught me where Lostwithiel and his like stand in relation to me and my like. Little one, when I came to Bradford I had no idea that I was stepping into anything like this. You must let me stay and see this through."

"If you can help, I shall be delighted," said Arnold.

"I'll help. I've begun helping. I spoke in your constituency – *your* constituency, my boy – last night. And this," he went on before the astonished Arnold could speak, "this – slapping the *Yorkshire Post*" – this is all they think I'm worth." His disappointment and anger broke out now. "But they shall see! Liskeard! Well, I've had the privilege of paying five shillings a week for years for one of Liskeard's father's hovels—"

"Your stepfather did, and your mother," Arnold put in dispassionately.

Hamer had risen from the table and was striding about the room excitedly. "It's the same thing, isn't it?" he cried, quite persuaded in his heart that Lord Lostwithiel had for years bled him white.

"And hovels?" said Arnold. "They're nice little houses, really."

Hamer stopped, and brought his fist banging on to the table. "Who's winning this election?" he demanded. "You or I?"

"Very well, then," he went on, when Arnold merely shrugged, "let me go about it in my own way. Can't you see this fellow is delivered into our hands?"

"Is he?" said Arnold, impassively buttering a piece of bread. "I'm not so sure of that. I've done a lot of work up and down these parts during the last couple of years. To get one man to see reason takes as much effort as to shift a ton of bricks from here to yonder."

"Reason! Reason!" Hamer cried. "You don't want 'em to see reason. You want 'em to see visions. They won't know what they're seeing when I've done with 'em. The point is, they'll vote for you. That's all that matters."

"I shouldn't have thought so," said Arnold.

He slowly finished drinking his cup of tea, then looked at this strange friend of his who had come back so different from the boy he had known. He looked at the fingers, drumming impatiently on the window-sill, at the flushed, impatient face, caught by the morning light falling through the panes. He thought to himself: "You're not one of us. There's something about you – I don't know what it is – but it's not the stuff we're made of – myself, and Pen Muff, and all the people we work with. You'll use us and them. 'They'll vote for you. That's all that matters.' That's it. That's all that matters – to you. You're honest, insofar as you believe what you're saying when you say it, and when you deceive us you'll be able to explain it to yourself, satisfactorily."

That is what Arnold would have said to himself if he had been able to crystallize and formulate the vague uneasiness that troubled his mind as he looked at Hamer.

Suddenly, Hamer wheeled round from the window and said: "You'll say next, in the fine sporting English tradition: 'I want a clean fight.'"

"So I do."

"My God! I'll bet Goliath didn't think it a clean fight when David did him in with a pebble. That was against all the rules of the good old ironclad. We'll have to think of a few tricks like that. For one thing, I want to gaze on the Lostwithiel home. It's not far from here, is it?"

"We can walk it in a couple of hours."

"Good. Let's start. I want a sense of contrast: Broadbent Street and—"

"Castle Hereward."

"That's it. Broadbent Street and Castle Hereward. We can get something telling out of that."

"First of all, we'd better get your box round to the hut. That's where you're staying."

Hamer could not but feel something cautious, something grudging and reserved, in Arnold's attitude. Arnold himself was perhaps unaware that this was mixed up in the bottom of his mind with

Ann Artingstall's backing out of the engagement to go with him to Keighley, and with his knowledge that she and Lizzie had, after all, been be-glamoured into going with Hamer to Four Lane Ends. It was this which troubled him, which caused him to see Hamer as an unconscious deceiver, one who swept people off their feet for his own purposes. Hamer was more aware of this mist between them than Arnold was. He turned now to Arnold with a face lit by friendship. "Think of it, Arnold," he said. "Broadbent Street, Old Suddaby, Birley Artingstall, those class-meetings with my father – we've had all that together. You and I are almost cut out of the same chunk of wood. There's been a break this last few years, but now it's beginning all over again. We've still got a lot to do together, you and I. I'm glad of that. It would help me to know that you were glad, too."

Arnold looked at the appealing face, the outstretched hand. He could not doubt so candid an approach. "Why, of course, Hamer," he said, taking the hand. "And our mothers still living together."

"Yes," said Hamer. "There's that, too."

Each took a handle of the box, and they carried it across the ling to the hut in the intake.

The sensation of the Royal Academy that year was Sargent's portrait: "Lady Lettice Melland, youngest daughter of the Earl of Dunford." Lettice Melland was twenty-three at that time. Hamer Shawcross, who in his later years collected a few pictures for his house in Half Moon Street, used to say that this was the only Sargent he would like to have. But it was beyond his purse, and anyway it was never in the market. He stood looking at it once in Lostwithiel's house, and said to Lettice: "That is how you were the first time I set eyes on you."

He had come across the moors with Arnold Ryerson, that day when he had first walked out to Baildon and they had carried the box to the hut between them. They were away before ten in the morning to gratify his whim to look upon Castle Hereward. They crossed the road to Dick Hudson's, where, on a winter day long before, Ann and Lizzie had eaten a memorable tea, and then they climbed the rough escarpment of the rock and heather that took them on to Ilkley Moor. On that tumbled and elemental height they felt on top of the world. There was nothing to be seen but the sky above them and the rusty brown of the bracken and purple of the heather about them. The sky never became a clear blue; autumn had breathed into the air, so that whether they looked upward or forward there was a gauze between them and clarity. The larks were numberless, but they were soon out of sight. In no time at all, heaven seemed to open to receive them.

They had nothing to say to one another as they strode forward, the winy air singing in their veins, their feet tramping the path that twisted in and out, hampered with tough heather roots and stones that were polished by the feet that had gone this way immemorially. Now and then their passing put up the grouse that went on heavy wings and with a startled chatter deeper into the moor.

Presently they looked down on Ilkley, neat and prim in its valley, with the charming Wharfe flowing through it, and beyond Ilkley they climbed again.

"Another ridge or two," said Arnold, "and we'll see it."

"See what?" Hamer asked.

"What we've come to see: Castle Hereward."

"Oh that! Good Lord! Let 'em keep it. I'd forgotten all about Castle Hereward. I was enjoying myself. All this, Arnold" – he flung his arms wide, embracing earth and air – "this is anybody's, This is ours. They can't take this from us."

Arnold grinned. "Spoken like a Shelley, Hamer," he said. "But *don't* be too certain. Can you hear the guns?" They listened, and heard them clearly. "And I don't like the look of this chap. It seems to me we left the path some time ago."

The path was clearly in the mind of this chap who was now rapidly approaching. "Now then, you two!" he shouted from a distance. "You're disturbing the birds. Get out of it. Get back on to the path, and keep moving on it."

Arnold turned obediently, but Hamer flushed suddenly a wild red and stood where he was. The man, a keeper with a gun under his arm, came up blustering. Hamer overtopped him by half-a-dozen inches. "Is that how you usually speak to people?" he demanded, dangerously quiet.

"It's how I'm speaking to you. Get out."

"Why should I get out?"

"Because you're trespassing."

"Then you'd better prosecute me and recover the cost of any damage I've done. Isn't that the legal procedure with trespassers?"

"Oh, a blooming lawyer! Get out, Mr. Lawyer, or I'll show you what our usual procedure is. These are Lord Lostwithiel's grouse moors, and I'm keeping the likes of you off 'em. Hop it."

"Come on," Arnold interceded. "We might as well get back to the path." He looked at Hamer's face, and saw that he was flaming with rage.

"Do you think I'm going to hop and skip because I hear this God Almighty Lord Lostwithiel's name?" he demanded. "I'll get back to the path in my own good time and in my own good way, and this dirty little hired scut with a gun can do what he likes about it."

"I'll pepper your backside with shot; that's one thing I'll do," the keeper threatened, himself now roused; and he raised his gun. This was not three feet away. Hamer strode forward, and with a swift and unexpected blow he knocked up the barrel and the gun flew from the keeper's hand. Hamer picked it up, pointed it into the air, and fired both barrels. Then, holding it by the barrels, he whirled it round his head and brought it smashing down on a rock.

"What do you do now?" he asked quietly.

For answer, the man flew at him. Never in his long career of jack-in-office had he been so treated. He, the trusty henchman of nobility, the guardian of the moor on which at that very moment, he knew, a prince of the blood was helping his master to slaughter grouse: *he*, defied and humiliated by a lout strolled out from the town! He flew upon Hamer like something loosed from a bow.

What should he know of all that boxing in an Ancoats bone-yard, or of the rough-and-tumble life that for years by land and sea had toughened the man before him and educated him in the use of his strength?

Hamer held him off for a moment almost playfully with one hand. "Listen, weasel," he said. "Listen, big boss who keeps people from breathing God's own air. I was enjoying the morning till I met you. You've annoyed me and upset me, but you've still got a chance to hook it."

"Me! Me hook it!" the man gasped. "I'll show you who hooks it off these moors."

He tried to come in again with flailing arms. Hamer let him come close, seized him by the body, and whirled him upside down. A thread of water dribbled nearby into a marshy hollow. Holding the man by the feet, Hamer dipped his head in the oozing pool – one, twice, three times. Then he dropped him. "I hope that's cooled you down," he said. "*Sic semper tyrannis*, if you know what that means."

A clatter of loose stones caused him, panting from the gigantic exertion he had put forth, and Arnold, white and apprehensive, to swing round simultaneously. A girl sitting sideways on a rough pony had reined up. Arnold removed his hat. Hamer, whose hat had whirled from his head in the struggle and whose tie was flying behind his ears, bowed stiffly. The girl ignored them both. She was dressed in tweeds and heavy shoes. She was very fair, with blue eyes and a complexion of what they liked to call in those days milk and roses. The fight had taken place in a little hollow. She had reined in on the edge of it, so that they looked up at her outlined against the vast blue of the sky. For all her loveliness, she looked as cold as ice; for all her youth, she seemed as hard as steel.

"Haslett, get up," she said. "You look disgusting wallowing there."

The keeper scrambled to his feet, his fingers wringing the ooze from his face. "I'm sorry, my lady. It was these men, my lady—"

Hamer intervened sharply. "It was not these men. It was this man." He lightly touched himself on the breast. "I assaulted this fellow because he was truculent and offensive. I dislike truculent jacks-in-office very much. If he wishes to do anything about it, he can have my name and address."

The girl looked at him coldly. "It is fortunate for you," she said, "that circumstances make it inexpedient to do anything about it."

Hamer was not aware what this meant: that the presence of a prince of the blood, popping away at the grouse less than a mile off, was incompatible with Lord Lostwithiel's troubling himself with common brawlers. He bowed again.

"You'd better get away and make yourself decent as quickly as you can, Haslett," she resumed, speaking as from a throne. "It was fortunate for you that a headache was causing me to ride back to the house. I came here because I heard shots. I didn't expect to hear shots here."

That was all she had to say. Her heel punched the pony's barrel, and he started forward. Hamer and Arnold stood aside as she bore straight down upon them without looking at them. She leaned slightly forward and with a switch she carried pushed Hamer's hat aside as though it might contaminate the pony's feet. In a moment she was gone.

"Thank you, Haslett," said Hamer, putting on his hat. "That was worth seeing."

The man looked up scowlingly from an examination of his broken gun. "Hop it, you bloody swine," he muttered. "And thank your Gawd it was Lady Lettice."

They found the path and went on. Ahead of them they could see Lady Lettice jogging along on the pony. "Lady Lettice who or what?" Hamer asked.

"That'll be Lady Lettice Melland," Arnold answered. "She's a daughter of the Earl of Durnford, and she's engaged to Lord Lostwithiel's son, Viscount Liskeard. I read about it in the *Yorkshire Post* last week. There's a whole mob of 'em at Castle Hereward for the shooting."

"Just a visitor, eh?" said Hamer. "And she told that keeper his business as if she were at least the owner of his soul."

"I expect she's like that. Some people are," Arnold replied. "And anyway, she will be one day."

"Yes," said Hamer. "The earth is the Lord's and the fullness thereof, and seeing that she's marrying the lord's son, it'll all be hers some day. Well, give me her damned supercilious sniff down the nose rather than Mr. Haslett's line of approach. I expect we shall see more of her, Arnold. I wonder what she would have thought if she'd known that one of the clods trembling before her cold patrician glance was going to have the nerve to say to the yeoman of St. Swithin's: 'Don't choose Liskeard. Choose me.'"

He slapped Arnold on the back as a rise of land showed them the house they had come to see. There could be no mistaking it: this must be Castle Hereward. "You are living in great days, my boy. Behold, you puny David, there stands Goliath. Sound a horn. Beat a drum. Fire a rocket. Do something. Castle Hereward. There it has been since Domesday, running us, ruining us, milking us, arranging the wars we should fight in and the dens we should live and die in. It's formidable, it's terrific; but we've challenged it, and we've won the first symbolic round. In the person of the armed flunkey, who says 'Keep off' it has received a punch on the nose, and we've got away with it."

Arnold was not so exuberant. The path went narrowly between two rocks before winding down to the valley in which Castle Hereward stood. Arnold sat at the foot of one of the rocks, leaning against it, looking at the great house. "That's been there a long time," he said. "It'll take some shifting."

The house lay the best part of a mile away. The land slipped down at their feet, a declivity of undulating purple, then, in the valley bottom, it flattened out into delicious green with the silver of the small river Hereward threaded through it. Beyond the river the green stretched backward, flat as a baize table supporting the gorgeous toy which was what, at that distance, the house seemed. The autumn sun winked in its windows; into the autumn air its innumerable chimneys gently exhaled blue spirals of smoke that soon were one with the blue sky. It was a building of vast irregular masses which had piled themselves together through the years, achieving a haphazard and careless beauty that brought turrets and chimneys, parapets and crenellations, towers, oriels and gables into a harmony that seemed to sing there on the greensward, between the shining river and the woods that climbed behind the house in a rich confusion of reds and browns and yellows to complete the picture with their fagged rock-infested line drawn across the mild blue of the October sky.

It looked as insubstantial as a dream, and Hamer knew that it was as strong as hell.

"Well, there it is," he said. "That's it."

"Yes, that's it," Arnold answered. He puffed at his pipe, watching the diminished shape of Lady Lettice Melland on her pony passing over a little humpbacked bridge that spanned the Hereward. "You came to see it. What do you think of it? It frightens me."

Hamer stood erect behind his sitting friend, and he glared down at the house. "Don't let it," he said. "See it as it is. Remember that it's made up of innumerable five shillingses drawn from innumerable houses in innumerable Broadbent Streets, and of royalties out of pits where men like you and me and our fathers sweat, and out of Darkie Cheap's bone-yard and the beer they drink in the Lostwithiel Arms. No, Arnold; don't let it frighten you. It's resting on our backs. It'll tremble when we stir. It'll crash when we stand upright."

Arnold allowed himself a wan smile. "That would go down well at a meeting," he said.

"Trust me," Hamer answered. "I don't waste my stuff."

He drew a breath of the invigorating air deep down into his lungs, and continued to stare almost with a mingling of love and hate at the mighty house. In the midst of the central group of buildings there was a great apse of glass, split up by the shafts of what he knew must be tall stone mullions. His fancy played with the immense hall, soaring up to a high roof, that lay behind that pile of windows, with the light quivering upon the floor in green and crimson stains where it had filtered through heraldic glass. "With it all," he said, "it's glorious." And added, to Arnold's amazement: "I sometimes wonder who my father was."

Those who in later years thought that Hamer Shawcross's oratory was worth analysis divided it into three phases. There was what they called the St. Swithin's period to begin with. It lasted long beyond the time of the St. Swithin's by-election, but it was that election which made the method known, and seeing that it turned out to be a famous election, as we shall presently discover, its name became a label for the early Shawcross oratory. Even after Hamer had been elected to Parliament and had said something frank on the floor of the House, a Tory member shouted across at him: "We want no St. Swithin's here." Hamer replied: "I readily understand that the honourable Member wants no saints here of any description. He is content to snore eternally in the company of those publicans and sinners, and occasional political harlots, who have contrived to make this House nothing but a shed for sheep-shearing."

That, in itself, was not a bad example of the rude hostility of speech that people were calling "St. Swithin's." It caused Hamer to be suspended from the sittings of the House, which was what he had wanted it to do. The most brilliant speech might pass unheeded: a suspension was always reported.

The second phase was the stateman's, clouding issues in rosy verbosity; and the third was the practised windbag's, the unending garrulity of a man who had always talked too much, who could not stop talking, and who could not himself have winnowed a peck of sense from the chaff with which he littered the floor.

But now he was young and eager, striding bright-eyed into his first arena. He was magnificent; he was inspiring; and he was nobody at all. He had not even invented the crude advertisement of "St. Swithin's." He was Hamer Shawcross, distributing handbills on an autumn night in the streets of a poor Bradford quarter, with Ann Artingstall walking on one side of him and Pen Muff on the other.

It would have suited Arnold Ryerson to join them that night, but he was not permitted to do so. He was worried and shaken: so much had happened in so short a time. Yesterday morning he had come pelting down from Baildon, feeling irresistible, convinced that, given the opportunity, he could ask Ann Artingstall to be his wife. A regular avalanche of events had swept upon him since then. He was to stand for Parliament; Hamer Shawcross had arrived; machinery had been set in motion all around him; and he, who prided himself on having a cool organizing brain, found that things were being done with no coolness at all, indeed with heat and dispatch, and yet as effectually as he could have done them himself. Worst of all, Ann seemed to be caught up and to be spinning in this vortex of energy with such momentum that he felt she would have no ear for the personal matters that were burning in his heart.

When he and Hamer turned at last from their contemplation of Castle Hereward he hurried into Ilkley and took train to Bradford. Hamer walked back to the hut. "I'll be at Ackroyd Park tonight," he said. "I've promised to distribute some bills."

It was a dullish afternoon for Arnold and Lizzie and Ann. They worked hard in Lizzie's study, writing letters, codifying information they would need for their campaign, studying a collection of the late member's speeches which Lizzie had carefully preserved and which would enable them to make a pretty contrast of his promises and performances. Tea was brought up to them, and they worked on. Towards seven o'clock Lizzie said: "I hope Mr. Shawcross will get here in time for dinner."

"Oh, surely he will!" Ann cried, on such a note of anxiety that Arnold could not bear to look at her face. He buried his head in his work, and said: "There's nothing for him to eat up there, anyway."

"At all events," said Ann, "I'd better go with him when he takes the bills. I must have some air and exercise."

"There's no reason why we shouldn't all go," Arnold volunteered eagerly. "We'll get the job done in no time."

But Lizzie quashed that. "Sorry, Arnold. There's too much to do here. You and I will have to stay." He looked crestfallen, and she added: "It's a shame, I know; and since you're to be the candidate, we'll have to take all this detail off your shoulders as soon as we can. But in the meantime, do you mind?"

What could he say? Nothing. And what could he do when both the women started up involuntarily, with brightened faces, on hearing

Hamer Shawcross's voice ringing out in the hall? Nothing at all. He smiled palely. "The moorland air seems good for Hamer's lungs," he said.

They all three stood, listening to Hamer's and old Marsden's voices downstairs. Suddenly there was a loud cackle of laughter. The women looked at one another almost in consternation. "I haven't heard Marsden laugh," said Lizzie, "since the day when we ran out of coal and every pipe in the house was frozen."

Marsden showed Hamer into the room, and when the door was shut Lizzie said: "You seem to have amused Marsden. It isn't easy."

"Oh, I was just telling him how to conquer women, with especial reference to a Miss Pen Muff. You remember her? She was on the list of possible workers that we drew up last night."

"I remember her all right," said Ann. "But I'm surprised that you do."

"I kept a copy of the list, and I went along to see her after writing my article."

"Article?" Lizzie asked.

"Yes. It occurred to me at the hut that I've got to live, so I wrote an article called 'We Shall Fight St. Swithin's – and Why.' I've posted it to London – to the *Morning Courier*. It's a Liberal paper, I know, but more sympathetic to Labour than any other. It ends with a couple of phrases that Arnold knows: 'Like a great castle, built stone by stone through the centuries, reaction looks solid and threatening. But we, the workers, know that it's resting on our backs. It will tremble when we stir. It will crash when we stand upright.' I've been to town to post it, and I called on Pen Muff on the way here. She doesn't like you. She doesn't like any of you. She hates your clothes, and she hates your bathroom, and she hates the way you ride home from Socialist meetings in stately carriages."

He gave Arnold a knowing smile. "But she loves our candidate," he said. "For him, she would wear a red cap, she would storm Bastilles, she would throw up barricades and fight behind them." He held up a quelling hand as Arnold started to his feet. "No, no! There have been no inquisitions and no confessions. All this I gather merely from a few tones of the voices, a few flashes of the eye. They were enough to convince me that Miss Muff's objections were not deeply founded, and that we could make her a good worker. She is going to join us tonight in the bill distribution."

"And how did you persuade her?" Lizzie asked. "I have always found her a difficult young woman – very obstinate, though full of the right stuff."

"I led her on with votes for women," said Hamer. "I persuaded her that neither the Liberals nor the Tories will ever give women votes, but that Labour is likely to be sympathetic. I drew her a picture of a wonderful world, with women voters, women Members of Parliament, women in all the professions, stopping wars, giving baths to everyone – you know."

There was something in the way he spoke those words "you know" that produced a moment's consternation. "But I *believe* all this," said Lizzie at last. "Do you mean you were telling Pen Muff these things with your tongue in your cheek? Supposing *you* were a Labour member. Wouldn't *you* work for that?"

Hamer saw that he had stepped into a morass. He recovered adroitly. Standing before the fire, he looked down at the others, smiling with all the power of his charm. "Votes for women," he said judiciously, "is one of the things I haven't gone into as thoroughly as they deserve. I shall not commit myself on the strength of vague talk and imperfect examination. It is likely that when I have time to go into the matter I shall reach your own conclusion. In the meantime, I believe so much in the Labour cause that I am ready to use any means" – the smile left his face and he looked intense end impressive – "*any* means to induce people to work for us. If I can do it by preaching a doctrine accepted by people like you, whose opinion I respect, isn't that common sense?"

His hand went straying through his hair. He looked a little uneasy till the two women's faces cleared. He did not notice that Arnold Ryerson's face remained perplexed. Arnold could see him standing that morning in the house at Baildon. "You don't want 'em to see reason. You want 'em to see visions." So it succeeded, the emotional bluff, even with a hard-headed girl like Pen. "I don't see," said Arnold, "much mirth for Marsden in all this."

"Oh, well," Hamer answered, "I was just fooling him generally with a picture of a woman's world."

Among the spoilt papers on polling-day there were seven which may be said to have ended Arnold Ryerson's ambitions as a candidate for Parliament. "These are interesting, Mr. Ryerson," one of the officials conducting the count said to him, and handed him the seven spoilt papers. There were the three candidates' names: Liskeard, Hanson, Ryerson. On these seven papers the name Ryerson had been crossed out and the name Shawcross written in, with the voter's mark against it. "He's our man. He's the man we *want* to vote for," these papers mutely cried; and Pen Muff, who was standing there with Arnold in the room full of excited people and buzzing gas flames, felt him wince, saw him look across at Hamer, whose bright excited face, with the hair falling down the forehead, was the most vital thing there; and she took his arm and led him aside, whispering: "Don't let that hurt you, Arnie. You mustn't – see!" – shaking him a little. "Promise me you won't."

He smiled and gave her arm a little squeeze. "That's all right, Pen. And give him his due, it's been his election. He'll sit for this seat some day. He's stolen my thunder. Well," he amended modestly, "he's introduced thunder where I would have rattled a can. There's something grand about him."

Pen wouldn't have it. "Grand my foot! Look at him posing. Look at him showing that Melland piece what a grand profile he's got."

"Don't you believe it, Pen. There's only one woman for Hamer and he can have her any time he wants her."

Pen looked at Ann Artingstall, breathlessly watching with all the others the papers pile up. Lostwithiel had come to be present at his son's entry into Parliament. He had (and need have) no doubt it would be that. He and Liskeard and Lettice Melland made an aloof collected trio; Ann, Lizzie and Hamer a trio by no means collected. Ann's face was almost strained with the excitement of the moment. She had forgotten the candidate; it was to Hamer's face that from time to time she occasionally lifted her eyes in a swift anxious smile.

"You were rather interested in her yourself at one time, weren't you, Arnie?" Pen asked.

Arnold had learned a lot about Pen Muff during the bitter weeks of the struggle. He did not have to blush and stammer with her now. "Yes, I was," he said. "But she'd never do as a failure's wife."

Pen turned on him roundly. "What do you mean – failure!" she cried hotly.

"I'm not going to win this election, you know," he said quietly. "I'm the loser here. It'll always be like that with me. Don't have any illusions about me, Pen old dear. I'm not a winner. Winning isn't my style."

She was annoyed into her roughest speech. "Don't talk like a daft old fooil," she said. "Tha's lost nowt yet, and onny road remember this: tha's not lost as long as tha's still fightin', and by heck! if tha weds me, tha'll have to fight till thi dyin' day."

Her sharp pale face fronted him aggressively, and he felt a warm surge of affection flowing about his heart. It was not the nameless ecstasy he had experienced when, on his favourite hill, or in the silence of the moor, he had thought of Ann and breathed her name. But it was something that he knew was good and durable – right Bradford cloth, if you like, he thought to himself with an inward smile, jannock stuff that won't wear out in a lifetime. He spoke to her in her own fashion of speech: "I was going to ask thee to take this ring, lass, if I were t'winner."

"Ah don't want thee," Pen said, "because tha'rt a winner. Ah want thee, win or lose, so long as tha'll fight."

"That's a bargain, Pen. Win or lose, for good an' all."

Pen looked about the room, feverish with mounting excitement, thick with tobacco smoke, overheated by the fire blazing in the grate and the gaslight flaring from a score of jets. "There's you and me," she said. "An' there's Hamer Shawcross and the Artingstall girl. An' there's yon Lord Mutton'ead and his piece. That's strange, Arnie" isn't it? Three young couples, all about to be wed. We're all starting from here. An' what different roads we'll go! I wonder what'll become of us all?"

Well, we know now, Pen; and it was to be something strange enough; but this was not the moment for speculation. The counters: were finished; the *bourdon* of talk fell to silence. Old Lostwithiel went on smoking his cigar, refusing to let the moment rattle him; Lord Liskeard, his young sunburnt face working with emotion, could not keep up the aloof pretence. He took Lady Lettice Melland by the arm and went up to the table where Arnold was standing with Hanson, the Liberal candidate, both drawn with excitement.

LISKEARD	7859
RYERSON	6001
HANSON	3213

It was amazing. Liskeard looked for a moment as if he had been struck a blow. Then his face cleared: after all, he *had* won. He glanced round, anxious to do the magnanimous thing. Arnold was standing at his side, but it was as though Liskeard did not see him. He strode towards Hamer Shawcross and took his hand. "You nearly beat us," he said.

Lady Lettice Melland held out her hand, too. She smiled sweetly. "But, after all," she said, "we won. *Sic semper tyrannis*, if you know what that means." He knew all right, and felt gratified that she had remembered.

Now, from the square outside the windows, cheering, booing, hissing and the noisy clatter of rattles told that the result had been made known to the crowd. Lostwithiel, of whom so many fantastic tales were told, Lostwithiel with his hair dyed dull black and the paint faintly touching up his parchment cheeks, and with the eyes that so few men cared to look at glowing like embers beneath his smooth high forehead, Lostwithiel who, it was said, had slept in his coffin every Friday and slept with the coffin under his bed every other day of the week since his wife died twenty-five years before, touched Lord Liskeard on the arm. "Better show yourself, my boy. Come, m'dear," he said to Lettice Melland. "Take my arm."

There was no one else in the room for him. Liskeard might condescend to smile at his Liberal opponent and shake hands with the man who had given him such a jolt, but Lostwithiel – no. He was a fantastic and legendary character. Born in the year before Trafalgar was fought, he could remember cheering at the news of Waterloo. As a boy of twelve, walking with his father in London, he saw the Prince Regent assaulted on his way to open Parliament. He had seen a man hanged for robbing a rabbit warren at Castle Hereward, and another, in a bitter winter, transported for life for cutting firewood from a tree. At fifteen he ceased to be Viscount Liskeard and became the Earl of Lostwithiel. His father's last words to him were that England was going to the devil, and Lostwithiel had believed this all his life. He hourly expected the time when the damned Radicals would not leave him a penny to bless himself with. He had fought in several wars, had shot a man in a duel, had trapped wild animals and found gold in Canada, had sailed round the world before the mast on a clipper, no one knowing that he was not Buck Roberts till the voyage was over, when he knocked the bullying skipper over his own rail into the East India Dock before humping his box and going ashore.

At sixty he married an exquisite child of sixteen, Lady Theodora Loring, youngest daughter of the Duke of Buckhurst. She died nine months later in giving birth to this young Viscount Liskeard who now, with Lostwithiel and Lettice Melland, was advancing to the open window through which the cries of the Yorkshire crowd came in out of the raw night.

After his child-wife's death Lostwithiel ordered his own coffin, set up a racing-stable, and became the most popular man on the turf. His popularity increased with the increase of his fame as a "character." His acceptability to the crowd, paradoxically, was heightened by his outspoken contempt for working people – "the scum," he said, "on which we lilies precariously float." Buck, the name under which he had served as a sailor, stuck to him. Crowds of workmen had been known to stop his four-in-hand when some classic race was near, shouting: "Give us a tip, Buck! What'll win next Friday?" He would shake his fist and yell: "You always want something for nothing. Never mind betting. Work, you— so. Racing isn't for the likes of you." He would drive on amid shouts of "Good old Buck!"

Now, at eighty-five, erect as in his cavalry days, and wearing the fashions of fifty years ago, his life was bound up in young Liskeard whom he had educated with all propriety, and who, he thought, might with luck be able to keep a couple of hundred a year when the damned Radicals had done with the country. At the moment, things were not so bad. Lostwithiel's royalties from South Wales coal-mines alone were worth something like £60,000 a year.

Hamer watched the three pass through the open window on to the balcony. This was Lostwithiel; this – incarnate at last – was the name that old Suddaby and others had dinned into his young ears as the enemy, that which must be defeated. It had seemed easier when it was just a name. This painted old skeleton affected him as Castle Hereward had done. Reluctant admiration tinged his antipathy.

The crowd was yelling for a speech, and Liskeard, no orator, gave them a few words. Then they started shouting: "Buck! Come on, Buck!" and Lostwithiel went to the front of the balcony and flourished his stick at them. "You nearly let him down," he shouted. "What do you mean by it, eh? you damned scoundrels. You'll have to do better than that, you know – much better than that."

But Arnold's supporters now took up the cry. "Get orf it, you old cockatoo. Let's 'ave the Labour man. Ryerson! Ryerson!" And when Arnold had spoken, someone shouted: "Shawcross!" and many voices took it up: "Shawcross! Where's Shawcross?"

The already familiar voice answered, to everyone's surprise from the midst of the crowd. Aware of dramatic values, he had slipped out unseen, and now shouted: "Where should I be except here among my own people? Thank you all a thousand times. This time we shook them. Next time we'll shatter them."

"That's reight, lad!" yelled an enthusiast. "We'd 'ave done it this time if it 'adn't been for t'bloody Liberal. Give Shawcross a shoulder. Shawcross of Peterloo!"

The name had arrived and stuck. He was hoisted aloft, and, high above all heads, he drew the sabre from its scabbard. For a moment before they bore him off in tumult, he could see the figures on the balcony. He could see Lettice Melland holding Liskeard's arm, and Pen Muff holding Arnold's. He flourished the sabre towards Lostwithiel and shouted: *Sic semper tyrannis!* He added: "And that means, boys, St. Swithin's for Labour next time."

That was the end of the fight: the victory to Liskeard, the glory to Hamer Shawcross, who disappeared amid a shine of torches. Lostwithiel watched him vanish round a corner, then turned to his son. "That's the enemy," he said. "That's the man you've got to watch." He waved his stick towards Arnold Ryerson and Hanson. "Never mind those two. They don't matter," he said in his penetrating grating voice. "But that other chap" – he wouldn't utter the hated name – it's a pity we didn't run him down. He's the one that'll lead the workers astray. Workers! What are they coming to these days? They're losing their guts. There was a time when hanging didn't frighten 'em. Now you can't sack 'em without their running to a union. The country's going soft. Come on. I want a drink."

They took him to the big railway hotel and left him in his room with a fire burning, a cigar in his fingers and a brandy-bottle on the table. "Get to bed," he said, "the pair of you. Lettie, come here. Give us a kiss. That's better. And look after him. He's got to *do* something. My father was in the government, and he'd better be, too. His mother would have liked that. She'd have been forty-three. Did you know that, Lettie? Forty-three if she was alive today. Run along now."

Lettice put a cushion behind his back, pulled the table nearer to his hand, and kissed him again on the high white forehead. She hated kissing his painted cheeks. Then they left him.

As soon as they were gone he pulled the cushion from behind his back and hurled it across the room, knocking over a spindle-shanked table. He took a comforting draught of brandy. Brandy was the stuff in all emergencies. It was the Prince Regent's tipple. "Harris, pray bring me a glass of brandy. I am not well." That was what the Regent said when he first saw Caroline, the blowsy German wench they had brought over to marry him. It went the rounds. He remembered his father coming home and telling the story with a chuckle. Yes, he remembered that and he remembered a lot more. He could remember Farmer George dying and the Regent becoming King, and old Silly Billy becoming King after him. He was already in his thirties when little Victoria came to the throne, and now there she was, a fat pop-eyed widow playing the deuce with the Prince of Wales, a decent feller who had just been shooting at Castle Hereward.

He remembered all that, and he remembered that right along the line there had been trouble, trouble, trouble. It was only by a fluke, b'God, that there was a monarchy at all. The Regent and his damawful brothers nearly finished it. Risings, demonstrations, Reform bills: always something seething under the surface. He could remember Peterloo that this feller – this Shawcross – had babbled about so much. A lot of fuss and nonsense about a few hotheads cut down. There were more killed in his own coal-mines any week, and no one raised a stink about that.

But with all the trouble and restlessness he had seen in his time, he felt he had seen nothing so deadly, so dangerous, as he had seen these last few weeks. He knocked the ash off his cigar and stared intently at the glowing end. "By God," he said, "I wish I had run him down and made an end of him." Because he knew, out of a vast, dark and intricate knowledge of men, that he had seen a leader, with all his *years* before him – all the years when Lostwithiel would be mouldering under the slab in the mausoleum at Castle Hereward, and this feller would be going on and on, and God knows what would be happening to England. "I could have done it," he muttered, "and made it look an accident." A number of strange accidents had checkered Lostwithiel's career.

*

Hamer was not the man to be caught with accidents like that. As soon as the fight warmed up he knew whom he was fighting: not Viscount Liskeard but the Earl of Lostwithiel and Lady Lettice Melland. That was the combination of unscrupulousness and cunning and fresh young brain that he had to meet. It would be Lettice Melland, no doubt, who stole his advantage over the donkeys. Arnold didn't want the donkeys, but Hamer was a showman in his early days and he thought they would be valuable. They were a counter to Lostwithiel's four-in-hand. Wearing a tall beaver hat and a tight-waisted caped greatcoat, the old man was a grand sight sitting aloft with the ribbons in his gloved hands, a cigar in his mouth, and Lady Lettice fresh as paint beside him. There was a man to blow a silver horn at intervals; and all who cared might read the inscription on the slender banner attached to it: "Liskeard for Peace and Plenty." The four skittish greys were soon better known than any of the candidates.

Hamer's four meek donkeys, attached to a flat cart with a man playing a mouth organ upon it, paraded the division carrying a placard: "We can afford nothing better till Labour rules. These donkeys are fed on oats. Lostwithiel's horses are fed on royalties from the mines he's never seen."

It went well till an opposition poster came out with a donkey's head in each corner, Arnold Ryerson's portrait in the middle, and the injunction: "Vote for the Asses' Party. Return Ryerson on St. Swithin's day and it will rain asses for forty days and nights."

Pen Muff brought a copy of the poster into the Labour committee room, shaking with fury. It happened that only Arnold was there. "How much longer are you going to let yon chap run you an' make a fool of you?" she demanded.

Arnold puffed steadily at his inseparable pipe, holding out the poster at arm's length and smiling gravely. "Not bad," he said. "We're learning something about campaigning, Pen."

"But this Shawcross—"

"Don't be unfair, Pen. Whether we win or lose, we're going to create a surprise in this division. And that'll be Hamer's doing – no one else's."

They got Keir Hardie down to speak for Arnold Ryerson. Randolph Churchill came early to speak for Liskeard, and when it was seen that the campaign was going badly Balfour came and packed St. George's

Hall, and Salisbury, the Prime Minister, sent a message. The Liberals sent an ex-Cabinet Minister or two to do what they could for Hanson; and when all these had come and gone none had left on the imagination of the St. Swithin's division the vital, red-hot imprint left by Shawcross of Peterloo.

Antics were part of his stock-in-trade, and the sabre was part of his antics. Soon after the campaign had opened, he attached to himself a youth who always preceded him on to a platform, bearing the sabre as a mayor's mace is borne. It would be placed on the table in front of the speaker's chair, and when the meeting was over the procession would retire in the same way: sabre-bearer first, then Shawcross, then the chairman and any other speakers who happened to be present. Hamer allowed no one else to touch the sabre. The fooling became earnest: his own mind developed a feeling about the thing which he could not explain. Whatever subject his speech was to deal with, it began with the sabre. He would hold it aloft and recite, as though it were a vow:

I shall not cease from mental strife
Nor shall the sword sleep in my hand
Till we have built Jerusalem
In England's green and pleasant land.

The first time this was done, there was great laughter in the Tory press; but you can't go on laughing when a trick is working. Lostwithiel found it working. He slipped into a back seat at a Labour meeting, watched this youth, handsome, flame-like, nearly as tall as himself, follow the sabre on to the platform; saw, when that vow was taken, that a great many people got to their feet and stood with bowed heads, and knew that something dangerous for him was starting here. "This is the sword of oppression," said Hamer Shawcross. "I shall tell you how it is being used against us today."

Landlordism was the theme that night, and Lostwithiel remained and writhed. "It was my fortune to be born and brought up in a street owned by Lord Lostwithiel. I can speak, my friends, with first-hand knowledge of the loving kindness of a Tory landlord. Whom the Lord loveth, He chasteneth. He must have loved us dearly, for he chastened us even as a tender father chasteneth his children. There was some slight reversal of the normal process, for in this case the children brought the bread and butter to the loving father. Any children would do, so long as they could contribute a scrap of butter or a crumb of bread. Black children as well as white. There was an old Negro whom we called Darkie Cheap..."

They listened to the tale of Darkie Cheap being thrown out of his bone-yard. Landlordism in the home. They listened to tales of lock-outs in Lostwithiel's mines. Landlordism in the job. They listened to the tale of Hamer Shawcross walking on the moor and being stopped by a keeper with a gun. Landlordism in God's own earth. And then a bit of good "St. Swithin's."

"Ah, my friends," Hamer cried, gazing straight towards the dark corner at the back which he knew Lostwithiel occupied, "it is inconceivable that this august being, whose roots go so far back in our history, spreading deep down out of sight and sucking their sustenance from the lives of so many simple men like you and me – it is inconceivable, I say, that even his ghost should venture to intrude into our midst tonight. But were the man himself here I should call him to his face an incubus that we must shake from our shoulders, a thief who intercepts the reward of our labours, a wielder under the cloak of legality of the ancient sabre of Peterloo. Have at him, and have done with him, in the person of this puny candidate that he and his like have the audacity to ask you to support."

He paused there; and the voice, when it began again, was pitched on a low emotional note – the note that made them "see visions."

"There was a night, a bitter winter night, when starving scarecrow children, clutching a few rags about their puny withered bodies, materialized like the ghosts of all the sorrows of the poor out of the side streets of Manchester. And, ah, my friends, the sorrows of the poor! Those children were the children of a Christian land. They were the kin of those to whom immortal words were uttered: 'Suffer little children to come unto Me. Of such is the Kingdom.' But, ah, my friends, there was no God to welcome them that night. They had come in the hope of receiving a little food. In this fat and opulent Kingdom – a little food! Some received it; some did not; and then the night swallowed them again with the pitiful tin mugs that they had brought to hold out like beggars under the bitter stars.

"How long, O Lord – how long, you men of St. Swithin's – shall these things be? Come, not as suppliant shadows stealing timorously through the dark with tin mugs in your hands. Come as men erect, come in the daylight, come with both hands open to the feast. It is you who planted. It is you who reaped. Gather then into your own barns and serve on your own tables – and eat!"

He stood silent and straight for a moment while the applause broke round him. Then he moved out after the sabre. He would never remain once he had spoken. He ended on his high note, and went. That was part of his technique. Nothing would make him stay. Already he was able to state his own terms.

That night Ann Artingstall stumbled out after him, as dizzy as if she had looked too long on radiance; and Lostwithiel, summoning his son to his room in the hotel, said: "You'd better get that Manchester agent – that Richardson feller – over here. Send someone for him tonight. At once. You're up against something, my boy."

Hamer Shawcross and Arnold Ryerson opened their eyes when they saw on a Tory handbill the name of Thomas Hannaway, Esq. "Find someone who's prepared to say anything for money." That was Lostwithiel's cynical command to Mr. Richardson. and Mr. Richardson turned with deep respect to Thomas Hannaway.

Thomas, at twenty-six, was already putting on flesh. Those days when he had boxed and run with Hamer Shawcross belonged to a past that seemed incredibly remote. Polly coddled him, fed him, kept him at her apron-strings. Once he had finished his day's work, he had no other thought than to rush home, eat his dinner, and play the parlour-games with cards and counters that Polly loved.

With dinner over, the hearth swept and the lamps lighted, they were playing one such game in their new, neat house in Didsbury when Mr. Richardson called. Mr. Richardson was impressed. There was a sense of prosperity about the place: in the capped and aproned maid, in the gasolier of elegant proportions hanging in the drawing-room, in the clothes that Tom and Polly wore. The conversation was brief. As soon as Tom knew that Richardson came direct from Lord Lostwithiel, he had no more to say to him. "I'll discuss the matter with his lordship." His lordship was nothing but a name to Tom Hannaway.

Tom sat with Mr. Richardson the next morning in a room in the Bradford hotel, and when his lordship entered he received a considerable shock. Lostwithiel had slept badly, and had just got out of bed.

He had put on an old red woollen dressing-gown, smeared colour upon his cheeks and shoved a comb through his lack-lustre hair. With his big thin white beak, he looked as gaunt as a sick eagle. There was a brandy-bottle in the sitting-room. He filled a glass with a hand that was a little unsteady, and when he had taken a drink he said to Mr. Richardson: "You can get back to Manchester."

Richardson bowed and backed out of the room as though from the presence of royalty.

All this startled Tom Hannaway a good deal. The haggard old scarecrow had taken no notice of him, was standing indeed with his back to him, gazing into the fire. It gave Tom time to think. He'd be damned, he thought, if Lostwithiel was going to treat him as he had treated Richardson. No one had got the better of him yet, and this chap wasn't going to, lord or no lord. In his bluffest Lancashire voice he said: "Ah don't suppose tha's dragged me all t'way from Manchester to give me the benefit of thi back. My time's money. What's tha want? An' Ah doan't mind if tha shakes hands."

Lostwithiel swung round, looking thundery. Tom held out his hand. It wasn't taken. One of Lostwithiel's hands held the brandy-glass; the other remained in his dressing-gown pocket. "Well, as tha likes," said Tom. "But come to t'point, and come quick."

He wore a watch in a fob. He hauled it up by the seal that dangled importantly, placed it on the table, sat down, and crossed one plump leg over the other. "Tha can go to t'devil," he thought. "At best Ah've got something to sell thee. At worst, tha' can't bite my head off."

There were two things that Lostwithiel wanted to buy. He wanted someone, who knew that part of Manchester which Hamer Shawcross came from, to go on to a platform and say that Hamer Shawcross was a liar, that Lostwithiel was an excellent landlord. And also, he wanted this man Shawcross to be privately approached and bought off. "Get him out of the place – today if you can. I suppose he's got his price."

Now Tom was at home. "First of all, let's discuss mine," he said with a grin.

"Five hundred pounds if this man goes at once."

"And if he doesn't?"

"Nothing."

"Now tha's talking daft. It'll cost me just as much time if he stays or goes."

"What do you want?"

"Nowt for myself. Ah want to put a bit o' brass in thi pocket." The old man glared at him testily. He hated to hear money mentioned. He did not condescend to reply; so Tom proceeded to develop his thought. He had a nice expanding business, he explained, next door to Artingstall's. Doubtless his lordship was not aware of the fact, but he owned the land on which both businesses stood. Anything which embarrassed Artingstall's, even in a slight degree, was to the advantage of Hannaway's. If Artingstall's rent were raised, say, by five hundred a year...

Lostwithiel threw the remains of the brandy down his throat and banged the glass on to the table with such violence that the stem snapped. "You and your damned drapers' shops!" he shouted. "I didn't send for you to have a talk as one bagman to another. You are an impertinent scoundrel, sir. By God, you appear to have a low opinion of me!"

"My lord," said Tom, using the title for the first time, and standing up red in the face like a fighting bantam, "you have asked me to bribe a better man than you or me. You must pardon me if my opinion of you is based on that fact. It is the only thing I have the pleasure of knowing about you."

He stuck the watch into his fob, picked up his hat and stick, and moved towards the door. His hand was on the knob when Lostwithiel said: "One moment, Mr. Hannaway. Don't be impetuous."

Hamer took a night off from the rigours of campaigning in order to listen to Tom Hannaway. Tom was not bad. Hamer had never imagined that Tom could speak; but he did well enough. No inspired orator, he nevertheless managed, with his carefully nurtured northern accent, to get on terms with his audience – men of the world – one man to another. That was the line.

"Ah've come to knock this chap Shawcross off his perch," he began. "Ah know 'im. We went to t'same school and played marbles in t'same gutter."

"Tha's stayed there ever since. That's t'difference," shouted a stalwart voice from the back.

Tom Hannaway accepted this good-humouredly. So far as he could see at the moment, his profits that year were going to be a thousand pounds. He had never touched that figure before. It wasn't an income on which one could run a racehorse, but there was something soothing and satisfactory about the sound of the words "a thousand a year." Money, always, was Tom's armour. So long as he had money, you could call him what you liked, and he would smile. He smiled that night. He didn't mind being told he was in the gutter. "Well," he replied, "if Ah'm in t'gutter, the interrupter and I can talk as man to man. How are we goin' to get out o' t'gutter?"

Why, by the good old method of entrusting one's fortunes to this famous family which for so long had stood for so much in British life. This Shawcross of Peterloo, as he called himself – God alone knew why, except that he'd bought an old sword in a theatrical outfitter's and made up some fancy tale about it – this fellow had been presenting the Conservative candidate's family as heartless vampires, sucking the blood of the poor. He had told what he imagined to be a damaging story about an old Negro, Darkie Cheap. Now what were the facts of the matter?

Tom presented the facts as he wanted his audience to see them, and drew an altogether delightful picture of the gay, carefree life of tenants under Lostwithiel's overlordship.

All this didn't worry Hamer at all. He could – and, by heaven! he said to himself, he would – answer it pretty hotly the next time he was on his legs. He leaned back in his seat, enjoying the relaxation after so many strenuous days and nights; enjoying, too, the companionship of Ann Artingstall who sat with him. As always when it was not in symbolic use, the sword of Peterloo was in its scabbard at his side.

Suddenly, he sat up, alert. Tom Hannaway had finished with Lostwithiel. "So much for t'record of his lordship. Now what about t'record of Mr. Shawcross of Peterloo? His lordship is the head of a great family. He fills his position with dignity and responsibility. What sense of responsibility has this man Shawcross got? Will you be guided by one who in his own affairs has no responsibility at all? Ask this Shawcross if it's true that his mother is still slaving at t'washtub, and he doing nowt to help her…"

Hamer suddenly felt sick. It was dastardly. But was it? Wasn't it the sort of thrust he would have liked to get in himself – less crudely, perhaps, less brutally. And it was true. He couldn't sit there and listen to Tom Hannaway developing that theme. He got up, sweating, and went out into the street. Ann followed, burning with anger, tender with sympathy. She tried to take his arm, but he shook her off impatiently, almost roughly, and went on with long strides.

"It's unpardonable," she said. "You must do something about it. You must answer him."

He strode another ten yards before he said: "Answer him? I can't answer him. It's true."

He seemed so distraught, so deeply wounded, that she grabbed his arm and compelled him to stand still. "Listen," she said. "It may be true. But it's not true in that crude way. I understand. Do believe that – I understand how such a thing could happen. You're overworked – you haven't had time to send her a little money – you're ..."

He cut her short harshly. "You understand nothing about it. What Hannaway said was true in the plainest and most brutal fashion. I just haven't thought about her because I'm the sort of man who doesn't think of other people. Since I've been here, I haven't even written to her. What do you say to that, with your understanding?"

"It's hurt you. It's hurt you terribly," Ann said. "It wouldn't have done if you had been merely the cold brute that man suggested."

"It's hurt my pride," he answered, "and that's all it's hurt – just my damned pride."

He stood there scowling at the pavement, one hand on the hilt of the sabre. She had never seen him look so desolate, so little the master of a situation. "Come," she said, full of love and pity for him. "Let us get back."

"No," he answered. "You go. Leave me alone."

There was nothing to do but obey. She walked on, and when she had disappeared into the raw damp night he ran to the railway station. "Can I get a train to Manchester tonight?" he asked.

"Be slippy. There's one going out in three minutes." He bought his ticket and fell into a compartment as the train began to move.

There were few people travelling at that late hour. He had a compartment to himself, smokily lighted by an oil lamp. He lit his pipe and lay back in a corner. This was the first time for weeks that he had been able to sit down and think. Talking, writing, attitudinizing, fraternizing, reading with an intensity which even he had never known before, he had learned in one hectic lesson what public life could mean. But it had been left to Tom Hannaway to teach him this bitter truth which now stared him in the face: that he could have no private life unless it was of a sort that could be exhibited in the daylight. He had learned that lesson in one swift flash of intuition as he stood with Ann Artingstall under the gas-lamp, his hand on the sabre's hilt; and with the speed of decision which was one of his characteristics he knew what to do about it.

He counted the money in his pocket. The *Courier* was paying him pretty well. The article he had sent them – "We Shall Fight St. Swithin's – and Why" – had been liked for its hard-hitting, uncompromising adoption of the Labour attitude. The attitude was still, at that time, something new; to find it so well expressed was unusual. Tied up though he was at all points with the work of the election, Hamer nevertheless suggested that he should send a daily report. This was agreed to; Lizzie was seeing that the paper had a wide distribution in the constituency; it was helping the Labour cause; and it was enabling Shawcross to live. All he had was in his pocket. He counted it. He could afford to buy Ellen a new bonnet and gown.

He had never bought her a thing. It seemed to him an appalling thought. As the train lurched and roared through the tunnel under the Pennines, his mind contemplated Ellen, and the hands that were so much harder than they had been when Gordon Stansfield was alive, and the face that was more deeply lined and that wore the mask of resignation and endurance that he knew so well on the faces of the poor. "And oh, my friends, the sorrows of the poor!" The words swam up out of his memory. The poor…the poor…What a convenient, anonymous lot they were! You could talk and talk about them, and they need not embarrass you. They remained – well, the poor.

The sorrows of Ellen Stansfield. That was another matter. He had never bought her a thing. Nearly four years away, and he hadn't carried back a handkerchief for her. And then, off he had run, to discover at last this fascinating, absorbing, compelling career, which he saw now was something that must go on and on. No more doubt, no more question as to what it was he had been preparing for through all the toilsome years. His mind reverted to the thought of the small boy, holding Gordon's trusty hand as they walked to chapel in Ancoats, a small boy watching the preacher face the packed audience of some anniversary occasion, and thinking as he watched how grand a thing this was: to be up there swaying, dominating, exhorting. Now he knew beyond a doubt that the small boy was right; for out of all the crowded emotions and experiences into which this adventure so unexpectedly had rushed him, none so exalted and fulfilled him as the exercise of this gift of speech which he now found himself to possess so abundantly.

He had rushed away from Ellen to all that, and he had forgotten her utterly in the sweet excitement of this impulsive dive into the sea that must now for ever bear him up. He roused himself, almost as if he were shaking the water from his eyes and taking stock after a literal dive. The train was grinding over the points outside Victoria Station. He got up, knocked out his pipe and put on his hat. Well, now they'd see. Thank you, Tom.

The sabre knocked against his leg as he strode down the platform through the mist that hid the high arch of the roof. He suspected that he looked a pretty fool. Well, let 'em think what they liked. He was wearing that sabre, and he'd go on wearing it. It meant so much: the old man lying babbling on his bed in Broadbent Street, and Gordon who had been with him when he brought the sabre back from the cemetery, and old Birley who made the scabbard and put such love into it. And Ellen.

It was only when he was walking up Great Ancoats Street through a cold and gritty wind, hard on midnight, that he began to consider Ellen's side of the affair. Till now, his action had been a swift reflex, in self-defence. He was aware that what had happened in the St. Swithin's division was not a common thing. He had long known that he was not a common man, but the knowledge had not disturbed him: it had been too far beneath the conscious levels of his mind. Now it was at the surface. Neither he nor anyone else could overlook the facts. Appearing out of nowhere, hurling himself into an unpremeditated situation, he was immediately the master of it because of the power that had been revealed in him to dominate the human material of which the situation was composed. To the people of St. Swithin's his emergence was even more dramatic than it was to himself, because they were not aware of the intensive preparation that had filled his years with labour, or of the dreams whose vague texture this occasion knit firmly into a prophet's mantle. What they took to be a lightning-flash was a dynamo that had been charging itself day in, day out, and was now for the first time harnessed to its job.

"I had got these people of St. Swithin's," says the diary with great insight, "so firmly in my power that I could see Lord Lostwithiel was both amazed and alarmed. His son, an amiable nonentity, was not capable of weighing up the situation. He had had no experience either of political life or of any other sort of life that mattered. Lady Lettice Melland was not experienced, but was extraordinarily quick-witted. She had a political flair, which would have made her at home, years before, in Holland House.

"But I wasn't afraid of either the earl or the girl. I did not think Arnold Ryerson would be elected, but I felt we could give the Tories such a jolt that the Labour cause would be enormously heartened, and that, from this point, we could go on to make inroads which would shake the seat into our hands at an election not far ahead. I was doubtful whether we could do this with Arnold as our candidate. As I saw it, some means must be found, once the election was over, to suggest to him that in the interests of the Cause, he should find an outlet for his talent in some other direction. I thought it not unlikely that I should then be asked to become the prospective candidate."

He had no leisure, while the election was in progress, to make daily entries. He dealt with this whole stretch of time in one long, considered summing-up on the very day when he had, in fact, replaced Arnold as the Labour hope in St. Swithin's.

The diary proceeds: "That is why Tom Hannaway's attack unnerved me. For the first time, something had happened that seemed to me dangerous. I do not think Tom Hannaway realized how dangerous. He would not have that much insight. But, hitting out in his wild way, he hit right where I could be damaged. The poor pride themselves on their family solidarity. 'It's the poor that help the poor.' If Hannaway had proved that I had rifled Lostwithiel's safe, been guilty of perjury, arson and highway robbery, he could not have injured me so much in the eyes of these people as by telling them that I had neglected my mother.

"I remember saying to Ann, in the first shock, 'It's true,' without realizing how right she was in emphasizing that only the pressure of unusual events had led to this apparent estrangement."

It must have been sweet to Hamer to write that last sentence. The whole entry is marvellously clear-sighted up to that point, where self-deception blurs it. "I realized that the very next day I should be questioned on the matter. Lostwithiel or Lady Lettice Melland would be quick enough to seize on this opportunity and to send hecklers to my meetings to bait me. I realized, too, what the answer must be, if I were not to lose all the ground that I had made. It must be simply this: 'Here is my mother. Ask her.' I went to Manchester at once, and it was only as I was walking up Great Ancoats Street, dark and empty, that I wondered what my mother would say about it. I might have known. Her love has never failed me."

There again, one feels that Hamer is making a concession to popular sentimentality, and to his own. True, indeed, Ellen's love never failed him. Often enough, in the years ahead, Ann was to see the old patient eyes of Hamer's mother baffled and perplexed. They were to be filled, too, with tears of pride and joy, but ever and again Ellen was to long for the old times, for the fire on the hearth and the sausage at door and window, the coarse red curtains drawn against the bleak Ancoats night, and Gordon's pen patiently scratching out the gentle exhortations to goodness that, from him, so little needed the shaping of sentence and paragraph. That was what she understood; that was where her heart felt at home. Her love never failed her son; but the meeting that night, when he so unexpectedly returned from Manchester, did not go off with quite the smooth acceptance of his will that the diary suggests.

The two old women had the house to themselves. All the young Ryersons were gone, the girls into domestic service, the boys into one mean job or another. They were all sending home a little; Arnold was sending home a good deal, and Mrs. Ryerson managed to get along. They were not old women so far as years went: Ellen at this time was fifty-six: but they had lived lives of labour and anxiety that put upon them prematurely the impress of the years' passing.

They had become great cronies in the last few years. During the daytime they were for the most part separated, each going to her own work; but when night came on they liked to have one another's company. Mrs. Ryerson could not read, and Ellen was no great shakes at it; but she had kept Gordon's books, and she improved as she pored over them; and for a long time now it had been her practice to read to Mrs. Ryerson in the evenings.

The longer this lasted, the more they looked forward to it. It became with them a pleasant mania. They asked nothing more, when winter besieged their street, than to be by the kitchen fire, with a pot of tea on the table, *David Copperfield* or some such novel in Ellen's hand, and the sewing or darning in Edith's. That was the arrangement they had come to: as Ellen Stansfield read, Edith Ryerson would do the mending for both, her sharp little eyes assisted now by steel-rimmed spectacles, her maimed hand quick and agile. She had never allowed it to worry her. There was nothing she could not tackle.

The characters whose acquaintance they made during these evening diversions became more real to them than the inhabitants of Broadbent Street. "That Heep!" Mrs. Ryerson would exclaim at breakfast, clicking her tongue and shaking her head; and Ellen would say: "Micawber'll get him yet."

They were usually abed by eleven at night, having two beds in one room for companionship, but on that night of early winter in 1889 they sat up late. They were nearing the end of *Great Expectations* – "Dear, dear! That Miss Havisham!" – and Ellen, flicking over the pages, saw that they were few, and said: "Let's sit up a bit, Edith. It's a long time since we sat up" – as though this were one of life's exciting, wicked diversions! – "let's sit up and finish it."

Mrs. Ryerson agreed by getting up, filling the kettle at the tap behind her, putting more tea into the pot, a little more coal on the fire, and spreading a shawl over Ellen's shoulders. "Go on," she said. "I want to know if he marries that Estella."

It was nearly eleven o'clock. Ellen read on in her slow, hesitating fashion, read on to the end: "The evening mists were rising now, and in all the broad expanse of tranquil light they showed to me, I saw no shadow of another parting from her."

Ellen closed the book and Edith stopped knitting. Two pairs of gnarled tired hands lay in two laps. There was nothing to be said about the tale that was ended. They loved it; they accepted it; it would stay with them always. They looked at one another with faint smiles, not speaking, but content – content with their simple lives and with one another.

They started to their feet as an urgent knock thudded the front door. They looked at one another as wildly as though it were the knock of destiny: as perhaps it was to these two women whose sons were being borne from them by strange currents. There was no light in the passage-way. Ellen took the oil lamp from the kitchen table and held it up, while Edith opened the door a crack and peered out into the misty night. Hamer pushed on the door and came in, seeming to crowd the narrow space.

"John!" Ellen cried. She could never bring her tongue to say Hamer.

She retreated into the kitchen, carrying the lamp with her, and when she had put it down he folded her in an embrace. Then he turned to Mrs. Ryerson and gave her his hand and his smile. She looked at him narrowly. "What brings thee home at this time o' neet? How's Arnie? Is owt wrong?"

"Arnold's fine," he said, sitting on a small wooden chair that creaked under him. "You're going to have a famous son, Mrs. Ryerson."

"*Going* to!" she said. "His name's in t'papers."

"Aye, but it hasn't got M.P. after it yet. That's what we want. That's what I'm working for, and that's what I've come home about."

Ellen pulled the shawl round her shoulders and looked at him from the depths of her old broken wicker chair. "I don't know what you're getting at – you and Arnold," she said. "I've read summat about it in t'papers, an' it fair licks me. The workers – the poor. What's wrong wi' t'poor? What's wrong wi' me and Edith? What was wrong wi' Gordon? If thi old politics could make a few more like him, there'd be some sense in 'em."

"The grace of God," said Hamer, who felt as if he were answering a heckler, "could make a man like Gordon in no time. It'll take ages for politics to do it – even Labour politics – and that's why we've got no time to lose."

He looked at her anxiously. Had he silenced the heckler? She seemed to be mollified, and he smiled. "Give us a cup o' tea," he said. That was something she understood. She was happily busy at once.

"Well, tha's not said why tha's come home," she said, putting the cup before him.

"Because I want you to help Arnold. I want you to come to Bradford."

"What! An' leave Edith? What's Edith going to do?"

"It's to help Arnold."

Mrs. Ryerson licked her lips. She spoke huskily. "Ah don't know nowt about politics," she said, "but if it's to help Arnie tha'd better go. I s'll manage, luv."

"Ah'll not go!" said Ellen. "Ah'll not! Ah'll not!" She wrapped her arms about her body, as though to detain herself forcibly upon that spot.

Hamer sipped his tea and said nothing for a moment. Then he said: "I shall be going back to Bradford first thing in the morning. Whether I shall ever return to Manchester I don't know. I can't say what's in front of me. But I'm asking you to come and share it with me, Mother – always."

Ellen said: "Ah'll not leave Edith. Ah'll n—" and then broke down in tears. When he saw them flow, Hamer got up and stood over her, his hand lightly on her shoulder. "We'll have to be away early," he said. "By half-past eight."

Mrs. Ryerson watched them go in the morning. All she said was: "Ah'm glad we stayed up an' finished t'book, Ellen."

She watched them turn out of Broadbent Street into Great Ancoats Street and then went back into the empty house to fetch her cap and coarse apron, her scrubbing brush and pail.

They were at Artingstall's, buying a hat and dress, at nine o'clock. They were in the train at ten. They were in Bradford at eleven-thirty; and by twelve Ellen was installed in the room that Arnold Ryerson had once used in Mrs. Muff's house. Hamer left her there, ran down to Manningham Station and took a train to Shipley. By one o'clock he was in his hut in the intake, stretched full length on the home-made bed, happy, relaxed, safe. He stuffed the pillows under his shoulders and looked about lazily. He could afford to be lazy; he could enjoy being lazy. He felt like a general who has made a stroke of incredible swiftness and averted a great danger.

The hut looked different from what it had been a few weeks ago. Considerate Arnold had removed all his own books and papers and clothes. Already the shelves were full of Hamer's books. He had arrived with none, but every time he came up to the hut he brought something that he had bought in a second-hand book shop. In place of the solemn, solid, reliable treatises, expositions, political histories, that Arnold had pored over, there were novels and poems in three languages, the *Anatomy of Melancholy*, *Urn Burial*, *The Compleat Angler*, and much else that Arnold found perplexing. "What do you get out of these?" he asked with a puzzled look, turning the books over; and Hamer said, with a wide smile: "Sweetness and light, little one, sweetness and light."

There was nothing to indicate political thought except a few Fabian tracts; and across the cover of one of them Hamer had written: "These parlour pussy-cats think they're terrible tigers. They'll move next door when we pinch their rug."

On the table his writing things were spread with great neatness. Those who were looking for such indications might find a hint of luxury in the pen-tray, pen-holder and ink-well, all of fine silver, delicately engraved. He had found them in Venice and could not resist them. They remained with him to the end of his life.

Also on the table was a small leathern casket. Years ago, one day when Gordon had taken him to see Birley Artingstall, the old man had given him this. He had put into it the curl of hair and the bloodstained ribbon that he had found among the Old Warrior's possessions. They were there now, together with a ribbon that Ann Artingstall had given him because she had no other present to give that far-off night when she came to his party.

Hamer lay there contentedly, looking round on these small intimate possessions. He must soon be up, get a mouthful of bread and cheese and beer at the Malt Shovel, and write something for the *Courier*. He was annoyed to see the window darken. It was not often that he was ditsturbed in the hut. The intruder, without so much as a knock, pushed open the door. "Ah, I hoped I'd find you in. I was told this was your den," said Tom Hannaway.

Hamer did not get up or hold out his hand. He put his arms behind his head and nodded to a chair. "Sit down," he said. "That is, if you can bear to make yourself at home in the company of something so contemptible as myself."

Tom Hannaway let out a guffaw. "Tha's been hearing how I basted thee last night. But that's nowt, lad. Tak no notice o' that. That was just a bit o' politics. Don't let it make any difference among friends. Thee an' me's run many a mile together. We'll run many another."

"You speak figuratively, I take it," Hamer could not resist saying, looking at his visitor's red face and plump body.

"Ah mean," said Tom, putting gravity into his words, "that there's a lot us two could do together." He joined his pudgy finger-tips and leaned towards the bed so solemnly that Hamer burst into laughter. "You look like a doctor who's given me an hour to live," he said.

"Ah'm giving you something much better than that. Ah'm giving you a chance in a million. Listen, lad." He rushed right to the point. "Labour hasn't got a chance in St. Swithin's. Labour hasn't got a chance anywhere. You're ambitious. You've got a certain amount of talent. No one denies that. And at the moment you're being a damned nuisance to a number of people. Now listen to me." He leaned forward again and poked a finger into Hamer's chest. "A nuisance has its value. It's like some damn' silly little shack standing where a great building wants to be. Consequently, it can demand its price. You've been clever, lad. You've created your nuisance-value. Now capitalize it. There's other parties besides Labour, and you'll find a future in 'em. Mind you, I name no names, but I can tell you this: You could get a safe seat as a member yourself, and be kept pretty handsomely while you're sitting in it, if you'd clear out of St. Swithin's; Dear old Ryerson don't matter. We know him. He's not like you and me. Now what d'you say? I'd like something concrete," said Tom, looking absurdly business-like.

During this speech Hamer watched him with a lazy smile. When it was finished he swung off the bed. "I think better with a pen in my hand," he said. "D'you mind if I clear this up? You interest me."

"Go ahead," said Tom, his face beaming.

He took the place on the bed and Hamer drew the chair up to the table. He sat down, took up his lovely pen, and, having gazed at the wall for a moment, began to write rapidly: "I, George William Geoffrey, Seventh Earl of Lostwithiel, being extremely apprehensive, to the extent even of blue funk, that Mr. Hamer Shawcross's intervention in the St. Swithin's by-election will be prejudicial to the chances of Viscount Liskeard, my son and heir, do hereby make offer to the said Hamer Shawcross of the following bribes, to be paid by me on condition that he immediately quit the constituency: (a) the sum down of £ ___ ; (b) the promise that I will promote his candidature in some seat selected by me, where he shall faithfully serve the interests of me and my class; (c) a sum, to be paid monthly, of £ ___ to maintain him while he sits in such seat. My hand and seal hereto attached testify that I will faithfully fulfil these conditions, should Mr. Shawcross signify his willingness to accept them."

He threw down his pen, blotted the sheet, and handed it to Tom Hannaway. "Here is something concrete," he said. "All that Lord

Lostwithiel has to do is fill in the blanks and sign it. With that in my possession, I shall be in a position to consider my next step."

Tom read the paper and tore it across angrily. "What sort o' bloody fool dost take me for?" he demanded, his face purple.

"The question is readdressed to Mr. Thomas Hannaway," said Hamer smoothly, opening the door.

It was an extraordinary day for Ellen. This Mrs. Muff with whom Hamer had made some rapid arrangements, and who seemed willing to do anything Hamer asked, even to the extent of shifting a wash-stand from in front of the fireplace and lighting a fire, brought up, later in the morning, a girl she called Pen, and Pen shouted down the stairs, and there was Arnold Ryerson.

"Mrs. Stansfield's lucky, isn't she, Arnie?" said Pen, pointing to the fire. "That's more than you ever got when you were here."

"John asked for it," Ellen said, and Arnold explained: "Hamer, Pen. His other name's John."

"Does he get everything he asks for, whoever he asks?" Pen demanded a little sourly.

"I think he does," said Arnold. "But don't forget, Pen, Hamer does more than ask. Unto him that hath shall be given. Did you ever think what that means?"

"Aye, I've thought about it plenty. It means if you've got ten thousand quid you can lay it out at five per cent, and live like a lord on ten quid a week."

"To apply it to what we're talking about," said Arnold in his grave pedantic fashion, "it means that a chap like Hamer has done so much to his own personality that other things – friendship, knowledge, power – just fly to him like filings to a magnet."

"Well, we'll be seeing a bit of you, I expect, Mrs. Stansfield," Pen said; and once they were outside the door she added: "I couldn't tick you off in front of his mother, but you make me sick, lad, the way you butter him up. And don't run yourself down, either. Don't be so damned humble. Think about yourself a bit more. Arnold Ryerson. It's a good name. Say 'I'm Arnold Ryerson.' And stick your chin up as you say it."

"I'm Arnold Ryerson," Arnold said, obediently, rather shamefacedly.

"You old fool," Pen said, nearly crying.

After lunch Arnold came again, bringing this time a stylish girl wearing a fur coat and a little round fur hat. "This is Ann Artingstall, Mrs. Stansfield," he said. "D'you remember her? She came with her uncle Birley to Hamer's party years ago. I'll have to leave you together. I've got a busy afternoon."

Ellen didn't remember the girl a bit, but she seemed a nice girl. Ellen considered her covertly. She must be very rich. Old Alderman Hawley Artingstall's daughter. She thought of the visit she had made to Artingstall's that very morning: walking along miles of carpet, past acres of mirrors, among regiments of bowing and scraping shop assistants. She had been scared out of her wits and had clung to Hamer's arm; but this girl, in whom all that commercial splendour should have been incarnate, did not frighten her. She talked about Hamer, and the wonderful things he was doing, and the certainty that he would have a splendid and important future. Then she said: "And now we must go and see Aunt Lizzie," and Ellen, who was wearing the Artingstall dress, put on the Artingstall hat, which was decorated with clusters of cherries made of thin red glass, and they set out for Ackroyd Park.

What a day! thought Ellen. She had been scarcely a mile from the centre of Manchester since she married Gordon; and here she was meeting all sorts of new people, walking through this strange hilly town which was as dirty as Manchester and yet more blowy and vital; and now she was taking tea in a room the like of which she had never hoped to sit down in. Often enough she had scrubbed and dusted and polished in such rooms; and once or twice when Mr. Wilder was the minister at Emmott Street he had asked her and Gordon to tea; but Mr. Wilder's house was nothing like this, with an old man wheeling in the tea on a wagon, and a silver kettle singing over a spirit lamp, and toast under a big silver dome. They didn't sit up to a table as she and Mrs. Ryerson did; and Ellen felt that everything might have been most awkward if this Mrs. Lightowler that Ann called Aunt Lizzie hadn't been every bit as nice as Miss Artingstall herself. She, too, seemed to want to talk of nothing but Hamer; and Ellen began to feel that she was the only person in Bradford who hadn't the pleasure of knowing the extraordinary creature who seemed to have created such a stir.

But it penetrated her consciousness bit by bit. She had time to think it over, for Mrs. Lightowler said: "Well, you must stay till Hamer comes. He always looks in for dinner. And now, excuse me and Ann, won't you? We're going upstairs to do some work." And despite Ellen's attempt to get away – "I must get back to that Mrs. Muff. She'll wonder where on earth I've got to" – she was put into a big easy chair and told to make herself comfortable. "Have a snooze if you like," said Mrs. Lightowler. "No one will disturb you," and with her own hands she made up the fire, and she and Ann went away.

They had drawn the curtains, and there was no light in the room but the firelight, and Ellen felt very tired, leaning back in a lovely chair. She thought, all the same, with some regret, of Edith coming home, as she soon would be doing now, to the house in Broadbent Street. Poor Edith would find it lonely, knitting by herself and now only for herself; and, despite all these new people she had met, despite Hamer himself, Ellen felt lonely, too, and wondered whether she would ever again live in any place she liked so much as Broadbent Street.

It was all so strange and sudden. She couldn't make the boy out. But it had always been the same. There was always someone who thought he was different from other people. "No mill for John," Gordon used to say; and Mr. Wilder had told her he might be a great preacher. "A very great preacher," Mr. Wilder had said, "a very great power, under God." And then there had been all that reading and writing that she couldn't make head or tail of, except that it kept him shut in his room upstairs, as unsociable as you like. And, dusting up there, sometimes she came on books in foreign languages, and even pieces of writing in foreign languages in the boy's hand, and she had wondered what it was all about, and he doing nothing but look after one of Tom Hannaway's shops and seeming to want nothing better.

She hadn't had much of him, she thought a little bitterly; and then off he must go, so that for nearly four years she had none of him at all. She wouldn't for worlds admit how much it had hurt her; but other boys didn't do that sort of thing. They stayed and kept a home for their mothers. Old Birley Artingstall was the only person to whom she had hinted these disquietudes. She couldn't help it, that day when they were walking back from the station after seeing him off.

"You come and have a cup o' tea this afternoon, lass," the old man invited; and over the tea he talked about the boy. He'd watched him grow up, he said. He'd watched many a boy grow up; but this was a boy worth watching. This was a boy who was going to surprise people. "Don't make any mistake about that, Ellen, lass." This sudden shooting off overseas. Well, the boy was after something. Perhaps he didn't know himself. The point was, he was seeking; and when he found what he was after – "why, lass, there'll be people in Ancoats who'll think the finest boast in their lives is to say 'I knew Hamer Shawcross.'"

Half asleep before the fire, dreaming of old Birley's prediction and of the things she had heard of Hamer that day, her mind inevitably streamed back and back, seeking some point to connect this present which as yet she could not grasp with the past in which its birth might be found. And once again she was at the point to which, now, her thought did not turn once in a year: the point where she stood, a silly girl, in a hall full of young people lit by firelight, sunk in fatigue. She saw again with extraordinary clarity the face whose contours she could never summon at will. She could not even remember his name. She felt a stab of jealousy and regret that Gordon had no part in this matter. No part? Why, if it hadn't been for Gordon...She fell asleep, and it was of Gordon she dreamed. She was in Gordon's arms, and she felt safe and warm and happy.

Ellen's extraordinary day was by no means over. This – though she did not know it – was the last day of the great talk. Tomorrow would be polling-day. Arnold's supporters had staged their biggest effort for that night. There was a derelict chapel in one of the streets of St. Swithin's. It was soon to be pulled down, but the furniture was still in it. Lizzie had succeeded in hiring the place for this one night. Bills for some days had announced a "great Labour rally" at which all the talent was to be assembled, including Mr. Arnold Ryerson, the candidate, and "Shawcross of Peterloo." This was the first time that Arnold and Hamer had appeared on the same platform. They had both instinctively avoided it. Pen Muff, too, would not permit it. She could not bear to think of Arnold being obliterated by Hamer's personality.

Dinner at Ackroyd Park that night was a hasty and restless meal. Ann and Lizzie, worn out by weeks of work and strung up taut for this last effort, were anxious to be off. Hamer was silent. He had scarcely a word to say to anyone. Ellen was in a dither with the unusualness of her situation.

A four-wheeler came for them at seven o'clock. It was a fine night, cold but starry. The chapel, they all felt sure, was a happy thought. So many of these northern artisans were chapel-goers. They would feel at home. As they were getting into the cab, Hamer said to Lizzie: "You've reminded the lantern-man?" and Lizzie nodded.

They were the last to arrive. In the little vestry of the chapel Arnold was sitting poring over notes. Pen was with him; and there was Jimmy Newboult, the tall, white-faced, red-headed fanatical youth whom Hamer had chosen out of many as his "sword-bearer." Hamer had a sure sense of the dramatic. He knew the value of Jimmy Newboult's face which, during the processional and recessional marches, was set and grim and dedicated. There were also present the chairman, a Bradford boiler-maker, with an efficient, hard-hitting platform manner, and a good solid trade-unionist from Leeds who was to speak first. Arnold was to follow. Hamer Shawcross would end the meeting. Jimmy Newboult reported that the chapel was packed in floor and galleries. A table had been placed on the platform beneath the pulpit, within the communion rails, with chairs behind it. At half-past seven they began to file out of the vestry door into the chapel. The chairman went first, followed by Arnold and Pen Muff. Ann and Lizzie followed. The man from Leeds deferentially stood aside for Hamer, this famous young person of whom he had heard so much. Hamer shook his head impatiently, and almost pushed the man after the others. He laid a hand on Jimmy Newboult's arm, detaining him. It was only when a slight but perceptible interval had separated him from the rest of them that he drew the sabre from the scabbard and laid it across Jimmy's outstretched hands. Then he took Ellen's arm, and, with head held high, followed the sabre into the hall.

If Ellen had been able to describe her emotions she would have said that she felt fair daft and dithered. She had never seen such jiggery-pokery in all her born days. That old sword that she used to clean on Saturday mornings with a cork dipped in moistened powdered bath-brick! She hadn't seen it for years, and now there it was, going in front of her into the chapel, carried in that extraordinary way by a young man looking like a ginger ghost. And John taking her arm! That was queer enough. He'd never done it before in his life, so far as she could remember. He'd be kissing her next. By gum, she thought, the chapel is crowded an' all! She had never seen Emmott Street, even on an anniversary day, so swollen with people. She longed for some quiet corner. The back of the gallery would do her fine; but there she was, wearing the new hat and dress, sitting next to John, with all those people gazing at her. She kept her eyes on the red serge that was stretched over the table.

There are people alive today who remember that meeting in St. Swithin's, and, indeed, anyone who attended it could hardly forget it. It started off as a commonplace Labour propaganda meeting. The chairman bellowed his hearty platitudes, and caused Ellen to colour with confusion as he expressed his pleasure in seeing, on the same platform with Hamer Shawcross, the mother who had been all in all to him. The man from Leeds followed with a witty, racy speech; and Arnold, whom Pen had implored to do his best, not to be left in the lurch, certainly did do his best: as good a speech as he had ever delivered. Pen flushed with pleasure as he sat down, and looked along the table toward Hamer Shawcross, as if to say: "Beat that!" Hamer did not catch her eye, and she was startled by the abstracted look upon his face, as though his mind were miles away.

Then the chairman called upon him, with a flowery reference: "Mr. Hamer Shawcross, the thews and sinews of the campaign we are waging in this constituency." Nearly everyone there knew him by this time, and when he rose a great wave of cheering broke towards him. In the midst of it, he turned, and to everybody's amazement, mounted the pulpit steps. This little action was so unexpected that the cheering died down, and by the time he faced them, leaning slightly forward with the weight of his body resting on the hands that grasped the pulpit rail, there was a profound silence into which his first quietly-spoken words fell with effect. "My friends. I have come up here because I am going to preach to you from the word of God."

He stood up straight, pushed back the wave of hair that fell across his forehead, and looked round the chapel: at the crowded floor, with people standing at the back, jamming the doors, at the galleries that could not take another man, and then down at the long table below him: Ellen's red glass cherries, Ann's hair coloured like white honey, the gleaming bald patch of the man from Leeds. Never before had he had such an audience. Only a fool would waste it by standing down there. Here he was commanding, isolated, Hamer Shawcross, Shawcross of Peterloo.

He took a Bible from his pocket, placed it on the lectern, and opened it at the twenty-first chapter of the Revelation of St. John. "I saw a new heaven and a new earth."

Before he was done, there was not a man or woman in the audience who had not seen it, too. There was no "St. Swithin's" about that address. It was only when he had finished that people noticed he had spoken for an hour. It was the longest speech he had made. He did not use a note. All the immortal promises of the chapter threaded themselves through a masterpiece of romantic oratory. He shall wipe away every tear. There shall be no mourning, nor crying, nor pain, any more. The old things are passed away. The old things. He went through them all – the old things that every one there knew too well: the sorrows of the poor. Passed away! They held their breath, those people. They saw the widow's tears assuaged, they saw a world of plenty and themselves living in it with freedom and joy. They saw Jerusalem come down from Heaven and dwelling among men, in England's green and pleasant land.

He didn't mention, as Pen Muff noted, a single thing that you could call a fact. He didn't mention the candidate or the party; but only a fool could have missed the implications of his splendid imagery. This was a possible world he was painting for them: let them go out and get it. They would get it when the old things were passed away.

They were spell-bound, and knew not whether they were listening to speech or sermon; but they felt they could listen for ever to this shepherd leading them to delectable mountains. The healing of the nations…no curse any more.

There are those who say that this was the greatest speech Hamer Shawcross ever delivered – and there were close on fifty years of speech-making still before him. There are those who say that it was pure fustian, a shameless harping on the emotions of lives starved of the beauty he promised them, desolate for the hope he conjured up, hungry for the food he spread as plentifully and deceptively as banquets laid before Tantalus.

He himself has left in the diary a comment on this occasion which, whatever else it was or did, gave him the reputation, which he never afterwards lost, of being the greatest romantic orator of his party.

"After Tom Hannaway had left me, I wrote what I had to do for the *Courier* and then I lay on the bed in Arnold's hut, thinking of the meeting that night in Selby Street chapel. I wanted to finish up the campaign on a high note, an appeal to the hearts of the people, because I believe that through their hearts, not their heads, one can get their votes. The fact of the meeting being in a chapel made me think of that twenty-first chapter. Rightly handled, the promises could seem heavenly or earthly. Years before, when I was a local preacher, I had dealt with this theme. I had liked it so much that I took it round: I preached on it in every chapel in the circuit. So it was firmly in my mind. I don't forget those things. I made no notes, but lay on the bed, half-asleep, half-awake, letting the thing saturate my mind and trying over some good phrases. Tom went at two. I lay on the bed till six, and then went down to Lizzie Lightowler's.

"As soon as I started I knew it was going to be good. There is some-times a resistance about an audience. You have to beat them down. This audience 'went under' at once. It was as though they were hyp-notized. And I myself felt, after I had been speaking for a little while, as though I were being used for the promulgation of truths that came from outside me. Often as I had spoken on this theme, never had I felt such conviction of the beauty and truth of what I was saying: so much so that I could almost literally see a world of peace and jus-tice descending before my eyes and displacing the stony streets of St. Swithin's. It was an experience of a peculiar sharpness and sweetness.

"Some time before this, I had come upon John Addington Sym-onds's great hymn and had made up my mind that the meeting should end, unexpectedly, with the singing of it. I believe in the value of such dramatic moments. So I had arranged with Lizzie Lightowler to have the verses of the hymn prepared on slides and to have a man with a lantern in the gallery. A screen was hung behind the pulpit, where the choir usually sits, and, though no one but me and Mrs. Lightowler knew it, there was a man in the organist's seat.

"I had not realized, when these arrangements were made, how well they were going to fit into the occasion. I ended by speaking of Labour's crusade for universal peace, because that's what I had to do – make these people feel that they were crusaders, not mere voters bought with a pint of Lostwithiel's beer or a Labour promise of ano-ther sixpence a week.

"When I had finished I stood where I was. Most of the lights were lowered, and the lantern shone the first verse on to the screen, as the organist played a well-known hymn tune to which it could be sung. When he began it a second time, they had tumbled to it, and started to sing:

These things shall be! A loftier race
  Than e'er the world hath known shall rise,
With flame of freedom in their souls
  And light of knowledge in their eyes.

"It was amazing. The hymn was, of course, the perfect conclusion to what I had been saying, and as I listened to its harmonies swelling through the hot crowded chapel, I knew that I had succeeded: that these people were seeing not a provincial by-election but a purpose to which lives might be dedicated.

"I stood there till the last verse began:

New arts shall bloom of loftier mould,
  And mightier music thrill the skies
And every life shall be a song
  When all the earth is paradise.

"I did not wait for the end of it. Half-way through the verse I walked down the pulpit steps. Jimmy Newboult saw me coming, picked up the sabre, and came to meet me. He walked before me to the vestry. When the others came in, I was too weak to stand. Pen Muff gave me a drink of cold tea out of a bottle. My mother was on the verge of tears. She said: 'It was beautiful. I wish Gordon could have heard it.' Ann Artingstall was crying without restraint. Arnold Ryerson took my hand and said: 'It was enough to make the very stones stand up and testify.'"

The Bradford boiler-maker and the man from Leeds went away together. Pen Muff took Ellen to the house in Thursley Street. Ann and Lizzie suggested supper at Ackroyd Park. Hamer merely shook his head, and they understood his mood and left him. Arnold said: "Are you walking up to Baildon, Hamer?" and Hamer said: "Yes – alone, if you don't mind, old man." Then Arnold went, too, and no one was left in the vestry but Hamer and Jimmy Newboult.

Hamer sagged in the chair, his long legs outstretched. Jimmy loitered about uncertainly, his lean face, that had those almost white eyebrows and lashes that often go with red hair, lit with livelier fanatical fires than usual. The sabre lay on the table.

Presently, Hamer got up. "Well, Jimmy," he said in a voice

utterly weary, "that's the end of it. That's all we can do. Thank you, and good-bye."

Then Jimmy did a surprising thing. He picked up the sabre by the point, knelt suddenly on one knee, and tendered the hilt toward Hamer's hand. Hamer divined the boy's intention, hesitated, wondering, perplexed. What would people say? Damn people! He looked down at the burning bush of Jimmy's bowed head, and laid the sabre lightly upon his shoulder. Jimmy got up. "Now I am your man," he said. "Call me when you want me." He seized his hat and rushed out of the room.

Hamer thoughtfully buckled on the scabbard, thrust the steel home. The little incident shook him, and uplifted him, more than anything that had happened that night. It might have been ridiculous, farcical. But it wasn't. He thought of Jimmy's white, dedicated face. No, it wasn't. It was beautiful.

A couple of hours later he climbed the wall into the intake. He leaned upon the cold stones and looked out over the moor stretching away in shadowy undulations beneath the stars. His exhaustion was gone. He felt the lightness, the joyful relief, of the creator when his task is done. He leaned there for a long time, the events of the evening defiling in a satisfying procession before his inner eye. Far off a star tore from its moorings and streamed across the dark ocean of the night. It made him think of the tears streaming down Ann Artingstall's face; and on the thought, he lifted his latch and flung himself upon the bed, dressed as he was, with the sabre girded to his thigh.

It was grand fun to have the noble lord for a coachman. You carried him on your back for years on end, and now, to show what a good sport he could be, here he was ready to take you in his drag to the poll.

A heartening morning, with the late autumn sun shining on the streets, and the early winter nip making the air as gorgeous as Bradford air can be, like a mouthful of wine. Heartening to the ears is the sound of the silver horn, spilling its music down these streets that hear little but the drone of the barrel-organ, the pom-pom-pom of solemn Teutons, blowing out red cheeks decorated with blond whiskers. Heartening the clatter of sixteen hoofs on the granite setts, as the greys lift their knees up and down with a pedantic precision, as though determined on voting day to put up an extra-special top-notch show for the benefit of St. Swithin's burgesses.

Heartening the sight of my lord, the God-knows-how-manyth Earl of Lostwithiel, sitting up here with the ribbons nattily gathered in one yellow glove, the whip curling round his grey curly-brimmed topper, the tight-wasted, long-skirted greatcoat enclosing more decrepit nobility than St. Swithin's is likely to see again for a long time. His hair, black and dull as indian ink, his cheeks neatly brought to the similitude of a June rose, a veritable rose at his lapel, he bestows the urbanity of his smile upon all who climb into the drag. "Good morning, Buck!" "Good old Buck!" they shout, and look enviously at the lucky dog who, being first in, has succeeded in sitting next to the Lady Lettice Melland, squeezed by the others into an unambiguous pressure of plebeian to noble thigh. O joy! O voting day!

The horn peals into the morning; his lordship touches the flank of a leader, drops the whip into its socket, and thus has a hand free to raise the grey topper to the housewives of St. Swithin's, standing, arms folded or akimbo, on the yellow-stoned doorsteps of their houses. Lordly salutation! How can you resist it? Bring out your husbands.

The urchins of the district run, with a clatter of clogs, alongside the horses. They sing:

Vote, vote, vote for good old Liskeard,
  Chuck old Ryerson out the door;
    If I had a penny pie,
    I'd dab it in his eye,
An' he wouldn't come to Bradford any more.

The horn-player plunges a hand into his pocket, pulls out a fistful of ha'pennies, and rains them down into the street. That'll teach 'em who their benefactors are! That'll educate the electors! Tally-ho!

The voters tumble out at the polling-booth. Lady Lettice Melland shakes out the coat which she will give to her maid tonight to be fumigated. The horn-blower places a cigar between Lord Lostwithiel's lips and holds a match.

So far as one can see, his lordship is in excellent humour. A grin stretches his lean face, tightens to whiteness the skin on his high beak, as they call him Buck. But his heart is chewing over an insult as he sits up there puffing serenely into the sharp air. A letter had reached him that morning:

"My lord: An agent whom I can assume to have come only from a person equally wealthy and unprincipled, called upon me yesterday and made proposals to which I replied in the terms you find here enclosed. He seemed to think that his employer would hesitate to put his hand to the document, but it would be an historical record of such interest and curiosity that I give you the opportunity to prove him wrong. Your anything but obedient servant, Hamer Shawcross."

There was enclosed a copy of the paper which Tom Hannaway had torn across, and which had been rewritten. Already, before the letter came, my lord had received reports of the Labour meeting in Selby Street chapel. Carried 'em off their feet. Had 'em crying and singing like Salvationists. Promising 'em the moon. My God! He'd seen plenty of that in his time, plenty of these chaps with dangerous tongues, but never one like this – such a good-looker, nothing of the hang-dog Radical-rebel cut.

And then the letter came, and the old man tore it angrily to shreds, chucked it in the fire. "Harris, pray bring me a glass of brandy!" He calmed his shaking fury, dolled himself up, and came down, outwardly debonair, to the service he had undertaken for the day. But he was seething yet. Run him down!

The greys were turned. The drag was ready to go back for more voters. He saw the man coming at the very moment when Lady Lettice said: "There's Shawcross!"

There were a number of lame and crippled voters in the St. Swithin's division. "I'll see to them," said Hamer, and made a note of all their addresses. He got a spinal carriage from a doctor who was in sympathy with the Labour cause, and he began his rounds. Ann Artingstall was with him.

The first house they called at was Jimmy Newboult's house. It was in a street that stood back-to-back with another street. There were regular Siamese twins of streets, indissolubly connected by their spines. You couldn't open a window at the back and let the air blow through. If you knocked a hole, you would be in the parlour of a house in the other street. At either end of the street was an earth closet, and it was Jimmy's duty, on necessary occasions, to take his father there. A shattered fly-wheel had hit Jimmy's father in the spine a couple of years before. It was Jimmy's ambition to be able to move to the end house, nearest the earth-closet; and the fact of his having to nurture an ambition so improbable and unromantic was, before all else, the cause of his dissatisfaction with things as they were. This one silly fact had started the fanatical fires behind Jimmy Newboult's pale eyes. The new Jerusalem that Hamer had promised last night no doubt meant many things to many men. To Jimmy it meant that inconceivably urbane fashion of living which did not compel an invalid to go half the length of a street to reach the closet.

Mr. Newboult was laid in the chair. Hamer took the handles. Ann and Jimmy walked on either side. They were in the middle of the road, nearing the polling-booth, when Ann said: "There's Lostwithiel!"

Hamer had had his gaze on the waxen face of Mr. Newboult, lying there with closed eyes, and with parchment hands folded on the rug. He looked up and saw the drag with the four-in-hand a hundred yards away. Like him, it was in the middle of the road. He drew over at once to his left. The horses began to come on, and to his surprise they moved to their right. They began to gather pace, and he paused, wondering what to do. There was not much time to move an invalid up to the pavement with the delicacy that would be necessary, so he swerved the spinal carriage to the other side of the road. The horses at once changed direction, coming now at a lick, and Ann Artingstall screamed. Hamer let go the handles of the carriage and shouted: "Hold it here, Jimmy!"

Jimmy was white to the gills, but he did as he was told, conscious of faces peering from doorways and of shrill warning cries adding themselves to Ann's shriek.

Hamer ran to meet the horses – ran as he had never run before – and reached them when they were twenty yards away from where Jimmy stood shaking and Ann was stifling her cries with fingers stuffed into her mouth. She was hardly conscious of the next few seconds' happenings. It was all to her a wild scuffle, as Hamer leapt at the head of one of the leaders, forcing the pair across the road. She heard someone shout: "Put on the brakes!" and saw what was happening as another voice answered: "God strewth! 'E's whippin' 'em on!"

She saw Lostwithiel's whip belabouring the horses, his reins striving to defeat the thrust that Hamer was making away from the spinal carriage. She saw the red distended nostrils of the frightened beasts as they hurtled past, just clearing her and Jimmy Newboult; and the next thing she knew was that she was running, running, to where, sweating and trembling, the four horses were at last standing in the road.

Hamer had been dragged a hundred yards, holding to the horse's head. The sole was hanging from one of his shoes, his face was wet with perspiration, and across one cheek an angry weal was burning. Ann had never seen such a blaze of fury as was in his eyes.

"You damned old blackguard!" he was shouting as she came up. "You tried to run me down. You did it deliberately, and you struck me deliberately with your whip."

Lostwithiel was fuming, too. Anger could not drain the roses from his cheeks, but his black eyes smouldered as he yelled: "Stand out of the way! How dare you interfere with my horses!"

Hamer continued to hold the horse's head. Get down to him. Horsewhip him in front of all these people. Humiliate him. The ideas ran through the old man's mind like fire. It wouldn't be the first upstart scoundrel he'd thrashed. He threw the reins to the hornblower, and clambered down as actively as a man half his age, the whip in his hand. Hamer let go the horse and took a pace towards him.

A crowd had gathered, licking its chops. It was not often provided with a spectacle like this. Shawcross looked a huge chap when he stood alone, but old Buck, straight as a ramrod, that big skirted coat flowing round his calves, the whip in his hand, overtopped him by an inch even without the tall hat. That made him look immense. He scowled like a gargoyle, thrusting his face into Hamer's. "You annoy me, sir," he said. "I don't like you. You are in my way."

"I should deeply regret it, my lord," said Hamer, "if there were anything in me that could take your fancy. Let's talk from an equal height."

He snatched the topper from old Buck's head and spun it into the drag. "That's better."

Never in all his life, not by one of his own class, had Lostwithiel been so coolly and publicly insulted. The blood surged before his eyes and he swung up the whip. At the same time Hamer pulled the sabre from its scabbard. He stepped back a pace and shouted: "I warn you, my lord! If you so much as touch me with that whip, by God, I'll cut you down, old man though you are."

Lostwithiel hesitated for a second, looking at the white resolute face on which the weal shone red. He had never seen such hatred and fury. It kept his arm from falling, and into the silence in which the gape-mouthed crowd stood and wondered there fell the voice of Lettice Melland, cool and quiet. "I beg you, sir, to come back. You are in the wrong of this."

The old man let the whip fall to his side. He turned back towards Lettice. "Wrong? Wrong, m'dear? There can be no right or wrong between us and these people. I've seen 'em hung. I've seen 'em transported…"

"Come back, sir," Lettice begged. "You are saying too much."

There was a guffaw from the crowd at the admission; and Hamer seized the point. "D'you hear that, men? Go and tell your friends. Tell them that Lord Lostwithiel strikes at Shawcross of Peterloo when he's hanging from a horse's head, and dares not strike standing face to face. Tell them that this outfit of his is a tumbril taking you to your own execution. Keep out of it. Use the legs God gave you. Walk to the poll, and vote Labour! If you're too lazy to walk, wait till I've got Jimmy Newboult's father back home, and I'll come and wheel you in a pram."

There was a laugh and a cheer and a few timorous boos for Lostwithiel. Buck had climbed slowly back to his seat, taken up the reins, and put on his topper. He clicked to his horses. Lady Lettice Melland leaned out and said: "Allow me at least to apologize. And congratulate you on a brave action."

Hamer took off his hat. "Thank you, my lady," he said. "It is kind of you to congratulate me. But I cannot accept apology for something you had no hand in. That should come from Lord Lostwithiel. However, I think he has gained us a few votes, richly as we all deserve hanging or transportation."

Lostwithiel swung round and growled: "Go to hell." The horn sounded, and sixteen hoofs went gaily clickety-click. The air was no less heartening, the sun no duller; but he felt he needed a brandy. He turned his head and said tartly: "You had no cause to interfere, m'dear, no cause at all. Insufferable swine! I'd have whipped the hide off him."

Lady Lettice was diplomat enough to make no answer, but she doubted it, and knew that Lostwithiel doubted it, too. She couldn't get Shawcross's face out of her mind. Clearly, he would have dealt with Lostwithiel as he would have dealt with a mad dog, with neither respect nor mercy.

Jimmy Newboult took the handles of the spinal carriage and pushed his father towards the polling booth. Ten yards behind, Hamer flip-flopped along on his broken sole, Ann Artingstall at his side. Last night he had seen her in tears. Today he had heard her shriek. He felt he was getting to know her. She was still shaken. She could see the four horses thundering by, with him hanging on, trailing, dragging, only by heaven's mercy clear of sixteen thrashing ironshod hoofs. She shuddered, stopped walking, and leaned against a wall, overcome suddenly by nausea.

"What is it, Ann?" he said, and his voice was full of anxiety and kindliness. It was the first time she had heard him speak like that. Always till now ironic badinage or dead seriousness. The kindly note brought tears trembling under her eyelids, ready to fall. She managed to smile through them, and said: "I thought you were done for. But there you are. You look solid enough."

She laid her hand on his arm, which was, goodness knows, solid enough. He placed a hand over it, detaining it there for a moment. "We could do a lot together, you and I," he said. "We want the same things, don't we?"

She felt her heart beating like an engine. "We must help Jimmy," she managed to say. "It's hard work for him – uphill."

"It's going to be hard work for all of us – uphill," he answered. "We'll all need comrades. Arnold will marry Pen. Had you noticed that?"

"What gossip for the busiest part of election-day!" she said. She tried to look severe, but he saw that her face was radiant. "I'm ashamed of you. Let's get on with our work."

"Very well," he said. "But I shan't be flinging myself under horses' hoofs every day. I thought I'd propose while you were blinded by admiration."

She had begun to run ahead, but at that she paused and waited for him to come up. "Blinded?" she said. "Oh, my dear, I haven't had to wait to be blinded. I've been watching you for weeks with all my eyes and all my love."

Chapter Twelve

On December 15, 1889, six weeks after election day, Lady Lettice Melland and Viscount Liskeard were married at St. Margaret's, Westminster; and Ann Artingstall and Hamer Shawcross were married at St. Margaret's, Frizinghall. There was a lot of éclat and orange-blossom at Westminster; and after the ceremony Buck Lostwithiel drove the young people to Victoria Station behind his four-in-hand. Thence they left for Italy, and he returned to an evening of lonely brandy-drinking in Belgrave Square.

The affair at Frizinghall was quieter. St. Margaret's is a little church whose only distinction is that Hamer Shawcross was married in it. It stands right at the bottom of one of the streets that run from Manningham Lane down into the valley; and at that time you could see from it not only a great deal of industrial grime but also a wide prospect of green fields and the strength of many hills.

When Ann and Hamer walked out of the church, man and wife, there was a light powdering of snow on the fields and hills. There was only a hired four-wheeler to drive them to Ackroyd Park. Hawley Artingstall, Lizzie and Mrs. Stansfield followed in another four-wheeler, and, squeezed together companionably in a hansom cab, Arnold Ryerson and Pen Muff made the tail of the procession. Jimmy Newboult had no part in the cavalcade. No one had thought to invite him to the wedding. Hamer was moved on seeing him in the church. He stood on the kerb waving as the little party drove away, and then set out to walk the miles to St. Swithin's.

It was a measure of Hamer's sudden fame that the *Yorkshire Post* reported the wedding: very briefly, it is true, but that was only to be expected. A newspaper-man stopped Hamer in the porch and said: "What are your plans now, Mr. Shawcross?" and Hamer replied: "To oust Lord Liskeard from St. Swithin's. It's only a matter of time." It took him eleven years.

Old Hawley behaved very well, considering the company he was in. All his life long, or at any rate from the time he began to "get on," as he liked to call it, he had belonged to the "Gentlemen's Party," his favourite name for the Tories. And here he was in this company which didn't include so much as one Liberal. They hadn't even got a party. "Labour," they called themselves; but what the devil did that amount to, the baffled old man demanded of his soul? There was no Labour Party: there was nothing but a handful of cranks and oddities bobbing up here and there, and that they would ever coalesce into anything that need be noticed he could not believe.

So Hawley couldn't pretend to find his company congenial; the more so as this young chap with the side-whiskers and the subdued respectable Nonconformist appearance had been reminding him of a number of things. He would never have remembered that this was the Artingstall errand-boy in whose house he had found Ann that night when all the trouble started which led to Ann's going away and Lillian's death. And now this chap had been standing for Parliament! A queer lot of birds, Hawley thought, Ann and Lizzie had got in with. He'd never get used to 'em – or even try to. It was bad enough meeting Ann and Lizzie after all these years.

Well, he thought, glancing down the table in Lizzie's dining-room at Ackroyd Park, Ann had turned out a fine-looking girl: nothing like him, nothing like bleak-nosed Lillian. He thought of his mother, that woman with the Viking touch who had come from the Northeast coast. She had probably looked like this on her wedding-day before the first "Artingstall-Leather" had brought her home to Great Ancoats Street.

There were two things he felt sure of about Ann: she loved this man, and certainly there was something about the feller beyond his grand size and proud looks. And Hawley was contented to know this. The other thing was, he ruminated, that exalted look about her – lit up inside. He wondered what would come of that. It wasn't what he would call a stay-at-home-and-bath-the-baby look. It was the look of someone who would fly off the handle one of these days. He wouldn't like to be in Ann's way if she got on the war-path. He had given her five hundred pounds for a wedding-present, which he thought was decent and forgiving in the circumstances.

He got up and proposed the health of the bride and bridegroom; and he didn't do it as well as he would have liked to do, because all of a sudden he remembered old Sir James Sugden doing the same thing – proposing *his* health and Lillian's – when all his pleasant striving days were yet in front of him, so many good things before he fell into the clutches of that red-haired bitch who now ruled his life and rolled his name in the mud, and to whom he must promptly return.

Lizzie had provided good wine, of which he alone had drunk generously, and he sat down rather fuddled and confused and self-pitying.

He was aware of his son-in-law speaking with gaiety and ease, referring to these other young people – this Ryerson and this Pen Muff – and hoping they would find in their own forthcoming marriage all the joy that he and Ann were going to find in theirs.

Well, my lad, old Hawley reflected, hardly realizing that he was filling his glass again, may it be so. I wish you luck, but marriage is a damned queer thing and women are damned queer cattle. If I were you, I'd watch that light in Ann's eyes. I'd watch it, my son, and look out for squalls when it burns up like a beacon.

Hamer and Ann Shawcross did not leave for Italy or anywhere so romantic. At half-past three they shook hands with the little party at Ackroyd Park and set out on foot for Baildon. The snow in Manningham Lane was a smear of sludge, but in the gardens of the houses it was white, virgin, untouched. "Like my life," thought Ann, "like my body"; and the exaltation that Hawley had seen in her eyes was there still.

Already the day was draining out of the sky. In the solid, grey stone houses lights appeared behind windows. As Ann and Hamer strode along, not touching one another, they could see fragments of many lives laid out for their inspection: a group round a tea-table; an old couple sitting on either side of a fire; a young woman walking out of a room with a baby in her arms. All sorts of things going on under the roofs with their fleeces of light snow. Small, insignificant particles of immense, significant life.

When they had passed through Shipley and were climbing the long hill to Baildon the snow began again, dumbing their footsteps, filling the air with grey wuthering flakes. They could not see the valley out of which they had climbed. They could see only themselves in a little cell full of whirling snow that powdered their eyelashes and coated their clothes: a cell out of which they never emerged, though moving always.

There was not a soul in the wide mouth of the village street when they got to the top. The old stocks had lost their outline; the Malt Shovel shone with hospitable invitation. They went on, through the short street, to the moor that had known so many winters, that had lain so deep in snow that many a time coffins carried on shoulders had passed, with no climbing, over the zigzag walls that now could be seen cutting their black lines into the deepening whiteness.

Then they left the path, striking away over the soft uncertain surface towards the intake wall. When they were nearly there, Hamer said: "Stay here." He went forward, losing shape with every swift stride, and it was nothing but a grey silhouette that she saw vault the wall and disappear from sight. In a moment the window of the hut sprang to view, a square of dusky crimson, barely visible, but stable, unmoving amid the air's confusion, bringing to her heart that immemorial comfort and reassurance with which a woman looks on her home.

She saw Hamer loom again, a gigantic insubstantiality upon the wall. He materialized through the flakes that were thickening and becoming bigger, and stood at her side, his arm round her, looking towards the light. "I wanted you to see it like that," he said, and she was glad he had thought of a thing so simple and beautiful.

Our shelter from the stormy blast
And our eternal home.

I know, I know, her heart cried, that those words have nothing to do with a window lit on Baildon Moor in a snowstorm. But why shouldn't they have? Eternal? The word daunted her, out there in the elemental night, on the moor that had never bowed to the mood of man, that had known neither ploughshare nor sickle since first it took form from chaos. So many lives had come and gone, leaving no more trace than there would be of the ling and bent-grass, when morning followed this night.

"My dear," she said, "are you certain?"

"Certain?"

"That this is for always and always."

"For always and always," he said.

"It seems such a little light."

"It is enough to love by."

He helped her over the wall, and they half-climbed, half-tumbled on to the other side.

"Open the door," he said, "and go in. Let love be there to welcome me."

He followed her in and drew a heavy curtain across the window in front of the red muslin through which the light had shone. He had put a match to the fire. Dry heather-roots and pine-knots were blazing and the coal was beginning to splutter. The lamp shone down from the ceiling. He took off her snowy fur hat and coat and hung them with his own behind the door. Then he took her in his arms. "We've hidden the light," he murmured into her hair that smelt like warm cornstalks and was their colour. "No wanderer can see us. We shall open to no one. This is the little warm space of our love. Tonight, it is for us alone."

He put out the lamp, and presently the roaring of the stove died down to a steady warmth. And the roaring of their hearts and nerves died down as they slept in one another's arms, with the snow falling soundlessly upon their roof and upon the empty miles around them – falling pitilessly, remorselessly, like the obliterating years that have so much to give, that they may take all away in the end.

Tyler, Ball and Company was begun the next day. They woke to a white world, which changed before their fascinated eyes to a world of blue and white. For as the day strengthened they saw that there was not a cloud above them, and when at last they walked out of the hut the sky was a milky blue arched over the radiance of the snow. The cottages of Baildon looked somehow smaller, crouching upon the white face of the earth, with blue smoke rising as if from humble altars.

They breakfasted in the Malt Shovel. No one else was there. Alongside a new leaping fire they ate their eggs and bacon and drank their coffee, and because of their great content had nothing to say to one another. They were thinking with satisfaction of the empty house, called Moorland Cottage, which they had just passed in the village street. It was the house where Arnold had lodged. Now his landlord was gone, and Arnold was back in his old lodgings at Pen Muff's, and Ellen was staying at Ackroyd Park. There had been a lot of shuffling about lately, Ann and Hamer had rented Moorland Cottage, and Hamer was wondering what would happen to the intake and its hut. Arnold's old landlord had rented that, and now he was gone – one of those sudden mysterious moves that poor people make. Hamer had been happy in the hut. It had been the base of his historic sortie. He hated the thought that any day he might be cleared out.

Suddenly he said: "I love this little place, Ann. I shall always want to come back here. Even after we go to London. As we shall. Look at that roof."

He pointed through the window to a spot where last night's snow had glissaded to the ground and the sun was shining on the roof of an outbuilding. It was made not of slates or thatch or tiles, but of oblongs of stone, an inch thick; and at the corners, where the searching wind might catch it, hooks of iron clawed the stones into the end of the building. "Solid," said Hamer. "There's something honest-to-God and no damned nonsense about that; and, though I dislike generalizing, I'm not far wrong in saying the people about here are like that, too. My poor little hut," he added with a smile, "is shameful in such company, but all the same I love it more than anything else in Baildon. I think I shall weep when I'm turned out. Especially after last night. Now it belongs to both of us. Now it's part of us."

"I know," said Ann. "I know how you love it." She handed him an envelope, and said: "Aunt Lizzie's wedding-present."

Hamer opened the document which the envelope contained and scanned its jargon: "All that part and parcel of land…comprising two acres bounded on the north…" He looked at Ann with a flushed face. "Then I'm a landlord," he said, "like Lord Lostwithiel."

"You're a landlord," Ann answered, "but not, I hope, like Lord Lostwithiel."

"But the hut," said Hamer. "That is Arnold's."

"The hut is Arnold's present."

He was more moved by that than by the gift of the land. The hut was something Arnold had made with his own hands, just as he had made, Hamer now remembered, those bookshelves in the house in Broadbent Street so long ago. "He's too good to me," he murmured. "Everyone's too good to me."

He sat there folding and unfolding the paper, then suddenly got up. "At least I can work," he said. "At least I can show they're not throwing themselves away on me. You'd better get down to Ackroyd Park. It's no good staying here. That furniture'll never get up through this. Tell Aunt Lizzie I'll walk down tonight and join you all at dinner."

It was not the way Ann had expected to spend the day. They had planned to arrange the furniture in Moorland Cottage. But Hamer was right. The snow was two feet deep on the road up from the valley and deeper far where it had drifted. The horses would never get a van through that. "Can't I help in the hut?" she asked, a little crestfallen. "What are you going to do?"

"I'm going to begin to write a book."

"So suddenly?"

"Not suddenly at all, my dear. It's been in my head for four years. I've chewed it over and made notes for it in every part of the world."

"It's nearly twelve hours till dinner-time."

"Can't help it. I've got a wife to keep. An obstinate Manchester girl. You'd never believe the arguments I've had with that woman in order to convince her of my devilish pride. She would have liked to keep us both. Never, I told her. I'll earn money somehow."

"Sounds a forbidding sort of person."

"She's not so bad when you know her."

"Would she mind if you kissed me? Because I must be off. My husband wants to work."

He gave her a hug and went to watch her start her floundering progress through the snow. Then he went in and paid his bill, and feeling extraordinarily uplifted in body and mind, he walked back to the hut. His hut! His field! He looked at the two acres of snow that were his domain, went in and lit his fire and began to work.

Tyler, Ball and Company had an extraordinary success. It was a history of popular revolt, threaded along the names of the people's leaders: Watt Tyler, John Ball, and all the rest of them down to the tale of Orator Hunt and Peterloo. Hamer's writing was like his speaking when he was making his hearers "see visions." Historical pundits could have picked him to pieces, but he wasn't writing for pundits: he was writing for the millions, and at least he reached the hundreds of thousands. Like Blatchford's *Merrie England,* his book came at a moment most opportune, voicing a growing unrest, feeding it, and giving it an objective. In its blue paper covers it made its way into the homes of northern artisans, of miners in South Wales and Durham, of chain-makers in Cradley Heath, and of seamen in a hundred ports. It showed him that he had a pen which could earn him bread, and, as important, it made his name known and talked about in the years while he was waiting to take up the work which he was born to build and to destroy.

*

"The rumours that Viscount Shawcross's health is seriously affected are without foundation. Lord Shawcross is well but tired, and as soon as Parliamentary business permits he will take a rest at his home in Yorkshire, for which he has a great affection."

It was late, towards sunset of Hamer's august day, when that was written. Everything was changed except his "great affection." The dusty old road he had so often climbed from Shipley was a gleaming oil-planished track and huge buses ground their way up to the top. Not far from the Malt Shovel, posters outside a cinema hit the eye like running wounds. All round the little grey village houses, red villas were gashed upon the landscape. The moor was a golf links. His house in the intake looked grey and immemorial, and indeed it must be forty years old. At any rate, he hadn't rushed upon the land and raped it, as everyone seemed to be doing now. The house was good-looking, of the local stone, with stone-mullioned windows and a roof of stone slabs like the one he had pointed out to Ann so long ago. There was a yellow lichen patching it, and houseleeks had taken hold here and there. The two acres of the intake were almost obliterated by the firs and larches he had planted. There was a big lawn in front of the house; a few flower beds were under the windows; for the rest, it was all enveloping trees; and in those latter days he was glad of that, because he could forget the scabs on the landscape, forget this brave new world that, God knows, he reflected, needs all the bravery it can find, and remember only his great affection.

It was a small house, still known with inverted pride as The Hut. "The Hut, Baildon, Yorks." That would find the Viscount Shawcross of Handforth. It was just three rooms up and three down – he had never set up to be a country gentleman – but it was big enough. It would have been big enough if it were still veritably the old shack that Arnold Ryerson had built and where Hamer had lain with Ann that night when the snow came down and they were babes in a dark world that still had all the cards up its sleeve. Yes, that old shack would have been big enough now that Ann was gone, and Charles was on the way to Spain with Alice Ryerson, and Jimmy Newboult was God knows where, after his white-faced bitter outburst: "You've sold us all! You bloody swine! You Judas!" And then had added, all anger gone, only his broken heart in his voice: "I'm sorry, Hamer. God forgive me.

God forgive you," and had rushed out of the house in Half Moon Street, to disappear utterly.

It was that day when Ann had gone down to Bradford and he was alone in the hut beginning his book that Jimmy Newboult came churning through the sun-bright snow. Hamer had gone to the door to take a breath of air, and there was Jimmy, lifting his feet high as his thin soaked papery shoes carried him across that silver-shining field furrowed with ridges that were like violet brush-strokes. He had brought a wedding-present, roughly wrapped but most delicately carried lest its fragile complications should be injured – a fretwork model of the House of Commons with clock-tower and all, and a clock which, he explained earnestly, really went, up there in Big Ben's place. From St. Swithin's down into the heart of Bradford, and through Bradford, and along Manningham Lane to Shipley, and up the hill to Baildon he had carried his monstrous work of love through snow and sludge, having no pennies for fares. And there it was, the wrapping taken off, planked down among the manuscript on Hamer's table, and Jimmy Newboult, having wound the clock and set it to the right time, standing back with his head on one side regarding it. "All to scale," he said. "It took a long time. My father helped me. It fills in the day for him. He made Mother a model of the Bradford Town Hall."

And Hamer said: "I don't deserve this, Jimmy. I don't deserve anything from anybody. But, by God, I'm going to. I'm going to be what you all think I am."   ⁂

Lizzie helped them to furnish Moorland Cottage. The house in Ackroyd Park was bloated with things she would never use. And there were things to come from Manchester, too. When Ellen went to live with Edith Ryerson she took the most cherished of her goods – the things that reminded her of Gordon – and sold the rest. She now declared that if Hamer wanted her to live with him he must find room for these things. It didn't come to much: the books, and the table at which Gordon wrote his sermons, a plush-framed photograph of Gordon, his holly walking stick, and a picture which he had liked of John Wesley addressing a field meeting.

Ellen was given the front bedroom of the cottage for a bed-sitting room. There she could be at her ease with Gordon's things about her, and a brand-new comfortable chair by the fire, and her new single bed against the wall. At her ease. It pleased Hamer to think that. No more scrubbing of offices, no more early rising and rolling of the coarse apron and donning of the old cap whose peak she had carried with an air. But he never thought what this ease would mean to Ellen. She had a nice fire, and a lamp on the table by her chair, and there were the books that she loved to read again and again. But, without Edith to share them, they didn't seem the same. She left them lying on the table, unread, and her knotted hands lay in her lap, unused, and she stared at the fire, and realized with bitterness that for the first time in her life she was helping nobody. She missed the very fog of Ancoats; she missed the comfortable familiarity of her slum, and the clatter of clogs by her window in the morning, and the shout of children playing by the canal in the evening. Here, there was nowhere to go. She hated the moor and seldom walked on it. She had never before felt so useless or so lonely, and she wondered why it had happened, why the son who had always seemed divided from her had thus suddenly swept upon her life, torn it up by the roots, and laid it down again here where there was so little to nourish it.

The back bedroom was his and Ann's. Downstairs, apart from the kitchen, there were only two rooms. In one they all met for meals. The other was Ann's own private room. She had a typewriter there. She was typing the book as Hamer wrote it; and when she wasn't doing that she was writing letters or reading. She seemed to be always up to the eyes, and Ellen had never seen so many letters as the postman brought to Moorland Cottage.

It was a strange household, Ellen thought. She liked a house where there was a day's work and then an evening's repose, with all the members of the family gathered together. But Hamer, she remembered, had never done that: he had always cleared off to his own room; and now Ann had the same trick. As soon as a meal was finished, in the evening as well as in the morning, Hamer would bundle a lot of papers into a bag and go off to that hut of his; and Ann would go into her own room, and Ellen, having washed up – and this, with cooking the meals, gave her some satisfaction – had nothing to do but go to hers.

Sometimes, dozing in her chair, she would hear him come in, and see to her surprise that it was eleven o'clock or midnight. She would hear Ann go into the kitchen to make tea, and she would long to go down and do it herself, but she never did. She felt that she would be expected to be asleep, but really she didn't want much sleep now.

She would be wide awake, listening to the clatter of the cups and the blurred sound of voices, urgent, earnest, going on and on. She never knew what it was all about; he never told her anything. She had only once asked him what he was doing in that old hut, and he laughed and said: "Oh, trying to knock out an old book. But don't you worry your head about that. All your worrying's over." Not like Gordon, who let her arrange his pens and papers, and once, when she had asked him what his sermon was about, had gone through the whole thing, explaining it most patiently, and asked her what she thought of it.

She heard them coming upstairs, and she could tell from the sound of their feet that they were on the same step, not coming up one behind the other but with their arms round one another's waists, their voices whispering. She wouldn't get into bed then for fear they should hear her and wonder why she hadn't gone to bed long ago. She pulled a shawl round her shoulders and dozed off in her chair.

So it went on when Hamer was at home, and often enough he was away, sometimes for a couple of nights, sometimes for a week. He would kiss her good-bye with some meagre explanation which Ann would fill out with talk of meetings, by-elections, conferences, at all of which, it seemed, he was someone who could not be permitted to be absent. And Ann would show her bits in newspapers – Mr. Shawcross does this, Hamer Shawcross says that – and, with her eyes glistening, would look at the paper as though she could see Hamer himself there on the page, doing wonderful things. When he came home she would greet him with rapture, and he would explain that he had been made a member of some committee or elected president of some council.

They were so wrapped up in one another and in all this work of which she knew nothing that sometimes she longed to shout: "Yes, but what about me? Talk to me. Tell me something."

There came a night in February when it was raining hard. Hamer, wrapped to the eyes in a greatcoat, with his papers tucked beneath it, had gone off to the hut, and Ann had gone to her room whence soon the staccato clatter and ping of the typewriter sounded. Ellen went up to her room and sat by the fire, listening to the wind whimpering down the lonely little street like something lost headed for the great emptiness of the moor. Occasionally the rain spattered her window sharply like a thrown handful of shot, and in her chimney a throaty rumble came and went.

She looked at Gordon's photograph on the mantelpiece, and at the table that had been his, and then she got up with a smile and began to layout the paper, the pen and ink, the Bible and the hymn book. She got no farther. Suddenly she stopped, realizing with a shock that made her heart give a painful thump that she had not willed to do this, that she was acting under some compulsion that she could not control. She was scared. She stood still in the middle of the room, both hands clutching her head. "I'm going mad," she muttered; and then, alight with fear, rushed to the landing, downstairs, and into Ann's room.

The fire was purring softly. An oil-lamp with a green shade hung down from the ceiling, throwing its light on Ann's typewriter and on the sheen of white silky hair as her head bent over a pile of manuscript. It was a tranquil and reassuring scene. Ellen felt that it was somehow miles away from her room upstairs, where she was so comfortable, so warm, so pensioned, so utterly useless and forgotten. She stood on the threshold staring for a moment at Ann, then a sob brought the girl to her side, strong young arms about her waist. "Oh, Ann, I can't go on," she cried. "I can't stand it. I can't live like it. It's driving me mad. It's killing me."

"Sit down," Ann said. "Let's have a good long talk. But first of all, let me make some tea."

Ellen cried eagerly: "Let me make it," and Ann had the sense to do so. There was always a kettle simmering on the damped-down kitchen fire, and in a moment or two Ellen was back with the tea and biscuits.

Ann clearly sensed the elder woman's need. It had been a cry of utter loneliness, a cry from beyond the pale wherein she and Hamer worked so happily, that had reached her from the door. It pierced her heart, bringing illumination, explaining a deepening mask of frustration that she, but not Hamer, had perceived to be growing upon Ellen. Unceremoniously, she swept up Hamer's manuscript and the pages she had typed, and threw them to one side, so that Ellen should see that these things did not matter tremendously. She dumped the tea-tray down where the papers had been, and refrained from fussing Ellen into the easy chair. Let her sit where she liked. Let her sit on the floor if she wanted to. She guessed Ellen had had fussing enough.

"There!" she said. "That's enough of that for tonight. A bit of a talk for a change will do me good. Will you pour out the tea?"

Ellen poured out the tea, and already she felt more tranquil. She did not feel now that something was driving her mad. "This is like the nights I used to have with Mrs. Ryerson," she said with a smile. "We used to drink tea, and she'd knit, and I'd read to her. Did you ever read *David Copperfield?* That Heep!"

Ann admitted with shame that she had never read *David Copperfield,* and Ellen's tongue was loosened in praise of the book.

"One of these days," said Ann, "you'll have to read it to me. On the nights when Hamer's away and hasn't left me anything to do. I feel lonely sometimes then."

"Now isn't that daft!" said Ellen. "You lonely down here an' me lonely up there! I never imagined you were lonely, Ann lass."

"Oh, yes, I am, when he's away," Ann said. "When he's at home he keeps me on the run and there's no time to be lonely."

"What does he keep you on the run *about?*"

For the first time Ellen listened to a patient, reasoned explanation of what Hamer was trying to do, of what his intervention in the St. Swithin's by-election had done for his reputation, of the way he now was here, there and everywhere, fomenting strikes, speaking at elections, growing all the time a figure of more and more significance.

"And one of these days," said Ann earnestly, "there'll be a real Labour Party, just like the Liberal Party and the Conservative Party, and when that happens the Labour Party may have to form a government. And Hamer would have to be in it. Goodness knows what he might be. He might even be Prime Minister."

But now Ellen felt she was entering the region of myth and fantasy. "Eh, Ann lass!" she cried. "Our Hamer? A lad out of Ancoats? Prime Minister, like Mr. Gladstone?"

Ellen was of those who said "Mr. Gladstone" as one might say Jehovah. Mr. Gladstone, the very chips of whose tree-felling axe none but the worthy and devout might receive and cherish! "Nay, nay, Ann. 'Ave a bit o' sense, lass."

"Mother – shall I call you Mother? I've never known what to call you."

"Aye. Call me that, lass. I'd like that."

"Well, Mother," said Ann with conviction, "let me tell you this. I know very well how you felt when you came down here tonight. You felt lonely and unhappy and neglected. You felt that Hamer had pushed you into that room to be out of the way, just as I'd push a hat into a box because I might want it some day but had no use for it at the moment. Didn't you?"

Ellen nodded.

"Yes," said Ann. "And you thought there was no sense or reason in it. And the reason simply is this: that your son is as important a man as Mr. Gladstone any day. If you think he's neglecting you, it's because his days are full of terribly important things. There's so much to do. Mr. Gladstone! He's got everything – a party ready-made, a tradition, an adoring mob. Hamer's got to *make* everything out of nothing. Don't worry him. Why, he's doing the work of two Gladstones," cried the passionate little advocate. "Don't you know he's wonderful? Don't you know there's no one else like him? Would Mr. Gladstone be where he is if he had started in an Ancoats back street?"

Ellen was borne off her feet by Ann's eloquence, her conviction, her love – inspired fervour. "Well, there's one thing I don't like," she said. "You shouldn't send out his washing."

Ann crashed down from her heights and dissolved in laughter. It was an old sore point with Ellen. Sending out the family washing had been one of the ideas for giving her a good time. "You let me do that washing," she now said. "I can turn out his shirts as good as anybody."

Ann, with her new insight, conceded the point. "Very well," she said, "if it will make you happy."

"Of course it'll make me happy – sittin' up there, gawping out o' t'winder at nowt."

"And, remember, next time Hamer goes away we'll have a good read. Will you come down here or shall I come up to you?"

"Turn an' turn about," said Ellen. She got up and put her arms round Ann, who so lately had put her arms round Ellen. She kissed her and said: "Tha's a good lass. I like thee. Tha mun stand up to everybody for 'im like tha stood up to me."

She went back to her room. The noise of the typewriter began to come up almost at once. It no longer annoyed her or made her feel isolated. She felt happier than she had been since leaving Broadbent Street, and with no agitation of mind she put away the pen and paper and books that she had laid out earlier in the evening. The rain on the window, the moan in the chimney, seemed to give her room a friendly, harboured intimacy. She mended the fire and said to herself easily: "I'll have a good read." It was *Dombey and Son*. That Captain Cuttle!

Chapter Thirteen

Mrs. Ryerson did not leave the house in Broadbent Street to which Ryerson had taken her on their marriage till she was carried out feet-foremost. But that was to be a long time hence. She was as tough as an old brier-root and went on tackling the business of living for many, many years. Soon after Ellen had left her, her eldest daughter married a monumental mason, a fellow whose infinite cheerfulness was undimmed by his daily occupation of chipping into stone and marble the records of human evanescence and mutability. It was almost as though he must make up for having death in his chisel by having laughter in his soul; and so he whistled as he worked, persuading pathos into a cherub's face, mournfulness into an angel's wing, and storing up in his mind the choicer epitaphs, to be retailed at night with appreciative laughter.

Mrs. Ryerson liked a good laugh, and she was delighted when the young people made their home with her. She knew that this would be a load off Arnie's mind. Arnie was always a one to worry about his mother – not like some, she thought darkly – and since Ellen had left her, he was worrying in every letter about what she was going to do. Well, now she was all right. He could look after himself; and it was her opinion that he needed looking after a great deal more than she did. He had mentioned a girl named Pen Muff more than once in his letters; and she was not surprised when he turned up in Broadbent Street, bringing this girl with him, after the election. She was a lean, tough-looking little thing, and Mrs. Ryerson liked her. She wouldn't have liked Arnie to marry anyone who was la-di-da; and Pen certainly wasn't that. "She's the sort that lasts," Mrs. Ryerson reflected. "They can't down that sort. She'll be able to tackle things as well as I can myself." It was a bit of a do, having two weddings on top of each other; and what Arnold was going to live on when he was married she didn't know. He said he had saved some money during the last few years, and that he and Pen were going down to the Rhondda Valley, where her sister lived, to look about them.

Neither of them had ever been out of the North, and on that spring day in 1890, they left the North behind them as the train slid out of the mean and sordid purlieus of Crewe. It was a transformation so sudden as to be dramatic. One moment, the soot-blackened station with the blasted trees, skeletons of trees, barkless, leafless, all about it; the next, the deepening green of the South. Both Pen and Arnold were accustomed to see field divided from field by walls of loose-piled stones, zigzagging for miles across the grey-green of northern grass. Now they looked on hedges as green as the rivers of paradise, foamed with hawthorn. In the orchards the apple trees were domes of pink and white. The sheep were whiter; the cows were redder; the whole cut and contour of the land had more fat to it. The villages lolled lazily in the shade of their elms, and the clouds were slow and immense, bowling across the sky as opulently as though for two pins they would rain milk instead of water.

The young middle-aged-looking man with the side-whiskers, the heavy broadcloth suit, the solid watch-chain, held the hand of the girl as scrawny and sinewy-looking as an old chicken. A half-hoop bonnet framed her keen enthusiast's face. Above them on the rack a yellow tin trunk rattled. Before their fascinated eyes the wealth of the English counties unfurled itself in mile upon lovely mile. Shropshire, Herefordshire, Monmouthshire.

"We'll soon be there," Pen said. "Nell will meet us at Pontypool Road. That's where we have to change."

Abergavenny, with the great hills towering. Hazel-copses with brown trout-water sleeping in pools, gurgling over pebbles, swirling round the hoofs of cows standing there with tails flicking at flies.

"Did you know it was so beautiful?" Arnold asked.

"It's not beautiful where we're going to," Pen said. "I've never been there, but I know what Nell's told me. Hills as big as that" – she waved a thin hand towards the flying landscape – "and once as lovely, but now with their insides torn out and left to bleed and rot. Streams that ought to be as sweet as this, but full of all the filth on God's earth. God's earth? That's a good one, isn't it, Arnie? Remember that Shawcross and his dramatic recitation – 'till we have built Jerusalem in England's green and pleasant land.' He ought to come an' have a shot at the Rhondda Valley. He wouldn't find it so green and pleasant, to begin with."

"Why don't you like him?" said Arnold patiently.

"Do you?"

"I think he's wonderful. I think when the Party is formed he'll be one of the greatest men in it – perhaps the greatest one of these days."

"You don't answer me," Pen persisted. "Do you like him or don't you?"

Arnold patted her knee. "Personal likings and dislikings get us nowhere in the sort of fight that's before us," he said. "Look how lovely this is. Let's enjoy it while we can."

"You don't answer me," Pen persisted, edging closer to him. She pulled off her bonnet, and with their cheeks together, they watched the fragments of beauty leaping to momentary life, streaming away relentlessly as time, and the hills of Wales darkening their crests against the incandescence of the western sky.

Nell Richards met them at Pontypool Road. She was not a bit like Pen. Mrs. Muff had had two husbands and had enjoyed, nevertheless, only two years of marriage. Her first husband, a platelayer, was killed on the line within three months of making her his wife. When Nell was a year old, her mother married again. Pen's father lasted for nearly two years. A weakness of the chest developed dramatically into what was called galloping consumption. Mrs. Muff, left with two small children, did not try a third time.

Nell had the generous build and ruddy colouring of her father. Her red hair was drawn back from a straight central parting and collected into an enormous "bun" on the neck, which was thick and white. Its heavy columnar strength did not seem inappropriate beneath the broad placid face with its generous mouth, large shapely nose and grey-green eyes. Nell looked like a rock against which the heaviest seas might rage without avail.

She enveloped the skinny form of Pen in an embrace, pressing her, as though she had been a child, against the firm bastion of her breasts. Her calm candid gaze, when she had put Pen away, rested on the pair of young lovers, as though she were weighing them up, assessing their chances in the long queer business of life that lay before them. Arnold, standing beside the yellow tin trunk, with a squarish bowler hat surmounting his grave face, felt extraordinarily vulnerable before that steady, mother-wise regard. "Well," said Nell at last. "Good luck to you. If you manage to keep as happy as me and Ianto, you'll do."

Their train came in. "Come on, now," Nell urged them. "I can't be away too long. Dai's all right with his grand-dad, but there's Pryce now. I can't leave him."

Pryce Richards. Aged three months. Dai's all right. Dai is nearly two. It's as well to be all right as early as you can in the Rhondda Valley.

Arnold carried the trunk into the compartment that Pen and Nell had entered. It was a dirty compartment. About them the countryside was green, but the compartment was very dirty indeed. It had come from a dirty place, and it was going back there. They had been travelling from north to south. Now they had reached the spot whence the valley rayed away to the west, as the spokes of a fan ray from the junction with the handle.

The train rumbled over the Crumlin viaduct, serenely trailing its plume of smoke behind it up there above the abyss. From below, it must have looked like a caterpillar traversing a taut clothesline. Arnold looked down with some apprehension. Never before had he travelled across so deep a gulf. These valleys, clearly, were valleys indeed.

"Down yonder green valley where streamlets meander." While Pen and Nell were cluckling away twenty to the dozen, he sat sunk in reverie, gazing at the darkening countryside, and the words of the song sang incongruously through his head. How green they must have been! he thought. What streamlets once meandered here! Nothing could alter the noble contours and proportions of the hills, but what infamy, what filthy degradation had been wrought upon them!

The pithead machines, with wheel turning against wheel in a dizzy dance of spokes; the synthetic mountains of black slag rising from the very backs of little cottages terraced on the hillsides, looking as though at any moment they might slide down and engulf them, and channelled with deep fissures that must in wet weather be conduits to sluice filth to the back doors; blear sidings, where now a light or two began to come out and the engines looked like little tubby dragons with their boiler fires eye-glowing and white steam snorting through up-ended nostrils; a stream choked with tins and done-for zinc baths and rotting baskets and smashed crockery and bloated long-dead dogs; and now, butting into the compartment at this station and that, the miners coming off the day-shift, chattering in high singsong Welsh voices, looking like infernal gnomes with their short, stooping stature, their faces coal-blackened and touched up grotesquely with red lips, white eye sockets, eyes that, shining through the ebon masks, seemed supernaturally keen and bright. They carried their tea-tins and their food-baskets. The slightest movement set a-dance about them the coal-dust with which their clothes were thick. Checked mufflers of red and black were at the throats of most, and their trousers were hitched up with yorkers below the knee. They filled the seats, they stood between the seats, they chewed tobacco, and they squirted the juice upon the floor.

Nell was unperturbed. She greeted some of them by name, and Arnold noticed that when she talked to them her voice tended to lose its customary intonation and to lilt and sing. Indeed, he might have thought, had his learning gone that way, whoever stayed here for long would be inundated, overrun, subdued, by these dark wiry midgets whose ancestry here in the valley went back to the halcyon age, the age when coal was undreamed of, when they walked on the green hills and watered their flocks in the flashing streams, the little dark people, the coracle men, earlier than the Romans, than Saxons or anything at all: the black Silures who were first called Britons.

And here they now were, clanking their tins, clutching their baskets, glaring fantastically out of their demoniac masks, tumbling with laughter out of the train, going with swift resonant hobnailed tread down the wooden platform, meagrely lighted by a few oillamps on which Arnold read the half-obliterated name Cwrndulais, He waited till Pen and Nell, both black-smeared in hands and face, had climbed out; then he followed with the yellow tin trunk and looked about him at the lights climbing here and there upon the hillsides beyond whose crests the glow of the day was now utterly gone.

From the station they climbed. Pen took one handle of the tin trunk, Arnold the other. Cwmdulais was a dimly lighted place. It didn't seem to Arnold to be a town at all. The houses were scattered, the shops small and few; but they had passed three chapels before Nell said "That's Horeb."

From the acclivity up which they had been toiling they had turned to the left, into a short street terraced on the hillside. Horeb stood at the end of the street, a stark forbidding building of blackened stone, without beauty, with great iron railings about it, as though it were the kingdom of heaven that must be taken by storm. A street lamp lighted up the front, glittered on the gold-leafed name Parch Taliesin Howells, M.A., B.D., and on HOREB cut in deep letters upon the grey granite lintel of the door.

"We're lucky to be so near to Horeb," said Nell; and Arnold, always shy with strangers, could not ask what luck there was in being near to that mammoth ugliness. He had yet to learn the place of Horeb in the life of the Richards family.

Horeb Terrace. He knew that was the name of the street which was their destination. They were half-way along it when a lively clatter of hobnailed boots behind them caused Nell to stop. "That's Ianto," she said; and at the same time there came a voice hailing:

"Nell! 'Arf a mo, gel. Well, well, so these are them!" said Ianto, hurrying to join them. "I can't shake hands with you, mun," he said to Arnold, a smile splitting the black mask of his face. "Look at the state I'm in. Wait till I've had a wash. We'll show you everything. Did you show 'em Horeb, Nell?"

Nell said she had shown them Horeb.

"And you're Pen!" Ianto ran on, falling into step with them.

"Well, indeed, you're not much like Nell. But there – who is? There's not another girl like Nell in all the Rhondda. We're little 'uns about here. I expect you've noticed that. Well, here we are."

Here they were, in a house not unlike the Broadbent Street house that Arnold knew so well.

"Leave the trunk there in the passage," Ianto sing-songed, "and come on in and see Dad. You're not nervous, are you, mun?"

The tin trunk blocked the little passage like a barricade. Ianto took Arnold's arm, gave it a reassuring squeeze, and drew him into the kitchen after Nell and Pen.

Richard Richards, Ianto's father, got up from a wooden armchair that stood on the rag mat by the fire. He was as small as his son. They seemed a race of jockeys. His forehead, like Ianto's, was tattooed with blue powder-marks, bitten irremovably into the skin, but you could not see Ianto's now for coal-dust. Old Richard had lost one leg below the knee. For ten years now he had walked on a stump of wood, rubber-shod, with a cuplike top to it, in which the relic of his leg rested, held there by a complication of straps. Ten years ago since the night shift in Cwmdulais Main heard the distant thud, paused for a moment in dread speculation, then heard the water, released from old workings, hurtling towards them. And hurtling before it came a train of trucks, shooting downhill, full of men fleeing the wrath to come. Richard Richards, running with others to the shaft, slipped and fell, and when the trucks had thundered past he hardly knew what had happened till he tried to pick himself up again. Then he crawled, and the water overtook him, and he crawled in the water, dyeing it red. Ianto remembered standing at the pit-head as a summer dawn was breaking, he a boy of sixteen, and watching the stretchers come out of the cage and disappear into the colliery office. Drowned men and shattered men were brought up, and now and then, as the stretchers passed, someone would lift a corner of the cloth and the word would go round the crowd. And another woman would not wait any longer, but go home. Now old Richard Richards did not work in the pit any more, but kept the little corner shop at the opposite end of Horeb Terrace from Horeb Chapel, with his daughter Blodwen to help him. Whenever Nell left the children, it was Richard, not Blodwen, who came in to look after them.

Arnold looked at the old man, whose wooden peg made him think of Jimmy Spit-and-Wink, but there was nothing but this piece of timber in common between the two. Richard Richards, for all his little size, and he stood not more than five feet high, had an air, a dignity, about him that could not be overlooked. His hair, growing unusually long, swept poetically back behind the ears, and his beard was long and fine, and neither in the beard nor on his head was there a grey hair. It was a lustrous brown, and his dark eyes had a penetrating quality.

Young Dai Richards was asleep in his grandfather's arms. Pryce was asleep in a home-made cot to the side of the fire. When the old man stood up, he held Dai easily in his left arm, and shook hands with his right. "They've been good," he said to Nell. "I'll take Dai up now, and you bring Pryce. Then I'll be off. You won't want me here any longer."

He turned to Pen and Arnold as he was leaving the room. "You must be tired," he said. "We'll have time to talk later." They heard his peg-leg thudding the scrubbed uncarpeted stair. Nell picked up the child from the cot and followed.

"Well, now, you two make yourselves at home," Ianto said. "Go and hang your things in the passage; then go into the front room. There's a fire there. Nell'll want to feed Pryce. Then she'll come down to scrub my back, and after that we'll have supper in here."

There were pans of water boiling on the fire. Ianto brought a big wooden tub in from the back kitchen and put it on the rag mat. He began to unknot his red and black muffler.

Pen and Arnold sat side by side on a yellow plush sofa in the front room. The fire was bringing out the earthy unused smell of the place. Apart from the sofa, there were two chairs with yellow plush seats, a table covered with yellow plush, ball-fringed, and a draping of the same material on the mantelshelf. A bamboo tripod in the window supported an aspidistra whose leaves shone metallically, as though they had been polished, as indeed they had. Nell was a great "fettler." The brass fender twinkled. The bits and pieces of mirror in the fussy contraption over the fireplace twinkled. The fireirons and the legs of the chairs twinkled. The wood of the harmonium in the recess alongside the fireplace shone like silk.

Arnold put his arm round Pen and leaned his head on her shoulder. He was very tired. "This is nice, Pen," he said. "Something like this will suit me better than something like Castle Hereward."

"Aye, lad, I expect it'll have to," Pen said practically. "It'll take a bit of doing to get something like this. And I'm not a good housewife like Nell. You mustn't expect me to scrub *your* back."

"I'd love you to," said Arnold with daring.

"It's all right for Nell," Pen said, ignoring the opening, "but it's hell's delight for some o' t'women in these valleys. Husbands and sons and lodgers, all on different shifts, coming into the house all the hours God sends, having to bath without baths, and slopping their muck all over t'place. And in yon house in Ackroyd Park, where no one takes a bit o' muck from year's end to year's end, they bath in a bathroom every day. There's no sense in t'world, lad. This 'ere Rhondda'll open thi eyes."

The northern speech came easily to her lips as her excitement mounted. She got up and stood kicking at the fender, glaring down into the fire. Arnold smiled his patient smile. He reached out for her hand and pulled her back on to the sofa. "You old warhorse," he said. "You're always sniffing the battle. Forget it all for once. This is our wedding night."

She hitched up closer to him. "Do I get on your nerves?" she asked. "Sorry you ever met me? Sorry you ever married me?"

He stroked her hair. "We're a grand couple," he said. "Pen and Arnold Ryerson. Made for each other. You're like a cart running downhill, and I've got a dull job. I'm just the brakes. Just to prevent you from smashing yourself to pieces at the bottom."

"Poor Arnold!" she said. "I expect I'll lead you a devil of a dance."

He closed his hand over hers. "Listen! That's Ianto having his back scrubbed."

From the next room they could hear the slop and splash of water. Then suddenly Ianto's voice burst out, singing in Welsh, a clear powerful baritone, shaken with sudden gasps which suggested Nell's powerful hand, clutching a soapy flannel, going over him with spasmodic vigour. "It must be grand," said Arnold. "I can't sing. but I'd try."

They went back into the kitchen as Nell was drying the stone floor with a mop and Ianto, clad in a shiny navy-blue suit, was emptying the tub into the back-kitchen sink. Ianto's clothes, like most men's clothes in the Rhondda Valley, had three phases of life. They began resplendently, worn on Sundays only to Bethel or Horeb, Ebenezer, Zion, or Pisgah. In those dandy days they had high company: a collar round the wearer's neck, a hard hat on his head, and something special in the way of boots upon his feet. Then they became houseclothes, to be worn as Ianto was now wearing his navy-blue, or in casual knockings about the town, or on a visit to Cardiff for an international rugby match. They were not likely now to know the companionship of a collar. Look at Ianto, and you will see that there is a stud in the neckband of his Welsh flannel shirt, but he is enjoying the ease of being collarless. Neither is his footwear stylish now. An old pair of boots with the uppers sliced off serves him for slippers. Finally, the suit that once perhaps had graced a deacon's pew or harboured a body ecstatic with Hallelujah shouts goes down the pit, accompanied by a muffler, is dropped at night like the dirt it is to the floor alongside the wash-tub, and thereafter its fate need not be too closely inquired into. It may be blown to pieces in an explosion, or rotted by firedamp, or swamped by a sudden inflow of water. An arm of a coat or a leg of a trouser may remain where it has been cut off to facilitate the amputation of a limb; and if it finally escapes all these vicissitudes, the suit at last will be washed by a miner's wife and either become part of a rag mat or go, via some Darkie Cheap, to the shoddy mills, to begin life all over again, resurrected and renewed, meet for Zion or Bethel or Horeb.

"Put the supper, Ianto," Nell said. "I'll show 'em their room."

First, they went into the room at the front of the house where the big double bed was that Nell and Ianto shared. At the foot of it was the cot where Dai was now sleeping, a thumb in his mouth, and at the side of it was the high wicker cradle where Pryce, looking with his crinkled peach-bloom face incredibly unlike a potential troglodyte, whimpered for one moment at the noise of entry, then slept again. Nell looked about the room, in the faint glow of a night-light burning in a saucer, with the pride of her housewifery. "Nice," she whispered, "Ianto likes things to be nice."

There were crochet-work hair tidies hanging on the supports of the dressing-table's swinging mirror. Everything on the table – brush, comb, glass candlestick, a bottle or two – stood on its own crochet-work mat. An immense photograph of Ianto's father was oak-framed on the wall over the chest of drawers, on whose top was a brass-bound Bible, with a crochet mat on it and a pink vase of paper flowers on the mat. Nell, so big and strong and practical, seemed to dote on all the knick-knackery. She swept it up in one loving regard, and "Nice," she repeated. "Come and see your room."

Theirs was the back room. The curtains were undrawn. A moon had risen, and faintly by its light Arnold could see the hill rising up behind the house, seeming to impend upon it. From Heaven, no doubt, the great moon-silvered mountain looked no more than a mole-hill, he thought; and pictured the work of the busy moles who, even now, as incessantly, night and day, were at their work down there beneath this very room wherein he and Pen and Nell were standing: the bells clanging, the telephone ringing, the cage shooting up, falling down, loaded tubs running to the shaft, empty tubs running from the shaft, blind ponies plodding, brattice doors opening, shutting, the main way, the radial side-roads, low, timbered, small lengths of spruce and fir holding up the mountain, maintaining intact (with luck) the dark ways of the warren where the miners walk crouching, with Davy lamp, with pick, shovel, to the face, where they crouch, slide in eel-like on their sides, hack and hew as they lie, sometimes in stony places, sometimes in heat, sometimes in wet, so that always the empty tubs shall run from the shaft and the full tubs shall run to the shaft. And someone owns the mountain, someone who isn't God looking down from Heaven on the mole-hill, someone named the Marquis of This or the Duke of That, who never carries a Davy lamp, who never has red lips and white eyes shining in a black mask, but who is the lord and master of all this coal, all this petrified vegetation that æons ago was trampled by mammoths and mastodons and drank in the light of a day before *Homo sapiens* began to squat on his hunkers. All that old sunlight transmuted into trees transmuted into leaf-mould transmuted into coal is theirs because they are clever enough to own the fruit of all the sunlight that shone on steamy swamps before the first man uttered his first grunt, clever enough to own the mountain they have never seen, let alone what is going on under it. And those who know what is going on under it, and do what is going on under it, like old Richard Richards, they must come up and wash as they can in a wooden tub in front of the kitchen fire, and have a nice little house – and be thankful for it – with a crochet-work mat on the Bible and a pink vase of paper flowers on the mat.

"D'you think it's nice?" Nell was asking.

He turned with a start from the window, from his contemplation of the moon-frosted hillside. "Nice? Yes, it's splendid. It's very kind of you to have us, Nell. Is Ianto a socialist?"

"He doesn't bother much with politics," Nell said. "He's a poet."

To be a bard seemed somehow to be more even than to be a poet. And Ianto was a bard. He had a bardic title. His peers did not say "Good morning, Ianto Richards"; they said: "Good morning, Ap Rhondda." Every Welsh village contains at least one boy eaten with desire to be a bard, as inevitably as every Scottish village contains a boy who wants to see "Rev." before his name and "M.A." after it. Ianto was the bard of Cwmdulais. Crushed away at the foot of a column in the *South Wales Daily News* you would occasionally see a few verses in Welsh, signed Ap Rhondda. At the Horeb Eisteddfod every year Ap Rhondda could count on carrying off the bardic laurels, and even at the august National Eisteddfod, when all Wales assembled and the Archdruid donned his fabulous robes and drew the bardic sword and called *A Oes Heddwch?* and the white-robed bards responded *Heddwch!* – even there the name of Ap Rhondda was breathed with respect.

You wouldn't think this to see Ianto standing in the kitchen at Horeb Terrace, Cwmdulais, when Nell and Pen and Arnold came downstairs; but among the little dark Silures the poet has never been a man set apart from the people, but a man of the people, singing of the people's hopes and fears and joys from the midst of their own toiling ranks.

Now that Ianto was washed, Arnold could see him more clearly. He was no longer an anonymous black mask, but a slim, sinewy Welshman, blue-jowled, dark-eyed, with hollow jaws and a thin straight nose. His close-cut hair was as blue-black as a crow's wing. In the temple, on the bridge of the nose and in one cheek the powder explosions had tattooed him.

He stood at the table with a saucepan in one hand and a big wooden spoon in the other, his fingers blunt-ended, broken-nailed. Not a poet's hands, but everyone in Cwmdulais and even farther afield knew Ap Rhondda's poem about hearing the skylark on coming up from the night shift. We go down to hell; you go up to heaven; but what better do you or we know than our nest on the common earth? You can't translate it: it is a lovely lyric in the Welsh.

And this was the sort of thing the poet was thinking of; this was Ap Rhondda's nest: the small room with the old-fashioned cooking-range, the table with scrubbed American cloth in place of fine starched linen, the heavy earthenware plates, this odorous mash of meat, potato and gravy that he was now dishing out, and his phlegmatic Nell of the white columnar neck and red-glinting hair to share with him and Dai and Pryce. Give him these, and books to read, and Horeb where he could listen to a good sermon and join in the harmonies of the back-bone-creeping Welsh minor hymn-tunes – give him these and the Eisteddfods at which he stood forth, the bard, in the eyes of all men, and Ianto Richards asked for nothing more.

When supper was eaten, they sat round the unaccustomed fire in the front room and talked. It was unlike any conversation that Arnold had expected to hear in the Rhondda Valley. Ianto, who could recite enormous tracts of Shakespeare from memory, propounded and at great length supported a theory that Shakespeare was a Welshman. Did Pen and Arnold but know it, Ianto could bring positive proof that any distinguished person, in any walk of life, had at least a drop of Celtic blood in him. It was one of his manias. Arnold could not interest him in Labour politics or in politics of any sort. He was too polite to try very hard, and he was relieved when Ianto said naturally: "Well, indeed, I'm gassing too much as usual. It's bed you two will be wanting."

There were two candlesticks, with a box of matches in each, on the bottom step of the stairs. Ianto went out into the kitchen, and Pen remained in the front room with Nell, who had taken her in a close embrace and held her there. Arnold lit his candle and went up to the back bedroom. The moon was cloud-hidden now, and the mountain was nothing but a greater mass of darkness against the darkness of the sky. He looked timidly round the small icy room, and set his candle down on a chair. There was little light from it, and much wavering shadow. He wasn't thinking any more about the restless life going on by day and night beneath the mountain. He was doing nothing but listen: to the loud alarming beat of his own heart and to Pen's footsteps climbing the wooden stairs which seemed so noisy and unreticent.

When Arnold woke, he could see from where he lay on his back the whole extent of the mountain, clear to the top, and the sky above it. A sky of spring blue, with a few light clouds upon it, a lovely sky that promised a lovely day. He lay with his arm under Pen's shoulders. It felt as dead as mutton, but he wouldn't remove it. To lie there, relaxed, with Pen's shoulders squeezing the life out of his arm, with the blue sky soothing his eyes – this was heavenly. Pen was frowning a little in her sleep, as though she could never wholly relinquish the problems and preoccupations of the day. Even now, dead to the world, she was a fierce-looking little thing, sharp as a needle overanxious to mend all the rents in the world's happiness. He smiled at her tenderly, moved his head round, and kissed her cheek.

She woke as Ianto began to stir in the next room, sighed, and moved closer in to Arnold's side. They heard Nell and Ianto go downstairs, and water splashing into a tin bowl in the back kitchen, and Ap Rhondda spluttering with delight at God's good gift of clean cold water. They heard him lift up his voice and sing, but they did not understand the words.

"It must be wonderful," said Arnold, "to speak two languages as well as Ianto does. I tried to learn French. No good."

"It's a pity," Pen answered, "that there's more than one language on earth. It's nothing but a cause of strife and division."

"I'm not so sure of that," said Arnold. "I don't want to kiss everybody who talks English."

"I never suggested that you do. Let's get up. It's a nuisance in a house if people don't eat their meals at the same time."

"This is very nice," Arnold temporized, slipping his arm round her waist.

"Yes. Nice for you and nice for me. But not nice for Nell." She slipped from his grasp and got out of bed. "Come on. I shall not encourage you in self-indulgence."

He smiled at her meagre righteous little face and pretended to protest. "This is our honeymoon."

"I know. But it isn't Nell's. You're not Lord Liskeard with a staff of servants at a house in Italy."

"I'll bet his night-shirt's no better than this," said Arnold, plunging out on to the cold floor.

Pen turned from the wash-basin and contemplated the long white sack that clothed her husband to the ankles. "By heck, Arnie," she said. "Get summat on. You look like Lady Macbeth."

The four of them had breakfast together, and Nell, Pen and Arnold went to the front door and watched Ianto, carrying his basket and tea-tin, go with his lithe springy stride down the street. He was whistling as he went, glad of the grand morning. At the corner, by Horeb, he turned and waved, then stopped, looking up into the sky. Something had attracted his attention. He gestured to them, pointing upward. They looked, and could see nothing, but could hear. It was a skylark, singing over the Rhondda Valley. They all nodded vigorously to let Ianto know that they had heard, and off went Ap Rhondda, round the bend, out of sight. Perhaps, in that last glimpse they were to have of him, his own whistled song suspended to hear the lovelier song above, he was thinking of his famous lyric, savouring the pride and joy of the bard.

Nell went upstairs to attend to the children, and Pen and Arnold washed the breakfast things. Then they went out together, to see this famous place whose products, pouring through the funnel of Cardiff, crossed the seven seas of the world. It was a fascinating mixture of loveliness and squalor. They walked for miles along dingy roads; they climbed hills and looked down on the rows of dismal slate-roofed houses, on chapels built like bastilles, on the railway lines curving through valley bottoms, opening out into sidings, running into colliery yards, busy with trains gorging themselves with the coal that day and night threaded its way through the subterranean galleries to burst at last into the sunlight which it had quitted æons ago. Steam of locomotives, steam of engine sheds, staccato stutter of shunted trucks. And everywhere the waste-product of the industry, hurled in filthy heaps, piling up year after year, obliterating the green bases of the hills, fouling, corroding.

"How d'you fancy this as a place to live in?" Arnold asked.

"It's not a question of what we fancy," Pen answered. "I suppose, if you're born here, and all your friends are here, you're blind to half you see. But we're seeing it with new eyes, and, by heck, it's awful. There's plenty to do hereabouts, and it'd be a job worth tackling."

"Tackling?" cried Arnold, amused to hear on Pen's lips the word his mother loved. "You make me think of my mother when you say that."

"I could make you think of plenty as is worse than her. In fact, if you want to flatter me, go on talking like that."

They were lying high up on a hillside. The sun was warm. "*Me* flatter *you*?" said Arnold. "Come here. Let me kiss you. D'you know you're worth ten or a dozen of me?"

Pen pushed him aside roughly and sat up, her hands pressing down to the earth on either side of her. "There's summat up," she said. "Look at all t'people running." She pointed down into the valley. The people looked very small, but there was no mistaking their agitation. They were pouring from all directions toward the entrance of a colliery yard. They were through the gates. All the scattered bits and pieces of them were congealing in a milling mass outside the colliery office. Pen and Arnold got up and began to run. They did not even know the name of the pit that Ianto worked in. They did not know upon which pit there had swooped the disaster that this agitation spelled for them. But both their hearts were frozen with a single thought: Ianto! Ianto!

Ianto called the pony Hugh Price Hughes. He himself did not know why. It was one of those damn-fool things that begin somehow, and then go on. Now the pony, a stubborn little beast, expected to be addressed by the full honorific title: otherwise it would not budge. Over its stall its name was written in chalk: Hugh Price Hughes, M.A., B.D., which Ianto would explain with a smile meant Master of Anguish and Bachelor of Docility.

Master of Anguish! Ap Rhondda had written a poem about Hugh Price Hughes, ambling blindly through the stone forest that once had been a green forest, pulling the tubs down the petrified woodland rides from which the gods had withdrawn, on which the sun neither rose nor set. The anguish, no doubt, was in the mind of the poet, not of the horse. But to Ianto, Hugh Price Hughes was a symbol of all that was condemned to loss of beauty for the sake of coal: a symbol of much in his own life, of the valleys degraded from the bearing of corn, of the streams that once knew the clean leap of trout into sunshine and that oozed now over the accumulated filth of an industry that never cleaned up its dirty leavings. Hugh Price Hughes, who had given his eyes without a murmur, summed all this up, the supreme Master of Anguish; and Ianto hoped in his poem that the good god of men and beasts would grant to the pony, stumbling in his blindness along the roadways of the pit, an inner life irradiated with green fields in sunshine and celestial colts gambolling in meadows star-bright with daisies.

Hugh Price Hughes seemed comfortable enough down there in his stygian stall that was odorous with dung and urine and knew nothing of winter's blasts or summer heats. He was temperamental. He was unhappy with anyone but Ianto, liable to kick viciously or to stand stock-still with invincible stubbornness unless the lilting voice of Ap Rhondda was in his ear. Ianto in the pit would sing for hours on end, and Hugh Price Hughes seemed happier for that. Ianto's pocket was always filled with bread crusts, to be doled out as the labours of the long dark day dragged on.

When the explosion rocked Cwmdulais Main the poet and the pony in one fell second found themselves encompassed by the same tomb. Ianto had not even the time to cry aloud before the aisles and transepts hewn through the coal were staggering in a ghastly disintegration. The little pit props, so carefully carried so many miles across the sea, so carefully placed upright to take, puny Atlases, the downward thrust of all the world, splintered like matchsticks holding together a toy on which a giant's foot had stamped as the giant shrieked in rage. One moment Ianto and the pony were ambling along, Ianto in full song; the next a mightier voice had drowned his singing; the mountain had heaved its shoulders; the world crumbled.

The bellow eased away to a rumble, a thunder's diminuendo, and then silence fell save for the uneasy creak and strain of huge dislodged masses settling down to new adjustments of thrust and counterpoise. By the light of his Davy lamp, Ianto could see that doors had been shut behind him and before. He had no tools to swing to test their thickness. He kicked with his hobnailed boots; he might as well have kicked against the granite bastions of Land's End.

Splintered trucks were strewn about him. Before him the pony lay upon his side. Hugh Price Hughes would kick no more; the fallen coal held him rigid in his final obstinacy. Soon now, if ever, his eyes would open on the fields of celestial colts. He had fallen sideways; all four legs were imprisoned to the knees in the forward wall.

Ianto knelt over the fallen pony. "Well, old butty," he said, and he could say no more. He knew he was done for as surely as Hugh Price Hughes. The yellow-slimed lips of the Master of Anguish were drawn back over his long yellow teeth. His blind eyes seemed fixed in an agony of appeal upon Ap Rhondda's face. The broken forward part of a truck was uneasy under the pony's shoulders and Ianto began to tug it away, so that the beast might at least lie easy. Hugh Price Hughes, as though divining the intention and resolved to assist it, heaved his shoulders up with a supreme convulsive effort. The truck came away and the pony sank down with a long sighing expulsion of the breath. "That's better, old butty," Ianto said, knowing that Hugh Price Hughes was dead and done for.

There was nothing now for him to do but sit and listen. He had listened in his time with joy to many things: to the singing of larks and the chuckling of streams over pebbles; to the moan of the wind and the rhythmic alternation of the waves' tumbling and their rasping backwash; to the thrust of bolts that meant that the day was done, with all well and Nell waiting for him upstairs; to the quavering cries of lambs and of his own new-born sons; to many voices upraised in Horeb in the greatest hymn-tunes the world has known, and to applause sweeping toward him, the bard, Ap Rhondda, ambrosial, sweet with the acceptance of his offerings to men. All these things he had heard and loved in his deep and simple fashion; but now it was not for these he was listening. He was listening, leaning back against the dead companion of so many labours, for the tapped-out code which would mean the swinging pick and crowbar, the sinewy assault of the saviours who, he knew, never by fault of their own left men to perish.

He never heard it. He did not know of the obstacle upon obstacle that lay between him and the mouth of the shaft. He did not for some time know of the gas seeping through this dead infernal forest as once the mist had seeped, twining about the trees that now were black brittle stone. But at last, through the tiny chinks and fissures of his cell it reached him, and numbed him and killed him, and those who know the strange secrets of the stone forest and never tell them found him with his arms thrown across Hugh Price Hughes's body and his face buried in his flank, as though he had cast himself down there and died weeping.

Fifteen hearses, and after each hearse three or four carriages, with black horses pulling the hearses and carriages, and many spring flowers piled on top of the coffins that were varnished yellow and glittered with bright metal fittings; and in front of all the hearses and carriages a colliery band with silver instruments flashing in the light of the spring day, a band that walked with the stilted unnatural gait of the living trying to be as near as possible to the immobility of the dead, while the silver instruments snarled their sorrow. The Dead March in Saul. And behind the band, and the hearses with their flowers, and the carriages with crape-veiled faces at the windows, came the anonymous many, dressed in the Sabbath black of Horeb and Zion and Siloam. Thousands of them, a procession one mile long, so that the last slow-stepping straggling tail could not hear the wailing of the silver trumpets or the solemn thud of the drum, but only the singing of the larks climbing above the Rhondda Valley to their celestial look-outs.

Nell and old Richard Richards were in a carriage; Arnold and Pen walked, he with his face fixed, dumb with misery, upon his slow-shuffling boots, she with her eyes lifted fiercely and resentfully to the sky.

There was a long way to go, and when presently the band fell for a moment to silence there was an indescribable poignancy in the sound of the feet. Nothing else could be heard. All the sounds of labour were stilled for the day. Along the roads the blinds were down, and those who were not in the procession were standing bowed in their doorways. And through the silence went the sound of the feet: not the purposive beat of soldiers' feet marching, not the gay staccato of feet going anyhow about their business; but a drear muffled unison, sorrow made audible, the texture and colour of crape translated into sound. It was, thought Pen, like humanity's slow march to some inevitable Calvary; and Arnold, who could not formalize his impression, wept quietly at the moment's content of unassuageable sadness.

Then the silver trumpets sang again, giving this time a theme that passed through the procession, inviting them all to take what consolation they might for the brevity and uncertainty of their days. The tune "Aberystwyth," with its almost unbearable agonies of hope and supplication, throbbed through the air among the mountains, and all the host began to sing.

Never before had Pen and Arnold heard the Welsh sing. Never do the Welsh sing so heart-rendingly as on such an occasion as that was. "Jesu, Lover of my soul," they sang in their own wild haunting tongue to that tune whose harmonies, embroidered by those thousands of untutored masters, could almost rend the heart from the body.

> Other refuge have I none,
> Hangs my helpless soul on Thee;
> Leave, ah, leave me not alone,
> Still support and comfort me.
> Thou of life the fountain art,
> Freely let me take of Thee.
> Spring Thou up within my heart,
> Rise to all eternity.

Silence again, and the dirge of the feet again; till the trumpets, passing within the cemetery gates, begin once more to dole out the muffled heart-beats of the Dead March.

The mile-long procession disposed itself in a ragged black circle around the fifteen graves. The Rev. Taliesin Howell, M.A., B.D., committed the bodies to the ground, and if bodies could ever be at home in the ground then surely these should be which had moved for so many years so familiarly through its secret ways.

"These our brothers..."

They would be for a while remembered for many things. Evan Hughes, the best three-quarter Cwmdulais had ever put in the field; Owen Rees, the adulterer and wife beater; Gwilym Price, a deacon of

Horeb; William Williams, who ran the gambling school out on the mountain; Henry Richardson, the Englishman, a huge flavoursome bawd and drunkard; Johnny Potham, who played the fiddle divinely; Ianto Richards, the poet, and all the rest of them, each with the mark and superscription of his own idiosyncrasy upon him. "These our brothers…" That is all that need be remembered at this moment. Brothers in the hardship and peril of life. Brothers in the uncertainty and brevity of days.

"Brothers," said Pen, as Arnold lay with his arms about her in bed that night. "What a time to call men brothers, when you're laying 'em in the earth."

They were speaking very quietly, drawn close together by the day's sorrow, which was with them still in the sound of Nell's smothered weeping in the next room.

"It's a beautiful service," Arnold said. "It's just as well to remember that death comes for the lot of us. We're brothers to that extent, anyway."

Pen grasped him tight and hid her face in his shoulder. "No, no!" she whispered fiercely. "Don't let's remember anything of the sort. Don't talk about death. I hate the thought of death. You can call men what you like when they're dead – these clods, these corpses. I want to walk about in Bradford and the Rhondda Valley, and think 'These our brothers.' Then's the time. And that's when people don't do it. And that's what we've got to do, Arnie. If Socialism doesn't mean that, it means nothing. What the parsons say over a coffin is all blarney and eyewash."

He could feel her body quivering with sorrow and anger. "Yes, yes," he said, soothingly.

She was quiet for a while, and then she said: "I think Ianto had a very happy life."

"I'm sure of it."

"But what Nell and the children will do I don't know. She was enough to break your heart tonight with those old poems."

She was enough to break anybody's heart. Old Richard Richards had come in, and Nell had produced from a drawer of the kitchen table the penny exercise book in which Ianto had written a fair copy of his work. "Read 'em," Nell said; and Richard Richards read them in the language that no one there but he could understand. But they could understand the rhythm and the lilt of the old man's voice; and Nell sat as white and rigid as a big statue, but with a fond silly smile on her face. It wasn't a smile of pleasure; it was a smile to wring the heart, because it was a smile that was an almost inhuman mask against human sorrow.

"This is the one about the skylark," the old man would say in English; and then the rippling Welsh would follow; "and this is the one about Hugh Price Hughes." Hugh Price Hughes, the Master of Anguish. Perhaps St. Francis would have counted him in with "these our brothers."

Nell put the book back in the kitchen drawer. "I'm glad Dai and Pryce will speak Welsh," she said. "It'll be nice for them. I'll get them all printed."

And when the old man was gone she said brightly: "Well, I'm going up now. Don't you two hurry."

They went up five minutes later and heard her smothered sobs coming from the big double bed in the room where the crochet-work mat was on the brass-bound Bible and the paper flowers were in the vase on the mat.

"Well," said Arnold, "we're having a queer honeymoon, luv."

"It's good for us," Pen answered. "Life's not a lot of silly stuff and flapdoodle, We've learned pretty soon what the Rhondda Valley is. We've learned summat about the price of coal. Let's go on learning, and let's do it here. What d'you say, Arnie? Could you stick this place?"

"Aye, I could stick owt with thee, lass."

She sat up and looked down at his serious face in the candleshine. "Owt? Ah believe tha would. Tha's a good old gowk, Arnie. Tha knows Ah luv thee?"

"Ah'm beginnin' to think there'd be nowt much to life if tha didn't, lass," he said, and pulled her down beside him.

Chapter Fourteen

"I know what men say of me. The favourite word is arrogant. Very well, I accept that. I am arrogant, if it is arrogant to have never been without awareness of my own worth. I am as God made me, and He made me with a sense of work to do and a sharp impatience with circumstances and people that got in the way of my doing it. Is this arrogance? Call it so if you like. I know that when Lostwithiel – Liskeard as he then was – defeated me in 1892, I felt as though he was holding up the march of history. As he was. Was it arrogance to be bitter then? I was bitter."

This belongs to a very late stage of the diary. In the early parts, the young man is content to record. Toward the end of his life, the old man, increasingly aware of himself as a personality, is apt to parse and analyse himself, and to justify his ways to men.

It was an understatement to say that he was bitter when Lord Liskeard defeated him in the St. Swithin's division in the General Election of 1892. It was the first substantial reverse of his life, and what made it worse was that his vote was only a few score more than Arnold Ryerson's had been. There was not much kudos in the fight, either. He had burst like a bombshell into the constituency when Arnold fought the by-election. The eyes of the country were on St. Swithin's. Newspapers would use what he had to say about it. This General Election was another matter. The fight raged throughout the country. There was no reason why the particular spot known as the St. Swithin's division of Bradford should attract attention. Old Gladstone, the Liberal warhorse, was uttering his last snort. This already legendary, rough-hewn, huge-beaked figure, eighty-three years old, with a Home Rule Bill for Ireland up his sleeve – he was the cynosure. In the light of that spectacular sunset, what happened to Mr. Hamer Shawcross was of small account. His defeat was unnoticed. Perhaps that was as bitter a thing as any. He was so convinced that he was by now a figure, as indeed he was. He was the author of *Tyler, Ball and Company*, of *Work without Wages* and *Wages without Work*, two books which brilliantly presented the lot of those who lived by working and those who lived on rents and interest. Besides these three enormously popular books, he was the author of innumerable tracts that brought him a steady income, he was accustomed to be consulted at every turn by those who hoped soon to bring an Independent Labour Party into being, and wherever there was an agitator's job to be done – and, goodness knows, in the conditions of the time these jobs were innumerable – Hamer Shawcross's eloquence was enlisted to blow up the fire. He and his sabre were here, there and everywhere, and he had indeed every reason to know that he was a national figure. But the cold fact remained that he was still battering in vain at the door of Parliament, and that Liskeard had slipped in again, and that, nationally, it seemed to matter to no one whether he was in or out. What caught everyone's eye was that Gladstone was in, to give the old Queen another bellyache, and that Keir Hardie was in. She wouldn't, of course, know what Keir Hardie meant, but Lizzie Lightowler knew, and Hamer and Ann knew. It put a pleasant coating on the pill of Hamer's defeat.

They walked home together through the summer night to Lizzie's house: she and Ann, Hamer and Jimmy Newboult. Jimmy's white fanatic face was strained with the work and worry of the last few weeks. He felt that the defeat was all his fault. Henceforth, whenever anything went wrong with Hamer Shawcross, Jimmy Newboult was to take it upon his own heart.

"No man was ever more faithfully served than I was served by James Newboult." This was the tribute of the diary years afterwards. "Our meeting was casual, at the time when I first went to the St. Swithin's division. When my friend Ryerson was defeated there and I was chosen as the prospective candidate, we began to build up a strong organization with Mrs. Lightowler as chairman of the committee, my wife doing the secretary's work, and Newboult as election agent. His father died soon after the election Ryerson fought, and Mrs. Lightowler removed Newboult from the slum he lived in and set him up in a small tobacconist's and newsagent's shop. He made a success of it, and all his leisure he devoted to my affairs. He would not, at that time, accept a salary, but he remained tenaciously concerned for my welfare up to the time when he became my parliamentary private secretary, on my appointment as Minister for the Co-ordination of Internal Affairs. That our long – and to me, lovely – association ended under a cloud has been a matter of gossip; but my conscience in the matter is clear, and if, contrary to my wishes, this private record is ever made public, this at any rate will stand daylight: that whatever, at the end, James Newboult thought of me, I have never ceased to think of him as a noble spirit, dedicated to the service of his fellows and tireless in heaping good upon myself."

What then – that hot summer night, walking up Manningham Lane with Hamer's hand laid across his shoulder – could Jimmy imagine. of what might happen "at the end?" He was a man of the passionate present moment, and all that he could receive into his mind was the bitter truth that they had fought – fought like the devil – and lost. He could recall Lostwithiel's painted sneer as he led his son to the window to receive the cheers of the dupes who could not see the light. "How do they do it? How the devil do they do it?" he demanded angrily, flinging down his hat in Lizzie's hall.

They went upstairs to the old den that had seen so many of their conferences, listened to so much of their hope and fear. Lizzie threw up the window and the air that flowed in was at furnace heat. She stood looking at the poplars drawn like black quills upon the luminous air, and at the hills beyond them, where a young moon was following the sun down the sky. "The baby helped," she said.

The baby indeed had been most opportune. The Viscountess Liskeard, who had done so well as Lettice Melland, did even better this time, canvassing for a few days, then taking to her bed, so that the rumour of her illness sent a wave of sympathy in Liskeard's direction; then allowing it to be known that the illness was but the prelude to a "happy event," so that sympathy changed to genial good wishes; and finally producing a daughter on the eve of polling-day. Old Buck Lostwithiel drove about in his drag, calling on the burgesses to "vote for the Honourable Molly's father" and distributing largess for the drinking of health to "dam and filly," as he gaily put it.

"We'll keep up the succession," he shouted into the torrid Town Hall Square when the result was known. "I suppose by the time the Honourable Molly's twenty-one, you'll have votes for women and women members doing their darning in the House of Commons.

I'll be in my grave by then – but not much before then – soh, no! – and my son will be in the House of Lords. Then you'll want a new member. Well, we've produced one for you on the eve of this happy day. You need never go outside the family."

"Yes," said Lizzie, "undoubtedly the baby helped."

They stood round her at the window, looking into the silent night. Hamer's arm was still on Jimmy's shoulder. He knew what Jimmy was feeling, and the friendly gesture said to Jimmy: "It's not your fault – not your fault at all."

"Well," said Lizzie suddenly, "I've always liked this view. I liked it the day my husband brought me here, and I've never got tired of it. But this is good-bye. There's nothing more to be done here."

"There's everything to be done," said Hamer. "There's St. Swithin's to be taken from Liskeard."

"That's your job," Lizzie answered. "And you'll do it. I'm not afraid of that. But Keir Hardie's in. Labour is in. Why are we moping? Why are we standing here as dull as cod on a slab? You, Jimmy Newboult, why aren't you singing Hallelujahs? Don't you all see what it means? The thin end of the wedge. Our people – Labour and nothing but Labour – are in Parliament. I'm going to London. The scene has shifted, my children, and I want to be in the middle of it."

Hamer, indeed, saw what it meant. He had seen it just as soon as Lizzie. But he was not yet ready to rejoice. It was still incredible to him that he – he! – had been rebuffed.

It was characteristic of Lizzie Lightowler that within a week of making up her mind to go to London, she was there. She found a little house in North Street, that opens off Smith Square in Westminster; she hustled the decorators at one end and the furniture removers at the other; and, when all was done, she looked ruefully at her new quarters that lacked the space of the square black Bradford house and that had no outlook on familiar hills climbing to the moors. But she could walk to the House of Commons in ten minutes; and, lying in her bed at night, she could not only hear the boom of Big Ben but almost feel his reverberation, which seemed to her like the breathing of history.

On the sixth of August Ann and Hamer travelled to London. Neither knew much about the place, and they had not been there together before. Arm-in-arm, they walked out of King's Cross Station into the dirty Euston Road which they looked upon with wonder that this wilderness of filthy brick and stone could indeed be the Babylon that they must capture.

They walked to Westminster: down Southampton Row, and along the Strand to Whitehall, and down Whitehall to the towers and pinnacles and crumbling stones: the Houses and the Abbey, Westminster Hall and St. Margaret's Church. Now Babylon looked another matter. They stood entranced, Hamer holding the small wooden box which had travelled with him through five continents, Ann with a sunshade tilted over her shoulder. Buses and hansom cabs and four-wheelers flashed and rumbled by; pigeons tumbled in the air above the towers that were so white upon the blue; from the river came the hoot of tugs and the occasional moan of a siren.

"So this is it," said Hamer at last; "this is what all the dusty work and drudgery means – to get through those doors."

Ann pushed the sunshade farther back so that she could look up into his face. She was conscious of a shock of surprise at its hungry concentrated stare. "It means more than that," she said. "Getting through those doors – yes, that's a beginning. But it won't be the end of the dusty work and drudgery. You've got to make 'em see in there all the dust and work and drudgery there is in the world, and make 'em see the people who endure it."

For a moment he did not answer. He continued to stare toward the House; then "Eh? What?" he said. "Oh, yes, there's all that, too."

Ann was aware of a little chill that struck her in the hot August street. "All that, too." Oh, *that* first and foremost and all the time, her heart cried; else what meaning is there in all I have been, all I have done, ever since the night I met you – the night that meant the loss of home, and parents, the swift change from everything I was till then?

Big Ben tolled two. "That's the voice of it all," said Hamer. "I hear that bell in my dreams. This is what Wordsworth was looking at, Ann, when he wrote the sonnet on Westminster Bridge, these very towers and spires. *Earth hath not anything to show more fair.* The Lake poet! Hasn't that ever struck you as strange? Here was the man dedicated to the beauty of nature, living among lakes and mountains, famous as the poet of solitude. And he puts it all second best to this – the very heart of a great city. And, by God, he was right! This is it. Earth has not anything to show more fair."

It was, Ann reflected, a typical Hamer observation. Often as she had read the sonnet, that thought had never struck her. "I don't think anyone but you would have noticed that," she smiled, tucking her arms in his. "Let's go. From Aunt Lizzie's directions, we can't be more than ten minutes away from North Street."

The day was good again, the little tug at her heart forgotten.

They found Keir Hardie in Lizzie's house. They had met him before, but Ann at any rate felt she was looking at someone she had never met. Hardie got out of his chair and engulfed her hand in his. "I feel we ought to be introduced," she said. "This is the first time I've met the most significant man in Great Britain."

His grave face softened to a smile, "Significant? No, no, Mrs. Shawcross. There's a rising tide, you see. I happen to be the first bit of flotsam it's pushed up on the beach. There'll be more – lots more. But the significant thing is the tide. Remember that, Shawcross."

He was thirty-seven – ten years older than Hamer. His face was of startling candour and integrity. Hair of a golden brown, already turning a little grey, curled above the broad serene forehead. The deep-set eyes glowed with purpose; the nose was beautifully shaped, and the beard failed to conceal the mingled strength and kindness of the mouth. He was a peasant. His face might have been a peasant's or an enlightened prince's: it was a man's.

Ann was aware of his fearsome struggle: working at six years old, in the coal-mine at ten, wresting knowledge how and when he could. All this was written in the deep lines of the forehead, and the triumph over it was in the serenity that shone from the man's face in an almost palpable emanation.

Hamer sat down and lit his pipe. "I'll expect to see you on the wagonette tomorrow," Hardie said with a smile.

"Wagonette?"

"Aye. It's a daft idea some of the boys have. They want to take me to the House in triumph. It doesn't run to a four-in-hand turn-out, so some of them have hired a wagonette, and we're driving to the House in that. I'll humour them, though I'd prefer to walk or ride on a donkey. But I'd like you to be there, Shawcross. After all, however we do it, it'll be Labour's first appearance in the House." He leaned forward and laid his hand on Hamer's with the extraordinary benevolence that was part of him. "That being so," he said, "you have a right to be present."

"I did not accept this invitation," Hamer wrote in the diary. "I have an enormous admiration for Keir Hardie, but I did not want to appear at his side, riding in a wagonette. I excused myself on the ground that others had done more for the party than I had, but the fact is that when I ride to the House I shall ride in my own chariot, not another man's."

But he was there with Ann and Lizzie to see the chariot arrive. Parliament Square was full of eager movement in the bright August sunshine. Hansom cabs and broughams and victorias rolled to the doors of the House, bringing old members who had been re-elected and new members making their first acquaintance with the solemnities of the senate. There were famous figures to catch the eye and hold the attention: Gladstone, Salisbury, Buck Lostwithiel, driving his drag with Liskeard and a party of friends behind him.

"And there's the Brummagem bagman," said Hamer, as Joe Chamberlain, wearing his property outfit of orchid and monocle, staring his stupid unintelligent stare, passed through the door. "The Radical! The awful bogeyman who used to frighten the dear old Queen! Well! He's lived and learned which side his bread is buttered on."

It was a relief to him to talk. The sight of Liskeard entering the House had caused his heart to thump. There, given the grace of God, might be I. But the grace of God was strangely withheld; and a moment later there was old Lostwithiel, driving the drag homeward, grinning like the devil he was, and pointing Hamer out with his whip to Lady Liskeard. "D'you want a lift anywhere, Mr. Shawcross?" he shouted, checking the pace of his horses. "Can I run you up to St. Swithin's? Plenty to do there, y'know."

Hamer's face flamed. He remembered this girl leaning from her pony to push with a stick his hat from out of her way, as though it were a piece of dirt. He remembered this vile old man charging upon him behind four horses in a Bradford street. He would have liked to throw something in their teeth. At that moment, strident in the hot air of the summer day, sounded the gay note of a cornet, and Keir Hardie's wagonette drove up. The cornet-player made the hot air ring. The two horses trotted gallantly; the group of men in the homely vehicle had an air of mild festivity, as though they were boys permitted an unaccustomed day out. Hardie sat sedate among them, wearing an old cloth cap, a tweed suit, a flannel shirt soft in the collar. He jumped down from the wagonette, and, amid a little spattering of applause from his companions and a final hearty cadenza from the cornet, disappeared into the House.

Lostwithiel and Lady Liskeard had both turned to stare. They did not need to be told who this homely fellow was, nor did they need any lesson concerning his significance. Lady Liskeard turned from watching the little comedy, her face lit by a smile not without humour and sympathy, but Lostwithiel had a grin that was at once malicious and rueful. "Cheer up, my lord," Hamer shouted. "Surely you can buy off a chap like that!"

Lostwithiel glared at him murderously, flicked his leaders, and drove away, with the wagonette hanging tenaciously to his tail.

"That's that," said Hamer. "Let's go now."

They began to walk back to North Street, and he saw that Lizzie Lightowler's eyes were full of tears. "He's so good!" she said. "I'm an old fool, a right old fool, but I feel so happy because our first man is such a *good* man."

Lizzie got them tickets to attend a session of the House. They listened to Gladstone rumbling. They looked down from their gallery upon the Government bench, upon all the faces that had been legend and were now become flesh for the first time; at members sprawling in the heat, hands in pockets, papers over their eyes, frankly asleep; at members strolling in and out as casually as though what was being conducted here were the affairs of a coffee-stall; at the wigged speaker, the sword, the mace. They looked at Keir Hardie, sitting there, saying nothing, absorbing everything, taking the measure of his opponents, biding his time.

It seemed to Hamer a slipshod, unimpressive business, if he judged it by the standard of his reason; but he knew that what he saw was only a casual, momentary foreground, and what he felt was an immense background whose drama and potency he could not withstand. "At the bar of the Commons." The words kept drilling through his head all the afternoon. Dull the House might seem, and at this moment pettifogging and parochial; but these were the common people of England. *"Ah, my friends!"*

Or were they? He looked again at Gladstone, Chamberlain, Hartington, Liskeard: out of the whole bang shoot of them, he thought,

I doubt if there's a man except Keir Hardie who knows the first thing about the common people save as a matter of bluebooks and statistics. These people the Commons? Yes, maybe, as a pleasant constitutional fiction. But a great deal would have to happen before the fiction had any relation to the facts.

"Looking at Hardie sitting there so lonely, surrounded by the hordes of the two great parties that had shared the sweets of office from time immemorial, I felt anew the *urgency* of our task. Pleasant though this brief London interlude had been, I hurried back to Bradford to take up anew the duty of pushing Liskeard out of the St. Swithin's division."

He never did push him out. That was always for Hamer Shawcross a sore point, almost a point of humiliation. Liskeard knew it. He could always touch Shawcross on the raw by reminding him of it. When they were both old men, and Lettice seemed twenty years younger than either of them, Hamer stood looking at her portrait by Ambrose McEvoy, hanging side by side with the portrait that Sargent had painted so long before. She had developed a wise and lovely face. Everything was in it except age. Her hair had retained the colour of its youth, and the painter had put a tiara in it, above the brow that had not a line to spoil its broad benevolence. The portrait hung in the great hall at Castle Hereward, and the evening sun, striking through the stained glass that filled the stone mullions, fell upon the floor in blues and greens and purples, and one pure ray shone directly upon the face of the portrait so that the diamonds in Lettice's hair seemed to sparkle.

The whole scene within the great hall was just as young Hamer Shawcross, with a wonderful precision of imagination, had seen it when, years before, standing on the edge of the moor with Arnold Ryerson, he had first looked on Castle Hereward and on Lady Lettice Melland riding a tubby pony over the humpbacked bridge.

And now he was inside, and dinner was over, and he knew that Lettice, who had a perfect apprehension of his moods and needs, had asked the other guests to leave him to himself. Tomorrow night he had a big speech to deliver in Leeds.

He strolled into the great hall, a fine figure in his evening clothes, his snow-white hair shining in the light of the summer evening, a cigar between his lips. On the walls about him were the Lostwithiels and their women from time out of mind. There was old Buck with his satanic grin, as Augustus John had marvellously seen him; and here was this latest one of all: Lettice by McEvoy.

Hamer was a connoisseur, and he was looking at the picture, head on one side, assuring himself in all sincerity that he preferred the Henry Lamb portrait of himself which had appeared at the same exhibition, when a soft footfall on the polished boards swung him round.

Lettice's husband removed the cigar from his lips and ranged himself with a smile at Hamer's side. Hamer would never have believed that young Liskeard could develop into this formidable Lostwithiel who stood beside him. Two wars, three important Embassies, a tireless interest in the game of politics, had made the young man Hamer once knew a figure that would have rejoiced old Buck's heart: oiled with the suavity of a diplomat, full of veiled power that was never turned on like the water of a torrent but pumped up endlessly at need like the water of a well. He didn't mind Lettice's interest in Labour cabinet ministers, though he never concealed from her his belief that the sooner the country was quit of them the better. Now his eyes looked out quizzically from his long bony face, and he said, waving his cigar toward the portrait: "Good, eh? You like it?"

"Within limits – yes," said the Rt. Honourable Hamer Shawcross.

"Excellent, excellent," Lostwithiel answered. "Within limits. Limits are so important. All through dinner I was thinking about the old days in Bradford. Bless my soul – how long it is since I saw St. Swithin's! I expect you still see a good deal of the place."

"Oh, yes; a fair amount."

Lostwithiel chuckled. "You never pushed me out, you remember. I'm not easy to push out." He paused as if to let that sink in. "Well, I'm told I musn't disturb you. Happy cogitations." He went in his discreet noiseless fashion, leaving Hamer staring at the portrait. "Not easy to push out." Now what the devil did the fellow mean by that?

It was Buck who really pushed Liskeard out of his seat and let Hamer into it. Hamer turned to look at the John portrait, one of the painter's earliest works, done in the year of the old man's death. The old villain to the life. John couldn't resist anything so racy, so utterly unique, as Buck Lostwithiel, boasting in his ninety-sixth year that the devil was not going to have him for a long time yet. There he was, grey hat at an angle, cigar at a slant, yellow gloves holding the ribbons, just as he must have looked when he set out to win his celebrated wager. Old Lord Carrickfergus, his bosom crony, had been visiting him at Castle Hereward. Lostwithiel was ninety-six that day, and at dinner, in the room from which Hamer had just emerged, he was in the humour of a skeleton elated at finding itself unexpectedly capable of locomotion. He kept up a crackle of reminiscence, aware of himself as a national institution, recalling episodes of a past so remote that the younger members of the party were tongue-tied with admiration, as though longevity in itself were an achievement. And, indeed, a longevity such as Buck Lostwithiel's was an achievement of no mean sort, for the creaking old skeleton could still touch its toes, and drink its brandy. and get through a day with no assistance from anyone. He and Carrick-fergus, ten years his junior, were bragging one against the other about what they could still do; and Carrickfergus was moved to say: "Well, Buck, I don't suppose you'll ever drive a four-in-hand again."

"Dammit, Ernie," Lostwithiel squeaked in his high falsetto, "I'll drive a four-in-hand this very night if you'll have the guts to sit beside me."

Carrickfergus received the offer with a smile, unfortunately for Buck a smile of disbelief. Buck tottered to his feet and cried: "I wager you five hundred guineas I'll drive a four-in-hand at a hell of a lick five times round the measured mile. Come with me or not. D'ye take me?"

"I take you, and I come with you. Give me a horn."

Carrickfergus, too, had now risen to his feet, and for a moment the table was held in the silence of consternation. Then Liskeard got up. "Father, I don't think you are wise—"

"'Wise?" said the trembling old man. "Who's talking about wisdom? Come along, Ernie. Here – Bellows," he shouted to the butler, "get the grooms. Get the drag out. Have the greys harnessed."

Then Lady Liskeard intervened, rising and laying a hand on his arm, while her husband appealed to Carrickfergus. "I beg you, sir!" Lettice said. "Please! It would be madness at your age. It's a bitter night."

"Can't I dress, gel?" he shouted. "Can't I get into something warm? Those damned horses have been eating their heads off too long."

There was now a regular hubbub in the room, the older people trying to restrain the two headstrong old men; the young thought-lessly clapping their hands and urging them on. "The sort of thing that happened in the Regency," one young fool was saying. "You'll be a legend, Buck," he added; and Lettice, white with anger, slapped him suddenly in the face. That was the second sensation of the night. The first was reported in every paper in the country; this one was not. But it started a feud which was never healed between two famous families.

When it was clear that nothing would deter the obstinate old men, Lettice made it her business to see at least that Lostwithiel was warmly clad. She went with him to his room, wrapped flannel round the frosty armour of his shirt, put a woollen muffler about his neck, and buttoned him into his celebrated bottle-green greatcoat with the capes and slender waist – there were two silver buttons at the back of it – and the flowing skirts. She took off his shining evening pumps and pulled thick bed-socks over his silken hose. Then she got him into his boots. She wanted to put on his head a deerstalker cap, and to tie the flaps over his ears; but at that he rebelled. "What, m'dear! Drive in that damned thing? And be a laughing stock for the rest of my days?"

"I'm thinking of the rest of your days," said Lettice patiently, standing there, the firelight falling on her in her low-bosomed dress of flamy silk, the absurd cap in her hand.

The old man was smitten with sudden compunction. He looked at her with admiration lighting the dark orbs that were sunk so deep in their sockets. "By God, Letty m'dear," he said, "you're a fine-looking woman. That boy of mine is lucky. Give him a son, m'dear, there's a good gel. Give him a son. We want sons – the likes of us – with the country in the damned state it is. Give us a kiss, m'dear."

She never could overcome her repugnance at the idea of kissing his lips or painted cheeks. She could not now – this last time when it would be possible to do so. He was tall and upright, and he bent his head, and she touched her lips to his forehead.

"You're sure you want to do this mad thing?" she asked.

He switched on his old grin. "Quite sure," he said. "Give us a decent hat, gel. Let's face my God like a gentleman."

She gave him his grey topper and yellow gloves, and, fully arrayed, he stepped to the long mirror and surveyed himself. He adjusted the hat half-an-inch to the left. "There!" he said. "That's how my father used to look when he drove down to Brighton to see fat George. That man was a bloody fool, m'dear. I've thought that all my life, and now I've said it. And a bore. And a boor. No gentleman. You'll see changes, Letty, lots of changes. They'll be due to fellers like that. They let us down."

He walked out of the room and down the grand staircase, straight as a reed, but a reed shaking a little.

Carrickfergus had been given a horn, and he greeted approaching Lostwithiel with a silver blast. He, too, had been packed up for the adventure, and the guests had put on greatcoats and cloaks and were gathered in an excited group outside the front doors of the house. A couple of gaslights in big round globes shed a glow under the *porte cochère*. Liskeard, sick at heart, saw his father come out, and said nothing. This *porte cochère*, he knew, was one of the danger points of Lostwithiel's venture. To pass under it was one of the constituents of driving the Castle Hereward measured mile. It had always been a favourite trick of Buck's, a consummate handler of horses even in extreme age. Another danger point was the humpbacked bridge, which Hamer Shawcross had seen the Honourable Lettice Melland cross on her pony. Every inch of the way was known to Liskeard, and as he now feverishly surveyed it in his mind, he thought of these two as the worst places. For the rest, the road was straightforward enough, through parkland, but dangerous in the dark where it ran, twisting, downhill for a quarter-mile through a pinewood.

Lostwithiel smiled at Lettice, impulsively shook hands with his son, and took no notice of anyone else. He climbed to his seat, and Carrickfergus climbed up beside him. "Let 'em go," he shouted to the amazed and frightened grooms who stood at the horses' heads. With the lamps shining on the flanks of the wheelers, Lostwithiel's whip tickling the leaders, the drag moved slowly out from the *port cochère* into the wind-whistling icy coldness of the night. It was eleven o'clock.

The grooms stood unhappily about. Liskeard, with dreadful providence, said to them, taking them out of earshot of the guests: "A couple of you get some stretchers. Get someone else – there'd better be four of you. Take them to the bridge. Keep out of sight. You'd better be under the bridge. You, Sutcliffe, get out a trap and bring Dr. Kershaw. Go on now. Move!"

He felt better at having done something, and rejoined the others. The night was moonless but starry. The wind was enough to blow the eyes back into one's head. The drag had come out of the pinewood. He could see the lights streaking swiftly across the blackness, and thanked God when they slowed down toward the bridge. Then they speeded up again, and the thud of hoofs came driven down the wind. He herded the guests back toward the door of the house, out of the *porte cochère*. There were fifteen or twenty of them crowded on the steps, the women holding their cloaks about them, the men with collars up to their ears and hands deep in pockets, all breathless, excited, a little afraid. They were beginning to feel that there was something terrible and superhuman in that old painted skeleton riding the wind.

Liskeard held his breath as the sound of the racing horses came nearer: sixteen hoofs frantically pounding the gravel, shaking the earth. He prayed that Lostwithiel would take the *porte cochère* with caution, as he had done the bridge; but there was a bit of a twist at the bridge. Here the track was straight for a few hundred yards. The dive under the *porte cochère* was something Buck could never resist. Now he was on them. It was a swirl of sweating horse-flesh, a quick music of jingling metal, a rush of wheels that seemed to miss the walls by inches, a spatter of gravel. The gaslight flared for a moment on grey plunging flanks, the yellow whirling wheels, the alert desiccated figure, leaning slightly forward with the reins seeming to flow ahead out of his fingers like the conduits of his energy to the racing animals. They had one glimpse of his face, all bony lights and shadows. "One!" he shouted; and Carrickfergus blared on the horn. Then they were gone, and you could hear the breath of the little group come out in one sigh upon the night.

The grooms did not get under the bridge till Lostwithiel had passed for the first time. With the other men they had brought, they crouched in the few inches that were to spare between the masonry and the water. The wind searched them out, whistling like a flight of cold arrows through and through the narrow retreat.

"Christ Almighty!" one said, smarting at having been roused from the side of a warm wife. "T'bloody old man's goin' off 'is rocker. Break 'is bloody neck – that's what 'e'll do. If I 'ad a bed like 'is, I'd be in it a night like this, not drivin' four poor bloody sufferin' animals to distraction."

"This is Friday night. 'E sleeps in 'is coffin on Fridays," another asserted, blowing his fingers in the dark.

"That's balls, that yarn is. 'E don't sleep in no bloody coffin."

"Honest to God, 'e do. Mr. Bellows told me 'imself."

"'E'll sleep in a bloody coffin tonight, all right. 'Ark! There they come."

They were silent then, and awed in spite of themselves, as the ground shook, and the bridge rumbled, and the drag, once over the hump, took up its speed and hurtled toward the house. They crawled out, and, on all fours like animals watching the sport of exalted creatures, they gazed at the two receding heads black against the stars: the head of Carrickfergus round and unimpressive within swathings of shawl, the head of Lostwithiel, exaggerated by the hat, tall and insolent upon the pricked darkness of the night.

In the pinewood a white owl coasted down the long aisle cleft through the darkness by the roadway. It uttered no cry, made no sound, but hovered, listening and looking, then drifted forward like one immense white feather. It had been seen often enough by the boy whose father now lay under the bridge with a stretcher. He was an imaginative boy, and the great white owl obsessed his imagination. He had dreamed of it night after night, and in his dreams it was a terrible thing, making no sound, but hovering always over his head, pure as he himself was not pure. He strove to overcome his impurity, but could not; and so he resolved to kill the owl.

In the wood there was a hollow tree, and the boy, escaped from bed when he thought his father was asleep, concealed himself in the tree with an air-gun. The owl did not come, but there came something that terrified him: the sudden sound of hoofs, the creak of harness and the musical ring of bits and curbs. He shrank back into the rotting phosphorescence of the tree, and all the echoes of the wood were awakened as the horses crashed by, panting and pounding, and a whip cracked, and a high inhuman voice chanted among the great pine-trunks: "On there! A-yah! On there!" There was a flash of lights in the boy's eyes, and he saw a tall man darkly against the greater darkness, and then the echoes were dying away and the wood was sinking back upon silence, save for the groaning of the sombre pine-arms rising and falling amid the wind's lamentation.

When the boy fingered his gun he felt stronger. He peeped out of the death-smelling fissure in which he was concealed. The owl did not come, but the boy was patient. In the cold windy darkness he thought of his impurity, and rejoiced that before this night was done there would be no white owl to hover over him, an incarnate reproach.

He nearly died when the four horses rushed again through the blackness of the wood. This time the crying of a horn added unearthly music to the stampeding echoes, the hammering, snorting, creaking, rumbling inexplicability of the whole matter. The imaginative boy had been reading the Book of the Revelation; and his night-dreams and the white owl and these four horses charging to a horn's music through the dark lamenting wood were tangled up in his unformed mind like the stars which he saw tangled among the branches writhing over his head. He waited for a few minutes to quieten the flutter in his breast, and then he began to run down the long aisle of the wood.

When he had run for some way, his flight inevitably suggested pursuit. He glanced over his shoulder, and the white owl was coasting through the darkness behind him. Terror nearly stilled his heart, but the need to kill the owl overcame the terror. He stepped off the path and crouched behind a tree, holding his gun. The owl saw or sensed him there, stopped itself upon the air, motionless and weightless as a great moth. Then the wings beat slowly; it approached the tree, passed it, and the boy, with shaking finger, pressed the trigger, of the soundless gun.

The owl gave a long angry scream, and then went beating forward on its way, swiftly, erratically, a damaged wing half-functioning, a sound one threshing the air to restore an impossible balance. This was the apparition that blundered, swerving madly, into the faces of Buck Lostwithiel's leading horses, already excited by the fury of the old man's driving. They reared and plunged, and all of Buck's cunning in emergency was of no use then. They swung the drag round; it crashed into a tree and went over and the wheelers with it.

Here was the end that Liskeard had not foreseen, and when he and others came running with lanterns they found Lostwithiel with his brains kicked out and one of the horses lying on its side with the grey topper, impaled upon a hoof, twirling round and round as the horse thrashed.

Carrickfergus, unscratched, was hanging from a branch that had pierced the skirts of his coat; and a boy with a gun was already deep within the wood, making a detour to his open bedroom window.

And so the Viscount Liskeard became the Earl of Lostwithiel and removed his presence to the House of Lords. He had represented St. Swithin's for a long time, for it was toward the end of 1900 that old

Lostwithiel died. The new Conservative candidate was a stranger; the Liberals did not fight the seat; and Hamer Shawcross was elected. Eight years had passed since he sat in the House of Commons looking at Keir Hardie, the sole Labour member. They were eight years of grinding toil; the Independent Labour Party was no longer a dream but a reality seven years old; and still the Labour members in the House of Commons were fewer than the years of their party.

"But I was in. I could have been in earlier for some other seat, but I had set my heart on St. Swithin's, and now Providence had removed the extraordinary person who had stood in the way. When the result was declared, it seemed strange not to see that legendary figure in the room, and Liskeard and his wife. Jimmy Newboult was beside himself with elation, but I felt flat now that I had achieved what I had worked toward for so long. The day happened to be my birthday. I was thirty-five, and I didn't feel young any longer. When the shouting was over, and I had finally shaken off Jimmy, I walked up to Baildon alone. Ann had not come with me. Charles was suffering from measles, and even the declaration of the poll would not part her from Charles at that moment, though my mother could have looked after the boy well enough."

Yes; there was now Charles. Charles was three, a child with an amazing constellation of names: Charles Gordon Birley Lightowler Shawcross. Hamer toiled up the hill from Shipley to Baildon repeating the absurd concatenation to himself. No mill for Charles. The phrase leapt at him out of a memory that already seemed, sometimes, incredibly far-reaching into the past: a memory of Gordon Stansfield and Wesleyan class meetings, of Birley Artingstall-Leather, and his odorous little shop; of Suddaby and his cat in the warm booky cavern shaken by the bells of Manchester Old Church. Tom Hannaway and the bone-yard and the fruit-shop with its synthetic dew, that girl – the parson's daughter – her name eluded him, but he could recall her sharp enthusiastic features; Arnold Ryerson, toiling in Hawley Artingstall's shop; boxing, reading, running a mile; the old ideal: the healthy mind in the healthy body.

Well, he still had that. He threw up his head, squared his shoulders, and took a deep draught of the grand Yorkshire air. He had never felt better. Three score years and ten. He'd done half of that; but, quickening his pace as he passed the old stocks and the Malt Shovel, he felt that everything was still in front of him: Hamer Shawcross, M.P.

He almost ran through the village street, dark and silent, for it was nearly midnight. Past the Moorland Cottage, now no longer his, out to the fringe of the moor. There, away to his left, he could see a light upon the darkness, a dusty red square that reminded him of the night when he and Ann had walked up to Baildon through a snowstorm and he had run ahead, leaping over the intake wall, to light the lamp in the hut. Now the house called The Hut stood on the field where the hut had been, and, frankly running now, he pushed open the gate at the spot where he had been accustomed to climb the wall, and hastened to Ann and Ellen – and Charles.

He was proud of the house. He had designed it himself and had it built out of money earned by his books. There was nothing much to it, except that every room was big. All his life he had lived in little rooms and suffered from their niggling suggestion of poverty. There was an entrance hall that was big enough to sit in, to stand about and talk in, to lounge in by a fireside. Apart from the kitchen, there were a dining-room, a large room which Ann and Ellen shared, and his own workroom. He had let his fancy go there on a huge fireplace. He loved to sit there reading at night, with his pipe on, the fire roaring, and the sense of the moor without filling in a satisfying background. Over the fireplace was the Old Warrior's sabre, and Ellen recalled the past by polishing it on Saturdays with powdered bath-brick. The room was full of books, and comfortably near the fire was a big writing-desk with the Italian inkstand upon it, and Birley Artingstall's leather box containing a curl of hair and a hair ribbon. One drawer of the desk was locked. It held a jumble of personal things, including a reproduction of Sargent's portrait "The Honourable Lettice Melland." Hamer thought it a fine work of art. The curtains of rich crimson velvet, and the red turkey carpet, were a gift from Lizzie Lightowler. With the deep leather chairs, they gave the room a great sense of well-being on a winter night, when the lamps were lit. There was not at that time any other lighting at The Hut.

But there was a bathroom, and there were three large bedrooms: one belonged to Hamer and Ann, one to Ellen, and one was the combined bedroom and nursery of Charles.

Charles, at three, was destined for the Diplomatic Service, though Hamer had said nothing of this to anyone, not even to Ann. To his constituents he said: "Ah, my friends, the dignity of labour! Old and trite as the phrase is, cast in your teeth though it may be as a cheap sneer, hold fast to it. Do not let go the deep security on which your status rests. The dignity of the arm wielding the riveting hammer, the dignity of the hand cunningly shaping the mould, turning the lathe, guiding the plough, the dignity of the back bent over toil in the town ditch and the country furrow; aye, and the dignity of the patient woman's eye losing its lustre over the stitch, stitch, stitch, beneath the lamp in simple homes: do not lose this dignity. It is your pearl, and with it, when the time comes, you will buy your ransom."

Whatever this may have meant, it had nothing to do with the Diplomatic Service for which Charles was destined.

Hamer was glad tonight, as he always was glad, to see the welcome light of his home shining across the darkness on the edge of the moor. It meant that Ann was up, waiting for him. He was still in love with Ann, though her political enthusiasms – or at any rate her political activities – had declined with the coming of Charles. No, certainly not her enthusiasms; for when they had discussed the education of Charles she had been all for sending him to the village board school. "I think he should mix with the children of working people. He'll meet them there."

Hamer did not want to make it a serious point of dispute. "It's just a question of expediency," he said. "Is it the wisest beginning, seeing that he'll probably go on to a public school later?"

"But, my dear, will he? Isn't there a perfectly good grammar school in Bradford? It's an excellent place. He could travel to and fro daily. And if he gets a scholarship, he could go on from there to Oxford."

Hamer smiled his most engaging smile. "I rather thought of his doing that anyhow."

"Well, I don't know," said Ann, perplexed. "I thought we didn't believe in that sort of thing."

"What sort of thing, my dear?"

"Why, making the universities the preserve of the rich."

"Rich?" He allowed himself an ironical laugh.

"Well, you'd be rich enough to send him, or he couldn't go," she said with unanswerable logic. "And we *are* rich, compared with most people, when we combine what you earn and what I don't. A lot of Labour people have raised their eyebrows at this house, I can tell you, my lad," she added playfully.

He lost his temper a little then. "A lot of Labour people are fools," he said. "Do they expect their leaders to live in hovels? That's the worst of the damned party. It thinks down instead of up."

"Well, we haven't settled Charles's future," Ann said lightly.

"There's time enough," he answered, and took up his pen with the gesture which she had learned to consider a dismissal.

It was all nothing much, but it left them a little touchy with one another for some days.

Charles was asleep. There was no need to worry about him. Ellen, nodding with sleepiness, had sat up long enough to take Hamer in her arms and kiss him. It was years since she had done that, and he was embarrassed, but she was not. It would never cease, for her, to be a natural gesture. She said nothing. Since the telephone message had come at nine o'clock saying that he was elected she had said not a word. In their big comfortable room Ann read and Ellen knitted. They understood one another perfectly, especially since the coming of Charles. Now and then Ellen would allow her hands to fall into her lap, and would sit for five minutes staring at the fire. Ann did not break in on her cogitations. She could guess they were little more than a vague wonder, a difficult acceptance of an incredible fact, a pride that would disdain to utter itself. After a while, the old hands would take up the knitting again and go patiently on. Ellen felt much happier about Hamer and his incomprehensible doings since she had met Keir Hardie. Hardie had sat here, in this very room, and she had given him a cup of tea. "Well, Mother," he said – and what a smile he gave her! – "thank you for the tea, and thank you for your son. You've given us a good boy." He didn't talk a lot of old politics like some who came there. He talked about his own mother, and their little cottage in Ayrshire. "A good place, Ayrshire," he said. "That's where Bobbie Burns came from." He recited a bit of Bobbie Burns's poetry, and the old lady was delighted, because this was perhaps the only poetry she would ever have recognized. It was a homely tag that Gordon had been accustomed to recite.

So she sat there nodding over her knitting, and thinking of "Mr. Hardie," and wondering what Gordon and Birley Artingstall would have said if they had lived to see Hamer write "M.P." after his name instead of "Rev." before it, which was what they had both wished.

And then he had come in, so tall, so much a man these days, glowing with his long walk, and she just kissed him and went off to bed.

When they were alone, he took Ann in his arms. She looked up at him with her eyes shining. "Well, my dear," she said, "it's been a long time. But now you're on the other side of those doors we looked at in London."

"How's Charles?" he said. 'I'd better go up and see him."

"I shouldn't if I were you. He's asleep."

"I won't disturb him. I can step as quiet as a cat."

They went upstairs together, and as they passed Ellen's door, which had been left slightly ajar, they had a swift glimpse of the old lady, kneeling by the side of her bed, with her hands joined as simply as a child's and her long nightgown falling in stiff folds about her. They were both queerly moved. "I had no idea she did that," Hamer whispered, inside Charles's room.

"I don't think she does as a rule," Ann said. "This is a special occasion, I fancy she's commending someone and his work very particularly to God's favour. She never talks to me about you, you know. If she believed in saints, I think she'd be asking Gordon Stansfield to intercede for you with the Almighty."

Her voice quivered and broke, and, by the dim light of the dip burning steadily with its little light painted sharply against its own halo on Charles's table, he saw a tear slide from her eyelids and trickle down her face. "You don't know, my dear," she said, "how proud she is of you. Me too."

She stood in the all but darkness with the feeble light concentrated in her glad troubled eyes. He suddenly felt humbled. "It's no great thing," he said, "that I have done. What I shall do now – that's what matters."

He put his arm round her waist, and they stepped the few paces together to the bed. They stood and looked down upon Charles.

The child was fair, like Ann, like old Birley Artingstall, and Birley's Viking mother. His face was flushed, and blue veins were pathetically clear upon the alabaster of his thin neck. Charles's hair had never been cut. It clouded his face and curled in tendrils upon his forehead. Hamer gently put a finger inside one of the tendrils and smiled to see the close coil stretch and then spring back when he took his finger away. Suddenly out of that crowded, jumbled, incongruous memory of his there sprang a thought. "I wonder whether the Old Warrior ever did that to the girl Emma who used to stand on his foot and then get on tiptoe to be kissed? I wonder whether he ever did it to the very curl that is in my box downstairs – the curl that the sabre sliced away?"

And, looking at the child, unstained as yet by the world's soiling touch, he thought of all the soil and staining of the world, of all the wrongs inflicted and endured, of all his own high resolves for the world's betterment, and the bustle, the business and the fuss that more and more obscured and hindered him. Suddenly, without pre-meditation, he did what his mother had done. At the side of the child's bed he sank to his knees and buried his head in the bedclothes. He could feel Charles's dainty feet beneath his forehead.

Ann did not kneel down. She stole from the room. When Hamer got up and found himself alone with the child, he did not know to whom he had prayed or whether he had prayed. But he felt stronger than when he had knelt down, clearer in his vision of the sort of world he wanted Charles to inherit.

He went down. Ann said nothing of what had happened upstairs. She came in from the kitchen with a teapot and two cups, and she put a log on the fire.

"This looks like a session," said Hamer. "It's past midnight."

"I know. But I think we're both too excited to want to hurry to bed. After all, in any man's life there's only one first day as an M.P. You should be thankful I've made you a hot cup of tea. If you'd married Pen Muff, it would have been cold tea out of a bottle."

"Why on earth should I marry Pen Muff?"

"Any man could do worse than that. I've been speaking to her tonight."

"Speaking to her?"

"On the telephone. Arnold rang up to know if you were in."

"An expensive call for poor old Arnold."

Ann poured out the tea and handed him a cup. "Not so much poor old Arnold," she said. "You always speak of Arnold as if he were one of the world's failures."

"I imagine he'll aways manage to be on the losing side."

"He's on the same side as you, isn't he?"

Hamer sipped his tea, laid it down, and began to fill his pipe, considering this poser. "What I mean," he said, "is that Arnold has that strange genius which can make a failure even of victory."

"I'm not so sure that you're right," she answered. "I can see Arnold making a victory of failure."

There was a silence of infinitesimal estrangement between them as Hamer struck a match and drew the flame into the tobacco. "Anyway," said Ann, "you'll have a chance to form a personal opinion. He's coming up to Bradford."

"After all these years? Whatever for?"

"Mrs. Muff is dangerously ill. He and Pen have been called to what looks like being a funeral."

"I'm sorry," he said lamely. "I like Arnold. Don't make any mistake about that."

"And another thing. I rang up Aunt Lizzie as soon as I heard you were in. Naturally, she's off her head with joy. She says that when you are up in town, North Street must be your home."

"For the time being, that will be excellent."

"Meaning?"

"Why, that we must have a house of our own in town as soon as we can manage it."

Hamer took up with the tongs a fine lump of coal and dropped it upon the fire. It smouldered for a while, then began to send out whistling balloons of gas, and finally, at a touch of the poker, fell into three pieces that blazed, duskily shining on the curtains and the red turkey carpet, the long rows of books, and the four people sitting in the comfortable leather chairs: Pen and Arnold, Hamer and Ann. It seemed natural to name Pen first of that couple, Hamer of the other. Hamer and Arnold were smoking their pipes; Pen sat doing nothing. Ann was fussing over a small tea-table that had been brought in to Hamer's room after dinner. Ellen had gone early to bed. There was no light but the firelight in the room.

They were all tired and overwrought. Hamer had sat with Pen and Arnold in the solitary four-wheeler that went slowly behind Mrs. Muff's hearse along the road to Nab Wood cemetery. It was a dreary day – a day of Bradford fog: cold and penetrating. Pen had never got on with her mother; to Arnold she had been little more than the woman who hired him a room; Hamer had scarcely even met her. There was something hurried and perfunctory about the way in which the poor woman was committed to the ground amid the swirling vapours and the dripping trees. And it was this very sense of the sadness of the woman's end, alone and unfriended, which they had done and could do nothing to mitigate, that set all their nerves on edge, and gave them, in place of the assuagement of tears, a dour wish that all might speedily be over, ending what could not be mended.

They did not go back to the desolate house in Thursley Road. At Shipley, Hamer dismissed the funeral cab and hired another – as decrepit and mouldy-smelling, but at all events untainted by the dolour of the day's doings. In this he took Pen and Arnold to The Hut, where they were to stay for the night in Charles's room. Charles's cot had been moved alongside his parents' bed.

At Baildon the air was clean and heartening, but bitterly cold; and there now they all were, relaxed before the fire, watching the crimson flame spurt through the blue woolly smoke.

"Best Welsh steam coal," said Hamer. "They produce good stuff in your part of the country, Arnold."

Pen's face, more pinched and wan than usual because of the experiences of the day, seemed to draw into a tight knot of anger. "Yes," she said, "it's good stuff is coal, when you've got nothing to do but warm your backside by it. But sometimes I never want to see a lump of the stuff again. If I were a miner, I wouldn't strike, I'd just walk out of the damn-awful valleys and let anyone who wanted coal go an' get it. How'd you like to do that? This is a nice room you've got here, a grand room for a Labour leader. The firelight's fine and romantic. How would tha like it," she demanded, falling in her excitement into the dialect, "if tha had to go down into t'pit and crawl on thi belly with a sweaty shirt stickin' to thi back every time tha wanted a scuttleful? Go an' ask 'em things like that in the House of Commons."

She lay back in her chair and glowered at the fire as if it were her enemy. Nobody answered her. There was silence save for the fluttering of the flames and the noise Ann made trying to cover embarrassment with the tinkle of tea-cups. It sounded as joyful as if castanets had clicked in the fog over Mrs. Muff's open grave.

"Tha's overwrought, lass," Arnold at last said gruffly.

"'Appen that's so," Pen admitted; and added reluctantly: "Ah'm sorry."

The admission cleared the air a little, and Hamer went to the tea-table, took a cup from Ann, and gave it to Pen. Then he gave one to Arnold, whose appearance, now that they met after the lapse of almost a decade, startled him. He wondered whether he himself looked so changed to Arnold. Arnold had put on weight and gravity. He had the look of a man who took no exercise and spent long hours stewing in an office over matters that puzzled and perplexed him. And that, indeed, was what he did, now that he was one of the leading trade union officials in the Rhondda Valley. His face had become pouchy. There were bags under his eyes; his side whiskers were greying, and the hair was falling back from his forehead. The large hands resting on his knees seemed to express, more than anything else about him, a tenacity and resolution, and also, somehow, an immense pathetic puzzlement that there should be need of so much effort to bring about changes that seemed to him so manifestly necessary.

He laid his great paw on Pen's fragile hand, and said: "I'll tell you, Hamer, what's the matter with this lass. She's a bit disappointed because we've seen nothing of you in the Rhondda."

"My dear Arnold, my dear Pen," Hamer excused himself, "I've been up to the eyes. Nursing St. Swithin's, travelling about the country, fitting in my writing – it doesn't leave much time for calls."

"Oh, I don't mean in a social way," Arnold explained, "though I dare say we could have given you a cup of tea and a bed to sleep in at Horeb Terrace. I mean, there's plenty to do in Rhondda, and a bit of help from a man like you would go a long way, It's not easy, Hamer, to see a great man in someone you went to school with, and played with in the streets, but perhaps I'm a bit clearer-sighted than some. I know what you are: you're one of the big men of the party; you're going to be bigger; and we could do with a bit of you in the Rhondda."

His face went graver as he added: "We can do with a lot of you in the immediate future. We're going to have a rough time. I've done my best, and I can't make our men see reason much longer. If I'm not mistaken, there's going to be violence at Cwmdulais before many days are over."

Hamer got up and stood on the hearthrug, looking down at the other three. "Why shouldn't there be violence?" he demanded. "There ought to be violence. There must be violence."

Now he was not a comfortable host, entertaining friends at his fireside. His eyes flashed; he was the storm-raiser who had stumped the country for years past, found always where men needed to be spurred to hot action.

"I may not have been in the Rhondda," he said, "but I've watched your struggle there. Ann knows that." He pulled a tall folio from the bookshelves and flicked over the leaves. "Here is your record. There's little that happens in the South Wales coalfield that you won't find here."

Arnold went and stood at his side, looked at the press cuttings, tables of statistics, manuscript notes, pamphlets, letters, stuck into the book. He noted that it had been taken from a shelf filled with similar books, and running his eye along the spines he read: Railways; Dock Labourers; Steel Industry; Agriculture; the Potteries; and every industry and subdivision of industry in the country. He marvelled at the industry and thoroughness of his friend.

Hamer laid the book on his desk. "You have been out two months. Your union funds are nearly gone. Your men are despairing. Your women and children are hungry. You are asking little, and the companies could pay it without turning a hair. What is left for you but violence? There are two courses open to you, and two only: go back, beaten by the well-fed who do not scruple to use starvation as a weapon, or take such action as will bring the eyes of the country upon Cwmdulais."

Arnold did not for a time answer him. He stood uneasily on the rug, his heavy body sagging, his pipe sucking emptily in his mouth. Presently, he said: "I hate violence. I believe in human reason."

The two women had put down their cups and sat looking at the two men, so manifestly fighting now the one to dominate the other.

"Arnold," said Hamer, "we have known one another for a long time, and God grant that for a long time yet we may be comrades fighting side by side for the same things. But we don't believe in the same methods. You believe in yeast. 'A little leaven leaveneth the whole lump.' I don't believe there's always time for all that beautiful fermentation. I believe there's a moment when you have to get your salmon with dynamite, not with a lot of exquisite rod-play. You've tried reason. You've tried to leaven the lump, and God knows the head of a coal-owner is a lump if ever there was one. You've failed. Admit it, man. You've failed, haven't you?"

"There's no failure except giving up," said Arnold doggedly, unconsciously repeating what Pen had said to him long ago.

"You've given up when your men go back," Hamer persisted. "You've failed then. You go back skinned alive; your funds gone, your men's fighting spirit gone, and every woman in Cwmdulais up to the eyes in debt to the corner shop. I know. I know the lives of the poor. And you leave the owners chuckling. That's the way to treat the dogs. If they won't gnaw on a meatless bone, take the bone away. That brings 'em cringing."

Arnold shuffled on his feet, knocked the dottle out of his pipe, and said: "I shall never accept the responsibility for violence."

Hamer handed him a tobacco pouch. "I don't ask you to," he said. He reached behind him and took down the sabre from the wall. "All I ask you to do is to allow me to bring this to Cwmdulais. Convene a meeting for me. Will you do that?"

The best Welsh steam coal spluttered and threw out flames that licked the shining surface of the sword. Arnold looked uneasily at Pen. "Do it," she said.

Arnold said: "Very well," and sat down beside her.

Hamer stood alone on the hearth with the gleaming weapon in his hand. His face shone.

He travelled alone to Cwmdulais. A winter night was closing over the valleys as his train ran through the pitiless desolation. There was just enough light left in the sky to show him tall pithead machinery etched above hill crests, the wheels motionless. On the seat beside him reposed the sabre in its leather scabbard. There were no homeward travelling miners to crowd in upon his solitude. He had the compartment to himself, and his impressionable mind soaked itself in the melancholy emanation of these hills whose very ruin now seemed pointless.

When he alighted at Cwmdulais, a dully smoky lantern or two scarcely permitted him to see the platform. A porter watched the train out, and it was not till it was gone and he had been left standing there alone for some time in the darkness that Pen Ryerson came as though she had been hurrying. "Sorry Arnold couldn't meet you," she said. "He's been busy all day at the union offices."

With no further words, they went out and climbed uphill through the raw misty darkness. It seemed to Pen now that there had never been a time when she didn't know that climb, and after a while, when they came to a solid block of a building slabbed upon the darkness, she said, as her sister Nell had said to her so long ago, and as most Cwmdulais folk said to visiting strangers: "That's Horeb."

At Horeb they turned left, walked a little way, and Pen said: "Well, here we are. It's not as grand as your place in Baildon, but it's got to do. My sister Nell used to live here with Ianto, her husband. He was a poet. He was killed."

Hamer liked the asperities of this tough uncompromising woman. "Yes, yes," he said gently. "I heard about that."

"There's a lot goes on here that you don't hear about. Well, come in."

The house was little changed since the days when Ianto shyly welcomed Pen and Arnold to it. The front room was used: that was the chief difference. In Ianto's day it had been closed on six days of the week, and on the seventh the fire was lit and, between sermons at Horeb, the harmonium was played and hymns were sung. The harmonium went with Nell and young Dai and Pryce when they took up their quarters with old Richard Richards at the corner shop. Now the front room was a den shared by Arnold and Pen. A bookcase contained the solid political treatises, the blue-books and pamphlets, that were all Arnold's reading. Hamer, at Pen's request, sat down by the fireside, and when she had left the room he let his eye range along the shelves to see if his own books were there. They were: the books and the pamphlets. Nothing seemed missing. He was gratified, but said to himself that he ought not to have allowed Arnold to buy these things: he should have sent him inscribed copies. That would have pleased Arnold. But what had he done to please Arnold in these last ten years? Precious little. A letter every six months or so. He blamed himself for that, and admitted wryly that he was always discovering means of beneficence when the opportunity was passed.

Arnold's writing desk was in the recess on one side of the fireplace; one which he guessed to be Pen's was in the other recess. There were a few photographs about the room: old Mrs. Ryerson, looking as tough and energetic as Pen herself; one of Hamer – again a swell of gratification made itself felt when he saw that; one of the Ryerson house in Broadbent Street. It might have been the house in which Hamer had spent his own childhood. Evidently, Arnold didn't want to lose touch with his origins. And what about me? Hamer asked himself. Would he feel pleased at seeing in the Baildon room among the crimson curtains and the red turkey carpets a picture of the house so crowded with memory: the sand sausages down to the doors to keep out the whistling draught, the red serge curtains drawn against the night, the firelight and lamplight, and the scratching of Gordon's pen, the lift of Gordon's head with the smile on his face, Ellen's needles ... click, click ... and a small boy who dragged his leg, looked interesting, and dreamed formless magnificent sustaining dreams. All this the photograph might have recalled; and Jimmy Spit-and-Wink tapping the windows in the grey light before dawn, and the rushing clatter of the clogs and the moan of the mill buzzer – ah, my friends, so much of the life of the poor! But, with it all, he knew that he would not like to see that photograph hanging at Baildon. He would rather take from his locked drawer the reproduction of Sargent's picture and frame that. But he wasn't sure how Ann would take it, or some of his callers, either. They might not see it, as he did, as a beautiful work of art.

It seemed to him, sitting for five minutes in that room which somehow impressed him with a sense of happy comradeship, fruitful common endeavour, that the very room had succeeded in conducting an inquisition into his way of looking at life, and living life, and Arnold's. It was a long time since he had taken such stock of himself.

He could not help noticing on Pen's desk, which was right at his elbow, a number of envelopes with the initials "W.S.P.U." printed on them; and when, presently, she came back, leading a little girl by the hand, he said with a smile: "You keep in touch with the firebrands, Pen? I see plenty of correspondence here from the Women's Social and Political Union."

"You'll see more than correspondence one of these days," she said. "This is Alice. Alice, shake hands with Mr. Shawcross. He's your father's greatest friend."

Was there a hint of irony, a touch of sarcasm, in that? He couldn't make up his mind, but told himself, in his mood of momentary penitence, that he had earned it if there were. This was Alice Ryerson, five years old now, and he was looking at her for the first time, as Pen and Arnold, a few days before, had looked for the first time at Charles. Alice gave him her hand without shyness and said: "How do you do, Mr. Shawcross?"

She seemed a self-possessed little creature, neatly dressed, with a round dark face that had round dark eyes and hair perfectly straight and black. "That's your photograph," she said. "Father shows it to me. It's like you."

He was good with children. They came to him eagerly, as a rule, as Alice came now, standing at his knee. "I knew your father," he said, "when I was a little boy younger than you; and now I've got a little boy younger than you. So that's a long time, isn't it?"

"Yes," she said, "your little boy is called Charles. Father told me."

"Yes, you must meet Charles some day. I think you'll like him."

Yes, indeed, she will like him. Look well at Alice. You are looking at a slice of your history.

"Well, bed now," said Pen. "I expect you'll see more of Mr. Shawcross in the morning."

The child put up her face to be kissed, and then took her mother's hand and went away without looking back.

Arnold came in soon afterwards, bringing Evan Vaughan with him. Vaughan was a small dark voluble man of thirty. His grasp made Hamer's hand feel as though a wire rope had tautened round it. "By God, Mr. Shawcross, there's glad I am to see you now," he sing-songed, "and you an M.P. That's something now to cheer up old Keir Hardie. It's men like you he wants. By God, it's about time you wass in the House. You've worked for it if effer a man did. All those books, too. By God, indeed now, mun, I don't know how you find the time. It's reading people we are in these valleys. Every one of your books I've read. It's an honour to meet you. And, By God, we need you. Have you heard the latest? Troops! Troops, by God, in the Rhondda! Shoot us down. With the bloody Boer war on and all! Isn't that shooting enough for 'em? Yes, indeed, it's time you wass here."

He stopped, still wringing Hamer's hand, and gazing into his face, as though he had met a deliverer. Arnold intervened. "Now let's have a bit of food," he said. "You can do with it, I know, Evan."

"By God, yes indeed I can now. The old woman's ashamed to show her face at Richard Richards's grocery. We've run up a bill there as long as a bloody elephant's trunk. Yes, indeed, I can do with some food. You make a note of that, Mr. Shawcross. It's without food we are in these valleys. Are they without food in Park Lane? Is that fair do's – people with full bellies fighting people without food? By God it's not! And now troops!"

And now troops. Troops! That was the word singing in Hamer's blood as he followed Arnold and Evan Vaughan into the kitchen, where Pen was waiting before a spread table. He had urged Arnold to make Cwmdulais a place in the eyes of all the country. Troops would do it. Troops, by God! as this voluble little man kept saying. Troops! The everlasting secular arm of the high priests who owned the earth. Troops – Peterloo – he perhaps would look on deeds like those which had made the Old Warrior an ancestral voice uttering the woes of the people. The people. The common people. The stock from which I sprang. It was always romantic dynamite to his imagination. He sat at the table, appearing as calm as anyone there, calmer than Evan Vaughan, but tingling with inward suspense.

Five thousand men, women and children. He had never before addressed such an audience. Old Richard Richards had come in to look after Alice, which meant no more than installing himself in the front room with his pipe going, a book in his hand, and his feet – one flesh, one timber – extended to the fire. There was grey now in the beard of Ap Rhondda's father, and his grave old face was set and drawn. The man who kept the corner shop, who knew that out of ten things passed over his counter only one was paid for: this man understood the depth of the disaster that had come upon Cwmdulais. He shook hands with Hamer, and looked with interest and speculation at so famous a man. "I'm glad to meet you," he said, "and I hope you'll do us some good. But I stand where Arnold stands, and where my son the bard Ap Rhondda stood. I am a man of peace."

"But, by God, Richard Richards – troops!" Evan Vaughan shouted. "Wass you wanting us to be shot down like dogs?"

The old man shook his head and did not answer. Hamer and Arnold, Pen and Evan Vaughan, went out into the raw darkness.

The Co-operative Hall was in the bottom of the valley: a vast grey-looming building of corrugated iron. At the back door a few men were hanging about. In the darkness there were confused and hurried introductions, and then they passed down a corridor, into an ante-room, and thence on to the platform. "I had never before," Hamer wrote, "felt so dramatically that I had been thrown suddenly to the wolves."

The hall was dimly lit by gaslight – so dimly that the backmost rows of people could not be seen. The audience thus appeared to recede into infinity, an infinity dense with tobacco-fog, and, when Hamer entered, vibrant with song. They were singing in their native tongue "Hen Wlad fy Naddhau," which Hamer knew meant "Land of My Fathers," singing with all their hearts and souls, harmony embroidered on harmony, with the untutored perfection of the world's greatest nation of singers. They did not pause when Hamer and the others filed on to the mist-blue platform, but, as though by way both of welcome and applause, swung back again into the chorus of their national hymn, sending the melody surging up into the unseen dome.

Hamer's histrionic gift told him at once that this was no occasion for a chairman, for all the platitudes and pedantries of procedure. Here was a people worked by their own emotion to a melting pitch on which he could at once make an impress. He laid his hand on Arnold's knee and said: "There's no need to introduce me," and sprang to his feet as the singing died away.

He waited for a few moments as the immense crowd rustled to silence, standing there poised above them on the edge of the platform: the foreground fairly clear: men in mufflers with caps on their heads, pipes or cigarettes in their mouths, thin dark little men for the most part with white intense faces, their women with them, and their children; and stretching back beyond these an immensity of diminishing white dots lost upon the darkness like stars upon a moonless midnight sky. He was moved and uplifted as he looked at them. He felt in his bones that this was going to be one of his greatest occasions.

"Land of my fathers," he said. "That is what you have been singing. I do not understand your language, but you and I have at any rate one language in common. We understand the language of the poor. We are one in the brotherhood of misery. We are one in detestation of the wicked power which permits a few to stand before the doorway of the granary and jingle the golden key before our eyes, and say how many or how few grains shall be doled out to us, and for how many hours of sweat and strain. Those are the conditions of our lives, the conditions of all of us who toil for our bread, and coming here tonight, expecting to hear the rumble of anger, the sharp accents of a common fury, what do I hear? 'Land of My Fathers.' Ah, my friends! I have a bitter message to deliver. What is this land you sing of? You have no land! It was the land of your fathers, indeed, but is it yours? Look into your hearts. Look into your larders. Look into the account-books of your old friend Richard Richards, and ask yourselves in the light of what you will find there: Is this my land? Let us reason this matter out. Let us take our points one by one and answer them. To begin with, let us answer this: Is this my land?"

The question rang out with all the oratorical challenge that he could put into it. There was a moment's uneasy silence, and then from behind him Evan Vaughan shouted: "No, by God, it is not. Not a bloody inch!"

The audience took up the answer, and Hamer knew that now he had them. No! No! No! came the shouts from all over the misty expanse that wavered in blue clouds before his eyes.

He took them through a catechism. Was it your father's land? Whose land is it now? How shall the people recover what once was theirs and what the few have filched from them?

"You know of only one way: you withhold your labour; and what is the reply to that? Troops!"

He waited, and heard rising from all over the hall the harsh murmur, the deep resentful suspiration, that soldiers used as oppression's Cossacks will always evoke. He turned to the table and took up the sheathed sabre, catching as he did so a glimpse of Arnold Ryerson's white anxious face and Pen's set jaw. He drew the sabre from the scabbard and held it aloft. "Troops!" he repeated. "Look well at this which I hold in my hand. It is what the troops bring with them. Look well, too, at this. It is what the troops leave behind them."

He took from his pocket a curl of hair with a ribbon attached to it. "This is too small for most of you to see, but it is so big that its infamy should fill the world. This is a curl of hair and a bloodstained ribbon that once was worn by a girl whom this sword, on a field in Manchester, cut down in the beauty of her youth. She was one of us – a worker – and her name was Emma. What her other name was I never knew, and why indeed should anyone know? Our names are not engraved on monuments. Our memorials are found only in such records as the Pyramids, and the Boer War casualty lists, and in the hollow roads and byways that make their network down in the darkness beneath the Rhondda Valley. So never mind who Emma was. I will tell you her story."

New to them, it was an old story to him, and he had learned to tell it with most moving power. It held them breathless, and when he had done there was a great silence. Into it he dropped his next words: "Troops! Such are the purposes for which troops are sent among the people. There are troops at this moment in your valley. What are you going to do about it?"

This was the moment. Pen looked sideways at Arnold, and her heart was wrung with love and pity to see the anguish in his face. The love was well-nigh to melting her, but she steeled herself against the pity. "By heck!" she thought fiercely to herself, "we should be dogs and less than dogs if all I have seen in the Rhondda this last few weeks did not make us rather die than go back crawling."

Hamer Shawcross's enemies always laid it to his charge that he incited the miners to violence. He always denied that he did anything of the kind. It is a point for casuists to settle. "What are you going to do about it?" he asked, and, sabre in hand, stood there and allowed them to answer the question for themselves. He knew that behind him was a hot-head on whom he could count, and when he had stood in a silence that seemed infinite and that lasted for ten seconds, Evan Vaughan's voice rang out: "We can march. That's what we can do. By God! Let us march now to the company's offices. Who can stop us? We are thousands strong. We can take possession."

In his excitement, Vaughan had risen and taken his place alongside Hamer on the edge of the platform. Was it a washing of hands, a public dissociation of himself from the decision now to be taken? "They decided for themselves," Hamer Shawcross always said, "and I should be the last to say their decision was a wrong one." At all events, he now left the platform to Evan Vaughan, put the sabre back into its sheath, and sat down.

Vaughan was in full harangue. "You have heard one of the great men of the Labour Party speaking to you words that are God's gospel truth. He has shown you the grip that capitalism has on your lives, and always has had. He has shown you how capitalism has used its power in the past, bringing the soldiers, by God, to cut us down if we want so much as to open our mouths. Are we going to put up with that sort of thing any longer? I said we could march. Well, can't we? There wass no harm in marching, wass there? We can march to the offices, and someone can go through the window and open the door. Then we can sit down. Here we are, we say. We wass reasonable men.

We wass doing no violence, but sitting here waiting for a peaceful discussion. Now come on then. Tell us why there must be hungry bellies in the Rhondda and fat bellies in Park Lane. That is all we wass wanting to know."

His verbosity streamed from him. Men began to shuffle, and Arnold Ryerson began to hope. The men had heard Evan Vaughan before. His torrential guff did not move them.

Then, while Vaughan was pausing for breath, a grave-faced man sitting on the platform, one of those whom Hamer had met at the door, got up and said very quietly: "My friends, our comrade Vaughan has made a proposal. There is no need for him to belabour it. The only question is: Do we march or don't we? I say Yes. I shall now leave this meeting and walk quietly towards the company's office. Let those join me who care to."

He casually took a swig from the chairman's glass, picked up his cap and walked out. Pen Muff followed him. Arnold gave her an agonizing glance, hesitated a moment, and went after her, exclaiming: "The meeting is ended."

There was no need for those formal words. Already the hall was an uproar of shuffling boots and arguing voices. Men were streaming through the cavernous doors on either side.

The other men on the platform began to go. They all looked grave and troubled, as though the matter in hand were not to their liking, but if it had to be put through, then they would be in it.

Hamer followed them out into the dark street in the valley bottom. Under the lugubrious heavens which held no light of moon or star, a great crowd was milling and fiercely disputing. The man who had walked out first was standing under a gas-lamp. He shouted; "All you women go home, and take your children with you. And if any man doesn't want to march with us, let him go home, too."

Gradually the crowd sorted itself out, thousands disappearing into the darkness: a formidable army, close on a thousand strong, forming up into rough marching order. Hamer strapped the sabre-belt round his waist, and wore his long overcoat above it. No one could see the sabre. He looked round for Pen and Arnold, and found them, with Evan Vaughan and the man whom he now heard, called Llewellyn, in the leading file of four. He ranged himself at their side, and the march began. One or two policemen had appeared; they walked quietly side by side with the demonstrators as though they were part of the show, speaking to no one. Presently a police inspector, appearing as if magically out of the humid night, was walking with the leading file. For a time he too said nothing. Then he said: "Evenin', Arnold."

Arnold said: "Evening, Shonnie."

Then again there was a silence in which the feet of the thousand went purposefully forward through the darkness measured off with a gas-lamp here and there. Presently Shonnie said: "Where are you off to, then, Arnold?"

Pen answered for him: "Just taking a walk. We're all ratepayers. We're allowed to walk in the streets."

Tramp…tramp…tramp…down over the level-crossing where the railway lines gleamed as if ruled in new-cut leaden strips; along the siding; moving steadily in a direction that Shonnie could not misunderstand.

"I'd tell 'em all to go home, if I was you, Arnold," he said.

This was not answered; and Hamer noticed, as they passed a gas-lamp that the inspector's face was kindly and troubled. "One of our men was in your meeting, Arnold," he said. "I'm not risking any trouble. I've sent for Parry Powell magistrate. If he reads the Riot Act you're done for. You won't get into the company's yard. The troops are quartered there."

Arnold said: "Thanks, Shonnie," and held out his hand. The inspector shook it, and then was gone as magically as he had appeared.

A pony-trap, driven at a lively lick, shot past the procession. "That's Parry Powell," said Llewelyn. "He'll read the Riot Act all right. He's got shares in the company."

Then nothing more was said till the great iron gate was reached which gave admission to the colliery company's yard. Suddenly lights shone in the yard, and the soldiers were seen, a posse of mounted men, sitting their horses negligently with great capes streaming from their shoulders down over the horses' flanks. Then the silence of the marching men broke. Again there went into the night a deep suspiration of anger and loathing. Whatever they had come for, with whatever intention, all was forgotten at sight of the statuesque figures sitting the animals whose heads tossed up and down, sending an opulent silver jingle into the night.

The ranks broke. The ordered thousand became a mob, storming towards the gate. Hamer, Pen and Arnold, Llewellyn and Evan Vaughan were jammed against it. Llewellyn took hold of the bars and shook them. "We demand to see some officials of the company at the offices," he shouted.

The horses' heads went up and down; the riders sat them with an infuriating watchful contempt. Llewellyn shook the bars again, well knowing that he might as well knock his head against Land's End.

Now other hands joined his. Everywhere the bars were seized, and Hamer, carried away by the delirium of the moment, found that he too was grasping the iron, rattling, shaking, thrusting menacing fists through the bars. The soldiers, looking as sculptured as the sculptured folds of their cloaks, sat their horses, and the horses tossed their heads up and down and pawed the ground. One of them whinnied.

It was Pen who turned and shouted back into the crowd: "What are we standing here for? Walls can be climbed, can't they?"

Then the thousand who had stood bunched behind the gate spread out to right and left. The air above the wall was bright with the light within; and now all along the length of it dark figures were silhouetted against the brightness, climbing, standing poised, gesticulating upon the air, dropping from view. Hamer stood back a little and watched that fantastic shifting frieze, and watched the men with backs bent on this side of the wall, others stepping upon those backs, climbing, leaning down then to hoist up the ones below. Most of the women melted away before this ordeal; but he saw Pen Ryerson appear suddenly, throw up her arms as though she were storming an aerie barricade, and vanish in a billowing of skirts and petticoats.

He went back to the gate and looked through. The soldiers had not moved. The time had not yet come for the secular arm, which sat there magnificently disciplined, not replying to any menace till authority gave the word. The crowd streaming across the yard ran between the horses, and chaffed the soldiers, and, exhilarated by what they deemed a victory, began to shout and sing. Now that they had their way, there was no harm in them. They ran happily towards the company's offices.

Standing at the gate, almost alone now, Hamer's heart suddenly turned over. He had seen this sort of thing before. He knew that the smooth surface of events was thin ice, which now might crack at any moment. He remembered the Old Warrior sitting by the fireside with shining eyes recalling the thrust and cut of the sabres as the crowd fled from the field of Peterloo. And he looked at the gate. Whither would these men flee? They would be like bullocks in a pen, with the slaughterer among them.

He turned to a man standing at the wall. "Give me a boost up," he said brusquely. The man bent; he stood on his back, and, such was his eagerness, he nearly vaulted to the other side. He ran here and there, shouting:

"Arnold! Arnold! Where's Arnold Ryerson?"

Arnold was standing with a few leaders outside the door of the office. "For God's sake," said Hamer breathlessly, "get that gate open before you do anything else."

The man Llewellyn saw quicker than anyone what was in Hamer's mind. "I can do it," he said, and ran back, twisting in and out of the crowd. "He's used to shot-firing," said Pen, for even yet Arnold seemed not to have grasped the point. "A lot of the men pinch the stuff and carry it with them."

But Llewellyn was not such a fool as to cause an explosion which might do more damage than the cavalry. He had a pistol in his pocket. There was one report as he fired into the lock. Then he swung the gate open. He came back as casually as though he had been away to wash his hands.

"Listen to me down there!"

Heads craned upwards. Arnold, Hamer and the others stood back from the door in order to look to the upper window whence the voice came. It was Parry Powell the magistrate.

"Arnold Ryerson, Evan Vaughan, Idris Llewellyn, I appeal to you three leaders of these men to take them away from this place."

"We have come in peace," Llewellyn shouted. "We demand to see officials of the company."

"There are no officials here," said the magistrate, a small red-faced man with glittering spectacles. He stood at the window importantly, took a pinch of snuff, and waved a yellow silk handkerchief before his nose. Shonnie, the inspector of police, and an officer of cavalry stepped forward from the darkness behind him. The milling and shouting in the yard ended abruptly. Everybody stood in silence to hear the colloquy between their leaders and the three at the window.

"Then where are the officials, by God?" Evan Vaughan shouted shrilly. "Isn't it here they should be, Mr. Parry Powell magistrate? Are they stuffing their fat gutses in Park Lane while we eat bread an' scrape in Cwmdulais? That's not fair do's, is it now? Give us fair do's, Mr. Parry Powell. We want to wait in the offices, that's all. There is no evil in us whateffer."

In comment on this, a stone suddenly shattered the window at which the magistrate stood. He did not blink an eyelid. His yellow handkerchief fluttered again, and he shouted: "Mr. Ryerson, be advised by me. Conduct these men to their homes."

Another stone was his answer, and then a small fusillade which broke several windows.

Parry Powell remained imperturbable. A glass splinter had jagged his cheek. He stanched the blood with his handkerchief and stood his ground. "I give you warning," he shouted, "that I hold this to be a riotous assembly. You are trespassing upon private property; you are unlawfully damaging it." He ducked before a stone, and went on: "Those of you who remain for longer than one minute may have cause to regret it. I shall regret it myself. One minute, Mr. Ryerson."

He took out his watch and laid it on the window-sill. Arnold was sweating. His palms were hot; his shirt was sticking to his back. Pen put an arm through his. "You can't back out, lad. You can't! You can't!" she whispered fiercely. "Let the swine do what they like. Let the country know what miners have to put up with."

Arnold did not answer. He was no leader in that moment. He stood mute and miserable as the inexorable seconds fled by. The noise in the yard had broken out afresh. Stones flew from all directions. Hardly a window had a whole pane left. A few men, finding a railway sleeper lying to hand, were beginning to use it as a battering ram upon the office door when Parry Powell took up his watch and shouted dramatically: "Time!"

But now the uproar was too deeply under way to be checked by a word. The men continued to shout and storm, to hurl stones, to batter on the door, so that few heard the magistrate flinging out the words of the Riot Act into the chaos:

"Our Sovereign Lady the Queen chargeth and commandeth all persons being assembled immediately to disperse themselves, and peacably to depart to their habitations or to their lawful business, upon the pains contained in the Act made in the first year of King

George for preventing tumultuous and riotous assemblies. God Save the Queen."

Parry Powell with a final flourish of his yellow handkerchief disappeared from the window. Hamer took Pen by the arm. "You'd better come away now," he said. "You know what that means?"

She shook him off. "Aye, Ah know as well as thee. This is where t'band starts to play."

There was a fierce joy in her face. Hamer, who had incited more than one riot, for the first time stayed and saw one through.

The pandemonium in the colliery yard was now so great that he did not hear the word of command given. The first thing he was aware of was that the statuesque soldiers were immobile no longer. The horses were pushing their way relentlessly between the wall of the office and the crowd yelling before it. The soldiers and horses seemed very patient. There was no wild charge such as his mind associated with Peterloo. Soon, by mere shoving, they had dislodged the ram-batterers and established a long cohort which now, perfectly disciplined, faced outward to the crowd. Then steadily, unhurriedly, they began to advance, and the crowd to fall back towards the gate. It seemed a mere sweeping up of light unco-ordinated refuse. The horses' heads went up and down and the bits jingled almost playfully.

Then Evan Vaughan turned and shouted: "Is it running away you all are, then? What wass it we came here for, by God? To run like bloody curs in front of a couple of fellers on gee-gees?"

Others turned with him. He stood his ground till a horse, thrusting remorselessly towards him, but at no more than an ambling pace, had its nose almost against his face. The excitement that had been simmering in the man all night blazed up. "Don't you poke your bloody nose in my face," he shouted, and, doubling his fist, he smote upwards with all his might into the soft flesh of the horse's lower lip. The creature reared. Evan Vaughan had a terrifying glimpse of a girthed belly, and of a pair of gleaming shoes suspended over his head, of genitals and the massy knots of hind legs. He quailed backward from that frightening primitive spectacle, and the hoofs crashed to the cobbled yard with a clang not a yard from where he stood. He had not seen the soldier draw his sabre. A smart smack with the flat on the shoulder made the little man reel. He saw the sabre then, and, feeling the pain in his shoulder, he yelled: "It's stabbed I am! By God, he's stabbed me!"

Many men were now streaming out of the yard gate, but many others paused on hearing the cry, turned and saw the sabre. Stones began to fly again. Horses and the men who rode them were struck, and now it was no easy-going tolerant pushing of the crowd. Saddle-leather began to creak urgently; now all the sabres were out, striking right and left, but striking always with the flat. The soldiers were out to inspire terror rather than to inflict injury. Hamer could see that, standing near the gate with a few men who feared the conflict but could not tear themselves away from the spectacle. The whole affair might have ended with bruised ribs and sore heads and bitter resentful memories but for Evan Vaughan.

Nearly everyone was out of the yard. There was a struggling angry knot at the gateway, obstinate, obdurate, having to be thrust out by the sheer weight of chest and swerving rump and the menace of the steel that had not once been fleshed. Vaughan ran outside the wall to a distant point, climbed over, and shouted: "Come on, boys, take 'em in the rear!" He dashed to the colliery office and began to climb through a broken window. A few soldiers detached themselves from the mêlée at the gate and spurred towards him. One reached him before the others and addressed him by name. The dreadful anonymity of uniformed terror had prevented everybody from recognizing a boy from this very valley. "Get out now, Evan Vaughan, you damn ole fool you," he hissed urgently. "No one 'ooldn't 'urt you, mun, if you'd get out."

Vaughan turned from the window. "Johnny Rees!" he shouted. "Johnnie Rees, by God! You bloody traitor you! Cutting off the breasts of your own women you are, and disembowelling your butties!"

He hurled himself at the youth, snatching at his bridle. But the others were up now, riding urgently, and one of them was the man whose horse Vaughan had struck. He himself was furious at having to restrain his passion while his own blood was pouring into his eye from a gash caused by a thrown brick. He saw Vaughan and recognized him, and his rage with this recalcitrant fool boiled over. He stood in his stirrups and rode at the man at a good lick, and struck. And this time it was not the flat smiting Vaughan's shoulder. It was the edge slicing his jugular and sending him down to gurgle out his life, by God.

"*Now* they know. *Now* they'll have to do something," Pen said. She was trembling, white with excitement, as she and Arnold and Hamer sat before the kitchen fire in Horeb Terrace. She was too overwrought to do anything. She lay back in a chair. "Murderers!" she said.

Arnold was not excited. He was miserable, and utterly and finally worn out. He had made a pot of tea. Three poured cups were on the table, cold, untouched. It was midnight.

"I can tell you exactly what they'll do, lass," Arnold said. "Nothing."

Five minutes later Shonnie came in and arrested him in the most friendly manner.

"Arrest me, too," Hamer challenged him. "I was in it, wasn't I?"

"I have no warrant for your arrest," said Shonnie. "Come on, Arnold."

Pen did not say a word as they went. When they were gone she went off to bed, still not speaking. Hamer did not sleep. He spent the night sitting by the kitchen fire. In the morning he returned to Baildon, and shortly thereafter he took his seat in the House of Commons, where the Tory benches greeted him with hisses. Arnold went to prison. The miners went back to work on their old terms. Nothing was done.

Chapter Fifteen

Hamer and Ann had no child but Charles. In 1905 Charles was eight years old. On an autumn day Hamer and Ann took him down to Graingers, the preparatory school for Hungerbury.

In the train on the way home Ann was very quiet. She could not get out of her head her last sight of Charles. The matron who was holding his hand was a kindly-looking woman, and Ann had no doubt that the headmaster, with whom she and Hamer had taken tea, was both kindly and intelligent. But to Charles, clearly, they might both have been Hottentots of an unaccustomed ferocity, but, as he stood, a frail-looking and forlorn little figure, backed by the virginia creeper flaming red about the school porch, it was evident that he had told himself that though they were Hottentots, he must not show his fear. A cab had come to take his father and mother to the station, and Ann's last glimpse of Charles, as she waved through the window, was of him standing there with a white smile on his face: the smile she had seen once or twice before: when he scalded his foot by overturning a kettle, and when a fool of a maid told him that the kittens had been drowned. Ann knew that this white smile was Charles's public face; and that, as soon as he found privacy, it would dissolve in misery. It was as heart-breaking to her as the thin shrill whistling in which the child indulged when he was afraid.

But it was not only Charles's misery that was on her heart: it was her own defeat. Charles had been from the beginning taken out of her hands. He had not gone to a board school, but to a series of little private academies. This arrangement had at least permitted her to see him every day. Now that he was gone, she felt empty. She and Hamer had two rooms in Lizzie's North Street house, and the run of the rest of it. Ellen, who was seventy-two years old, was living a superannuated life at The Hut, with a maid ministering to her needs, which were few, for she was hearty and active. And Ann, standing on the placid country station, looking forward to the years ahead of her, felt super-annuated too. So long as she had had Charles she had felt a person of some importance, and she had not bothered with active political work. She didn't feel that it would be easy to pick it up again. She was forty-one. Hamer was forty.

She stood on the platform in a white silk dress, very tight in the waist, very billowy in the skirt, which was all aerie flounces, and she carried a white folded sunshade in her hand. She did not open it, for the heat was gone out of the day which was now marked by a tender luminescence. The station flower-beds were full of dahlias, coloured a deep burgundian purple, and of Michaelmas daisies, big top-heavy sunflowers, golden-rod, and many flowers she did not know. The colours were muted in that late autumn light, and they held for her the sadness of all things whose youth is ended and whose dissolution is at hand.

So she was quiet in the train, sitting opposite Hamer who took a book from his pocket and began to read. Now and then she looked at him with the pride that the years had deepened. The moustache was gone now; the face had taken on the contours that the years would do nothing but engrave and confirm. The wing of dark hair falling across the broad brow had a line or two of grey in it, and occasionally his old childish gesture asserted itself: he swept it back with an impatient hand. His big sombrero hat was tossed on the seat at his side. A black silken bow was at his neck. The Spanish cloak he affected had been thrown on to the rack.

This was the man who had defeated her, and as the train ran through the bloomy dusk, stopping at all the little stations that seemed no more than flower-gardens, and he read on, marking a passage here, making a note there, she knew that a thousand such defeats would not change her pride or abate one jot of her love for him. The Diplomatic Service! He had at last broken his precious secret to her, and she had said Yes, Yes, to it all, knowing in her wise heart how long are the years, how fragile is the planning of men.

Hamer at last put down his book. "Well," he said, "I think he took it like a little man. He should be happy there."

"I think he will," said Ann, "once he's got over his first few weeks. He's a sensible child."

"I feel I've done my best for him. The board school – all that sort of thing – I think you were wrong, my dear." He leaned forward and spoke urgently, laying a hand on her knee. She felt he was justifying himself. "I'm as good a Labour man as the next, but I think I see farther than most of them. D'you mind a little boasting?"

She smiled and shook her head.

"They think Labour's always going to be what it is now," he went on. "They can't see it as anything but a handful of working men in the House of Commons, perpetually in opposition, perpetually arguing about an extra ha'p'orth for the poor. That's wrong, utterly and absolutely. I see Labour as a great party, a successful party in fewer years than you may think, a party in office, not haggling about ha'p'orths but handling the finances of a nation, administering all the great offices, conducting this country's relations with the empires of the world. That's coming – coming soon. Balfour's weakening. This Government won't see the year out. It's coming all over again," he smiled. "A general election. Another fight in St. Swithin's. I'm not afraid of that. I'm dug in there now. It's going to be a Liberal Government next time. Take that from me."

She gave him her serious attention, but she was smiling in her heart at his urgency. He was still the bright confident creature who rushed so surprisingly into her life and Lizzie's that day when she had gone with Arnold to meet "the boy Shawcross." He was like this even then. "Take that from me." Well, he was usually right, and, right or wrong, she could take a lot from him.

"Yes," he went on, "a Liberal Government, but a great many more Labour members in the House; and that's a step to what will come as sure as the sun is going down behind those chimneys. I mean a Labour Government. We've got to be ready for it. We must breed and train the men for it. We must be ready for dignity, responsibility, power. We've got all the trade union leaders we need, plenty of Ryersons and Jimmy Newboults. What we shall lack is statesmen."

"Poor little Charles!"

"Fortunate little Charles! But, believe me, all this is going to happen long before Charles is ready. He will not be one of the creators of it, but one of the inheritors."

"Meantime, there's Charles's mother, now out of work, in a manner of speaking."

"There's work enough to do, God knows."

The train was joggling over the points, edging into the dark cavern of the station. Hamer got up, put on his hat, switched his cloak down from the rack. He would put it on to stride up the platform. It was part of his inseparable outfit. The newspaper cartoonists loved it. The porters on the station would recognize it and nudge one another. "Hamer Shawcross."

"Yes, work enough," he repeated. It was a saying often on his lips: "So much to do. So much to do."

She had not intended to tell him just yet what it was that had come to her mind as she sat, surveying her own lonely estate, watching the purple twilight deepen over the land. But suddenly she said: "Lizzie and I have always believed in votes for women. That movement is about to take a lead in political affairs. Take that from me."

He jumped down to the platform with his youthful agility, and held out a hand for her to follow. She saw that his face had darkened. "Keir Hardie believes in it," she said.

Her pattering stride went with his swinging gait along the platform. He looked down at her sideways. "Well, I don't," he said flatly.

"Will you say that on a platform in St. Swithin's at the general election?"

"I'll say it anywhere, at any time. Why?"

"Because I shall go to one of your meetings and put the question."

"You wouldn't dare!"

"I would and I will. Let me tell you."

It was another of his sayings. She threw it at him half-playfully; but as they came out into the bustle and chatter amid the bright lights of the fruit stalls and bookshops she saw that his face had tightened, and she felt her resolution tightening, too.

"We must take a cab," he said. "I've got so much to do."

He was falling into the habit of taking cabs. He would not have dreamed now of walking from King's Cross to North Street.

He held up his hand and a hansom stopped at the kerb. The cabby saluted with his whip. "Evenin', Mr. Shawcross."

The recognition pleased him, but he remained silent as the cab sped through the London evening towards Westminster, with the lamps coming out and hanging their soft chains of radiance along the violet dusk.

*

The autumn morning was chill in the north. Old Hawley Artingstall stood on the hearthrug at The Limes in Fallowfield and warmed his dwindling shanks. He gazed through the window at the white rime lying on the grass, tightening the edges of the fallen chestnut leaves. It was nine o'clock. The Artingstall diligence was not a thing you could set your watch by in these days. Hawley's body was shrunk and his mind was sluggish. He went up to town when he felt like it, and sometimes he didn't feel like it at all.

He was a disappointed man. He had hoped for a knighthood, if not a baronetcy. It would have been attractive: Sir Hawley Artingstall. He had contributed liberally to the Conservative Party funds, but his ample bribes had not had the hoped-for and customary result. His second wife, the red-haired Hilda, had left him. Both the children she had borne him were dead. He was not only disappointed: he was lonely. He sometimes thought with regret of his early days with Lillian, and a deepening tenderness was in his memory of Ann.

He often sat in this room and dreamed of the mornings when he and Ann had gone up to town together, she so fair and eager in the victoria at his side, he so keen, alert, ready to scowl if Haworth were half-a-minute late bringing the carriage to the door. He hadn't it in him now, he admitted. His business, formed years ago into a public company, had been going downhill, and that chap Hannaway had been as steadily going uphill.

Mr. Councillor Hannaway. He often glowered at the fellow across the floor of the Council chamber in the Town Hall: he the alderman glowering at the councillor, who never returned the look save with a cheerful impudent grin.

Only the other day, walking across the mosaic pavement of the Town Hall landing with his shoes clicking loudly on the stone, he had found an arm through his, and there was Hannaway, dressed up to the nines, a rose at his buttonhole, a silver-headed malacca cane in his hand.

"Well, Artingstall, come and have a look at this."

He led him down the stairs, out into Albert Square, and at the kerb was one of those newfangled motor-cars, with a driver sitting high up in front.

"What d'you think of it?" Councillor Thomas Hannaway asked.

"Ah reckon that'd give thi owd diligence a start and beat thee to t'post."

Hawley had little to say. He couldn't get on with the fellow. He didn't like his business methods: Hannaway had set up a chain of drapers' shops all over England. "Hannaway's." You saw it on some fascia wherever you travelled, and you knew it meant the same thing as cheap and nasty.

"Remember t'first time tha met me?" Hannaway asked.

Hawley remembered it well enough, because this fellow was always reminding him of it: how he had told a street urchin to call him a cab, and the brat had been full of back-chat, even going so far as to hint that some day he might buy Artingstall's.

"I remember well enough, Mr. Councillor," said Hawley with pompous formality. "When are you going to buy Artingstall's?"

Hannaway got into his chariot which shivered and rattled and finally shot off in a blue stink. "Ah've bought it!" he shouted.

And, by God, he had! By God! By God! Hawley swore to himself when in the privacy of The Limes he discovered the hidden machinations of Thomas Hannaway. Using all sorts of people for his cover, he had been busily buying in the Artingstall shares, till now he owned more than Hawley himself, more than all the other shareholders, till he was, in effect and practice, Artingstall's.

It was the final blow to old Hawley. It left him spiritless and lethargic, not caring much whether he ever went to town again. At ten minutes past nine, when in his vigorous heyday he would already for some time have been making the fur fly in the shop, he succumbed to the odour of the coffee and kidneys, and walked into the dining-room, where the *Manchester Guardian* lay folded on his plate.

Hawley was not deeply interested when a headline told him that there had been a "Fracas at the Free Trade Hall!" and that women had been thrown out into the streets. These women! They were at it everywhere. Sir Edward Grey, Winston Churchill, and a few other Liberal leaders were stumping the country, telling the people how sweet the world was going to be when this Conservative administration was swept away and a Liberal Government reigned in its stead. And wherever the expositors of the Liberal gospel went, wild women leapt up and demanded to be told whether votes for women made a part of the promised Liberal paradise. They screamed. They kicked up a fuss.

And usually a few stewards got them by the scruff of the neck and threw them out into the street. It was all very undignified; Hawley could not believe that votes for women would come this way, and, for himself, he hoped they would not come at all.

He put a succulent forkful of kidney into his mouth, and was flicking over the page with impatience when, incredibly, his own name flashed upon his sight at the bottom of the report. He turned back and read: "Mrs. Shawcross is, of course, the wife of Mr. Hamer Shawcross, the Labour Member for the St. Swithin's Division of Bradford, and the only daughter of Alderman Hawley Artingstall of Manchester. Mrs. Lightowler is her aunt, sister of the late Mrs. Hawley Artingstall and a daughter of the late Sir James Sugden. Mrs. Ryerson, the third of the ejected women, is said to be the wife of a trade union official in South Wales."

Hawley could not believe his eyes. Ann chucked out of a public meeting, manhandled like a Saturday night drunk? It couldn't be true! And that old fool Lizzie Lightowler: the woman must be over fifty! So far as he was concerned, she could do what she liked, the tough old hen. But Ann—!

He didn't know much about Ann. They had drifted hopelessly apart. At Christmas time they sent one another cards with snow, holly and glowing lanterns on them, and for the rest she sent him two or three letters a year. There was one not long ago. It was not often she opened her heart to him, but he could read between the lines of that last letter that she was distressed at the thought of losing Charles. She had not wanted him to go: it was this chap Hamer, a climber if ever there was one, Hawley thought to himself.

He finished his breakfast and sat in an armchair by the diningroom fire, trying to get this incredible affair straight in his own mind. His thoughts wandered back through the years – back to the wedding breakfast in Ackroyd Park. He remembered how Ann had seemed to him exalted, and how he had ruminated that one of these days she might fly off the handle.

It had been a long time coming, but it looked as if it had come. Somehow, it gave him satisfaction to reflect that this would be one in the eye for Hamer Shawcross. He couldn't believe that this was what Shawcross would want. Well, he had asked for it. He had forced the girl's hand where the child was concerned. He had left her in a dead end, and he must thank himself if she took her own way out.

Suddenly, to the old man, the affair seemed not so disgraceful as it had at first appeared. He chuckled as he sat in his chair, He lit a cigar and smiled at the glowing point. This would shake up that complacent young devil Hamer. Good for you, Ann! It was a Viking stroke. They'd called old Birley the Viking. It was a long time since he'd thought of old Birley, dead and gone so many years. He thought of him now with reminiscent affection, and of Ann with pride. The warmth of the fire took possession of his old limbs. The cushions were soft and the frost still sparkled without. There was a time when he would have rejoiced to be out in it, feeling his blood tingle. But not now, not now. He let his head loll backwards and stubbed his cigar. The housekeeper who came to clear away the breakfast things tiptoed out on finding him asleep. Hawley Artingstall asleep at half-past nine in the morning! Ichabod! Ichabod! An hour and a half ago the stinking rattling chariot had taken Mr. Councillor Hannaway townwards.

"Take it from me." You could usually take it from Hamer Shawcross. His flair for the political situation was uncanny. As he had predicted, the Conservative Government crashed that year, overburdened with the disgraceful debris of the Boer War. Campbell-Bannerman formed a Liberal administration, went to the country and came back triumphant. And in this new House of Commons there were thirty Labour members. "There's a rising tide. The tide is the significant thing. Remember that, Shawcross."

That was what Keir Hardie had said, and Hamer didn't need to be told it. A man might join the Conservative Party or the Liberal Party, old and slow-moving both of them, and in twenty years be where he was at the beginning. The party of the rising tide was another matter. Not – he shook his hair back impatiently, as though he had caught himself out in a treasonable thought – not that that had anything to do with his choice of a party. Ah, my friends, I know the bitter lives of the poor.

Well, here the tide was, still gaining inch by inch. Thirty members in the House, and he one of them, he one of the leaders of them. There had been no trouble about holding St. Swithin's, even though this time both Liberal and Tory had come up against him. It would have been one of the happiest elections he had fought, but for the incredible behaviour of Ann.

He had left her at The Hut at Baildon, and come up to London alone for the opening of the new Parliament. To find a small house, too, He had quarrelled with Lizzie Lightowler, told her he would use her North Street place no longer. He walked his quarterdeck and told himself it was past belief that the two women who owed so much to him should behave in such a fashion. Pen Muff he could understand. She had been in it, too.

His quarterdeck was the terrace along the Thames, opposite the House of Commons. He loved to come here and walk and think. On one hand the blackened time-smoothed granite parapet with the lamps springing out of it. Beneath his feet the long stone pavement, running forward in a lovely vista and almost always unfrequented. On the other hand the silver-grey Portland stone wall of St. Thomas's Hospital with the plane trees rising above it, and above the plane trees the windows of the hospital in tier upon tier. They were lighted now, and the lamps springing from the parapet were lighed, and, on the other side of the river stirred by a cold winter wind, the windows of the House were lighted. In front of him Westminster Bridge and behind him Lambeth Bridge carried their lights across the dark water sucking and gurgling under their arches, and beyond Westminster the lights of great hotels and offices built up a fantastic faëry façade diminishing in a perspective that he could never look upon without emotion.

The great city! He loved it. He watched the barges forging down the wide roadway of the river, and the lighted buses crossing it on the bridges, and the twinkling lights of hansom cabs dancing like fireflies along the farther shore, and here, where scarcely a soul seemed ever to come, he could be private, swinging along in the cold January night with the Spanish cloak about him and the big sombrero hat crowning his splendid head. He was aware of himself as part of this metropolitan magnificence, this show so brave though superimposed, as he knew, not a few hundred yards from where he walked, upon the black misery of the Lambeth slums cowering under the medieval splendour of the Archbishop's palace. But his back was to the slums, and he looked across the water to the wintry sky that, above the discernible and manifest lights enchanting the eye, pulsed and quivered with emanation of unseen mile after mile of lighted opulence and gaiety. A brave show. He had found himself of late coming again and again to his quarterdeck to look upon it. Never had it seemed lovelier.

Never had it been more pregnant with allure, with the invisible and intangible promises that wove themselves so deeply into the tangible prosaic conflict of his daily life.

> And when the strife is fierce, the warfare long,
> Steals on the ear the distant triumph song;
> And hearts are brave again and arms are strong.

Often on a night like this he heard the song. This immense pulsation of light over the unseen anonymous millions of London seemed the song made manifest. And of what triumph did it tell? What quality of conquest did he discern at the heart of his dreams? *Quality* of conquest? He never knew the mood which can parse and analyze laurels. He pressed forward. Or was pressed forward. "I felt sometimes that if I had hesitated in the course that from the first lay so plainly open, some influence would have blocked retreat and pressed me forward, willy-nilly." (The Diary.)

That is at least honest. That was his accustomed mood; but tonight the mood was darkened because he was still smarting from Ann's defection.

They had travelled north together: he and Ann, Lizzie and Charles. This was Charles's first holiday from Graingers, and already the boy was a little apart from them, wrapped, though as yet ever so lightly, in the silky cocoon of an environment alien to them. For the first time in his life Charles had had experiences which they had not shared, could fall back upon memories in which they had no part. In the train he had gently contradicted something which Ann had said, giving as sufficient reason: "Old Robbie says so." Questioned as to Old Robbie's credentials, he would vouchsafe only: "Oh, he's a chap."

Ann was hurt by the small encounter, and reflected that now there would be an increasing procession of Robbies, vaguely anonymous and wholly authoritative chaps, from whom there could be no appeal. It must be so, of course it must be so, she told herself. No one but a fool could hope or wish to remain sole custodian of a growing child's integrity; but this thought only threw her back the more sharply upon her resolution to guard her own integrity, too, and to sacrifice to Hamer not an inch of her political conviction.

He had pretended at first to take her woman's suffrage work as a joke, an ebullience of spirit, that would boil over soon and be done with. Even when she and Lizzie had gone to Manchester to heckle a speaker who was certain soon to be a Liberal cabinet minister and had been ignominiously seized and roughly thrown into the street, he refused to take it seriously. But he read her a lecture: for the first time in their married life he talked to her like a Dutch uncle, begging her to remember the dignity of his position – that was his word! – and the derogatory effect her conduct was likely to have on his public position.

There had been an all-night sitting of the House. Lizzie had already gone out when Hamer came home, tired and irritable. He and Ann sat down together to a meal in the pretty North Street dining-room, with the pale winter sunshine falling on an importunate organ-grinder who, throughout their dispute, kept drooling "Good-bye, Dolly Gray."

It was when Hamer referred to his dignity that Ann boiled over. She threw John Ball and Wat Tyler in his teeth, and every man jack of the agitators down to Keir Hardie, down to Hamer himself. Had they stood on their dignity? Was she doing anything they hadn't done?

Ah, but these were working for a possible cause, for a reasonable end. Did she suppose that women would ever get the vote, that women, outnumbering men as they did, would ever voluntarily be granted the vote by men?

She seized on that word voluntarily, and told him she expected nothing of the kind. That was why the suffragists must do as they were doing. Would Gladstone have *voluntarily* brought in a Home Rule bill for Ireland? Would the Tories have *voluntarily* enfranchised men like Hamer Shawcross and Arnold Ryerson and Jimmy Newboult and Keir Hardie? Voluntarily! She gave him back his word with scorn.

He left his breakfast untouched, bathed and shaved himself, and, without sleeping, went to his work-room and was soon immersed. So much to do! So much to do!

The memory of the hot debate was between them as they travelled north but they had patched up a truce, and he could not believe that she would intervene in St. Swithin's. He saw little of Charles, for the general election was upon him. Jimmy Newboult was at the station in Bradford to meet him, trusty as ever, forgetting none of the things that would minister to his leader's comfort. He had a couple of cabs ready to take the little party and the luggage across the town to the Midland station where they caught the train to Shipley, and at Shipley two more cabs were waiting to take them through the deepening winter dusk up the long hill to Baildon. At The Hut Ellen had tea ready in the big firelit drawing-room, and as soon as tea was over Hamer took Jimmy off to his study where the fretwork model of the House of Commons stood on a low bookcase.

So it was all through that Christmas holiday. Charles had but fragmentary glimpses of his father, usually at breakfast, and he did not see much more of his mother or of the woman he knew as Auntie Lizzie. Those two were in and out of Bradford every day, not, as had been their way in the past, to work for Hamer, but to make a nuisance of themselves at meetings and to organize meetings of their own. And so Charles was thrown more and more into the company of Ellen.

There was a perfect understanding between them. The old lady, whose life now was almost wholly in the past, had lost asperity and became very gentle. Charles, when the weather was too bad for them to go out, would sit for hours on the floor at her feet, reading a book. Sometimes she would stroke his hair; sometimes she would doze right off; not often did she have much to say; but sitting there close against her black skirts, the child felt as happy and secure as if he were sitting on a summer day at the foot of an old tree that had known the storms of many winters.

Occasionally she would put on her spectacles and read to him her favourite bits out of Dickens, and tell him about Gordon whose books these were, and about the Old Warrior whose sabre was over the fireplace in Hamer's room, and about Hamer himself, a little boy playing in the Ancoats streets, working in an Ancoats greengrocer's shop, boxing in a back street bone-yard. Once started, reminiscence flowed from her. It was as though a river, feeling already the pulse of the nearing tides, had begun miraculously to retrace its course, to rediscover, before the last engulfment, the slow twist and loops through green mature meadows, the dartings and sparkling leaps down the sunny slopes of infancy.

From all this Charles learned much that he had never known before about the nature of his own inheritance, and began to apprehend a background immensely different from the background of Robbie and other heroes of Graingers who were occasionally called for by rustling dowagers riding in carriages behind cockaded servants. He began to be aware, too, of his father as a public figure. He was a precocious reader, and whenever the name of Hamer Shawcross, M.P., struck his eyes in some public print he would devour what was said. The picture he built up was rebellious. This Mr. Shawcross seemed always to be getting reproved by the Speaker in the House of Commons, or addressing great meetings of discontented men, or predicting the overthrow of all that Charles, even after one term's experience, dimly apprehended to be meant by Graingers.

This rebellious person fitted in well with the boy whose early years Grandmother Ellen sketched in for him, but not so well with the father he knew. "Hamer Shawcross" sounded to him almost like a character out of a book, a defiant, truculent, heroic character. Father wasn't like that. There was a vague and undefined territory between these two characters that troubled him because he could not bridge it.

In her lonely time, when they lived in Moorland Cottage and she had that room, so little desired, to herself, Ellen had assuaged her solitude by cutting from the newspapers all the references to Hamer that she could find and all the reports of his speeches. She had hidden them in a drawer, saying nothing to him or Ann, and had read them again and again.

One day she produced this pile, and, to find the child some occupation, she told him to stick them into an exercise book. In the kitchen she made paste out of flour and found him a brush, and for a couple of hours he sprawled on the rug at her feet, absorbed in his task. When it was done, she told him he could keep the book. He took it up to his room and put it in a drawer. Day by day thereafter he read it, until some of Hamer Shawcross's utterances were as firmly woven into his mind as familiar proverbs or as Ellen's sayings. "Never mind what people call you so long as they don't call you pigeon pie and eat you." That was one of them. There had been a time when he sweated with apprehension lest one of the workers, going home through the winter dusk from the little grey stone woollen mill in Baildon, should pounce upon him and proclaim him to be pigeon pie.

In the room where, long before, Tom Hannaway had publicly charged Hamer with neglecting his mother, Hamer faced his friendly election audience. He had no fears. St. Swithin's had long since taken him to its heart. His own flair told him that all was going well this time, and

Jimmy Newboult, with a practised finger on the pulse of the constituency, had assured him that his return was certain. Jimmy wouldn't say a thing like that merely to flatter.

He saw Ann and Lizzie Lightowler come in and take seats at the back. This was the first of his meetings they had attended, and seeing them sitting so quietly there his mind jerked back to a day long ago when he had joked about votes for women with old Marsden, now gone to his rest in Nab Wood cemetery, and Lizzie had asked what the joke was, and left him flat by her passionate assertion: "But I *believe* in all that."

Well, if they had come to make trouble, let them have it, He wasn't the dependent boy he had been in those days. He was Hamer Shawcross, and the knowledge that Hamer Shawcross didn't believe in votes for women had been efficacious in the Labour Party. Except Keir Hardie, there was no man of influence in the party wholeheartedly espousing this cause – nor in any other party, if it came to that; and he flattered himself that, so far as his own party was concerned, his was the influence that kept them where they were. Hardie was the leader of the party, and here was the first important issue on which his influence was greater than Hardie's. For that very reason, he felt a fanatic resolution to hold on, not to budge an inch.

He started to speak, wondering when and how the trouble would begin. He knew the game the women were playing up and down the country. They did not wait till question-time and put their questions in an orthodox fashion. That would be too tame; that would attract no attention. They jumped up early, popped a question, and, if it were not answered, or if the answer were not to their satisfaction, they tried to wreck the meeting.

He was going along well enough, but the sight of Ann and Lizzie sitting there teased and harassed him. He felt as though he were looking at a bomb which he knew must go off, and it was almost with a sense of relief that he saw Ann rise suddenly to her feet. He stopped speaking in the middle of a sentence. The audience looked round in surprise as Ann shouted: "Does Mr. Shawcross believe in votes for women?"

She was almost as well known in the constituency as he was, and there was a moment's surprise, almost consternation. Then, as Ann remained standing, all the heads swung back towards the platform. If any one had thought that this was a put-up family show, arranged to air a question, the sight of the two dispelled the notion. Ann's face was white and tense, Hamer's dark with resentment.

He said: "If the speaker will put her question at the proper time, I shall then decide whether it is one that need be answered."

Ann sat down, and Lizzie got up and shouted: "It's easy to say Yes or No."

Hamer's chairman sprang to his feet and said: "I decline to allow any questions to be put to the candidate till question-time."

Ann and Lizzie, in reply to that, stood up side by side and at the tops of their voices yelled the words that were growing into a mighty chorus up and down the country: "Votes for Women!'" Then they left the meeting.

It was the tamest interruption perhaps that any speaker suffered at the hands of the suffragists, but it left Hamer quivering with annoyance. The very fact that they had made their point and then let him down lightly, "walking almost contemptuously from the scene of their exploit," as the *Yorkshire Post* said the next day, getting the utmost juice out of Wife Heckles Husband – this very fact the more deeply incensed him.

When the meeting was over, he felt he could not face Ann that night. But at the same time he could not forget the white tension of her face. He did not underestimate the nervous torture it must have been to her to outface him like that in the midst of so many who knew them both. Admiration and resentment battled in his stubborn heart, and when his damned dignity took a hand, resentment won. Walking the miserable streets in the cold drizzling rain, he finally hardened his heart, turned his back on this cause which, if he had espoused it, would have been the one cause of the many he advocated to which, in his old age, he might have looked back and said: That, at all events, came off. Though so much else was wind and water, that endured, that came through.

But what, then, would it have mattered? From beneath the glory of his coronet, his mind, tinged as it was with philosophic irony, might have reflected that he was now in an hereditary place where votes do not corrupt, and where even the overwhelming vote of the women could not break through nor steal a safe seat on the lordly crimson benches.

*

But that was a long way off, and Ann was very near and very dear, so that when he came, close upon midnight, to The Hut, his heart was a bitter mixture of outraged tenderness, of wincing wounded self-esteem, and of self-righteous conviction that now he was a martyr stabbed with arrows on his own hearth. Since Charles had gone to Graingers, his room had been sometimes used for visitors. A spare bed had been moved in there, so that two people might be put up for a night.

He remembered this. There was no one stirring in the house. A lamp had been left lighted for him in the hall. He took off his cloak and great hat, and walked upstairs with the lamp in his hand.

Ann was sitting up in bed, the sheet drawn to her chin. Her hair was as beautiful as ever: the same white-honey glistening cascade that had fascinated his youth. It was streaming about her shoulders now. He noted all that, with resentment and hurt dignity in the ascendent, blowing cold over the deep tenderness of his heart, and noted, too, the white tension still in her face.

"Oh, my love!" she said, almost in tears.

The words abased her and glorified her. It was surrender. She was his at that moment on any terms. He said tonelessly: "I don't understand you. You are trying to destroy me."

It was monstrous, absurd, outrageous. And he knew it was untrue. He added with bathos: "I have come for my pyjamas."

He walked to the bed and fumbled for them beneath the pillow. Ann shrank away, holding to the sheet lest he should see her nakedness. He saw it, and was shaken. But he would not give in. He took the pyjamas, unhooked his dressing-gown from behind the door, and said: "I shall sleep in Charles's room."

Then he was gone with the lamp, and the click of the shutting door sounded in Ann's ears like the snip of fatal shears, She sat for a long time, with the sheet drawn up to her chin, staring at the darkness. Her body was hot with shame, and her heart was cold with anguish. For a long time her mind talked to itself. "I said 'It seems such a little light' and Hamer said 'It is enough to love by.'"

She had never forgotten that. It was a Hamer phrase, a lovely phrase, and always it had been able to evoke the rapture of that night in the old rickety hut when the iron stove was blazing and the snow was falling on the moor, so that they woke to a wide white world seamed with little valleys of bluish shadow. "Enough to love by."

Now he was gone out, carrying the lamp with him, and she wondered whether life could ever be the same again.

Not quite. The breath that clouds the mirror clears, and the reflection is bright again; but the mirror is tarnished at last by breath upon breath till the image is leaden, not crystal.

Hamer liked sleeping with Ann. The physical contact of their bodies, lying limb against limb, was pleasant to them both, and salutary, and tranquillizing to their minds.

During that December night the drizzly weather changed to frost, and he woke in his single bed unconsciously clutching the clothes tightly about him, aware of a sharp discomfort in one knee. He had felt it before, and it annoyed him beyond its cause. He was vain of his perfect health, his magnificent physique. "A touch of rheumatism" seemed to his mind, supersensitive in such matters, the first touch of blight in the bud, of worm in the oak, of rust in the steel. He hated illness, and, without opening his eyes, he lay there magnifying the rasp of the knee, suddenly aware of what had brought him to this single bed where his enemy had got at him, and blaming Ann for a day that was beginning badly.

At last he opened his eyes and saw Charles sitting up in bed with a dressing-gown on, writing by candlelight in an exercise-book. Another exercise-book lay on the bed.

Seeing his father awake, Charles put down the pencil whose end his small white teeth had pocked with nibblings, and said: "Hallo! What are you doing here?"

Hamer kept his face averted as much as possible from the child. This was another of his sensitivities. Charles had never seen him unshaven, unkempt. During his travels he had spent many nights in the homes of Labour leaders who appeared at the breakfast-table with scrubby chins and in shirt-sleeves. He hated it. So he averted his face from Charles and said: "I was very late getting home last night. I didn't want to disturb your mother."

Charles said nothing for a time; then he asked: "Do you like big words?"

Hamer permitted himself to laugh. "You bet I do, Charles," he said. "Don't you ever listen to people who say that writers and speakers should always use short words. Perhaps at school one of these days you'll learn something about Anglo-Saxon. Then you'll find a lot of fools who will tell you that good English is only written in simple Anglo-Saxon words. Listen to this..."

In his eagerness, for he did not often have a chance to talk with this intelligent son of his, he forgot his reticence and turned towards the boy. He intoned: "'The multitudinous seas incarnadine.' How d'you like the sound of that?"

Charles considered it, and said: "It sounds rich – like the fire shining on your curtains."

Hamer laughed outright, well pleased. "Yes," he said. "I think it's better than 'redden the many seas' which is what it means. Oh, yes, big words can be grand things. They can make nothing very much sound pretty good. They can be like coronation robes on a piddling little king."

"My word doesn't sound very grand," said Charles. "It's 'environment,' but I can't spell it."

Hamer spelled it out for him, and the boy wrote it painfully. "What are you writing?" Hamer asked.

"An essay for school," Charles said. "We've got to do a long essay in the holidays on anything we like. I'm doing one on the early life of Hamer Shawcross, M.P." He read: "Our hero's early environment was most meagre, for he played in bone-yards, and while still a child was a greengrocer's boy near the canal which bounded the outskirts of his humble home, from which he sallied forth to the markets in the dewy morn ere many were risen from beds of sloth."

Hamer ceased to smile. "Where did you learn all this?" he asked.

"From Grannie. And about the sword and the Old Warrior, and Gordon and Darkie Cheap, and your wretched estate."

Charles's hair had been uncut since the holiday began. It had begun to arrange itself again in tendrils, on his forehead, There he sat, blue-eyed, angelic-looking, nibbling the pencil, unaware that he had wrung his father's withers.

"You know," said Hamer reasonably, boiling within, "I don't think it is usual to write essays about living people. I don't think they'd like it at Graingers."

Charles looked dismayed. "I've done a lot," he said.

"That's a pity," said Hamer, "but I'm sure Alexander the Great or Cæsar would be better. I can give you a good little book on Alexander."

He left the child dubious, but dutifully consenting to enlighten his headmaster concerning the exploits of Alexander.

Ellen couldn't be kept out of the kitchen. She did not sleep much, and always before seven o'clock she was up and dressed and pottering about with preparations for breakfast. These winter mornings she wore an old blue woollen gown and a grey shawl hooded over her head, held under the chin by a safety-pin, Small as she was, she had achieved a serenity, a dignity of which she was unaware.

That morning, she was surprised, on coming out of her bedroom, to hear voices in Charles's room. She recognized Hamer's voice, and went downstairs full of perplexity. She was assembling cups and plates on a tray in the grey light when Ann came into the room, her face as grey as the morning. "Let's have a cup of tea, Mother," she said.

Ellen soon produced it, and Ann sat at the kitchen table, holding the cup in both hands as though to warm them, and sipping the tea occasionally.

"Don't lay a place for me," she said. "Tell Lizzie I've gone straight up to Bradford. She'll know where to find me."

"Not without a bit o' food in you you're not going," said Ellen warmly. "There's some queer nonsense goin' on in this house, it seems to me."

"Nothing that won't soon mend itself," Ann answered without conviction. She refilled her cup, nibbled a few biscuits, and, despite the old woman's entreaties, went out.

Lizzie went, too, soon after breakfast, a silent meal. Hamer scarcely spoke. He permitted himself to be absorbed in the newspapers, and Charles had a book on Alexander the Great propped open by his plate.

When the meal was done, and Lizzie gone, and Charles retired to his room to meditate on Alexander, Hamer said: "Mother, could you spare me a moment?"

How many moments she would have spared him! How, day after day, and year after year, saying nothing to anyone, she had felt the uselessness descend upon her because he did not want her moments any more.

She went before him into his room, on the way picking up from the table in the hall a half-knitted sock of Charles's. She did not sit in one of the deep leather chairs but on a rigid wooden one which kept her back straight; and the frosty sunshine fell through the window on to the blue gown and the grey hood of the shawl as she began at once to work.

She did not lift her eyes to her son, but was aware of his restlessness, his mental unbalance, as he stood towering above her on the hearthrug, filling his pipe with nervous fingers.

"How do you get on with Charles?" he asked when he had lit his pipe.

"He's a dear child," she said simply.

"I was having some talk with him this morning. He was telling me about an essay he's writing to take back to school."

She smiled as her busy fingers flashed, "Such nonsense! Why harass the child's carcass when he's on holiday?"

"It's necessary," said Hamer. "It's a good thing for him. I'm trying to have him brought up in such a way that he won't have to harass his carcass as I did – working all day and studying all night. I want him to miss that atmosphere altogether. I don't see, myself, why he should ever be troubled by the knowledge that I grew up that way."

For the first time, she raised her old eyes and looked at him, her hands ceasing their busy motion, and there was that in her regard which made him add hastily: "I mean, of course, not just now. It stands to reason that he'll know, and that I'll want him to know, later on. But he's only a child. He's in a new environment, and I don't think it's good for him to imagine that he and his people are different from the boys he's meeting there."

"Whatever he imagines won't alter t'facts," Ellen said sharply. "Of course we're different – different as chalk and cheese. That's the fact, lad, and facts'll out sooner or later. Don't thee forget Broadbent Street, or thee'll come a cropper."

Hamer puffed angrily at his pipe for a moment, then said: "Never mind me, Mother. We're discussing Charles, not me, Charles's mother didn't come out of Broadbent Street, and half of me didn't either, for that matter."

As soon as the words were out of his mouth he cursed the anger that had forced them from him: cursed, too, that hidden preoccupation with his own origins that often teased and excited his mind. He would not have been surprised if Ellen had got up and walked out of the room or if she had railed at him fiercely. She did neither. Her fingers let go the knitting which lay in her lap, and her hands folded above the knitting in her immemorial attitude of patience and endurance. She looked at her hands for a long time as if considering what to say; then she said, using the name he had not heard for years:

"I'm only an ignorant old woman, John, and you're a great man. I don't grudge it to you, lad. All credit to you. But give me a bit of credit, too. I may be ignorant, but that don't mean I'm a fool. I've lived for seventy-two years, an' that counts. I can put two and two together an' see what's what. I don't think I've done anything to hurt your Charles, and never in this life, God help me, have I done anything to hurt you. And never will you make me change my opinion that everything decent in you – an' that's a lot – came out of Broadbent Street. Who your father was don't matter all that. But when you've done thanking God for Gordon Stansfield you'll be past hoping for."

Hamer knelt suddenly at her feet in a swift impulse of penitence and sincerity. "And for you, Mother," he said.

"That's as may be. I haven't been of much account to anybody – except perhaps to Gordon. Go on with you now. You've got your work to do. Go and leave me."

It was his own room, and he had much to do there, but he said nothing about that. He went out of the room, and presently out of the house, and the urgent business of life caught him up from her again. Ellen sat for a long time, utterly without motion, living over every second of that strange interlude which somehow left her feeling moved and uplifted and happy. They had talked together, again, face to face.

As he walked his quarterdeck with the night wind moving about him and the London lights pulsating in the firmament, he was thinking of all these things and the things that followed. Pen Muff, whose name was becoming known throughout the country as one of the most savage of the women suffragists, had turned up with a cohort of Amazons, and with bells, rattles and catcalls had wrecked a meeting. As a suffragist, she had dropped the name of Ryerson. "Miss Muff," "Pen Muff," and in the more facetious papers "Little Pen Muffet" was getting into the public prints everywhere.

Ann and Lizzie often accompanied Pen Muff on her wrecking expeditions, not only in Bradford but all over the north of England. Sometimes they were away for days on end, and once Ann came back with her face bruised and her hands scarred from trampling feet. Lizzie had always kept her hair cut short, and to his horror Ann also appeared at The Hut one day with her hair gone save for a boyish vestige, which was grotesquely parted at one side and brushed across the head. "It's not so easy for men to grab hold of," she said.

She and Lizzie had left his meetings alone after their small symbolic interference. The truce was back, uneasy and tantalizing, yet workable. But, so far as Lizzie at least was concerned, it couldn't go on. He felt that once the House was reassembled and he back in London, he couldn't go on living in this atmosphere of constant strain and conscious accommodation. He told her so. "Don't be a fool, man," she answered brusquely. "We're fighting for what we believe to be right, as you've always done yourself. If that makes us impossible to live with, there's something wrong with your liver."

He quickened his steps. He must get back to North Street. He was still living there, unable to find a house within his means. He was approaching the steps leading up to Westminster Bridge when a woman, who seemed in the dim light vaguely familiar, began to come down them. She came with a light tripping step, almost dancing, and her cloak breezed out like wings. Then he recognized her. They had never spoken, except during that brief encounter on the moor and in the course of polite formalities while votes were being counted at St. Swithin's. He swept off his great hat, and Lady Lostwithiel paused on the pavement at the foot of the steps. Then she came forward and held out a gloved hand. "Good evening, Mr. Shawcross. So St. Swithin's has sent you back again. May I congratulate you?"

Her hand was small, firm and warm. He held it for a fraction of time longer than he needed to do. The cold night air was suddenly alive with her perfume, as though a wind had stirred a bed of flowers. The light of one of the spherical lamps, rising from the wreathed dolphins on the parapet, fell on her lively face and dancing eyes.

"This is a lovely place for a walk," she said. "I always take a little air here after visiting St. Thomas's."

She had begun to walk, and he turned in his tracks and walked at her side, hugely overtopping her, back towards Lambeth Bridge.

He hoped politely that no one of importance to her was ill in St. Thomas's.

"Not unless you call a maid important," she laughed. "I do, as it happens. She's a good gel." She had old Buck's pronunciation of some words. "I come to see her every Friday. And – oh, dear – I forgot to commiserate with you. The suffragists seem to have given you a bad time."

"Yes," he said. "But that sort of thing can't last. They are an excited and misguided set. They'll fizzle out."

Her laugh was very clear and silvery, "Oh, Mr. Shawcross! And I've always considered you a prophet! I've always told Lostwithiel to take note of what you do and say. Do you know, I've always thought you the most dangerous man in England? And so did old Papa Buck."

He accepted the compliment placidly. "Dangerous to us, I mean" of course," she added. "Wind-bags and ranters and scrubby trade unionists will never do us much damage, but you—" She shrugged her shoulders.

"And now, as a prophet, you're letting me down. This suffrage movement is going to win, you know. I've tried to drill it into Lostwithiel. The Conservative Party ought to support these women tooth and nail. Because women outnumber men. Give them the vote and the future is ours. For, you see, women are naturally conservative creatures. I really believe that you understand this, and that that is why you oppose the suffrage."

"You believe right," he said grimly, letting the reasons that had dwelt in his heart out into the light of day for the first time, "But you can't tell Hardie a thing like that."

She stopped and looked at him sweetly. "No, I suppose not," she said. "He's utterly upright. However it worked, he would see it as a matter of right and wrong – wouldn't he? He wouldn't ask if it suited the party book."

Hamer winced. "I am a politician," he said bluntly. "I want to see my party in power."

"You will," said Lady Lostwithiel. "Don't doubt it, you will."

They came out upon Lambeth Bridge, and there she said: "Would you mind calling me a cab?"

He did so, and held the door while she climbed past him in a scurry of perfume. He shut the door, and she gave him her hand through the window. "We've talked nothing but politics," she said. "I'm afraid that's been very dull for you. We must meet again. There are so many other things in the world."

Then she was gone, and though he had so much to do, he did not hasten to North Street. He went back and paced the quarterdeck. A week later he remembered that she had said she always came on Fridays. Perhaps the maid – that good gel – was better. Lettice did not appear.

Hamer remained in North Street. His resentment could not stand against Lizzie Lightowler's gusty humour or Ann's silent pleading, Lizzie was enjoying the crusade. Ann was not, She did not know how long, how bitter, the way was that stretched before her. Had she known, she would have trodden it just the same, But she hated it. She hated the public odium, the rude manhandling, the dust and wounds, She suffered in spirit as well as in body; but Lizzie seemed to thrive in spirit almost in proportion to her physical suffering. These were her great years.

Years! Hamer would never have believed it, Few people would have believed it; but the incredible struggle went on, increasing in ferocity, for longer than most wars endure. Throughout that time, Hamer and Ann led lives that lay apart. They shared the same house, but neither knew when the other would be in, where the other would be. There were days and weeks when they saw nothing of each other. Hamer got used to most things: he got used even to Ann's being in prison: the finest women in the country were in prison: but when the hunger-strikes began, here was something he could not get used to. Never so long as he lived did he forget the first time the cab drove to the door, and Ann got down and tottered and fell. He ran out and picked her up, wondering at the lightness of this pitiful white-faced wreck of a woman he held in his arms, her eyes deep and burning, her sunken cheeks flushed. He carried her in and laid her on a couch. She was barely conscious, and when she could speak he broke out in an anguish of supplication. "My darling! Must you go on with this? Must you?"

A pallid smile dawned in her eyes, and she began to murmur: "I shall not cease from mental strife, nor shall the sword sleep..." and then she fainted again.

He knew what she meant. She was reminding him of the verse he himself had loved to quote long ago when they were fighting side by side in St. Swithin's. It was the verse he had always recited with the sabre in his hand. What mental strife had he endured, what ardour of body, to compare with Ann's? He stood looking down at her, distraught by the impotence of his own compassion, Poor Ann! Poor Ann! What did she imagine would come of it all? Jerusalem in England's green and pleasant land? Did that come through giving votes to women? Did it come through giving votes to anyone? Did anything worth while ever come from the schemes and machinations of politics?

Looking at Ann, short-haired, haggard, the mere husk and dry shell of the girl he had loved, he was visited by a profound seizure of pessimism. For a moment he hung over a gulf where he and his like, all the makers of windy promises, the pedlars of paradise, swirled like a handful of inconsiderable dust. He saw with clarity that the immortal aspirations of men for freedom, truth, beauty, equality, could never know a secular satisfaction, and that this very fact made both the glory and the tragedy of human life. And all this, he confessed in that moment, was outside the sphere wherein he daily exercised himself.

He knelt down and drew off Ann's shoes. The soles of her stockings were in rags, She was neglecting herself, Her feet were all but bare. He kissed them, knowing them to be the feet of a martyr.

But in 1906 all this was still in the future. The war of the women, and the politicians' savage and bestial war upon the women, were hardly begun. Hamer for one still regarded the whole matter as one that would blow over, fizzle out, obligingly accommodate itself in one way or another. Scuffles and scrimmages round about the House of Commons were frequent; they were not unknown within the sacred precincts; and so he was not surprised, when walking through the lobby one October day, to find a knot of excited women waving their arms, shouting at the tops of their voices, denouncing the Government for its callous disregard of their claims. Policemen were roughly pushing the women out, and Hamer would have hurried on, thinking the matter of small importance, if he had not noticed Ann and Lizzie Lightowler among them. Ann's arm was held behind her back in a grip that would have meant torture had she resisted. She was hustled out of the House, and Hamer followed to see how the matter would end. It did not end, as he had hoped, with the women being told to go home. In police custody, they were marched away through the mild October sunshine. Hamer turned back, whitefaced, into the House. This was the first time he had seen his wife manhandled.

*

Ann woke with a start in the prison cell. A grisly light was filtering through the grated window. She could just make out her surroundings. Lying on a hard board covered by a mattress coarsely stuffed with what felt like wood shavings, she looked at the cold stone walls of this tiny domain in which a tall man could not have lain down straight on the floor. The door was of iron, pierced by a hole. An eye peering through at her had been one of the horrors of the night before.

She had come, after sentence, in a dark van, jolting through the crowded streets of London with as little knowledge of her journey as if she had been a corpse in a hearse. She had no idea what would happen to her in prison. She had stood in the dock white-faced and stony-eyed, unable to summon up the wild bravado of some who yelled their battle-cry "Votes for Women" even into the teeth of the law's majesty. She couldn't do that sort of thing. She could only suffer, while shrinking from suffering with every nerve of her being.

It was still to her, staring at the grey morning wall, and shivering in the stony cold, a confused incredible nightmare: the stripping of her clothes, the hustling into coarse serge daubed with broad arrows. She drew great clumsy boots upon her feet, looking with wonder at the stockings on her legs, grotesque things ringed in black and red, as though she were about to play some farcical pirate part.

All this was jumbled in her memory with the sound of the boots clumping through stone corridors, and the jangling of keys, and the clang of the iron door. Then the long doleful night, rustling with strange alarming noises, made horrid with the sense of an eye at the peep-hole, Thou God seest me. Then fitful sleep, full of dreams: Charles, Hamer, Haworth in his happiest mood driving her through the leafy lanes of Cheshire. They were happy dreams, and she clung to them tenaciously, lying there in the grim half-light, till bells jangled, lights snapped on, and the routine of the jail caught her up.

Looking back upon it, Ann thought it an easy time. Scrubbing the board that was her bed, scrubbing the plank that was her table, scouring her few pots and pans with bath-brick, marching at the word of command down the clanging corridors to Divine Worship – her own mind ironically supplied the capital letters – exercising in the yard – round and round so drearily, round and round, with tall forbidding walls about her and a glimpse of pale autumn sky as remote and inaccessible as mercy – reading the Word of God, provided by the Christian authorities at a cheap cut rate which ensured small eye-destroying print, eating her skilly and loathing it: she got through the days somehow.

It was a time of dreariness and boredom, and she filled it with dreaming – dreaming awake and dreaming asleep – and with scratching upon the wall of her cell. She scratched with the point of a safety-pin taken from her clothing. "I shall not cease from mental strife." It was something to do, and it made the verse her own. It was Hamer's war-cry, and therefore it was doubly precious to her, for never had she loved him, never had she yearned for him, as in these days of their separation. He was wrong, woefully wrong, about woman suffrage; but who, she asked herself loyally, was not wrong about something?

Early on the morning of Ann's release Hamer was walking the pavement outside Holloway Jail. He was not wearing his cloak and sombrero. He knew what happened on these occasions. There would be a crowd of suffragists waiting to hail the new martyrs, possibly to form a procession and march away on some new exploit which would land more of them in jail before the day was out. There was no end in those years to the candidates for martyrdom. Up and down the country the women were roused, hundreds of thousands of them, gentlewomen and harridans, peeresses, seamstresses, laundry girls, professional women: it was a great unifying wave of feeling, productive of a willingness to suffer which no uprising of men had seen in the long course of English history. There was no party allegiance about it. In all the parties the women were deserters, declaring their readiness to support any candidate who would take up their cause. Senseless, heroic, unheedful of consequences, the movement rolled on, sullied by violence, by arson, by every kind of destruction, advertised by anguish, by suicide, but redeemed by the quality which is rare and precious: the willingness to hand over, for a faith, body and soul to the torturer.

Women of this breed would be at Holloway, and Hamer did not want to recognize them. So he left at home his famous attire and lurked in the background. October was fading towards November, but the morning retained the quality of autumn, mild and melancholy.

Hamer paced a regular beat from one corner to another, and suddenly, reaching one of the corners, he collided with a man who turned out of a side-street. It was Arnold Ryerson, rather shabby-looking, stout and flabby and grey. He had shed his side-whiskers, but retained a heavy moustache. More than ever, he looked like a tired engine-driver, soiled by contact with his locomotive.

Arnold's face lighted up with the affectionate smile Hamer knew so well and he held out his puffy hand. "Well, Hamer!" he said. "Quite a great man you are these days!"

"My dear Arnold," Hamer replied, "this isn't very nice of you. Why didn't you tell me you were coming up? You could have stayed with me."

"No, no," said Arnold, "I couldn't bother you. Anyway, I've been travelling all night. I haven't got much time to spare, you know. One of Pen's little friends is in there." He nodded towards the prison. "Coming out this morning. I've to take her back to Cwmdulais for a bit of a rest. She's a nervous little thing – wouldn't like to travel alone."

Isn't that like them? Hamer thought. Nervous little things who don't like to travel alone, and they defy the State and all its majesty.

"Ann is in there, too," he said, "and I don't like it."

"What – the idea of being in jail? Pen's been in more than once. We don't mind. We're used to it in our family. Don't forget, I've been in myself."

There was no reproach in his voice, and anyway it was a long time ago – that night when Evan Vaughan gurgled out his life. "They've got as much right to citizenship as we have," said Arnold. "The means they adopt are their affair."

"I thought you didn't believe in violence?"

"I thought you did."

Hamer had no reply to that. They walked in silence for a while, then Arnold said: "It's a long time since I heard you called Shawcross of Peterloo. I liked that name. It had a ring about it."

"They die out, these old nicknames," said Hamer. "I suppose it's inevitable.

"Aye," Arnold said simply. "We grow old. The kick goes out of us. It's taking our women now to remind us of what we once were ourselves."

He filled a pipe and stood heavily on the corner, sucking loudly as he applied the lighted match, Hamer saw that he was unshaven, and guessed that probably he had not had breakfast, He thought of saying: "Look, Arnold, come and have some food with me and Ann, and bring your little friend with you." He was still thinking of saying it when Arnold shouted: "They're opening the gates," and rushed across the road.

Hamer did not rush with him. He stood where he was and watched the women carrying their banner "Votes for Women" close in on the gates. They clung to the heavy iron railings, waving bouquets, shouting their slogan, held back by policemen from the tree-shaded forecourt of the prison. When the prisoners came out through the big wooden doors and walked down the forecourt towards the gates there were delirious cries of welcome and applause. The crowd closed about them, formed a procession about them, began to march away as with victors. When the street was nearly clear, Hamer saw that Ann had let the tide slip round her and past her, and that she was standing alone, looking a little bewildered and bemused. Then she saw him, and came across the road with an eager run, and fell into his arms.

"I wondered if you'd come," she said.

"You darling. Why did you wonder that?"

"You're not ashamed of me – a jailbird?"

"Would it make any difference if I were?"

"All the difference in the world," she said. "Hate what I'm doing if you must, but love me, my darling, go on loving me. Is that too difficult?"

She looked pale and ill, and her face was full of wistful pleading. He smiled at her sadly. "Very, very difficult," he said. "But not impossible."

"I dreamed and dreamed all the time I was in there," Ann said. "I still feel giddy and as though I were seeing visions. I actually thought I saw Arnold in the crowd."

"You did. He came up from Cwmdulais to meet a friend of Pen's."

"Oh, but my dear, you should have stopped him. You should have taken him home with us, It's years since I've seen him."

"He was terribly pressed. He had to get a train at Paddington."

"Well, let us go. Can we afford a cab?"

"We can do better than that. See what's coming."

A motor-car stopped at the kerb beside them, a vehicle rare enough in those days to excite Ann's wonder. She got in, and as they drove away Hamer said: "Lady Lostwithiel's. I went to an art show the other day in Bond Street. She happened to be there. Did you know? she's very much in sympathy with your movement. She insisted on sending the car."

"It was very kind of her," said Ann. She lay back in the cushions.

After her prison bed, it was like reclining on clouds. She looked at the car's silver fittings. After the prison grey, they were charming to the eye. And she tortured herself all the way to North Street with the thought that while she was eating her skilly and moving round and round, round and round, in the exercise yard, Hamer was enjoying himself in Bond Street, and meeting Lady Lostwithiel who was so kind and so much in sympathy with the movement.

Chapter Sixteen

He had never expected anything like this. His wife was a notorious woman. The Pankhursts, Annie Kenney, Pen Muff, Lizzie Lightowler, Ann Shawcross: these and a few other names, day by day, week by week, month by month, blazed across the public prints. Campbell-Bannerman went; Asquith became Prime Minister, and the warfare went on. Mammoth processions; wild wrecking tactics at public meetings; throw 'em out, send 'em to jail, tear 'em, beat 'em.

In the House, discussions, promises, evasions, nothing done. Outside the House a growing pandemonium. Right Honourable gentlemen, immaculate between banked flowers on public platforms, suddenly not immaculate. A paper bag of flour, sailing through the air, bursts upon the Rt. Hon. gentleman's head, drenches him in penitential white, sets him spluttering and sneezing. "Throw her out!" The stewards – used to the game by now – pounce like hawks upon their pigeon. Heels beating a tattoo on the floor, Ann is dragged, screaming "Votes for Women!" along the gallery, down the stairs, bump, bump; and hurled out into the street. She leans, half-fainting, against a doorpost, listening to the pandemonium within. For now, at her signal, there is the devil to pay. More flour bags hurtle through the air, explode on striped trousers and platform-ladies' elegant creations. Stink-bombs nauseate the senses, rattles whir, bells clang, and the frantic stewards, rushing hither and thither, find now that the pigeons are not all docile. Walking-sticks and dog-whips flail and lash. The audience, sympathies divided, yell encouragement or abuse, lend a hand with the chucking-out or, incensed by the stewards' rough tactics, hurl themselves in rugby tackles round necks, legs, bodies. The hall is filled with the noise of the fight. "Ladies and gentlemen!" The chairman, white-faced from flour like the clown he probably is, is attempting to make himself heard above the uproar, "This meeting is closed."

It certainly is.

*

Hamer had given up meeting Ann when she came out of prison, For one thing, he couldn't travel all over the country, and she was in jail in Manchester or Birmingham as often as in London. And it had gone on so long: 1906, 1907, 1908, and now they were in 1909,

She had turned into a fierce flame of a woman. Her body was being consumed. She was gone to a shadow, but out of the shadow her eyes burned and her mouth showed tense and grim. When they met, she no longer ran to him as she had done when first she came out of Holloway. Her bodily needs had abated: even her need to be comforted.

So when they went North together with Charles in the summer holidays of 1909, the child was aware of tension, of personalities estranged, not touching, not mingling. And as they had grown away from one another, so he had grown away from them. He was twelve years old. Four years at Graingers had filled his life with new ideas, new occupations. He was a quiet, introspective boy; and as the train rattled north he found plenty to think of in the silence: Hamer reading as usual, Ann busily scribbling some propaganda stuff on a writing-block.

Charles looked forward to meeting his Grannie. With her at least he had never known restraint. The old woman and the child had always met on the footing of a simple human acceptance of one another.

But this resource was now to be denied him. Ellen, who had no fear of death, had often chuckled over a remark Charles made when, as a child of five, he had been going away for a week-end. Looking at her with his candid blue eyes as he stood in the doorway holding Ann's hand – oh, how different an Ann! – he said sweetly: "Goodbye, Grannie. I expect you'll be dead and gone by the time I get back."

Well, Ellen looked now as if she would soon be dead and gone. To Ann and Hamer it seemed as if the very desire of life had gone out of her. Her energetic step was changed for a slow creeping, and her body, always small, had shrunk till she seemed like an old withered nut that you could rattle in its shell.

There was nothing wrong with her, she insisted: and indeed there was nothing wrong except that her years were now too many and that for too long she had been of no account. Alone in the house, with a maid to minister to her against her will, she had no recourse except to decline upon Death, to whom she went nostalgically down the long road of her past, rather than with a forward glance. She was unloosening all the strands of her life backwards.

She spent the mornings in bed, and Charles would go and sit at her bedside, but he did so only from a sense of duty. This was not the Grannie he had known, She would talk to him a little, become disjointed and incoherent, and end in a mumbling that turned to sleep. Then the boy would creep out, and, being left now to his own devices, would run gladly in the sunshine on Baildon moor, or, sitting against a warm pad of whin and heather, while away the day with a book.

It was thus that Ann found him when she came one day, running and calling his name. But the old woman was dead before they got back. Only Hamer was with her. He had found her sitting up in bed, talking wildly, and had sent the maid to telephone for the doctor, Ann to find the boy. Then he sat at the bedside, and as he took her hand she lay back gently on the pillow. Her little claw-like hand, even now, as he clearly saw in the sunlight streaming through the window, seamed with the ineradicable lines of labour, tightened upon his with a grip that did not seem to want to let go.

He said: "Mother!"

She opened her eyes and looked at him, and was now calm and rational. "What's the matter with you and Ann?" she said.

"Nothing, Mother, nothing," he said. "Don't worry about us."

"I've done nothing but worry about you all my born days," she said. "It seems to have been my job."

Then she closed her eyes again, and he felt the tension of her grip relax. Once she murmured: "Put it right. Put it right," but whether she meant his relations with Ann he did not know, She seemed to be talking to herself. Whatever she meant, it was the end of her talking. This was the first death-bed Hamer had ever known. It seemed to him incredible that she should be so unobtrusively gone; but he knew that she was. It was almost as though to the last she had considered how she might spare him trouble. Just as, when he was a boy aloof from her in his own little study, if she had to go out into the night, she was careful not to bang the door.

Now Ellen was under the ground in the graveyard on the edge of the moor; Charles was back at school; Hamer in London for the opening of the new session of Parliament; and Ann in Manchester.

It was strange to be at home again. For a long time The Limes had not seemed like home; but now she found a great friendliness in it, so crowded was it with memories that assuaged the bitterness of her present life. She wished she could stay for a while, but she knew that she could not. Tomorrow there was one of her savage jobs of work to be done; and she would no more have turned back from it than a good soldier would shirk the firing-step.

Pen was with her. Pen no longer remembered the girl in whose house she had taken a bath after the long ago Battle of the Amazons, the girl who, one night in Bingley, had carried Arnold off in a victoria. The two were now good comrades. They had shared danger, felt wounds, been beaten and abased in one another's company. Ann's beauty was gone, but to Pen she was fair to look at; the exaltation of her thin face was more lovely than loveliness.

Look well, Pen, at the face of the comrade you have come to love, for soon you will look no more on this face or any other.

Hawley was gentle with the two women. Age and adversity had brought him if no great wisdom at any rate a little understanding. They said nothing of the night when he stood swelling with rage before this very fireplace because Ann had brought home from Ancoats a book by Robert Owen. A Radical! How he had spat it out! But now it seemed to him not to matter much that he was entertaining the wife of the boy who gave Ann the book – herself a Radical more deeply dyed than Owen ever was. He was a lonely old man. His business was dominated by Tom Hannaway, who out of pity allowed him to dodder about the office. His daughter had come home with her friend and he was glad to see them, That was all it came to.

So they sat by the fire and talked, and the two women allowed their strained nerves to relax. As they went upstairs together Ann stopped Pen with a hand laid on her arm. "I've made up my mind," she said. "This time I shall do it."

"It will kill you," Pen said.

They stood and looked at one another, each with a heart brimming over with tenderness for the agonies the other had endured and must yet endure. Then they went to their rooms,

Old Hawley had no idea of their business when they set out together the following day after lunch. Each carried a muff, and concealed in each muff was a large jagged rock of flint. They walked the few miles to town. When they were out of jail they walked all they could to keep their bodies fit for further endurances.

It was three o'clock when they came to Market Street. The day was bright and cold, and the street surged with people. Ann and Pen walked from one end to the other, taking note of the men and women who had arranged to be there in support. These silently, unobtrusively, gathered behind them, mingling with the crowds.

"This will do," said Ann.

Pen looked at the shop, the magnificent expanse of plate-glass glittering in the cold sunlight. "Yes," she said, "Now don't stop and think. Do it."

While their resolution was hot, they stood back half-a-dozen paces, took out their flints, and hurled them into the window, The startled people looked round to see the two women surrounded now by a bodyguard unfurling the familiar defiant banner: "Votes for Women!" The words fluttered on the banner, and were cried by a score of voices, almost before the last fragment of glass had tinkled to the stone.

Then broke out the familiar pandemonium. Cheers, catcalls, voices pro and con. Someone yelled: "It's the bloody Suffragettes again!" and there was a rush at the little band which had now begun to march down the road, Ann and Pen in the van, with the banner over their heads. The Suffragettes were fair game for anyone who wanted to manhandle a woman. Ann and Pen were used to free fights in the street, and that day they had a fierce one. They were struck in their faces; they were kicked and buffeted; and before the police took effective charge their blouses were hanging in ribbons and Ann was holding her skirt in position with her hand. But it was all in the day's work – all in the work of the weary years – and still there were more years to go than yet had gone! Derided and reviled, looking like a couple of drunken harlots who had been at one another's throats, their hats slanted over their eyes and their faces clawed, they tottered between the policemen to the police-station.

Alderman Thomas Hannaway, Justice of the Peace – yes, alderman now – sat upon the bench. Ann did not know that this was the man who had supplanted her father; but Tom knew that Ann Shawcross was the daughter of old Hawley and the wife of that stuck-up devil Hamer Shawcross, who was once employed to sprinkle the dew on the cabbages and lettuces.

Tom was glad that he had no part to play. He merely sat with a few other magistrates on the bench, leaving it all to the chairman and the magistrates' clerk. Tom was no sentimentalist. But he would have hated to send this woman Shawcross to jail, or this woman named on the charge-sheet Penelope Ryerson. He understood she was the wife of Arnold Ryerson, who used to play about Broadbent Street with him and Shawcross.

As it happened, it was Tom's very first day on the bench. Polly had made him dress with unusual care, and, sitting there with his plump little legs crossed, he certainly thought he must be the very picture of a successful man. He looked at the two women, so weary and heavy-eyed, still bearing scars; he thought of Polly in the new and bigger house he had bought in a better part of Didsbury; and he pitied Shaw-cross and Ryerson. Poor devils! He wouldn't be in the shoes of either. Well, this would be something to tell Polly tonight over a game of bezique. Two months' hard? 'Strewth! That would mean Christmas in quod. He called that pretty rough. He and Polly were going to spend Christmas at a big hotel in the Lakes. They'd take the bezique with them for the dark nights.

Now the moment was come that Ann had often envisaged, She had thought out to the last detail what she should do. She would get books from the prison library, and she would read and read, and when she wasn't reading she would sleep and sleep. And so she would slowly dec-line, waste away, till at last, she supposed, she wouldn't be able to read any more, and her sleep would have the quality of unconsciousness. Then they would have to let her go. These were the chief points in her programme, and another one was that to her hunger and thirst strike she would add a speech strike. She would utter no word to anyone.

The plan went wrong from the beginning, She left her breakfast skilly untouched. Her wardress asked what was wrong with it, and Ann did not answer. The woman went away, and it occurred to Ann that she could not have books to read unless she asked for them. She resolved to do without the books rather than speak.

She must, above all things, conserve her strength. She did not want to become a crying, protesting wreck: she wanted to pass out gently, peacefully. So she lay on her bed, trying to empty her mind of all thought, to forget Hamer, Charles, Hawley, even Pen, who, somewhere within these grim walls, was facing her own ordeal. But she was not left long undisturbed. The wardress returned, carrying her dish of skilly, and with her came a male official of the prison. Ann remained lying on the bed.

"Get up!" said the wardress.

Ann did not speak and did not stir. The wardress put the skilly on the table, bent down, and with arms beneath Ann's armpits hauled her erect in one muscular movement. The jail official waited till she was standing facing him; then he looked at her like a father deploring the recalcitrance of a child, He pointed to the skilly and asked: "Are you abstaining from food for some ulterior purpose?"

Ann did not answer.

"To put it plainly: are you hunger-striking?"

She did not look at him; she kept her eyes on the floor; she did not open her mouth,

"I must warn you," he said, "that hunger-striking is a misdemeanour. It will cause you to lose many privileges. You will have nothing to read and no writing materials. Nor will you be permitted to take exercise." He smiled most winningly, though she did not see the smile. "Is it worth it? Isn't it better to serve your sentence quietly, and give no trouble?"

Then they all went: the official and the wardress and the skilly, but when Ann left her midday meal also untouched, that did not go. It remained on the table, meat congealing in fat. It nauseated her to look at it, so she lay down and tried to go to sleep.

She could not. Footsteps echoing in the stony corridors, keys jangling, doors slamming, occasionally a sudden outburst of hysterical crying and banging on a door; worst of all, footsteps going by furtively, as though felt-soled, so quietly that she wondered if she were imagining them: there seemed no end to the noises which once she could happily have ignored, but which now all seemed moves in a gigantic conspiracy to keep her nerves on the stretch.

She looked forward with a passionate longing to the night, when she would sleep by habit. Night came and she could not sleep. She had desired sleep too long and too earnestly, She began now to feel the pangs of hunger, The emptiness of her belly made her cold. She lay on the planks and shivered, her eyes, wide open, staring into the darkness. She felt as though she had never been so wide awake in her life, and she got off the bed and began to walk about in the darkness: up and down, to and fro, missing the few objects in her stony cage because even so little time had taught her every inch of its mean dimensions.

In the morning she was stretched on the planks. She did not remember lying down, She felt deathly with weariness.

When her breakfast came, her craving for food was so intense that she lay on her back and with both hands gripped the sides of the bed. She shut her eyes so that she should not see food that normally would have offended her taste. The wardress leaned over her. "Now sit up, dear," she said. "Just stay in bed, but sit up. I'll hold the basin and you take the spoon."

Ann sat up. She could hear her own heart beating, feel flames behind her jaded eyes. The smell of the skilly reached her nostrils and they flared hungrily. She looked at the stuff, at the warmth-promising steam rising in invitation to her cold famished stomach. She took the spoon, and the wardress smiled.

Suddenly, to Ann, all the world's contempt was in that smile. The woman who said she could do it, and couldn't; the martyr who recanted at sight of the faggots; the traitor who sold the pass at the whisper of a bribe. "A mess of pottage." The words were too dreadfully apt, and as they came into her mind she struck up sharply with her knees and spilled the basinful. Then she lay back, utterly collapsed, but knowing in her heart that now she had won.

She was removed that day to the hospital cells. They were like any other cells except that she had a mattress instead of planks. Let it never be said that Authority did not understand the chivalry due to women who were prepared to starve themselves to death.

It was luxury to lie upon the mattress. She stretched her limbs and closed her eyes. But she could not sleep. She felt light-headed, as if she were floating out of her body, but all the time her body was beneath her and she was aware of its fever, its racking torment. She wondered when she would pass through this to the phase of blissful nothingness, that nirvana which always had buoyed her resolution when she contemplated the act which she was now executing.

She came to herself with a start at the sound of voices, and sat up. She was sweating, and yet she felt cold. "Put it there." It was the official who had visited her before. The wardress came behind him, carrying a tea-tray, daintily arranged. It was actually spread with a fair white cloth, and upon it was a brown teapot, steaming invitingly through the spout, a cup, milk, sugar, and uncut cake. The wardress put the tray on the table, and the official cut a segment out of the cake. Ann, sitting up on the bed, watched him fascinated. He broke a morsel from the fat piece he had cut and put it into his mouth. He chewed it over, savouring it slowly. "Yes," he pronounced. "Delicious! Pour out a cup of tea for Mrs. Shawcross. Sugar?"

She stared at him, grinning idiotically, but she did not answer. "Well, we'll leave it. Help yourself," he said.

Then they went, and Ann sat looking at the cake and the dainty china, and sniffing the aroma of the tea. It was the most devilish torture. Tea! Oh, the teas she could think of! Tea with Arnold Ryerson in Broadbent Street that day his mother's finger was caught in the mangle; tea at The Limes with the firelight playing on the gold fluting of the white chair legs; tea with Lizzie at Dick Hudson's when the snow was on the Yorkshire moors without; tea in the den at Ackroyd Park as they talked and talked. Her mind whirled dizzily round the subject of tea, the drink she craved above all others, and she stared at the steaming cup that was hypnotizing her, drawing her from the bed to the table. Tea! Cold tea in a bottle, smashing angrily on the pavement at Bingley that night when she took Arnold away from Pen. Oh, Pen, Pen! Somewhere here in this very prison, enduring her own anguish, confident of Ann's loyalty and steadfastness to the end. Tea, smashing, smashing! She was hardly aware of what she was doing, as she hurled the teapot against the wall, crashed the tempting cup to the floor, threw the cake after it, and trampled it in a frenzy on the stones.

When they rushed back at the sound of the smashing she was already on the bed again, burning and shivering.

Now if only I could sleep. I will imagine I am walking up the hill from Shipley to Baildon, past the long grey loose-stoned wall with sloping field above it, touching each stone as I go, counting them. One, two, three, four, five – catching fishes all alive – catching Suffragettes – God knows why – they only want to be citizens – a citizen of no mean city. They saw beautiful city of Cecrops, but I saw beautiful city of God. Beautiful city of Zion. Zion and Carmel and Horeb, where Ianto the poet loved to hear the singing. Now why did I stop counting and concentrating my mind on the grey stones? Six, seven, eight, nine…

She got off the bed again. The prison was dark, silent, bitterly cold. She could hear her heart beating. All day long she had been aware of it. Now, in the night, it was pumping like a rapid piston. She leaned against the door and put her hand over her heart. She could feel it: pump, pump, pump; then a staggering flutter like a bird in the hand.

If only I could sleep! And then again in the morning she was asleep, sitting on the cold stone, leaning against the door. It was still dark. She crawled to the mattress and lay there, and sleep came again. She woke to find that daylight had come and that her table was spread.

At first this seemed a dream, a mirage. Sitting up in the bed, with her hands pressing down into the mattress on either side, she stared incredulously at the table. It was covered with a cloth. There was a plate with a few slices of white chicken-breast, some bread and butter wafer-thin, an orange, peeled and alluring with all its juicy segments fanned out. There was a carafe full of water, and a glass. She reached out her hand and touched the things. They were real! She lifted the carafe and was surprised to find how heavy it seemed. Her wrist bent. But she filled the glass, dipped her finger into the water and was about to suck it. Then she wiped it impulsively on the bedclothes, pulled the clothes up over her head, and lay still. Her tongue, with that temptation near, seemed twice its size, hot and cracked. She swallowed convulsively and felt sick. Her tongue nearly choked her.

No one visited her till the evening. She slept fitfully, and when she was not sleeping she tottered about the cell. She felt now that she could not eat. The food was no temptation. But again and again, as she brushed against the table, she stopped, gripping its edge, looking at the water. At last she took the carafe by the neck and slowly tilted it on its side. The water soaked the cloth, dripped to the floor. Suddenly she threw herself down, lay with her back in the pool and her mouth gaping beneath the dripping hem. The drops of water fell upon her tongue: one, two, three, before she staggered unsteadily to her feet, her heart racing.

Traitress, traitress!

She lurched to the mattress, collapsed upon it, and pulled the clothes over her head. She lay shivering, blinded by tears, and passed off into nightmare-ridden sleep.

She came to with a start at the sound of the cell door opening. The light flashed up, dazzling her. Two men she had not seen before were standing diffidently on the threshold, wearing the conventional garb of their profession: trousers neatly creased and striped, black coats, stiff collars, butterfly-winged. One wore a stethoscope round his neck.

Ann stared at them in affright. Never in her life, save when Charles was coming, had she had any commerce with doctors. She had an unreasoning fear and hatred of them, and she shrank from these two as though they were undertakers come to measure her for her coffin.

The doctor with the stethoscope came over to the bed. She shut her eyes as he bent above her and took her wrist, feeling the pulse. Then she felt his fingers at her breast, opening her clothing. She seized his hands and struggled violently, her vow of silence breaking down. "Let me alone!" she gasped. "Let me die."

"Please be reasonable," he said politely, taking his hands off her.

She opened her eyes and looked at him. He seemed a decent man, very grave, rather sad. She ceased to resist and lay still, crying feebly. He applied the stethoscope to her racing heart; then his colleague sounded her too. They stood apart, talking in whispers, and then the first of them came to the bedside again, swinging the stethoscope.

"You would save yourself and everyone else such a lot of unpleasantness if you would take a little nourishment," he said reasonably.

Her head rolled slowly to and fro in negation. The doctor sighed heavily, looked down at her in commiseration. "You have quite made up your mind?" he asked.

She did not answer. "Very well," he said. "We cannot have you dying on our hands, We shall have to feed you by force."

When they were gone she could not sleep again. She got up and tried to walk, but body and soul were exhausted. She fell full length on the stone floor, crawled to the bed, climbed upon it, and lay still.

If only they had said when it was to be! Waiting was the horror: waiting in the cold darkness, with the furtive footsteps passing and repassing in the corridor, with the sudden alarming cries tearing at her nerves, with the keys jangling. Ah! those keys! As long as she lived Ann could hear them: the most devilish of all the noises that distracted her, the symbolic noise of the whole prison gamut, the noise that branded her an animal, dangerous, locked away out of sight and sound of the lovely radiant world.

So she waited, hot-eyed in the dark, stringing her nerves up to resistance, to conflict, to the wild-cat struggle that was all she now had left to oppose to Authority that debased her. But hour followed hour, and as she lay there taut as a wire, with the wind of her emotions twanging it madly, she could not have said whether she had lain there for moments or months.

She lay there till the next morning, The grey grudging light, all that ever penetrated the cell, was present again like the sad ghost of day when she heard the keys jangling outside the door. She leapt off the bed, quivering with fear. Leapt! She did not know how it had happened. Last night she was crawling, But now she leapt, sprang to an angle of the cell wall, and waited, her breast heaving, her eyes wide, her fists clenched.

She had expected the doctors. They did not appear. She counted the women who filed silently into the cell: one, two, three, four, five, six. Muscular Amazons, unsmiling, watchful-eyed. They closed upon her in a half-circle. They came so slowly, so inevitably, so doomfully, not looking her in the eyes but watching every movement of her body, that she could not wait for them but sprang forward, striking out with her fists, kicking with her shoes. They were not six separate women: they were one force against which she was pitted with all her strength of body and will. She was seized; she writhed, squirmed, twisted, gasping and panting; once she actually escaped from the twelve clutching hands, stood for one second upright, eyes flashing, breast heaving; then was overborne. By head and heels she was carried to the bed and dropped upon it, and before her struggle could begin again the six women flung themselves at her. She was pinned down: by the ankles, the knees, the thighs, the wrists, the elbows, the forehead. She closed her eyes, felt the warm breath, heard the quick panting, of the women above her. It sickened her.

"Try and open her mouth." She must almost have lost consciousness. The words brought her back with a start, She did not open her eyes, but instinctively her teeth gritted together and her lips firmed their line. She felt a hand on her face, and knew it was a man's hand. It smelled soft and soapy, slightly scented, nauseating. She felt the hand manipulating her lips, trying to force them back over her teeth, as though she were a mare whose age must be ascertained. She resisted, clenching her teeth till she felt that her jaw would break. Her heart was racing madly. Surely they could hear its wild alarum? Surely they knew that this would kill her?

"No good," the voice said softly.

"Give me that," said another voice. "No – the other."

She felt steel forcing her lips apart, grating on her teeth. It searched along the line of clenched teeth, slipped, cut into her gums, She tried to heave her body up, to escape this awful indignity, but the six heavy women were leaning down upon her, so that she felt as if she were buried under a fallen building.

One of the voices spoke again. "Look! There! There's a tooth gone."

The steel moved through her mouth, found the breach in the defence. It slipped through, touching her tongue. She tried to draw her tongue back, retching. She could hear the rasp of a screw, The noise seemed to fill all her head. Pressing hard against the inexorable lever, she felt as though her jaw would be pulled off her skull. Her lips, her gums, her tongue, were torn and bleeding, and now that her mouth was open she could taste the salt of her own blood dribbling down her throat,

Slowly the screw forced the jaw open. The voice said: "That'll do. Quick! The tube."

Now Ann was more dead than alive. She felt the tube in her throat which convulsively contracted with nausea. Then the blessed nirvana came for which she had so desperately hoped, When she came to herself she was alone in the cell. She sat up on the bed, drenched with perspiration. Her whole being heaved suddenly as though she were disrupted. She leaned sideways and vomited. Then she fell back on the bed and lay there staring at the wall, listening to her heart trying to tear itself out of her side. Her legs and shoulders burned with their bruising, but worse than that was the wounding of her mind. She felt obscene, disgusting, like a woman brutally raped.

All day long she did not stir from the bed. In the later afternoon she awoke from sleep, aching in the body, twitching in the wounded mouth, but feeling a little easier in her mind, Now at least she knew the worst that could happen, and she had triumphed. Now she would be left in peace for a while. Peace and quiet. The very thought of them was balm, and she felt beneficent rest flowing down her weary limbs, soothing her tortured mind,

Then she was wide awake, upright on the bed, shivering like a frightened horse. Steps! They stopped at her door. The keys jangled. The six doomful women entered, this time the doctors were close behind them, carrying their instruments. Ann did not stir; she could resist no more; but she let out a great screech that echoed through the cold inhuman corridors of the prison. Then she lay back, feeling the sweat break out and drench her again, and let them do as they would. The six women were not needed. She was held passive by her own broken heart. She was sick while they were still in the room, and when they were gone she turned her face to the wall and cried like an abandoned child.

Now all was gone except her resolution. She did not wake up now expecting a little peace. She woke up, emaciated, bruised, swollen-eyed, praying for the day's strength. Beyond the day she could not look. Every morning and every evening the agony was forced upon her. Sometimes she was wild and fighting-mad, and the women pinned her down like a butterfly on a board. Sometimes she shrieked; and sometimes she was an inert log into which the odious injection was made. But always she was sick, automatically rejecting the food that was poured into her.

At last there came a day when the two doctors entered the cell alone. She knew they were there, but she did not open her eyes. She did not know whether this was their morning or evening visit. When after some time there was no touch of offensive hands, no rasp of steel, she opened her eyes. They were looking at her ponderingly, with interest and commiseration. They sounded her with a stethoscope; they felt her pulse; tapped her chest; lifted her eyelids and peered into her eyes.

"Mrs. Shawcross," one of them said, "my colleague and I have decided that an application for your release must be made to the Home Office."

She was too apathetic, too dazed, altogether too far gone, to notice for a moment what they were saying, One of them put an arm round her and raised her gently, as if she were his own sick child, and said: "Do you understand? It is all over."

She understood, and she cried a little very quietly, and nodded.

"It must be some days before your papers come through from London. While we are waiting for them, will you take a little nourishment – now that you have – er – won?"

Again she nodded. It did not seem to matter that she had won or that she might take food again. She was so feeble, sitting there in the bed, that one of the doctors remained with an arm about her shoulders till the other returned with a small cup of broth. Small as it was, she could take only half of it, the doctor feeding her with a spoon. Then she was laid back gently on the bed, and the bedclothes were tucked round her, and the doctors went. They gave her the impression that they felt as though they were glad to be finally stealing away from the scene of a crime.

Peace and quiet. Peace and quiet at last. She slept, and in the morning she drank a little warm milk. When she tried to get out of bed she staggered and fell, but there was a wardress ready now not to pin her down but to pick her up. On the third day she crawled feebly round the exercise-yard. It was not till the fifth day that she was free. A wardress accompanied her in a cab to the railway station and remained till the train drew out.

Ann slept the whole way to London. She felt as if she could sleep for ever. At St. Pancras she got into a cab and was taken to North Street. That was the time when Hamer rushed to the door and picked her up and called her his darling. She lay all that day in North Street, feeling broken, shattered. She wondered if ever again she could bring herself to endure an experience so devastating to body and mind. She did, not once or twice, but many times.

It was not all jam, Tom Hannaway discovered, being a Justice of the Peace. You could get publicly into hot water. You could innocently cause a national outcry. What you imagined to be a brilliant inspiration might have to be apologized for in Parliament by no less a person than the Home Secretary, son of the great W. E. Gladstone, and denounced as a "grave error of judgment." All through that wretched woman Pen Muff.

Pen had never wanted to sink into a state of nirvana. She had spent all her life in a tough, fighting atmosphere. She was renowned as the most bellicose and destructive of the Suffragettes, always ingenious in devising new means of being a nuisance. She resolved to join Ann in her hunger-strike, but there was no speech-strike in her case. Every time food was placed before her, she hurled the vessels at those who brought it, denounced and abused them.

She hunger-struck for five days, and at the end of that time was not broken. She slept little, prowling her stony cage like a starved she-wolf, ready to snap and bite. She was horribly emaciated; her bones, always prominent, were almost through the skin, and her face was like a skull, balefully lit by dark staring eyes.

Then they began upon her with their jaw-prising instruments and their tubes. She smashed a wardress's face with the heel of her shoe before they got her on her back, and then it was like holding down a squirming snake. When the doctors forcibly handled her, she had no sense of shame, of outrage, like Ann's, only a blind, passionate fury that she vented in a torrent of abusive speech. They never left her cell without being white, shaken and ashamed.

For four days she endured the torture which did not so much nauseate as infuriate her; and the doctors and wardresses alike marvelled at the end of that time that her physical resistance still seemed sustained by some quenchless flame of the spirit. She never stumbled or staggered or crawled. Always when they entered the cell they found her upright, wary, untamed, all their brutal work of subjugation to be done anew.

On the morning of the fifth day she was brought back from the lavatory, and said nothing when the wardress who accompanied her locked her by mistake into a cell that was not hers. One cell was like another to Pen. She began at once her hungry, tigerish prowling round it, then stood still, staring at the floor, The cell had not been used for some time; a spare plank bed had been pushed into it and lay there alongside the one that was the normal furniture.

A ghastly grin broke out on Pen's face. Here was a chance to make trouble! She heaved one bed head-on against the door, placed the head of the second to the foot of the first. Still she hadn't quite filled the space between door and wall; still they could force her fortress. So she placed the legs of the wooden stool against the foot of the second bed, and found that now, sitting with her back against the stool's seat, her own feet reached the wall. That was the barricade: two beds, a stool, and a starving, outraged woman. When all was arranged, Pen crouched, waiting.

She had not long to wait. Soon came the well-known odious jangling of the keys and, when the door did not yield, a wardress's voice. "Open the door! Let me in!"

Pen tensed her knees, thrusting her feet with all her might against the wall. She said nothing, heard the key turn, locking her in again, and the sound of feet echoing down the corridor. She relaxed, smiled, waited.

They could not budge her. They came and shoved till she felt as though her back would break, as though her tensed knees would snap or her feet be driven into the wall. But some superhuman strength was vouchsafed to her: she held on, with the veins in her sunken temples swelling with the magnitude of her exertion.

They wheedled with soft promises; they tried to frighten her with threats of punishment; she answered nothing to threat or promise but sat grimly on the floor, knees up, feet to the wall.

At last they went away again. She heard the key turn and took a deep breath, But she did not get up. She smiled, and waited.

Alderman Thomas Hannaway, J.P., was in the prison. He was a Visiting Magistrate, and with other visiting magistrates he was assuring himself that the law of the realm was being administered without fear or favour. To the visiting magistrates now came the perplexed, perspiring officials to report that a woman had them at bay.

The magistrates walked along the cold corridors, pondering the problem that had been laid before them. It made Tom Hannaway wrinkle his brow. Here was a test case; here was the opportunity for a magistrate to prove his sagacity and worth. His eye fell on a hose-pipe, neatly coiled, ready for use, all spick and span with penal brightness, white linen and sparkling brass.

Tom paused and pointed to the hose. "Drown her out," he said tersely.

The other magistrates concurred, looking at Tom with respect. Simple, practical, brilliant! Drown her out.

They were away a long time, but Pen had no illusions. They would be back. She couldn't win. She could only make trouble. Very well then. She would make all the trouble she could. She still expected the assault to come from the doorway, and was startled to hear suddenly a shattering of glass and to see that the cell window had been stove in. She was wondering what this portended when a jet of water struck her in the middle. It was terrific, like the kick of a horse, and she gasped, putting her hand to her side. She looked up and saw the nozzle.

Already she was drenched from head to foot. Her clothes were clinging to her as though she had emerged from the sea, and the icy shock of the water set her skeleton frame shivering, She got up from the floor and climbed upon a bed, but the nozzle found her. It quartered the tiny room. The water whacked into the wall and fell back on her in showers. It hit the ceiling and descended like a thunder-storm. It sprayed up from the floor like a fountain. Pen lay face downward on the bed with her hands over her head, spluttering and gasping. So small was the room, so powerful the jet, that the water fell upon her as though she were in a shower-bath, and so narrow was the vent under the door that it began to rise upon the floor. She peeped over the edge of the bed at the encroaching water, rising so rapidly that now terror at last seized her. They had found her one fear: fear of water. She lay still, her heart pounding. This little cubic box would fill. She would be drowned! Already the terror of imagination was upon her. She was struggling, choking, going down, down, down.

But she would not cry out. She bit her pallid lips till they bled lest a sound of surrender should be torn from them. It was not Pen's voice but a voice without that cried: "Stop!"

The cold bombardment ended. Her teeth chattering as if with ague, her hair streaming in sodden rats'-tails down her face, Pen heaved herself up on hands and knees and stared about her. There were six inches of water on the floor.

Then suddenly the pressure on the door was renewed. Now there was no last human link in the chain of defence. The beds swung away over the slippery floor, and they entered to look upon their victory. They saw a woman on hands and knees, sodden, battered, wild-eyed, leaden-lipped, glaring at them over the head of a bed. None of them ever forgot that burning stare of loathing and contempt. "You bastards!" she gasped after a while. "You dirty, rotten, bloody bastards!"

These things were not done in a corner. The case of Pen Muff caused a national outcry; the sufferings of the forcibly-fed were notorious throughout the land. Year followed year; 1909 became 1910; 1911 and 1912 went by; the warfare continued, The women were carried face downwards in prison by their arms and legs, their faces bumping on the floor; they were chased over roofs like burglars; they were struck by doctors and reviled by magistrates.

The country was dizzy with argument. In the House, Bills, Conciliation Bills, amendments to Bills; promises, easily made, easily broken.

Bills and talk, talk and Bills, and at last an Act: the Cat and Mouse Act. Ah, my friends, a glorious Act this! An Act to bring a glow of pride to the face of British statesmanship. Consider how it works. Take one woman (hereinafter to be referred to as the Mouse) and one policeman (hereinafter to be referred to as the Cat). The Mouse is arrested and thrown into jail. She refuses to eat and at last is forcibly fed. This legal saving of her life is so well calculated to bring her to death's door that it can be only a matter of time before the cage is opened and the Mouse is allowed to go free.

Hitherto, that had been the end of the matter until the Mouse committed some new offence. But now when the Mouse leaves the cage the Cat follows. The Cat sits down before the Mouse's hole, watches the Mouse vigilantly until satisfied that it is now a restored Mouse, fit to go back to the cage. Then the Cat pounces and bears away the Mouse to complete its term of incarceration; but as the Mouse will immediately refuse food, be forcibly fed again, and soon be out once more, possibly with days or weeks added to the sentence for prison misdemeanour, the Cat will have a busy time chasing the Mouse to and fro, and the Mouse, poor fool in search of the illusory cheese of politics, will endure weeks and months of alternating starvation, outrage and recuperation.

A Mouse called Pen Muff crawled out of a London jail on a morning of late summer in 1914. A taxicab took her to the house in East London where she lodged. She went to bed at once, but she was up early the next morning. The resiliency of her body and mind was extraordinary, Ann Shawcross by this time was morose and neurasthenic, enduring with a sullen acquiescence what Pen still encountered with passionate aggression.

For a long time Pen had lodged in this East London house. She got on well with her landlady, whose husband was a stevedore at the East India Docks. Her landlady was proud of her. She was a character in the district. As she went by people would point out the woman whose exploits now included an attempted suicide in jail, arson and a horse-whip assault on a Cabinet Minister.

Pen was tired of being a Mouse. Even at this moment, for aught she knew, the Cat was behind the curtains of a hired house opposite, waiting the moment to pounce. Well, this time the Cat would be sucked in, Pen reflected grimly.

At ten o'clock a baker's delivery van drove up to the door. A youth sat in the driver's seat with another beside him. A sad and sorry person, this other, with a raging toothache that necessitated the comforting of his face with a woollen muffler. He got down from the van and carried a basket of loaves to the front door.

"Whatever's the matter with you?" demanded the stevedore's wife, and the poor wretch pointed to his face and groaned.

"You'd better come in and drink a cup of tea. That'll ease you," said the stevedore's wife; and the youth in the driver's seat shouted: "Don't keep him long, Ma. And bring me a cup while you're at it."

Yes, a pretty comedy altogether for the benefit of any Cat who might be licking his whiskers in the neighbourhood. Pen, all prepared, was wearing nothing but a dressing-gown. She whipped it off as the young man began unceremoniously to shed his clothes. The exchange was soon made, and the young man, slender as Pen herself, carefully tied on the muffler,

"There! You look fine, Mother," she said. "That hides your face."

Pen, carrying the basket, came out as the stevedore's wife was recovering her cup from the driver. She climbed up behide him; he clicked to the pony; they turned a nearby corner, and then went spanking along with remarkable unconcern for the delivery of bread.

It was not till the bread van had been returned to its owner, one of Pen's admirers and supporters, that she turned to him and said: "Thank you, Charles. You did well."

Charles Shawcross blushed with pleasure. The child who had built up in his mind the hero, Hamer Shawcross, was now the boy who was vividly following the exploits of the heroine, Pen Muff. It was in the nature of Charles, gentle and unassertive, that he must be led. This seemed to him a grand romantic way to be spending one of the earliest days of the long school holiday – the last, as it happened, before he went up to Oxford.

"It was splendid of Alice," he said modestly.

"Let's go on now to the teashop on the corner," Pen said. "I could do with a cup, and Alice is going to meet us there."

For the moment, Ann Shawcross was not a Mouse. The house in North Street was not under observation. Pen was to spend a few days there, quietly regaining her strength, and then she was going to take a holiday in some remote place where Mice could circulate freely without fear of Cats. It had been difficult to persuade her, but Ann and Lizzie Lightowler had made her see reason at last. After all, for anything they knew, this barbarous warfare might go on yet for years. It was to be a communal holiday: Lizzie and Ann and Pen, with Charles and Alice.

Nothing of all this had been said to Hamer. Hamer was having a very busy year. It was the year of the Independent Labour Party's coming of age, and for one thing Hamer was writing a book that was to blow a fanfare of praise for the emergence of true democracy. He had announced that he would go to Baildon when the House rose, and complete the work in solitude at The Hut. Writing books had once been a high-spirited affair for Hamer, an affair of glad co-operation between him and Ann. Now it was a solemn matter. Jimmy Newboult, who was in the House as member for an industrial division in the North, came in to look up references, check data, do all the donkey-work; and also once or twice a week there was a girl to do the typing.

Hamer was at work in his room when Charles arrived with Pen and Alice. He was standing at the window, looking down into North Street, a figure to catch and please any eye that beheld it. He had given up all eccentricities of dress. There was no more of the Spanish cloak, the fluttering bow, the wide sombrero. The mad divagation of Ann and Lizzie from the normal tended to throw him in self-defence back upon normality; and a remark that Lady Lostwithiel made on that charming morning when they had talked so happily together in Bond Street finished the matter for him. It happened that the pictures they were looking at were chiefly of Spanish subjects. They stood for a long time before one that showed a piratical-looking fellow dressed so much as Hamer then was that Lettice could not resist a little titter. She referred to her catalogue and said: "No, it's not you." Then, after a pause, and with a sideways glance at him: "Somehow, they don't look right – don't you think? – these gay raffish ruffians? Too Barnum altogether."

Hamer was no Barnum now. He dressed with an exact English correctitude, and to see the six-foot-two of him in full evening fig was a sight for sore eyes. There had been a dinner – some affair arranged by the Lostwithiels with a pseudo-philanthropic purpose – some jabber about combining all parties so that differences might be forgotten and a common ground agreed on for helping the unemployed. Keir Hardie had been invited, and instead of a formal declining had published the invitation in the *Labour Leader* – the new guise of that old *Miner* which Pen used to hand to Arnold in Thursley Road. "They ask," Hardie wrote, "that all differences may be forgotten. Let me tell you what the differences are. For every ton of coal Lord Lostwithiel graciously permits to be dug out of his mines he receives fourteen pence, while the miner who goes down into the bowels of the earth to dig it and send it to the surface receives sevenpence. I do not accept your invitation, my lord, because I do not want this difference to be forgotten. I want it to be remembered and at last abolished."

Hamer went, and Lettice said to her husband that night: "Did you notice Shawcross's shirt-front? It was crying aloud for the ribbon of the Garter."

Very correct, very conventional, but seeming by his magnificent presence, his greying hair, his commanding eye, to make convention itself romantic: that was Hamer Shawcross at forty-nine. He liked to wear a dressing-gown when he wrote, and standing there at the window in North Street, pondering on the chapter in hand, with the garment of severe black silk upon him, he wondered who the thin youth with the wrapped-up face could be, entering with Charles and Alice.

Alice was a problem that puzzled him. He pretended to himself that he was keeping an open mind about her, but he knew that in his heart he disliked her association with Charles. It had all begun in the most natural way. Charles had gone on from Graingers to Hungerbury, and Hungerbury, with a new headmaster priding himself on modern ideas, was full of social activity. The boys were taken to view, from their privileged pedestals, the lot of those less fortunately circumstanced; and Charles, at sixteen, had been one of a squad taken to examine life in the Rhondda Valley. Hamer could do no less than suggest that the boy should stay for the week-end with Arnold Ryerson.

Charles never forgot that week-end. He liked Arnold, and, as Pen was away on some Suffragette exploit, the two spent the first evening in the den at Horeb Terrace, where Arnold boiled over on the subject of Alice. It was remarkable to Arnold that Alice, off her own bat, had been able to do for herself all that Hamer had done for Charles. But she had. With scholarships she had passed from Cwmdulais to a secondary school in Cardiff. With more, and more brilliant, scholarships, she had passed from Cardiff to Oxford. Her first year at Somerville was just ending; she was expected back at Cwmdulais the next day.

That day, the Hungerbury boys went down a coal-mine: the mine where Richard Richards had lost a leg, where Ianto had died, crying, with his arms round the neck of Hugh Price Hughes; the mine where Evan Vaughan had toiled, by God, nourishing on sweat resentment against oppression. But the Hungerbury boys, in neat little bogus suits of dungarees, knew nothing of all this as they excitedly chattered along the dark roads, swinging their lamps and furtively daubing their faces with coal-dust so that when they emerged into the light of day they should look like real miners.

When they came up, Arnold was waiting to meet Charles, and he had Alice with him. Charles ran to him in his boyish way, eager to show himself off in all the glory of this grimy panoply; and while Arnold smiled gravely at this attractive eagerness, the girl with him broke into a merry, mocking laugh that showed her white teeth and red tongue. Her mockery comprehended the whole Hungerbury squad thinking that it was learning with this one little sip something about the bitter draught of a life which she herself had known so long and so deeply.

"Well," she said, as she took Charles's grimy paw, "I suppose you know the Rhondda now, inside out?"

There was the trace of a Welsh lilt in her voice, and now, whenever Charles thought of his own adventure into Oxford, so soon to come, he heard Alice's singing tones and remembered with pleasure her white teeth and red tongue.

Hamer went downstairs to see who the boy with the muffled face might be. In the narrow passage-way which was all the North Street house had for a hall he stopped, for there was a knock at the door. He opened it himself. Keir Hardie stood on the threshold. He was wearing his customary tweeds and rough woollen shirt. He looked Hamer up and down, his shrewd eye taking in the silk dressing-gown, the cared-for hands, the gleaming brush-back wing of hair. "Ye're looking bonny, lad," he said dryly. "The auld leddie up at Baildon would have been proud of you. May I come in?"

Hamer loked at his old leader, the man whose life had been all fighting, and whose fighting was nearly done. Hardie's hair and beard were white; his eyes were troubled and sad and weary. He looked, as he was, sick to death. Hamer's heart had a sudden motion of reverence and envy for an integrity which, he knew, he could never emulate.

He stood aside silently, and Hardie entered the passage, throwing down his cap on a chair. "MacDonald's just come from Asquith," he said. "He was sent for."

Hamer paused with his hand on the handle of the drawing-room door. "There are some visitors," he said, "and Lizzie and my wife are both in, too. If it's anything private—?"

"It's nothing the world won't know soon enough," said Hardie. "And if Lizzie's in I'd like to see her. The auld body always cheers me up."

They went into the drawing-room together, and Hamer's face darkened when he saw Pen Muff, her bandage gone, sitting there in her boy's clothes. There was no love lost between them. "Good morning, Mrs. Ryerson," he said stiffly.

Pen replied, with a hint of mockery: "Good morning, Mr. Shawcross. I hope I shan't incommode you during the few days I stay here."

Lizzie was warmly greeting Keir Hardie, introducing him to Charles and Alice; and she turned now to Hamer and said: "We ought to have explained all this to you before, I've no doubt. But you've been so busy and we've been so busy, there's been no chance to talk about anything. All it comes to is that Pen's a Mouse, and she's hiding here so that the Cat shan't jump. We're all packing off for a holiday together in a few days – the whole lot of us – Charles and Alice and all – while you're up in Baildon finishing your book. So that ought to be satisfactory all round."

She got it all out in a rush. It was growing on her, this habit of gushing speech; and now she turned to Hardie and appealed to him: "Don't you think a poor Mouse should use any trick to dodge the Cats?"

"I have publicly expressed the view," said Hardie, "that the Cat and Mouse Act substitutes murder for suicide, and that the only alternative is to give women the vote. But I know I don't go fast enough or far enough for some of the ladies. I believe Miss Pen Muff herself has used a stick on me."

He stated this truth without rancour. Pen remained silent; and Hamer, fearing that the discussion would trickle into the endless channels of the suffrage question, broke in. "The point is, Mrs. Ryerson is breaking the law. Whether you like it or dislike it, the Cat and Mouse Act has been passed. I do not see that a constitutional representative government can afford to repeal any Act under the threat of force. I for one am not willing to be a party to such an endeavour.

You make me a party by bringing Mrs. Ryerson here to my house. I cannot consent to this."

Lizzie raised her eyebrows, "Your house?"

Hamer stammered. "The house I live in. I cannot be dragged into this. All this violence creates a precedent that could be used against our own party when it takes office. There are other ways out if Mrs. Ryerson wants to evade the consequences of her own actions. You know that Lady Lostwithiel is organizing a regular network of get-aways for Mice, as you call them. Get in touch with her."

"Aye," said Pen, speaking for the first time, "she's a grand lass. She's doin' everything for t'cause except go to quod. And when women have got t'vote she'll say: 'Remember what Ah did for thee. Be a good lass, an' vote Tory.' Nay, keep thi Lady Lostwithiel. And keep this house, too. Come on, Alice lass. Ah'm off back to t'East End. Ah wouldn't offend Mr. Shawcross by evading the consequences of my own act-ions. When Ah invite people to riot, Ah riot myself, and Ah tak the consequences of riotin'. As Arnold did at Cwmdulais," she shot over her shoulder.

Alice followed as Pen went impulsively out of the room. The front door banged. Charles would have gone after them, but Hamer gave him a look which said: "Stay where you are," and the boy obeyed.

Keir Hardie sighed and shook his white head. "There's so much to be done," he said, "and for me there's such a little time for doing it, and all about me, in the Party and out, I see nothing but quarrelling and dissension, men and women swelling up their chests with their own little ambitions and interests. Hamer, my boy, do you ever think what a fine figure you'd cut on the Government front bench?"

"I've never given the matter a thought," said Hamer.

Hardie looked at him sorrowfully. "Ye're a liar," he said.

Hamer stiffened. His handsome face went red. Hardie stilled the ris-ing outburst with a wave of the hand. "There was a youth in the Bible," he said, "who went out to find the lost asses, and he found a Kingdom. I'm talking to you as a dying man, Hamer, and I tell you that's how Labour must find its Kingdom – by getting on with the day's work. There's a certain virtue" – he smiled – "in lighting your own fires, and cleaning your own boots, and cooking your own food, as I do in my wee place behind Fetter Lane. There's more virtue in that than in hob-nobbing with the Lostwithiels, who are robbers of the poor, or in turning that poor misguided woman out of your house on a barren point of legality."

"The law must be the law, to Labour people as to everyone else," said Hamer. "And as to hob-nobbing – are we to divide the world into hostile camps?"

"It is so divided," said Hardie.

"I place myself second to no man," Hamer declared, "in my attack on abuses, but I think personalities should be kept out of debate."

"In a sty of starving pigs," Hardie said whimsically, "the abuse to be attacked is not the abstract idea of fat hoggishness but the particular fat hog who has cornered the food."

"I am busy—" Hamer began, and Hardie interrupted him. "The world will be busier soon. We are on the brink of war."

There was a sudden silence in the room. Hamer had been expecting the news. To the other three it came with the shock of a thunderclap.

Looking utterly grey and worn, Hardie went on: "Asquith has sent for MacDonald, as leader of the Party, to know what his attitude, and what the Party's attitude, would be. As to my attitude, I suppose you can be in no doubt."

"No," said Hamer sincerely. "No one could be in any doubt about that."

"Thank you," Hardie said. "I shall stand by what I have always preached." He added with prescience: "I am prepared to be mobbed, hooted, called a traitor. Before it is all over, I suppose there will be jobs in the Cabinet for Labour men. They'll be willing to pay for our support. But on our side there'll be no pay. We have to choose."

He sat sunk in his chair, his white beard in his chest. It was a long time before he ventured to say, almost timorously: "Where will you be, Hamer? I am not asking you now as your old leader. As a friend, tell me, where will you be?"

He was almost afraid to look up into the bright handsome, ambitious face. When he did so, he said sadly: "I see."

"It is not a thing that can be decided off-hand," said Hamer. "There are a thousand considerations."

"There is one consideration," Hardie answered. "Thou shalt not kill."

He got up wearily and held out his hand. "Good-bye," he said, "Think of me at cock-crow."

Part Three

Sabre in Velvet

Chapter Seventeen

The dining-room of the house in Half Moon Street was small and cosy. The walls were painted a creamy parchment. There was only one picture, a good Duncan Grant. It looked well over the marble fireplace, with a strip of concealed lighting above it. The long curtains of rough texture and oatmeal colour, the sage-green carpet, the Sheraton table and chairs, all seemed good to Hamer as the fire-light shone upon them. It had cost him a pretty penny – this room and the rest of the house.

Well, why not make it the house he had always intended to have? It was the last house he would live in. No more moves after this. That was pretty certain. It was January, 1924. He would be fifty-nine before the year was out. If Ann had lived, she would already be sixty.

Old Pendleton came in with the coffee as a clock on the mantel-piece chimed eight. He brought *The Times* and the *Manchester Guardian*, too, and laid them beside Hamer's plate. There was a tremulous ear-nestness about his actions, his soft-footed tread, his deferential stoop. He had not yet recovered from the shock of finding himself in such luck. He was not so old as all that, but Hamer always thought of him as old Pendleton because two years without work had put their lines on him. He was a Bradford man. Jimmy Newboult had found him and brought him and his wife to see Hamer when the new house was being prepared. Now there they were, the sole staff.

"There's a parcel, sir. Will you see it now?"

Hamer said he would, and as soon as Pendleton brought it into the room he knew what it was. "Unpack it," he said, "and then bring that old sabre that's in the hall."

When the thing was unpacked, it was lovelier than he had hoped. It was an oblong box, beautifully carved, standing on four claw feet. The side that faced you as it stood up was of glass, and this side was

furnished with little gold hinges, so that you could let it down and get
at the interior, lined with velvet of a rich royal blue. Set in the velvet at
the back was a small gold plate, inscribed: Peterloo, August 16, 1819.

Old Pendleton had brought the sabre, and Hamer hung it on the
hooks let into the case to receive it. Then he shut the door and pressed
in the little catches. He was so pleased with the thing that he took it
up at once and carried it to his study. There he placed it on top of a
low bookcase that he had had in mind all along as its destination. He
stepped back and looked at it admiringly.

"Well, what do you think of it?" he said to Pendleton, who had
followed.

The old man stood with his head on one side for a moment before
pronouncing: "A reg'lar museum-piece, sir, if you ask me."

That was what Lettice Lostwithiel had said, Hamer reflected as he
walked back to his coffee and newspapers.

It was so long ago since that night when he had met her on his quarterdeck and she had predicted that the Labour Party would govern the
country. So many years, and so full of war and death and disaster that
they seemed twice as many as they were; and then, when he had met
her last week she had remembered. "Well," she said, "have you got any
secrets to tell me? Am I talking to the Foreign Secretary? I've had to
wait a long time, but I was right, you see."

She did not know that she had touched him on the raw. Foreign
Secretary. It was what he wanted. It was what he thought he ought to
have, but didn't know yet what he was going to have. All he knew was
that Ramsay MacDonald intended to be Foreign Secretary as well as
Prime Minister.

He gave her some non-committal reply, and they walked on side
by side through the Green Park, where he had overtaken her, with
the roar of Piccadilly on their left. It was a dull afternoon, deepening
toward winter dusk. The lights were coming on in the buses and the
shop windows. "I don't know," he said, "whether you'd care to look at
a picture I've got – a Duncan Grant?"

It was a safe appeal. They shared this passion for pictures and had
met more than once at art shows. They crossed over into Half Moon
Street, and he apologized for the confusion of the house. The workmen were still in it, and the rooms were cluttered with furniture,

draped and unarranged. But the dining-room was already finished, in order; and Lady Lostwithiel, standing before the picture, approving it, approved the room, too.

Pendleton brought in some tea, put it on a little table before the fire. Lettice walked about the room, admiring this and that, pausing now and then at the table to sip her tea. The sabre had been thrown down on a chair, and alongside it was the leather casket that Birley Artingstall had made so long ago. The lid was up, and she looked curiously at its unexpected contents: a curl of brown hair, an old, faded, dirty ribbon, and a ribbon that looked a little newer. Hamer came over and stood at her side. Very delicately, she put a long white finger inside the close convolutions of the curl and lifted it out of the box. The dirty stained ribbon came too, attached to it. She turned to him, holding it up for his inspection. With a rather malicious smile she asked: "An old flame?"

The girl Emma, the Old Warrior's little love who had stood a-tiptoe on his foot to kiss him. Dead already for nearly half a hundred years before Hamer was born, And yet it was true enough. She had been a flame, filling his days with passion, giving pith and point to his early crusading years. He gave a light laugh, took hold of the ribbon and lifted the curl off Lady Lostwithiel's finger. He shut it back into the box. "A family relic," he said. "It goes back further than I do. I'm afraid it could recall no flame of mine unless I were Methuselah."

Then she took up the sabre. "Now this is something I *do* know about," she said, and mockery was dancing in her blue eyes that the years had done nothing to dim. "I remember how you threatened to cut down old Buck with this. What a ruffian you were! I believe you would have done it for two pins."

She picked up the sabre, and the weight of it bent her slender wrist. She put her other hand to it, holding it out straight before her.

"How did you come by it in the first place?"

"I told the story often enough in St. Swithin's."

"Ah! St. Swithin's! What a long time ago that is! We lived in different compartments then. I don't remember that I ever heard the story."

And Hamer, who had told the story so often, who had known how to infuse it with pity and passion, told it now in bald, bleak words that tinkled emptily in the comfortable room.

"You shouldn't let it lie about like this," she said when he had done. "I don't suppose there are many genuine Peterloo relics left. It's a museum-piece. Let me have a case made for it. I'd like to do that. I'd like it to be my contribution to your new house."

She was full of pretty enthusiasm, and called on Pendleton to fetch a two-foot rule. Very businesslike, she took the measurements, wrote them on a piece of paper and tucked it into her muff.

"There!" she said. "I'll put that in hand at once." He walked with her to the door and she held out her hand. "You know, don't you," she said, "that I wish you the very best of luck? I should feel happier if you were in Downing Street instead of that man MacDonald."

So should I, he thought, as he walked back to have another look at his picture. So should I.

But he wasn't going to be at No. 10, or even at No. 11. He knew now that he was Minister of Ways and Means. The Rt. Honourable Hamer Shawcross, P.C., M.P. It was a good enough job, a job that would demand all he could put into it, seeing that the Labour Government had inherited not only office but the messy clutter of drift abroad and trouble at home that the Coalition had piled up. He opened a letter or two, thinking ironically of this Coalition Government that was going to hang the Kaiser, squeeze as much out of Germany as the Spaniards had squeezed out of Peru, make an England buzzing with work, larded with plenty, Well, the Kaiser's neck was still unstretched, Germany was a dry sponge, and England was indeed a land fit for heroes to live in: fit for nothing else, as he had said during the election, because if you weren't a hero you might as well die as try to live in the conditions the Coalition had created.

He looked at the postmark "Cwmdulais" on a letter, recognized Arnold Ryerson's handwriting and put it aside. There were so many letters from Arnold lately, all telling the same tale of grief and woe in the coalfields, expecting the Labour Government to wave a wand and magically cause barns to burst and purses to overflow. Well, it wasn't going to be so easy as all that. They had damned the Coalition up hill and down dale all through the election, and now, for the first time in history, it was Labour's turn to rule in Britain. The lines that the years had put into his face deepened. No, it was not going to be so easy as all that. The soap-box Socialists were going to have a shock.

He got up as the silvery chime of the clock told him that it was half-past eight. (Not the clock in the fretwork tower that Jimmy Newboult had carried over the snow to Baildon. That was in Pendleton's bedroom.) Pendleton helped him into his coat in the hall, gave him his black felt hat. He took up a dispatch-case and stepped out into the still grudging light of the January morning. The wind was blowing shrilly in Half Moon Street, rushing in wild eddies hither and thither in the Green Park. He walked very upright, a tall inspiring figure that people turned to look at, across the Mall and St. James's Park to the back steps into Downing Street. He took them at a run, almost as enthusiastically as he had done his morning mile thirty-five years ago. A press photographer was ranging Whitehall and snapped him as he went up the steps to the Ministry of Ways and Means. Nine o'clock had not yet struck. It was his first morning in attendance at the Ministry. He was going to show the civil servants that an era of activity was upon them. So much to do!

Pendleton put some coal on the fire in the study and asked if there was "anything more."

"No, no!" said Hamer. He flashed the smile that lit up all his face, that made you think all his concern was for your particular well-being. "No, no! You go to bed now."

The old man permitted himself to say: "You ought to be there yourself, sir."

"I'm all right. I'm not a bit tired." He smiled again, this time dismissively. Pendleton went out and shut the door quietly.

No; he was not a bit tired. He sat down in the creaking armour of his evening clothes and rejoiced in his strength. It was midnight. A table-lamp by his chair and the firelight on the hearth were all that illuminated the big book-filled room. He looked out into the gloom: at the rows and rows of familiar volumes; at Ann's portrait half-seen on the distant wall; at the sabre in its velvet lining catching a comfortable glint of fire-shine. He pulled a big foolscap book on to his knee, took out a fountain-pen and began to write in his firm, flowing hand: "Charles was at the dinner tonight. There was no opportunity for us to speak."

It had been a day! At the Ministry, in the House, at Downing Street, back at the Ministry, home to change, on to the dinner at the Hyde Park Hotel. Hovering behind the chairs at the top table was a big chap wearing a boiled shirt and an evening coat of huntsman's pink, who bellowed at the right moment in a voice that made the glasses rattle: "Ladies and gentlemen: the toast is Literature, coupled with the name of the Right Honourable Hamer Shawcross, Privy Councillor, Member of Parliament, His Majesty's Minister of Ways and Means."

"My friends," he said, "I am coupled to Literature by the frailest links. The Muse so many of you here so worthily serve would disdain, as merely utilitarian, the small offerings I have myself from time to time laid at her feet. But there is one link which I cherish in my heart – not utilitarian but creative. I am if not the father at least the grand-father of a masterpiece – Charles Shawcross's *Fit for Heroes*."

Well, he would let Charles see that he knew how to hand him a bou-quet: rather an overblown one, for he knew well enough that Charles's "proletarian" novel was a long way from a masterpiece, though it had created a bit of a stir. He waited for the applause to die down, for the necks that had twisted round toward the blushing Charles to come back in his own direction, and then went on: "But if Literature owes me little, I owe Literature much; and no doubt the most appropriate thing for me to do tonight will be to tell something of the enchanted flasks I have drained, the magic doors by which I have been permitted to travel occasionally in those realms of gold wherein you are the priv-ileged citizens and ministers."

How it flowed out of him! Suave and easy and honeyed, the words cascaded from his lips: the cavern in Manchester – "piled like some fantastic Aladdin's cave with jewels whose worth it would be beyond the wit of man to compute" – the little bookshelf in an Ancoats back-bedroom – "Ah, my friends! the bitter life of the poor, adding penny to penny like some diligent church mouse as much entitled, surely, as any other mouse to run free and delighted in the granaries where you creators spill your grain in the careless profusion of genius."

They liked it. Sometimes, in moments of frank self-recognition, he was amazed how easy it was to make them like it. There was no one else in the Labour Party, except Ramsay MacDonald himself, who could do this sort of thing. Assemblies of architects had listened with apparent deep appreciation to just this kind of diffuse and woolly gen-eralizing about their art, and on his engagement list, he knew, there were dinners of artists, librarians, teachers, who would all expect – and not in vain – to find him breathing over their particular Edens like a roseate and ambiguous dawn.

There was "no opportunity" for him to speak to Charles. In the break-up of the gathering, with earnest hands pressing his, with thanks for his wise words raining upon him, he saw Charles disappearing toward the exit, doing nothing to make the opportunity. Charles was dragging his legs and looking interesting, not in the fashion of a small boy with blue veins in his long delicate neck, hovering on an Ancoats doorstep long, long ago as the boxed-up body of the Old Warrior came bumping down the narrow stairs. Charles dragged his leg because it was made of wood, cunningly jointed with aluminium, and he looked interesting because the most careful surgery had not quite made the shot-away side of his face resemble the other.

"At one time," Hamer went on, writing in the deep night hour, undisturbed by any sound but the silvery chimes telling the quarters, "I hoped that Charles might enter the Diplomatic Service."

It was the first time he had put on paper the old dead dream. It did not die slowly. It was stabbed to death with one sharp blow that day when he and Ann had gone to see Charles in the charming hospital set up in a country house not far from Graingers, where he had been at school. It was on an autumn day in 1918, a day that seemed in every particular to recreate the occasion when they had taken the child and left him standing against the virginia creeper flaming on the school porch. They travelled down the same line, and actually to the same station. The day had the same autumnal quality as the train stopped at the little stations blazing with late flowers and then puffed forward between orchards full of ripe apples. They were retracing their steps into a past flushed with the deceptive glow of a time that seemed in retrospect as though it had known nothing but happiness. It was almost as if, at the end of the journey, they would find the eager boy who so often had run to meet them when they came down for the half-term holiday.

Charles came to meet them, but he did not run. He had not yet been furnished with a charming imitation of a leg. He swung slowly down the drive on two crutches whose ends were matted with autumn leaves. His face was still raw and repellent. When he saw them coming, he waited, leaning heavily on the crutches, unsmiling, his features full of pain. Ann felt her heart would break. She wanted to rush forward and throw her arms about him, but you can't do that to a man swaying uncertainly on crutches. So she stopped in her tracks, gazing at him in a turmoil of love and impotence, till Charles broke the spell by saying with a bitter grin: "*Vive la guerre!*"

Then Ann and Hamer went up to him, standing there with a thin shower of golden leaves shaken down upon him by a little wind, under the blue sky, between the hedges full of honeysuckle and the red berries of guelder roses. It was a scene set for idyll, and Charles got his right armpit bedded deep down on the crutch so that he could hold out his hand and achieve an awkward shake. "I'll show you round," he said. "All very charming, don't you think? The tennis lawns are in excellent condition."

Ann wanted to cry out: "Oh, my dear! Don't let it make you bitter. Don't let it get you down!" as Charles sardonically told how easy it was to learn to play tennis with one arm, and how every day the doctors had new stories of one-legged dancing instructors and other heroes triumphing over the worst that could happen. But Ann did not say that, because she knew what man could do to man; she knew the bitterness in her own heart, planted there by the savagery she had suffered to achieve the vote which she knew now she would never use, the vote which seemed to her, now that it had come, as significant as one of these yellow leaves spinning slowly through the blue hazy air. She had trusted men, and fought them, and seen her cause triumph, and learned in bitter wisdom that the triumph was a pop-gun pellet fired against the walls of Jericho. So she walked at Charles's side, holding her peace, as his crutches crunched on gravel, and dully smote the turf, and sounded sharply on the flags of the ancient terrace where they had tea looking out towards a view of Graingers' roofs and chimneys infested with the white doves whose nests a two-legged Charles had once been agile enough to raid.

But Hamer winced occasionally at Charles's acid sallies, and when the time came to go he said: "Well, bear up, my boy. You know you can count on me."

Charles leaned on the crutches, his head sunk in his shoulders and thrust forward, a predatory mask. "Can I?" he said.

It was spoken so sharply, it was so unexpected, that even Ann looked up in surprise.

"Come," said Hamer. "You know you can."

"I'm not so sure of that," Charles answered. "Mother and Pen Muff thought they could count on you, didn't they?"

"Please, Charles, please!" Ann intervened. "That's all over and done with. Your father took one view, and if I took another, that was no reason for him to change."

"I agree with you, Mother," Charles said. "That's exactly what I have in mind. I don't expect to count on Father if my views are different from his. Why should I? I don't ask to."

"Put it all out of your mind for the moment, my boy," Hamer said with unusual gruffness. "Just give your thought to getting well."

Charles let out a harsh cackle and looked down at his pinned-up trouser-leg. "Get well of this?"

"Get strong. Get your nerves right. Get as well as you can," said Hamer. "Then will be time to talk. We'll understand one another, never fear. What have you got in mind? What do you want to do?"

"I want to go on where you left off," Charles said.

That sentence was the one sharp stab that killed the dream Hamer had so long entertained for his son. It was spoken so firmly, out of so deep a sense of conviction, that he recognized its final and inescapable quality. On the way back to town he saw that Ann was crying quietly from time to time, and he did not know with what words to comfort her. He had lost the way of it. He talked of the hopeful wonders of surgery, for all the world as though he were replying to a toast at a surgeons' banquet. "Don't you doubt it," he said. "Charles isn't finished. He'll walk without crutches, and his face'll show nothing but a few scars. It's not surprising that he's too out of spirit to think of his own future. We shall have to think for him. I wonder what he'll do?"

Ann dabbed a handkerchief to her eyes and looked out of the window at the landscape darkening to a plum dusk. "I expect," she said, "he'll do like the rest of us. He'll do what he wants to, till the time comes for him to wonder whether it was worth doing. But don't think you've only got to get his body right. It goes deeper."

Well, Ann should know something about that. They had got her own body right enough. She no longer started up in the night with evil dreams, crying aloud that she heard the jangling of keys and felt the nauseous suffocation of unwanted food pouring down her tubed throat. Through all that time she had slept in Lizzie's room. The women's campaign ended when the war burst on the country, and Lizzie, unharmed in mind or body, gave all her time to nursing Ann back to health. But Lizzie knew, and Hamer knew, that Ann's mind had been poisoned with bitterness. That, at least, is what they thought, but the bitter cup had cleansed, not poisoned, her. It gave her an astringent wisdom whereby she saw the triviality of the shadows that the other two pursued, and an understanding that the things worth having in life are few, and easy to get, and not to be got by striving; above all, that truth, wisdom, beauty, justice, are there, absolute, neither to be implemented nor destroyed by the haggling of politicians.

She did not want to declare these things. She nursed them secretly in her heart, and her life grew in upon itself. She continued to sleep in Lizzie's room, and Lizzie more and more treated her as she had treated, with a special consideration, the small child who came to Ackroyd Park, hurt by those who should have loved her, so many years ago.

And so, when Ann and Hamer came home to North Street that autumn day after visiting Charles, Lizzie was waiting, rosy, stout, white-haired, to pack Ann off to a warm bath, and then to bed, where she ate her dinner and read Marcus Aurelius, who fitted all that she now understood of life so much better than pamphlets and blue-books. She read, and she laid the book on the counterpane, staring at the fire and thinking of Charles. She thought of the day when Ellen had died, and she had run out to bring Charles in from Baildon Moor. They who had thoughtlessly seen so much of the old woman's life were not in time to see the last moment which their imaginations blew out to a disproportionate significance, and Charles had said ruefully: "I wonder if someone will be too late when I die." Well, he had died his first little death, and she wondered in what guise he would be resurrected. She imagined that that would depend a good deal on Alice Ryerson. She took up her book and read again, and presently fell asleep with her strange white glistening hair spread like an aureole behind her head. She had let it grow again. She did not have to fear now that men would seize it, and haul her through the streets like a trull, and beat her, making her heart quake with fear and her soul stiffen its armour for the fantastic, heroic, senseless crusade.

She had been asleep a long time when Hamer came in to say good night. She had not put out the light, but had tilted down the shade, so that a golden glow was upon her features that were extraordinarily tranquil. It moved him deeply to look at her, so near but so inaccessible. That was the word that fitted more and more what he thought of Ann. She said nothing, did nothing, to create that feeling. What she was, not what she said or did, had raised a barrier between them. "And yet, that was untrue," he has said, for he recorded this moment in his diary. "She had raised no barrier. I am incapable of explaining the subtlety of what prevented me from understanding Ann as I had once done."

He did not ask himself whether the whole thing might not be that she had gone forward and left him standing. He knew only that this sleeping tranquil woman seemed nearer to him than Ann, awake, ever seemed now. He bent down and kissed her, and, without waking, she crooked an arm round his neck, smiled, and pulled his head down to hers. She murmured "Always, always." He disentangled himself gently, put out the light, and tiptoed from the room.

The outcome of his visit to Charles, and his deep sense of spiritual estrangement from Ann, left him feeling restless and unhappy. He went to the room which Lizzie had given him for a study, and took up the diary which more and more, as the years flowed by, provided an outlet for his self-questioning. "Have I been happy at all since the war started? Sometimes I think it would have been better if I had followed Ramsay MacDonald into the wilderness."

Now he was getting down to it. Now he was probing the matter to the bottom. He had never been convinced of the war's necessity or justice, and he had got nothing for his acquiescence. He had been offered no post in the Cabinet. He had been courted, flattered, used. He had been sent on missions up and down the country, and the Prime Minister had publicly in the House referred to the importance of his work in getting the South of Wales miners back into the pits in July 1915. In 1916 he supported the Compulsory Service Bill and received an ironical telegram from Charles at Oxford: "I've joined the army today. I'd hate to be kicked into it." It made him wince, but it was not so bad as the wire that had come the year before from Cwmdulais on the day when the Prime Minister thanked him. It was signed "The Ghost of Evan Vaughan" and said simply: "Bravo, Peterloo." He never knew who sent it. It was the sort of thing Pen Ryerson might have done, but Pen was committed to the war as deeply as he was himself.

That was the strange thing, he reflected, sitting there that night in North Street at odds with himself: the war had split them all up, set them off on unpredictable courses. He would have expected both Lizzie Lightowler and Pen Ryerson to take the extreme pacifist view. They had done nothing of the sort. The frenzy which had carried them along in the suffragist campaign was canalized into the new national direction. Lizzie's days and nights were filled with a jumble of activities in canteens and sewing-classes, and Pen found work in a munition factory. Arnold, his daughter Alice, and Charles were the pacifists. It was that which made Charles's telegram from Oxford the more bitter. All Hamer had to set against it was Lady Lostwithiel's approval. She wrote to him: it was the first time she had ever done so. "I cannot say how pleased I was with your speech in the House yesterday. The support of men like you and Mr. Arthur Henderson is of immense importance, especially as one hears that Sir John Simon is likely to leave the Government on this issue."

He wondered whether to reply, and did so. He did not say how near he had been to opposing the Government, but now he had waded in too deep to go back. He sent a note of polite platitude. He was a little distrustful of her. He remembered the occasion in 1915 when he received a card, decorated with a coronet, whereon the Countess of Lostwithiel requested the pleasure of Mr. Hamer Shawcross's company at dinner.

It was a warm summer night, and he was aware of a mood of exaltation as the taxicab took him through the London streets to Belgrave Square. He would have been more, or less, than human if he had not recalled the circumstances of his youth. "On the way there, I thought of my youth, and hated it." We have his frank confession, and can fill in for ourselves the images that his mind evoked as he drove that night to Lady Lostwithiel's: the Lostwithiel Arms on the corner of an Ancoats street; Mr. Richardson, the Lostwithiel agent, calling on a Monday morning, when the back yards were fluttering with the week's wash, his pocket stuffed with rent books; Darkie Cheap, living on his tiny corner of Lostwithiel property, thrown out to disappear no one knew where. So powerful this name of Lostwithiel had been in his childhood; and perhaps his imagination plunged forward to the time when he first found it incarnate in the splendid house that he and Arnold Ryerson had gazed on from the moor-top, and in the legendary Buck Lostwithiel who crossed his path in St. Swithin's.

Now, stiff in evening clothes, renowned if for the moment almost neglected, learned as few men in his own or any other party were learned, handsome and commanding in any company, he was on his way to the lair of so much that had then been ogreish. "I must confess to a relish of this situation – perhaps it was no more than ironical amusement – as the cab put me down at that redoubtable door."

Never before had Hamer crossed a noble threshold in the capacity of invited guest. Never before had he seen Lettice Lostwithiel as she was when she received him in the great drawing-room: so radiant, so gracious, the brief train of her wine-dark dress hissing upon the carpet as she came forward to shake his hand. Diamonds were sparkling at her throat above the white swell of her breasts. He was sharply aware of her as a beautiful woman, seen for the first time against her indigenous background.

There were a dozen people at dinner. Lostwithiel was not there. 'He was commanding a division in France. Lady Lostwithiel invited Hamer's opinion of Orpen's portrait of him in regimentals, and a Royal Academician was pleased to concur with one or two criticisms that Hamer ventured to make. There was a prelate of the first eminence, who complained of the strain which outdoor speaking was imposing on his throat. He had been, only that afternoon, addressing a recruiting-meeting from one of the lions in Trafalgar Square. There was a general, and a famous novelist who for years had jeered at kings and nationalism, but was now a happy convert to better manners; and an editor whose weekly article had a patriotic surge so imposing that its backwash might sink a liner. There was a member of the Cabinet who greeted Hamer with a wizard smile and oiled him with the unction of his approval.

Though the summer light still lingered without, the curtains were drawn in the dining-room. In the rosily-lighted gloom long-dead Lostwithiels looked out of their frames, and no doubt they had seen so much in their time that, if each man jack of them were alive and kicking, he would not bat an eyelid at seeing Hamer Shawcross in that company, sitting there on Lady Lostwithiel's left, talking with fluent ease to her and the Cabinet minister on her right. On Hamer's other side was a rich American woman who had given her Scottish castle for use as a hospital and who now hadn't a European roof over her head except a villa at Cap Ferrat and a suite at Claridge's.

Lady Lostwithiel was brilliant. She was sure, she said to her Cabinet minister, that, occupied as he was with the war all day long, he would welcome the chance to forget it for an hour or two. "And that applies to you, Mr. Shawcross, too, I'm sure."

The Cabinet minister said that he, too, was sure of it. The Labour members who were supporting the Government had taken up a tremendous burden, and the way they were carrying it was not likely to be forgotten.

And so for a long time they talked of everything except the war. It was incredible what they talked about: they discussed pictures, of which the Cabinet minister knew nothing, and books, which revealed his love of going to bed with a thriller, and whether Wesley had prevented a revolution in England on the model of the French revolution, and whether, had the United States not revolted from the British crown, the British Empire would now be impregnable, so colossal a power that Germany would not have dared to raise a fist against her.

And then Hamer was aware that skilfully, almost insensibly, this had led back to the war which they were not to discuss, and that the Cabinet minister was deploring the outlook in the South Wales coalfield. It was not to be endured that at a time of such enormous national peril the miners should think of striking, but there seemed no doubt that they would do so.

"Forgive me if I'm side-tracking the matter," said Lady Lostwithiel, "but a point of personal interest struck me the other day. I noticed from the newspapers that one of the men's leaders down there is named Arnold Ryerson. That's the name of the man Lostwithiel had against him when he first went to St. Swithin's. I wondered if it were the same man. I think it must be. It's a rather unusual name."

She turned inquiringly to Hamer, and he nodded. "Yes. He's been down there now a good many years."

"You and he were hand-in-glove against my poor husband," she smiled. "You must know him very well."

"I haven't kept in touch with him," said Hamer. "Not closely, anyhow."

"Ah! but to some extent?" It was the Cabinet minister, smiling and alert.

Lettice Lostwithiel stood up. A moment later she and the other women were gone, Hamer and the Cabinet minister, smoking their cigars, had left the table and moved over to the privacy of a nook by the fireplace.

"It really was extraordinarily lucky, Shawcross, that I should meet you tonight and discover that you know Ryerson in a personal way. I've watched Ryerson for a long time. He's a man I admire for many things. I think he's a man who would listen to reason from a friend."

Hamer pulled judiciously at his cigar. "Ryerson's idea of reason wouldn't agree with yours in this matter, believe me. I know him."

The famous smile flashed at Hamer. The Cabinet minister's hand was laid on his arm. "You know him. And you know what your country needs at this moment." The voice sank to a pitch of gravity. "I say no more about it. Except that to have met you here tonight seems almost as though Providence had intervened."

As he was leaving that night Lady Lostwithiel gave him the feeling that he was being singled out for special favour. "Good-bye, Mr. Shawcross, You must come again. I always felt we should know one another better, understand one another's point of view."

He travelled down to Cwmdulais the next day.

Never before had he felt so furtive and ashamed. He was oppressed, choked, by a sense that he was being basely used. He believed that the miners were in the wrong, but that was not the point. He had not come voluntarily to tell them so. His visit had been contrived by people who would have been against the miners wrong or right,

He had not telegraphed to Arnold Ryerson. Through the fading end of the stifling summer day he climbed the hill from the station and, unannounced, knocked at the door of the house in Horeb Terrace. Arnold, coatless, his shirt sleeves rolled up, his shirt collar unbuttoned, himself came to the door. His hair was untidy and his fingers were inky. His big sagging body looked tired and his pouchy face was grey with a desperate weariness. He looked at Hamer for a moment, as if unable to believe his eyes, then held out his hand. "You're too late," he said. "They're coming out tomorrow."

A blow in the face would not have surprised Hamer more. Walking up from the station, he had wondered how to introduce his business. There was no need to introduce it. Arnold had divined it, writing him down instinctively as a messenger from the enemy camp.

"Come in," Arnold said. "I'll make you a cup of tea. I'm all alone here at the moment."

He led Hamer into the front room, where the two desks were

littered with papers. "Sit down," he said, "and make yourself comfortable. Light your pipe. I won't be a minute."

He went out into the kitchen, and Hamer could hear the clatter of cups, the poking of a reluctant fire. He lit his pipe and looked about him at this room so different from the room to which he had been bound at this very moment last night. It was smaller and meaner than he had remembered. It was intolerably stuffy, and seemed untidier than when he had seen it last.

Presently Arnold came in and put down a tin tea-tray among the disordered papers on his desk. He poured two cups. "Pen's out," he said apologetically. "She goes down to Cardiff every day to work, and she's staying tonight to see a film."

They sipped their tea for a while in embarrassed silence. Then Arnold got up and walked to the window and looked down into the evening gloom, thickening in the valley bottom. "There's one thing," he said without turning his head, "that I shall never live to see. I thought I was going to see it, but I never shall."

Hamer pulled on his pipe and waited for him to go on. "I shall never see you Prime Minister of England. I thought I should. But you've missed the tide, lad. The tide turned in August 1914, and you missed it. The right way was out into the darkness, and Ramsay Mac took it. This war seems very terrible. It *is* very terrible, as every war is. But there's a sense in which every war is just flim-flam and flap-doodle, a dirty boil, and the real business comes after. When the real business comes, the man we'll follow will be the man who always said that war was flim-flam and flapdoodle – as you did – but who went on saying it even when the war was there."

He turned round from the window, and in the obscurity of the dingy little room his features could not be seen. "I wanted to say that, and I've said it, even though it's not a nice thing to have to say. But there are so many things that are not nice. I don't think it's nice to see Arthur Henderson and Billy Brace in the Government. It sounds all grand and glorious, but I tell you, apart from anything else, it's a dead end. You think Ramsay MacDonald's in a dead end, don't you? You'll see. You're a better man than he is, Hamer, but you've handed it all to him on a plate. There – I've finished. It's your turn. Tell me what I ought to do to stop this strike."

Listening to the flat toneless voice coming out of the faceless body,

Hamer was intolerably oppressed. He felt as if he were listening to the voice of doom, and he recognized the inescapable accent of truth. He jumped suddenly to his feet. "Let's get out," he said. "Let's walk. It's so hot."

"Are you staying the night?" Arnold asked.

"I'd like to, if I may."

"Very well, then. We'd better go and get our supper. I'm no cook, and Pen won't be back for hours."

Just as he was, sleeves rolled up, collar open, Arnold went out into the passage, took down a cloth cap from a hook, and put it on. They went downhill, to the long village street in the valley bottom: the street along which Hamer had last walked in company with Evan Vaughan and a thousand marching men. Arnold pushed open the door of a fish-and-chip shop. "This is the best I can do," he said.

The place was furnished with deal tables, scrubbed till the grain stood up in ridges. It was stiflingly hot, full of blue fumes and the stench of sizzling fat. The great cooking-stove and its cowl of aluminium shone with cleanliness. Arnold brought two plates of fish and chips to a table which was provided with a tin salt-caster and a bottle of vinegar. He bestrewed his plate with these and began to eat, picking up the food with his fingers. There were no knives or forks.

"I always come here," he said, "when Pen doesn't come home."

Hamer followed Arnold's example, picking up the greasy food with his fingers. He did not eat much. He was glad when the meal was over, but he had to wait till Arnold had eaten doggedly through his portion. Then they went out, and the night air was gratefully cool after the mephitic fog of the little saloon. They climbed uphill again, past Horeb Terrace, and still up till they were beyond the highest house in the place, among the ling and the bracken that recalled the ancient peace and loveliness of the Rhondda. They sat down where the heather cushioned a rocky buttress, and they lit their pipes and watched the tip of the full moon beyond the opposite hill climb till the whole orb was clear, swimming in silvery luminescence.

And there was nothing to be said. The tobacco smoke scented the air; the clank and stutter of shunted trucks came up to them, but remotely, without urgency; the moonlight bewitched every common object; and they lay back against their stone, still warm with the sunshine of the long summer day, and for a long time said nothing at all.

But at last Hamer said: "You're quite right, Arnold. I came down to do what I could to stop the strike."

"You can do no more than I can," said Arnold, "I've tried, hard enough to stop it myself. But I'm not God Almighty."

"You tried to stop it?"

"I did. I can understand what the men feel. The fat will get fatter out of this war. You know that as well as I do. The men know it, too, and if they get off the rails and try to force an advantage for themselves out of a situation that's enriching so many others, I for one don't blame them. I understand them, I don't blame them, but that's not to say I encourage them. Whether I like the war or not, it's there. There's no hope for you or me or the miners, or anything we stand for and have worked for, till the damned thing's over. Surely to God, Hamer, you know I'm realist enough to see that? There's no need for you to come down from London to tell me that?"

He spoke with unusual urgency, and Hamer, who had come prepared to say so much, had nothing to say.

"Very well, then," Arnold went on. "Industrial disputes will hang the thing out. I don't want them. It's not the time for them, but," said Arnold, getting up and knocking out his pipe on his heel, "you can tell your friends in London this: that once this dirty business is over we'll fight 'em, by God, yard by yard, inch by inch, till we get what's due to us out of this industry or smash it to blazes in the process."

Hamer lay still, quietly pounding with a stone at the smoulder Arnold's tobacco had made in the heather. "Meantime," he said quietly, "the strike begins tomorrow."

"The strike begins tomorrow, and if you want any kudos out of it," Arnold said bitterly, "I'll see that you get a public meeting where you can tell the men what you think of them."

"I'd like that."

"All right, You can have it. Come on now. Let's see if Pen's back"

Pen was not back, but she came in presently, a strange haggard woman, yellow as a canary from the fumes she worked in. She seemed to Hamer to have lost much of the old keen edge, to be softer and quieter, and he guessed that this was because she and Arnold differed about the war. It lay between them, but they knew how to step over it. They treated one another with an exquisite consideration. More tea was brewed, and they sat drinking it in the sickly yellow light of an incandescent gas mantle, with the window flung open upon the hot night. Pen would not discuss the war, or her work, or the strike. She talked about the film she had seen, and about the high old times she and Ann and Lizzie Lightowler had had when the suffrage crusade was blazing, and about Alice, who was teaching in a secondary school in Manchester. But she did not say much about Alice, because she knew that Alice was a sore point with Hamer. She seemed to be blessed tonight with a fine sensibility that he had not known in her before. He remembered that the last time he saw her was when she had come, a persecuted mouse, to the house in North Street, and he had as good as shown her the door. Her magnanimity pleased and surprised him.

He did not sleep much that night. His bed was in the back room wherein Pen and Arnold had spent the first night of their married life, the room that looked out on the slope of the mountain running up to the sky that now had lost the moon's lovely and mysterious light. Clouds were banking up in a hot accumulation as if all the heat that had tortured the valley throughout the day were sucked up and there made visible. He lay with nothing but one sheet over him, thinking how long it was since he had slept in such a room as this, and listening to the low rumble of Pen's and Arnold's voices clearly audible through the thin wall. He had hardly dropped off into a light troubled sleep than he was awake again, listening, taut, to the clang of thunder and watching the fiery zigzag of the lightning draw infernal hieroglyphics upon the black sky. He had once feared thunder intensely, and still disliked it, and the strangeness of the little room, his isolation from all that had now become customary and familiar, tinged the present dislike with the old infantile fear.

Perhaps it was because he was lying now in just such a room as the room in which his fears had visited him, the room into which, he knew, lying awake and shivering, Ellen would surely come to sit by the bedside till he was asleep and the storm was rumbling to extinction in the far fringes of the town. Whatever the cause, he lay unhappy and aware of a slight sweating, as the room flickered into startling clarity and then fell upon darkness again, and the thunder boomed and rocketed with increasing violence among the hills.

Presently there was a flash so startling that he persuaded himself he heard the hot sear of it, and then a stuttering crescendo of thunder that ended in a disruptive explosion more violent than any he had ever heard. He would have got up and lit the gas, but the house in Horeb Terrace was so curiously provided that the gas was in the downstairs rooms only. He leaned out of bed and was fumbling for the matches and candle he had placed on a chair alongside it when a shuffling of footsteps sounded and his door opened. Arnold was standing on the threshold, and a lightning-flash coming at that moment picked him out with the clarity of a spotlight. A long white night-shirt trailed its hem about his feet encased in large worn carpet slippers, and over this he had thrown on a raincoat that reached his knees. The flash faded, and the yellow shine of the candle he carried in a tin candlestick was thrown upwards on to his tousled hair, his grey heavy troubled face, whose dominating note, Hamer saw in that illuminating moment, was an immense kindliness and a rock-like steadfastness. There was comedy in the figure Arnold cut at that moment, but Hamer did not see it. He felt about twelve years old, and in Arnold all the protective and comforting influence that had been about his childhood was suddenly incarnate.

"Are you all right, lad?" Arnold asked. "I remembered you didn't like lightning."

"Aye," said Hamer, dropping into the easy tone, "I'm all right, Arnold, but thanks for coming."

Arnold walked over to the window and pulled the heavy serge curtain across it. "That'll keep it out a bit," he said. "Pen's gone down to make a cup o' tea."

Oh, the everlasting tea of the Ryerson household! But as the storm continued to roar, there was something comforting in the sound of Pen moving about downstairs, and when presently she came up, as queerly dressed as Arnold was, with tea and biscuits, Hamer enjoyed the midnight picnic, and they were all more happy and easy with one another than they had been for a long time.

They talked for half-an-hour of old days in St. Swithin's, and then Pen gathered up the tea-things and went. Soon Arnold followed her. First he pulled back the curtains and looked out into the night, "It's takkin' up, lad," he said. "Ah can see t'moon, and thunder's nobbut a belly-rumble."

He held his candle aloft and looked down with what Hamer divined as a sad anxious affection. Then he went, shutting the door softly behind him. Hamer was soon asleep, his mind bemused with thoughts of Ellen: not old Ellen dragging out her days at Baildon, but an Ellen younger than he himself was now, who had seemed so long ago to be all that he understood by providence.

When he came down in the morning, Pen was gone and Arnold was frying sausages in the kitchen. It was a lovely summer day, fresh and cool. After breakfast Arnold went out, and Hamer sat in the front room, reading the newspapers and writing letters. He made a few notes of what he would say when he met the miners. By eleven o'clock Arnold was back. He had arranged for an open-air meeting to be held at three.

It began as a turbulent and disorderly meeting. Hamer spoke from a lorry. Arnold was his chairman. No one else stood by the two as they climbed up to espouse their unpopular cause. Arnold did not say much. "Now, you men, you've known me long enough, and you know my one concern is for your interests. And you know, too, that I think you're playing the fool in coming out now. When I'm with you I tell you so, but when I'm against you, neither you nor anyone else is going to make me pretend I'm not. However, you know all about that. I've told you often enough, and you're not here today to hear it all over again. So I'll shut up now and ask Hamer Shawcross to talk to you."

The men listened to Arnold quietly, interrupting with nothing but affectionate back-chat: "All right, Arnold. Sit down, mun, an' let's hear the big bug." "Come orf it, Arnold. You ought to be down here, mun, not up there. We'll have to get a new leader, boyo."

They were not so quiet when Hamer got up. Before he could open his mouth there were shouts from all directions. "What are the bosses paying you?" "Why don't you bring the soldiers?" "Who's backing up the war?"

Hamer did not treat himself to any preliminary niceties. He stood there quietly watching for his chance, and seized it at once when that last shout came. "Your leader Arnold Ryerson isn't, for one," he said. "He wants to see this war ended because he believes it should never have begun. Who is getting in his road? You are!"

This renewed the uproar. "To hell with that!" "We don't want the bloody war!"

"Whether you want it or not, you've got it," said Hamer. "What an intelligent man asks is: How can we end it quickly? That is what my friend Arnold asks. Last night I sat at his fireside: the fireside of a man

I have known and loved from childhood. I listened to what he had to say, and I divined that his heart was well-nigh broken at the thought that what he has worked for among you for so long was in danger of being torn to pieces. My friends, think twice before you destroy the work of a man like Arnold Ryerson."

They were quieter now, and someone shouted: "Never mind Arnold, Arnold's all right."

"Of course he's right. That is all I have come to tell you. He is right, and you are wrong. Let me tell you how right he is."

He went on to expound the views which Arnold had expressed the night before. They had heard it all from Arnold, but Arnold was not capable of giving it the cogency it now assumed.

The interruptions had died away, and Hamer went easily on to an emotional conclusion. He pictured the minesweepers heaving on their little ships through the dark of a winter night, wondering if their fuel supplies could be maintained. "Ah! If only our friends in the Rhondda had not betrayed us!" He made them see the infantry among the rotting sandbags in the front line going over the top unaided by an artillery barrage. Why was there no barrage? Because the shells were not coming up. Why were the shells not coming up? "Ah, my friends, why indeed! How shall the great factories roar, how shall the shells they make reach the coast, how shall they cross the seas in ships, how shall they go from the base to the line if you deliberately snap the first link in the great chain? And so it may well be with their last breath that your brothers in the front line cry: 'Ah, if only our friends in the Rhondda had not betrayed us!' You can deliver them. But no! You have chosen to be like some doctor with the life-saving medicine in his hand who says to the dying man: 'I can save you but I've raised my price!' Stand out then for your thirty pieces of silver, and spend them with the world's contempt muttering in your Judas ears."

It was a consummate rhetorical effort. Not a cry was raised against him when he had finished. What contribution was made by this widely-reported speech cannot be precisely assessed, but the strike ended in a week.

Newsboys were running down the streets as Hamer and Arnold climbed from the lorry. They wore like aprons news-bills of the *South Wales Echo*: "Munitions works explosion. Many dead."

Arnold heard their shrill cries, read the disastrous words they carried, and a chill premonition struck him to the heart. He remembered the far-off spring day when he and Pen had lain in the heather on the hills, and looking down had seen the crowd milling into the colliery yard. Their hearts were shaken by a common dread: Ianto! Ianto! Now, not knowing he had spoken, Arnold muttered: "Pen! Pen!"

Hamer had already snatched a paper from a boy and torn it open. Arnold read over his shoulder. It was very brief. The factory was the one where Pen worked. Many dead. Many injured. Cause unknown. No names. That was all.

Arnold was trembling, and Hamer put an arm about him. "Where's the nearest telephone?" he asked.

It was at a public-house round the corner. He rang through to the Cardiff Infirmary. Arnold stood at his side, grey as a ghost, supporting himself by holding on to the corner of a table. Hamer would not use the word death. Not yet. Not unless it was necessary. Now he was through. "Is Mrs. Arnold Ryerson among the injured?"

There was a little delay, someone scanning a list. "Penelope Ryerson."

"That's it. Are the injuries serious?"

He listened to the reply and hung up. Then he laid a hand on Arnold's shoulder. "She's alive!"

Arnold stood up from the table. "Thank God!" he said, There was sweat on his forehead.

"They can't tell me much more. I expect they're at sixes and sevens, still receiving people."

"I must go and see her." He looked at his watch. "There's no train for an hour."

"Never mind the train. We'll get a taxi," said Hamer. He sought out the landlord and pressed a coin into his hand. "Get through to a garage," he said. "Have a car sent up to Mr. Ryerson's house at once."

"Very good, Mr. Shawcross. Arnold, I'm sorry about this, mun. I hope it's nothing much." He grasped Arnold's hand, and instinctively Arnold pulled himself together. He walked firmly with Hamer up to Horeb Terrace. Hamer put his few things into his bag. "You won't want me in the way now," he said.

The car was at the door, and so was a group of men who had drifted up from the meeting. "Good luck to you, Arnold." "Bring back good news, boyo." They crowded round him, trying to shake his hand, patting him on the back, giving him their affection, sharing his grief, in the only way they knew. "Thank you, boys, thank you," he said. "I'll give Pen your love."

Then they were away, purring through the heat of the summer afternoon, with the windows down but stifled none the less by the dingy odours of the ancient cab. There was nothing they could say to one another. They knew too little and too much. Hopes and fears shuttled to and fro amid their blank uncertainty.

They reached the infirmary in the early evening. The waiting room was full of scared anxious people, some of whom did not yet know whether their relatives were living or dead. From time to time those who had been called out of the room came back to pick up a hat, a stick, a bag, and those who were left scanned the faces as though in the joy of some or the white blank misery of others they could read their own doom.

It was very hot. Half-an-hour passed, three-quarters, and then the door opened, and a thin dark young man looked round it. Arnold at once got to his feet and his choked-back anxiety took him across the floor in a stride. Hamer alongside him. "Why – Dai!" he said.

The young doctor took them into the passage and shut the door. This was Dai – the child of the poet Ap Rhondda and of Pen's sister Nell, young Dai of whom Pen had talked to Arnold so long ago in the house in Thursley Road, Bradford. Dai the darling baby was now in command; Arnold stood humbly before him, looking imploringly at David Richards, M.B.

"I didn't know you'd be at the infirmary, Dai," he said. "I'd have tried to get you on the 'phone."

"It's bad business," Dai said. "They've raked in all of us they could get."

"How is she?"

"I attended to her myself. You shall see her, but you can stay only for a moment."

Hamer's heart quickened as he noted the evasion. They were following David Richards down a corridor, up a flight of stairs. "May I see her?" he asked.

"Oh, this is Hamer Shawcross, Dai," said Arnold.

Dr. Richards stopped and tapped his teeth with a finger-nail, considering. "All right," he said, "but you mustn't talk to her. And, Uncle, the less *you* say the better."

They were setting off again when he stopped once more. "Oh, and look here. Don't go back to Cwmdulais tonight. You stay with us. Go straight along there. I'll come when I'm through. I've 'phoned to May to expect you. You'd be lonely up there in that damned hole. It may be some time, you know, before you get Auntie Pen back."

All these warnings, Hamer thought. All these dark foreboding hints!

They were at the door of a ward. Dai pushed it open and beckoned with his finger. "Sister! To see Mrs. Ryerson. Only a moment, mind."

He went on down the corridor, and Arnold and Hamer tiptoed into the hushed ward. The evening light was filtering through the trees that grew without, wavering in watery patterns on the wall. There was the faintest touch of rose and gold in those dancing beams, and that was the only colour that broke the snowy purity into which they advanced. The beds were like snowdrifts on a plain of snow, and on the last snowdrift of all was a higher pile of snow that was Pen beneath the white bedclothes. But here, at last, was an incongruous and pitiful touch of colour: Pen's yellow hands resting on the coverlet, the lower half of Pen's yellow face looking strange and inhuman, as though it were not part of a face at all, beneath the bandages bound round and round her forehead and her eyes.

They thought they had advanced as quietly as death into that polar purity, but as they halted by the bed Pen whispered: "Arnold!"

He knelt down by the bedside and put his face close to hers. "Yes, luv," he said.

She spoke in a tired far-away voice. "I've been listening for you for hours. I heard those old boots. I told you to oil 'em."

"Yes, luv," he said again, and took her thin yellow hands in his pudgy paws.

She let him hold her hands, and did not speak for a moment. Hamer saw that Arnold's eyes were streaming with tears, and presently they began to fall on Pen's hands. Then she took her hands from his grasp and weakly felt his hair, his face, his eyes. She rubbed his eyes as though she would wipe away his tears, "Eh, lad," she said, "don't be a great fool. It's only my eyes. It'll be all right. It's only my eyes."

Then the sister tapped Arnold on the shoulder. He got up clumsily, and, crying without restraint, went with Hamer out of the ward.

*

When Hamer looked back at the war years, each one had its poignant emotional content. Nineteen-fourteen was the year of his great decision, and though he appeared to make it easily, he made it with deep foreboding. He was not to be gulled with easy phrases. "The rights of little nations" didn't take him in. He was well enough read historically to know that no great nation had ever thrown away its wealth out of love of a little one. No; it was fear of the further aggrandizement of a powerful nation that set the works going. The fatal hour inexorably came; and it was pretty to pretend that the gilded figure on a clock had struck it. But he knew better.

He knew that the cause for which he stood would receive a shattering blow in every country that took up arms. He wondered where his own party would be found, and was deeply comforted that so many of its leaders were prepared to join him in toeing the national line. By the end of the year, the sound of the new note in his own voice had ceased to surprise him. If no one else could fool him, he claimed the right to fool himself.

Nineteen-fifteen was a tangled complex of emotions, public and private. Again and again his nerves were wrung with humiliation as he realized that everybody with plums to offer must know that he had put himself in the market, and yet no one hired him. At least, no one gave him what he thought should be the full tally of his hire. He was used, and thanked, and left on one side till it was necessary to use him again.

And that was the year, too, of Pen Ryerson's blindness. He stayed in an hotel in Cardiff that night, and suddenly, after he had got into bed, he broke out into a sweat at a thought that leapt into his mind. What if Dai Richards had not asked Arnold to stay with him for the night? What if there had been no Dai Richards? How easily Hamer had packed his bag in Cwmdulais! "You won't want me in the way now."

His vivid imagination pictured Arnold, had there been no Dai Richards, returning distraught in the dirty Rhondda Valley train to the unkempt little house in Horeb Terrace and sitting there through the long hot hours of darkness in lonely meditation, in agonized reliving of the moment when he stood before the sightless wreck of Pen.

He got out of bed, unable to sleep, thinking how, the night before, the flash of the lightning had brought Arnold eager with all the strength he had to offer. How much more, now that a more terrible lightning was searing Arnold's sky, should he have been there to comfort and support his friend! It was a long time since he had so poignantly confronted himself. "My God!" he groaned. "What am I becoming? What sort of man am I?"

In the morning, in the London train, he read: "The Rhondda Strike. Shawcross Castigates the Miners," And on the same page was the dire story of the explosion: the long list of the dead, the longer list of the injured. "Mrs. Ryerson, wife of the Rhondda miners' leader, has lost the sight of both eyes." There was no connexion between the two things, but that casual juxtaposition jarred him, and he threw down the papers impatiently. Lady Lostwithiel rang him up in town that night. She said she thought his speech was splendid. Charles, who was down for the long vacation from Oxford, was not at home, Ann said that he had telegraphed to Alice Ryerson, as soon as he read of Pen's injury, and was gone to meet Alice who was travelling from Manchester to Cwmdulais. Hamer saw little of Charles that holiday. Pen had to stay for a long time where she was, and Charles and Alice took Arnold away, That was the end of Alice's school-teaching. She remained at home, when Pen came back, to guide her mother's footsteps, as her mother had once guided hers.

It was altogether a nerve-racking year, Hamer thought, and 1916 was little better. That was the year of compulsory service, of Charles's joining up, the dead despairing middle of the war, when retrospect and prospect alike were lurid with hate and bloody haze. This was the time when he was most tempted to walk out, to go, though late, into the wilderness, to withdraw from a scene in which all that he had stood for appeared to be foundering in a sea of blood and fire.

It was Jimmy Newboult, of all people, who prevented him from taking that step: an incredible Jimmy Newboult, another of the war's enigmas, a Jimmy Newboult wearing a colonel's uniform and several decorations for gallantry in the field, commander of a mob that had gained some notoriety as the "Wool-Winders' Battalion."

Pacing the streets between the House of Commons and North Street – the dark wartime streets with the searchlights crossed upon the peace of the sky like naked blades shutting the gates of paradise – this Jimmy, home on leave, listened as Hamer laid bare his soul, came near to confessing that he had sold his birthright for a mess of pottage, and was waiting for the pottage still.

Jimmy came to a stand under a blacked-out street-lamp, and its little trickle of light dribbled down upon his face, white and fanatical as ever, but ennobled now by his daily consorting with death. "No!" he said. "*You!* When you betray a cause, Hamer, may God strike me dead."

There was such devotion in the man, a depth of loyalty so rich and unsullied that Hamer was moved to the very marrow, as he had been when the fantastic scene was enacted in Bradford and Jimmy Newboult became his man.

"Nay, Hamer. You're tired. You're wearing yourself out. You're doing too much. No, no. Nothing's given away. When this is over, by God they'll be able to deny Labour nothing. Stand by us boys, and when the time comes, we'll stand by you."

And Hamer said, as he had said once before: "I'll try to be what everybody thinks me, Jimmy."

Nineteen-seventeen was always muddy in his memory with the filth of Passchendaele, where Charles was; tragi-comic with the coming, that year, of votes for women. He listened in the House with ironic detachment to the easy platitudes with which those who had persecuted Ann and Pen made their recantation. Well, little enough Ann would want the vote now she had got it, or Pen, either, for that matter, he suspected.

It all seemed to him to be the more childish, without real significance, because in this year had come an event which he recognized as among the most significant of his times: the Russian revolution. His Labour colleagues were dazzled, delighted, gloriously aware of a new star in the East. His own heart was filled with doubt and fear. He was impatient alike with the optimism that saw the millennium rising unsullied out of the revolution's bloody lake, and with the baser notion that it would be easy, by force or fraud, to keep Russia toeing the Allied line. He knew that Russia had gone her own way, finally and beyond recall; and he knew that it was a way he did not want to follow.

It was a little personal point that had given him his deep knowledge of what was happening. He was attached by a living link to this new act in the ever-shifting drama of mankind's agony. Old Suddaby, sleeping by the fire in his Manchester cellar, Sheba the white cat, the silent catacombs of books, and the bells of the Old Church steeple shaking the air: all these were woven into his apprehension of the trend of events. These gave it human point and substance: Suddaby and Engels digging out their statistics in the Manchester streets and factories, Engels dispatching them, with the week's dole, to Marx, hypochondriac and morose, piling up in London the fabulous documentation of his humourless paradise.

Five hundred books! Many a time in that troubled year Hamer, walking his quarterdeck, now war-darkened and oppressive, with the river black and turgid and mysterious sliding by: this river on the one hand, symbol of the eternal restless roll of time, and on the other the rectangular blocks of the great hospital dark against the sky, crowded with sick humanity, brief transient man dying there with every swing and turn of the tide: many a time in that year, walking there broodingly, he thought of the five hundred books that Suddaby, dying, had bequeathed him. Moved by an impulse to explore all that had been so powerful and dynamic in the old man's life, he had sought out the shelves where Suddaby had garnered all that Marx and Engels had written, all the commentaries thereupon, all the dark and intricate imaginings of those who, blinded by the world's injustice and the cruelty of men, pictured the white lilies of love and law springing from a soil watered with the blood of their enemies.

It was a most compendious and illuminating library of Communist literature. He did not delve into it for many years, and in the meantime he added to it whatever books on the subject he could come by. At last, reading in three or four languages, he explored that colossal edifice, wandered in its dark corridors and dungeons, surveyed its huge speculative chambers, climbed out where its minarets pricked up among fantastic and implorable stars. And he saw that it was all founded upon a fallacy: the fallacy that man could be just to man. And in 1917 he knew that, whatever any politician might do, he would witness one more of man's superb and pathetic aberrations: the endeavour to apply this fallacy to the government of the race.

Somehow, by the destruction of one set of men, written down for the purpose of the argument as bad men, there would flourish a worthier race of men automatically good. He didn't believe it. Walking in the darkness between the river and the hospital, he knew that this weak and fugitive creature man, compounded of good and bad in every instance that had lived and breathed, would climb, if at all, by infinite slow organic degrees, not stream magnificently to heaven on the tail of a fiery bloody rocket.

*

And this, for one thing, was what Charles meant when he said in 1918: "I shall go on where you have left off," Looking back upon it, Hamer thought that few things in his life had been more poignant than Charles's endeavour to find in this new and bloody movement of the human tide a point of contact with his father.

There had been so few points of contact. They had missed it somewhere. While the boy was at school, he had seen too little of him, and when the moment came which might have remedied that, Charles fell desperately in love with Alice Ryerson.

Ann and Hamer had gone on a winter day to meet Charles at Paddington, returning from his first term at Oxford. He was tall and slender, fair and blue-eyed, and there he was coming along the platform with a suitcase in each hand and a gaily-coloured muffler thrown carelessly round his shoulders. The girl with him was short, but beautifully made. She was hatless, and a square-cut bob of black hair swung about her vivacious face in which everything was dark and sparkling. Her very complexion, dark as a gypsy's, seemed to sparkle with health and vigour, and her eyes were as black and shining as onyx. Every movement of her body and turn of her head seemed to radiate purpose and energy. Charles, loping along at her side, had the look of a tall sailing-boat that would do well if the winds were light and with him; and Alice's snub-nosed, dark pugnacious face made one think of a tough little tug that would ask no favours but would thrust its shoulders forward, into and against any wind and weather.

"Father – Mother – this is Alice."

There was something naïvely proud in the announcement, as Charles put down Alice's suitcase and his own and shyly kissed his mother. "This is Alice." No need to say more than that, for his letters had been full of Alice, and looking at her now Hamer did not need to be told who would lead whom if those two walked together. They did not see much of Alice that time. She went straight away on some business of her own which had brought her briefly to London. Then she went back to Cwmdulais. But Charles's words remained in Hamer's ears. They sounded like the fateful announcement of a new important player appearing on the scene. And so they were. This is Alice.

That was the time when Ann and Pen and Lizzie Lightowler were in full cry, and Alice was with them heart and soul. So, therefore, was

Charles, and this was where the somewhat puzzled estrangement which had kept Charles and Hamer apart, a passive feeling, not quite aware of itself, took the definite turn towards active antagonism. The boy who had wanted to write a hero-father's life did not want to do so any more. It was not that Alice consciously depreciated Hamer in Charles's eyes, but she was too honest to pretend to think him a hero. Just as Charles had sat at old Ellen's feet and learned of Hamer's boyhood, so now he learned more of that same story from Alice, who sketched in the part that Arnold Ryerson had played, and left Charles feeling a vague uneasiness, a sense that Hamer had subtly slipped away not only from friends but from allegiances. The war clinched the matter. It was, to Alice, outrageous that a Labour man should betray what she called the world solidarity of Labour, and Charles, without bothering to notice that this solidarity was as solid as a quagmire, went about depressed by a secret shame. Charles was of an age and under an influence which prevented him from seeing that, compared with his father at that same age, he was an uninstructed and half-baked fledgling. When Hamer faced his own heart, unobscured by the thickening golden mist of ambition, it was not the threat to the dubious solidarity of Labour that made him see the war in its naked horror: it was the crime of man against man.

Always, it seemed to him, he had been going to meet Charles or seeing Charles off. Taking the child to the station and putting him on the train for school; meeting the boy come down for the Oxford vacation; waiting for the overdue train bringing the youth from Cwmdulais. And now he was at Victoria, on a day late in 1917, waiting for the man returning from the wars. And there the man was, pushing his way with a mob of others through the barrier, where the free tea was given away to the heroes cluttered with packs and rifles: there was Charles with his second-lieutenant's star on his shoulder, his clothes caked with mud, his eyes pathetically blue and childish in his thin immature face. They went in a taxi-cab to North Street, and when Charles had bathed and put on civilian clothes he looked less than ever like a soldier.

It was when they were half-way through dinner that Charles burst forth suddenly, as though something he had been keeping bottled up would out willy-nilly: "I say, sir—"

"Damn it, Charles," said Hamer impatiently. "I'm not your commanding officer."

"I say, Father, this Russian business is pretty good. It puts a different look on things."

"In what way?"

"Well, in every way, surely."

"Charles, I try to use the word 'surely' sparingly. The longer I live the less I feel safe in saying surely this, surely that."

"But surely," cried Charles impetuously, "nothing but good can come of the workers' overthrowing a bloody tyranny."

"I can imagine a great many things coming of it that are not good at all," said Hamer reasonably. "It's many a long year since I've done a day's work as the Communists understand it. Possibly a man who has spent all those years cleaning out cowsheds or driving an obsolete Russian engine would therefore make a better hand than I would at running a government department, but frankly I doubt it."

Charles pushed aside his plate impatiently. "You throw cold water on everything that's young and courageous and experimental," he said, flushing.

"Cold reason, if you like," said Hamer. "Have you read Karl Marx?"

"I don't need to read Karl Marx to know that this is a grand turning-point in the world's history."

"*I have* read Karl Marx," Hamer went on relentlessly. He smiled; "When I talk to my colleagues, and to people in other parties, too, I think I must be the only man in the country who has done so. May I put you right on one point?"

"You don't want to put me right. You want to put me in the wrong," Charles declared.

Ann intervened. "Charles, Charles! Do you know there actually are moments when I think it would have been good to follow your father's advice? There's a confession now!"

Hamer leaned back in his chair, one hand in his pocket, one twiddling the stem of his glass. "The last thing I want, my dear boy," he said, "is to check the things that you call young and courageous and experimental. But there's nothing experimental about what is happening in Russia now. It was all laid down years ago, and we shall see an attempt to apply a cut-and-dried scheme of living worked out by a tired old mole who hadn't the first idea of living himself. You say the workers have overthrown a bloody tyranny, That's one way of looking at it. Another is to say that they have cut a nation's throat. You don't do that with impunity, Charles. Believe me, you let out a lot of good blood as well as bad. I'm for handing the sick man over to the doctors – drastic doctors if you like, with keen scalpels and deep cutting – but not to the slaughterers."

"Figures of speech!" said Charles. His thin face was working with a furious dislike. "You're an expert at them."

Hamer looked at him sadly, and felt a very old man. "As you like, Charles," he said with resignation. "But I've lived for more than half a century, and I've come to believe that there is more in life than bread-and-butter for what you call the workers, I believe they can have it – plenty of it – without destroying free art and science and letters. But you can't have a dictatorship without destroying those things, and if you can tell me how millions of men who have run riot can be controlled without dictatorship, I shall be glad to hear what you have to say."

But Charles had nothing to say except: "I thought you were a Socialist?" and to that Hamer made no answer.

So Hamer did not run after Communism, as so many Labour men did. What it had destroyed was clear. He waited to see what it would build, and had a pretty good idea what that would be. He wrote one of his swift journalistic pamphlets: "The Labour Highway and the Communist By-Road." It was scathingly reviewed by Alice Ryerson in a Labour newspaper. That was his first indication not only that Alice was writing but that she had a dangerous effective pen.

But he didn't mind this. His ambition was still restlessly stirring, and he hoped his stand against Communism, a doctrine which he knew would deeply infect his party, might draw upon him the eyes he still wished to attract. Arthur Henderson had resigned from the Cabinet. His sympathy with Russia had been too acute and too obvious. There was room for a Labour man of the first rank. When the year was a few months old Hamer gave up hope. And that was what 1918 was to him in retrospect: the end of what he had come to look upon frankly as a self-chosen degradation, the beginning of a series of attacks upon the Government, growing sharper and sharper as the year wore on through the despair of spring to the hope of autumn; this, and the return of Charles; and at last the end of the whole matter: the dawn of a peace which he envisaged with none of the delirium, none of the frantic hope, that turned London on November 11 into a whirling pandemonium.

Chapter Eighteen

"Come ye out from among them and be ye separate."

That was Hamer's war-cry as 1918 wore to a close. Once more he felt free and happy. He had cast off the shackles; he would run his own race.

Now while the country was still giddy with victory, not yet knowing the victory for bran and chaff, now while all things seemed possible and the prostrate enemy could still be looked upon as Golconda to be infinitely mined, the Government flew opportunely to the polls. "We have given you the victory. Now give us *carte blanche*. Keep our glorious Coalition in being. And if any candidate is against the Coalition, let him beware! We will not pin our coupon upon him, and then let him see what will happen to him."

And Hamer replied: "To hell with coupon and Coalition. Let Labour stand once more on its own feet. Come ye out from among them and be ye separate." And Labour came out, and was smitten hip and thigh. The Coalition went back with 478 members to back it. Labour had sixty-three. And Hamer Shawcross was not among them. After so many years, St. Swithin's turned him down.

"You're feeling better, my dear. You're looking better," Ann said, as they sat at breakfast in North Street. She smiled in the patient understanding way that had grown on her during the war. "I think you're feeling more honest."

Hamer looked up from the newspaper that was folded open beside his plate. He gave her back her smile. He liked this new Ann. She was not the girl he had married, in the sense that he was still, unchanged and unchangeably, the man who had married her. And she was not the disturbing, estranging person who had flamed into being when Charles went to school. He had come at times dangerously near to disliking that woman as certainly as he had loved the other. But this new

Ann – and not so new: she had been growing before his eyes for some years – was neither to be loved nor disliked. "The angel in the house." He had always thought it a clap-trap phrase; but it came as near as any to fitting this patient, tranquil woman, who, he felt, had not expended her fires but was diffusing them in a general spiritual warmth rather than blazing them away at a point of action.

"I think you're feeling more honest." She seemed to understand him as well as ever. "I am," he said. "Not that I ever felt very dishonest. There was need for Labour to be represented in the Cabinet, and I should have liked the job."

"Were you very disappointed?"

"Yes, I was. But now I think it's all for the best. Not to have been in the Cabinet may be an asset to a Labour man in the days that are coming."

She smiled again at his frank opportunism. "Well," she said, "I've no doubt that if you'd been in the Cabinet you'd have made an asset of that, just as you'll make an asset of not having been in it."

"All my assets will be no good," Hamer said. "I shall be slaughtered in St. Swithin's."

At that she opened her eyes. "Oh, my dear! I hope not! Surely not!"

"Do you remember," Hamer asked, "the little lecture I gave to Charles on the use of the word surely? No, no, my dear. Surely nothing in this wicked world. You know, you've lost touch, lost interest, with this game I'm playing. You don't appear to know that nine people in ten are going to hoot like Yahoos for this miraculous Government which has given them the victory. Bill Jones who lives by the gas-works at Bethnal Green isn't going to realize that it was he, sticking in the muck on the Western Front, and Tom Smith, and all the rest of them, who did the trick. He and his missus and all his pals were going to vote for the victorious Government, and we poor fools who tell the Government what to do with their coupon, we're going to get it in the neck."

"Oh, Hamer! I hope not."

"That's better. I won't deny you the consolation of hope." He poured himself more coffee. "You don't know the cream of the joke so far as St. Swithin's is concerned." He picked up a letter from beside his plate. "I got this this morning. It tells me the name of the coupon candidate – Coalition-Tory, to give him his official title – who's going to boot me out of my dear old seat. Would you like to guess?"

"How can I?"

"Alderman Sir Thomas Hannaway of Manchester."

Ann's hands, resting on the edge of the table, involuntarily clenched into white-knuckled fists. Her face darkened. She got up, walked away from the table, and sat down in a rocking-chair by the fire. I must not hate that man. I must not hate him. The words swam through her mind. She strove philosophically to see Tom Hannaway as a human soul in error, deserving her pity and understanding.

It was he who had ordered that the hose should be turned upon Pen. It was he who had insinuated himself into her father's business. She would never forget the pitiable state of old Hawley the last time she had seen him: fat, lethargic, dozing throughout the day by the sitting-room fire at The Limes, having nothing to do, conscious of impotence, uselessness, unimportance. That was in the early days of the war when she was recovering her health. She and Lizzie had gone to Manchester. She had been like a child, seeking a comfortable, known, secure environment, and what she had found had shocked her and made her worse. The old man was bald and paunchy and his face was mottled and ugly. She understood with poignant force the old phrase "senile decay." Lizzie had taken care to get her away as soon as possible. Hawley died soon afterwards, and she heard later with inexpressible disgust that Thomas Hannaway had bought The Limes and was living there. It seemed to her like a triumphal dance on old Hawley's grave.

And so Tom's Rolls-Royce was accommodated in the stable where she had so often watched Haworth grooming the horse that pulled the Artingstall diligence to town with an eager fair-haired child sitting beside her alert father, and in the drawing-room, whose gilt-fluted white chair-legs were inseparably mixed with winter afternoon teas in childhood, Tom's Polly spread out the table-games with cards and counters for Tom's delight.

All that Tom did was sumptuously in keeping with his Rolls-Royce; and army clothing contracts, executed in his own factories which he had set up long since to supply his multiple shops, had enabled him to lavish the gifts to his party and to wartime charities which had now been appropriately rewarded with a knighthood. The twenty thousand pounds – all his fortune – which Hawley left to Ann would have seemed small change to Tom.

This was the man. I must not hate him. He had injured Pen. He had injured Hawley. And now, Hamer said, he was likely to injure him. "Well," she said. "I should never have thought he was the sort of man you'd fear."

Hamer laughed. "No, my dear. I'm not afraid of Tom Hannaway. But I shall not be fighting against Tom Hannaway. 'We fight not against flesh and blood, but against principalities and powers, against darkness in high places.' Are you coming to see me slaughtered?"

"What shall we do about Charles?"

Lizzie and Alice Ryerson answered that between them.

Charles was at home, and was daily attending a hospital. Lizzie had made him her charge. All her life long Lizzie had flung herself into cause after cause. Now she flung herself into the cause of Charles. Well on towards seventy, as hale as a well-kept winter apple and as wrinkled and ruddily-pleasing to look at, she announced suddenly that she had bought a motor car and had learned to drive it. She made herself Charles's chauffeur, drove him to and from the hospital, and ran him about amid the last of the year in the Home Counties. That bobbed hair of hers which had been white and pleasing as a dandelion clock before she was thirty blew about her head, unconfined by any hat, as she drove and laughed and chattered, refusing to be overcome by the silent, emaciated, embittered young man by her side. She had fought so many fights: she was not going to be beaten in this one. At home she helped Charles up and down the stairs, put him to bed, helped him to dress. She would hardly suffer even Ann to give a hand with these things. Once, as he lay in bed, and she had brushed his long fair hair and given him a book to read, he suddenly put an arm round her neck and kissed her. He hadn't done that since he was a child, and the old woman's heart fluttered with joy. "D'you remember old Grandmother Ellen?" Charles asked.

"I should say I do," said Lizzie. "I remember how your father rushed over to Manchester one day and brought her back to my house in Ackroyd Park. That was the first time I set eyes on her, She didn't know what to make of him or me or life in general. We took her to a big political meeting that night. Eh! Those were days!"

Charles ignored her reminiscences. "You remind me of her," he said simply.

She knew what he meant. Charles had always been a clinging child.

He had clung to Ann, and he had clung to Ellen, and now, she thanked God, it looked as if he might cling to her. He had never been able to do without a woman who was stronger than he was himself. And so, when Ann raised the question of going North with Hamer for the election, Lizzie said: "Don't worry about Charles. You can leave him safely with me."

She drove Ann and Hamer to King's Cross, and when she had seen them on the train she wired to Alice Ryerson at Cwmdulais, inviting her to stay in North Street. It's my house, she said to herself. I can ask whom I like to stay in it. She was as tough as an old war-horse, but she wouldn't last for ever. Charles would want someone to cling to when she was gone, and she couldn't imagine anyone better than Alice Ryerson. Alice had all of Pen's independence and vigour, all of Arnold's solid reliability, and she fused these inherited qualities into something of her own, something heightened and made finer, polished and pointed in schools and college.

It was a drear December day, but before going back to North Street Lizzie drove about in the parks, full of dripping black naked trees and crawling mists, with lights springing up in houses and hotels, though it was not yet noon. She thought of her own happy runaway match, and of all she had seen since: young awkward Arnold Ryerson mooning after Ann, and Hamer Shawcross nipping in and carrying the girl off her feet, and now here were Arnold's daughter and Hamer's son ready, if she were not mistaken, to go on with this everlasting fascinating game of living that was much of a muchness whatever causes one fought for, whatever, for the moment, seemed the triumphant or the losing side. She laughed at herself as an old schemer who should know better, not seeing how thoroughly and swiftly her schemes were to work to their end.

Not that it mattered, she said to herself when Charles and Alice came in radiant a week later. Whatever she had done or left undone, this would have happened. It was only a matter of time.

Alice had borrowed the car, saying she would like to take Charles for a drive, and they came back from a registry office married. Lizzie looked at Charles hobbling on his crutches along the narrow passage of the North Street house, his face, raw and ugly, twisted by a smile, and at Alice, so small and tough, preceding him as if pushing a way for him; and she knew that this was a good thing, that whatever Charles might do could never be done alone, but must be done in the protective shadow of some woman stronger than himself.

"What will you do when you are beaten?" Ann asked. It was taken for granted now that Hamer would be beaten. His diagnosis of the situation had been accurate enough. Tom Hannaway had come primed with all the paradisaical promises, and Hamer had little to set against them except the bleak fact that he refused any longer to support the government that made them.

Ann took no part in the election. She remained at The Hut. She would not have even a daily maid in to help with the work. She had come up here not for a political fight. She didn't want any more political fights. She wanted rest, quiet, the loneliness of the moors, and all of Hamer's company that she could get. She got a good deal of it. She had never known him take an election as he was taking this one: it was almost as if he could not take it seriously. There were days when he did not address a single meeting, did not so much as bother to go up to Bradford. "This is not my time," he said "I shall come back when their bellies are empty and their jobs are gone, and they know a thing or two about the facts of life. They're not getting those from Tom Hannaway."

So after dinner they would wash up their dishes and make up their fire, and Hamer would read aloud, or they would sit quiet, listening to the wind blowing through the firs and larches he had planted when the house was built and which now ringed it in with a dense plantation.

Thus they sat one night, he reading and smoking, Ann sitting on the other side of the hearth. Presently he looked up from his book and covertly watched her. He had marvelled of late at her capacity to be still. She would sit for an hour at a time without moving or speaking. But now she caught his eye, and they smiled at one another, and he said: "What were you thinking about?"

"I was thinking how we rush into things," she said, "how we don't wait. I've been such an impetuous woman." She dug out an old affectionate phrase they used once to bandy between them: "Sorry you ever met me?"

He shook his head. "No. If it all had to come over again, I wouldn't want it any different. Would you?"

"I'd want myself to be different," she said. "I would want not to rush into things so. I was never anything much, you see, but I always acted

as if I were – as if what I thought and believed were terribly important.
Do you know this?" She recited in a low hesitating voice:

"Only since God doth often make
Of lowly matter for high uses meet,
I throw me at His feet;
There will I lie until my Maker seek
For some mean stuff whereon to show His skill.
Then is my time."

"That's very beautiful," Hamer said. "Who wrote it?"
"George Herbert."
"It's very beautiful," he repeated.
"We need to do less," she said with apparent inconsequence. "The
world is dying of causes and committees. Why can't we just love one
another and leave one another alone?"

.She did not seem to expect an answer. Her eyes turned back to the
fire and she fell again into reverie.

This was the last long evening he spent with her in The Hut, and
it seemed to him, whenever he was there in the years that came after,
that he could never exorcise, even should he wish to do so, the two
memories that so poignantly remained: the memory of the girl who
came to the place when it was a hut indeed, the girl so eager for sen-
sual life and struggle, with whom he had lain through the long snowy
night; and the memory of the woman with her life all but done, nostalgically dreaming of another world, under the delusion that she was
thinking of a possible life in this one.

When he was in Bradford conducting his half-hearted campaign Ann
walked alone far and wide over the winter moors, taking her meals in
the tough stony Yorkshire cottages, coming home flushed and tired,
more tired than she cared to admit, flushed with more than exercise.
Hamer noticed her exhaustion; and it was with this in mind, that,
when she asked what he would do when he was defeated, he replied:
"Take you for a long leisurely holiday. I've been working hard now
for a good many years, and while the Government is making a mess
of things I think I shall clear out of the country. You must come with
me. We'll go abroad and stay abroad. We'll wander about for a year."

She raised the old objection: "What about Charles?"

Hamer was quite willing to leave Charles in Lizzie's care; and then came the letter from Lizzie to Hamer, and a joint letter signed by Alice and Charles to Ann.

Ann suspected that all but the signature had been composed by Alice. It was a sensible letter. Alice had given up three years of her life to Pen, and now Pen herself, having learned to feel her way about every nook and corner of Cwmdulais, was anxious for the girl to go. It all sounded true. Ann could imagine how Pen would wrestle with and overcome her disability and how she would hate to have the girl, for whom she and Arnold had planned so much, tied up in the Rhondda Valley. "I can find plenty of journalistic work," Alice wrote, "and I can keep Charles occupied and interested."

It was all without rhetoric or emotion, and when Ann had read it she said: "This has made me feel very happy, my dear." Hamer did not feel so happy, but he kept his opinions to himself and was glad at least that there would now be no obstacle in the way of their holiday. On polling-day he went up to town armoured with irony, cynicism, philosophy – what you will – prepared to be without a job on the morrow. As he was leaving, Ann said: "I've never met Sir Thomas Hannaway. Would you like to ask him to lunch tomorrow? Then we could get back to London in the afternoon."

He had expected to be defeated, and the defeat was crushing. He was out by 12,637 votes. In the very enormity of the figures there was a sort of consolation. He wanted a rest. Well, this justified one!

It was very dull in the counting-room. He recalled the first time he had stood there, with the gas and fire blazing, when he was young and impulsive, buoyed upon visions that enabled him to ride gallantly over the crests without suspecting, as he so often did now, the dark engulfing deeps beneath them. Ann had been there, and Lizzie Lightowler not even middle-aged, and Pen and Arnold and little fanatical Jimmy Newboult. Old Buck Lostwithiel was still alive and kicking like the devil, and Lettice Melland, who had not yet married Buck's son, was lit like a flame with youth and beauty. And now none of them was there but himself, and all this business which had seemed so romantic had faded into routine, something tiresome that he was anxious to have done with.

When the result was announced, Tom Hannaway smiled and put

on his big overcoat with the fur inside, and Polly put on her big coat with the fur outside, and the three of them stepped on to the balcony. The cheers surged up toward Tom as he moved to the front to say his few words; and then there were a few half-hearted calls for Shawcross. He remembered how, that first time, they had borne him off, shoulder-high, in the light of torches. Well, he knew what they would like now: they would like to put torches to his pyre because he had told them the truth. Groans and hisses filled the night when he stepped forward, and here and there men shouted "Traitor!" He had difficulty even in getting a hearing, and when he did his words were few: "Men and women of St. Swithin's: Many years ago, with the help of you who are now shouting against me out there in the night, I won this historic seat for Labour. Historic! You and I between us have made history here in St. Swithin's. Now, for a moment, you have put back the clock. The clock of history is not like the clock in this tower above me. It goes backwards as well as forwards. It will not be long, my friends, before you awaken from your dream and find that the clock is slow. Then you will want me again. I shall be ready. Good-bye now for the moment. I shall be back."

This was a true prophecy. Five years were to pass. Then he came back, and St. Swithin's was faithful to him till the coronet was placed on his head and the Viscount Shawcross of Handforth needed to trouble himself with votes no more.

Sir Thomas Hannaway liked to drive his own Rolls-Royce. He liked to see Polly in her fine feathers leaning back among the crimson cushions surrounded by ivory fittings. The car made a cavalcade in itself; and it was Jimmy Newboult who once said, looking at Tom and Polly in the sumptuous interior, that it was a cavalcade of ivory, apes and peacocks.

"One can't really dislike him – or her either," Ann said, when the cavalcade had come and gone the next day. "I'm glad I've met them. They're so childlike."

To be Thomas Hannaway, whose face had launched a thousand shops, was something. To be Sir Thomas Hannaway, up to the eyes in affairs, with The Limes to live in in Manchester and an Elizabethan house in the green Cheshire countryside, with Consolidated Public Utilities growing under his watchful eye into something vaster than even he had dreamed of controlling – this was much more; but to be Sir Thomas Hannaway, M.P. – this was almost more than Tom could bear.

He was kindness itself to Hamer. He gave the feeling that his tender heart was nearly broken at having done him out of his seat. Anything he could do, Sir Thomas let it be understood, he would do with all his will. His concerns had ramifications from one end of the country to the other, and there were plenty of niches where he could fit in a man of talent.

"No, Sir Thomas—" Hamer began.

"Damn it, lad," said Tom magnanimously, "Hannaway to you." "Well, I was going to say," said Hamer, "that I'm a sort of professional politician. I've never mixed things, and I'm afraid it's too late for me to start now."

Lunch was over, and Sir Thomas produced a crocodile-skin cigar-case stuffed with cigars of magnificent proportions. "What are you going to do then?" he demanded, "look for another seat? You're in the wrong party, you know, lad. I warned you years ago, when I came to the old hut you had up here."

"No," Hamer answered, "I shan't look for another seat. St. Swithin's is the only seat for me, and I warn you, Hannaway, I'll have you out of it at the first dawn of reason. Meantime, I shall take a holiday."

"Eh, Polly, listen to that! 'Oliday! When did I last take an 'oliday?" And Polly, playing up to the vision of a hard-driven Tom, ignoring his three-day week-ends in Cheshire or the Lakes, shook her head, sadly, wobbling the jelly of her neck and setting her earrings atremble. "Not for years and years!"

"Yes," said Hamer to Ann when they were gone, "they're childlike, I agree. They're a couple of greedy gluttonous children, gorged with sticky sweets."

"There was no reason," Hamer wrote in his diary, "why Ann and I should not have waited for the spring weather before setting out, but, once we had made up our minds to go, something urged us to go quickly. And so I can look back with inexpressible joy to those few months alone with her."

It was better every way that they should go at once. Hamer admitted to himself that it would be embarrassing to Charles and Alice to have him about the house. It was Lizzie's place, and she could please herself what she did with it. Clearly, she wanted the young people to stay with her, just as she had wanted Ann in Ackroyd Park and him and Ann here in this house when they first came to London. When he got back, he would do what he had wanted to do for a long time: find a London house for himself and Ann.

Ann was quietly happy, like a self-possessed child on holiday. She had spent very little time out of England, and the mere foreignness of things was enough to please her. During the winter months they moved about without rush or bustle among the smaller, less frequented places of the French Riviera. They were received as eagerly as the first swallows. It was delicious to wake up in the mornings and to find the sun so often shining on blue water and to smell the growing mimosa that she had never before known except as a feathery joy in shops or hawkers' baskets. Through the advancing year they wandered along the Mediterranean coast into Italy, and from Venice Hamer wrote to Ernst Horst in Berlin. He did not tell Ann that he wanted Horst to see her because he was one of the greatest European specialists in tuberculosis. She knew only that Horst was a Socialist whom Hamer had met before the war at international conferences. They had liked one another and had corresponded in English and German until the war came.

It was a long time before Horst's reply reached them, and while they were waiting for it Ann enjoyed the sunshine of the Lido and became brown and vigorous-looking, but by now Hamer was in a ferment of worry. This hale skin did not deceive him. A little effort exhausted her, and at nights she coughed unceasingly. He would steal back into her bedroom after she had left it, and examine her handkerchiefs in the laundry-basket, looking for the tell-tale flecks of blood. At last he found them, and then he hurried to the telegraph office and sent an urgent wire to Horst. When he got back to the hotel, Horst's letter was there. It came from a village in the Harz Mountains that Hamer had never heard of, and said that Horst would be delighted to renew an acquaintance which he had never ceased to think of with pleasure. They left Venice the next morning.

Of the many books that Hamer Shawcross wrote, the only one that was not in some way political was the memoir of his wife. He wrote it to assuage some need in himself. It was Charles who induced him to publish it: Charles who had inherited so little from his father save the artist's touch which in the older man was never given free play. We must go to Hamer himself for the story of Ann's last days and death:

From the time we left Venice (he wrote) I knew in my heart that we were moving towards her grave, and so, I am sure, did she. But she did not complain. She never lost her tranquillity. It was early in May. We travelled through orchard-lands that were like foaming seas of pink and white breaking upon the green background of the land, and no regret was forced from her that she must soon be leaving a world capable of so much enchantment. All she said was: "You know, my dear, Browning shouldn't have longed to be in England in April. I think it's wiser to take beauty and happiness where you find them. We should just thank God for allowing us to be alive in a world of such lovely appearances, and have done with it."

It was late one afternoon when we reached the little station which Horst had told me was the nearest to his village. Ann had been sleeping for an hour, and when I awoke her she started up violently and sprang to her feet. "Oh, I overslept," she cried, and before I could stop her she reached up for her heavy dressing-case and swung it off the rack. It slipped from her hand on to the seat, and she suddenly leaned forward, collapsed upon it. I saw blood trickle from her lips.

Horst was at the station, dressed in very old and shabby clothes of a professional man, and with him were two tall young men wearing German country clothes: stained leather shorts, jerseys, and feathered hats. They all three clicked their heels and bowed, and he introduced the boys as his sons Axel and Georg.

I explained what had happened, and while Horst and I helped Ann on to the platform Georg and Axel took the luggage. Ann was laid flat on the table in the little waiting-room. Horst took off his old frock coat and placed it under her head. I saw that his shirt was thin and worn, torn here and there. He bent over Ann and murmured: "Be tranquil, *Liebchen*." She was tranquil enough.

Presently the two boys, who had disappeared, returned and whispered to their father. They went out again, and when they came back they carried a few planks nailed together, with a thick feather-bed resting on them. They gently lifted Ann and placed her on this stretcher, then carried it out to where a small rugged horse stood attached to a flat cart. The stretcher was laid on the cart. All these improvisations had happened with speed and without fuss. Horst left his coat folded under Ann's head on the mattress. Without self-consciousness, he took the horse's head and we started off, Georg and Axel carrying a suitcase on either side of the cart, and I walking behind.

We walked for about three miles, adapting our pace to the slow amble of the horse. It was uphill all the way, at first through tidy vegetable gardens and orchards, through blooming hawthorns and laburnums. The sun was shining strongly and the air was full of the song of birds. Then the acclivity sharpened and we were in the woods, dark with firs, silent, and resinous to the smell. The sun did not reach us and the sky was a blue strip unwinding over our heads. I saw that Ann's eyes were open, fixed on the shining of this inaccessible heaven.

It took us nearly an hour to reach the village where Horst lived. It stood on a plateau cleared in the forest. All the cottages were wooden. You stood there and looked down steeply over the dark heads of the trees climbing up from the valley below, and then, looking behind you, you saw the forest climbing still to the distant blue of the sky.

There was something enchanted about the place. All the German fairy-tales I had read as a child seemed incarnate in this forest, in these wooden houses, in these two grave blue-eyed boys walking on either side of the country cart, in the geese on the green, and in the tall fair-haired girl who came towards us out of one of the cottages. Horst briefly introduced her as Marta. Then he spoke to her urgently and rapidly, and she ran back to the cottage.

Ann was lifted from the cart on the stretcher and laid upon the rough lawn, surrounded with flowering apple trees that stood before the cottage. The two boys, in that silent purposeful way of theirs, went in with the luggage. Their father followed them, and I was left alone outside with Ann. Her eyes were shut now. I sat on a corner of the feather-bed and took her hand in mine. It was limp and unresponsive. The sunset was washing over the valley down below me, and near at hand a blackbird was singing in an apple tree. Presently he flew away, shaking down a little flurry of over-ripe petals. I thought of what Ann had said about taking beauty where you find it; and I realized why beauty made Browning wish to be somewhere else. We want to escape from our own mortality which beauty mocks.

Horst came out with Georg and Axel, and they carried Ann into the house. A great bed had been dismantled in an upstairs room, brought down, and set up just inside the window of a downstairs room looking on to the orchard. Then we all went out, and the girl Marta remained to undress Ann and put her to bed. Axel and Georg went away together to return the borrowed horse and cart and feather-bed. Horst and I were left alone. He had put on his old shabby coat. I noticed now how worn his shoes were, how drawn and grey and anxious he was. I had not seen him for about six years. Then he had been debonair, self-confident, with the look and manner of a man who knew himself the master of his job. All this was gone. We sat in a room at the back of the house, and for a long time not a word was spoken. Then he rose to his feet and said: "So! Where now are our dreams, my friend?" He stood between me and the light, looking out upon the darkening climbing forest; then abruptly he turned and walked out of the room. I could hear him and Marta moving about next door, talking occasionally in low tones.

In a few moments Marta came into the room where I was. "*Sprechen Sie deutsch?*" she asked. "*Ja,*" I said; and she then apologized for having left me so long without food. She brought me coffee and bread, and neither was good. Then she went back to Horst.

I felt intolerably lonely, and when I had eaten I left the house and walked down towards the road by which we had come. I longed for someone to talk to, and hoped I might meet Georg and Axel. It was now dark among the trees, and a river of stars was flowing down the lane of the sky. Now and then I could hear the furtive scurry of nocturnal creatures and the melancholy calling of owls. The night was warm, and I sat on a log and waited for the boys.

Presently, far off, I could hear the sound of their feet, marching to a tune plucked out of a mandolin. It was a sad nostalgic tune. I could not distinguish the words they were singing. When I got to my feet and hailed them the music stopped. They greeted me with grave politeness, and when I urged them to go on singing they did so self-consciously for a verse or two and then stopped altogether. We returned in silence to the house where now candles were burning. On the threshold they simultaneously clicked their heels, bowed, said: "Excuse, please," and disappeared I know not where. I saw nothing more of them or of Marta that night. I learned later that Marta spent the night on a pallet bed in Ann's room.

I endured an agonizing hour in the candle-lit back room before

Horst came in, shut the door quietly behind him and drew the curtains. He took a half-smoked porcelain pipe from the mantelpiece, lit it, and sat down. "So!" he said. "I have done all that I can. She is asleep. She is comfortable."

He said no more for a time, and I could not put to him the question that was in my heart. But he knew it was there, and presently he said, looking past me into a shadowy corner of the room: "You will understand, my friend, that there is not much I can do. I am not the great Dr. Horst. I do not dispose of the resources of a famous hospital. No. I am a poor man in a poor country. I have lost everything – except my knowledge, you understand."

He pulled for a time at the gurgling nearly-empty pipe, and then went on: "Shawcross, my friend, I could say to you: 'Send her to Switzerland.' I could tell you: 'In such and such a sanatorium in Switzerland there is the great Dr. So-and-so.' I could tell you what he would charge you, and I could describe to you every detail of what he could do to make her live, and how long he could make her live. My friend, it would not be long."

It would not be long. I remembered a night in our North Street house when my wife, sleeping, put an arm around my neck and murmured: "Always, always!" Time crumbles our everlasting covenants: this was the end of always.

"Here," said Horst, tapping the dottle from his pipe and laying it carefully in a tin, "here it would not be so long. We have not much food, not much butter or milk or eggs. And I – I have not the resources, you understand. So! You will decide, my friend. What I have is yours."

I got up and took his hand. "Horst," I said, "you and I were never enemies, nor can we ever be enemies."

"I am no man's enemy," said Horst. "If I am the enemy of the wickedness in myself I am busy enough."

He went out to look at Ann, and then he made some more of the bad coffee. I put a tin of tobacco on the table, and he half-filled his pipe diffidently. We talked far into the night. Marta, he explained, was Axel's wife. She would look after Ann. She was a trained nurse. Axel was an artist – "but I ask you, friend, what is an artist now? There is a Chinese saying: 'If you have a loaf, sell half and buy lilies,' but if you have only lilies, like Axel, who will buy them that you may have bread?"

Georg wished to be a farmer – "like my father," said Horst. "Yes, before I am a famous doctor I am a farmer's son, and I am glad for Georg. It is good to love the land."

It was Georg who had found this cottage, where he had a few goats and geese and a pig, and here he had brought Axel and Marta when both were near to starving, and here Horst himself had come. I never discovered what misfortune had overwhelmed so celebrated a man.

Our talk ranged away from the family, but I could not get him to discuss political matters. That one abrupt exclamation: "Where now are our dreams?" had given me a glimpse into his disillusion, and it was only when the night was all but done and he was taking me upstairs to bed that he said: "There is no peace, you understand, Shawcross, no peace anywhere except in a man's own heart."

I did not expect to sleep that night, but I did. I was exhausted in body and spirit, and I slept heavily. When I awoke I was surprised to hear sounds of music. I looked at my wrist-watch and saw that it was nearly eleven o'clock. I jumped out of bed and ran to the window, to see a surprising sight. Ann, on a long wicker chair on wheels, was reclining in the sunshine under the apple blossom. Over the back of the chair was a blanket boldly striped in green and white and yellow. Axel Horst lay on the grass at her feet, plucking at the strings of his mandolin and humming softly. Down below them the dark green fleece of the forest fell away to the valley full of morning sunshine. It was a scene so unexpected and idyllic that my heart jumped with joy. All that had happened yesterday seemed like a nightmare from which I had awakened to a beautiful reality. Then I heard Horst's footsteps coming up the stair. He knocked at the door, looked into the room, and came over to stand at my side.

"That is lovely," he said. "You will remember this, Shawcross: that you brought your dear one to an old friend's house, and it was a very poor house, but the good God made many lovely things instead of the things that your old friend would have given you if he could."

We stood in silence for a moment, and then I asked him if Axel would paint Ann's portrait, as she was there, under the apple-blossom with the green grass at her feet and the gay spring sky of blue and white over her head. And, working throughout the next week, which was a miracle of blossom and sunshine, Axel did this, so that always now, for me, Ann sits there with the gay bold rug behind her shoulders, her hair, which never lost its lustre, clouded against the apple tree, and

Axel's mandolin thrown in for signature, dropped carelessly against her feet as though, playing, she had tired and lain back to rest. It is there to remind me always that Ann died among friends.

She chose to die there. Horst and I told her the alternatives, and she said: "Why should I give up so much peace for a little more life? Dr. Horst, you have heard the saying that man is a soul dragging a carcass about with him?"

Horst was sitting on a chair at her side on the grass, his finger on her pulse. He nodded gravely. "So!" he said. "Epictetus is right."

"Well," she said. "I'm tired of dragging. Let me drop my old carcass here."

Horst put her hand down gently and looked at her with infinite tenderness. "Not old," he said. "Not old." He himself cannot have been much older than Ann. He looked like her father.

She did not last long. May passed into June, and the disease went its way of attack and recovery. Sometimes she was out in the sunshine, wan and exhausted; and sometimes day followed day when she was on her bed indoors, with Horst and Marta hardly leaving her side. The boys, shy elusive creatures, came and went, doing every conceivable office. They cleaned my shoes and tidied my room, and if I found them at it they coloured, said, "Please, excuse!" finished what they were at, and disappeared. Now, thinking of these things, remembering that brief period when love and death went hand-in-hand, I sometimes wonder whether politics, which should implement the best desires of humanity, do not rather come between men and the untutored goodness of their hearts.

We had reached mid-June, summer's height, when Ann died. The apple-blossom had all fallen and the roses had come, and still the wonderful weather held, day after day of beneficent sunshine and birdsong and gentle winds. Ann, on her reclining-chair, had been moved out into the garden. She had had a number of bad hæmorrhages and was very weak. I lay on the warm grass beside her, drowsy with sunlight. Georg's geese came strutting on to the green, and Ann struggled to a sitting position to look at them. She began to laugh. "Look at the way they go," she said. "So pompous, so political."

The silly creatures, as though they understood and resented her words, turned with fatuous waddling dignity and began to retire in single file. There was something so comic about this solemn recessional that Ann's laughter seized me, too. "The delegates are leaving the platform," I said. That made her laugh the more heartily. It was so long since we had laughed at anything together. Horst, who was watching us from the window, came hurrying out. "No, no! Please!" he cried urgently; but Ann had reached the point of paroxysm: she could not stop laughing. Her whole body was shaking, and presently she began to gasp for breath. I put my arms round her. I was holding her, in the sunshine, under the roses, when her life spouted out.

Georg made the coffin. His hammer sounded through the long-drawn-out twilight of that midsummer day. The next day Horst and I lifted her into it, and Axel and Marta covered the coffin with roses laid upon sombre boughs of fir which they brought from the forest. The day after that Axel came up the hill, leading the same rugged pony, drawing the same flat cart, which had carried her from the station. He had pulled boughs from the firs on his way up, and the coffin was placed upon these, which strewed the cart. Then he brought out of the house a great bunch of roses, tied with green and white silk ribbons which I had seen fluttering from his mandolin. He laid this on the coffin.

Then we went, Horst leading the pony, I behind the cart, and behind me Marta, Georg and Axel walking together. The forest was cool and full of resinous scents, and the little spear-tips of the trees were lifted into a sky as blue as the periwinkle-flowers that Ann had planted at The Hut.

Down in the valley, we jolted over a level-crossing near the station and came soon to the cemetery. It was a peaceful place, near a stream, with willows growing along the banks. We stood there till the grave was filled, and then Axel stepped up to me and handed me the big bunch of roses, tied with green and white ribbon. "Excuse – please!" he said, and bowed. I took the flowers and laid them on the loose earth, and I stood there for a moment looking down at the alien grave of one who had been so dear and familiar. Alien? I remembered what Ann had said a few weeks ago: "It's wiser to take beauty and happiness where you find them."

Horst laid a hand on my shoulder. "My friend," he said, "your poet Meredith has this line: 'Into the breast that gave the rose shall I with shuddering fall?' So! All the world is the vesture of God. In Germany also we have roses. Leave her with us."

*

Hamer was glad that he had been alone with Ann at the last. He had written to Charles and Lizzie, but there was no possibility of their travelling to Germany. Charles's wounds were still too serious for that, and Lizzie would not leave him to Alice's sole care. Alice was already busy, doing what she could to earn a living for them both, and she was helping Charles to forget his pain and bitterness by encouraging in him his one talent, which was a writer's. There was something in Charles's nature which caused other people to make plans for his future. You had not to know him long before you realized that whatever talent he might possess would have to be stirred up; and just as Hamer had planned for him a diplomatic career, so Alice now planned a career in letters. She did not imagine that Charles would ever write successful popular books; his talent was small and twisted with bitterness. She was prepared to make the money if he would make the reputation; and now, as well as her left-wing journalistic work, she began a novel. Even Charles knew nothing about it. If he had seen the title-page, he would have read: "Death Speaks Softly," by Gabrielle Minto.

The letters from Charles and Alice were not very informative, and Hamer knew nothing of all this. Nor did he go home to find out. At first, he thought of returning to England. Dr. Horst, with Axel, Georg and Marta, walked with him down to the little station on the day after the funeral. Horst and Georg waved good-bye. Axel and Marta travelled with him as far as Hanover. They were beside themselves with delight. Hamer had insisted on paying Axel fifty pounds for the portrait of Ann. He knew that this was the only way in which he could make any of them accept a recompense for all they had done. Axel seemed as if he could not believe there was so much money left in the world, and now he and Marta were going to scrounge for paints and brushes and canvases, and buy presents for Horst and Georg.

Hamer said good-bye to them when they reached the city, and the next day he took train for the Hook of Holland, intending to cross to Harwich. As the train stood in the station at Utrecht, he leaned out of the window, and there walking down the platform with his nose in a newspaper was Vanderwinter, the Dutch Socialist, whom he had met many a time before the war. They began to talk hastily, as people will when the whistle may blow at any moment. "Ha! Horst! I've lost sight of him," said Vanderwinter. "Where is he? What's he doing?"

There was so much that Hamer wanted to say to this excellent old friend, that he suddenly pulled his cases off the rack and leapt to the platform as the train began to move. "I'm not in a hurry," he said. "I'm not in Parliament now, you know. I'll stay here for tonight."

He stayed for a week. There were so many people Vanderwinter wanted him to meet, there was so much to discuss, there was a whole social cosmogony to be mapped amid clouds of tobacco smoke and endless talk.

"You ought to find time to go to Antwerp and see Der Groot," Vanderwinter said on the last night of his stay in Utrecht.

Hamer laughed. "And Der Groot will want me to see Claesens at the Hague."

"Why not?" Vanderwinter asked. "You're a rich man without a job."

Why not? The next morning Hamer set off to see Der Groot, with Vanderwinter's "Why not?" still in his ears. He would perhaps never have a chance like this again. The tide would swing back in England. He would oust Tom Hannaway from St. Swithin's. He felt that in his bones. Then all the fret and hurry would begin again. So much to do. So much to do. There might even be a Labour Government next time. Looking at the flat landscape streaming past the window, he meditated on this supreme ambition which was never far from his mind: to be a member of His Majesty's Government. Foreign Secretary. He sometimes thought he would rather be Foreign Secretary than Prime Minister. All these distracted lands of Europe, all the lands of the world, the places he had seen as a youth. They began to flow through his mind as the landscape flowed past his eyes: scraps of half-remembered experience: the mad old Spanish woman with her fountains and parrots in Buenos Aires; that chap Carradus with whom he had worked in the mines of South Africa. Before he had reached Antwerp, he had resolved to travel again, as extensively, and even more intensively. That was one thing a Foreign Secretary should do. If he didn't do it now, the chance would never come again; and, as Vanderwinter said: Why not?

Vanderwinter had called him a rich man. He did not know how rich he was. Ann's will reached him at The Hague, posted by Lizzie. Ann had inherited £10,000 when she was twenty-one, and she had never used more than the interest of this money. On Hawley's death she inherited another £20,000. Her will was in one sentence: "I bequeath all I die possessed of to my dear husband, John Hamer Shawcross." He read the date on this will with inexpressible emotion. It was the date of the day after their marriage. Sitting in the lounge of his comfortable hotel, with the music of a dance-band in his ears and the heat of the summer oppressing him, he could recall every shade and detail of that morning. There was heavy snow on the ground at Baildon and they plunged through it from the shack to take their breakfast at the old Malt Shovel inn. They had intended to bring up the furniture for Moorland Cottage, but the snowdrifts were too deep, and he had gone back to the hut and begun to write *Tyler, Ball and Company*. He had sent her off to her Aunt Lizzie's in Bradford. She was sad to go, and all her thought had been of him. She wanted to pour out upon him, whom as yet she knew so little, all that she had. And so she had written this. He looked at the faded ink, the signatures of the two witnesses: Lizzie Lightowler and old Marsden, who had been in his grave long since. "My dear husband." He thought of the many times he had vexed her, and of the bitter years when they had run so far apart. But she had let it stand. "My dear husband." Always, always. More than ever, he did not want to return to England. He wanted to travel and forget.

He was away for nearly four years. It was a different journey this time. He travelled as far east as Japan, as far west as California. Wherever he went doors were open. He talked with politicians of every breed and brand, with scientists and teachers and journalists, with artists, writers, dockers and workers in the mines and fields. His pocket was full of journalistic contracts. For the serial rights of *World Survey* an American syndicate paid him a sum that many good writers do not make in a lifetime. He came back a richer man than he set out: richer in money, in knowledge, in contacts with the great figures of the modern world. Now, even more than when his first odyssey ended, he could say: "I know what I'm talking about." It was during this journey that he wrote his memoir of Ann. Throughout the last of these four wander-years he had the company of Jimmy Newboult. Colonel James Newboult was as poor as a church mouse. Outside his own country, he knew nothing except what the landscape looked like between two hedges of barbed wire in France. In that year there was a great deal which he wouldn't have chosen for himself: all these theatres and concerts and visits to picture galleries; these week-ends with people who, Jimmy felt sure, could teach him nothing about "the working-class angle," which was all he thought mattered; and when, taking his courage in both hands, he asked Hamer what he was getting out of it, Hamer laughed and said what he had said so long ago to Arnold Ryerson: "Sweetness and light, Jimmy, sweetness and light." He added: "Those are not things that have greatly distinguished British Foreign Secretaries. I wonder what effect it might have had on the mind of Lord North if he had sat in American drawing-rooms and knew what the Americans were painting and writing and singing?"

Jimmy scratched his blazing head. "You get the craziest notions, Chief," he said. "And 'oo the 'ell was Lord North?"

"The man whose birthday all good Americans should observe as Founder's Day," said Hamer. "He gave America away with a packet of tea."

"Ah, the Boston Tea Party!" cried Jimmy. A cliché always cleared his mind.

But if Jimmy was sometimes perplexed, he was always sensitive to his good fortune, and when he had seen the great ports of the American seaboard, and gone down into the Southern States, and crossed the desert to California, and gone up into Canada, and so home along the St. Lawrence and across the Atlantic to Liverpool, he was filled with a new devotion to the man who was still, to him, the crusader, the liberator, the youth with the blazing sword – Youth itself with its blazing sword – consumed with a passion to burn out the tares from England's green and pleasant land.

From Liverpool they did not go straight to London. They arrived in June 1923, and a name in the *Liverpool Echo*, which Hamer was reading as they took lunch at an hotel, changed his plans. "Jimmy," he said, "I don't think I ever told you that the first time I appeared in St. Swithin's – that time when Arnold Ryerson was the candidate – they tried to bribe me out of it?"

Jimmy shook his head. "That's nothing new. They tried it on Keir Hardie in Mid-Lanark."

"The gentleman who came to me," said Hamer, "was Tom Hannaway, now Sir Thomas, who holds the seat. I am reminded of it by seeing his name here. Sir Thomas has a horse running in the Derby today. He calls the beast St. Swithin's. If it's beaten I shall regard it as an omen – a bad omen for Sir Thomas, and I shall go straight through to Bradford and have a meeting, June or no June, and tell people why Sir Thomas is going out at the next election. It's time I made a speech in England again."

St. Swithin's was beaten that afternoon, and Hamer rang through to the secretary of the St. Swithin's Divisional Labour Party. He held his meeting the next Saturday night. The years had done their work, as the years will. He had been content to take them for his allies and leave it all to them. Now he stepped in and pointed the moral of what they had destroyed, constructed and subverted. There were no shouts of "Traitor!" There were few cheers. He did not play for them. He played for gravity, for warning. Five years of peace – and where was the flow of gold that was to be tapped out of Germany's anæmic veins? Five years of peace – and where were the jobs that were to put butter on their bread? Five years of peace – and who, in a world restless, troubled, feverish, would dare to say that in five more years peace – even such a moulting, poverty-stricken peace as they had – would still be with them?

"I come back to you after four years of journeying through the earth. I have been out like Noah's dove scanning the face of the waters. Now I come back, and ah! my friends, I do not come back with an olive-branch. The waters are not abated. Look where I will, they are high with menace. Our ark is still adrift; the rain of misfortune still pelts. You know that. You are soaked to the skin. Four and a half years of Coalition government, and the chill drops still fall: strikes, unemployment, less coming into your pockets, more going out of them, and over it all the thickening cloud of international distrust. Are the nations nearer to one another than they were in November, 1918? Ask your member. You will find him somewhere on the road between Epsom and Ascot. You will find him in a green paddock, wearing a grey top-hat, with a carnation in his buttonhole and spats on his feet. Go to him, and ask him what he has been doing during the last few years to learn of the chill winds that are rising throughout the world and that are about to fall on you with blizzard force. I have not come to you with comfortable doctrine. I have come to warn you, my friends, to look out for squally weather and to say to you: Choose your pilot well. I have seen the world. I know what I am talking about. Well, then. There will be an election soon. I shall come here, and this time I shall stay here."

This was the man who, that January morning in the following year, walked out of his house in Half Moon Street: Hamer Shawcross, P.C., M.P., His Majesty's Minister of Ways and Means.

Chapter Nineteen

Pen Ryerson came out of the house in Horeb Terrace and turned her sightless face up to the sky. Grey clouds hung low over the valley, and the wind had a knifey edge. Pen's face was as grey as the clouds, as sharp-edged as the wind. She was not one of those whose blind eyes retain the illusion of sight. You had only to look at the perished balls to know that she was blind; and this seemed to intensify every other feature of her face. You could almost see her listening: her head had a way of turning to this side and that to permit her ears to catch every whisper of sound. Her nostrils were sharpened, pinched in, as if with incessant sniffing of the breeze. The blindness did not dim the alertness of her look. She seemed on the strain to use to the full the senses that were left to her.

Now, with her face upturned to the sky, she listened to the wind and sniffed the air, and could picture as clearly as though she saw it the landscape of Cwmdulais: the pithead machinery with its wheels not turning; the empty sidings down on the railway; the rows of squat cottages with grey slate roofs and the grey clouds pressing down close upon them. She could imagine the wind blowing all in one direction the smoke that curled out of the chimneys, smoke from coal that the men got by burrowing into the hillsides and making lucky strikes. And she could picture the men themselves: sitting by the fire, lounging at the corners, queueing up at the Labour Exchange that had no labour to exchange, with their hands getting soft and their minds getting bitter and their feet getting cold. It was all there, clear as daylight in Pen's mind. She turned back into the house and shouted: "I'll go and meet 'em now. It's going to snow."

Arnold came to the window of the "den" they shared, the window of the front room. It gave straight on to the street. There was only a pane of glass between him and Pen. He always came and stood there when she was setting out on some errand, all his love aching to be her eyes, her hands, her feet. But he knew that she did not want him with her. It was a point of pride, and he was careful, now that she had lost so much, to leave her her pride.

She had set about in her own way to master her darkness. She was wearing a cloak and hood of thick red woollen material. In the summertime she wore a similar cloak and hood of a lighter make. The red cloak, as she had intended, became known up and down the Rhondda Valley. "That's Pen Ryerson." You couldn't mistake her. Everyone gave her room, and, if she needed it, gave her help. She carried a stout white-painted stick with a bicycle-bell fastened to the crook of the handle. When she wanted to cross a road she did not wait for someone to take her arm. She held out the stick in the direction she intended to go, rang the bell, and went, keeping the stick horizontally forward till she was across.

So she went now, a striking figure, with one hand clutching the cloak about her, the other holding the stick that tap-tapped along the pavement's edge. There was hardly a soul in the desolate streets: the Rhondda seemed as cold and hopeless as the Russian steppes, and presently the snow that Pen had predicted began to fall. At the corner by the grim forbidding tabernacle Horeb, immense and ugly as sin with the white silent snow falling around it, Pen waited a moment, holding out her stick, then rang her bell and crossed. Down the hill. she went, where her feet were like eyes, knowing every furrow and joint in the stony way. She felt with her hands to see that the level-crossing gates were open, and Gwilym Roberts signalman leaned out of his box into the wuthering snow to shout, "All right, Pen. Go ahead."

She crossed to the station, where the icy wind was cutting along the platform, carrying the snow with it in a horizontal drive, and she sought the waiting-room for shelter. There was no fire in it; it was as cold as the grave; and Thomas Hughes porter put his head in and said: "Come an' wait in our room, Pen gel. There's a bit of fire there. God knows we want something to warm our backsides in the Rhondda these days."

So she went into the porters' room and stood there with the fire thawing the snow off her red cloak till the rumble of the train from Cardiff was heard. Then she went out on to the platform again, cocking her head sideways to listen to the opening and banging of doors. There was not much of it; few people seemed to make Cwmdulais an objective, but soon Pen's ear caught what it was listening for: the quick eager run of Alice's feet and the slower awkward advance of Charles slightly dragging his wooden leg. It was not a wooden leg such as old Richard Richards, Ap Rhondda's father, used to wear when he was alive – an honest-to-God peg-leg – but a new-fangled, up-to-date, utterly scientific contraption, which Charles cursed daily none the less.

They had got out from a compartment at the end of the train, and Alice's run took her right ahead of Charles, so that he looked on from a distance, coming slowly up, as Alice's black bobbed head bent over Pen's red-hooded sightless face, and the two women clung together, kissing.

The spectacle moved him deeply. As he approached, Pen disengaged herself from Alice's arms and turned up her face for him to kiss, too. He did so, simply and without embarrassment. "Mother!" he said.

The snow had thickened while Pen waited for the train, and the daylight had declined. It was nearly four o'clock. As they left the station and turned to the right on to the level-crossing the wind came at them with a cold snarly howl and a drive of snow. It made them stagger and plastered them white all down one side. "You shouldn't be out in this, my dear, You should be sitting by the fireside, warm and comfortable," Alice wanted to cry; but she said nothing. Like Arnold, she had learned to respect Pen's pride. But she took her arm: that was permitted – but only to Alice: and they breasted the steep hill, going with muffled heavy steps. Then they were past Horeb, walking along the terrace, and Charles stopped for a moment to look down into the valley, a pit of darkness filled with the swirl of the snow and made intolerably desolate by the little ineffective pricks of light that looked as though at any moment they would be swamped, overwhelmed, submerged, blown out for ever, like hope abandoned.

"God!" he said. "And when I was a school-kid I thought a weekend visit had shown me the Rhondda! How much did you say, Alice, the Marquis of Mool was getting out of the coal trade?"

"A hundred and fifteen thousand pounds a year," said Alice with grim deliberation.

"God!" Charles repeated. "That's one thing they didn't tell me when I was a kid."

Pen stood between them, leaning on her white stick, her blind face turned towards the valley, "Ah, well," she said, "I sometimes think the Almighty himself has got summat to learn about what we're puttin' up with down here. But come on now. Arnie'll be waiting with a cup o' tea."

When he had seen Pen go tapping her way down the bitter street, Arnold tidied up the papers on his desk and went into the kitchen. So much of his life was spent between these two rooms, especially now that Pen was blind. He looked after their simple cooking. That was one thing she must not be permitted to do. At first, she had insisted on trying, and he had lived in terror of coming home and finding her burned to death. Now she left it to him. He would not have changed these rooms for any others. In this kitchen – Nell had scrubbed Ianto's back while he and Pen, raw youngsters, had sat in the parlour. Here he had met old Richard Richards, now dead, and the babies Dai and Pryce: Dai the doctor, Pryce who was a bit of dust, for ever England, blowing in the sand of Suvla beach. They were all gone now except Dai: Richard and Ianto and Pryce: he had seen those three generations pass: and Nell, who had wept so much over Ap Rhondda's poems, had married again and gone to Patagonia. She had forgotten the poems. When she was gone, a lot of old rubbish was found turned out of boxes and drawers and left pell-mell on the bedroom floor. Arnold discovered the poems there: Ap Rhondda's heartbreaks about the songster over the valley and Hugh Price Hughes drawing the coal-tubs where sun and birdsong never came: the Master of Anguish. Arnold felt as if he were picking up a living thing, and he had a clear vision of Ianto walking down Horeb Terrace with his food-basket and tea-tin, pausing to look back and point to the sky, that last time they had seen him. He took the poems and locked them in his desk, renewing their short lease from oblivion.

The poor little house was full of these memories, and they were with him now as he filled the kettle at the kitchen sink, lit the gas, and put the black-and-red check cloth on the table. He proudly took down from the dresser the tea-service of "cottage pottery," decorated with a bold design of flowers and foliage, that Alice had bought. If most of the memories in this house came to a dead-end, his thoughts of the little Alice, the punctual cheerful scholar, flowed happily forward. Her presence was all about him: in this china and tablecloth, in the typewriter Pen used, knocking out with blind uncanny accuracy the letters and notes which he dictated. The typewriter was one of Alice's grandest ideas; it helped Pen to overcome her feeling of uselessness. All these things, and many others, Alice had bought, and Arnold knew that she could well afford them. There had always been between him and Alice a particular depth of intimacy which even Pen had not shared. Neither Charles nor Pen knew what Alice had confided to him: that she was the author of the detective novels of Gabrielle Minto. Arnold knew little enough about detective novels or any other sort of novels, but he soon discovered that Gabrielle Minto wore a halo. Even reviewers who damned the school to which she belonged admitted that she alone might have redeemed it, because of her good writing, her true psychology, her scrupulously accurate detail. Dons and deans, bishops and Cabinet ministers, all freely acknowledged themselves to be readers of Gabrielle Minto, little knowing that this celebrated person was Alice Ryerson who at the general election of 1923 had stood as a Communist candidate and polled twenty-nine votes out of an electorate of 260433.

Arnold felt that Charles at least should be let into the secret, but Alice would not agree to this. "Not on your life, Daddy! It's nice for Charles when people say: 'You know Alice Ryerson is the wife of Charles Shawcross who wrote *Fit for Heroes*.' It wouldn't be so nice if they began to say: 'You know Charles Shawcross is the husband of Gabrielle Minto.' Charles needs all the pride he can have."

Alice was very careful of the pride of those she loved.

Arnold heard the train come in, and put the tea into the pot. He made up the fire, smoothed out the red-and-blue Indian rug that Alice had bought to replace the old rag mat. He looked round him, well content. He had cut two plates of bread, and there was a good currant-cake, butter, and a small pot of fish-paste. This, in the firewarmed kitchen, seemed to him all that anyone could want. If only everyone in the Rhondda could be certain of so much! Ah! the Rhondda! The thought of his people overwhelmed him. His face saddened, and he drew the red serge curtains against the black snow-dancing night as Pen's brisk knock sounded at the door.

Arnold poured out the tea. "Whenever you're home, Alice," he said, "I want to start meals with grace. You know, Charles, we always did that in Broadbent Street when I called to have tea with your father. Gordon

Stansfield, his stepfather, always said grace. You would have liked that man. He was one of the best men I ever knew."

"I don't like thanking God for what I've got when there are so many who've got nothing at all," said Pen. "I can't believe I'm all that of a God's favourite, Spread some fish-paste on my butter, Alice. No, it wouldn't seem right. 'Thank Thee, God, for this fish-paste, but why hasn't Mrs. Morgan got any at all, and why has Lord Muck got caviare?' You'd start summat if you began that road."

"I hope we'll soon start summat any way," said Alice. "We don't want to ask the Almighty those questions. We just want to ask our own common sense. However, that's enough of that. You hate us Communists, don't you, Daddy? That's one thing Charles and I have in common: both our fathers hate our political ideas like poison."

She was kneeling on the hearth, toasting the bread at the fire and handing it to Charles, who spread the butter and fish-paste on it. Arnold did not answer her, and she went on: "Ah, well, Daddy, don't think I'm blaming you. No doubt when I'm fifty there'll be plenty of young things to call me a Tory. After all, you did bust out of the Liberal Party, and so did Hamer Shawcross. We give you that."

"Thank you, my dear," Arnold said gravely.

She got up, gave the last piece of toast to Charles, and ruffled Arnold's scanty hair. "But don't be too proud about it," she said. "There's a difference. The line of advance had stopped with Liberalism, and you carried it forward. But it was the same line. Don't forget that. We go off on a new line: that's the difference. You still believe that politics can put all this right, don't you?" She waved her hand towards the window, comprehending all the desolation and misery of the workless coalfields.

"I'm as sure of that as I'm sure that I sit in this chair," said Arnold stoutly.

"And I'm as sure that it can't," said Alice. "When you were a boy, you met Friedrich Engels. I've often heard you say so."

How long ago it seemed! When you were a boy! When Shawcross was working in Tom Hannaway's greengrocery shop, sprinkling the dew on the lettuces, and the pair of them used to go down to Suddaby's cellar, looking for book bargains. He remembers well enough the day he had met Engels there. Old Suddaby had told him it was a day he must never forget. Now, when he thought of Alice, when he pondered on some of her activities at which he only half-guessed, he knew that Suddaby was right: he would never forget that he had met Engels.

"Yes," he said, "I remember him very clearly, sitting by the fire in the old book-shop I used to go to in Manchester. He was a bearded man, very melancholy, with little to say."

Alice laughed. "He had plenty to say. And what it all boiled down to was simply this: that political action was no good. He believed that the fight between the rich and the poor would have to shift to another ground. And that is the ground I stand on."

Arnold sighed. "That is a matter for you to settle, my dear," he said. "I know you took high honours in history, and no doubt you have satisfied yourself that revolutions have proved themselves in the past to be successful in filling the bellies of the poor. I have reached no such fortunate conclusion from my limited reading."

When Arnold's usually blunt speech took this rather rotund turn Pen recognized it for a danger signal. "That'll do now, Alice," she said. "We've always had politics enough in this house, and when you and Charles are home we can give 'em a miss."

"All right," said Alice. "I've brought Father a nice safe book that'll cause no trouble to anyone: Gabrielle Minto's latest novel."

"Well, I'm damned!" said Charles. "What you see in that woman! You buy every book she writes."

"You're just a high-brow," Alice chaffed him. "You with your four years' work on one little book. You shouldn't despise poor Gabrielle. She does a useful job in the world."

"I'd like to know what it is," said Charles.

"Well, she gives the dear old dons of Oxford and Cambridge, and all the stuffy old canons lurking round the cathedrals of Britain, a chance to read what they really want to read. Most of them stopped thinking thirty – forty – years ago. Since then their minds have just gone round and round in circles. They're sick to death of the antiquated stuff they once learned and now teach. They like to get down cosily at night to a shocker or a thriller, with the latest publication of some learned society ready at hand to take up as they stuff the thriller under a cushion when an undergraduate comes in. But now, with Gabrielle, they needn't do that. They've conspired to make her an intellectual fashion. She actually had a passage from Sophocles, in the original Greek, opposite the title of one of her books, and occasionally she slips in a Latin tag. She knows her stuff. She's got all the old boys on toast. She's saved their hoary souls from deceitfulness and pretence. She's the toast of the senior common-rooms, and her seven-and-sixpenny editions can count on a sale of thirty thousand copies. D'you call this nothing?"

"*Fit for Heroes* sold thirty-five thousand," said Charles haughtily. "So it did," said Alice. "You do it every year, my lad, and then you can start to run down Gabrielle."

She and Charles washed up, and Pen said: "Let's go and sit in the front room."

"No, no," said Alice. "This is the most comfortable room in the house. I like an evening by the kitchen fire."

They humoured her, and Arnold carried in the old wicker chairs from the front room. He and Charles put on their pipes and Alice produced Gabrielle Minto's new novel, "This one interested me very much," she said, "because it's set in a mining valley. The cage starts for the pit-head with its load of tubs, and there are four witnesses to prove that it contained nothing but tubs. Propped among them when it comes up is the body of the under-manager. As usual, Gabrielle's detail is absolutely right. I can't find a flaw in it."

She read a few chapters aloud, and when she had done even Charles admitted: "Well, she *can* write. I never said she couldn't *write*..."

It snowed, off and on, during the three days of their visit to the Rhondda. It was awkward weather for the crippled Charles to get about in. For the most part, he remained in the kitchen, helping Arnold with the cooking, doing the washing up, and, between times, writing at Pen's old desk in the front room. "I can write anywhere," he would boast; and so he could, but, wherever he wrote, the work was snail-paced.

As the snow continued to fall, the wind dropped; and a great deal of Charles's time was spent standing at the front window, which gave an upper-circle view of the white stage set in the valley, For hours he would stand there ruminating on the few trains that filled the cold wet atmosphere with their low-hanging steam; on the relentless snow that fell dumbly upon the smoking roofs; on the grey silence, the suspended animation, through which the winding machines rose up like gaunt unanswered prayers. This once green valley; this valley which, after it had ceased to be green, had been pulsing, vibrating with the labour that scourged and scarified it; now neither green nor vibrant, but lying in the silence and rigidity of death under the falling snow. Then he would go back to his chair, and stretch his awkward leg straight out under the desk, and write a little more, with all this for the grey background of his mood.

When Pen's white stick hammered on the door, he would hasten to open it, to greet her and Alice, letting life into the deathly chill of his meditations. Alice, with her dark pugnacious face whipped by the cold, with her sloe eyes shining and her black bobbed hair looking electric with energy: he longed to take her there and then to the cold little back bedroom with its window giving upon the white acclivity of the mountain, and amid all this winter death to lie on her warm breasts and feel the flood of her abundant life flowing into him, renewing him. The wounded side of his face would twitch with the urgency of his need, and over Pen's blind head he would jerk his own head demandingly towards the stairs. Sometimes Alice's love responded to his mood, and she would nod and run up the stairs. Charles climbed slowly on his wooden leg, and almost before he was there she would be waiting for him, and he would forget the snow, and death, and the manifold miseries that nested in his heart like black crows in a ragged tree.

What Alice did with her time Arnold did not fully know. He knew that she was renewing innumerable acquaintances, calling on all sorts and conditions of people, making for her journalistic purposes an inquiry as thorough as only she could make it into the slow death of the Rhondda. But there was much else: she was spending time with people whom he distrusted, and what schemes they were hatching he could only guess. There was a barrier here, cutting short the confidence between them. He had been at one time inclined to think her Communism a girl's generous impulse, a fancy of youth that facts would dissipate. But her standing as a candidate against an immensity of odium had made him change his mind. No; Alice was running true to character. He had never known her to take up a thing lightly. He remembered the day when she won her first trifling scholarship, and he stroked her black hair and said: "There's a fine little scholar now! Wherever will you end!" And Alice said firmly: "In Oxford University." He and Pen had laughed, and Alice did not even bother to reply to their laughter. She went on with her work. So it had always been with her; and whatever she might now conceive to be her work, she would go on with it.

It was on the last evening of their stay that Arnold said: "Well, there's one thing: we *have* got a Labour government now. Once they get into their stride things should begin to improve."

"Why should they?" Alice demanded. "The most your friends will do is patch up the old tyre. What we want is a new car, a new road, and a new driver. For myself, I doubt whether they'll even do the patching up. I'll take a bet with any of you that unemployment won't fall under this Government."

Pen surprisingly said: "I'd like to see your father, Charles. I'd like to ask him point-blank what the Government's going to do for us, and I'd like to tell him how much there is to do in this part of the world. We're forgotten. We're off the map. They've allowed a curtain to come down, shutting us out, because they're ashamed for the world to see us."

"Why don't you *make* the world see you?" Alice asked. "London won't come to the Rhondda. You can bet your boots on that. Let the Rhondda go to London. Walk there. Show yourselves in Whitehall and Downing Street and Piccadilly. Go to the House of Commons. There you are. There's a programme. There's something to do. It's better than sitting here till the snow covers you."

"Well," said Pen, "it may come to that. And if it does, I shall march with the rest. But in the meantime, I want to see Hamer Shawcross. I've got every sort of right. I worked alongside him when he was nobody—"

"He was never that," Arnold put in in his grave, just way.

"Well," said Pen, "when nobody thought he was anybody, and I worked alongside Ann, and one of these days he and I may have the same grandchildren."

"No!"

The word burst from Charles with an explosive force that startled Pen and Arnold. Pen could not see that Charles's face had gone white and that his lips were trembling. Charles dreaded the thought that a child might absorb from himself some of Alice's ministering love.

"No," said Alice. "No grandchildren, my dear. Charles and I are the only children you two and Hamer Shawcross and Ann produced, so the decision is absolutely with us. And we'll bring no children into the world because the world is not worthy."

"It's a coward's decision," said Pen stoutly. "Why, God love us, Alice, the world has been pretty tough on me. And if anyone said to me: 'D'you want it all over again, Pen Muff, just in the way you've had it, blindness and all?' why, I'd say: 'Aye, and again after that, as often as you like.' It's not a perfect world for children that matters, or that you'll ever get: it's children to work for a perfect world. No, no, Alice, believe me, there's going to be no harps and wings here below. By heck there's not. But when we stop working for 'em, God help us."

"That's your view, Mother," said Alice, as Charles sat looking at her, white and tense, "but it's not mine."

No more was said. Arnold had got up. He stood at the window with all the weight of his years on his sagging shoulders. He looked down at the valley where his life's work lay dead, and at the snow falling quietly upon its grave.

"Is that you, Father?"

Charles! It was the first time Charles had rung him up since he had lived in Half Moon Street. He had felt hurt about it. Let Charles go his own political way. No one could complain about that. But the boy, on the few occasions when they met, went beyond this. He left a feeling of personal resentment. This was easier to understand in the first bitterness of his return, so badly hurt, from the war. Hamer had never forgotten – felt he never could forget – that day at the hospital when Charles broke out against him, almost openly charged him with breach of faith. But though he could not forget it, it did not weigh with him. And it was more than five years ago. Now Charles was happily married. He was, in his own circle, looked up to as a successful man. The world had not been so hard on him as his little essays and stories in the precious weeklies would make one suppose. He could have gone back to finish his course at Oxford, but he wouldn't have that. He said he would feel a fool among all the green youngsters. It seemed to Hamer that he lost no opportunity to nurture his quarrel with humanity.

"Well, my dear boy," said Hamer, "how are you? What are you doing? Are we to have another book?"

He was proud of Charles's book. He had no illusions about it. It was a hit of the moment, and only of its moment. It lacked a fundamental understanding of the perpetual pathos of life, and so it was a grumble rather than a tragedy. But all the same, Hamer was proud of it. Charles was an author, and he had great respect for authors, for artists of any kind. Despite all the books to his name, he never thought of himself as a man of letters, though, in that line alone, Charles would never catch him up.

"Oh, I'm working – slowly," Charles said. "But I've been busy."

That was typical of Charles's attitude. He liked to pretend that his writing was something he turned to casually now and then in the intervals of being "busy" with large and undefined affairs. "I've been down to the Rhondda with Alice," he said. "We've been making a survey of conditions down here. We brought Pen back with us, and Arnold sends his love. I wondered if you'd care to see Pen."

"By all means, my dear boy. I shall be out this afternoon, but I'll be back here at tea-time. Could you come at half-past four and bring Pen and Alice with you? – and Lizzie, too, if you like. It's a long time since we all met. I'd like that."

"Very well, Father. At half-past four. Good-bye."

It was a lovely afternoon, clear and frosty, and Pen said she'd like to walk. So they set off at half-past three, Pen wearing her red cloak and hood and carrying her white stick. But now she had to give up her independence. This wasn't Cwmdulais that she knew inch by inch. She took Lizzie's arm. Alice and Charles walked behind the other two. Lizzie chose the route, along the Bird Cage Walk, past the front of Buckingham Palace, and down the Mall. At St. James's Palace a little crowd was gathered, and Lizzie, who had been acting as eyes for Pen, telling her of all they passed, explained: "There's a levee on, Pen. The people are just coming away. D'you mind if we stand and gape for a moment? I'll tell you the names of all the bigwigs who come out."

Charles and Alice would not have been attracted to a levee. They would have gone straight on, Alice with a fierce conviction, Charles following her with his nose obediently in the air. But they stayed for Lizzie's sake. "There's nothing much left for me now but standing and staring," Lizzie used to say, "and to be frank, I like it. If you two don't, run along."

So now they stood and stared, and Lizzie, who had an encyclopædic knowledge of personalities, named the admirals and generals and prelates who came hurrying out in their fine feathers, leapt into cars, and were borne away.

Now she whispered excitedly: "Here's Ramsay Mac, and" – hardly able to control her emotion – "Hamer's with him."

Pen, Charles and Alice all stiffened. Lizzie alone allowed herself to be uplifted by sheer delight. "Where are they? Where are they?" poor Pen demanded; but Alice and Charles said nothing. They stood as if frozen to stone, looking at the two men.

They were two men worth looking at: the two handsomest public figures in Great Britain at that time. Each carried the cocked-hat of his ceremonial dress under his arm. Hamer was a little taller than his chief. The intelligence of both the faces, each topped with grizzled hair, was remarkable. They stood for a moment talking with animation, the crowd looking on from a little distance. Then two cars pulled up. MacDonald got into one which drove off towards Downing Street; Shawcross, bending double, his hand on the hilt of his sword, into the other which turned into Piccadilly.

The silence lasted for a little while; then Alice said bitterly: "And that is Labour in office!"

Lizzie turned on her, with a face still radiant. "That is a bloody miracle!" she declared, carried away by her emotion. "That is Hamer Shawcross, of Broadbent Street. And if that means nothing to you, it does to me. I've seen it all happen, and I tell you it's a miracle – a bloody miracle."

The old lady's indecorous enthusiasm broke Alice's grim humour down into laughter. "Come on," she said, "or you'll be getting run in. Your hat's askew. You look like yourself in your Suffragette days when you didn't love him so much."

"Love him or hate him," Lizzie declared, "I admire him. You've been looking at something that doesn't happen once or twice in a generation."

"Thank God for that," said Alice. "And that goes for the pair of 'em. Come on. I hope his tea's as gorgeous as his trousers."

It couldn't be done. Hamer had hoped to be back from St. James's in time to change before tea, but the clock in the taxi said 4.20 as he got out and ran up to his front door. He didn't mind wearing these clothes. They had caused a scandal in the party. They seemed, to many, a betrayal. Labour was in office, but what of that? Keir Hardie had driven up to the House in a wagonette, wearing a cloth cap, acclaimed on a plebeian cornet. Why shouldn't Labour members continue to be humble? Why shouldn't Mr. MacDonald smoke a clay pipe and why shouldn't Mr. Shawcross wear a cloth cap? Even a dinner jacket was suspect; full-fig evening dress was impious; ceremonial uniform, with swords and cocked hats, was almost blasphemy. These matters had been seriously and hotly debated. To many simple souls, these ceremonial swords were traitorously plunged into the breast of Labour.

To Hamer, it was all very amusing. He frankly liked the look of himself in these clothes which he carried as if born to them. He intended to have his portrait painted wearing them. But they were a matter indifferent; and because fundamentally, as he told himself, they meant nothing to him, it delighted him to scare and alarm the austere sackcloth-and-ashes members of the party. He would tell them with gravity of silken underclothing which he was obliged to wear beneath the uniform, and how the Gentleman of the King's Bedchamber had to inspect it personally each Monday morning when it came back from the wash. Ramsay MacDonald's, he said without a smile, had a Greek key pattern of gold lace round the legs of the pants.

But he didn't want Charles and Alice to find him in gorgeous raiment that day. It seemed inappropriate for a family tea-party. But there wasn't time to change, so he went into his study and waited for them.

It was the room he liked best in the house, a room of rich deep colours punctuated startlingly by Axel Horst's portrait of Ann over the fireplace. Axel had put in the rug behind Ann's head in vivid Van Gogh slashes of green and white and yellow, and the whole composition had a freshness and gaiety that sparkled amid the dark furniture and the sombre books. Tea was set on a couple of low round tables between two couches of old red leather running out at right angles on either side of the fire.

In physical appearance, Hamer Shawcross did not change much from the man you see there, now in the last moments of his fifties. He stood between the couches with his back to the fire, the tight gold-braided trousers on his long slim legs, the toy sword at his side. He was as straight and clean-built as the sword, broad in the shoulders, carrying with an air of authority the noble head whose grey hair, almost white, hung in a picturesque wing across his brow. The face was full without being fleshy, hale and ruddy in colour, with deep lines running from the straight nose down to the mouth. It was that rare thing: a face which is both intellectual and handsome. The intellect seemed almost literally to flash in the dark eyes whose brows remained black when the hair of his head was white. Here no longer was the battling agitator, the man who was prepared, if it would advance his cause, to play the mountebank in clothes and actions. Here was the statesman, equipped for the part, enjoying the part, as ready to savour its trivial amusements and worldly pomposities as to endure its responsibilities and ardours.

He unbuckled the sword and laid it on one of the couches as he heard the bell ring. Old Pendleton, eager to do everything as it should be done, was at the door, half-way through his formal rigmarole: "Mrs. Lightowler, Mr. and Mrs. Charles Shawcross—" when Hamer was across the floor gathering them all into the room and as it were into the welcoming warmth of his smile.

"Well, Charles, my dear boy, there's so much I want to show you here. Come in, Alice. Ah, Pen, my dear. Let me take your arm. Your hat's crooked, Lizzie. Take it off, for goodness' sake."

"Charming, charming," Alice thought. "The Great Irresistible. I wonder what he'll have to say about the Rhondda." She picked up the sword which he had laid on the couch. "Don't let this come between us," she said. She looked round for somewhere to lay it down, and saw the case containing the sabre of Peterloo. She bent to read the inscription on the little gold plate. "Ha!" she cried. "Your old swashbuckling weapon is a curio now, I see. We'll lay this on top as an appropriate epilogue to its story."

Hamer was used to Alice's ways. She loved to bait him, but he would never fall to her assaults. "You wait, young woman," he said. "One of these days I'll present you with a miniature bomber to place as an appropriate epilogue over your sickle and hammer."

He passed her over with a laugh, and carefully led Pen to a place alongside himself on the couch. "Well, Pen," he said, "that's a striking costume. Who are you supposed to represent – Ceridwen?"

"Who's Ceridwen?" Pen asked.

"Oh, dear! Have you lived all this time in Wales and not heard of Ceridwen? She was a rather distinguished Welsh witch."

"Oh! I'm afraid I'm nothing so romantic as that," said Pen. "I'm just an old blind woman. We don't learn much about fables in the Rhondda nowadays. The facts are too much with us, and they're too bitter.

Do you remember a long time ago when Arnie and I spent a night with you at Baildon?"

Hamer remembered it very well: it was the only night they had ever spent there. He motioned to Lizzie to pour out the tea. "Why, yes, Pen," he said. "It was when you had come up to bury your mother, and Arnold invited me to go down and talk to the men in the Rhondda."

"You invited yourself, and I backed you up. Arnie didn't want you. But let that pass. I remember you produced a great book stuffed with all the facts about the coal trade. I was wondering whether you'd kept it up-to-date."

"Pen, there's nothing you can tell me about the Rhondda. No doubt you could fill in a bit of human detail here and there. When I tell you how many people are out of work, you can tell me that the people are Griffith Hughes and John Jones and so forth. You know them and their wives and children, and that makes the problem the more poignant to you. But I know as well as you do what the problem is, how appalling its dimensions are."

"Well, answer me one plain question," said Pen. "I told Arnie I'd put it to you, and I'd like to give him your answer. What's this government going to do about it? He's got a right to know. He's given his life to those men and he hasn't got fat on it. And the men have got a right to know. They voted for your party, most of 'em, and they voted in hope. They've heard your candidate say again and again that the Labour Party had a cure for unemployment. Where is it? And what is it? I came to London to ask you."

Hamer was aware of Alice watching him with malicious amusement and of Lizzie Lightowler covering her embarrassment with hearty eating. "The unemployment you speak of, Pen," he said, "is a consequence of conditions going back through decade upon decade of history, aggravated by the greatest war the world has known. Think of that on the one side. On the other, think of this. The Labour government has been in office for only two months. It's a minority government at that. We have 191 members. The Tories and Liberals can muster 424. At any moment they can combine to throw us out."

Pen interrupted sharply: "If you can't *do* anything, what does it matter to us whether you're in or out? If our bellies are to stay empty, we don't sing Hallelujah because they're empty under a Labour government."

"There are some things we *can* do," said Hamer, "and I believe Mac-Donald will do them in foreign politics. On the strength of what we *do*, we may hope for more seats next time. We may hope at last for an absolute majority. Only then can we turn to more of the things we would like to do. That, as I see it, is the situation."

"A lovely situation for the Rhondda," said Pen bitterly. "It's practically a life sentence. By heck! What a game politics is!"

"I admit," said Hamer, "that it's a matter of getting the most out of the second best. If all things were working for the best – why, there'd be no need of politics at all, Pen. I suppose the very word means not what we want but what is expedient."

"My God, Father!" Charles broke in. "We began with starving miners and we've got on to the Shorter Oxford Dictionary!"

Pen repeated: "'Getting the most out of the second best!' Well, well. I can remember the earliest days in St. Swithin's. This isn't how you talked then."

"One lives and learns," said Hamer sadly and frankly.

"Aye, one does an' all," Pen said, falling into her broad accent.

"An' one thing Ah've learned, lad, is not to trouble thee again wi' our sorrows. We'll grin an' bear 'em, an' when we can't even grin any more, why, we'll just bear 'em."

She groped for her stick and stood up. Alice took her arm. There was nothing more to be said.

When they were gone, and Pendleton had cleared away the trays, Hamer went upstairs and changed. The visit hadn't gone as he had hoped. He would have liked to show them over the house, talk to them about the things he had gathered there, feel like a man with his relations around him. But they gave him no chance. They seemed to regard him all the time as a target, almost an outlaw. He came back to the study, meditating unhappily, and called Pendleton. "Don't bother me with dinner. I've got too much to do. Bring me in some sandwiches and coffee at eight. And I can't see anyone or talk to anyone on the telephone unless it's government business."

He set out the papers neatly on his desk, filled half-a-dozen pipes, and put them in a bowl ready to hand.

They didn't understand. They thought a government, even a minority government, was an almighty juggernaut that could plough down the tremendous façades that had been built up through the centuries. Blow the trumpets and down comes Jericho! Ah! if it were as easy as that! The Rhondda! Yes, whatever Pen might say, he knew all about the Rhondda. He had seen the scarecrow poor reaching up their arms to the soup wagon under the bitter stars in Stevenson Square, Manchester, and having seen that, he had seen poverty and hunger wherever they might be. He took up Ann's copy of Marcus Aurelius, which he kept now always on his desk, and turned to a passage she had marked: "Men and manners are generally much alike. All ages and histories, towns and families, are of the same complexion and full of the same stories. There's nothing new to be met with, but all things are common, and quickly over."

Quickly over, Pen, the good things as well as the vile, the lovely as well as the loathsome. Meantime, one did what one could, and acknowledged – yes, it was true – that it could be only a second best.

It was not till midnight that he got up from the desk, yawned, and sat down on one of the red couches by the fire to write in his diary. He smiled to himself tiredly as it struck him for the first time that the couches had the same colour as the seats in the House of Lords. They were very comfortable.

Chapter Twenty

Charles and Alice went to Russia. They went as some simple soul of the Middle Ages, knowing nothing of the politics behind the crusades, might have gone to fight in the Holy Land, thinking it was all for Christ and the Cross. Certainly there were politics enough connected with this Russian visit, but they were not politics as Liberals and Tories, or even Labour men, understood them. They were Truth revealed. They were the Word, wherein was salvation.

So at least it seemed to Alice, looking with generous enthusiasm at the experiments of a backward people, exclaiming with delight at infant efforts to achieve the buds of civilization which she had long enjoyed in its flower.

"Worthy and commendable perhaps these efforts are," Hamer wrote in his diary on the night when Alice and Charles had dined with him in Half Moon Street and poured out the spate of their enthusiasm. "But they are clearly the efforts of a nation which should be led and educated. These young people talk as though all the schools should be put under the direction of the class for backward and defective, if hopefully striving, children. And for myself, I am still full of doubts as to what these children have in mind against the time when they are grown up. Oh, why do not these young Marxists read Marx and Lenin and Engels? I am not convinced that it is necessary to knock down Notre Dame before beginning to build a tin tabernacle."

He liked the phrase. He had used it to Alice. He couldn't help admiring the girl for all her antagonism. He knew what was the matter with Alice. Her heart was too sensitive to the sorrows of the world. She saw the ulcer and was convinced that the patient was at the point of death. She was too impatient to work for a cure. Off with the leg, the arm, even the head! He liked as well as admired her. She looked well, sitting there on his right hand, with the parchment-shaded electric table-lamps between them! Her firm energetic body was well set off by a dress of dark red lustreless silk – as darkly red as the carnation at the buttonhole of his dinner-jacket. Charles was wearing flannel bags and an old blue tweed jacket he had had since his Oxford days.

They went into the study to drink their coffee. Charles declined a cigar as though he were making a religious renunciation, and lit an evil briar, chipped round the edges, with an air of applying the sacred fire to an altar. Standing up before the hearth, piercing his own Havana, Hamer noticed that the boy's finger-nails were dirty and his clothes unbrushed. He wished that Alice, who seemed to influence Charles in everything else, would take his toilet in hand, make him as groomed and shining as she herself always was. He wondered if they were hard up, and whether Alice would jump down his throat if he offered to help them. Charles couldn't be making much money. *Fit for Heroes* had perhaps netted him a few lucky thousands, but he had done nothing since and was not likely to do much in the future. As for Alice, she was a prolific journalist, but for the most part her writing was not published in papers that paid well.

He poured out the coffee, then stood up again, looking down on the oddly varied but so well-matched young people, sitting opposite one another on the red couches. He drew appreciatively on his cigar for a moment, then said: "How is it, Alice, that you always manage in these days to look as if you had come into a fortune? Is the *Red Pleb* paying twenty guineas a thousand words?"

For the first time since he had known her, he saw Alice lose her self-possession. Her ruddy cheeks went a deeper red, then paled a little. "My God!" he thought. "I shouldn't have said that. I've stepped on something there," and watched her narrowly.

"The *Red Pleb* isn't the only paper I write for," she said, recovering. "There are intelligent weeklies and monthlies, and one or two dailies as well, that are ready to give space to views that are not precisely their own."

Hamer nodded, glad to let her out. "And Charles must have made a pretty packet out of his book," he said.

"Yes," Alice assented eagerly. "And the poor lamb doesn't waste much on himself. And don't forget that Aunt Lizzie doesn't take a penny of rent from us. We pay for nothing but our food."

All the same, thought Hamer, all the same, I'd like to know what you paid for that dress, my pretty proletarian.

"Forgive my question," he said. "It was due entirely to my admiring your – er – ceremonial uniform."

He sat down alongside Alice and looked across at Charles. "What about the new book?" he asked.

Charles was not often willing to talk about his writing, but now he confessed that he had abandoned, or put aside for the moment, the novel he had been working on for two years. He had begun a novel about Russia while his impressions were still fresh.

"Might one ask what the title is to be?"

"*The Good Red Earth,*" said Charles proudly.

Hamer considered this, looking at the glowing end of his cigar. "People might think that was something about Devonshire, in the Phillpotts vein," he objected.

Charles did not like criticism. He shuffled uneasily on the couch, and said: "Of course, if you can suggest a better title?"

"Why not just *Phoenix?*" Hamer suggested. "You know, something winged rising from ashes and desolation. It's simple, and somehow – er – proud. Don't you think?"

Charles seemed surprised to find his father taking even an academic interest in his work. He made a few quibbling sounds, but Alice broke in eagerly: "Yes, *Phoenix* is a much better title. You must use that, Charles, unless you think of something better still."

"Perhaps *Red Phoenix,*" Charles slowly conceded.

"Have the brute red if you must," Hamer laughed. "I was thinking of spirit, not pigment."

He poured out more coffee, and turned to Alice. "Well, we've been in office now for seven months. What do you think of us? Have we done anything at all to earn your favour? How much longer do you think we can hold out against the combined hosts of the Liberals and Tories?"

"Go and sit over there by Charles," Alice said, "where I can look at you, and you can look at me."

He got up good-naturedly and crossed to the other couch.

"I want to talk to you straight, Hamer Shawcross. The more I see of you the more I like you."

Hamer waved his cigar airily. "The way of all flesh, my dear," he said.

"You're a great man," Alice went on. "You've achieved great things. I give you that. I know how great they are because I've seen plenty of people start from nothing and stop short because they haven't got that little extra flip that men call genius. Old Lizzie Lightowler the other day was carried off her feet when she saw you in fancy dress for the first time. She said it was a 'bloody miracle.' So it was, in a way."

"That was the day Pen came here to tea," Charles unnecessarily amplified.

"Yes," said Alice. "She had you in a corner, Father."

Hamer's heart gave a little jump. Father! She had never called him that before. He wondered what this attractive vivacious creature was getting at.

"You couldn't get out of it," Alice went on. "You knew you couldn't, and I admired your honesty in admitting that you could do nothing for those poor men my father works among."

"I admitted," said Hamer, "that we couldn't do everything at once."

"You admitted that you were in a dead-end: the same dead-end as the Liberals and Tories. And that's what makes you and your party so damned dangerous. We know where we are with the Liberals and Tories. But there are thousands of misguided working men who think you're different. But you're not. You're for tinkering and patching. You're the chief danger. So now, when you ask me how much longer do I think you can hold out, I say: Not a moment longer than I can help. I want to see the Tories back, so that we can have a visible enemy."

Thank you, Alice," said Hamer gravely. "Like you, I prefer to know my enemies – politically speaking at the moment. But when you say not a moment longer than *you* can help, are you speaking personally? Have you fabricated some weapon to blow us sky-high?"

Alice did not answer the question directly. "I give you another three months at the outside," she said.

The Government was out within the three months that Alice predicted.

"The Red Letter settled us," says the Shawcross diary. "We had gone to the country on another matter. Almost on the eve of the poll this mine exploded under our feet and blew us sky-high. Much has been written, and much will be written, about this celebrated epistle, but the facts are simple. We were forced to go to the country at the moment when the Russian Treaties were on our hands. MacDonald had no more love for Communism than I had; but when has it been a rule of politics that statesmen must love the nations with whom they negotiate? 'Agree with thine adversary quickly whiles thou art in the way with him.' That was what MacDonald and I felt, and certainly the Russian Treaties did not bind this poor nation like sickles on a war chariot, as Edward Grey's continental understanding had done.

"Well, there it was. We should have had a hard fight in any case against the hysteria and loathing that the name of Russia called up in millions of minds. An unclouded atmosphere was necessary for the explanation of our intentions. Then came the letter, filling the air with darkness. The letter was published in the newspapers on the Saturday before the poll. It was signed by Zinoviev, the President of the Third (Communist) International, and it was addressed to the Communists of Britain. It suggested that MacDonald had been pushed into the Treaties by Communist pressure, and that much more push must be applied. It advocated revolutionary instead of political action, with insurrection in the Army and Navy.

"There was much else that I need not go into. This was enough. We were beaten, though our votes increased by over a million. The Tory votes soared far beyond our figures. I managed to hold on in St. Swithin's.

"Now the country is full of questions. Was the letter a fake, the dirtiest political dodge ever engineered? I have respect for historical method, and dislike conclusions founded on guesswork. Therefore I shall merely suggest an explanation of this affair without insisting that it is the correct one.

"The letter, of course, would have done us no harm if it had not found its way to the Foreign Office, and to the newspapers. How did it do that? It was 'in the air,' floating about for some time before it was published. I myself saw a copy of it. I called at once at North Street. Mrs. Lightowler and my daughter-in-law were out. Only my son Charles was at home. I asked him where Alice was, and he said that she had gone to Fleet Street. She might be away the whole afternoon. She had left a telephone number in case she was urgently wanted. He gave me this number, and when later I discovered from it what newspaper Alice was visiting, a suspicion that had already entered my mind began to sharpen. I remembered what she had said to me at dinner a few months earlier: 'You will not be in a moment longer than I can help. I want a visible enemy.'

"I took tea with Charles and led the conversation to his visit to Russia.

Had he called on any of the political chiefs? No; he had spent his time looking round factories and crèches and culture parks. Alice had seen a lot of people, though. She did more conferring than sightseeing. Had she seen anything of a chap called Zinoviev? Charles scratched his head. For all his Communism, he was not well up in Communists. Then he got it. Yes! that was the fellow! Zinoviev! Alice had a long pow-wow with him one day while Charles was examining a super concrete-mixer.

"I have no more facts than these. Alice is a convinced and resolute Communist, not a follower of fashion in Charles's shilly-shally way. She is a woman of original and inventive mind, intellectually capable of devising this plot for giving her party a 'visible enemy.' She had predicted to me the date of our downfall. She had been in close consultation with the alleged author of the letter. At the critical moment of the whole matter she was engaged in some secret negotiations in Fleet Street.

"I leave it at that. Whether hers or another's was the hand that struck us down, down we are, and we pass on to Mr. Baldwin the sorrows and distractions of this England."

Sir Thomas Hannaway came back on the Tory wave as Coalition-Conservative member for one of the seats in his native Manchester. For the first time he and Hamer Shawcross were simultaneously members of the House of Commons. Jimmy Newboult lost his seat, which was a serious matter for him, for he lost with it £400 a year. It was at this time that he became a member of Hamer's household. There was room and to spare in the Half Moon Street house, and Jimmy was given a bed-sitting-room in which he did secretarial work for his Chief. Chief was the name Jimmy had himself invented, and if it hadn't been for the Chief he would now have been in Queer Street. As it was, he had food to eat, a roof over his head, three pounds a week to spend, and plenty of work to do. It tided him over the next five years, till 1929, when his party's triumph took him back into the House, and the beloved Chief entered the second Labour Cabinet, this time in the immensely more important office of Minister for the Co-ordination of Internal Affairs.

During those years when he lived so near to him, Jimmy Newboult was often surprised, sometimes staggered, and once or twice a little hurt by the frankness with which Hamer expressed himself. There was a day when he asked in his naïvely eager way: "What do you think the main qualification for success in a politician, Chief?" and without seeming even to consider his words Hamer answered: "Why, just this, Jimmy. While appearing to have nothing but his country's interest at heart, he must be an expert at appealing to panic, passion and prejudice. When these do not exist, he must know how to create them at the right moment."

"I should resent it if anyone suggested that you had conducted your life on those lines, Chief," said Jimmy, taken aback.

"Then you would be wrong," Hamer answered. "What threw us out last time? The Red Letter panic. What will take us in next time? The panic, which we shall carefully foster, in the public mind at the state of things at home and abroad. The international situation going from bad to worse. At home, appalling unemployment, the general strike last year, these marching miners now in London. All these things are symptoms of a terrible disease, and it will be our business to throw the patient into a panic, to persuade him that he's going to die unless he takes our medicine."

"And so he will," said Jimmy stoutly. "Don't you think we've got the cure?"

"I think," said Hamer, "we know the right road, and if we could persuade people to walk along it far enough and for long enough we might get somewhere. But frankly, Jimmy, I don't believe we can."

"Chief!"

"Do you know what I'm coming to believe, Jimmy?"

Jimmy shook his red head.

"That the world's going to the devil, literally and with increasing momentum, and that you and I can do precious little about it."

Jimmy looked up, amazed, and was comforted to see that the Chief's face was serene and smiling. "You always were a one for your joke," he said. "You gave me quite a start."

These marching miners now in London.

The words that Alice had spoken in Cwmdulais long ago had borne fruit. London would not go to the Rhondda; London would not look at the Rhondda; and so the Rhondda came to London. The little dark men, the men from the beginning of things, civilization's troglodytes who had hewn and sweated in the darkness to spread light and warmth and power in the land above: they flowed down now out of their valleys, on to the English plain, and they presented themselves at the gates of civilization. They surged through London, singing their hymns and songs, talking their lilting musical speech. What will you do about us, London? Home of the Mother of Parliaments, hub of the Empire on which the sun never sets, behold thy children who ask for no more than this: work where the sun never rises; work in the dust and heat, work where the water drips, work on our naked backs and bellies, squeezing through crack and fissure, work with the risk we will gladly take of sudden death from flame and flash, falling roof, rushing water and crawling gas, work that gives us these little bending bodies, these pocks of powder, and that sends us home day after day and night after night carrying our filth to our bathless houses: work! Will you hear us put our case? We have come a long way to do it.

And Downing Street forgot the Bantams' Battalions, made up of little men like these, shouldering their packs, singing their ironical songs, jesting in the very article of death; and Downing Street said: "No. We cannot receive your deputation. Your conduct is utterly unconstitutional. Go away, please. We are very busy considering the problem of unemployment."

Charles and Alice Shawcross, Arnold and Pen Ryerson, marched with the Cwmdulais contingent. It was cold November weather when the 275 set out. Pen wore her red hood and cloak. The miners carried their safety lamps. It was good copy for the press-men: a fancy-dress parade, a carnival, with little Red Riding Hood for the star turn. Alice Ryerson, the now thrice-defeated Communist candidate, was a good mark, too. This notorious woman who seemed able to spend as much on her campaigns as any other candidate, who could forfeit her deposit with indifference, was only a journalist. Where did she get her money from? It was Red, every cent of it.

Fine fun the correspondents of the London Tory papers had, marching day by day with the singing, patient column. Here is Charles Shawcross, son of Hamer Shawcross, still the oracle of a little clique, though, since the lucky hit of *Fit for Heroes*, all his books have flopped. And who is this Arnold Ryerson, the husband of little Red Riding Hood, the father of the Little Red Candidate? Isn't he the man who went to jail for inciting miners to riot?

In London Hamer read the papers and ground his teeth with rage. He thought of Pen's blind eyes – blinded in the country's service – and of Charles's leg, a bit of England left overseas, and of Alice with her fierce, honest, sorrowful heart. He thought especially of Arnold. He could see Arnold, getting too old and heavy for that sort of thing, plodding with his arm through blind Pen's doggedly along the wet November roads, under the ragged clouds in the chill showers: Arnold whose life from boyhood had been sublimely sacrificial and unmindful of self. He remembered Ann saying long ago that Arnold was the sort of man whose very defeat would have the quality of victory, and surely, he thought, it would be for men like Arnold, rather than for those who went down to death amid the splendours of obsequies, tombs and epitaphs, that all the trumpets would sound upon the other side.

"Chief," said Jimmy Newboult, when the marchers were within a day or so of London, "you ought to go and meet 'em. It would be an enormous leg up for 'em. Ramsay Mac ought to do it. You both ought to do it. You both ought to march into town at the head of 'em, and lead a deputation to the Prime Minister."

Jimmy paused, and looked for a moment wistfully at the Chief, standing tall and elegant in a favourite pose, his back to the fire, a red couch on either hand. And a red carnation at his buttonhole. It was delivered regularly every day now from a florist's in Shepherd Market.

The Chief was sunk in thought and did not answer. "There was a time when you'd have done it. There was a time when you'd have gone to the Rhondda and marched every yard of the way. And I'd have been with you. I'd have carried the sword for you. That would have been like old times: the four of us – you and me, and Pen and Arnold."

Hamer looked at him sadly: the faithful old hound making a last bid for puppy-tricks. Still he did not speak. He looked over Jimmy's head at the sabre in its case, but he was not seeing it. He was seeing the marching men, and the fog that was falling upon London, and Pen tapping her way forward with her white stick, the fleece of her cloak dewed like an old reddled ewe's in a winter field. And he was thinking of Arnold's letter in his pocket, asking him to do just this thing that Jimmy Newboult was asking him to do.

"Chief, for God's sake," said Jimmy, alarmed at Hamer's strange absent look, "you're not going back on us? You're not going back on all we stood for—"

"No, Jimmy," Hamer said, "there's no going back. We must go

forwards, not backwards. We stand for the things we always stood for, Jimmy, you and I; but now we see that different times demand different methods. When the bird is nearly in the hand, go carefully. Don't shout and bluster. And the bird is coming our way again, Jimmy. Mark my words. That's what we're after. Give us office, with power, and then something can be done. In the meantime, we mustn't scare the bird."

"So you think my idea's a bad one?"

"I think it's inopportune."

"I suppose you're right," said Jimmy; but for the first time Hamer wondered whether, in his heart, Jimmy did not think him wrong.

My dear Hamer: As you see, I am writing this en route. We expect to enter the outskirts of London in a day or two. It has been a long and tiring march, and I should like something to happen to cheer the men at the end of it. Nothing would do this so much as the presence of some first-rate Labour leaders to meet us. After all, Hamer, we *are* Labour. If we are not, the word means nothing. Then what is wrong with some leaders of the Party coming to meet us? I write against my will, because we have all felt that it should not be necessary to make this appeal. We have hoped day after day to receive a message saying that we would be met. It has not come, and the men, who felt overlooked and neglected in the Rhondda, feel even more so now that they are in strange places, meeting few friends.

I ask you, Hamer, to come and meet us. We have known one another for half a century. Have I asked you for anything before? I do not think so. I am not asking now for myself. I cannot imagine anything that would cheer up this November weather so much as the sight of your face. If you could induce Ramsay M. to come with you, so much the better. But at all events, come yourself for the sake of all that we hold in common and of memories which, I hope and believe, are not without affection.

A lot of the men have worn out their boots. Pen asks to be remembered to you. She has stood the journey well enough so far as her spirits go, but I can see that she is very tired. I shall not be sorry to get her under a roof. Ever yours, Arnold Ryerson.

My dear Arnold: How unnecessary your letter would have been, how I should have hastened to meet you and your men, had I thought there was the slightest hope of my presence achieving anything useful. Ah, my friend, we have been in tight corners together. We have fought side by side. You know, therefore, that I should have thought no effort too arduous, no labour too great, if it could have served your interest.

For the sake of the old times of which you remind me, and because of present affection, too, I must say frankly that I think this march on London is ill-advised. Your miners are not medieval beggars that they need to show their sores at the street corners. There are doctors about. There is the Party. And within reasonable time the Party will once more form a government. Then will be the moment when any aid I can offer will be effective, not merely spectacular.

Think of the position, my friend. You know that concerned with your march are elements which the Labour Party cannot counte-nance, elements frankly Communistic. If I, or any other leader of the Party, marched into London associated with those people, we should be giving to our political enemies a handle which they would use against us at the very moment when we might hope to be of help to you. Remember what Communism did for us at the last election.

You must believe, then, that I am acting in what I think your own best interest when I refrain from meeting you. I am acting, in short, as a friend – I hope you will come to see, a wise and experienced one.

My thoughts have been much with you during this trying time. In spirit, I have marched by your side every step of the weary way. I am distressed to learn that Pen has found the journey tiring, and though you are too self-sacrificing to speak of yourself, I can well imagine that it has been no easy time for you. Will you, then, while you remain in town, make my house your home? – you and Pen. I should be more than delighted. You will be comfortable here, well looked after, and able to rest at the end of an enterprise which I can deeply admire though I cannot share. Ring me up and let me know that you are going to give me this pleasure. If I am not in, Jimmy Newboult will take a message and make all arrangements. Ever your friend, Hamer.

My dear Hamer: I write this on the eve of entering town. I am naturally sorry that you cannot see your way to help us, and of course, if you think the way you say, you must act accordingly.

Pen and I thank you for the offer of hospitality. We had already been asked by Charles and Alice to use their rooms at Mrs. Lightowler's, but we think we ought to stay with the men. We have led them all this way, and they might misunderstand if we now went into comfortable quarters. They are all staying out at Bethnal Green. I am not sure where that is, but at any rate I shall go with them. Pen too. Yours sincerely, Arnold Ryerson.

P.S. If you have any old boots that you have grown out of, perhaps Jimmy Newboult could make arrangements to send them to Bethnal Green. No doubt he could discover where we are staying.

Hamer read the postscript several times, with knitted brows. He had never known Arnold Ryerson guilty, or even capable, of irony. He decided that he had read more into it than was warranted.

It was a week of rain and fog and misery. From their quarters in Bethnal Green the miners marched into the city. They sang their hymns and songs, they held open-air meetings, they passed through Downing Street and Whitehall. They showed their sores at the street corners. In Trafalgar Square they drew a crowd six thousand strong. A pipers' band marched them in. They were a good turn, and they won a rain of pennies. They sang their everlasting hymn-tunes to the crowd surging round the stony-faced lions; and as the dusk of the November night deepened, they lit their miners' lamps that glowed through the murk at the foot of the column whereon, hidden in darkness, Nelson went on expecting every man to do his duty.

For the first few days, wherever they went Pen went with them. They liked her to go with them. She was valiant, and had won their affection. She was picturesque, and helped their show. Her hood and cloak, her white stick and her bicycle-bell, all built up into something that had character and idiosyncrasy, the power to attract attention and sympathy. But bit by bit she wilted; her spirit fell away; and Arnold was aware that though she still marched with the processions, hummed the Welsh hymns whose words she had never mastered, her faith in the enterprise was gone.

She was a tireless walker. Blind though she was, she would not use the buses, or the taxis that the miners now and then offered out of the meagre sums they collected. Lizzie Lightowler wanted to place her car entirely at Pen's service, but she wouldn't have that, either. "Nay, lass," she said, "Ah've walked all my days, an' Ah guess Ah'll go on walking till Ah'm carried."

She herself knew that her mind had lost its grip on this business. So many things suggested not the matter in hand but some happening of the past. This offer of Lizzie's for example. As they walked away from her house, Pen's arm tucked within Arnold's, she squeezed his arm to her side and said: "D'you remember, lad, when tha wanted me to ride in state, coachman art' all?"

He remembered well enough. There in the November chill of London, with yellow fog billowing by in visible waves, with the street-lamps wearing wan haloes and the buses crawling by, blind, bewildered, half-seen monsters in this forest of a city that he hated, he remembered the summer night at Bingley when Ann Artingstall appeared at his meeting, and, with the air of a princess announcing that a pumpkin had become a coach, said that there was a victoria waiting at the door. The recollection of the moment was still for him an enchantment. All his youth seemed focused at that point. Now, thinking back to it with an intolerable nostalgia, it appeared that even as he sat in the carriage, bowling through the warm summer dusk, unable to exchange a word with the girl at his side, with the Cottingley beech-boles silver-grey under the immense droop of their sleeping branches, he must have known that his mind was in pursuit of a bright illusion, that this exquisite moment was poised between his hopes and dreams and desires and the humdrum way of hard struggle and small achievement that the fates had written down for him.

"Aye, luv," he said with a rueful smile, "Ah remember well enough."

"Eh, but Ah were mad!" said Pen with a little laugh. "Ah smashed t'tea bottle wi' a great wallop on t'pavin' stones. Ah could've killed Ann that neet. T'devil were in me. Poor Ann."

Poor Ann! It provided for Arnold the last touch the moment needed, the last reminder that desire and dream, toil and failure alike with toil and honour, are fugitive ripples, restlessly resolving back into the underlying flow of time. Poor Ann, the bright girl with the lustrous hair, the girl who had shared his tea in the Ancoats kitchen, who had at so many points illuminated his own dull dragging way, was dead long since and lying far from the memory of all that, living, she had seemed to charge with her life.

They walked on in silence for a while, Arnold observing what Pen could not see: the strange transformation of London wrought by this foggy weather. Naphtha flares were lit in the middle of the roads, insubstantial silvery bursts of flame, like a succession of little false dawns breaking through the mephitic night. Policemen carried their lighted lanterns, trying to guide the traffic into some sort of order, and the whole yellow-surging world within vision was a chaos peopled by ghosts that loomed for a moment and floated away, and by ruddy eyes that crawled out of the darkness, glowed transiently and were suddenly put out.

"Pen, lass," Arnold said at last, "we'd better take a taxi. We'll be late for the march this afternoon."

"Ah'm not gain' to march," Pen said.

Somehow, he had been expecting that. "You're tired," he said. "You've done too much."

"Ah, Ah'm tired," Pen agreed. "An Ah'm tired of bein' part of a circus. That's what we are, lad. We're a music-hall turn. We've done what we could, an' it's come to nowt. Well, Ah'm not on exhibition any more." She was silent for a moment, then burst out in sudden passion: "Let the God-damn fools spit on us if they want to. They've got their Bank of England stuffed wi' brass, and enough shows an' faldelals to dress a forest of monkeys. But by heck, that's not enough. They'll live to regret the day they let the workers get soft and stale in their bodies an' bitter in their hearts. They'll want us some day, an' I hope to God we'll have the guts to say: 'Go on wantin'. Dig the bloody coal yourselves wi' your Gold Sticks and White Wands and Black Rods. We've 'ad enough.'"

She had stopped dead in her tracks. Her words rang out like a challenge through the pall that hung mourning over the metropolis.

Then she began to cry, clinging to Arnold there in the thick evil-smelling darkness, and his heart was melted to see the tears welling out of the sightless sockets. She cried loudly, with deep distress of soul, and he put his arms about her and comforted her, saying: "Hush, lass, hush. Us'll go on fightin'. Never fear. Never fear."

"It's your work," she sobbed. "All you've lived for, all you've sweated your guts for. I can't see, Arnie, I can't see, but I can feel the darkness all about me, an' I can smell it. It smells evil. All your work, lad – it's ended in a darkness smelling of evil."

They were standing under a plane tree, its blotched peeling winter trunk wet and grimy, and drops of congealed fog fell upon them from the bare branches whose spectral lace vanished in a chill infinity.

Pen leaned back against the trunk, and Arnold wrapped his arms about her and kissed her as though they were young lovers glad of the dark.

"I shall fight on, Pen," he said. "Win or lose, I shall fight on. It were thee taught me to do that. Years ago, Pen, tha said to me: 'Ah don't want thee because tha'rt a winner. Ah want thee, win or lose, so long as tha'll fight.' Remember that, Pen? Remember that?"

"Aye, Ah remember that, Arnie. But the years are so long, lad, an' so many of them are bitter. Ah were a young thing then, an' now Ah'm nobbut a blind old woman far from 'ome. Ah've not got so much as a decent pair of eyes to weep with."

They clung to one another, and Arnold was near to tears himself. "Let's not go back to Bethnal Green," he said. "Let's find some place handy, an' have a bit o' food where it's light an' warm."

"Aye," she said simply. "Let's do that, old luv. Let 'em look after themselves for once, an' let's be alone together."

They were not alone in the busy popular restaurant that Arnold found, heavy with the steam of human bodies, noisy with talk, strident with profuse light shouting defiance to the enveloping gloom. But at least they were away for a moment from their cares. Arnold led Pen tenderly in and out of the crowded tables topped coldly with white marble, and presently they sat down, not facing one another but side by side, their bodies touching, as though they needed the warm reassurance of this physical contact. Arnold looked at the bulky silver watch he had carried ever since the days he was Lizzie Lightowler's secretary. Lizzie had given it to him. It had belonged to her husband. He saw that it was five minutes past one. They went out again at twenty-five minutes to two. Arnold was never to forget that half-hour. Nothing notable happened in it, except that, in relaxation from unusual stress, they felt warm, closer together than they had been for a long time. He remembered the shelves of long, coloured glasses containing virulent-looking drinks, the clatter of cups and saucers and the tinkle of cutlery on the table-tops, the smell of food: tea and fish, buns and steaks, chipped potatoes and fried eggs and mashed potatoes, a lavish blending of all the meals of the day. He remembered the endless coming and going, the shrill clash of a hundred conversations, the whole noisy glitter amid which Pen sat patiently, hardly speaking, in her red hood and cloak, "alone," as she had said, with him. He remembered the door swinging open now and then, letting in a clammy blast and a sight of a subaqueous world in which the shadows of men swam through a grey tenuous element, as though he and Pen and the others were imprisoned in a bright glass bubble sunk to the bed of a sea that was rolling sluggishly over the earth.

He remembered it all because this was the last half-hour he was to spend with Pen, with whom he had spent so many hours and years, and so much of life that was beyond the computation of time.

They went out: a shabby, more-than-middle-aged man, a blind sharp-faced groping woman who would have attracted no attention but for her outlandish dress, and they stood for a moment irresolute on the pavement's edge, drowned in the silence and mystery of the fog. Then they heard, piercing with a heart-breaking poignancy the cold oblivion of the afternoon, the sound with which they were now so familiar, the sound they had first heard when they walked side by side behind the coffin of Ap Rhondda winding its way with so many others, amid the silver sorrow of the trumpets, to the hillside cemetery: the sound of Welsh voices singing the dirges that had the power to cleave to the very marrow of grief. Always moving, the hymn now, sung in this alien place, coming out of throats unseen in the darkness, was heavy with exile and longing. Arnold felt Pen's arm clutch with a sudden convulsion closer upon his own. "It's the boys!" she cried. "Come on! Ah'm not tired now, Arnie. We'll march after all. We'll stick wi' 'em to the end."

She broke from him, and he held out a hand to detain her, saying: "Steady, lass, steady. It's black as pitch." But in Pen's world of darkness, darkness was one, summer's noon and winter's midnight. She thrust out her stick, rang her bell, and fairly ran. He clutched at her cloak, but she was beyond his reach. She was beyond his reach for ever. He was not aware of the car that had stopped. It was lit inside with a rich golden glow, a little rolling world of luxury that had brushed her out of existence. He was aware only of the red cloak, spread upon her like a pall where she lay face-downwards, and of marching feet coming nearer, the hymn-tune dying suddenly out in a consternation of Welsh voices. They all seemed to be crying with his own heart: "Pen! Pen! It's Pen!"

But it wasn't Pen any more. It was the husk of unregarded valour, the clay of a little lamp whose flame had never wavered but was blown out suddenly by a casual wind.

*

Jimmy Newboult brought the news to Half Moon Street. "Pen! God A'mighty, Chief, I remember 'er when she was a slip of a thing 'elping Arnold in St. Swithin's. She goes back a long way, Chief. She goes back to the beginnings. Christ! I can't believe it. Poor Pen!"

Poor Ann! Poor Pen! Poor humanity that must bow the neck and take the blow at last, with much or little done.

"Go away, Jimmy. Go away, there's a good chap."

Jimmy went, leaving the Chief gazing into the fire, his head on the arm draped along the mantelpiece. "Best Welsh steam coal." He remembered the altercation with Pen in his study at Baildon, and the visit to the Rhondda that had followed. He saw her clambering the wall of the colliery yard, silhouetted against the light that flared within, as it were storming an aerie barricade. She had always been like that: an impetuous flyer toward her objectives. Even her blindness had not stopped her. But she was stopped now. Somewhere in the miscellaneous junk of memory were a few lines that he had written when looking out from The Hut upon a rigid winter landscape. They stirred now.

How little snow on Baildon Hill
Makes all the flowers and grasses still.
How still the dreams within the head
One second after we are dead.

How still the dreams! "Where now, my friend, are our dreams?" Old Horst had said that a week or two before Ann died. Ann and Pen. He had heard from Arnold how they had rushed together into their first fight, laying about them in a rainy Bradford street when a pack of factory girls had gone for Arnold. Well, it was all over for both of them. Oblivion without laurels.

He did not go out. He remained in his study, hoping that Arnold would ring him up. It became an obsession with him. He would feel a pardon in Arnold's telling him of Pen's death. But what was there to pardon? He had always acted in the clear light of reason. But he wished Arnold would ring up. If not Arnold, then Alice or Charles. But there was no message from any of them. It was not till after dinner that Lizzie Lightowler came to see him. The old woman was limp with lamentation. For once in her life, she was not only verbose but almost incoherent. He gathered that Arnold had said: "Tell Hamer"; but Charles and Alice had looked stony. "I'll tell him nothing," Alice had broken out at last. "He should have been with us. He should have been here to know for himself. We want men who *know*, not men who need to be told." And, in an atmosphere of misery, no more was said. It was left at that.

Old Pendleton helped him into his thick fleece overcoat. He turned up the astrakhan collar and pulled the brim of his black felt hat down over his eyes. In the street the abominable weather showed no sign of breaking. From his side of Piccadilly he could not see the railings of the Green Park. He got into a taxicab and was taken at a crawl toward the streets about Paddington. He got out and waited, and had not long to wait.

They were not singing as they came two by two, their tread slow and muffled, their lighted miners' lamps pricking the yellow obscurity. The hearse came first. Two horses drew it, breathing smokily in the chill street. This was Pen – all that was left of Pen – lying there with the red hood and cloak draped over the coffin. An unlighted miner's lamp stood upon the coffin, symbol of her swift extinction, symbol of the lightless years through which she had battled valiantly.

Crowds of sightseers stood bare-headed on the pavements, listening to the hobnailed boots shuffling through the gloom, looking at the swaying points of light that emphasized but did not dispel the darkness. Arnold walked behind the hearse, his shoulders bowed, his hat in his hand, his thin hair dewed with vapour. Behind him Charles walked in his old tweeds, wearing no hat or overcoat, looking starved and fanatical, with Alice on his right hand and Lizzie Lightowler on his left. Behind these came the miners, two by two, the lamps swinging in their right hands. There was no sound from the rubber tyres of the hearse. There was no sound at all but the sound of the mourning feet.

Hamer walked on the pavement, level with the hearse. He was not bowed like Arnold. He walked with his shoulders square, his head up, his eyes staring with angry defiance before him. But they fell on nothing but the wreathing fog, the phantasms and insubstantialities that appeared and beckoned and melted and were gone.

The station was cavernous, resonant, cold, choked with the confluence of engine-steam and evil vapour. The hearse came to a standstill, and Arnold, Charles, Alice and Lizzie stood, too. The miners marched on, broke their double line, and in a single file stood with heads bowed, lamps hanging in front of them in joined hands, along the platform before the waiting train. Standing thus, at length they began to sing. The lovely harmonious voices lifted to the hidden roof, sending their aspiration up to a heaven that had never seemed so far removed. It was the hymn they could not resist, the hymn they sang in joy and sorrow, "Jesu, Lover of My Soul," to Parry's incomparable tune. And as they sang, Hamer, standing behind them, saw the red-palled coffin coming down the platform on the shoulders of four little bowed men, with Arnold and the others crunching slowly behind it. When it was abreast of him, he turned down the collar of his overcoat, took out the dark carnation that was in the buttonhole, and broke through the miners' line. "Hide me, o my Saviour, hide," they were singing as, hatless, he dropped the red flower on the red pall, his eyes so blinded with tears that the long box and the people with it went by in a moving blur, and he did not know whether they saw him or not.

Only when the singing had stopped, and the four living and one dead were aboard the train, and the engine gave a great deep shuddering cough and began to move, did he come to himself. Then he ran forward, searching the windows of the compartments and crying "Arnold! Arnold!" But the train slid by, and he did not see the face he sought, and presently the gloom swallowed all up and left him lonely and desolate, as though he had witnessed the burial of his youth.

Chapter Twenty-One

Two cities had conferred their freedom upon him; he was an LL.D. of one university, Rector of another, D.Litt. of a third. He was a Privy Councillor, His Majesty's Minister for the Co-ordination of Internal Affairs in the second Labour Government, and he was sixty-five years of age. It was December 20, 1929, his birthday, and he had asked the Earl and Countess of Lostwithiel to dinner. He had also asked Charles and Alice. Unlike the Earl and Countess, they had found some reason to decline, but Lizzie Lightowler would be there, and a foreign ambassador with his wife, and a much-talked-of sculptor with a lovely girl who probably was not his wife. Eight, Hamer thought, looking in at the dining-room was the perfect number for an intimate dinner.

The room had never looked so enchanting. He had been in Half Moon Street for some years now and had acquired some lovely things. The picture by Duncan Grant that he had once asked Lady Lostwithiel to see had three or four companions. He was particularly fond of an oil by L.S. Lowry, a painter not so well known, he felt, as he deserved to be outside Manchester where he lived. This picture showed a steep unlovely street, one whole side of it occupied by a mill wall, and it was full of clogged feet whose clatter you could almost hear and of grey shawls drawn over heads that you knew, without seeing them, were grey with labour. The lives of the poor! One should be reminded of them.

He had found the long refectory table in a Yorkshire farmhouse. Generations of bucolic elbows had brought its surface to the sheen of satin. He looked with satisfaction at the firelight catching its edges, shining in the deep hollows worn in the rungs. It would be a shame to put a cloth on such a table. He walked round it, touching here and there the Jensen silver that had been laid out, re-arranging with a sure touch the flowers that had come round from Shepherd Market. In each of the finger-bowls on the sideboard floated a few petals of syringa. The china waiting for use was a reproduction of the Copenhagen Flora Danica set.

He stood before the fire for a moment, looking on all these things that satisfied in him some deep need for beauty. The wall-lights glowed behind their shades of golden parchment. A hired cook was in the kitchen, for Mrs. Pendleton was not to be trusted with such a dinner as this, and there would be two hired waiters. Old Pendleton would have nothing to do but announce people and look after the coffee and cigars. It was all going to cost Hamer a pretty penny, but he could well afford it. He had discreetly inquired of Lizzie Lightowler concerning the finances of Charles and Alice, and no help from him was needed there. There was a mystery about the business – Lizzie herself did not know where the money was coming from; but it was coming, clearly, in comfortable quantities, so that he had no one to provide for but himself.

He balanced his tall body up and down on his heels, chewing over that reflection and trying to be pleased with it. No chick nor child. Stupid old phrase. But in the quiet house, filled with exquisite inanimate possessions, he was seized now, as he was more and more often seized, with a loneliness, a sense of living in a cosy vacuum, that would have been a little frightening if he had allowed his mind to dwell upon it. Charles, now. Charles saw more of Arnold Ryerson than he did of his own father. Wherever the money was coming from, Alice was spending it freely on Arnold since Pen's death. Arnold would not leave Cwmdulais, but almost every week-end either he came up to town or the young people went to the Rhondda or to some South Wales coast resort where Arnold joined them. All out of that money that Alice mysteriously commanded.

When Arnold came to town, he did not see Hamer. There seemed to be a conspiracy to keep them apart. But from one thought he drew satisfaction. Lizzie Lightowler, his informant in family matters, told him that Arnold had insisted on the red carnation being left on Pen's pall. Solitary, it had jolted through the night to the Rhondda. Hidden beneath masses of flowers, it had lain upon her grave, and tied to its broken stem was a card, written in Arnold's hand: "From Hamer."

The well-conducted, deep-carpeted house was so quiet that he heard the faint silvery chime of the clock in his study telling the quarter-hour, relentlessly marking the march of this new year of his life, eating already into the hours of this anniversary of the day when, sixty-five years ago, he had been born in circumstances of what ignominy who knew?

His restless heels had come to a stand. He remained for a moment, tall and brooding, teased by the unresolved enigma of his life, a little resentful, a little proud; then, shaking himself, he went upstairs to bath and change. Full fig. He adjusted to perfection the white butterfly tie, put the carnation into his buttonhole. His studs and cuff-links were of square-cut onyx, unadorned. He preferred them to any metal or jewellery. He went down to wait.

Ramsay MacDonald, a widower like himself, ambitious like himself, as interested but not so deeply instructed as himself in cultural matters, had been there once or twice to dinner, and they had enjoyed the opportunity to forget "the Party," the eternal playing up to a crowd, and to talk about books and pictures, to exchange an occasional appreciative anecdote about a peeress. They were much the same type of man: they got on well together. MacDonald was struck one night with the amusing idea that had entered Hamer's own head. Looking at the red couches by the study fire, he said: "What do you do here, Hamer: practise sitting in the Lords?"

Hamer laughed it off; but MacDonald said: "It may come to that, you know. The Liberals had to pack their men into the Lords, and we may have to do it, too. I don't think Philip Snowden would mind. What about you?"

Hamer drew himself up to his great height and said jocularly: "Look at me. I was made for ermine."

The subject fizzled out on a half-facetious note.

There has been these little dinners with one friend, or two or three, but this was the first time he had "entertained" in a grand way. But he was easy in his mind, waiting there for Lizzie, who would be with him to receive the guests. He had chosen his company well. The sculptor was a witty talker who was anxious to sculp his head, and the girl with him was desirable for her startling decorative value. Hamer liked the company of handsome women. The ambassador was a sardonic fellow with no illusions. His conversation was salted and astringent. Hamer welcomed his abhorrence of sentiment and humbug. Believing that Europe was hastening to the devil, he would say so with always some new mordant twist, opening the way for endless talk and speculation. His wife was a dowdy nonentity. Lostwithiel, who was once accredited to her country, could look after her.

Lostwithiel was the dubious member of the party. Hamer was without self-deceit where Lostwithiel was concerned. The man tolerated without liking him. It was Lady Lostwithiel who seemed not only willing but almost anxious to cultivate him. "She wants to cut your claws, Chief. That's the long and short of it," Jimmy Newboult dared to say one day; and in his heart Hamer was prepared to admit that perhaps in the beginning that had been part of her intention. But now, he believed, she had some personal feeling for him; and he didn't care who knew that he liked her. She had retained her beauty, she had deepened her humanity; her voice had lovely tones. He wouldn't have minded, he sometimes extravagantly thought, if the tones of Lettice Lostwithiel's voice told off his passing like the silvery bell on his study clock. Notes were frequent between them: about books and pictures, affairs in countries that both knew intimately, about this and that. He had not destroyed one of her notes. They helped a little with the half-regretful feeling that he was made for ermine.

Lostwithiel was another matter. The years had changed the ineffective youth of St. Swithin's into a small, dry, formidable man, profoundly versed in all the chicane and trickery of government. If to meet these Labour chaps helped, if it would do anything to keep them quiet and docile, then so far Lettice had better have her head. That was his view, and Hamer knew it.

He led Lady Lostwithiel into the dining-room. She sat at his right hand, the ambassador's wife at his left. Beyond the ambassadress sat Lostwithiel, who screwed a glass into his eye, gave a searching sardonic glance at a Labour interior, then, as it were with a startled jerk of the eyebrows, caused the glass to drop abruptly.

"Didn't Keir Hardie toast his own bannocks, Shawcross?" he asked loudly.

"He did," said Hamer suavely. "Would you call that a virtue?"

"In a way – yes."

"Well," Hamer smiled, "it's open, I suppose, to anyone of us to practise it?"

The ambassador, the Count of Fuentavera, stroked his small silvery pointed beard, and said across the table to Lostwithiel: "It's a virtue I commend especially to you, and to myself. We shall all be toasting our own bannocks soon – if we have any bannocks to toast, and any fire to toast them at."

Lostwithiel laughed harshly. "Your ears, my dear Fuentavera," he said, screwing in his eyeglass to look critically at his soup, "are tone-deaf to everything but disaster. If a hen cackles you think the foxes are rampant. If a twig snaps you imagine the forest is coming down."

"My dear Lostwithiel," said the count, "you will pardon my telling you that the English are the most obtuse people in the world, and you, my dear sir, as I have told you many times, are the most obtuse of the English. Is it a hen cackling in the United States at this moment? Half Wall Street would be glad of bannocks to toast. Is it a twig snapping in Austria? Or here in your own country, with your millions of unemployed, with your National Insurance Fund as bankrupt as Wall Street itself? These things are the beginning. Let me tell you that in five years from this time—"

They were happily away on their hobby-horses, and Hamer turned with contentment to Lady Lostwithiel.

"I'm going to be a nuisance to you," she said. "I expect a lot of your friends ask you to read their books?"

"As a matter of fact, no. I'm not a man of letters, you know," he said, believing that firmly. "I've written a lot in my time, but it's all been propaganda stuff. Why should people want my opinion about books?"

"Oh, anyone's opinion goes nowadays," she laughed. "I saw a publisher's advertisement on Sunday, giving a comedian's view of a very serious novel. So why not a Cabinet minister's?"

A Cabinet minister's! He liked to hear her say that. There were times, even now when his name flared at him from every newspaper in the land every day, when he couldn't open his mouth in public without seeing a dozen reporters taking out their note-books at a table in front of him: even yet there were times when he could not get over this fact of being a Cabinet minister. With his anxious attention everywhere: watching critically the silent dexterous waiters, noting that Lizzie and Sanderson the sculptor were getting on well together, taking in appreciatively the beautiful bare shoulders of Sanderson's girl as she drooped back on to her chair a slip of a fur cape: with all these preoccupations of a host and connoisseur, he found a space within his mind to marvel that *he* had called this elegant and successful little occasion into being: he, Hamer Shawcross, Privy Councillor.

"You are too modest," Lettice Lostwithiel was saying, "though, of course, this is the only matter on which you have any modesty at all. You are as vain as Lucifer, and look it."

"Lucifer wasn't vain," he corrected. "He was proud."

"Have it how you like," she said. "But I do want you to read a little book I've written. You remember old Buck?"

Did he remember old Buck! The waiter's black sleeve came across his shoulder, and he watched the rosy wine rising in the glass. So rosy, so tinged with reminiscent sentiment, was the thought of old Buck now – a strange, ogreish, legendary creature out of a tale read in youth, a tale that had caused a shudder but now was powerless to affright. He raised the glass to his lips and sipped the wine. "Yes," he said. "What a man! They don't breed 'em now."

"He was obsessed," said Lettice, "with the idea that all he stood for couldn't last. It was on his mind the night he died. I wrapped him up before he went out for that idiotic drive, and he talked about it then. He said he hoped I'd have a son. We'd need men, he said. Well, I didn't have a son."

She sighed, and Hamer knew well enough what the sigh was for. Surely…Surely…He had always distrusted that word. You could be sure of nothing. All he had hoped for Charles had come to the rather pathetic end of the unsuccessful writer in papers with high ideals and low circulations. As for Lostwithiel's daughter: he remembered old Buck announcing her birth, telling the burgesses of St. Swithin's that she would be ripe to represent them when Liskeard had moved into the Lords. Well, she had proved ripe for other things than that: over-ripe, rotten-ripe, in those few crazy years after the war when barricades of morality, usage, tradition, spectacularly crashed. Drugs, drink: there was the crude truth. Her movements into and out of discreet homes in the country, which "cured" her for a month or two, were known and talked about. She was a beautiful girl whose photograph looked well in the viler newspapers. That was the worst of it. "Back again, after a vacation in the country, to add colour to the lives of London's brighter young people." It was heartbreaking. Hamer knew that the great house on which he and Arnold had looked down so long ago, watching Lettice Melland jog over the humpbacked bridge on her barrel-bellied pony: he knew that that great house rested now on sand. They had looked on it as the incarnation of the might against which they must pit themselves, Goliath with all his brazen breastplates defiant before their puny slings; and time had done what they had been unable to do. Their pebbles had not been needed. This dry, tough, able and, he felt, unscrupulous man, sitting a few paces away, was the deadend of the Lostwithiels. Buck had been an only child, and so was this Lostwithiel. It was a strange family that had run to only children, and this time the child was a daughter, and bad stock.

All this was behind the sigh that fell on Hamer's ear as he sat there fingering the stem of his glass. When you got old, he reflected, so much could lie behind a gesture, a turn of the head, a lift of the shoulder, a word, a tear. But Lettice Lostwithiel was not one to parade things, and especially this thing. She went on: "I think Buck was right. It's all going – all that he knew. Half my friends seem to have estates in the market." She smiled. "You know, you Socialists have won."

Lostwithiel, who had heard the end of the conversation, turned to say: "Yes, a grand victory, Shawcross. You've handed over England's green and pleasant land to the jerry-builder. That's the Jerusalem you've built. You'll want that cornland and pasture one of these days. When the next war comes, it'll be a great help to have ten thousand stockbrokers' clerks living on an estate like Castle Hereward."

"The next war, my friend," said Fuentavera, who could never resist the subject; and they were off again. Hamer turned once more to Lettice: "And your book is about all that?"

"Yes. It's just the story of my own childhood. I've tried to put on record what it was like to be born and brought up in the great houses. It was all rather lovely, you know, in its way. The hunting and shooting, the Christmas parties at places like Trentham, the speech-days at Eton, and the cricket matches and races. All the boys and gels I knew…"

All the boys and gels I knew. That was it. That was the essence of any story, and the story was much the same whether they were chimney-sweepers or golden lads and lasses.

"I'd love to read it," Hamer said. "Have you found a publisher?"

"No. I don't know anything about that sort of thing."

"Leave it to me," he said confidently.

"Oh, but I couldn't bother you. With all your work."

"I'll deal with it." He could find time for *that*!

*

She had brought the typescript with her. They were alone for just a moment when she handed it to him. She thought he looked very happy, and guessed that the evening had been a little triumph for him, a bolster to his esteem. Not his vanity, his pride. She accepted the correction. She noticed again how handsome he was. The years had obliterated a certain raffishness, a swashbuckling quality that had been in the good looks of his youth. His hair now, falling across his forehead, was quite white and lustrous. He pushed it back with a characteristic gesture as he took the parcel and laid it on his writing-table. "You are very good, my dear," she said. She took his hand in one of hers and patted it in brief affection with the other.

When they were all gone, he sat with his legs up on one of the couches, ready to read. Most of his reading now had to be done after midnight. Old Pendleton came in and suggested anxiously, as he so often did, that it was more than bedtime. "No, no. Off with you and get your beauty sleep," Hamer said, flashing on his smile. "And thank you. Everything was splendid. Tell Mrs. Pendleton so."

Everything was splendid. "You are very good, my dear." An old woman whose life was so far behind her that she had already memorialized it, and an old man whose youth was a dream, whose hates and animosities were dying embers. A touch of affection between the two. That was all. But everything was splendid.

He began to read. He began to discover the young Letty, the girl who existed before he had set eyes on her, the girl who was riding her first pony round the paddock while he was trudging from Broadbent Street to school. Great names resounded through the pages. Half the Cabinet ministers who had governed before the Liberal uprising seemed to have been her uncles, godfathers, or what not. And all these names were woven into a story of grooms, guns and gaiters, the summer meadows, the autumn woods and fields, with the shadow of the great house in the background. It was all like a pretty embroidery on a page of English history. And fundamentally he knew that it *was* English history, that the stuff historians wrote missed the point, that for each one of us history is neither more nor less than what happens to me. And to "the boys and gels I knew." Most of those that Lettice had written about were gone. Those that remained were already legends of the prime, lingering on into the present dissolution and decay.

The reflection startled him. He put down the typescript and lay back with his eyes closed. His clock struck three. It was so quiet that he heard the distant boom of Big Ben, repeating the small clear notes that had fallen into the room. Dissolution and decay. Was that what he thought of the world he was living in? Yes, it was. He had lived to see all that Shawcross of Peterloo had fought for nearer to attainment than he had ever believed possible. The dying Liberals had bequeathed an immense achievement in social legislation, and the Labour Party had twice held office. Lettice Lostwithiel had said: "You Socialists have won." That was nonsense: what remained to be done was immeasurably greater than anything done yet. But, all the same, his cause had prospered, and it had brought him into a world which seemed to him dull, stale, flat and unprofitable, lacking the heroic temper and the individual genius of the world he had known. Perhaps it was simply that he was growing old. Whatever it was, he went slowly up to bed, thinking of the past with regret, of the present with distaste, and of the future with a grey foreboding.

Perhaps he was growing old. He was beginning to like his comfort. He could work as hard as ever. He could read till three in the morning and be up at half-past seven, and feel none the worse. But he would have hated to get up if Pendleton had not brought his morning tea. From a hard day's work in Whitehall and the House of Commons he could go on, fresh as paint, to speak after a dinner, but he wouldn't have liked the bother of putting his studs in his shirt. At the recent election he had worked in St. Swithin's with furious energy and had found time, too, to go and speak for Jimmy Newboult and other candidates. But he had taken Pendleton with him, to look after his creature comforts. "Remember Pen Muff wi' the cold tea for Arnold?" Jimmy asked with a grin. He slapped Hamer on the shoulder: a gesture few of Labour's rank and file would have used in those days. "Yon chap Pendleton's your cold-tea bearer. You used to have a sword-bearer; now you want a cup-bearer, a blanket-carrier, a foot-warmer."

Jimmy spoke jocularly, but Hamer was not misled. Jimmy was not his man in the full and dedicated sense that he once had been. He was prepared to criticize. He was on the look-out for sun-spots. He had gone to Pen's funeral at Cwmdulais. He had followed her body up the winding road on which Ap Rhondda and Richard Richards and Evan Hughes had preceded her. He had left the house in Half Moon

Street soon afterwards, and had never been quite the same since. Now Hamer had made him his Parliamentary private secretary. He loved the job and did it well. They were closer together again, and Jimmy said "Chief" with the old devoted intonation. But Hamer sensed the jealousy in his heart: the jealousy of a lover who fears, after many years, the straying of the beloved.

And so, as Hamer stood at the window looking into Half Moon Street on the morning after his dinner party, he thought of Jimmy. He wondered what Jimmy would say of this car, now sliding to a standstill outside the house. It was not the most expensive car in the world, but it was a nice-looking thing, and a liveried chauffeur sat at the wheel. He had brought it round from the garage in a nearby mews. Over the garage was a small flat where the chauffeur lived. He was a good-looking boy. He couldn't be more than twenty-five – one of those public school men who could not find a footing in this queer modern world. Jimmy would hate his accent.

Well, Jimmy could think what he pleased. Perhaps I'm getting old, Hamer thought again. Anyway, this was another of those comforts that he liked because, he persuaded himself, they allowed him to get through so much more work. This very morning, for example: he could nip round to his literary agent's office with Lady Lostwithiel's typescript and still be in Whitehall no later than usual. He would miss his brief morning walk across the Green Park, but in this life you can't have everything.

"The car, sir," said Pendleton.

The olive-green car stopped. Chesser – Stinker to old Wykehamists – leapt down from his seat, glad to be doing his first day's work, and opened the door. Stinker Chesser's grandfather had been a Cabinet minister under Salisbury. His sister was now a manikin, and his mother lived at *en pension* rates in Harrogate. Stinker stood bolt upright holding the handle of the door, his face as grave as a carved marble of Apollo. Hamer came out bent double, stood upright, and said: "It's a lovely morning. You are permitted to smile." He himself smiled as he knew well how to, and Stinker obediently lighted up, with crinkles round his deep blue eyes. He preferred to smile, if only this damned world would let him. He had been haunted by the fear that this Labour chap might make him feel a worm, take it out of him. He looked at the tall figure disappearing into the office, and began to whistle. It *was* a lovely morning, now he had the heart to notice it. He took out a duster and rubbed a spot of dirt from the car.

It did not take Hamer more than ten minutes to convey to his agent his own enthusiasm for Lady Lostwithiel's book and to suggest who should publish it. Then, eager to justify his car by being at Whitehall on time, he went briskly out of the office and ran down the stairs. There was a sharp turn half-way down, and it was there that he collided with Alice. She was coming up slowly and quietly. He heard nothing, and was on top of her, spilling the papers she carried, before he could check himself.

"Oh, I'm sorry, most terribly sorry."

Then he recognized her. "My dear, I hope I did no damage."

"None at all." She seemed dour and cross, and bent to pick up the scattered papers.

"No. Let me do that. I'm sixty-five, but I can still touch my toes."

He gathered up the newspapers and a book which had fallen open among them. It was the sort of book which few people see: a proof copy, in paper covers. He saw printed across the top of the open page the title: "Fall to Your Prayers, Old Man," and here and there in the margin, written in Alice's bold thick unmistakable hand and in the green ink she always used, were one or two corrections. Hamer looked up at Alice in surprise. "Hallo!" he said. "You turned author?"

He couldn't make out what was the matter with her. She was leaning against the angle of the stairs looking pale and distressed. She was not at all her usual self-possessed woman. He closed the book and handed it to her, and then his eye fell again on the title printed across the paper cover and on the author's name, Gabrielle Minto. For a moment this perplexed him, then he gave a surprised "Oh!" of complete realization. "Oh!" he said. "So that's it! I thought you looked a bit off your stroke, my dear. Are you terribly annoyed at being found out?"

She continued to lean against the wall, as though glad of its support. "It's not that," she said. "Charles has left me."

Lizzie had gone for a walk. Alice was in Fleet Street. Charles was alone in the rooms they occupied on the first floor in North Street. He was so untidy that he might almost have been called ragged. The cuffs of his tweed jacket were whiskered and his flannel trousers were spotted with grease. He wore no tie. His shirt was open at the collar. His finger-nails were dirty and his face was not properly shaved. There had been a time when all this might have been written off as the affectation of a picturesque rebellious boy. But Charles was a boy no longer. He was thirty-two. He looked, and was, a careless, slipshod, unsuccessful man, angry with a world which had failed to see in him the character he imagined himself to be.

Angry; especially at this moment, with Alice. He looked round the room, and everything in it screamed at him: Alice, Alice, Alice! The desk he wrote at, the beautiful simple modern furniture, the carpet on the floor, the pictures on the wall: Alice had bought them all.

He stood at the window, pushed aside Alice's curtains impatiently, and looked down into the street, gnawing his nails already bitten to the quick: looked down at the bright affected little doors of red and green and yellow, the brass knockers, the painted railings, all trying their damnedest, in a toy-shop fashion, to seem cheerful and happy under the grey sky into which the chimney-stacks cut their shapes with uncompromising realism.

He was beginning to loathe it all. He was beginning to see it as an Ibsenesque doll's house in which a woman had shut him up. He walked away from the window, turning the thought over in his mind. An amusing inversion: there might be a play in it. He had never tried a play. But the thought soon faded out of his mind, dissolving in his general misery like the pale blue smoke of the chimneys dissolving against the grey of the London sky.

Even the harping, carping, cavilling articles that he supplied to some of the weeklies were beginning to be turned down. "Look here, old man" – this was Rossiter of *Intelligentsia* – the disgruntled old sweat attitude is played out. The next war's too near for us to keep on the sympathetic stop for the sorrows of the last war's victims."

That was bad enough, but for Alice to back it up: that was too much! "There's something in it, my dear," she said. "I don't think anything worth while was ever created out of mere resentment."

"But damn it all, Alice!" he burst out. "Don't you resent the world you're living in? Don't you think ninety people in a hundred are trea-ted like hog-wash for fat swine. Don't you want to bring it all down with a crash?"

She looked at his pale thin weary face – the face of this man so utterly dependent on her – and her heart was wrung with compassion. "Yes," she said, "you're quite right about all that; but there is also this: I enjoy every minute of my life." She reached across the table and laid a hand on his. "I wish you could do that, Charles. When you've got a long, long journey in front of you, what's the sense of storing up your joy till you get to the end of it? You may never get there. So try to get some fun out of the road."

He pulled away his hand impatiently and stood up. "My God! Quite a little philosopher!" he said with a sour grin.

She was hurt by that. "It was a philosophy good enough for my mother," she said. "Her life was no easier than yours, but she enjoyed the fight. Even when she was blind, up to the very end, she was happy."

"Well, I'm not," said Charles. "I'm sick of my spoon-fed bloody existence." He got up, strode to the window, and stood, hands in pocket, glowering down into the street.

Alice looked sorrowfully at the bowed head, the narrow shoulders, silhouetted against the pale diaphanous net of the curtain. She could feel the tears behind her eyelids, but she would not let them fall. She knew well enough what was the matter with Charles. His love had turned to bitterness because it could not pour out the gifts of its own generosity. He would have been happy had he been able to do for her all that she had done for him. She was oppressed with a sense of crisis as she watched the defeated figure slouched brokenly against the pearly-grey light. Suddenly he turned round and demanded in a high excited voice: "And where does the money come from? That's what I'd like to know? *I* know what one gets paid for your sort of journalism, and it doesn't buy all this." He waved his hand round the room. "You're seeing a damned sight more than I like of Pappenheimer. The place stinks of his hair-oil."

She felt as though he had stabbed her. She understood the desperation and despair that had led him to make a suggestion so horrible. But all the same she wondered if she could ever forgive him. She stared at him stonily, saying nothing. He came round the table and seized her wrist in his cold bony clutch. She had never seen him look so wolfish and ravening. "He's rich, isn't he?" he demanded. "He can give you everything. Some bloody Communist, Mr. Pappenheimer! I don't like him. I don't want to see him about the place any more – understand that? When I come in, I don't want to smell the trace of him. It makes me retch. He's – unsavoury."

She could not be angry. She could only be overwhelmed by the desolation that was in her heart. She could only be numbed by sorrow that life had brought Charles to this. She got up and shook him off easily but kindly. She walked into the next room and took from her desk a little book in which she had kept a record of all the financial and other concerns of Gabrielle Minto. Then she put on her hat and coat. When she went back, he was standing again at the window. She put the book on the table and said: "Charles, I have to go out. I'd like you to examine this while I'm away."

He did not turn round, but when she was in the street he craned his neck hungrily to catch a glimpse of the trim little figure walking along the pavement.

Alice's bookkeeping, like everything else about her, was clear and straightforward. It did not take Charles five minutes to discover all that she wanted him to know. Since their marriage she had written eight novels. None of them was out of print. Even the first was still selling freely in cheap editions on the bookstalls. "Peter Paul Perkins," the most successful of them, had sold nearly 100,000 copies in its most expensive edition. One way and another, she had never made less than between £2,000 and £3,000 a year since she began to write; in some years more.

Charles put down the book and sat with his head in his hands, his temples throbbing, his hollow cheeks twitching with a tic. He couldn't understand her. She was not only rich: she was famous. It wasn't the sort of fame he would have liked for himself. Some carping jealous reserve wouldn't allow him to admit that. But he did admit, sitting there twisting his nervous fingers into his hair, that he himself had desired above all things to be a famous man. Some fatal indecision, some native deficiency, had defeated him. And Alice all this time might have enjoyed the popular applause, the public acclaim, that he himself had savoured: savoured for a flashing hour to which, as to a bright oasis, he looked back with increasing gall and bitterness as he journeyed deeper and deeper into arid deserts of impotence and nonentity.

He couldn't understand her. And then he understood her with a sudden searing clarity that brought him to his feet with a curse. God damn her. She pitied him! She was hiding her light under a bushel lest it put him in eclipse. All his self-pity, all his resentment against a world which held him cheap, blazed and danced around him. He loathed the very clothes he wore, rags though they were. Alice's money had bought them. He had a small pension for the loss of his leg; he earned a guinea here and a guinea there. That was all. And the guineas were becoming fewer. His last novel, the one after *Phœnix*, had not found a publisher, and he had never tried another. A failure was fatal for him.

And what confronted him now was not a failure. It was Failure's very self, in all its grinning immensity and finality. Pitied! Pitied by Alice, as he had been, he swiftly persuaded himself, pitied by everybody: his father, Lizzie Lightowler, Pen, Arnold. He thought of the old woman Ellen, his grandmother. His vision of her was tinged with the sentimental rosy clouds of distance. She hadn't pitied him. Hers, he said, was the only breast on which he had happily lain.

To spare his feelings, so that he should never have to come to her for money, Alice paid all she earned into an account opened in their joint names. He had only to go and draw what he wanted. But his pride made him keep such calls on the account down to a miserly sum. That was why he wore his clothes to rags. She understood that, and never urged him to buy new clothes.

Now he took out his cheque-book. "Pay self £50." It wasn't much. A cheap price for getting rid of a grave liability, he reflected bitterly. He put on the overcoat and hat which he did not often wear, went out into the grey street, and limped slowly away.

A week later he had not returned, and it was with all the weariness and anxiety of that week in her face that Alice met Hamer on the stairway and said: "Charles has left me."

"Come with me to The Hut," Hamer said.

He and Alice had eaten dinner together in Half Moon Street. Usually, she was self-reliant; there was almost a defiance about her; but, leaning against the angle of the stairway, she seemed, for the first time in his knowledge, shaken and indeterminate. "You must come and have some dinner with me," he said. "You're looking like death, girl."

"I'm feeling like death," she admitted.

"You ought to have let me know about this long ago," Hamer protested. "Why hasn't Lizzie rung me up? You'd better ask her to come along with you tonight."

"Please," said Alice. "D'you mind if I come alone?"

"God bless me! Mind? Why, I shall be delighted. I didn't know that you'd want to dine alone with a shady character like me: that's all."

"Don't think me horrid and ungrateful," she said. "Lizzie's done a lot for me and Charles, but I'd welcome a chance to get away from her."

"Lizzie's done a lot for everybody," he said. "She did a lot for me, and she did even more for your father. But I know what you mean. Poor Lizzie! Very well, then. I'll send the car for you soon after seven."

For the first time she smiled. "I like you," she said. "You're old, and yet you're like a child. Charles is so childish, and yet so old. However, don't bother about your new toy. I'll walk. I'd rather walk."

She began to go on up the stairs. Hamer called her: "Alice! If you want this Minto business kept secret, you can rely on me. But I'm glad I know. I'm very proud of you. And not only for writing the books. You're a grand woman."

He was late at Whitehall, and before sitting down to his desk he stood before the fire thinking that he had been lucky in knowing his share of grand women: Ellen, Ann, Pen Muff, Lettice Melland, and Alice Ryerson. Lizzie? She was a good old stick, but her excessive busy-ness had never hidden a woolly streak in her. She was cake, not good crusty bread. Poor Lizzie!

When Alice came to dinner she looked better than she had done in the morning. He was glad to see that she had taken pains with her appearance. When he was alone he often had dinner in his study, at a little table close up to the fire, and he did this now, so that Alice should feel cosy and at home. After they had eaten, he said: "Now, my dear, tell me what you've been doing today."

"Well, first of all, I went round to Fleet Street to blow the gaff on myself."

She produced an evening newspaper. There was her photograph – very attractive, too, Hamer thought – and the identity of Gabrielle Minto at last revealed.

"It will be amusing to see what effect that has on my sales," she said. "The books are harmless, but seeing that they come from a notorious Communist candidate, the old ladies may turn sniffy. However, it doesn't matter, for I don't suppose I'll write any more of them. I'm going to Moscow."

"Moscow!"

"Yes, as a correspondent."

"Ah, Pappenheimer's job!"

"That's it. I wish Charles had been as good a guesser as you are." Her face saddened. "I've known Pappenheimer a long time. He showed me everything and introduced me to everybody when I was in Moscow with Charles. He always called when he was over here on holiday. Now that he's resigned the job out there, he's been seeing me nearly every day, trying to persuade me to take it on. I didn't want it, so long as Charles had his little bits of work to keep him busy here in London."

"You'd have liked it, though?"

"I'd have jumped at it. To live in Moscow!"

"What a damned fool the boy is!" Hamer exploded.

"No, no!" she protested. "He's a child, but not a fool. It's I have been the fool. There must have been some way...I must have gone wrong somewhere..."

She looked up at him in a sad perplexity, as if out of his wisdom he might find the word to tell how she had lost her way. He shook his head. "I can't help you, my dear. You know, he left me, too. Did we both fail him, or did he fail us both?"

"The world failed him," she said. "It was never a good enough place for the likes of Charles."

"Don't blame the world too much," he advised her. "When I was young, I was as ready as you are to blame everything on to 'the world.' It's such an easy target till you come to shoot at it. Then you find, to your perplexity, that it isn't there to be shot at. I'm going to preach to you. I'm old enough to be your father-confessor."

She gave him a smile. "I am beginning to think," she said, "that there are few people whose sermons I'd rather listen to. So preach away."

"Well, the older I get, the less I believe that a change in what we like to call 'the world' will have any effect on the things that belong to our peace. An old German said to me, about the time my wife died: 'There's no peace except the peace in a man's heart.' I believe that that is true. When we politicians talk about changing the world, we mean no more than bringing in a few of our own fashions to replace certain fashions that we dislike. To ninety-nine people in a hundred it means nothing whatever. Both we and the people we have replaced might just as well have never existed so far as the essential things of most lives are concerned. By essential things I mean such things as have been between you and Charles. You say the world was not good enough for him. You think that if you had had a Communist government here in Britain you would have changed the world. I don't believe it would have made two-pennyworth of difference to Charles. He would still have had a loose-ended mind, incapable of coming to conclusions, and that's the root of your trouble. He has shot off now because he received a final blow: the blow of discovering that through all these years you were his superior in a sphere wherein he thought you couldn't touch him. These are the things that make the bed-rock conflicts of life: not whether women shall vote or Parliaments dissolve. No government that ever will be can do more than maintain a clear framework within which the essential acts of private life may go on. The more a government confines itself to that, and keeps out of the way of the lives of the people, the better government it is; and that is why I think your dream of turning everything upside down and setting the world by the ears is more than wicked: it is useless. It's no good to sit down excusing our deficiencies while waiting for a world that's worthy of us. Let us be worthy of a better world, and then, by that very fact, the better world is with us and within us. Even a politician should realize that the more virtue we have the fewer treaties we shall need."

Alice smoked her cigarette in silence for a while, then said: "Very persuasive. But what does it all come to but *laisser-faire*? I'm surprised you don't adopt Lord Melbourne's motto: 'Why not leave it alone?'"

"There are things that must not be left alone. All I ask you to believe is that in this life you must not expect certain consequences to follow mathematically from certain actions. Assuredly not reformation from revolution."

"We seem to be a long way from me and Charles."

"That is what I am emphasizing. You think that a different sort of world would have made Charles a different sort of man. I am pointing out that I don't believe it. It has taken me a lifetime to find out that the sort of people I want to see prospering are to be found in every party and every walk of life, and that neither the party nor the walk of life has anything to do with the qualities I find admirable in them."

"It only means," she smiled, "that you've dawdled into the lazy tolerance of old age."

"I hope so."

"I'd like to hear you utter these sentiments on a Labour platform."

"You never will. I'm a politician to the marrow."

She looked at him with narrowed eyes, her blunt intelligent face sharpened by the scrutiny, as he stood before her, back to the fire. "I'm going to make a prophecy," she said. "You know as well as I do that this country can't go on as it's going on at present. You Labour people are having your second shot at pulling it out of the mess. You're not succeeding, and you will not succeed. Again, you know that as well as I do. The poor are becoming poorer. The unemployed are so many that they could destroy you by their very numbers if they took it into their heads. Something will have to be done about it, and within a very few years. I know what it will be. It will be the old patriotic act: sink your party differences, rally as one man to save the Empire. The Liberals and Tories will be only too ready to rush into that breach. What about Labour? I will tell you, and this is my prophecy. Labour will be smashed to pieces, like a barrel smashed by the waves against a rock. The Labour Party has come in your time. You saw its beginnings; you helped to make its beginnings – few men more so. And you will help to make its end. That also is my prophecy. You do not believe any more in the thing you made. You are going to destroy it, and before you are many years older thousands of men and women will be cursing your name."

He was shocked. In his time he had heard many hard things said about him and to him, and he had gone his way with a smile. But now he did not smile. Her words disturbed him profoundly. He stood looking down at her with a frown, not answering for a long time. Then he said simply: "I'm sorry that you think that of me."

"What else can I think?" she demanded. "It screams out of every word you've just uttered, out of every action you've taken for years past. Look at that sword!" She pointed to the elegant cabinet containing the sabre of Peterloo. "My father has often talked to me about it. He's told me how you once literally confronted tyranny with that sword in your hand and threatened to cut it down. Look at it now. Does it please you?"

"It's done its work."

"No, no! If you feel that, give the sword to me."

"And what will you do with it?" he smiled. "Whirl it round your head as you walk through the Moscow streets?"

"I'll tell you what I'll do with it," said Alice. "I'll return it to you if in five years' time my prophecy is not fulfilled. The empty case should help you. It will remind you how shocked you were, how unthinkable my suggestion was. Is that a bargain?"

"Yes."

"The first day you opened your mouth in a Labour meeting you carried that sword and called yourself Shawcross of Peterloo. I don't care tuppence about the prosperity of the Labour Party, but I do care about men like you and my father remembering the dreams of their youth."

"What do you know about my dreams?" he asked. "You know only my words. My words have been for others. Am I not allowed a dream for myself?"

She dismissed the whole thing with a laugh. "Ah, well," she said, "so long as you don't dream that the moon is made of green cheese and the earth of beautiful Tories."

Chesser drove her home, and she took the sabre with her. She had promised to travel with Hamer the next day to Baildon. The House was up for the Christmas recess. She would spend a week with him, then pay a farewell visit to Arnold before returning to London to complete her arrangements for travelling to Moscow.

Alice had never before been in Bradford, and for her it was a week of pilgrimage. From Pen and Arnold, from Charles and from Lizzie Lightowler she had heard so much of the place that her mind was full of things she wanted to do and see. Harner was delighted to use this means of keeping her mind off her loss. "I had never before realized that Bradford was a shrine," he laughed, as they stood looking at the ugly old house in Thursley Road where Pen had been born and Arnold had lodged; at Lizzie's old home in Ackroyd Park; at The Hut itself, near the site of Arnold's shack.

"I wish you had left it," she said. "You could have built your house alongside of it, instead of over it."

"Why," he teased her, "you're a sentimentalist, after all. And what a text, if I wanted to give you another sermon. I thought you were all for the clean sweep and the brand new building?"

They were walking in the copse of conifers that had sprung up on the old intake field. A cold blue winter sky was above them. The air had a nip and northern tang.

"You've got me there," Alice said. "I admit the debating-point, but spare me the sermon. Hallo! Here's quite a little house."

The path had led them to the corner of the small estate. The little house was at its end. Hamer took her arm and stayed her. From twenty yards away they looked at the little house. "That is it," he said.

"You kept it, after all?"

He nodded. He was too full of memories to speak. As a rule, he avoided the little house. In these days he did not care to see it. Now his mind rushed back to embrace it as it had been: when it stood in the bleak corner of the field, with none of these trees to hide it, with the blackened stone wall standing between it and the bare noble sweep of the moor; the wall over which he and Arnold had often climbed together; over which he and Ann had come to on their wedding-night, and Jimmy Newboult had clambered the next day with his fantastic wedding-present. That was the day when he had begun to write his first book. So many first things were bound up with this sorry little shack mouldering under the trees at the end of the path: his first parliamentary campaign, his first book, his first night with Ann. Now its roof was matted with a thick brown carpet of needles from the trees, a few of its boards were falling askew, and one of the windowpanes was broken. Even from where they stood, they could see that the woodwork was green and mildewed from the cloistering of the trees and the lack of paint.

"I had almost forgotten it was still there," he said at last.

Alice seemed to be as moved as he was. "So that was Father's little place," she said. "He sometimes talks about it as though it were the loveliest thing."

Yes, no doubt Arnold, too, had been happy here, because here Arnold too had been young.

"You ought to have it put in order,' she said.

"No, no!" he answered almost testily. "Leave it as it is. It'll last my time, and then it won't matter to anyone. Let us see if we can get in."

A piece of string was all that secured the door of this shrine. Inside, the place smelt fusty. A gardener had left a few tools propped against the wall: a rake, a spade, a hoe. Festoons of bast were hung on nails among the festoons of cobwebs. A lot of junk had been thrown in and littered the place: old bottles and newspapers and empty cans. The poor furniture had never been shifted. It seemed to Hamer incredible that this draughty hut – so small, it appeared now, that he might by stretching out his arms span it from wall to wall: it seemed incredible that this had ever for a moment been a place of illumination and beauty. The very bed was still there, tumbling to pieces, with a great loose load of hay thrown upon it, and he started in revulsion from the sight of that desecration. This scarred and dirty piece of deal was the table at which he had sat to write his proud defiance of Buck Lostwithiel. This was the chair; those were the shelves on which he had accumulated his books. "Sweetness and light, little one. Sweetness and light." He stared at the rusty, oozy tins of weed-killer and insecticide that cluttered them now. Once the place had been clean, bracing and defiant, wide open to the light and the wind. Now he could hear the faint scratch of drooping branches on the roof, and feel the crapulous encroachment of mouldering time.

It was unbearable. "Let's go back," he said. "Tea will be ready."

But Alice was fiddling about, lifting this and that, and now she pulled out the table drawer. She picked things from it fastidiously and laid them one by one on the table: pens and pencils, damp papers holding together with blue-grey clots of mildew, and presently a roll of cuttings tied with tape. She pulled out the knot, but the cylinder of paper did not unroll, so long it had been imprisoned there. She flattened it out with her hand, cutting after cutting concerning the career of Hamer Shawcross, old Ellen's hoard that she had given to the infant Charles. In the middle of the roll was a sheet of foolscap paper, and written in pencil on it was the heading, "My Father, Hamer Shawcross, M.P."

Alice placed weights to hold the roll open, and in the dark green obscurity they stood side by side looking as it were down a tunnel of years at this pathetic piece of salvage. She did not know, as he knew, what occasion had called it into being. He remembered how he had come home from Bradford, burning with anger against Ann, and had picked up the lamp standing in the hall to light him to their room. She was in tears, and had reached out her white arms to him, and he had taken his night-clothes and left her. He slept in Charles's room, and in the morning he found the boy writing by candlelight. This paper, that had lain here rotting through the years, was what Charles had written. He remembered his annoyance: he had advised the child to find another hero. Well, Charles had done that.

He was beginning to hate this place. It was a charnel-house where too much of his youth was dissolving into mould. "Let's get back," he repeated gruffly. "I didn't know Charles ever used this place."

And then Alice was crying on his shoulder, crying as if her heart would break. "Look at his writing," she sobbed. "It hasn't changed. He still writes like that. Even in his writing he's remained a child."

He put his arms round her and comforted her. "Is it so bad, so bad?" he murmured.

She could not answer. She could only go on crying with convulsive gasps that shook her. At last he led her away to his cosy fire, and tea, and calm reassuring talk. But that night, when the weather changed, and a wind arose to lament in the trees about the house, he could not sleep in the room which he had shared with Ann. His mind raced on and on, living again its memories. How much now of life was memory! And how much of memory would for ever be centred on the rude hut, whose door, he remembered, he had left unfastened, straining, as he lay with hot sleepless eyes, to hear its far-off rattle in the wind. And to all the memories gathered there – of Ann and Arnold, of Jimmy and Tom Hannaway, of love and loyalty and ambition – would always now be added this: of Alice crying in his arms for the child who had strayed from her keeping.

Chapter Twenty-Two

Sir Thomas Hannaway knew better than to leave his money in vulnerable places. Early in the Great War he got his fingers into shipping, and took them out, larded with profits, before shipping went to the devil. When the war was over he bought up cotton mills in his native Lancashire, and when the price reached a point of insane inflation Sir Thomas sold out, was over the hills and far away, leaving spinners and weavers and all poor fools who lived merely by working to face the lean gaunt years when Lancashire was for sale.

These, and such like, were his flying piratical ventures. His normal operations were in things that people must have. He never paused to analyze his career. Had he done so, he would have seen that from the beginning he had subconsciously been attracted to that course. Small boys must have white rats. Small householders must buy cabbages and potatoes. People must have clothes on their backs. From these early stages he had gone on to the vast ramifications of Consolidated Public Utilities, and before drawing any new venture within that colossal net Sir Thomas always assured himself that it was concerned with something for which the demand never faltered, be it so humble as a button or so exalted as a ducal domain, ripe for developing as a pleasure park, greyhound racing track and dancing rendezvous. Hamer Shawcross did not know it, but at least one of the great houses of which Lettice Lostwithiel had written in her book – that book which had succeeded beyond her hopes, which the critics said might well become a "little classic" – was now, at Tom's behest, a stamping-ground for the crowds who rolled up in motor coaches, wearing paper hats; and nightly fireworks dazzled the sky that had been for so long the exclusive canopy of the golden lads and lasses.

All this was fortune, but it was not fame, and Tom had no mind to spend his life in a golden corner. He leapt into the spotlight with the adroitness of which he was a master. It was the year in which his horse

Darkie Cheap won the Derby, and as he led the beast in, with all the cameras snapping his rosy beaming face, the great thought sprang to his mind. Inevitably, the question came from the reporter, note-book in hand: "How do you feel, Sir Thomas, on winning this classic event?"

Sir Thomas removed his grey top hat and said reverently: "I am delighted, but no credit is due to me. We must thank this superb animal, this fine jockey, and Almighty God."

The reporter gasped, and Sir Thomas continued: "For many years it has been my ambition to win this great race, and I have prayed that I might do so. I prayed during the race. God has answered my prayer."

The praying racehorse owner! God answers an Epsom prayer! Here was meat beyond the usual. But even now Sir Thomas had not done. "I shall express my thanks to God by giving two million pounds to charity!"

There! It was out, and Sir Thomas didn't know whether to be glad or to damn his folly. It had come over him like an inspiration. He thought of all he had heard about public benefactions, and he could not remember one case of two million pounds being given away in a single fling. More had been given piecemeal, but this gesture of his, he felt, would rock the country.

It did. Sir Thomas sprang to fame overnight. He was besieged by reporters seeking details of his colossal beneficence, and ten thousand charitable institutions, begging societies and widows of clergymen rang him up or wrote asking for an opportunity to heal the sick, redeem the oppressed, or give their sons a last chance in Kenya.

Tom played his publicity well, kept the newspapers guessing for a fortnight; and when he showed his hand it was found that universities and hospitals were the beneficiaries. "Hannaway wings" sprang up about the country, and in common decency a few universities placed caps on Tom's head, and tricked him out in fancy gowns, and permitted him to call himself, if he wanted to do so, Doctor Hannaway.

It gave him a *cachet* he felt he had lacked. He had bought it all, cash down over the counter, and so far from being abashed by that, he derived a satisfaction from it. When he opened his new house in Eaton Square, he was able to invite people he had never hoped to meet. Lostwithiel wasn't there. Tom would have liked him to come, and Lostwithiel himself was in a difficulty, because he was Chancellor of a university that had pocketed close on a quarter of a million of Tom's money. He accepted the invitation on behalf of himself and Lady Lost-withiel, but on the day of the housewarming he said: "You go, m'dear. Tell the feller I've got a cold."

Tom had not hired footmen for the night. He had footmen of his own; and Hamer Shawcross heard one of them bellowing his name as he reached the head of the staircase. A vast mirror was behind Tom and his Polly as they stood there receiving their guests, and Hamer saw himself looking down upon them, overtopping hugely the fat waddling little woman, who had grown with the passing of the years absurdly like Victoria Regina in her last phase, and the rosy robin, puff-chested and big-footed, that was Sir Thomas Hannaway. He saw himself, the dark red flower, the jewel of the Order he loved to wear shining under the white butterfly of his bow, the white hair that he wore now affectedly long, the whole impressive broadside of a superb and famous dominating personality. He saw the chattering crowd away beyond Tom and Polly; he felt the surge of more and more people coming up the stair behind him; and he wondered, as he bent low over Polly's pudgy hand, with the rings cutting into the flesh and the diamonds sparkling like decorations on a little pudding, and as he murmured: "How do, Hannaway? Hope you'll have many happy years here" – he wondered why on earth he hadn't stayed at home. There were so few evenings when he could do as he pleased; it would have been agreeable to spend an hour with Ann's charming old edition of Marcus Aurelius: a wise bird who'd got all this stuff and nonsense properly weighed up for what it was.

There was no need, he reflected, as he passed on, for this footman to be shouting his name to Tom Hannaway. Didn't they know one another well enough? Tom, there on the landing, had given him a swift vulgar wink, as if to say: "A long way, this, from the dew on the lettuces. Remember?"

He remembered: that little shop in an Ancoats back street, the book propped open on an orange-crate up-ended, that parson's daughter – what the devil was the girl's name? – Wilding? Wilberforce? – who had taught him to pronounce the verbs. J'ai, tu as, il a. What a game it had been! What a fight! And now it was all over. He realized with a swift intuition that it was all over. No more splendid fights, no more struggles, no more conquests. He was clogged with all the fame he could hold, as Tom Hannaway was clogged with golden guineas. From the old bone-yard in Ancoats they had set out together, and this was as far as they would come.

"Too many pictures in the society papers, Chief," Jimmy Newboult had complained; and though he had received the rebuke coldly, he knew there was something in it. He blinked as a photographer's magnesium bulb flashed in his eyes. The royal garden party at Buckingham Palace; Goodwood; the opera; the opening of the Royal Academy show. He enjoyed it all with the aloof relish of a connoisseur. It didn't bluff him; he knew it all for what it was; but he enjoyed it none the less. Even tonight, this flashy affair of Tom Hannaway's. After all, he'd known the man a long time. It would have been curmudgeonly to refuse; and there was something amusing in the spectacle of an Ancoats go-getter with a disintegrating society bowing over his boots. When nothing else was left, there was always the superb irony of life.

Leaning over the balustrade, he saw Lady Lostwithiel coming up the stair, a white-gloved hand holding her skirt clear of her twinkling shoes. He heard her name sung out, and what a name Lostwithiel was! The loveliest name in England, he thought, a name like a trumpet, rallying to a forlorn hope.

"Well, my dear!"

He could say that easily now, and she as easily could smile back at him and lay a hand affectionately on his arm. They passed on together, and if here and there a knowing smile was exchanged, an insinuating wink flashed from eye to eye, that did not disturb them. They were happy and comfortable together: they had come from poles apart to a common ground of humanity.

Presently they found Lizzie Lightowler, sitting alone and neglected under a palm tree. She was very old, no more now than a spectator of life, vast and amorphous, and, Hamer felt with a pang, lonely. Now that Alice and Charles were gone, the house in North Street must be a dull place. But who wasn't lonely? It was the business of the years to take away bit by bit all that they had given.

The old woman got up tremulously, scattering bag and handkerchief. Hamer recovered them, and gently put her back into her chair. "Well, Liz!" he said. And to Lady Lostwithiel: "You know Mrs. Lightowler? She goes back a long way, don't you, Liz?"

That was all. They left her nodding and dreaming there, and now her dreams were happy.

"You know," said Lady Lostwithiel, "she doesn't really go back much farther than I do myself."

"Exactly one day."

He remembered precisely. He had come home from his travels and gone to Bradford to see Arnold. That night he had slept at Lizzie Lightowler's, and the next day he and Arnold had gone to look at Castle Hereward.

"You were very disdainful that day," he said. "You shifted my hat from in front of your pony's feet as though it would soil the brute."

"I may have looked disdainful," she laughed, "but I was terrified. I was not used to great hulking men rising out of the ground, lifting up gamekeepers as if they were dolls, and dipping their heads in the mire. Oh, yes! You had me trembling from the first. And that shout you let out: *Sic semper tyrannis!* That was what the assassin shouted as he shot Lincoln. Fortunately, I'd just been reading about it, or I shouldn't have known what on earth you meant. They didn't educate us gels."

They went in to supper, and in the crush at the door brushed shoulders with Fuentavera. He was quickly swept apart from them, but as he went he turned his head to say: "Ah, dear Lady Lostwithiel, let me be the first to commiserate with you."

"That man has a genius for smelling out disaster," she said. "I didn't think it was known, but Castle Hereward's in the market."

Hamer felt as though he had been struck a bitter personal blow. Castle Hereward, the house which had been the incarnation of all he had sworn to destroy; Castle Hereward, where he had been but a few months ago a guest, courted and played up to; Castle Hereward that, in one form or another, had stood with its feet dug into the Yorkshire soil since before the Normans came: Castle Hereward was in the market. If she had said England was in the market, he could hardly have been more shocked.

"But how on earth—?" he began.

She smiled, and seemed little disturbed. "We shan't starve, you know," she said. "It's not so terrible as that. Belgrave Square isn't so bad, and there's quite a pleasant dower house that we shall keep at Castle Hereward. That is, if we don't have to keep the lot, whether we want it or not. It's not so easy in these days to sell a place like that. There don't seem to be even rich Americans any more."

"I can't believe it!" he protested. "It seems monstrous."

She laughed outright at his solemn face. "We should have been a bit more patriotic," she said. "But Lostwithiel got very nervous about the state of England under a Labour government. When you first came in – in 1924 – he began to shift investments to America. Well," she shrugged, "you know what happened to investments in America."

"I'm sorry," he said, but she rallied him gaily. "Why should you be? Under your Labour government unemployment pay is being cut down: the only income of people with a few shillings a week. You're not going to weep, are you, because Lostwithiel's dole is cut? I'm not weeping. For all the practical and reasonable purposes of life, this makes no difference to us whatever. Perhaps, even, it relieves us of a burden."

They had moved to a quiet corner of the room, and he stood there stock-still at her side, gazing before him. Then he pushed the drooping hair back from his forehead and said: "Rich and poor alike, the knife is at our throats. Rich and poor alike, we shall have to make a stand. We are spending more than we earn, and I tremble to think what the consequences of that will be on our credit abroad if it goes on much longer."

"My dear," she said, "you know I'm a non-political woman. You must not make speeches to me. But if your little speech means that you think party strife is folly, do, for God's sake, make it in the proper quarter."

He had not heart for lingering at Tom Hannaway's jamboree. He went home early, profoundly depressed. It was a late summer night in 1931. London lay under the soft bloomy dark that he had come to love. The trees were full-leafed against the violet shining of the lamps, and, as he glanced through the window of the car, everything looked normal, solid and reassuring. But he knew that all this was only a seeming, a crust of prosperity spread upon chaos.

All his life long he had preached redemption through the Labour Party; and he had now to face the fact that under the government of the party the country was wallowing, like a ship without a rudder, in seas of darkness and disaster. Lady Lostwithiel had had to remind him that, even from the desperately poor, pennies were being retrenched. And he had to face the further fact that what, more than anything else, had moved and disturbed him, was a blow at the citadel which, in his youth, had been for him the lair and covert of evil.

In Piccadilly he stopped the car so that he might walk the rest of the way home. He put back his shoulders and drew the air gratefully into his lungs. He thought of the days when he and Tom Hannaway would run a mile before breakfast. Tom looked now as if a hundred yards sprint would make him drop down dead. Well, Tom had got what he wanted out of life. Have I? Have I? he asked himself. And he knew that he had. Clear of all evasion and self-deceiving, he knew that what he had wanted was nothing more than the fame that now was his; and he knew, also, that if the mighty upheaval which he sensed approaching should offer him the alternatives of going down into oblivion or riding the storm under the victors' banners, he would be found confronting the comrades of a lifetime, throwing all the resources of his heart and mind into destroying the building which he and they together, brick by brick and painful course by course, had raised from nothing to be the pedestal from which he now must leap.

He turned into Half Moon Street, pondering Lettice Lostwithiel's remark: "For God's sake, make it in the proper quarter," when he saw Arnold Ryerson coming, on the other side of the road, from the direction of his house. Arnold was walking head down, sunk in thought, and he started when Hamer, crossing the street swiftly, accosted him: "Well, Arnold!"

They stood confronted for a moment, ill-assorted: Arnold, wearing an old alpaca jacket against the summer warmth and with a cap on his head, shortish, stout and uneasy; Hamer tall and debonair, his light open overcoat showing the splendour of his raiment. Then their hands met, and for a long time remained warmly clasped.

"I hope you've got an hour to spare, Arnold," Hamer said. "Come along home with me."

Arnold swung round, and they walked up the road together. "I've just come from your place," Arnold said. "I'm in London on a bit of business, and I find it weary, now Alice is gone. Old Lizzie Lightowler is out, too. I went round there."

"Shame on you," Hamer laughed. "Am I always to be your last option?"

"Well—" said Arnold; and Hamer read a world of meaning into the grudging monosyllable. He put Arnold into the study while he went upstairs. He came back, having shed his coat and the jewel of the Order, wearing a black silk dressing-gown. "I've just been visiting an old friend of yours, Arnold – Tom Hannaway."

Arnold, with a match at his pipe, grunted: "Him! D'you know what I think, Hamer? A chap that can give away two millions without feeling it ought not to be honoured: he ought to be impeached."

Hamer laughed. "Poor Tom! I wonder what he'd say if he knew that you despised him and I pitied him?"

"I don't care what he'd say," said Arnold. "There's too much else to think about. What the hell *is* going to happen to this country, Hamer? You ought to know. Down in the Rhondda they're desperate, going Bolshie hand-over-fist. I reckon any Communist candidate down there today could rake in ten thousand votes. That's something to make you think, lad. If that sort of thing goes on, it may do more to break down the Labour Party than anything the Liberals and Tories have ever done between 'em."

"The Labour Party will break down, anyway," said Hamer. "The Labour Party, Arnold, is finished. At least for a long time to come. It may have a resurrection, but I don't imagine that you and I are going to live to see it."

Arnold looked at him, dumfounded. "No Labour Party! Then what in hell are we going to live for, Hamer – you and I? Why, good God, lad, we made it. It's been the breath of our beings."

It was a cry from the heart. There would be many such. Hamer had no illusions on that score. This old friend was a touchstone of the millions like him: the men who had fought without heeding the wounds, laboured without counting the cost. In Arnold's anguished face he saw prefigured all the pain and sorrow, the bitterness and disillusion, that would soon be let loose.

"The party will not be killed," he explained carefully. "All I am saying is that we cannot expect it to survive in its present strength. We made a force of it, Arnold, a tremendous force. Well, it will remain a living thing, a thing that will continue to demand all we can give it, but as an individual force it will go, as the Liberal Party will go. There is enormous virtue in the Labour Party, and that virtue must for the time being forget its own private demands and merge itself into the general effort of the country. You ask me what is going to happen to the country. Well, *that* is going to happen. Isn't that something to stir the heart? Isn't it a great thing to be able to say that this force, which you and I, and Pen and Ann, helped to create—"

Arnold broke in brusquely: "For God's sake! You needn't go on.

Don't practise out election speeches on me. Before I'd sign myself 'National Labour,' or whatever fancy name you invent, I'd cut my throat. And I'd think that a better action than to cut the throat of my life-long principles."

This was deadlock. Looking at Arnold's worn heavy face, tired with the work and lined with the sorrows of a lifetime, and acutely disturbed by what he had just heard, Hamer knew better than to go on. And he knew that through Arnold's lips he had listened to the answer that most of his colleagues in the Government, most of the men and women in the Party, would make when his scheme was propounded. There were some he felt he could count on. He was pretty sure that Ramsay MacDonald would go his way; probably Philip Snowden, possibly one or two others. But Arnold Ryerson had answered uncompromisingly for most of them: "I'd rather cut my throat."

A heavy silence fell between them. Suddenly, they were worlds apart. This quietly gorgeous room, this elegant little clock that tinkled through the warm summer air the news that it was eleven o'clock, the deep carpets and the splendid curtains, seemed active agents, the summary of all that had grown bit by bit into the chasm that could not be leaped, the gulf that separated the two who long ago had walked so closely side by side.

It was Arnold who broke the silence. His pipe had gone cold. He got up and knocked out the dottle against the bars of the empty grate. Then he turned to Hamer, sitting there on one of the red couches. "Well, lad," he said, and Hamer was keenly moved to hear the old familiar appellation. "Well, lad, there's not overmuch time left for either of us. I'm hard on seventy, and you're not all that younger. I suppose I've got set in my ways. I'm an old dog and can't learn new tricks. Alice'd like me to go Bolshie, and you'd like me to go summat pretty near Tory. Well" – and with him, as it had done with Pen in moments of stress, the old Northern accent came out: O Gordon! O Birley! and tough, tackling, Mrs. Ryerson! "Ah'm not saying there's virtue in bein' an old stick-in-t'muck, but that's how Ah'm made. Such wits as God gave men made me believe t'Labour Party were t'reight party for me. If the earth were crumblin' Ah'd still think as our Party were best to stop t'rot. Maybe tha's been converted, lad. But, wi' me, Ah wouldn't be a convert. Ah'd be a renegade. An' if Ah were that, Ah couldn't think on Pen again.'"

Arnold paused, his voice caught on a tremble at Pen's name. He cleared his throat and went on: "Pen were all right. They starved her an' drowned her an' blinded her, but she were Pen all t'time. They couldn't take an inch off the height of her. And, with apologies to you, lad, when it comes to a question like this, Ah'd rather follow Pen than follow thee. An' Ah know what road Pen'd take now. So that's my road, too."

He held out his large, fleshy, blunt-nailed hand, the hand that had knocked together Hamer's first bookcases, that had rummaged with his for twopenny bargains in Suddaby's basement. "So Ah reckon it's good-bye, lad."

Hamer got up. They stood confronted for a moment, their hands, clasped. They were both in the grip of a deep emotion. Hamer said: "Arnold, I'd like to tell you something that Ann once said about you. She said that for a man like you even defeat would have the quality of victory."

"Ann were a good lass," said Arnold simply. "An' Ah'll tell you summat as Pen said: 'Tha's never beaten so long as tha goes on fightin'.'"

He picked up the cap he had thrown on a table, and moved towards the door. They did not speak again till they stood at the front gate. Then once more their hands met and Hamer said: "Well, good night, Arnold."

Arnold said; "Good-bye."

Hamer stood at the gate, watching the heavy ageing figure move slowly away. He hoped that Arnold would turn, wave, shout something; but Arnold plodded on towards Piccadilly without once looking back.

As soon as Arnold was out of sight Hamer went back to his study and called Pendleton. "Bring me some coffee, and go to bed." He sat down at once at his desk, lit a pipe, and began to write: "Some immediate considerations that call for the formation of a National Government." Early in the morning he hurried round to 10 Downing Street. Two months later, it was all over.

It was all over with a completeness, a finality, that numbed even the mind which, more than any other, had set the thing in motion. He had once said to Jimmy Newboult that the successful politician must appeal to passion, panic and prejudice; and never had this been done as it was done now. Never before had he fought so strange a fight as this, speaking from Tory platforms decorated with the Union Jack, supported by the Party he had spent life in opposing, bitterly denounced by the comrades of half a century, who in blind confusion, baffled, puzzled, strove in the dark waters into which Shawcross and MacDonald had thrown them.

And even as they strove there, knowing that they were doomed, they must listen to the clamour of denouncing voices, telling them that it was *they* who had mutinied, they who had scuttled the ship, they who had betrayed the country. That was the poignant, the almost bestial, element of the whole matter: those who knew they must sink, and those few leaders who had opportunely leapt to the safety of the grand new "National" ship, shook their fists at one another, abused and spat on one another: this band of brothers, these co-builders of the Party of comradeship.

At all costs, be National. That was the advice of Hamer Shawcross, making his last urgent campaign up and down the country. If you are asked to choose between a National Tory and one of your old comrades, a man who has given you all he ever had to give, then vote for the Tory if that Labour man refuses to call himself National Labour. Such virtue in a name!

Shawcross was too great a man now to be allowed to fight quietly in his own corner. His reputation was powerful: he must be used to the last ounce of energy. He who remembered the small beginnings: the soap-box and the street corners, the sparse meetings in little parish halls: now assisted in the splendidly theatrical obsequies of the end. Night after night found him in the roar and turmoil of crowded meetings: the shuddering organ – "Land of Hope and Glory," the tempestuous thousands, dimly seen through the haze of their smoking; the rostrum trimmed in red, white and blue; the microphone, the great trumpets of the amplifiers hanging in the blue smoke like metal lilies in a tropical haze.

Ah, my friends! It's all glory and little hope now; but I remember the time when it was all hope, and glory seemed far away. You didn't shout then, for us or against us. You left us to do the donkey work, to sweat our souls out: me and Ann, Pen and Arnold, all the pioneers, all the comrades who cut through the undergrowth, and made the road, and built the blockhouses. You cheering, emotional, excited fools. You rallied to us at last, but even then not enough of you. You didn't give us the numbers or the passion that we wanted. And so here we are tonight to hand over our swords to the conquerors.

So he might have spoken, as the crowds roared when he walked on to the platform: tall, stern, tired-looking, not giving them a smile, the famous man with the crimson flower on his coat. But he did not speak like that. For the last time the sword of Peterloo gave him matter for oratory. He told of its inheritance and of its influence in his life. "I was born a Labour man, my friends, before the Labour Party was born, I have lived a Labour man, and I shall die a Labour man. Would I use my sword to kill the thing I love because I, as much as any man, made it? Would I choke the tree round which I have twined the branch of my power and the tendrils of my affection – even of my love – all the days of my life? God forbid!

"What then am I doing? Let me tell you, my friends. There are three houses on the edge of a forest. In each live people with their own concerns, with their own views of how their common affairs should be conducted, ready it may be to oppose one another tooth and nail in this matter or in that, Their interests are not identical, for in the Tory house live the enclosers of much land thereabouts. They have proved in the past a rather rapacious family, and the people in the Labour house have scores to settle with them.

"But the moment to settle scores is not when the forest is on fire. Bend your ears, my friends, to the winds of the world, and you hear the dread crackle of the flames, you hear the crash of forest giants that might have been expected to stand for ever. Thrones and parliaments, currencies and customs, the ancient loyalties and allegiances of common men, are melting in a fiery flux. The world is in the grip of a dissolution the like of which has not been paralleled since Rome herself dissolved. The smell of the smoke is drifting our way; the reek of danger is in our nostrils. Is this the moment for parish pettiness, the moment to do anything but rush out of doors and man the engines, fighting side by side with anyone – let him call himself by what name he may – who will range himself with us in the hope that we may even yet be not too late.

"Ah, my old friends, my old comrades of many a well-fought fight, my heart bleeds and breaks that in this present fight we are not still one in mind and hand. But dawn follows the night, be it still or fiery; and in the calm that will come after this hot roaring we shall find that a long tomorrow stretches before us, with all our old familiar tasks lying ready to hand. I at least shall take them up again, and even now I anticipate with confidence history's verdict: that the man who helped to save his country was thereby strengthened to the task of saving his Party."

But he knew that the Party would not be saved; that in his time at any rate it would not recover from the savage wounding blows that he and a few of his colleagues were dealing it; and when, on the morning of October 29, he sat with the newspapers before him at the breakfast table, there was one headline to which his eyes were drawn again and again: "The Cyclone Passes." "We write," said the correspondent of the *Manchester Guardian*, "as after the passing of a cyclone, and there is little to record save the survival here and there of a few fragments of the English political scene."

To all intents and purposes, the Liberal and Labour Parties were destroyed. The Government might as well sit with no Opposition at all. It counted 551 members against 57. Of the 551, 470 were Tories, but they bore the blessed tag of National Conservatives, and so Hamer Shawcross, who had come through safely in St. Swithin's, could sit down happily with them, for he, too, carried the blessed tag of National Labour.

The man who had loosed the cyclone did not eat. He threw the papers suddenly to the floor, drank a cup of coffee, and went into his study. He stood with his back to the fire, still as a statue, looking down the long perspective of the years, seeing the men and women who had worked with him, admired him; loved him – some of them; made him what he was; and he thought of them torn by this cyclone that had passed, prone like dishevelled corn-stooks that have been ravaged by a gale. He knew that most of them would never be erect again. Their political lives were finished.

Well, so was his own. He had known that, all through the fight. He had gone, when it opened, to St. Swithin's. St. Swithin's was dear to his heart. He said so, and this was one of the things he meant. There were not many politicians who, all through their careers, had represented but one constituency, who could go back, as he now went back, an old man, to open the last fight on the scene of the first.

It was dear to his heart, but he was glad that the call to a wider field made it unnecessary to linger there. Too many ghosts for his comfort walked the streets of St. Swithin's. "This for me, my friends, is holy ground. My dear wife and my dear comrades here supported me and guided me when many of you who face me tonight were in your cradles, like the party we then were nursing and nourishing."

He meant that, too. The ground of St. Swithin's was as full of memories as if each paving-stone were the lid of a tomb, inscribed to some dead occasion of his youth. And, knowing that this was the last of all the occasions, he was anxious to get it over, to quit the spot where at every turn he was outfaced by the most disquieting ghost of all: the fiery boy who had believed in perfectability, in a loftier race, the light of knowledge, the flame of freedom, Jerusalem in England's green and pleasant land.

The rigid figure before the fireplace stirred and sighed. He walked to his desk and took up his pen. "Dear Ramsay: My congratulations on your stirring personal victory in Seaham, and on the stirring victory throughout the country as a whole. While the fight was in progress I did not wish to trouble you with a matter which is the reason for this present letter. When you are called upon to form your new Cabinet, do not consider me eligible for any office. Perhaps there will be other ways – perhaps there will be some other sphere – in which I can serve the Party and the country; but I have made up my mind not to accept office again."

He felt as though, by the mere writing of the letter, he had slipped the arduous harness of a lifetime. Perhaps there will be some other sphere...He went back to the fire, and stood pondering between the familiar comfortable red couches.

Pendleton tapped on the door. "Are you able to see Mr. Newboult, sir?"

"Bring him in."

Another of the ghosts of St. Swithin's. The pale, thin, ageing ghost of a red-headed young fanatic, kneeling in a room in Bradford. "Now I am your man."

"Well, Jimmy—"

Jimmy's eyes were tired. He had fought and lost. He was one of the multitude for whom Arnold Ryerson had spoken: "I'd rather cut my throat." His long sandy jaws were twitching with emotion. He kept his fists clenched and his arms straight down his sides, ignoring the hand that Hamer held out as he advanced to meet him at the door. Hamer took the stiff obstinate arm and led Jimmy to a couch.

"Sit down," he said. "It's very early. Have you had breakfast? Shall I get you something?"

Jimmy did not sit down, and he shook his head.

"Not even some coffee?"

Jimmy did not even bother to shake his head. He stood, so clearly fighting back tears that Hamer turned away his face. "At least, put on your pipe, Jimmy," he said.

Jimmy did not light his pipe. It was evidently all he could do merely to stand there, struggling with his feelings. His pale eyes were misty with pain. His fair aggressive eyebrows jutted out in perplexity and dismay. At last he said: "Why did you do it? If it had to be done, why did *you* do it?"

"If it had to be done, Jimmy," Hamer said gently, "why should I not do it? It was necessary."

"And necessity knows no law," Jimmy bitterly replied, clinging to a cliché to the last.

"Necessity *is* law," said Hamer. "There is no other law."

That was too much for Jimmy Newboult. "Christ Almighty!" he suddenly burst out. "You stand there uttering clever sayings when England from top to bottom is littered with the men and women you have slain! Yes, slain! Aren't they dead when all they stood for is dead? Does a man go on living when his hope is blown out, and his faith is betrayed, and every principle he ever worked for is trodden in the mud by the very boots he would have blacked, the very feet he would have kissed? Why, by Christ, man, there was a time when I worshipped you, and up to the last I admired and respected you. I'd have run to the ends of the earth at your bidding. And now the sight of you makes me sick. I wouldn't want an honest man to see me in your company."

"I'm sorry, Jimmy."

"Sorry! What have you got to be sorry about? You've won, haven't you? You've got what you wanted. And now there's no end to what you can have. The enemy pays high for traitors."

He stood trembling whitely for a moment, his fists clenching and unclenching; and then suddenly he sat down, almost collapsed, upon the couch and buried his face in his hands. His shoulders heaved. "There's nothing left," he said in a stifled voice. "The beauty and the glory – they are gone."

The beauty and the glory. Hamer had never expected to hear such words from Jimmy Newboult. They moved him as he had not thought anything could move him now. This was Jimmy's youth breaking up through the crust the years had laid upon him. This was not the shabby man, trembling on the couch: this was the boy in his pride, bearing the sword, announcing the liberator.

Hamer looked down for a moment at the broken figure, abandoned there amid the shards of hope; then he laid his hand lightly on Jimmy's shoulder. At the touch, Jimmy winced like a galled horse and leapt to his feet. "Don't do that!" he shouted. "You touched me on the shoulder once, and I'd have followed you to kingdom come. And now, by Christ, I find I was following a bloody Judas. You're a traitor to the men and women who made you. They won't even want to tell you that. They'll shun you like poison. So I'm doing it for them. You've sold us all. You've betrayed us."

Jimmy's voice had risen to a harsh excited pitch. He stopped, and stood there shaking; then said in flat tones: "That's all." He kept his pale eyes lowered. He did not look at Hamer again, but turned mechanically and went out of the room. Hamer remained with his chin sunk upon his chest, his hands gripping one another behind his back. "That's all." Well, he thought grimly, it was enough. He wondered what Jimmy really knew about the state of the world, on what basis of evidence he, and those for whom he spoke, imagined that the Labour Party had any effective medicine for the convulsive fits and burning fevers that were shaking mankind to the depths. For himself, he had no illusions that a Government calling itself National would be in much better case. His profound knowledge of foreign affairs was like a delicate finger on the pulse of the world, and he didn't like the tremulous message he received. He was aware of a vast Tory jubilation up and down the country. Well, that was a buzzing of gnats that would die out when the cold winds blew. He looked into the future, and he was sure they would blow. Let the gnats dance and ululate! They would soon change their tune and their measure. The fact was, he told himself frankly, that he had lost faith in anything that could be done by those who called themselves statesmen, to whatever party they might be attached. He asked himself bitterly whether statesmen might not be the true pests and cancers of human society. They had controlled the affairs of the world for centuries, and the affairs of the world seemed to him now beyond any control at all. He could not think of any matter of statecraft that was not conducted with more complication, less honour and simplicity, than would go to such a matter between a few private human beings. It looked as though the time was coming when mankind would have to devise sharper and more stringent means of controlling those who conducted its business.

He raised his head and glanced across the room at the portrait of Ann by Axel Horst. "Love one another and leave one another alone," Ann had said. Was that, too, a dream, like all the rest? Where now, my friend, are our dreams?

He sealed the letter to MacDonald and struck his bell sharply. "Take this to the post at once," he said to Pendleton.

Now a man could rest a little. Now a man could look about him, and think, and read, and not be always worried by the thought: So much to do! True, there was still St. Swithin's to be represented in the House, but after such years as he had lived that was a little thing, and even that would not be there to worry him much longer. He felt like a man taking a holiday in an Indian summer. There were days when he did not go to the House at all, but gave himself up to the joys of such gorgeous freedom as he had not for years experienced. He would linger late over breakfast, spend the morning reading and writing in his study, and get Chesser to run him to some inn in the Chilterns for lunch. Then he would walk his eight or ten miles in the crisp winter weather, rejoicing to find his body still supple and responsive. The car would pick him up at some prearranged spot, and he would be home in time to bath and change, eat his dinner and go to theatre or opera. And, also, he had time now to feel lonely, and therefore he saw more of Lizzie Lightowler than he had done for a long time. The old lady was no companion for country walks, but they ate many a meal together, and for her sake he endured much in the theatres. She had a great taste for light farces, and would sit throughout a whole play with her loose amorphous body shaking with silent laughter. It was a tribulation to her, this body. All the faculties within it remained keen and bright, but they were like blades in gelatine. Hamer always took her home after the theatre, and sometimes went in for a bite and a chat in the house that was so closely knit up with Ann and Charles and the old days of hope and striving. It was from this house he had gone out to see Keir Hardie drive up to the Commons in a wagonette; it was to this house he had come as the young member for St. Swithin's. And now, although St. Swithin's did not know it, he knew that in a few weeks he would be done with St. Swithin's for good.

Lizzie liked to fuss him. She had always had someone to fuss till Alice went away, and now she wrapped herself round Hamer. She liked to see him sitting by her fireside smoking one of the good cigars she kept for him, and drinking a glass of the weak toddy that she concocted with whisky, hot water, lemon and sugar.

So they sat one night when that December of 1931 was half-way through. They had dined at a restaurant and then gone to a cheerful play, and when they came out the snow was falling. North Street, so quietly tucked away in the midst of the city's turmoil, seemed an enchanted place, with the flakes falling quietly through the golden haloes of the lamps. The church roof at the end of the street was a cold even white under the grey of the sky. The roadway was dumb with the snow.

"You go home to bed," Hamer said to Chesser. "I'll come along in a taxi."

Ten minutes later he was cosy beside Lizzie's fire, with the cigar lit and the toddy in his hand. On the other side of the fireplace she sat stirring the tea in her pot. She liked some "body" in it, she said. Her skirts were drawn back to let the warmth get at her stout old legs. Hamer contemplated her with the warm affection in which there was always a tincture of amusement. The old warhorse! Out to grass at last. He wondered lazily how old she was. She was the youngest, he knew, of a family of sisters – at least ten years younger than Ann's mother. Lillian was about twenty-six when Ann was born, so that made Lizzie sixteen years or so older than Ann. If Ann were alive, she would be sixty-seven, for she was a year older than he was. And that put Lizzie well on into the eighties.

She poured herself a cup of tea and looked across at him sharply with the eyes that were almost black, and so looked startling under the white mass of her hair. "I still like snow," she said. "I'm romantic enough for that. It's a damned nuisance to all concerned, especially if you've got leaky boots and an empty belly; but I like it all the same. It snowed the day you and Ann were married. D'you remember that? Yes; the boys were tobogganing down the roadway in Ackroyd Park that night."

She reached across for the decanter, and poured a little whisky into her tea. "Old Hawley, you know, was a bit tight. When you and Ann went, he wouldn't come in. He stood in the porch looking at your footsteps in the snow, winding away through the laurel bushes. He kept on saying: 'Poor li'l footsteps. Poor li'l footsteps. I wonder where they'll end up, those poor li'l footsteps in the snow?' I had to take him by the arm and drag him in. 'I'll tell you where they'll end up, old son,' I said. 'They'll end up in the House of Commons. No argument about that.'"

"You were wrong, Liz," Hamer said. "They'll end up in the House of Lords."

One pair of them would, anyway. The other pair had ended long ago in a field with a stream flowing by its edge, and willows by the stream, and fir-covered scented hills rising up over all. There was something to him exquisitely poignant in the thought of Ann's footsteps starting off on the road of their long adventure through the snow on Lizzie Lightowler's garden path.

"What's that?" said Lizzie. "House of Lords? What are you doing: guessing or telling me?"

"I'm telling you," Hamer answered. "But keep it to yourself. Look out for the New Year honours."

The old thing got up from her chair and kissed him. "There!" she said. "You've gone the whole way. You've gone as far as it's possible to go."

"That's exactly how I feel about it myself, Liz, but there's this: at one time I thought it would be possible to go a long way farther. It was Parnell, wasn't it, who said no man had the right to fix a boundary to the march of a nation. Well, there's no need to fix boundaries: they're there all the time, not only to nations but to all men. *Homo sapiens* is a circumscribed species, Liz. That's the chief thing I've learned in life. When I was young I thought there were no boundaries to the adventure of the spirit; now I think I was mistaken. Even now, I think perhaps there are no boundaries to the adventure of the brain, but that's another matter. Television and great air liners, the cinema and all the rest of it are not, to me, more significant than two fleas leaping over one another's backs. Bunch them all together, and they don't shift man so far from the tiger as he is shifted by one tear of pity or one sacrifice of love."

"That's very far-fetched," said Lizzie, "but I think I see what you mean."

Hamer got up. "I have a feeling, my old dear, that before this decade is out a great many people will see what I mean. Well, I must go and look for a taxi."

Lizzie heaved herself to her feet, finished off her tea at a gulp, and said: "I still keep the rooms, you know, as those two poor young things had them."

"Alice wouldn't thank you to call her a poor young thing," Hamer laughed. "She's a very self-sufficient young woman."

"No she's not. She's no more self-sufficient than the rest of us. She was as dependent on Charles as Charles was on her. Well, there you are, you see," she added, throwing open a door on the landing. "That's their sitting-room: the room you and Ann used to have. They've altered it a bit. It's ready for them when they want it. They'll come back all right."

There was something very touching to Hamer in the thought of the old lady in her lonely house, waiting for the return of the young life on which she had always expended herself. He put his arm round her big lax waist, and kissed her. It occurred to him that she had had to make out, in her long life, with very little love. "Look here, Liz," he said suddenly. "There's plenty of room in Half Moon Street, you know. Why don't you come and share with me? Then we could sit up half the night talking and I wouldn't have to go out into the snow."

The old black eyes lighted up with pleasure. "My dear, that's sweet of you. How many people I've looked after in my time! And you're the first who's offered to look after me. But go on with you now and find your taxi. It's high time you were in bed. You don't want an old thing like me about the place."

"Really, Liz, I'd like it."

"Well, you can't have it. No, no. This is the only house I've had in London. My roots are down here. Now off you go, and I'll put a bit of coal on the fire and have a read. I don't sleep much, you know, nowadays."

He let himself out. She waited till she heard the front door bang, and hard upon that came deep-throated Big Ben chiming the hour and following that with one sonorous stroke. She had spoken truth: she did not feel a bit like sleep, though her large body was physically tired. She dragged it back to Charle's and Alice's sitting-room, and wandered about there heavily, touching this and that. "The dear children," she murmured. "The dear children. I must be here when they come back."

*

Liz, who had arranged so much in her time, could not arrange that. As it happened, that night out with Hamer was the last night out they were to have together. She rang him up on the first of January and congratulated him on his viscountcy, then made public. "It's a terrible thing you've done to Alice," she wheezed into the telephone. "Charles will be the second viscount, and Alice will be a viscountess. She'll never forgive you."

"Oh, I don't know," Hamer laughed back "She's been in Russia a long time now. That's a pretty good cure for Bolshevist notions. And what's the matter with you, Liz? You sound like a leaky bellows."

"Well, I'm in bed, you know. The doctor's keeping me here. Bronchitis, or something, I suppose. He doesn't say much."

"Now that's a plague, old dear. I was going to take you out tonight. We ought to celebrate the hop into Debrett."

"I'm terribly sorry. Get someone else. It's high time you did: someone nice, and ten years younger than yourself. You ought to have married again long ago. You can't conceive how thrilling and vital you look."

"Fie, Liz! I had no idea you were such a wicked old woman." He could imagine the humorous sparks crackling in her old black eyes. "No, no. It's you or no one. On an occasion like this I realize I'm a pretty lonely man."

"Well, come and see me, then, if it's as bad as that. I feel exceedingly reminiscent. And I don't have a viscount to talk to every day of my life."

He put down the instrument, smiling. But there was nothing to smile about when he got to North Street that night. Lizzie's maid said the doctor was with her, and Hamer waited in the warm little sitting-room where, of late, they had had so many homely talks. Presently the doctor came in: a young man, looking very serious and worried. He knew at once who this tall impressive white-haired man was who got up at his entrance, and he had evidently read the day's newspapers. "Mrs. Lightowler is gravely ill, my lord," he said.

"Not too ill for me to see her, I hope?"

"I am afraid so. She is in a very high feverish state. I – I'm afraid of pneumonia."

Hamer was shocked. He looked at the young man before him, and suddenly his mind went back to a night long ago: a stifling summer night when he and Arnold Ryerson, waiting in the Cardiff Infirmary, met Dai Richards. Dai, then, was no older than this young man, but he had that about him which cheered them both. The young Westminster doctor did not look like Dai Richards. Hamer guessed that this was one of his earliest cases, and that he was terribly perturbed at the thought of a patient dying. "Sit down, Doctor," he said. "I suppose you're arranging about a nurse to come in tonight?"

"Yes. I shall do that at once. I shall telephone from here."

"Mrs. Lightowler is a sort of relative of mine, you know. I married her niece. I'm naturally anxious that everything should be done. Would you think me very interfering if I suggested calling in my own doctor?"

The young man's face lightened. "Frankly, sir, I'd welcome that," he said.

"Very well. When you've telephoned for the nurse, I'll ring him up: Sir Bassett Milnes."

The young man looked even more relieved. Clearly, he would be delighted to shelter under the shadow of Sir Bassett Milnes.

Hamer called in the maid-servant, a young thing devoted to Lizzie, but not, he imagined, a person to manage the house now. He told her how ill Lizzie was. "You're going to have a very busy time, I'm afraid. Cooking for the nurse, and one thing and another. There may have to be a day nurse and a night nurse. I think it would be a good thing if you had some help, don't you, my dear?"

And the little maid, who would have hated to be told "I'm sending someone round to run this show," was only too glad to have someone to help her. Hamer rang up his house. "Pendleton, Mrs. Lightowler is very seriously ill. You and Mrs. Pendleton pack your things and get Chesser to bring you along here. Pack a bag for me, too. Leave it on the way at my club, and tell them to have a room for me tonight. I'll stay there as long as you have to be here."

Pendleton and his wife arrived within the hour, and soon afterwards Sir Bassett Milnes came, and went with the young doctor into Lizzie's room. While they were there, the nurse arrived, and then Hamer felt that he had done all he could. The organizing side of his brain switched off, and he sat by the fire, waiting for the doctors and thinking of poor Liz. Twelve hours ago she had been rallying him gaily. Now...He heard the doctors coming out. Sir Bassett Milnes wore his famous beaming smile. You could never read from his face whether he was going to sentence you to death or send you away rejoicing. "Pretty bad, pretty bad," he said. "Oh, no, you can't see her. Oh, dear, no. Well, Dr. Musson, we meet here tomorrow at nine-thirty, eh? Good night, Shawcross. Oh, by the way, congratulations."

"Congratulations?" Hamer asked blankly.

"Good God, man, you haven't forgotten you're a peer?"

For a moment he genuinely had. While waiting for them, he had been so far from Debrett. He had been an arrogant unlicked young giant, just arrived in Bradford, just meeting Mrs. Lightowler, so formidable, it seemed to him, so vital, strong and full of purpose. She had given him so much, and he had repaid so little. One was late in realizing such things.

"Oh, thank you, Milnes, thank you," he said; and the young doctor stood diffidently in the background, envying the great ones of the earth who could look on death and smile, who could wake up and find themselves translated mysteriously from commoner to noble. Hamer ran down the stairs and got into the car as into a refuge. Congratulations! Ann and Pen dead, Lizzie dying, Arnold estranged. Alice miles away in body and spirit, and Charles God knows where. Congratulations!

He didn't see Liz again. He saw the coffin sliding slowly on the rollers towards the big metal door inscribed "Mors Janua Vitae." He saw the doors open, the coffin disappear, the doors close. His heart was uncomforted. The gaping doors seemed like the maw of death itself, visibly opening and swallowing its prey. His last memory of Ann, he felt, would be tenderer. "Into the breast that gave the rose." Old Horst had quoted that. Somehow, though all that was Ann would long ago have disintegrated and decayed, he could think of her as lying at peace beside the willows, as he would never be able to think of Liz at peace after this fiery end.

She had been lonely at the last. Only a scattered handful of people attended at the crematorium. As Hamer came out of the church into the bleak January afternoon, he saw ahead of him Arnold Ryerson making off swiftly, as though he did not wish to be overtaken. Hamer had not seen him in the church. He must have come in late, and sat at the back, and gone out quickly.

Hamer let him go, slackening his own pace till Arnold's black over-coat and bowler hat were swallowed up in the raw mist of a day that was ending without having seen the sun. Hamer could not remember the first time he had seen Arnold Ryerson. The earnest boy, a little older than himself, seemed always to have been there in those earliest years to which his mind could go back: the years of Ellen and Gordon, and the chill grey Ancoats streets, and the happy domestic life behind the red serge curtains, by the fireside, with sausages down to door and window. But if he could not recreate the moment of Arnold's coming upon the stage, he knew in his bones that he had witnessed his going off. The curtains of mist that had fallen silently behind him would not rise again. And with the going of Arnold it seemed as if so much of himself was gone that for a moment he was tempted to run, and call, and postpone a moment so heavily charged with consequence. But he checked the gesture, recognized the futility of the impulse. He looked around for Chesser, and was glad that Mr. and Mrs. Pendleton would be back in Half Moon Street. It looked like being a filthy night. He would spend it at his own fireside. He felt very lonely, and as the car slid away from the crematorium he thought: "Good-bye, Liz. I shall miss you, old dear."

Chapter Twenty-Three

In December of 1935, on the day when the Viscount Shawcross of Handforth was seventy years old, a large gilded basket of red carnations was delivered at his door in Half Moon Street early in the morning. The card tucked into the flowers said: "How beautifully you stand up to the years. *Sic semper tyrannis*. Lettice."

Pendleton, very old and white, stood the basket on the breakfast table. He looked to the fire, switched on the table light, for it was a drear morning, and then listened for Hamer's footsteps. They came, as he knew they would, punctually at eight. "Good morning, my lord. Many happy returns of the day."

"Thank you, Pendleton, thank you. Ha! Flowers?"

It was still the old enchanting voice, still the tall, unstooping figure, the hale face, the clear eye. He sat down to the table and pulled the card out from among the flowers. Yes: he had known they would be from Lettice. He was eager to ring her up and thank her at once, but glanced at the clock and desisted. He pulled one of the flowers out of the basket and put it in his buttonhole. "You shouldn't do it, you know. You can't really afford it." But he was very glad, very glad, that she had done it.

It was a bit extravagant, perhaps, to say she couldn't afford it. But she hadn't the money to fling about that she once had had. Her world had gone upside down. That wild daughter of hers had run off with a Dago prince and sickened of him in six months. He had demanded a fortune before he would consent to a divorce, and Lostwithiel had paid it. Then he had gone to fetch the girl home from Antibes. She insisted on driving herself, in a racing car in which she had terrorized the countryside. Something of old Buck's lunacy was in this girl's blood; and perhaps, as Lostwithiel roared along the country roads towards Paris at his daughter's side, he remembered the far-off night when he had sent the grooms to wait with stretchers beneath the bridge at Castle Hereward. So Buck's father had driven down the road to Brighton; so Buck himself had driven; and so Buck's granddaughter drove now. "I'm gettin' very bored with this, Daddy," she shouted in his ear. "You'll have to buy me an aeroplane – something that moves."

He looked askance at the fair helmeted head, the eyes wild with excitement, the thin nervous hands playing with the wheel. He wondered in his heart at the mystery of his life: that he could love this daughter so much while hating everything she did. His love for her was profound, and by that much more a torment.

They died together. No one saw what happened. In the morning they were found beneath the car at the foot of an embankment. In the last extremity of his love, Lostwithiel had got his arm about her neck; her wild unruly face was pulled close to his.

That was two years ago. When Lostwithiel's complicated affairs were straightened out, his widow found herself poorer than she had expected. But she was nevertheless a very rich woman. If she gave up the mansion in Belgrave Square and took a small house in Green Street, that was only because she did not want any longer to be bothered with estate; and if, when she went north, she did not live in the dower house at Castle Hereward but in a house that had belonged to the bailiff, she did that for the same reason. "I'm just an old widow, my dear, whose days are nearly done," she said to Hamer. "I won't be worried with big places and lots of servants. I've never felt my soul was my own so much as I do now. If my hopes are gone, so are my illusions, and that's the great thing, after all."

Yes, it was the most utter nonsense for him to say that she couldn't afford a bunch of carnations! But it pleased him to imagine that she would have made that small sacrifice for him if necessary. He knew that she would. They had never seen more of each other than they did now; they had never understood one another better. She never omitted him from the small, unpolitical dinner-parties that she liked to give in Green Street, and occasionally they had a dinner tête-à-tête, there or in Half Moon Street. Each felt there was something wrong with the week which had not brought a meeting.

Pendleton came in with a telegram. "Many happy returns. I'm coming to lunch. Alice."

He got up from the table with a quizzical smile. "What do you think of that, Pendleton?" he said. "A man can live in this world for seventy years and have only two greetings on his birthday: one from a countess and one from a Bolshevist. What d'you make of that?"

"Well, my lord," said Pendleton, with a brave attempt at humour, "it seems to me like making the best of both worlds, as one might say."

Hamer looked at him sharply. "Yes, yes, there's that about it," he said, and went into his study.

He felt as if he were dropping – had dropped – out of the world in which he had battled for so long. Not one of his old political colleagues had remembered his birthday. You stepped off the stage and you were soon forgotten. New players arose to earn alike the hisses and the applause. The play went on, and now he was merely a spectator of its accelerating rush. He thoughtfully pierced a cigar, as he stood before the fire, thinking of this play in which his interest had never waned, though he had chosen to withdraw from the stage to a seat in the stalls. The rise of Hitler, the Italian march into Abyssinia, the rush of Europe to rearm. His ear was as acute as ever, and he heard afar off the roar and turmoil of the battle that 1918 had halted but had not ended.

Framed in *passe-partout* and hanging over the fireplace behind him was a cartoon by Will Dyson that he had clipped out of the *Daily Herald*. It was drawn on the occasion of Philip Snowden's receiving a peerage, and showed Snowden as a candle, his arctic face roughly adumbrated in the tallow. The candle was guttering, and, reaching out of the vast dark of the background, came a hand placing over the flame an extinguisher shaped as a coronet. "Out, out, brief candle."

It was a superb piece of work, and its mordant truth had greatly appealed to Hamer, none the less because he had known that he himself would shortly be in the same case. He turned now and looked at the bitter caustic lines of the drawing, and he knew that in his case at any rate it was not wholly the truth. No, no. The coronet had not extinguished *him*. "No, by God, it hasn't," he swore softly to himself. An observer of the game could be as alert as the foremost player, and never had his own brain been more sensitive to the subtle and hidden drift of mankind towards the precipice whose boiling waters filled with dark premonition his sense of the years to come.

"My dear, you look radiant," he said when Alice came. "I didn't know you were in London. Did you come over specially for my birthday?"

She kissed him with real affection. "I'm forty years of age," she said. "Reserve your flattery for infants."

"Forty? Good God!"

It was incredible. He did not feel old except in these moments when he realized the age of people he had known as children. Alice was forty! He looked at her keenly, holding her by both hands at arm's-length. There was a grey strand or two in her dark hair. Around the eyes, black as onyx, creases were deepening their channels. Charles, then, is thirty-eight, he thought; and he said: "The most radiant forty I've ever seen."

"And you're a fine mellow old seventy," said Alice.

"'Mellow old seventy.' Sounds like the name of a ripe port."

"You rather look like that, you know."

He laughed, and led her in to lunch. "Well," he asked, "how's Russia?"

"A country of human beings, like any other."

"Ha! Now there's an admission! You're the first Bolshevist I've met who's admitted that a Bolshevist could sin. We differ from the beasts in being able to sin and in knowing that we are sinning."

"Whenever we meet," said Alice, "you treat me to a sermon."

"You forget that I was once a local preacher."

"Yes, you've been that too, haven't you? You've been everything: politician, author, traveller, preacher, linguist, proletarian and peer. You really are a rather remarkable person."

"Now you see one of the advantages of being forty. Your eyes are beginning to open."

"Well, go on. Give me the sermon. I can see you're dying to do it. But keep to the headlines."

"I'm glad you see that Bolsheviks are human. The Communist usually sees them as inspired by a more than human wisdom. Whatever they do *must* be right. This feeling is getting a hold in Germany, too. And don't fly at me when I tell you that Germany and Russia are tarred with the same brush. In both countries is this self-worship, this refusal to admit the possibility of error: that is, the possibility of sin. It is quite literally true that the fear of the Lord is the beginning of wisdom, because how can we fear the Lord unless we are conscious of sin? That is, unless we admit that we can go wrong? The refusal to make that admission permits any abomination to be committed in the name of our own infallible godhead. Which is a myth, my dear – at the moment the most dangerous myth in the world. Admit that we are human, that we can err, and half the battle's won. Then we look round for a cure. We don't go blindly on, smashing and crushing, as Germany and Russia will smash and crush, if they get half a chance, for a long time to come. That's all."

"You are quite right," Alice said – rather surprisingly, Hamer thought. "Quite right, anyway, in your general notion. I differ from you on two points. I don't see a ha'p'orth of similarity between Germany and Russia, and I still feel that Russia, though I can see the faults of the country and of the men in it, is on the right track. Russia, I have learned, is no paradise, but show me the land that is. I have been disillusioned in much that I have found in Russia, but I am not disillusioned about Russia's direction. To say that Russia would smash and crush into other countries is utter nonsense. If it did, my heart would be broken. The foundations of all I believe in would crumble. But I don't believe it. Russia is huge, still blundering, but benign. If necessary, I would die for Russia."

She spoke so earnestly that Hamer could almost imagine tears behind her eyelids, And what, he wondered, is the meaning of that? So he had seen and heard mothers passionately defend their children. though troubled with an unadmitted doubt of their integrity.

"Well, well," he said, rising from the table and leading her into his study, "come and sit down here and tell me all about yourself. I'm willing to let politics look after themselves for an hour or two if you'll do the same. What's your happiest news?"

"I've heard from Charles," she said.

Charles, whom Hamer and Alice had long since given up mentioning in their letters to one another because in each heart the pain was too deep, too keen; Charles, whom he and she never through these years had ceased to track to the farthest limit of any possible hint or clue, but always in vain; Charles, who had succeeded in so little, but had succeeded past belief in dropping from sight like a stone dropped into the sea: she had heard from Charles!

Hamer stood arrested, with a lit match burning down towards his fingers. He threw the match into the fire. "Where is he? How is he?"

"He's in South America, and he seems to be happy."

"Well – well—" he exclaimed impatiently. "Go on."

He held a light to her cigarette and she saw that his fingers were a little unsteady. She was glad of that. She would not have liked news of Charles to be coldly received.

"I got his first letter about a year ago," she said.

"What a woman you are! Why on earth didn't you let me know?"

"Because Charles asked me not to let anyone know. You yourself once described the root of Charles's trouble. He's been surrounded by too many successes. You were a success at your own game. I was a success at mine. I suppose Charles's mother and Auntie Lizzie were successes, too, in their way: they had learned to live successfully. After his one little burst, Charles was a failure among all of us shamelessly successful people. I think perhaps the little burst with Fit for Heroes was the most unfortunate thing of all. Charles knew what we were all enjoying. He'd tasted it, and he couldn't get a second helping."

"Yes, I see that," said Hamer. "Well?"

"Well, in the first letter he wrote to me he was contrite about running away, and burning with shame for what he'd said to me before he went. You never heard what that was and there's no reason why you should. I knew it was just lunacy, that he didn't in his heart believe a word of it; but it was the sort of lunacy that haunts the person who utters it rather than the person who hears it. Though I did not for a moment believe he meant it, yet through all these years he'd thought I did."

"Yes, yes, I understand."

Alice moved up closer to him on the couch. He took her hand and held it and looked at the rings: the wedding-ring and the diamond engagement ring. "I've never met anyone," she said, "who *understands* so much."

Ah, my dear, he thought, if only that were true! This engagement ring: how he had hated the thought of Charles's association with Alice! How little he had understood then!

"Well," he said, "I suppose what made him write was that he was beginning to find success coming his way at last in whatever it was he took up?"

"Yes, and would you believe what it was! Aeroplanes!"

"What? Is he flying?"

"He wasn't when he first wrote. He was just finding his feet as a representative in South America for an English firm of aeroplane manufacturers. That was the very first thing he wrote about: he was doing well in the job, and he was full of hope. What he'd been doing before that I don't know. Having a thin time I should think, but anyway he'd learned Spanish. Then his letters became more frequent. I don't know how on earth one sells aeroplanes, but he was doing it with increasing success. His firm gave him a wider and wider commission, and now he's going from one South American state to another, selling to private companies and to governments. He mentions his first big success in selling to a government in the last letter I got." She took the letter out of her bag. "'If you're ever in London, you can tell my father. I don't know who the supreme chief of our show is in London, but whoever he is, he seems to like me. It's almost as though there's some influence at work pushing me on. Anyhow, there it is. I'm on my feet. On my foot, anyhow. The one that's missing doesn't matter on this job. I can fly without it. I'm working for my pilot's ticket now. You'll see me soon, my dear, showing War Ministers over the Andes and selling them a consignment of "buses" soon afterwards. If José goes to Europe soon, I expect to be able to wangle leave to accompany him. Then, my love—'" She folded the letter hastily.

Hamer got up. "Extraordinary!" he said. "To think that his talent, after all, was a sort of commercial-cum-diplomatic mix-up. Well. And José. Who is José?"

"José Esquierra. I don't know much more about him than you do, except that he comes into every letter Charles writes. He's a pilot, too. I don't think Charles has ever had a man friend before. This José is on his brain."

He patted her hand. "Now I know why you're radiant. This has made me too very happy, my dear. Tell me – what is the name of Charles's firm? Do you know?"

"No. But their aeroplanes all have fancy starry names: Pleiades and Capricorns and Orions and so forth. Why, are you going to hunt down Charles's benefactor? I think it's a myth. He's succeeding because he's found his job. That's all there is to it."

"No. I was just interested," Hamer said vaguely. But when she was gone he sat for a time by the fire. He could not say it to her, but he hated the whole thing. He detested aeroplanes, whether for civil or military use. He considered them the major curse of all man's meddling inventions. He remembered the letter which John Galsworthy had written to the newspapers after the last war, urging the nations to destroy once for all, and for all purposes, this thing that they had made. He was convinced to the bone and marrow that there had spoken the voice of wisdom.

Selling aeroplanes! He would rather sell poison to a murderer.

Presently he took up the telephone and rang through to an address in the City. In two minutes he knew what he wanted to know. Pleiades, Orions and the rest of them were all within the vast ring of Consolidated Public Utilities.

Then, with a succession of calls, he ran Sir Thomas Hannaway to earth at his club at four o'clock in the afternoon.

"Look here, Hannaway, I just want to say a word of thanks about what you're doing for that boy of mine."

Sir Thomas was in a jovial mood. He laughed huskily into the microphone. "Eh! Tha's rumbled me at last, lad," he said, doing his best Lancashire imitation. Then he became the responsible man of the world. "There's no reason why the boy should know anything about it, Shawcross."

"He doesn't. I made a lucky guess."

"Well, you know, by the merest fluke I found that he was doing some little bits and pieces for our people out there, and I told 'em to give 'im 'is 'ead. That's all."

"It was good of you."

"Well," said Tom. "I don't forget things, you know, Shawcross. The old lettuces, eh? There's a lot between us two. And that night you turned up in Eaton Square. You were a Cabinet Minister then, and that meant something to me. Why should I deny it? I'm a simple man. I don't forget those things."

"You mean to say that influenced you with Charles? Good Lord, Hannaway. You're a caution."

"I 'ope I'm a Christian," said Tom with simple dignity.

"I hope you are," Hamer thought as he hung up and returned to the fireside.

This José, this Esquierra, with a face almost as black and wrinkled as a pickled walnut, this short, long-limbed, ugly little monkey of a man, whose superabundant vitality sparkled in his dark eyes and flashing teeth, was tickled to death that his dear friend Charles should be the son of Viscount Shawcross. José had an immense knowledge of European statesmen: their biographical records and their achievements in office. José was an anarchist from Barcelona. One of these days, he hoped, all these Jacks-in-office, tee'd up above the generality by no more than the little piles of self-esteem they sat on, would be swiped into the rough, and stay there. His restless animal vitality was equalled by his fierce and unreflecting animal courage. He had himself tried a bit of swiping with a few home-made bombs. Spain became too hot for him. Enrique Valdar found it necessary to disappear; and so this José sprang up in South America, Enrique's reincarnation. He knew how to knuckle down to authority when authority had anything to give him or teach him. His job in Barcelona had been that of motor engineer, and he laid his talents humbly at authority's feet in South America because he wanted to learn all about aeroplanes. It seemed to him that, singing through the air in an aeroplane, and dropping death on his enemies, he would find the deepest satisfaction life could offer. The moment for this, José believed, would surely come, and he lived for it with the simple intensity with which a child lives for a promised picnic, counting off the worthless days between. On the great day when he mounted up with wings like an eagle, he would sing the song of life and know why he was born. It gave him great pleasure at the moment to be the viper warming in the bosom of those he would destroy.

José's straightforward uncomplicated fanaticism was fed from his old organization in Barcelona. Hardly a week went by without his receiving some seeming-harmless letter or newspaper whose import he understood. Daily he longed for the import to be what he knew some day it must be: Come home. The moment is at hand.

Charles Shawcross walked briskly across the blazing aerodrome. He had thought he would never walk briskly again, never do anything briskly again. It was the slavish subjection of his mind to other and more successful people that had brought him to South America. His father, he knew, had landed in South America and set out thence to conquer the world. So to South America he went himself. But Charles found the world a hard place to conquer. His thin embittered personality did not expand in this sunshine, did not cheer in the dry harsh startling colour of his new environment. He dragged his old life with him like a heavy corpse. His heart was full of blended love and hatred for Alice, almost of pure hatred for his father, of hatred undiluted for "them" – the vague, undefined powers that had turned down his pretensions to a writer's excellence.

His life for a long time was miserable and poverty-stricken. His old ambitions dogged him. He found an unexpected aptitude for Spanish, and tried to sell articles and stories, written in Spanish, to the newspapers. He began a novel, in English, of South American life: a self-pitying autobiographical novel of a worthy soul rejected by fools and struggling desperately with fate. It limped along, till he began to loathe the record as much as the life it recorded. One night he burned it and threw his pen into the fire in a gesture of desperate symbolism. He never tried to write again.

Within a week, abandoning all pretensions, he was working as a clerk in an English house. He was surprised to find that at once he felt happier. Miserable and mechanical as his work was, he was its master and his soul was uncankered by the old disastrous assaults upon an impossible objective.

A year later he entered the office of Sky Traffic. Here his work was more interesting and more responsible, though it was still unimportant enough. But again he was the master of it, and he received a number of small promotions. Then one day, out of the blue, came a promotion that he had not expected. It meant responsibility in a real degree, and money that, for the first time since the writing of *Fit for Heroes*, left him something to play with.

If failure in the midst of success had been the bane of Charles's life, this success was the wine he needed to warm his heart. Merely to walk into the office, to pass by the room of undenominated clerks in which he once had worked, and to enter the room with "Mr. C. Shawcross" painted on the door: this squeezed the gall out of him and left him a sweeter and more reasonable being. He went home that night and wrote to Alice. He felt for the first time in his life that he was not a child.

And then came the day when he was told to fly to a neighbouring country in order to conduct a business negotiation that would need every pennyworth of his powers. He walked briskly on to the aerodrome. His leg didn't worry him. An observer would not have known anything about It. An aeroplane came taxiing toward him, and under the pilot's goggled eyes gleamed the white teeth of a man he had not seen before – José Esquierra.

Charles had not flown before. The sky was cloudless: a hard light-blue enamel. They soared towards it, and he discovered that his emotion, concerning which he had been troubled by some doubts, was one of supreme elation. Merely to watch the altimeter pointing to eight, ten, twelve thousand feet was exhilarating. To look down on the green seas of prairies, on the inconceivable remoteness of towns and villages, on railways drawing their slender lines into infinity: this was to have experience heightened to a pitch he had not imagined possible. So this was an aeroplane; this was what he had to sell! His commission presented itself in a new romantic light.

In this exalted state of mind, it seemed to him a natural thing that José Esquierra should turn to him and say: "You permit, señor, that I occasionally sing?"

Charles laughed outright. "Sing your head off, man, if you want to," he said, and above the roaring of the propellers José lifed up his voice and sang. Thus José loved to be hurtling through the air, imagining, as he pulled his levers, that he was operating at last the switch that would drop his lethal eggs upon the enemies of the people. He sang, but it was only a rehearsal of the great song of life that he believed he would sing one day as he sowed the instruments of death.

For the last hour they flew with the sea on their right hand. José brought the machine down low, and Charles could see the waves sewing their lacy fringe for mile after mile along the calm blue quilt of the water. White and pink villas clustered at the mouth of a stream flowing into the sea; gardens; bathers running up the beach; little yachts, mere pleasurable toys, scudding before a propitious wind in a pygmy contest towards a painted buoy.

It seemed years to Charles since such sights as these had given him pleasure; and when at last the aeroplane touched the ground and he stepped out into late afternoon sunshine, he turned to José and said: "Thank you. I enjoyed that. I hope we'll have many trips together."

A taxi was waiting to take him to his hotel. He had not realized that now he and José would part. Rooms had been booked for Charles at a resplendent white hotel overlooking the sea, as befitted one who on the morrow would interview members of the government. The company's knockabout pilot, the aerial taximan of Sky Traffic, could hardly hope to share such quarters. José was not perturbed about this, but Charles was in an expansive mood. "You must at least come and see me after dinner," he said. He didn't want this glorious day to end in loneliness.

José, out of his aeroplane, looked a different being. Charles found him at the time appointed in the hotel lounge, wearing a blue suit off the hook, cracked glacé leather shoes, a lilac shirt with a yellow tie. He was rolling a cigarette, bending his inquisitive monkey face over the task, and the light caught his hair, shining as synthetically as his shoes. Charles asked him to have a drink, but José declined. He was a teetotaller. He did not tell Charles – not at that time – that he had taken a teetotal vow until his great mission was accomplished. His eye and hand must be steady. He was capable of such a dedication.

They wandered out into the street together. Though the sun had set, the night was as warm as an English midsummer noon. Charles had not been in the town before, but José knew it well. Charles asked him about the possibilities of amusement, and José detailed them with a frankness that was startling. Charles gave him to understand that he had not asked his company as a pander. José was at once contrite, and for a time silent. Then, bridging with one leap the gulf between the exotic and the hygienic, he suggested that they might bathe. They had come out upon the seashore. To right and left the esplanade ran, hung with lamps whose coruscation dwindled to a violet darkness where the two horns of the bay pointed inwards. Before them the moon was riding high, trailing a dance of glittering sequins upon the water. The sea came whispering in as though its voice had never known the tones of thunder.

Charles was tempted. He had been a magnificent swimmer. Of all the forms of sport, this was the only one he had mastered and enjoyed. But since he had lost his leg he had not tried to swim. Alice swam as well as he did, and he would sit on the shore watching her with a furious envy, his pinched heart refusing to allow him to join in the sport in which he knew she must now master him. Standing that night with the warm foreign air blowing about him, with that exquisite moon-lacquered sea sighing at his feet, and watching the bathers running along the beach with towels draped over their shoulders, he felt so painful an urge to go in and swim that he burst out resentfully: "Damn it all, man! How can I swim? You know I've got only one leg."

José was overcome. He had known nothing of the kind, and said so volubly. He said further that he had known men with one leg aye, and women with one arm – such magnificent swimmers that clearly Señor Shawcross was making something of nothing. He, José, could say without boasting that he was veritably a fish in the water. He detailed his life-saving achievements at length, holding back nothing of the beauty, grace and gratitude of some of those whom he had saved from death. Even if Señor Shawcross found himself in difficulties – which he refused to believe was possible – he would stake his own life that no harm should befall him.

Charles succumbed to this overwhelming onslaught. They took a taxicab back to the hotel and procured towels and costumes. Then the taxicab ran them to the end of the esplanade. Charles, again full of misgivings and hating the thought of being stared at, insisted on walking a mile to a spot where the beach was utterly deserted. When he had undressed and put on his costume, he felt overcome with shame. A few doctors and nurses and Alice: no one else had seen him in that condition. He started absurdly to try to hop on one leg towards the water, thrusting away pettishly José's offers to help. But José good-humouredly persisted, encouraging him with loud cries, and at last Charles found himself concluding the hop with one hand on José's shoulder. He hopped till the water was round his thighs, and then José with a shout of "Hola!" let him go. Charles fell over on to his back. The sea bore him up. The old sense of happiness and well-being came flooding in. He lay finning gently with his fingers, staring up into the serene face of the moon. The warm water lulled him, buoyed him. He felt as safe and content as if he had resigned himself to maternal arms.

Presently, he floundered over on to his breast and struck out. It was not easy. He had to invent, to improvise, but he swam, he progressed; and José, making circles round him, encouraged him, declared that he had never seen such mastery of a handicap, all the time as watchful as a duck over a duckling's first swim.

When they came out, Charles was tingling with well-being. He made no bones about allowing José to help him up the beach. José, a grotesque long-limbed, little-bodied creature, glistening in the moonlight, went first, and Charles, with a hand on each of his shoulders, hopped behind, shouting with laughter at his own clumsiness when, once, he nearly fell. He allowed José to hold him up while he towelled himself, to help him into his clothes; and then he lit a cigarette and blew ambrosial smoke through his nostrils while José dressed.

José was delighted. "It was as I said, eh, señor?" he kept on demanding; and Charles as often replied: "I didn't want your help, eh?"

"No, no, señor. Before the misfortune you must have been a fish, an electric eel. Even now—" and José spread his arms expressively.

Charles slept soundly, and awoke full of a happiness that seemed an unreasonable consequence of so slender a cause. But he had conquered something, and mainly he had conquered his own shrinking from enterprise; and therefore, going out that morning on a task whose like he had not undertaken before, he went with more than usual confidence and buoyancy of spirit. His negotiations lasted for three days. He did not swim with José again, for his evenings were now caught up in hospitality given to his clients and received from them; but he saw José from time to time when the pilot was called on to explain and demonstrate the machine; and when finally he took his seat for the return journey and José said: "We have sold the aeroplanes, señor – yes?" he replied wholeheartedly: "Yes, Esquierra, *we* have sold the aeroplanes."

"I will teach you also to fly them," said José; and that, in due course, happened. Charles represented to his firm the advantages of his practically understanding the machines, and, the hidden influence from London still operating, no obstacle was put in his way. He expressed a preference for Esquierra as his instructor, and Esquierra was attached to him. Charles's success in selling the areoplanes had made him a person of greater consequence than ever. His desires now carried weight.

Charles could never remember what slip of the tongue, what lift of the eyebrow, what small unguarded trifle first revealed that he and José were, equally, political rebels. But that day came, the day when, except before some third party, he ceased to be Señor Shawcross and became Carlos, and Esquierra became José. Once that intangible barrier was down, it was not long before José, the stronger spirit, was the dominant partner in their friendship.

In the darkness of night José would come to Charles's rooms, and night after night Communist and Anarchist talked their hearts out. Now that Charles was in communication with Alice again, his flagging political beliefs stiffened. Left alone, he would have soon forgotten them, for they were not so much beliefs as absorptions from a personality overflowing into his. He was surprised to find how little he knew of the confused welter of sect and passion and opinion in which mankind found itself.

"But I don't understand, José," he said one night, "why you are not back in Spain. Spain's a republic now."

José spat: one of the unpleasant habits he permitted himself in this new intimacy. "Pah! How little you understand, Carlos! It is this republican government that I fly from. Have you not heard then of the Anarchist rebellion in Aragon in 1931? The dog Azafia, leader of the republic, put us down. Firing-pom-pom-pom," said José, his little eyes sparkling with anger. "Troops – the troops of the republic – they maimed us and killed us. One hundred of us were sent off – deported – to the desert. I escaped."

He rolled a cigarette, brooding angrily. The room was drowsy with heat, blue with tobacco smoke, a waving chiaroscuro like Charles's mind which was hazy with names: Anarchists, Communists, Socialists, Advanced Liberals: all at loggerheads in a tormented country which till now he had conceived, as he conceived the world, to be a clear-cut field for the simple opposition of Right and Left, which to him meant Right and Wrong.

One day, early in 1936, José was not at the aerodrome. He was not at his lodgings. "When I go, Carlos, I go – like that!" he had once said to Charles, doing a disappearing trick with a coin. "There I am! There I am not! Like that."

And now he was not. The company was perturbed at the loss of its best pilot. Charles kept his peace. He had not expected any farewell letter, even any farewell word, from José. When the newspapers announced that all the parties of the Left in Spain, including the Anarchists, had united to form a Popular Front, he knew where José was headed for. He was lonely and unhappy, and looked the more eagerly for Alice's letters, pouring out passion in reply.

Six months later, the army rebellion was launched against the Popular Front. Charles often thought then of José. Whether he ever sang the song of life and death over the riven body of Spain Charles never knew. José, so important in Charles's life, was a cipher in the life of the world. His deeds, if there were deeds, did not create an echo.

Chapter Twenty-Four

It seemed a very strange thing to the Viscount Shawcross to be up at half-past five on a dull May morning. But a great many strange things had been happening of late. A King had died, and another King had reigned for a little while and then put by the crown, and £1,400,000,000 were to be spent on armaments by Great Britain, and another King had taken up the crown his brother had laid down, and this morning, May 13, 1937, would see his coronation.

It wasn't a nice morning for a man getting on for seventy-three to be up at half-past five. Hamer pulled aside the curtain and looked Half Moon Street in its unpleasant face: cold, raw, misty. If so much as a gleam of colour came through before the day was out the papers would talk about royal weather. But it wasn't: not a bit of it.

He turned from the window and went into the bathroom. When he came back, Pendleton was reverently laying out upon the bed the Viscount's robe of red velvet and ermine. The coronet reposed on the tumbled pillow.

"Have I got to wear these things to breakfast?" Hamer grumbled.

"I think it would be advisable, my lord. There will not be much time afterwards."

With Pendleton's assistance Hamer arrayed himself, tucked the coronet under his arm, and went downstairs. The fire was lit and the lights were on. It was a cold and miserable six o'clock.

At half-past six Pendleton came in with a linen bag, fastened at the neck with a draw-string. "Mrs. Pendleton thought, sir, you could conceal this by pinning it inside your robe. Coffee and sandwiches, sir."

Hamer pulled the string and peeped into the bag at the thermos flask and the parcel of sandwiches. He roared with laughter. It tickled his humour to be going to a coronation like a boy to a picnic with his packet of sandwiches. He would sit amid the splendour of Westminster's crumbling stone, amid the tiaras and coronets, gold sticks, tabards, the aigrettes springing from jewelled turbans, the admirals and the generals, the Lord High Chancellor and the coped ecclesiastics, under the very shadow of the throne itself, and he would feel Mrs. Pendleton's good hot coffee warming his heart.

Pendleton produced a safety-pin and pinned the bag in place. "Thank Mrs. Pendleton," said Hamer. "Tell her it's a splendid idea."

"She has been making inquiries, my lord. It will be generally done. Some of the peeresses will carry their sandwiches in their coronets."

Chesser came with the car at seven o'clock. Hamer drove to the Abbey through the streets lavish with crowned poles, fluttering with pennons and bunting, embellished with enthusiastic mottoes, thronged with thousands who had been up all night, astir with troops and soldiers marching to their posts. In the grey grudging light the old Abbey did not know itself, with bits and pieces stuck on here and there for the purposes of this day's ceremony.

Nor was there much of the Abbey to be seen within. The whole place was transformed into a splendid theatre for the playing out of the timeless ritual. A man carrying a scarlet stick preceded Hamer up the nave. Normally, when he had walked here, it was through an emptiness of grey echoing stone, with the names of the illustrious dead on the floor beneath his feet, their monuments, epitaphs and effigies crowding the walls on either hand. Now, walking behind the scarlet stick, with the coronet under his arm, with the hem of the robe whispering on the ground behind him, his footsteps made no sound, for carpet deadened them, hiding the stone lids of the tombs; and to right and left, reaching up from this narrow muffled lane in which he walked to the very roof, rose tier upon tier of receding seats, concealing the monuments, cloaking the dusty imitations of mortality, with thousands in gorgeous uniforms and with drapings of rich sombre colour.

The floor of the Abbey was of blue and gold: blue in the nave, and elsewhere a rich mat golden carpet on which the light of the hanging lamps fell flat and even. The blue and golden floor stretched along the nave, and forward into the sanctuary, with branches to right and left into the transepts north and south: a huge cross of blue and gold: that was what everybody was looking down upon from the piled seats crowding close upon every point of its body and arms. At the junction of body and arms the day's play would be enacted; and there, edging the steps up to the two thrones, the gold was touched with crimson.

The scarlet stick bowed the Viscount Shawcross to his seat in the north transept. There was little that Hamer could see now. The nave was hidden from him, and so was most of the sanctuary. He could see little but the cleared sweep at the intersection of the arms of the cross, and beyond that the south transept piled with the crimson and ermine of the peeresses, as this side was with peers.

These two thrones on which the King and Queen would sit while ecclesiastics and ministers wove the complicated dance of ritual about them faced inward to the sanctuary, and just within the sanctuary itself stood the coronation chair on which the King alone might sit. Amid all the glitter and glamour of the occasion, amid the blue and silver, the gold and crimson, of the splendid fabrics that cloaked the Abbey's cold stone, the chair, it seemed to Hamer, had an incredible and poignant austerity and loneliness. He had, before now, seen it close at hand, and knew it for what it was: an old wooden chair with a high pointed back, casually scratched and scrawled upon by the generations like the lid of a desk at school, an old chair such as you might find standing in some farmhouse ingle-nook. But there it was, as it had stood when Edward the First was crowned upon it, when armies fought with arrows, and Marco Polo was wandering in China, and Kublai Khan was organizing Tartar hordes. Plantagenets, Tudors, Stuarts, Hanoverians: such sanctity as immemorial succession might give, they had imparted to this old chair. It stood there, very lonely, the oldest thing in the Abbey, save the Stone beneath it whose history and antiquity none rightly knew.

The building was filled with the rustle of the eight thousand souls who crowded it: men and women from the five continents of the riven world, assembled here for a moment, he reflected, in the amity of a great ceremonial moment, but divided perhaps even more deeply, he thought, than when the chair came new and glistening from the hands of the village carpenter who made it. Behind this brave new face of the Abbey, engraved upon marble, chiselled in stone, related in elegy, epitaph and superscription, was the epitome of this empire's history: the whole glittering and precarious edifice built up of service and sacrifice, violence, cunning and chicane, valour and endurance, with greed and subterfuge following their footsteps, the dreams of poets and of tale-tellers, the certitudes of science, the promises of religion and the schemings of statecraft. Such, too, was in the rough, the history of every state here represented: for it was the history of restless man himself, deaf for the most part to such intimations as came now with the suspiration of this great uneasy gathering, filling the ancient church with the sound of an autumn forest, of leaves about to fall.

It was all too ornate, high-wrought and over-jewelled for him to remember it in sequence. His memory, afterwards, was of a medley of emotional and æsthetic appeals: a fanfare of trumpets sounding suddenly outside the doors, the sharp, clean, classic notes piercing through the romantic jangling of bells; the surge of organ music that seemed to creep into every crack and crevice of the ancient abbey and rumble there; the slow crescendo of a procession through the standing thousands: swords and crosses, copes and tabards, gold, silver, feathers, jewels, bowed backs and pious hands of priests stiffly encrusted with vestments; orbs, crowns and sceptres and all wherein do lie the dread and fear of kings; the chanting of shrill-voiced boys; the strutting of little pages, scarlet as robins, with their toy swords stuck out behind them like tails.

These things he remembered, and the endless, dazing piling up of ritual on ritual, ceremony on ceremony, the presenting, the anointing, the crowning, the nation's symbolic man sitting there at last in the old wooden chair while a bald priest twiddled the crown in his hands to get it the right way round. And when the crown was on, the lights increased their power, shining down strongly on the golden floor, scintillating in red and green and yellow sparks as they caught the jewels of the crown. From without, the boom of distant guns was heard announcing to the people that another king had been crowned in the chair; and, within, Hamer with all the other peers put on his coronet and joined in the shout "God Save the King."

Hours by now had passed since he followed the scarlet stick to his seat: hours of sitting and speculating, hours of splendid colour and sound and movement; and he was weary and restless, stuffed and sated with the gorgeous occasion. He dozed and nodded; the buzz of a sonorous priestly voice became a lullaby; he started awake again when the voice droned off into silence, thinking: I'm getting too old for this sort of thing. I wish I was home."

In the transept opposite there was a white flash of peeresses's arms, raised in unison to put on their coronets. So the Queen had been crowned. Splendid, he thought; now we're getting on. He was very hungry. He felt Mrs. Pendleton's bag pinned inside his robe and smiled.

It was not till half-past two that he was able to take the bag out. Then it was all over. Then the vast crowd remaining in the Abbey became once more a collection of individuals with human needs. The peeresses in the transept opposite were munching from paper bags; conversations had broken out everywhere. A peer whom Hamer did not know, who had been sitting morosely on his right all through the long hours, turned to him suddenly and said: "By God, Shawcross, I'm starving. What've you got there?" Hamer gave him a sandwich, and they shared amicably, swig for swig, from the tin cup of the thermos flask.

He was a burly, red-faced chap, this peer; and now in his loud commanding voice he hailed a scarlet stick: "Here! I've been here too long. Where's the place?"

"This way, my lord," said scarlet stick gravely, and Hamer followed the peer with relief.

When they returned to their places, Hamer's neighbour said: "They ought to be calling us out soon. It's gone three o'clock. I shall go soon, call or no call."

There was no call. All the Abbey was divided into lettered blocks, and it had been arranged that a loud-speaker should call the occupants of the blocks, letter by letter, telling them by which exit to leave. Simultaneously, telephone calls would apprise the chauffeurs in the car park which bore the same letter. The cars would proceed to the door named; cars and car-owners would smoothly meet.

But all broke down, and what Hamer remembered most clearly of the day was its disastrous ending. There was no call for him, and at four o'clock he found himself in a jam of people intent on getting home somehow. They had been up since dawn; they were tired and hungry. They were in a narrow passage leading out of the Abbey, wigged judges and robed peers, generals and admirals, with their womenfolk, all pressed and jostled together, all aware that it was raining furiously. A stream of cars rolled up unendingly to the door and a voice shouted down the passage, calling for the cars' owners. But all was in confusion. Thousands of chauffeurs, who had waited hours to be called, had tired of waiting and had come to any door they fancied, seeking their employers. None of the employers seemed to be in this jam in which Hamer found himself, and the cars by hundreds rolled away empty.

Someone desperately suggested: "Let anyone use anyone's car, and then let the cars come back. That'll clear the place."

Hamer was tickled by this far-sighted Communist idea; but did not wait to see whether it was adopted. He elbowed his way to the door and, tucking the hem of his robe under his arm and jamming his coronet on his head, he stepped out boldly into the deluge.

Westminster was awash. The gutters ran with the downpour, and the pavements were white with the shattered raindrops. He was not alone. Peeresses ran with their robes pulled up, their slim ankles soaked with rain. Scarlet and ermine, fur and feather, walked disconsolately beneath the weeping sky, scanning the procession of rain-glistening cars that crawled by without cease, bonnet to tail-lamp, all empty.

It was so complete, so glittering a fiasco, that Hamer, catching a countess's distracted eye, as he strode along with the rain dripping from his coronet down his nose, laughed aloud. The spectacle of all the serried pomp within the Abbey reduced by a touch of nature to this common necessitous level was almost perfect in its symbolism. And there was symbolism, too, he thought, in the sumptuous cars on the one hand and the people who could not use them on the other, need cut off from its satisfaction by a superb piece of over-reaching organization.

He pushed his coronet jauntily to the side of his head and strode along, down Millwall, over Lambeth Bridge, for somewhere in that direction, he knew, his car should be. And for every yard of his walk the constant stream of cars flowed past him towards the Abbey, and soaked disconsolates stood piteously scanning the faces of the chauffeurs, stern with the integrity of men who knew their own masters.

At last he found Chesser, a ripple on the endless stream. He threw his coronet into the car, and climbed after it with his scarlet and ermine soaking round him like an old bath-robe. Chesser dodged out of the stream, made some clever cuts, and had him home by five. Hamer strode into the house shouting for Pendleton. "Turn on a hot bath. Light the fire in my bedroom. Bring me some hot soup and toast to bed. And if anyone wants me say I'm engaged with Marcus Aurelius."

"Marcus—?"

"Aurelius."

"Very good, my lord."

*

This was better. This was very nice indeed. For the first time in his life a public event had exhausted him. It was good to be in bed with some warm food inside him, the warm blankets over him, the fire whispering in the grate, and the subdued light above the bed shining on the pages of his beloved book. Ann's book. And, before her, goodness knows whose. "Printed for Richard Sare, at Grays-Inn Gate in Holborn. MDCCI." Seventeen hundred and one. He leaned back against the propped-up pillows, with the brown leather book in his long hands, and on his nose the horn-rimmed spectacles that he used now for reading and writing. For nearly two hundred and fifty years this old volume had been knocking about the world. It was a long stretch of history. Steele and Addison were writing and Marlborough was fighting when somebody first picked up this book. North America was a dutiful colony of the British Crown. The French Revolution was undreamed of and Napoleon was unborn. His mind ranged over the long passage of time, a quarter of a millennium: political revolutions, industrial revolutions, revolutions in thought and custom. But was mankind, for all the sound and fury of its strife, for all the ingenuity of its mechanical contriving, any nearer to the thing which, in his youth, he had imagined the few flying years of his own life would see: the loftier race that Addington Symonds had sung about, men inarmed as comrades free, the pulse of one fraternity? He thought of Germany and of Spain, of the ominous writing on Britain's wall: £1,400,000,000 for arms. No, no. The priest might lay the unction thick on such a ceremony as he had seen today; but mankind's ceremonies were still played out upon a cross.

He was very tired: more tired than he cared to admit. He laid down the book, and the spectacles upon it, and closed his eyes. He was dozing off when a knock brought him upright. Pendleton put his head round the door and said in a subdued voice which he kept for the bedroom: "Mr. Charles is here, my lord."

Instantly Hamer was wide awake. "Here? Mr. Charles?" "Yes, my lord. Downstairs."

"Then bring him up. Bring him up at once."

Charles did not wait to be fetched. He came into the room as Pendleton was turning from the door.

"My dear boy, my dear boy!" said Hamer. He stretched out both his hands, and Charles took them. For a long moment they held one another in a close scrutiny, and then Hamer said: "You're looking well. You're looking fine, Charles."

"You're looking better than ever, Father," Charles said, and Hamer was pleased. The bed-light was falling full on his long white hair and ruddy healthy face. He was vain, and glad that he could stand his son's critical inspection.

"I'm as good as most at seventy-three," he boasted. "But you look magnificent, Charles. You've grown up. You've filled out. Pull up a chair. Sit down. I think I ought to get up."

"No, no," Charles protested. "Pendleton's been telling me what a barbarous day you've had. Please stay where you are. I've just been looking at your velvet and ermine drying on a clothes-horse by the kitchen fire. The coronet is on the hob." He laughed, and Hamer was glad that there was no malice in the laughter.

Charles brought a chair to the bedside. He was brown, tough and wiry. He had grown a moustache, clipped in close military fashion. His blue eyes were harder, mature. He was wearing a grey chalk-striped lounge suit that fitted him perfectly. He looked altogether like a lean young subaltern in mufti. He did not look his forty years.

"What about dinner?" said Hamer. "Ring for Pendleton."

"I've had dinner. It was not easy, believe me, to get dinner in London tonight, but I managed it."

Hamer eyed him fondly. "You know, Charles, you look as if you do manage things now. Well, what about a drink?"

"No, sir, thank you. I never touch it."

"Neither did I till that villainous Lizzie Lightowler got me into the way of it. And damn it, I'll have one now. You'll join me in a cigar?"

"I'd love to. Let me get your drink. What do you have?"

"Pendleton will show you. It's a harmless brew."

Charles went out, and Hamer lay back again. Well, men were fools, inquisitive and acquisitive monkeys, the constant enemies of their own peace. But there were still the old loyalties. There was still the peace of the individual heart; there were still lovely moments. A moment such as this, when a man could say: This my son was dead and is alive again, was lost and is found.

Charles came in with the toddy on a tray and the box of cigars. "Pendleton says I am to remind his lordship that he has a nearly empty stomach."

"His lordship has been a pretty safe custodian of his own stomach for a good many years now," said Hamer. "Well, here's health. Have one of these. D'you know where they came from?"

Charles shook his head.

"Old Liz. She used to like me to go and sit with her and have a smoke. She laid them in specially for me. I don't think I smoked one a week with her, and there were five hundred found after she died. The old dear must have expected to be immortal."

They smoked in silence for a while; then Hamer said: "Well, what are your plans? Have you got a long leave? Are you going out to join Alice, or is she coming over here, or what? She ought to give up that Russian job now for good. And you could get fixed up here in your firm's London office. I should think something could be arranged," he said, thinking of Sir Thomas Hannaway. "It would be very nice, you know, my boy, if we could all be together again. There aren't many of us left now." He blew out a spiral of smoke and considered it attentively. "Precious few. Precious few."

Charles did not reply for a long time. Then he said: "That would be very nice, Father. In many ways, I'd like that as much as you would, and perhaps some day it will be possible. But it isn't possible now."

"What – you're going back?"

"No. Alice and I have both resigned our jobs. She's travelling home now. We're going to Spain together."

Neither spoke for a moment. Hamer finished his toddy, and put down the glass with a steady hand. But his heart was not steady. He felt as though an uncovenanted blessing had appeared suddenly within his reach, and then been snatched away. It was Charles who at last broke the uneasy silence. He said: "There doesn't seem to be anything else for it, believing as we do – Alice and I."

"What exactly do you believe?" Hamer asked. "About the contest in Spain, I mean – a country that has always been seething with political unrest, whoever happened at a particular moment to be in power. You and Alice will go out, of course, because you are Communists. Supposing your side wins: what do you think the outcome will be?"

"I can't say what Alice would answer to that. As for me, I don't know and I don't care, except that here is clearly a case of right against wrong, and if I have helped the right to win, I am ready to let it settle its own fashion of exploiting the victory. What is your view?"

"Simply this: when somebody wins, and whoever that may be, the common people – the people in whose name both sides are fighting – will say 'Thank God that's over,' and, a good deal poorer and sadder, they'll settle down till another saviour comes along to ruin them. If I could be sure of having one prayer answered I would pray for this: that for fifty years, throughout the whole world, politicians of all breeds would leave the people alone. We might then have a better world. We couldn't have a worse one."

Charles got up and began to walk restlessly about the room. Hamer watched him for a while, thinking he did not now look so assured and confident as he did a few moments ago. "I believe, Charles," he said, "that there are too many damned reformers in the world, too many people who are certain they know what life's all about, and are prepared to tear the world to pieces just to show how nicely they can put it together again. Do you ever read this fellow?"

He took up the book from the bed and handed it to Charles. "It was your mother's favourite book at the end," he said.

Charles turned over the pages and handed it back to his father. "No," he said. "I've never read him."

"There's a passage here," said Hamer, "that seems to me to have some common sense. 'I would not have you expect Plato's Commonwealth: that draught is too fine, and your mortals will ne'er rise up to it. As the world goes, a moderate reformation is a great point, and therefore rest contented. If we can but govern people's hands, we must let their hearts and their heads go free. To cure them of all their folly and ill principles is impracticable.'"

He laid down the book, took off his spectacles, and looked fondly at his son. "If someone had read that to me when I was your age, Charles, I know what I'd have said; and you can say it to me now if you like."

Charles looked relieved, and smiled again. "I must confess, Father," he said, "that I still find it a bit difficult to follow a man who once demanded the Millennium and now says he'll make do with Pleasant Sunday Afternoons."

"Go on demanding the Millennium, my boy," said Hamer. "God help us when we cease to do that. But don't expect to get it, and, above all things, don't try to shove it down other people's throats. If the Millennium pays a penny in the pound, you'll be lucky. Now, tell me what you've been doing, and what you're going to do. How long have I got you for?"

"Only a few days, I'm afraid. Alice is going straight through to Cwmdulais to see her father. He hasn't been well for a long time. Then, when I hear from her, I shall join her in Cardiff. I believe we sail from there. We are going on a cargo boat."

Hamer lay back on the pillow, and Charles ran on. Once launched, he had plenty to say. Hamer was glad to hear the voice which for so long had not spoken to him at all, and for so long before that had spoken only in tones of estrangement. But of all the things that Charles said, only two remained in his mind after his son had wished him good night and put out the light: Charles was staying for but a few days and Arnold was ill. Arnold would be seventy-five. If Arnold went, no one but Tom Hannaway would be left, and somehow Tom Hannaway didn't count. There would be no tie at all with those days that seemed at once incredibly remote and so near that he felt he could reach out his hand and put it confidingly into the hand of Gordon Stansfield. He passed to sleep through a turmoil of vague confused thought in which he hardly knew whether he was on the pallet bed in Broadbent Street with the Old Warrior's sabre on the wall, or in Half Moon Street with the coronet on the hob.

Down in the valley the spring was covering the scarred earth with green hopeful things, and workless men sat at their doors soaking themselves in the benign weather. The King who had resigned the crown had been among them, his young-old face puckered and creased at sight of this ghastly fragment of his Kingdom. He had been their prince: the Prince of Wales. While yet a child he had been presented to the Principality in a gorgeous ceremony at Carnarvon. And now he was their King. They had always liked him. They believed that he understood common men, and felt with them, and suffered with them. They would give him simple gifts when he came among them. And now he had come and walked through their streets with that hurrying nervous stride of his, and he had sat in their kitchens and looked about with his quick, shy glance, and he had gone away, exclaiming: "Something shall be done."

And through the valleys there was hope again; the years behind did not seem so desolate, nor the years before so empty. But now he was gone. He had laid aside the crown, and his word of hope fell flat in the valley like a singing bird shot in flight. Nothing was done.

So the old men sat by their doors: they could at least absorb God's unrationed sunshine: and the young men played ping-pong in the charitable institutes, and scrounged Woodbine cigarettes, and went at night to have three-penny-worth of Marlene or Myrna.

And in the front bedroom up at Horeb Terrace, where the ironic sunshine fell through the window all day long, Arnold Ryerson sat up in bed, the bed he had shared with Pen that night long ago when they had come down from the north and sat shyly in the parlour, listening to Ap Rhondda singing in the kitchen as Nell scrubbed his back. Nothing seemed changed in the little house: there was still no bathroom; there was still no gas up here on the bedroom floor; but it was not the same house to Arnold: it was a place enriched with living and suffering, with birth and death. Almost as much as his body, it was his earthly tabernacle.

His body had let him down at last: the tabernacle was in dissolution. He had never given it much thought. It had become gross and heavy, and now had suddenly fallen away, slack, flaccid. He sat with the pillows piled behind his head and shoulders, and the face that looked down into the valley was ashen-grey and shrunk. The big purposeful hands had gone white, blue-veined. The eyes were large and brooding. From time to time he muttered to himself: "Ah'm tired." "Ah can't be bothered." But he was not speaking to any one in particular, or about anything in particular. His mind was rambling, already half-absent from the cumbering flesh.

Dai Richards came quietly into the room: Pen's nephew, Ianro's son: Dr. David Richards, with the long string of degrees after his name, with the Rolls Royce car and the Rolls Royce manner, the physician that all Cardiff was running after. But it's no good to run after David Richards when you're far gone as Arnold is, and Dai knew it.

Dai rubbed his hands together in his hearty O-Death-where-is-thy-sting manner. "Well, Uncle, it's a grand day for the journey. Look at that sunshine! Healing in his wings!"

Arnold did not turn his head. He gazed dully through the open window. "Ah'm not going. Ah can't be bothered," he said.

Dai, rather portly, superbly dressed, with a thin gold chain across his stomach, looked down at the shrunken husk of the old fighter. "No one's going to bother you," he said. "You'll travel like a prince.

Think of the most comfortable journey you ever had, and then you can bet your boots this will be easier. Well, I'll be back soon."

He went out, the fairy godfather who was going to conjure up the pumpkin coach; and in the darkness deepening through the recesses of Arnold's mind there stirred a train of thought that Dai's sprightly words had called into being. The most comfortable journey you ever had…That night driving home from Bingley with Ann…The tall shapes of the beech trees wavered like sombre banners against the darkness of his mind; the clippety-clop of the horse's hoofs, the jingle of brassy decoration on the harness, sounded faint, far-off, like something heard and not heard as ears strain in the night. Ann, Pen, Hamer…they were the three great names that had been trumpets to his ears, lamps to his feet; and now they came back, but only as a dying echo, a just-seen glimmer over the edge of extinction.

The glimmer strengthened, and suddenly with the clarity of a picture seen in a small mirror his mind focused round the moment when he had shaken hands with Hamer Shawcross and said goodbye. He saw again the tall handsome man, felt again the surge of mingled admiration, love and regret which, in their latter years, had always filled him in that presence. "Defeat which would have the quality of victory." So, Hamer said, Ann had summed the matter up. Well, it was defeat all right. His cloudy mind, which for weeks had been brooding over the valley, had no doubt about that; but by heck! – as Pen would have said – by heck! it needn't be a craven end. He struggled up and shouted powerfully: "Dai! Dai!" and when David Richards came running, he said simply: "Ah'm ready to go, lad. Ah want to go."

Dai did not understand that the small avowal was a victory.

Do you remember the day, Arnold – it was a hot summer day and there was a war on – when you heard that Pen was hurt, and you and Hamer Shawcross waited in this house for the taxi to come? And the colliers were standing outside the house to say: Good luck, boyo. Bring back good news.

It's your turn now, Arnold, and Dai Richards and Alice are waiting for the big cream-coloured ambulance with the balloon tyres that Dai is having sent up from Cardiff. He's a good-hearted man, is Dai, though perhaps a bit bumptious, and he can't leave you here any longer. There was a time, Arnold, when Pen talked to you about Dai:

a time when you and she were boy and girl in Thursley Road and Dai was a baby-in-arms in this very house in Cwmdulais. You could laugh then at the thought that Dai could mean anything to you, one way or the other, and now here you are, a log, a hulk, and Dai must make the decisions.

Give him the thanks that are his due. The rooms in his private nursing home cost ten guineas a week, and he's going to give you one for nothing, and take you there on balloon tyres. The big cream-coloured ambulance is even now climbing the hill to Horeb: the hill that you will not climb again. And that won't matter much to you now, because it's all over: old Richard Richards is gone, and Ianto is gone, and Pen is gone; and when you are gone, too, Alice will not come back here any more. She will bang the door and walk down the hill to the station, and perhaps in this little old house someone else will start a new story. But your story is finished. There is no more room in the Rhondda for you or the job you tried to do.

The miners are at the door again, as they were when you waited here with Hamer Shawcross. They see the two big male nurses carry you down, wrapped in blankets, on a stretcher; they see the stretcher slide into the handsome ambulance, but you now know nothing about this. The sombre banners that were moving in your dark mind have melted into the blackness of oblivion. You do not see Alice watching the doors of the ambulance close upon you, as you yourself not so long ago watched the doors closing upon the coffin of old Lizzie Lightowler. *Mors Janua Vitae*. Well, it may be so, Arnold. It may be that somewhere Pen is waiting with a golden trumpet, and if she is, by heck, she'll blow a blast, because she won't be disappointed in you. Perhaps, in that place, they'll give her back her eyes; and if they don't, she'll want no better guide than you to the city that stands four-square: as four-square as you are yourself, Arnold.

The sun sloped to the west, and the shadows of the old men sitting at the doors lengthened, and the shadows of the tall, idle winding-machinery lengthened, and the synthetic stars blossomed on the bosom of the Super Cinema de Luxe. They were pale in the dying light, but they strengthened as the shadows lengthened, and at last they were fiery, dominant, a glamorous halo against which the black silent bulk of Horeb stood out like a grim abandoned citadel.

Alice had gone back into the house as soon as the ambulance was out of sight. The house where she was born. She could have walked blindfold through every inch of it, as she had taught Pen to do. But after tonight she would walk through it no more. Dai Richards had said that Arnold would never come back, so now she was going through the house, assembling the few personal things she wanted to keep, destroying papers, documents, this and that. She must leave the house anonymous; then those could come in to whom she had arranged to give the furniture. They would strip it bare, and then her home would be that pathetic thing an empty house.

All through the afternoon the smoke floated out of the chimneys as she burned in the kitchen, the front room, upstairs and down. There was an old exercise-book in Arnold's desk, the leaves written upon in brown faded ink, the language Welsh. Though born in the valley, she had never learned Welsh, and she did not know, as she tore up the pages and dropped them a few at a time upon the clogging flames, that there went Ap Rhondda's immortality, following his mortal bones to dissolution.

When nothing more was to be done, she cleaned the kitchen fireplace of its crackling refuse, laid a clear fire, and put on water to boil. Then she pulled out the old tin bath that Pen had washed her in as a baby, and that Pen and Arnold had bathed in, too, and she undressed herself and bathed. She dressed in clean clothes and made herself up carefully. The evening now was come. She began to prepare their supper.

It was not an easy day for Alice: a father going, a lover-husband returning. A lover, no doubt. No doubt at all about that. It was excess of plagued love rather than its lack that had driven Charles away. That was the hope and faith by which she had lived. Sometimes of late she had laughed at herself, called herself an old woman – too old for love. But the sweet warmth of her body told her that this was not so.

It was a long time since she and Charles had eaten in this kitchen. She remembered the occasion well enough. She and Charles had declared that they would have no children, and Pen had flared up, calling that a coward's choice. It was no good trying to choose a world for our children, Pen had said: we must let them do as we had had to do: take the world as it was. No harps and wings here below, but we must work for them all the same.

She stood at the window, looking out at the scarred slope of the mountain running steeply up to the sky that was greenish, luminous, with one bright star palpitating upon its forehead; and she thought of her mother, and of Pen's unquenchable gusto for life. Love of life. That was a better word. If someone had offered it to her over again, just as it had been, blindness and all – so she had said that night – she would jump at the offer.

Well, you can't do that, Pen. But you live in me. And I told you that night that you'd die in me, too. It seemed an easy boast then, a gallant emancipated gesture, but now you are gone, and soon Arnold will be gone, too; and, considering where Charles and I are going to, we may be gone as well. Even now, it may be too late.

She went upstairs and laid and lit a fire in the little back bedroom that she and Charles would occupy that night. While the fire drew up, she stood silhouetted against the window, with the dark mountain beyond her and the star above her head, shining like mercy over the abyss.

She did not go to the station to meet Charles. She was as shy as a maiden when she allowed her thoughts to dwell upon him: this new Charles whose photograph she had seen, a confident lean-faced sun-burnt man: a stranger, almost, so far as the flesh went: and yet Charles, her lover. She could not bear to meet him where strangers' eyes might see them.

She remembered how, the last time they had been here together, he would hurry to the door at her knock and over the blind head of Pen make signs of love to her. And now here was *his* knock, and she was hurrying down the flagged oil-clothed passage, and there were no years at all between. There was nothing but Alice and Charles and their love. And these three were one thing, heightened in her mind by the thought of the bloodshot threshold on which their lives now stood.

For a moment they did not speak. He had dropped his bag to the ground, pushed to the door, and taken her in his arms. There was no light in the passage. They stood in the darkness, close in a long embrace. When they did speak, their words seemed foolish and pointless. She inquired about his journey, apologized for not meeting him. He asked about Arnold's departure, brought her greetings from his father.

"Now go and wash yourself," she said, "and I'll put the supper on the table."

She was anxious to escape into commonplace words and commonplace actions. It gave her time to think, to re-establish her emotions; and when supper was over, and they had washed up together and sat one on either side of the kitchen fire, she was glad to hear Charles say: "You know, something like this is what I've been longing for. Just to be sitting down, with you, at peace. When you come to think of it, it's the thing I never did. I was always in and out and up and about, torturing my guts over impossibilities. If I'd had a lot more of this, I'd never have cleared out."

"You weren't ready for it," Alice smiled; and she thought how long it took most people to be ready for wisdom. He hadn't called her my love, or my dear, or my darling. But he had said: Just to be sitting down, with you, at peace. And they *were* at peace. She had feared at times, pre-figuring this meeting with Charles, lest its emotional content should overwhelm her. But they had slipped together as simply and complet-ely and with as little fuss as two raindrops meeting on a window-pane.

Charles lit his pipe, and Alice made coffee, brightened up the fire, and turned out the gas. They sat in the dancing light of the flames, and Charles said: "You needn't have put the light out, you know. You're still good to look at without benefit of a romantic glow. You're no different, to me at any rate, from what you were the first time I saw you. D'you remember when that was?"

Yes; she remembered the tall, fair schoolboy, coming up out of the mine, proudly displaying his dirty overalls, and imagining he knew a lot about the Rhondda. Do you remember? Do you remember? Soon they were unlocking the chests where all their common memories were stored: Cwmdulais and Oxford and North Street.

"D'you remember the day when old Lizzie first saw my father wear-ing his ceremonial uniform? A bloody miracle! A bloody miracle!"

Alice laughed, and then sighed. "I don't think I'm quite such a prig now as I was then," she said. "I'm still with all my soul after the things I want and believe in, but I don't think I could ever again be so sniffy about what other people believe in. Poor old Liz! Your father was her hero. She found it hard to see spots on him."

Charles got up and knocked out his pipe. "It may be a confession of approaching senility," he said with a smile, "but I myself don't see so many as I used to. In fact, during the last few days I've come to the conclusion that I have a rather remarkable sire."

"He's as God made him," said Alice, "and perhaps he's not so bad at that. Anyway, he's the last of them: Pen and Ann, Arnold and Hamer. Take them by and large, we needn't blush for those who made us."

She remained for a while sunk in reverie, then started up suddenly. "Let's go to bed," she said.

Charles had left most of his luggage in Cardiff, and Alice had sent hers there during the last week or so. They left the house in the morning carrying only a small handbag each. They had got up while the light was still grey. They had little to say to one another, filled as they were with a sense of last things. Charles boiled the kettle on a fire of sticks. Alice laid the table, and when they had eaten she washed up the few things and put them on the dresser. She would never come back to this house: it was almost an act of piety to leave all in order, spotless. She went upstairs, folded the bedclothes, and left them on the bed, neatly piled. Then she walked through the rooms of the house, looking round her for the last time. It did not take her two minutes. "I can remember the time, my love," she said to Charles, "when this place seemed full of distance, mysterious recesses, and when I was in bed in the dark, Father and Mother seemed miles away. Well, there it is: four little boxes with a ladder going between the pairs."

She had always seemed to Charles the embodiment of the practical, the efficient, the unemotional. It moved him now to see that she herself was moved, and he knew that she was saying good-bye not to the four little boxes but to the spirits that her mind would for ever conceive as haunting these humble walls: the fierce, life-loving restless spirit of Pen, the sober resolute spirit of Arnold, and the young ghost of her own childhood, looking out of these windows upon the valley and the hills and the beckoning illimitable world beyond the hills.

"I'll go on," he said. "You catch me up," and he stepped out into the morning, leaving her to her farewells.

He had not got half-way to Horeb when he heard the door bang and the eager following of her footsteps. He turned to wait for her, and saw her wiping her eyes and blowing her nose. They went together down the hill to the station.

There was a holy quiet about the moment in which they looked their last at Cwmdulais. It was not yet seven o'clock. There was no roar and rattle of work; no smoke or steam was to be seen anywhere in the valley, and there was no one about the streets. The sunshine of May was falling silvery, without heat, and even the posts of the railway signals had a fresh and virginal look, as though they should be wreathed with garlands. Blackbirds and thrushes were pouring out wild songs. Only the men and women, sleeping in all the little sleeping houses, were unawakened by the miracle of May. The writhing old hawthorn that grew on the station platform was a dome of scented snow.

Charles and Alice stood under the old tree, waiting for the train, breathing the clear incense of the morning and of the blossom. When the locomotive swung slowly round the bend, Alice said suddenly and urgently: "Kiss me now. Kiss me under this old tree. We'll never kiss again in Cwmdulais."

Charles kissed her, and when the train had started Alice leaned out of the window, thinking of a little pig-tailed girl leaning out in just this way thirty years ago, watching the old tree fade from sight and hearing behind her the chant of all her school-fellows bound for Cardiff:

Kiss a man under the old may tree,
And you've kissed the father of your first baby.

Such rubbish! Such rubbish! she thought, and Charles saw, when she withdrew her head and sat down at his side, that her eyes again were dewy with unshed tears.

All the arrangements had been left in Alice's hands. Charles moved through the day like an automaton, with nothing to do but follow. He knew that they were to go to Valencia. There they would meet other English men and women who had offered their arms and their lives to the government of Spain. He was a good air-pilot, lacking the verve and dash of José Esquierra, but cool enough, and efficient. Here was the service in which his false leg would be no hindrance. Alice did not know what she would do. The circumstances must decide. She was a capable nurse, a good cook, and she could drive a lorry. With these talents, she would find something.

They lunched with Idris Howells. "It's all influence, you see," Alice laughed. "Idris wouldn't refuse me a thing, would you, Idris?" Now that Cwmdulais was behind them and there were things to do, she had recovered her spirits and her practicality.

Charles found himself shaking hands with a short, tough, bearded man in a blue suit and a bowler hat. He might have been any age up to sixty, but it appeared he was just as old as Alice herself. They had gone to an infants' school together at Cwmdulais, and Idris had stayed in Cwmdulais long enough to have much the same political views as Alice. Clearly, he was one of her great admirers. The Communist candidate and the author of Gabrielle Minto's novels were alike wonderful in his eyes. Idris had been apprenticed early to the sea, and was now master of the *Mary Marriner*, loaded with a miscellaneous cargo for Valencia, and ready to sail that night from one of the Cardiff docks. She would go out on the tide just before midnight.

They parted from Idris Howells after lunch, and spent a strange wandering day, a day of sunshine and cool airs, visiting the places that Alice wanted to see again, and wanted Charles to see with her: the school she had attended, the parks she had played in, the noble group of white municipal buildings with domes and towers reaching into the blue sky and the spring green of the trees about them rushing into ecstatic life. They sat there for a long time: it was the loveliest place in all the city to sit.

When the light was going, they got up and went to a café in Duke Street, and after they had eaten they went to a cinema, winding up the inconsequent day with the wildest of all inconsequence. At a quarter to ten Alice said: "Come now," and Charles's heart gave a leap, for he knew that with those words the inconsequence was ended, and that, as they stumbled over the feet of embracing lovers, they were leaving that somnolent and stifling air for the harsh wind of reality.

It seemed prosaic to be meeting Idris Howells by appointment on the corner of St. Mary Street. There he was: dark, reserved, uncommunicative as he had been at lunch, but emanating nevertheless a sense of loyalty, a sense of a man who would be staunch and dependable at need. Prosaic to be climbing on to the electric tram, to hear the ting of the ticket-punch as though they were passengers bound on some pennyworth of unromantic travel, not mixed with concerns of life and death.

Once they had left the tram, the moment heightened for Charles, who was in a quarter he had not visited before. From a quiet, almost deserted, road they ducked under a low dark arch. They came upon the leaden gleam of stagnant dock water. They stepped over hawsers and stumbled on railway lines. They heard the quiet conspiratorial plash of water, caught the minute glow of a cigarette, as someone dimly seen paddled himself ashore in a dinghy. Against the dark sky the darker mass of the coal shutes stood out, and here and there an arc lamp burned down with a violence of light that made the surrounding shadows as black as a midnight forest.

The *Mary Marriner* was lying at a dock wall under the long darkness of a warehouse. A light or two was burning aboard her, but she had an abandoned lifeless look. A few spectres flitted about her deck; at the head of the gangway a man loomed to life out of the shadows and said "Good evening, sir," to Idris Howells. Idris nodded without speaking, and Charles and Alice followed at his heels along the deck. He took them to a small cabin with two berths, one above the other, a wash-basin let into the wall, a small chest of drawers, a screwed-down swivel-chair, and nothing else. "This'll do, I suppose," he said. "There's your things. I had them all collected this afternoon. Keep out of the way now till we're at sea. I must go." He went, shutting the door behind him. He sounded brusque and impatient; but Charles and Alice, sitting side by side on the lower berth, knew the shy solicitude behind his words.

As for them, for a long time they had no words at all. They sat still, looking about them by the light of the raw bulb, caged in wire, burning over their heads. A sense of inevitability held them both mute. Here they were, in this unremarkable ship. For this, Alice had come from the East and Charles from the West, travelling across half the world. For this: to meet here in this little cabin, stuffy with new white sickening paint, the cramped vehicle of their adventure towards an horizon which, in the imaginations of both, blazed with the fires of truth consuming the dark pretensions of a lie. It seemed an endless time since Alice had banged the front door and run along Horeb Terrace to overtake Charles: endless as time must be that marks the fateful division between the intention and the act.

"I feel very tired," said Alice. "I think I'll lie down. Switch out the light."

She lay upon the lower bunk and Charles spread a blanket over her. In the darkness he stood at one of the open portholes, gazing at the obscurity of the warehouse wall: unanswering and enigmatic as his fate: mere blackness on which blacker shadows moved from time to time, and in which voices occasionally spoke so low that they seemed to be revealing secrets not intended for his ears.

Suddenly he was overwhelmed with loneliness and premonition. He turned towards the bunk, whispering urgently: "Alice! Alice!"

"Yes, my love," she said. "Come and lie down now. I can make room for you here."

She understood his doubt and his need. With her arm about him, they lay squeezed together on the bunk, and they slept uneasily. They were more emotionally exhausted than they had known, and they were not aware when the *Mary Marriner* throbbed to life, slid out of the dock, and pointed her nose westward into the grey water of the Bristol Channel.

Alice always remembered that it was a lovely voyage. Heaven at least granted her that. Years of separation, but only days of love renewed. But they were days to treasure in memory for ever. Not a moment of them but was lovely, from their waking up to the first light of morning on the dancing sea, to the last moment of all, which also was in the morning, virginal and lovely.

They might have been going on a honeymoon too long delayed. Charles, indeed, said so, standing right aft that first morning, looking over the stern of the *Mary Marriner* at the glister of sunrise on the wake. A hopeful morning of May, fresh and sane, with the men going about their simple tasks as God and common sense intended men to do. And soon, said Charles, this would be all over. The task they had put their hands to would be completed, and then, with no home in Cwmdulais, no home in North Street, they would begin as he wished they had begun long ago, with a home and long years yet before them.

So Charles spoke in the keen fresh morning, with the wind playing through his hair and whipping with its salt sting Alice's eager face. He stood with his arm about her, all the doubts and premonitions of the night blown away like darkness when a shutter is opened on the sun.

Only once again did Charles see England: a far-off cloudy glimpse of the country about Land's End, a white house or two, a glint of green fields, the last lonely outposts looking westward across the Atlantic. He was young and happy, and Alice knew that he had no real understanding of the hazards before him. He had fought in a great war, with half the world embattled, and his mind conceived the affair in Spain as a parochial brawl that would soon be over.

She did not utter what was in her heart, but accepted his mood, and she was to be glad that she did so. Only once did a moment of darkness deepen over the serenity of those days. He was in the cabin, and she had come down to find a scarf, for the evening was cool. She lifted the scarf out of a trunk, and Charles saw, before she could prevent his seeing, that it was wrapped round a revolver.

"Hallo!" he cried. "What on earth is that for?"

Alice tried to pass the matter off with a laugh. "Well, if we get short of food I can shoot pigeons," she said.

Charles had taken up the revolver and was examining it expertly. "A useful thing," he said. "I'd like to have this myself. I don't imagine either of us will want it, but I'm more likely to do so than you are."

"No – please – let me have it," said Alice.

"You bloodthirsty Bolshie," Charles bantered, slipping the revolver into his pocket. "I don't believe you know a thing about revolvers. You're not to be trusted with it. You'd be a public danger."

"Charles!" said Alice, so sharply that he looked at her in surprise, to see that her face was white. "I could hardly miss with the barrel at my own head," she said, and then threw herself on the bunk, trembling.

He knelt at her side, his arms about her, instantly filled with contrition. "My darling," he said. "My darling."

"Oh, Charles!" she sobbed. "You're still such a child. I don't think you know the world you're living in. It's a filthy world, full of filthy things. Things that men had grown out of have come sneaking back – dirty beastly things like torture. Torture is again a part of the technique of governments and armies. I could stand most things, Charles, but *that* I could not stand. Give me the revolver."

He gave it to her, and ran out on to the deck, feeling sick.

Even the Bay of Biscay was kind to them. They met none of its traditional evil weather. Day followed placid day, with the little *Mary Marriner* chugging happily through temperate seas. They ate their meals with Idris Howells, the first officer and the chief engineer. For the rest, they lazed in the sun all day, went to bed early, and got up late. They passed Gibraltar and steamed north, with Spain's eastern coast on their port, and the sunny Mediterranean Sea dividing with hardly a ripple before their bows.

They were leaning over the starboard rail that night, facing the full moon rising out of the sea, when Idris Howells, who had been pacing the deck, stopped behind them. "Well," he said, "we'll have you there tomorrow. I reckon we should make Valencia about noon."

They swung round from the rail. "Thank you, Idris," Alice said. "You've been a good friend."

Idris took the pipe out of his bearded jaws and looked thoughtfully at the glowing tobacco. "Well, Alice gel," he said, "I dunno that there's anything to thank me for. You've got to find that out yet, haven't you?"

She put her hand impulsively on his. "Idris, don't let that worry you," she begged him. "Whatever happens – you understand, *whatever* happens – we wanted most dearly to come, and you must have no regrets."

"All right, gel," he said gruffly. And, resuming his quiet pacing, he added over his shoulder: "Not that we're there yet, mind you."

Alice turned to Charles, and with a little gesture of clenched fists she said: "I feel excited! For the first time since we started, I feel excited. Spain! That is Spain!"

They crossed the deck to the port side and looked over the intervening moon-washed sea at the faint loom of the coast. That is Spain! That is the new Holy Land. Tomorrow there will be another, and another the day after that.

"I wonder what will happen to us?" Charles said with the simple wistfulness of a child. "You know, we'll have to separate."

Alice looked towards the land with her dark eyes shining. "Who knows what will happen to us?" she said; and murmured in a low voice:

"It may be that the gulfs will wash us down.
It may be we shall reach the happy isles
And see the great Achilles whom we knew."

"And who may that be?" Charles asked practically.

"Oh – God, or whatever you like to call it. Whatever it was that thundered into my ears from the time I could think that there was a job for me to do and that I must get on with it, helping to clean up the greedy makeshift mess that halfwits call civilization." She turned to him laughing. "D'you think that's too tall an order for a little girl from the Rhondda?"

"Well," said Charles, like a good boy repeating a lesson, "we must do our best. But, you know, my father—"

Alice laid a hand on his arm. She turned and leaned against the rail, with the white light of the moon falling full on her face. "Yes," she said.

"I know his views. They're an old man's views, and as such I can tolerate them and even respect them. But, remember, Charles, there's an impulsive wisdom of youth as well as a cautious wisdom of age. The views he's been giving you weren't his views when he was as young as we are now. Those were the high romantic days when he carried the sabre. I wonder whether he was ever anything but a romantic at heart? I think that would explain him better than anything else."

She remained pensive for a moment, then said: "There's no job now for romantics. We, on our side, have got to be as dispassionate as a sanitary squad, cleaning up a dirty mess. And we've got to be quick, because it's spreading, and soon it'll poison and suffocate every decent thing and instinct. Stay there a moment," she added, and broke from him and ran to the cabin.

When she came back, Charles saw to his surprise the glint of moonlight on steel. "This is it," she said. "This is the sabre of Peterloo."

She stood for a moment looking at the light playing on the curved blade that had known so many vicissitudes: the blade that had slashed the life out of the girl Emma in a Manchester street, that the Old Warrior had maundered over, that Ellen had polished with bathbrick, that Hamer Shawcross had used to carve his way to the notice and the applause of the people, that Jimmy Newboult had worshipped, and that Lady Lostwithiel had embalmed in velvet. Alice stood looking down ironically at its gleaming length as the *Mary Marriner* sighed and gently rolled through the placid moonlit water off the coast of Spain. "I wondered why I brought it," she said: "But now I know. The world is face to face with reality. It is time to make an end of romantic gestures."

She stood away from Charles, whirled the sabre in a shining circle once round her head, then hurled it far out into the radiance of the moonlight. Silently, as if spellbound, they watched the silver splash of its fall, an Excalibur that no hand was lifted to receive.

For a moment neither spoke; then Charles said quietly: "That was the most romantic gesture I have ever seen."

Idris Howells himself came banging at the cabin door early the next morning. He carried two mugs of hot over-sweetened tea, which he put down on the chest of drawers. "Get this into you," he said, "and then come up on deck. This'll be your last chance this trip to see the dawn over the Mediterranean."

They climbed, yawning, out of their bunks, drank the tea, and pulled on dressing-gowns. They pulled overcoats on top of the gowns and went out into the fresh air that seemed to smack their faces, so stuffy the little cabin was, with its still-odious smell of new paint.

The eastern sky was trembling with a pearly suffusion that, as yet, could hardly be called light: a blue-grey-pink of such delicate loveliness that Alice held her breath. The sea was carpeted with a woolly texture of mist, a carpet that swayed and lifted, wove itself into ropy patterns that twisted and dissolved. It reached away infinitely like a smoke of milk.

From the sea-floor to the zenith was a miracle of insubstantial form and colour, and even as they watched, it faded like a cock-crow phantom. The grey and blue drained out of the sky. The pink deepened to red: red banners flung out suddenly like breaking standards, and the forehead of the sun peeped over the rim of the water. The mist rose quickly, hurrying to nothingness like a million ghosts caught out too late, and soon there was only the Mediterranean sun burning down on the blue Mediterranean sea and falling in rays of long level light upon the eastward face of Spain.

"Well," said Idris, who had remained silently smoking at their side, "that's God's idea, gel, of how to start a day. And I wish to God I was in Valencia, because hereabouts are people whose ideas are not so lovely."

He swung on his heel and walked to the bridge, leaving disenchantment in both their hearts. Charles gave a short ironical laugh. "He does well to remind us that this isn't a honeymoon," he said; and Alice: "Yes. It's grim, isn't it, when we must tell God Himself that the day of romantic gestures is ended."

They went to the cabin and dressed, and then they began to pack their things. Charles was kneeling at the task; and Alice, sitting on the edge of the bunk, began to stroke the close crisp curls of his hair. Remaining on his knees, he looked up at her smiling, his blue eyes full of that faith and confidence and surety that he seemed to know most deeply when with her.

"Charles, my love," she said, "you're quite sure about this, aren't you? You wanted to come? You believe in what we're doing?"

"I believe in you," he said. "So long as you're living in Spain I'll live and fight there happily; and if you die in Spain, then, by God, I feel

I should want to soak the place in blood for having robbed me of the chance to redeem all those years when I was a fool."

She took his head between her hands and pulled it on to her lap, and sat there stroking his hair and gazing before her at the blue emptiness drifting by the porthole.

It was while they sat thus, close together, their bodies touching and their minds resting confidently each in the love of the other, that the torpedo struck the *Mary Marriner* amidships, below the water line. The little boat stumbled and staggered. Alice pulled Charles to his feet, and they ran out to the deck The morning was as placid as ever, but already they could feel that the deck was at a tilt beneath them. Idris Howells was on the bridge, shouting down the tube to the engine-room. Even as they watched him, clinging to one another, he got his answer. A rumble in the bowels of the *Mary Marriner* roared swiftly to climax: an explosion that blew a great rent in her from engine-room to daylight. A rush of scalding steam screamed into the air and with it came a shrapnel-burst of flying metal bits. There were two men in the engine-room. Both were killed. So was Charles. When Idris Howells came running down from the bridge which was blown crazily askew, he found Alice squatting on the deck with Charles's head again on her lap. Her lap was dark with the blood draining from a hole drilled into his temple by a flashing steel bolt. Only a few seconds had passed since the ship was struck. Charles and Alice had not exchanged a word since those last words in the cabin.

Chapter Twenty-Five

It was very dark out on the moor, and the wind was rushing there with shrieks and howls. It sounded as though the world were about to founder in chaos.

The clock with the silvery chime struck nine. It was up here now at The Hut. London didn't see much of the Viscount Shawcross, and though he still kept the house in Half Moon Street, he had taken his most treasured possessions north. Axel Horst's picture of Ann was over the mantelpiece, and, striking what a stranger might have thought an incongruous note, there stood in a place of honour a fretwork model of the House of Commons, with Big Ben in the tower, all complete. Old Pendleton was dead; his wife had gone to end her days with some young relatives; and the clock was found when their rooms were being rearranged for Chesser.

And now here Chesser was, with the nightly glass of hot toddy. He placed the tray on the table alongside Hamer's chair: a table which already contained a box of cigars, Marcus Aurelius, *The Observer* and *The Sunday Times*. The papers were of that day's date: Sunday, December 3, 1939.

The old man got up from his chair while Chesser was mending the fire. He was thinner; his hair, long and fine, had the glister of white silk. He stooped a little, with his hand in the small of his back. "It is a great satisfaction to note from the papers, Chesser," he said, "that Japan deplores the Russian invasion of Finland. A Japanese newspaper thinks it an inexcusable crime, and in the next column I see it is reported that two Chinese cities have been heavily bombed by Japanese airmen. You know, Chesser, the most extraordinary thing about this world that you are living in and that I am dying in is that nations are not aware of the wickedness of their own hearts. They really *do* believe that a ghastly crime committed by someone else is a permissible national gesture when committed by them."

"Yes, my lord, I suppose that is so," said Chesser. He got up from the hearth, pierced a cigar, gave it to Hamer, and held him a light. He was used to these little speeches. For weeks on end he was the old man's only audience.

There was not so much power and resonance now in the famous voice. It had gone thin and silvery, like his hair, like the chimes of the clock.

"Things are being done today, Chesser, by the governments of great nations that their ancestors of two hundred, three hundred, years ago would have thought beyond the barbarous reach of cannibals. You think you've got the laugh of me, young man, because you're stepping on to the scene and I'm sliding off. But, by God, I don't envy you. No, Chesser, I don't envy you."

He let himself down carefully among his cushions and stretched his long legs towards the fire.

"That's better. I get stiff – just a bit stiff, you know, Chesser, sitting here."

"Is there anything I can get you, sir, before I go?"

"Yes. You can get me that big book over there. The Bible Designed to be Read as Literature, they call it. Though it seems to me a matter of common sense that the Bible was designed to be read as the Bible. You read the Bible, Chesser, and Marcus Aurelius, with an occasional dip into Shakespeare, and you won't hurt."

"Yes, my lord."

"And I shall be sleeping in the hut tonight."

"But, sir, it's a terrible night! Hark at the wind!"

"You do as I tell you. You can light the stove."

"I don't really think—"

"I know very well what you think. You think you can do as you like. You know I'm very fond of you. You know I'm dependent on you. And so you try to annoy me. Well, I won't have it, you understand? You do as you're told, my boy."

"Very good, my lord. I'll wait up to see you're all right."

"I don't want you to wait up. I can still get to bed without help, thank God."

"I'd feel easier in my mind, sir—"

"Very well, very well."

He smiled when Chesser was gone. He liked the fellow, and he liked being fussed. It was lonely without Alice, and he hoped she wouldn't be long away. She wouldn't. No, she wouldn't. He knew that – not with young Gordon here in the house.

It was extraordinary, he reflected, how the coming of another generation blew on the sparks of dying hope. Because of that child, not yet two years old, sleeping up there where Charles used to sleep, the world seemed worth saving. Letty Lostwithiel had driven over that afternoon from the bailiff's house she lived in at Castle Hereward. Like him, she did not trouble London much nowadays. The child's nurse had said it was too wild and blowy to take him out on the moor, and they had gone up and looked at him lying in his cot: this child of Alice and Charles, grandson of Pen and Arnold, as well as of himself and Ann, this child who carried the Christian name of Gordon Stansfield. So much seemed to meet and to be embodied in this bit of flesh.

They had tea in Hamer's study, which was already darkening, with the pines and firs lashing in the blast beyond the windows. "You're a lucky man, my dear," Lettice said. "You used to think, didn't you, that Castle Hereward and the name of Lostwithiel were almost eternal things that even you could hardly blow out of existence. Now you know how frail such things are. It's worked out like that: I am an end; you are a beginning."

He hadn't thought of it like that before, but there it was: England had seen the last of the Earls of Lostwithiel, but upstairs was the second Viscount Shawcross, with a world of sorts in front of him. Not that the title mattered, but the hope of an immortality of the flesh was, irrationally, a comforting thing.

He and Lettice Lostwithiel had not discussed the state of the world. For the last few years the tempo of its Gadarene rush had accelerated, and now here they were at war again, all furnished with Gadarene snouts to put on, and with holes in the ground to run to like foxes. But he and she were so far beyond surprise that they could leave all that aside and be happy in talk of personal trivialities. In their own now restricted circle, they were the only two survivors of an age. It was an age in which no good had seemed impossible, and now they accepted the age in which no evil, no bestiality, no treason or treachery seemed incredible.

This was the age of which Gordon Shawcross, aged one year and nine months, was the heir, and, sitting there after Chesser was gone,

Hamer found the age more tolerable in contemplation because Gordon would inherit it. It was the old fallacy of human hope. He knew that well enough. "While there's life there's hope," and that was true not only of each man's life but of the life of man. He remembered something that Arnold Ryerson had told him long ago: Arnold whose photograph, with Keir Hardie's and Pen's and Ann's and Letty's and Lizzie's, stood on the mantelpiece under the Axel Horst portrait: a sort of "Who's Who in the Life of Hamer Shawcross."

Arnold had said that one night in Bradford, when he went out – his first venture – to speak to the factory girls, they had rushed on him and Pen under the street-lamp in the rain, and had torn and gashed them, stripping away their clothes and their skin. And Arnold had said despairingly when it was over: "They're not worth saving," and to that Pen had answered: "Men and women – they're all we've got to work with. 'Appen they're all God Almighty's got to work with, come to that."

Well, He hadn't got so far with His work. With whimsical blasphemy, Hamer reflected that if his own life's work – entered on with such high hopes, with such banners and trumpets – had been a failure – and he admitted it was – he need not feel unduly cast down since God, with all eternity to scheme in, had not been more successful. Never had the idea of God been more widespread. You couldn't sink a drain, or launch a cruiser, or go into battle without the ever-present priest. It would not be long before Hollywood had its corps of clerks in Holy Orders to bless each film as it first flickered on to the screen. But old Marcus Aurelius had, as usual, got pithily to the root of the matter: "The gods had much rather that mankind should resemble than flatter them." The flattery of imitation was not yet widespread. We were still at the rudimentary age in which too many priests had little to do save show that God was the Yes-man of the State.

Young Gordon Shawcross was sleeping upstairs, a puny and insufficient cause for hope in all conscience. Yet as each generation was launched from the womb of time, men would go on hoping that it might be the ultimate wave, the final undermining surge to loosen the strong bastions of evil and bring them crashing down.

But they would not come crashing down. Three things were immortal: good and evil and the hope in men's hearts that evil would be overcome by good. There would always be the battle, with the promise of unachievable victory swaying this way in one generation, and in another generation that way. For himself, he was not sorry that his own part in the everlasting warfare was nearly done. Disillusions and despairs went at last the same way as dreams and desires. One came in the end to an equipoise, to an acceptance of all that life could do or give or take away.

He put down the dead cigar and leaned back, looking at the portrait of Ann, glowing as brightly as on the day when Axel Horst painted it. He was glad that Ann died when she did. It was still possible, then, to believe in faith between man and man, in reason going its slow patient way, building with its small but well-laid bricks.

The picture took his mind back to those days in the sunshine of the Harz mountains. Even then – even then – the premonition of the world's calvary was present in old Horst's cry: "Where now are our dreams?"

Such dreams there had been! Dreams of Jerusalem in England's green and pleasant land, and extending therefrom to the uttermost coasts. The solidarity of Labour! The old man's face twisted with a weary smile. What was solid now? All the earth was quagmire because no longer were men's words their bond. Faith was gone, snuffed out like a candle in a hurricane, and with it hope and charity were gone, too. From the western coasts of Europe, eastward through Russia and the waste places, even unto China and Japan, the world was embattled and the ancient foundations were crumbling. The statesmen with their childish diction talked of the grave deterioration of international relationships; and so grave, indeed, so shocking to all decency and good human feeling was the present state of the world that it was easy to fly for refuge to the belief that God Himself was afflicting mankind. Rather, mankind was afflicting God, afflicting the Godhead in the human soul; for if one thing was so certain as to need no demonstration it was this: that a good or a bad state in human relationships was the consequence of the actions of good men doing good things or of bad men doing bad things, and of nothing else.

In the silence, above the crying of the winter trees around the house, he heard the drone of aeroplanes: deep, resonant, like mighty harpstrings vibrating in the sky. They seemed to him the very voice of a world in which he had lingered too long: the vainglorious voice of Satan's host sweeping to a new revolt against the majesty and the authority and the peace of God.

He got up a little unsteadily from the chair, and stood listening, supporting himself with his hands on the arm. From upstairs he heard a whimper, rising to a cry, and while the throbbing of the aeroplanes was still there for all to hear, he ceased to hear it, all his being concentrated suddenly on listening to the voice of the child.

The child had been born in this house. The house already was becoming an historic place. Here his mother had died; here he himself soon must die; here his son had been born and his grandson.

Alice did not so much as land in Spain. The small crew of the *Mary Marriner*, all packed into one boat, rowed away as the little ship settled down in the water through which, but lately, she had been ploughing her way. The three dead men went down with her: so swiftly Hamer's son followed Hamer's sword to the deep oblivion in which all gestures, romantic or realistic or springing from whatsoever part of the restless spirit of man, are done with for ever.

A British steamer, homeward bound from Valencia, picked them up at noon. Hamer met Alice at a London dock and took her home to Half Moon Street. Soon afterwards, she knew that the child would be born; and then they went to Baildon, and they had rarely been out of it since. Alice had little to say of politics during those years, and little of Charles. She was a quiet ageing woman. She went on writing her novels.

Rarely – very rarely – she mentioned affairs in Russia, with a growing doubt, a deepening apprehension. That morning she had left The Hut to travel by the Sunday train to London in order to keep an appointment early on Monday morning. She said nothing when she read the Sunday papers with their tale of Russia's blow at Finland. It was not till the car was at the door waiting to take her to the station, and she was saying good-bye to Hamer in the hall, that she exclaimed bitterly: "It is nice of them to be so frank. They have at least left me in no doubt what Charles died for."

"My dear, my dear!" he said, the old silvery man bending over the grizzled head that he had known so black and smooth; but she would not wait to be comforted. She rushed from the house, the car door banged, and she was gone.

Who sees his dream fulfilled? he wondered, sitting back in his chair when the crying of the child ceased, and the aeroplanes had passed over, and nothing could be heard but the wind lamenting in the loneliness. Perhaps only a fool. Not Ann. Not Pen nor Arnold, not himself nor Alice. Tom Hannaway perhaps.

It was time for bed. He got up and walked out into the hall where Chesser was sitting by the fire reading. Chesser looked at him reproachfully. This business of sleeping in the hut was something he could not understand. It was not the old hut any longer. It had been renovated out of recognition. It was dry and weather proof, electrically lit and warm. But still it answered some need in Hamer's mind. When Chesser had wrapped him up in an overcoat and muffler and lighted him down the path and seen him comfortably settled and had then gone away, Hamer gave a sigh of relief. Now he was alone, and, with a little imagination, it was the old hut. The deal table and chair and the rough bookshelves were untouched, and this was the old stove, though polished and more safely housed.

If his dreams were dead, here at least he could be near their ghosts. He did not even need to shut his eyes to call them up, for they were within him. They were an indissoluble part of him. They had made so much of him that he was already, he thought with a smile, three parts ghost. What scenes he had haunted! What hopes he had known, what triumphs and what despairs!

Here, in this little room, they were all about him: this little room to which he had come with Ann so long ago. He switched off the light and lay back listening to the wind hectoring hungrily about the world. A little light, he had said to Ann, is enough to love by. O little light! Come to the world! Come to the world that is so full of wind and darkness!

He fell asleep there where he had known his love that night when the snow fell upon the hut pitilessly, relentlessly, like the falling of the years which give so much that in the end they may take all away.

Pinner, Middlesex: September, 1938.
Myler, Cornwall: January, 1940.

About the author

Howard Spring (1889–1965) was born in Cardiff. He began his writing career as a journalist, working for the *Manchester Guardian* and the *Evening Standard* before becoming a full-time writer of novels. His first major success came with *My Son, My Son* (1937), originally titled *O Absalom!*, which was adapted into a successful film in 1940. He is best remembered today for his novel *Fame is the Spur*, a fictional account of a working-class Labour leader's rise to power.

About the introducer

Born in 1974, Tristram Hunt teaches modern British history at Queen Mary, University of London. He writes political and cultural commentary for the *Los Angeles Times* and *Time* magazine, and has authored numerous radio and television series for the BBC and Channel 4.

More from Apollo

NOW IN NOVEMBER
Josephine Johnson

> *Now in November I can see our years as a whole. This autumn is like both
> an end and a beginning to our lives, and those days which seemed confused
> with the blur of all things too near and too familiar are clear and strange
> now.*

Forced out of the city by the Depression, Arnold Haldmarne moves his
wife and three daughters to the country and tries to scratch a living
from the land. After years of unrelenting hard work, the hiring of a
young man from a neighbouring farm upsets the fragile balance of their
lives. And in the summer, the rains fail to come.

BOSNIAN CHRONICLE
Ivo Andrić

> *For as long as anyone could remember, the little café known as 'Lutvo's'
> has stood at the far end of the Travnik bazaar, below the shady, clamorous
> source of the 'Rushing Brook'.*

This is a sweeping saga of life in Bosnia under Napoleonic rule.
Set in the remote town of Travnik, the newly appointed French consul
soon finds himself intriguing against his Austrian rival, whilst dealing
with a colourful cast of locals.

THE MAN WHO LOVED CHILDREN
Christina Stead

> *All the June Saturday afternoon Sam Pollit's children were on the lookout for him as they skated round the dirt sidewalks and seamed old asphalt of R Street and Reservoir Road that bounded the deep-grassed acres of Tohoga House, their home.*

Sam and Henny Pollit have too many children, too little money and too much loathing for each other. As Sam uses the children's adoration to feed his own voracious ego, Henny becomes a geyser of rage against her improvident husband.

MY SON, MY SON

Howard Spring

> *What a place it was, that dark little house that was two rooms up and two down, with just the scullery thrown in! I don't remember to this day where we all slept, though there was a funeral now and then to thin us out.*

This is the powerful story of two hard-driven men – one a celebrated English novelist, the other a successful Irish entrepreneur – and of their sons, in whom are invested their fathers' hopes and ambitions. Oliver Essex and Rory O'Riorden grow up as friends, but their fathers' lofty plans have unexpected consequences as the violence of the Irish Revolution sweeps them all into uncharted territory.

DELTA WEDDING
Eudora Welty

> The nickname of the train was the Yellow Dog. Its real name was the
> Yazoo-Delta. It was a mixed train. The day was the 10th of September,
> 1923 – afternoon. Laura McRaven, who was nine years old, was on her
> first journey alone.

Laura McRaven travels down the Delta to attend her cousin
Dabney's wedding. At the Fairchild plantation her family envelop
her in a tidal wave of warmth, teases and comfort. As the big day
approaches, tensions inevitably rise to the surface.

THE DAY OF JUDGMENT
Salvatore Satta

> At precisely nine o'clock, as he did every evening, Don Sebastiano Sanna
> Carboni pushed back his armchair, carefully folded the newspaper which he
> had read through to the very last line, tidied up the little things on his desk,
> and prepared to go down to the ground floor...

Around the turn of the twentieth century, in the isolated Sardinian
town of Nuoro, the aristocratic notary Don Sebastiano Sanna reflects
on his life, his family's history and the fortunes of this provincial
backwater where he has lived out his days. Written over the course
of a lifetime and published posthumously, *The Day of Judgment* is a
classic of Italian, and world, literature.

THE AUTHENTIC DEATH OF HENDRY JONES
Charles Neider

> *Nowadays, I understand, the tourists come for miles to see Hendry Jones'*
> *grave out on the Punta del Diablo and to debate whether his bones are*
> *there or not…*

A stark and violent depiction of one of America's most alluring folk heroes, the mythical, doomed gunslinger. Set on the majestic coast of southern California, Doc Baker narrates his tale of the Kid's capture, trial, escape and eventual murder. Written in spare and subtle prose, this is one of the great literary treatments of America's obsession with the rule of the gun.

THE LOST EUROPEANS
Emanuel Litvinoff

> *Coming back was worse, much worse, than Martin Stone had anticipated.*

Martin Stone returns to the city from which his family was driven in 1938. He has concealed his destination from his father, and hopes to win some form of restitution for the depressed old man living in exile in London. *The Lost Europeans* portrays a tense, ruined yet flourishing Berlin where nothing is quite what it seems.

THE STONE ANGEL
Margaret Laurence

> *Above the town, on the hill brow, the stone angel used to stand. I wonder if she stands there yet…*

Hagar Shipley has lived a quiet life full of rage. As she approaches her death, she retreats from the squabbling of her son and his wife to reflect on her past – her ill-advised marriage, her two sons, the harshness of life on the prairie, her own failures and the failures of others.

HEAVEN'S MY DESTINATION
Thornton Wilder

> *One morning in the late summer of 1930 the proprietor and several guests at the Union Hotel at Crestcrego, Texas, were annoyed to discover Biblical texts freshly written across the blotter on the public writing-desk.*

George Marvin Brush is a travelling textbook salesman and fervent religious convert, determined to lead the godless to a better life. With sad and sometimes hilarious consequences, his travels will take him into the soul of 1930s America.